ESMERALDA'S WEB

Book 2

J.R. GONZALEZ

Matchstick Literary
1-888-306-8885
orders@matchliterary.com

Photograph by J.R. Gonzalez

THREE BULLETS FOR HER LOVER

Sometimes grown-up women are just little girls in adult clothing.

-J.R. Gonzalez

FLACO AND SABRINA MET AT Sangrona's for coffee and because she called and told him that he needed to see him, that she needed to talk, and when she told him that over the phone she cringed because that would have been enough to send Stephon away for a while "on business" though she knew he just didn't want to hear it.

But to her delight and surprise, though not entirely unexpected because of the way he'd been up to now, he was happy to hear from her and was ready to listen to whatever she had to say; he must have thought or sensed that it was something serious because he said he would listen and not interrupt or try to "fix what he couldn't" which sounded so great to her that she almost cried when she heard him say that.

Although there were others from the school there; some that they knew and some that they didn't, they felt as though they all left them alone; that it was their world on that day, and it was never so clean or so beautiful as it was that day.

Because of that, they never noticed the others that were quietly watching them; had been there earlier and were waiting for them to show, there were three other places where Stephon placed his boys as places they might show up at, and these guys were the "lucky ones" that found them, and just as Sabrina was sitting down, one of them nodded to the other and then he left without a word while the other one stayed to watch them in case they left.

As Flaco tried to talk to her, he called the server over to order something for them to drink when he noticed that her cheeks were drawn and her eyes puffy and red; her nose runny, all signs that she'd been crying and it tore at his heart because he thought he did something wrong, yet could not imagine what it was, but he tried to apologize anyway.

The server came over and he apologized and said they'd need another minute and asking her, "Que Paso mi Corazon?" he said gently, he was focused entirely on her now and she liked that, he wasn't accusing her of being too girly or anything like Stephon would have done; he didn't act embarrassed that she was crying, but rather concerned.

She started to cry again and then leaned forward and put her head on his chest; she reached around him and pulled him close, she was so afraid that what she was about to tell him was going to cost her his love, though she didn't think he was that shallow but she didn't know for sure; she'd seen other girls in this situation dumped as quick as the guy could get up and run away, you just never knew with men.

All she could do was hold onto what they had before, and she wished with all that she had that she knew what he was going to say when she told him; she was feeling so alone and helpless and yet she knew that she had to tell him; she felt as though the world was about to come crashing down on her at any moment.

After several more tense moments, she worked up enough courage, it was one of those "shit or get off the pot" kind of moments and thinking about it that way almost made her laugh in spite of her fears, she finally leaned back so she could look him in the eyes and then whispered, "I'm pregnant!" and she was going to say, "with your child" but she knew that she didn't have to tell him that because he'd already know, and she remembered that when she told him that she was a virgin he wanted to wait but she insisted and he gave in.

"De veras?" he asked her, "Are you sure?" he said, she noticed first of all, that he didn't look at all angry or indignant and she was afraid that he might be; instead he looked so very happy, as if it was the best possible news she could have given to him and he hugged her close to tell her how happy he was because he didn't know what to say.

He was trying to find a way to tell her how happy he was, what he felt in his heart; but for only the second time in his life words failed him and so he held her close and hoped that she would understand how he felt.

Under normal circumstances, the smile on his face when he saw her warmed her heart, no matter what else was going on, good or bad; but this time it was exactly what she hoped for, she knew that he wasn't going to ask her to kill it, never question who the father was and that this wasn't going to be easy but they could do it together, she knew that now.

She looked deep into his eyes then, at that smile that she'd seen so many times since they met and it always gave her hope; he made her feel that he wanted the love that only she held in her heart, for the woman that was inside and he was not trying to impress anyone except her.

He whispered that he would take care of them, that his parents would be upset at first; but they would forgiveand help them as much as they could, because they would do the right thing and it was their grandchild after all, and life would go on as it was meant to.

Speaking of his happiness, he told her that they would tell them and then be married before the baby was born, and she was crying even harder now but it was okay because these were happy tears now, he could see it in her eyes; she was beginning to think that it was going to be alright after all, that they would get away from here and start a new life together, far away from Stephon and his friends.

She was just starting to wonder how this would work and how she could ensure that her nana would be okay when she heard a voice that she knew all too well say, "What the fuck are you doing with this pendejo?" as she heard Stephon asked her angrily; he'd been watching them for a few minutes and could stand no more.

All the color was drained from her face at the moment, along with all the hope she held in her heart; her knees shook and she almost fainted, and although he heard the alarms going off in his head and he saw all the red flags, Flaco didn't know who the hell it was, or why she was suddenly so afraid of him, but he wasn't going to let anyone talk to her that way.

He stood up and turned towards Stephon, trying to say something when one of Stephon's friends hit him in the back of his head with a two by four, there was a small flap of skin peeled back and his eyes rolled back just before he fell to the ground, unconscious.

Though he was out and couldn't fight back, and bleeding from the scalp wound, three others closed in on him and began to kick him in the head and back, they tried to kick him between the legs but they couldn't; she screamed at him then, looking at my brother as he lay helpless and begged him to stop, "Por favor Stephon! Please make them stop, he didn't know!" she cried, but her pleas fell on deaf ears.

Stephon looked at her for a moment, as if he was considering it; and then spit on the floor in Flaco's directionand then turned away; the other's took that as a sign to continue so they did, and they seemed to enjoy the sound of their feet kicking his body; they kept it up until they got tired, and then they walked away, laughing.

Sabrina screamed his name twice, trying to make Flaco get up or to see him move and know that he was still alive but then Stephon grabbed her by the blouse and slapped her hard on the face before grabbing her arm again and pulling her along as she tried to get to him.

She fought against him, and ran to Flaco, used her body to shield his even though they weren't kicking him anymore; he grabbed her again, this time by the hair and then he punched her hard in the stomach and all she could think of was that was where her baby was sleeping as she grabbed her stomach with both hands.

Her breath flew out of her with the punch and now she was trying to think of a way to save Flaco and their baby; she didn't want to raise it without the father and she was never going to give Stephon a baby unless they held her down while he raped her, she thought that, even if they if they crippled or disfigured him when they beat him, that was still her love and the father of her baby and she would still love him as much and they could still have a life together.

Then her knees buckled again but this time she did fall, one of them tried to catch her before she fell but he was too slow and she fell hard, "Mi Flacito!" she whispered to her stomach, she saw the look in his eyes and knew that it was all over now; he wasn't going to let him live and he would never allow her to have another man's baby.

He would have to kill them all because she would not stop fighting him with everything that she could to prevent him from killing either of them, she didn't much care about herself anymore, knowing that she'd never see her love again and didn't want to live without him and the bay anyway.

She didn't think he could ever be that cold-hearted with her, but seeing that look in his eye told her all that she needed to know; she didn't want to live in a world where she had no choice in what she did, where all she was in his world was someone to use and then leave for a while and she couldn't feature that in any way.

Disgustedly, though he was trying to help her; she pushed the man away from her and stood up on her own, which she didn't mean to be symbolic and yet that was what Stephon saw, her trying to prove that she didn't need him and he didn't like that either.

She looked at him with renewed hatred in her eyes, and at that moment, she could have enjoyed knowing that another man took his life; she might have even enjoyed watching it at that point because she hated him so much, she showed him a side of her that he thought she was not capable of and it hurt him to see it and especially to feel it in his heart.

Since no one was holding her, she stepped closer to Stephon and brought her claws out, she wanted in the worst way to scratch his face off, but the guy that hit my brother with the two by four did it again; this time he hit Sabrina, she fell to her knees and fought to stay awake, but she quickly fell down face-first before anyone could react.

Stephon yelled at the man, then shot him twice in his rage; he was reacting as a boyfriend, and yet he was fighting against himself over what he already knew he was going to do to her; part of him still held a lot of love for her and that was driving him crazy too.

But as soon as he shot the guy, he regretted it, it was a knee-jerk reaction and too late to take it back, he stepped forward as if to apologize to him as he fell, and then he struck his own forehead with the butt of his gun and shouted at her, "See? Do you see how crazy you make me? The things you force me to do?" as the others looked at each other, they were seeing him as weak for the first time and it surprised them.

"Pick her up!" he shouted at one of the others and he ran forward and did, and she started to come around at that time and reached out once more with her claws out, she reached for his eyes but never made it and passed out again from the effort; he looked at her once more, and even lying in the dirt as she was; she was still beautiful.

All he wanted at that moment was to hold her, to tell her how much he hated doing this but that she forced his hand; he wanted to tell her how much he still loved her but it was all out in the open now; everybody knew and they were all watching to see what he was going to do about it, if he didn't do what they thought of as "the right thing" it would be open season on him and he would be fair game, even to his own men.

5

He looked at his men again, they were all standing there and watching him closely now, waiting to see how he was going to deal with this; in the early days, he would have already been dead and they would all be having fun with her now; but this wasn't the old days and this was the new Stephon, they weren't sure that they liked it, but some of them knew at that moment that it was over and they'd have to find a new guy to follow; some of them saw the weakness and wanted to kill him now; he saw it in their eyes and yet they had to wait to find out first.

He spit on her and then turned away, and he never looked back, as badly as he wanted to, but he couldn't turn around because he was starting to cry once more; and they didn't see it because they were down there, trying to pick her up and some were "taking stock of the goods" and were too busy to see the last of the humanity in Stephon's heart as it died.

No one had orders for Flaco, so they left him lying on the street, they didn't care about him and though there was nothing he could do, the cops wouldn't take it serious, would stall the investigation until the trail was cold and no one would talk anyway; they even joked that, "If the cops asked him who did it, all he could do was describe the kind of shoes we wore!" and they laughed about that for a long time.

They took one last look around, but everyone that remained from the crowd that was there before looked the other way immediately, they knew that no one would tell anyone anything about what they saw, so they tossed her unceremoniously into the trunk of their car and drove off.

They took her to Stephon's and tied her to a chair, and as she regained consciousness, she started looking around for Flaco and panicked because she couldn't see him anywhere, she hoped for a moment that he was left behind and forgotten for the moment, "he will live!" she whispered to herself; even though in her heart she knew that there was not going to be a happy ending for any of them.

She knew that if he wasn't already dead, that he would be soon, there were too many of them and he was all alone; her baby stirred in her stomach then, and yet she felt that it was also dead to her now, and she couldn't wait to join them and be together in the next world, where she was sure there would be no one like Stephon because he was bound for hell and they all knew it.

Thinking of better times, over the years she'd sat in this room, looking out that window on the far wall and admired the view of the ocean, a sparkling jewel in the night, and a million glittering diamonds during the daytime, and she wanted to see that view one last time; it always gave her a feeling of hope and goodness in the world and she could use taste of that right now; but it would be false hope and she already knew that too.

All she wanted was for this to be over, she only wanted to die now and get it over with; she was far beyond consolation and then she started thinking that if she pushed him hard enough, Stephon would have no choice and he'd have to kill her, it wouldn't matter if he wanted to or not at that point.

Stephon was standing there, waiting for her eyes to open and wanting so badly to change all of this for her; it wasn't too late, if only she would show something like remorse instead of the defiant stance she was taking; she was making this easy and he thought she didn't know; he expected her to beg for their lives, but that was before he found out what they were talking about.

He was looking for a sign of remorse; something that said that she felt bad for what she'd done to him, and yet he still could see nothing but contempt in those eyes.

"How could you betray me this way?" he asked her, still trying to keep his anger in check, "I trusted you! I gave you everything that you asked for, and some things that you didn't have to ask for were yours for the taking, and you thank me like this?" he spat at her again.

The look in her eyes at that moment froze his blood, he was about to say something else when he saw that look and stopped because it actually scared him, she looked evil and it seemed almost as if she'd shrunk within herself as he watched her, and yet she scared him and he waited for her to do something with trepidation that he hid from his men; who also felt it and were hiding it from him.

"I'm carrying his baby!" she hissed at him with as much venom and hatred as she could muster, it actually hurt her throat as she said it, but there was no way she was going to stop or that anyone was going to stop her.

She had no idea of what he had in mind for her but that whatever it was, there was little or no room for forgiveness or mercy, she was remembering something her nana told her long ago, something that she never forgot; she told her, "When you are dealing with men, especially arrogant men and also especially Mexican men, if you want to hurt them, or you simply want to get their attention, you have to go for the huevos!" she said.

"Not if you want to be nice to them, mija!" she said, "If you feel the need to hurt them, I am sure they deserve it, because you have a good heart!" she told her grand daughter and then smiled.

"You can't be nice to them anymore, and you must remember to hurt them in the place that they treasure the most!" she said and then she laughed hard at that thought for a moment.

But as she watched her nana that day, Sabrina got the distinct impression that her nana had kicked more than her share of huevos in her day; that this just wasn't something that she'd heard about; she was speaking from experience.

He stepped in and slapped her again, this time it was so hard that it left red welts on her cheek, "Hija de puta!" he said to her and then he spat at her but saw that she was smiling back at him; blood was flowing from her mouth and staining her teeth as well as the front of her blouse, she spit it back at him and then stuck her chin out so he could hit her again, telling him that he couldn't hurt her anymore.

"Puto!" she seethed at him, "You hit like a girl!" she said and then started to laugh at him, and once she started; she could not stop; she started laughing hysterically at him, pushing him harder because she knew he was so close to that edge.

He clenched his fists and then grabbed her by the throat, he wanted to rip that smile off her face but then he stopped as if she was the one that was dirty and took his hand awayand wiped it on his pants as if he couldn't stand it.

The horrified look on his face would have surprised her if she was jot fighting so hard for air, she leaned back then, as if she was going to surrender at last; she knew that she'd taken her best shot and could see that it worked.

He relaxed then, he thought that was giving in and was resigned to her fate; ready to admit that was his and there was nothing else to be said about it; her life was in his hands and then he let his guard down, just enough and she saw that window open and went for it with all that she could muster.

Putting all her weight into it; she swung her right leg up and caught him square in the balls with her ankle, he fell like a stone, grabbing and coughing at the same time.

His men stepped in quickly, but even they were as surprised, as caught off-guard as Stephon was; none of them saw that coming but they remembered the lesson of the two by four and didn't know what to do next, they held her back but she wasn't fighting them either; they were all watching Stephon and waiting for him to tell them what to do; none of them was going to rub his balls to make them feel better, and they were having a hard time not laughing at him as he coughed his way around the floor.

He sat up as much as he could and then said, "If she's going to be his whore, then she can be everyone else's too!" he said between gasps of air as he tried to steel his heart for what was next, he was trying to kill off whatever was left of his feelings for her and he hated her for making him do this.

He tried to leave then, and turned to his men, hoping that he looked and sounded more confident than the felt; he said, "Hector! Give her a taste!" out loud, while inside he was angrily thinking, "the bitch won!" as he left to look for some ice for his aching balls, he started to turn one last time but thought it better to remember her in better times.

She took great satisfaction in watching him limp away; she didn't know what a taste was, and yet she was as sure that she wasn't going to like it as she was that him saying she could be everyone's whore which also put the fear of god into her heart, they weren't going to kill her after all.

Sabrina knew that she cut him, deep into his soul if he had one, and the only thing that would have made it more satisfactory would have been seeing one of his own men as he killed him right now; she'd exposed him as weak and knew they would do it, if he couldn't protect his own balls from a girl tied to a chair then what kind of a leader could he be after all.

She knew that she was going to miss her nana and they wouldn't let her go see her either; but she as hoping that this was enough and they were going to leave her alone, she as an old lady after all, and what harm could she do, even if she went to the police, they wouldn't do anything when she would mention Stephon's name.

At that moment, she began to cry for them; she was thinking of the three of them so hard that she could almost see them all walking together, hand in hand on cloud covered ground, no sings, no harps and no halos but at least they were all together and that was all that mattered.

Stephon's men thought she was crying for herself, that she knew what they were going to do with her and one of them thought she really did feel bad for what she'd done and was crying for Stephon, but it was nothing to do with him.

Sabrina cleared up that misconception in a hurry, she wasn't feeling bad for anyone and she wasn't done yet, she looked at them and shouted, "Hijo's de putas!" at them and then spit out some of her blood on the floor defiantly.

"You will all burn in hell for this and the other crimes you committed, a TODOS!" she shouted at them and then she began to laugh at them again; the look in her eyes made them stop for a moment, as if they were thinking that she was just crazy enough to hurt them because there was nothing else left.

She took the best Stephon could bring and was actually asking for more, she was full of fight and it scared them and at the same time they started to admire her strength and courage; grown men would be crying and begging for their lives, offering anything for another day, but she was ready for more.

Sabrina thought that she was ready for whatever was next, she thought if they raped her she would laugh at them and make them feel "less than adequate" until they gave up and went home; she felt that she was ready for that kind of abuse, but she didn't know what levels Stephon would slink down into, though they never saw such strength in a woman, they were excited and scared at the same time.

Then she saw Hector heating up the spoon and the fixings in front of him laid out for her and felt them tying a rubber strip around her arm and realized what they had in mind by a "taste" and she started kicking and screaming, fighting for as long and as hard as she could because she wanted to die, not become a crack whore or addicted to some drugs so they could have their way with her.

Because she was sure that was what they meant now, they were going to get her addicted and then have her turn tricks for them, but she would rather be dead than become a ten dollar whore and work the streets, there had to be something else on the table and yet she could see nothing but that awful needle; soon she would be under its influence and they would all take turns with her and she would be unable to fight them off or even laugh as she planned.

She couldn't let this happen and yet she had no plan, this was her body and she was a mother now, and she would do whatever she could to avoid that but it didn't look good for her at this moment; she could die there, the baby first and then her, she thought Flaco was already dead and then she saw the needle closer to her but instead of feeling it in her arm; she felt it pierce her heart and at the same time, the heart of her baby, and they would both die from it.

Still fighting them, she tried to scream and pull away as they plunged the needle in; kicking and squirming as hard as she could manage, the needle was cutting her arm at the same time because she wouldn't be still and though it hurt; she wasn't going to stop as long as she had fight in her, one of them then grabbed her neck and pulled her one way, another grabbed at her shoulder and pulled another way until she stopped.

As she felt it course through her body she went slack and they released her; here eyes rolled back and her head lolled over to one side, she felt it poison and kill its way through her body and was still trying to fight it even then, to kill it off but there was no way she could and she was slipping away fast now.

She felt it work it way through her and could feel it killing off her organs and it slithered along, some parts of her were already dying as it flowed beneath her skin, shutting down forever and she cried as she sat there, she hoped this would be enough for them and muttered "Abuelita" hoarsely and felt her senses slip deeper into nothing, her head felt like cotton and her throat was dry, she was parched, she tried to swallow but couldn't.

"What did she say?" one of them asked and then leaned in closer to her when no one answered him because no one else heard her either, he thought she was going to beg for mercy or something but instead she spit in his ear and the others all laughed at him.

"You will be the puta at the end if this day!" he whispered to her as he wiped away her spit, "You will see!" he said, nodding his head; "You will beg for mercy, but there is no such thing here today, not for you!" he said menacingly.

Then he stroked her hair gently and said, "Then you will wish that had been kinder to me today!" he said, then he grabbed her by the hair and pulled her face closer to his; her answer was to try and spit into his face, but there was no spittle left and she had no strength left either so it just dribbled down her chin.

That was when her mind started to drift off; instead of the men that were still there, she thought that she was a million miles away; and with her family now, they were all together and having a picnic lunch in a park that she'd never seen before, she had no idea where she was but they were together and that was all that mattered.

As she looked around her, she saw a sign that said, "Echo Park" and then, just under that, it said, "City of Los Angeles" with a seal that made it official, all these things she didn't understand, they were having fun and all, but she didn't remember going there, didn't know how she got there and, just as important to her; why they were there because something about it just didn't feel right.

She knew this wasn't Mexico though; and she could smell the ocean, but faintly, and there were other odors that were not at all like anything that she remembered, and the people around her looked and dressed differently too, though nothing solid, nothing that she could see clearly and know what it was.

Everything that she saw told her that she was in California, and she was looking around her then, trying to find someone that she could ask how she got there, but the question sounded so dumb that she couldn't find anyone that she could ask; it also felt as though she was enjoying the moment and no one seemed to notice her trying to get help because no one would stop, they all kept going as if they couldn't see or hear her.

Then, as she was trying to savor that feeling; that sense of calm and being together as a family kind of bliss and real, true happiness, but she also felt the other side of that coin and it scared the hell out of her; she felt her heart racing, her pulse was jumping all over the place, weak and thread one minute, then too strong the next but never exactly right where it should have been, she feared only for her child though, she remembered that Flaco was dead and thought she was too.

Nervously, she looked around her again but everyone around her was enjoying the moment, laughing and having fun with their families as if nothing was wrong and yet that seemed worse than if they were all panicky; it made her feel more alone than ever, even though there were a lot of people there.

Flaco was there with her, and she was holding the baby close to her chest; she could see it, wriggling under the blanket as they rented a boat so they might enjoy a leisurely spin around the lake. Then she saw nana on the far shoreline and thought that everything was going to be alright; she was waving to them with a toothless smile on her wrinkled old face and she could the cackle of her laughter from all the way back there.

There were others, feeding the ducks and playing catch with everything from a frisbee to a football; and one man was trying to fly a kite but there wasn't enough wind and it wouldn't take off; the grass smelled as though it had just been cut and somewhere nearby she could not only smell barbecues that were cooking all kinds of meat that wafted across her on a breeze, but she could also hear the feint sounds of a Mariachi band nearby too.

Then a hard wind swept in and it took off, the kite shot up so high that it was quickly a tiny speck high above them; there were a lot of cars speeding by as well, and further down from there, the freeway raced along, all normal sounds and indications that everything was okay, but it still didn't feel right, she could hear Flaco's voice as he was talking to her, but not what he was saying; it was as if he was at the far end of a long tunnel and talking through a cardboard megaphone.

They were now in the middle of the lake, and then she felt stronger pangs of fear sweep over her then; again, she knew that something was very wrong and yet the scene was idyllic and that made no sense; she didn't know what to do and was starting to panic.

Flaco must have felt the same thing at that moment, because he suddenly started rowing faster towards the shore as he kept looking back, towards the center of the lake as if he expected a large shark, a whale or some kind of big fish that was coming there to swallow us all.

They finally made it to shore and got out of the boat quickly, she could tell that her baby was feeling to too, because she could hear baby crying and yet even that didn't sound right; it reminded her of a cat that attacked her once, when she was very young, he was small and all black and meowed at her the same way, and she hadn't thought of that incident in a long time.

Others joined in now, looking towards the water as if something was going to come out of it and attack us, and as she stood there, looking from Flaco's concerned face to the water and back again; she noticed that now everything was quiet, even though Flaco was telling her something and pointing, she could see nothing when she looked and no sound came out of him.

Now the baby was screaming at her, hungry or scared or both; it didn't seem to matter and it was the only sound she could hear as he struggled in her arms as if he couldn't wait to get out and see what was going on for himself.

Maybe that was why they never heard Stephon, as he snuck up behind them and stabbed Flaco through the back; Stephon's hand, and the knife that he held in his hand was sticking through to the other side of him, covered in blood and reaching for Sabrina and the baby through him.

She stepped back from him then, to protect her baby and then he pulled the knife out and Flaco was reaching for her as he fell and then died, Stephon left her alone then; that was enough for him as left walked away when my brothers body hit the ground, he stopped only long enough to lick some of the blood off the blade as he smiled at her, but he never laughed, though she did hear the sound of laughter now and thought it was the devil, watching them and enjoying their suffering.

Sabrina had never seen him smile that way in all of the time that she knew him and it scared her more than anything else he'd done up to now, a smile on his face was rare enough; but this smile didn't hold humor; it showed her how far gone he was, how insane he must have been and who knew for how long, that was anyone's guess; but it was a certainty that he was never going to return from that state of mind.

Seeing him leave then, she thought at least her and the baby were safe for now, and she pulled back the blanket to tell her baby, then she was going to see if there was anything she could do for Flaco, but as she pulled the blankets back on the suddenly motionless baby; she found that they baby was dead too.

She remembered feeling the baby moving around as they got into the boat and while she was trying to make sense of things, she even heard it cry, she thought; and yet she was now holding a rail-thin caricature of the baby she thought was in that blanket only moments ago.

What she was seeing now was something that hadn't been alive for a long time; empty eye sockets and skin that was blackened and stretched out over the tiny bones, now it seemed that it really hadn't moved in a long time and she was wondering what she felt before and thought then that she was losing her mind too.

His eyes were long gone and yet he almost seemed to glare at her, and most would have shrunk away in revulsion at what she was seeing, a long dead corpse that might have once been her baby and yet she didn't remember delivering, or when they came here or why they were there.

But even if the baby was dead, it was still her baby and she had nothing but love for it; she would not drop, nor toss away her baby, but she did scream; a long and piercing scream that came from deep in her soul and yet still, no one heard a thing and they were all enjoying themselves, oblivious to what was happening only a few feet away.

She was shaken back to reality when she felt them untie her and they were going to take her upstairs and have some fun with her, she didn't want to help them and thought that was why her legs wouldn't move and she couldn't get up, she felt as though she was there, and also a thousand miles away at the same time; she could hear them as they talked about what they were going to do but she couldn't hear them, and when she looked back to where the chair they'd tied her to was, she could see herself standing there, screaming at the world that was too busy to hear her.

As they tossed her onto the bed and began to rip at her clothes and tear them away, there was a cleaning woman that was walking through the hallway and heard the commotion; she stopped to see what it was and was going to leave because she didn't want to see it but something made her stop and take a close look at Sabrina, who wasn't moving.

She pointed towards the bed and Sabrina's lifeless form and said, "One of you idiots overdosed her, look at her cabrones! Pendejo's!" that woman is dead, you guys are sick!" she said as she turned to leave because she really didn't want to see that kind of sickness.

They pulled her hair away from her face and saw that her eyes were open but there were no lights and no one was home anymore; though she still had that defiant smile on her face that was covered with foamy drool and her arms still caressed the dead baby in her womb.

Stephon told them to get rid of the body before it stunk up the place, he didn't feel what he was saying and it hurt to know she was dead, though he was done with her; he did it so the men would think he was that tough and it worked, they threw her body back into the trunk and buried her outside of town in what was becoming Stephon's graveyard with so many buried there already.

About an hour after that, Flaco finally came to; he was alone and it was dark now as he sat up and felt his wounds gingerly, looking around to see what had happened to Sabrina when he remembered why he was on the ground to begin with.

He looked around for anyone that might tell him what happened, but most were gone home by then and the few that were still there wouldn't look at him, they were clearly afraid that he would bring them into it, and yet when he looked around, he saw no one holding a gun or acting menacingly so he thought they were too afraid of what happened to him, but he wasn't going to hurt them, he just wanted to know what happened to Sabrina; where she as at that moment that he could go find her.

He reached for his wound gently as it came back to him; he noticed that there were not as many people as he would have thought would be there at that time; usually it was alive with conversation about school and what some of them were going to do this weekend, the beach seemed to be the most popular.

Tonight there was only about seven or eight people, and that included the server who was standing nearby, waiting for someone to call him over and order something or ask for the tab, and instead of openly discussing whatever they normally would be, they were leaning together and talking quietly among themselves as if they were discussing their deepest secrets.

As he looked for someone to give him any answers; he unwittingly ran into one of Stephon's boys, he was sent back there to deal with him and was just waiting for him to wake up and open his eyes because killing him while he was out didn't seem like much fun.

He told Flaco, as he helped him to his feet, "They threw her in the trunk of a car!" he said, as if he was aghast at what they did but it didn't escape

Flaco's attention that he didn't look as though he tried to stop them either, "I don't know where they took her when they left, but I think since they put her in the trunk that way, I'm sorry to say, if she was a friend or relative that she is likely…dead!" he told him sadly.

My brother muttered "Thanks" and turned in that direction and then Hector took out his gun and fired two rounds in the back of his head, he made sure to use a '22 caliber so that the bullet would do the most damage once it got inside his skull and started to bounce around; the force of the bullet would get it in, but it would lose steam quickly and not come back out and he as dead before he hit the ground.

When word got to my father about what happened, he wanted to run out and kill Stephon and whoever was with him with his bare hands, he was so hurt and angry that they killed him, but he looked at his pregnant wife and soon to be child and knew that he couldn't leave them alone and he would surely die along with them if he did that.

He was sure that they would come there next and kill him and anyone else that they could find, he stayed long enough to bury my brother and then left town, they took a chance and crossed the border because to stay was to die there; doing it the legal way would have taken too long and they be dead before anything would be done.

For those of you that look for the "ying" to the "yang" in life, or balance, a rival drug dealer did kill Stephon, it was a few months later and too late to do Stephon or Flaco any good, but her prayers were answered just the same.

Stephon died all alone with a bullet to the back of his head, but they didn't bother with destroying his brain, that wasn't good enough, they used a '45 caliber at close range, blowing out the front of his face so he'd have to be buried in a closed casket, no last look for anyone that cared to, he was found with his beloved dragon knife shoved into his ass for emphasis.

That was done by his friend Hector, who was tired of hearing about how special that blade was, and then Hector was called over to Hernando, who was going to be the new boss, and Hector thought it was to thank him for delivering Stephon so they could get him.

"Hey Hector!" he called, "How long did you work for him?" he asked, and the way he asked sounded innocent, and yet it froze hector's blood, probably because he knew right then what was coming; he'd been Stephon's right hand man ever since the beginning, even before the stabbing.

As he started to answer he got a bullet to the back of his head too, and they used the same '22 that he used to kill my brother with, it might have eased her mind a bit, maybe even both of them; but then, neither of them was that evil-minded.

I learned a lot of things that summer and the following school year, things that might make me a better man, but not a smarter man; at least more of the guy my mother always hoped I would be, but whatever I did learn that year, nothing else stood out or was important enough that I even noticed; it just bothered me that I had a brother like that and I never got to meet him, and I couldn't even get even for him because those guys were dead, though I didn't know that.

Now I knew the deep secret they hid from me for all of this time and why we left our home like thieves in the night; and I knew why they were afraid to tell me as well; because my first thoughts were of revenge for the cold-hearted murder of my brother that I never even got to speak to even once while he was alive.

It sounds crazy when I think of it that way, and yet I can't see it any other way; nothing else explains the loss I felt when I found all of this out about him, I missed the camaraderie we would have had, the time we would have spent together, the trouble we could have gotten into and doing the kinds of things that only a brother could understand.

I could see it, we would both drive our parents crazy with worry when we got hurt while playing sportsor riding a bike down the street and going too fast, skidding down and getting raspberries on our knees that itched like crazy when they scabbed over and took forever to heal.

Making them worry when we went out on dates, what kind of girls we would date and the kind we might bring home; how mom would cry when we went out the door but not in front of us because she was sentimental when she wore a fancy dress and I wore a tuxedo and looking like a penguin.

I wondered if he would have played baseball in the park like I did, or maybe basketball; what sports he might have liked and what he could have taught me about catching a fly or scoring a touchdown, to make sure when I shoot the basket that there's a proper rotation to the ball when I let it go; all of those things I felt that I'd missed out with my brother because he fell in love with the wrong girl and it cost him his life, but I wondered if it was worth it to him, because it seemed as though he was truly happyand so was she from what I learned about them.

Knowing the little bit that I knew of him, I know that he would have gone head-on into that anyway, even if he knew the danger, and if he'd been given a fair chance it would have turned out a lot differently I think, he would have kicked Stephon and Hector's ass in a fair fight, but he never had a chance.

The price of love didn't seem to be something he shied away from or wasn't prepared to pay if it felt right to him; and maybe deep inside, he knew that it was headed that way because it was too perfect in all other aspects; they both fell in love so easily that it felt as though they'd done it before and were simply going back to old habits.

Revenge, or avenging his death was something that I thought about, they were right about that; but not knowing they were dead didn't make me feel any better and I even wondered how they thought we'd be safe here when they could always cross the border as well and maybe find us anyway.

POMP AND CIRCUMSTANCE

In a mad world, only the mad are sane.

-Akira Kurosawa (1910-1998)

WHILE WE SLEPT, MARIA AND I began to have even more bizarre nightmares, and they were more complicated and harder to understand as well; and some of the worst involved a small black cat who seemed to always be where the evil was, and though it looked innocent enough; we could both tell that there was something "not right" about it and that it looked or simply felt bad.

He would look at her with those yellow-green eyes that seemed to glow in the dark, and then he would "meow" just like any other cat, and then he would begin to change; not in his appearance, but in his manner, as though he was impatient with being stuck as a cat in this world.

She felt as though he as going to change and reveal his true self, which was nothing to do with being a cat and she felt afraid because she wasn't sure just how bad that could be and he seemed to be more than just menacing and she didn't know how she came to feel that way, but she kept thinking that he was too damned intelligent to be a cat.

When he came around, she would suddenly see him, watching her every move, every gesture, everything that she did was being weighed and measured by a house pet and it was being balanced against something that she might have done in another life for all she knew.

In another dream, she was watching him; it was early in the morning and he was sitting in the street, down below her window and preening when he stopped suddenly, his tongue still sticking out a bit as he looked around for moment.

Then he turned and looked right at her, as if he knew what she was thinking and then he opened his mouth again, and she heard him clearly say, "Asmodeus" instead of meow as she expected; and though she had no idea if she actually heard that or thought that she did, it caused a deep fear that she felt as it resonated all the way down until she felt it deep in her bones.

She turned away from the window, and pressed her back tight against the wall because she was afraid to see anymore; and yet she felt that she needed to know what was next, she knew without looking that he was still there, that even if she stood in the back where the shadows were the deepest or stayed there, hiding behind a solid wall; he could still see her, or maybe he was getting a sense of her where she stood but she felt his eyes on her everywhere she stood in that room, though he was below her and on the street he was right there with her because there was no place to hide.

She also knew that he was waiting for her to look, because he knew that she would because she couldn't help herself; and they once told her that she suffered through some terrible nightmares as a child and she couldn't remember any of those until now; they thought she'd outgrown them because they stopped a long time ago but now she remembered some of them, and it was as though the gates were opened now because she felt surrounded by images of death, gore and dismemberment, flames as high as the mountains and oceans of blood, flashes of lightning and screams of terrible pain, those were the things in her head as she tried to sleep.

When she woke in the morning it was as if she'd never slept because she was so tired, this was so real and vivid that she had a hard time convincing herself that they were not real and just her imagination; that it was nothing that could hurt her and it wasn't real or anything that she needed to be afraid of.

She got older and could speak about those images and things and they brought her to a therapist that showed her how to channel her thoughts and images to a much better result if only she believed in it; and she was desperate and tried so hard that it hurt, and it worked for a while but was not permanent.

The therapist told her that if she thought about nice and pleasant things; told her self "stories in her mind" about things that happened during the day that were vexing her and imagine them with a much better result or outcome, and it made sense to her, that's why it worked for the time that it did.

But the thing about it was that, when it didn't work, the nightmares were far worse than before; they became even more bloody and violent, they were very intense, and they stayed with her long after the sun came up.

She felt at times as though the nightmares knew that she was trying to do and they were furious with her and punishing her for trying to make them stop, and those were the times when nothing could keep them away and she was so terrified that she would stay awake for as long as she could.

The good thing was that it was happening less and less until they stopped altogether when she dredged up imaginary thoughts about her parents; and since she never saw them or met them; and no real idea of what they might be like, or even how they would treat her, the values and ideals they would pass down to her so she made up her own ideas and images of them.

Sometimes she would look deep into the mirror before she went to sleep, she did that for two reasons, for one; she was trying to what she thought she might have, her mother's eyes? Her father's nose? She thought about that a lot and the other reason was so she could imagine their features and "project" them into however she imagined them to be.

Of course, in her dreams they would love her totally and unconditionally, and they would always make sure that she knew that about them, that they were there to love and support her with all they had because that was how they were; and they would never, ever give her up; or give up on her.

When she thought about it; that was really all that she ever wanted in this world, she would joke about it at times and then ask herself, "Who could ask for more?" and then laugh about it…or cry about it until she fell asleep.

On this night, she was thinking about that sensation that she'd been feeling and hoped that it would not lead her to another confusing nightmare that led to nowhere, yet she thought that this was the only way she was going to get answers, and she didn't know where else to go.

Then, as she fell asleep; her mind drifted off to her childhood, and she started off by remembering some memories of one of the few girls that she'd ever thought of as a friend as she grew up.

She forced herself to drift even further back; and she saw a baby that she thought was herself as she took her first steps and falling on her bottom; it all seemed so real that she felt she could almost remember that day and what happened later.

The tile floor with those small black and white squares, polished to a high sheen and slippery beneath her feet as she tried to walk, and that was why she fell so much; not because she was clumsy or learning how to walk but of course, she couldn't tell them that.

But then, she crawled out of her crib and wasn't supposed to be there in the first place; she was out in the main hallway now and then saw a face that she remembered with great fondness, she thought it might have been her nurse and namesake, Maria; the nurse lifted her off the floor and started rocking her back and forth gently until they were both laughing together.

That made her sad then; it reminded her that she never got to know her mother, and then she tried to force her mind back even further, she was hoping to catch a glimpse of her as she dropped her off that day at the orphanage.

It occurred to her that she might also see her father, sitting in a car down the street, maybe smoking a chain of cigarettes as he waited impatiently for her to return, sand baby of course; hoping that they wouldn't be seen as they made their escape and then she wondered what made them do it; maybe that wasn't her father and he just didn't want to raise another man's child, she had no idea but it bothered her; what made them give up on her without even getting to know her.

As she saw several different visions in her mind sweep by and try to attract her attention; she saw something that she'd seen before and it made her nervous that time as well; every time she saw it, she wondered about its significance in her life.

She saw a baby that she was certain was her, lying in a crib and she could clearly see the note that her mother pinned to the basket when she left her behind and again she wondered why; she thought she heard her mother sobbing as she walked away and it started to make her cry in her sleep.

Trying to change her mood, she went back to the time she saw Maria as she was making her rounds one night, she was making sure that everything was locked down and put away for the night, and when she came to the baby's room, she flicked on the lamp in the corner and took a quick look around.

As she turned to leave, she switched off the lamp and stopped at the door again because something "didn't feel right" and she went back to the crib to check the baby again, just to make sure that she was alright and she seemed fine; her diaper was dry and she was sleeping soundly.

Maria pulled her thumb out of the baby's mouth and laughed when she slowly placed it back in her mouth, as if she were awake and being defiant, she didn't need to be changed, she was sleeping and yet something still felt wrong and bothered her, tugged at her mind and wouldn't let go.

Smiling down at the baby, Maria she felt so happy around this baby, they did have a bond almost as strong as though she was her own; she would spend hours sitting in the corner and reading, watching the little chest rise and fall as she slept.

She touched the baby on her cheek, gently and tenderly and then checked her diaper again and it was still clean, the last thing she did was to pull the little coverlet over the baby and then leaned into the crib to give her a kiss on her cheek before she was finally ready to leave and felt it would be okay.

Maria was finally pulling the door closed when she felt, rather than saw something move furtively out of the corner of her eye; and though it was far too dark for her to see anything, there was a chair on that far side of the room, she sat in there when she read, and also while she rocked the baby to sleep.

Right next to that chair was a vent, for the heater that never seemed to work right; when it clicked on, it would hum loudly for about five minutes, a smell would rise out of the vent, like something metal was heating up, it would blast cold air into the room for a minute after that; and then it would turn off and start again later.

When it did work, it would heat the room excessively and they would have to open the window to let cool air in until it felt normal, and the heater decided when it was needed, no one had to turn it on so they joked that it was haunted.

Maria walked back into the center of the room again, and then walked over to the corner where the vent was and saw a large spider crawling out of the vent and into the room; it turned and seemed to be staring at the baby's crib for some reason.

If it wasn't for the way she felt about all of this, and the spider didn't seem to be focused on the baby which was really weird and then that the baby wouldn't wake up by it; she would have turned on the light to make finding the spider easier, she was thinking she could just kill the spider and flush it down the toilet and then leave.

Then she found that the closer she got to the spider, it would sense her there and become more elusive; it would run under a chair or table and kept getting away from her, it almost seemed as if the spider knew where she would look next and hid somewhere close but not right there, and then she heard the baby crying and didn't know why because she'd made very little noise if any at all.

At first, she tried to ignore the baby, thinking that she could fix this problem and then comfort her back to sleep, but then she looked at the crib and felt the urgency in her crying; it was as if the baby knew that she was in danger, though there was no way she could see the spider down below her crib as she was still lying on her back.

Then she went back to her search and couldn't find the damned arachnid, she was frustrated and getting angry that it was so much effort, and threw one of the chairs across the room and saw the spider at last, it was more than halfway to the crib already, the spider went all the way around behind her, hugging the wall until it was past her, and now she could see it.

Maria saw the spider's leg coiled under her and thought it was getting ready to leap at the crib and she could almost swear that she heard it scream as it sprang off the ground and towards the baby, and, because of that; she almost waited too long to react.

As crazy as it sounded, even to her; she felt as though the life of the baby as well as her own were at stake or she would have looked for something to swat it with, she acted quickly and jumped at it, slapping at the spider with her bare hand; she sent it flying into the far corner and heard it plop against the wall and slide slowly down the wall until it dropped into the vent.

Maria saw these things that had happened such a long time ago, she was remembering those things now; she saw Maria walking towards the crib but looking at the carpet with a serious expression on her face, now she knew why.

Whatever it was she was looking at or searching for; it must not have been something nice or some new game that she was playing with the baby, whatever it was, it seemed to be quick and elusive because she could see the nurse getting angry and frustrated because it kept getting away from her somehow.

She saw the nurse trying to step on it then, it seemed that either she missed it a lot or it was invincible and she couldn't kill it that way; and then she saw it; a huge black widow that was crawling along the wall behind her and towards the crib and that was when she started screaming.

Even to the baby, it seemed odd to see that spider so determined to get to her crib; every time it was "redirected" by the nurse and away from her, it somehow found its way ever closer to the baby who was now screaming her head off.

As she watched it, through her tears she could almost feel it; the arachnid was trying to find a way to get to her without getting stepped on by her nurse;

she started screaming even louder then, even she knew there was a reason it was coming for her and she had a good reason to fear it.

As it got closer, she saw that its head was larger than normal too, but as a baby that wouldn't matter, but it was clearly looking angrily at her now; ready to jump those last few feet between them; it would get there at last.

She looked at her nurse and knew that she was trying to ignore her, that she was thinking it was because she was wet or uncomfortable and had nothing to do with the spider; but the urgency in her screams made the nurse turn and she moved closer to the crib, trying to peer over the side and see what she was crying about, making sure that the spider wasn't in there with her already.

Maria's nurse had never in her life had a fear of spiders in her life, but she was determined to get this one, even over her fear that it wasn't a normal spider, it seemed too smart and too crafty in how it moved and eluded her, it had more than "bug instinct" it had intelligence.

The way it moved, hard it worked to try and get to her; and then, to make it even worse; she heard that damned cat and it made her think of that black cat she saw outside of her window, she hadn't seen him since that nightmare so she'd forgotten about him, but hearing him now made everything surreal and added to her fears.

Now, instead of focusing on the "spider search" as she was, she was trying to figure out the cat would have found its way there, it sounded as though it was in the vent somehow and it was watching them, she could hear it growling at the nurse when it got in the way and stopped whatever it was they were trying to do.

When it was finally over, she felt the nurse lift her off the crib and start to rock her gently; cooing in her ear until she calmed down and then she gently laid her back into her crib, adjusted the blanket and made sure she was fine, all the while keeping her eyes on the vent.

Now, she could swear that the cat was right there; his face pressed hard against the slats as he tried to squeeze through and get into the action, and when her nurse saw it; as the cat was all black and there was no light in the vent, it seemed that those yellow-green eyes were following her as she soothed the baby and moved about the room, she stepped closer to chase it and then it was gone, it vanished as quickly as she moved towards it.

"You're safe now mija!" she told the baby gently; but she was still looking towards the vent; all of this had a supernatural feeling about it, and she wasn't sure how much of it was real and how much of it came from being too tired and having a vivid imagination; but it sure felt real.

Before she left the room, she placed a large, heavy book over the vent, and then, feeling that it wasn't enough; she found two large phone books and a brick doorstop that the others would be looking for in the morning but she didn't care about that right at the moment; she just wanted to make sure that if the spider came back that it wasn't through that vent.

Maria woke then, she could see the nurse as she left the room that night but the image faded as she opened her eyes; she knew now that what happened was real; that it happened when she was very young and forgot about until now; and she knew that it was important as well, that through memories such as this one, she might be able to find some of the answers to her many questions.

Esmeralda however, had a totally different view of that day, it burned into her memory and she swore that she would never forget it, "that interfering bitch!" she swore at the nurse.

She vowed that day to "eat her heart out!" before she was done; she cursed her as she slid down the vent and down to her hiding place. That day she was out looking for food when she "felt" something different and it was so strong that she couldn't ignore it, which is what she was trying to do because it led her to a part of the building she wasn't comfortable with; there were lights and activity there, people moving around and people would always try to step on her so she normally avoided them.

But she had to stretch out her comfort zone lately, food was becoming scarce as the source of it was getting smart enough to stay away and she'd already eaten or chased off everything that was close; she followed the draft up the vent because then she could see what was going on without being seen.

It led her to that room with the baby, and though she had no use for babies, for some reason this one intrigued her; she could see no more than the back of her right hand because the baby was on it's back, but for some reason it looked delicious to her, as if she would feel invigorated and refreshed if she took a bite of that delicate little hand.

Since she had never been this high above the furnace level; she wasn't even sure where she was at that moment, but she felt that she could not quit until she got some answers, she felt something tugging at her, drawing her ever closer to that crib on the other side of the room.

She also had a sense of Asmodeus, he was urging her to get over there too, and maybe he had a better sense of the nurse on her way or something because even though he wasn't right there with her, she felt him coaxing her to get over there now, that it was safe for the moment.

There were so many scents and odors in that room with all that wenton in there that it was driving her senses crazy; she was ready to run out of there if anything changed or she felt more danger and yet she ignored that strong sense of danger that was already in the air, she started to look around the room more and then saw the nurse enter the room and lean over the crib to kiss the baby and then turn to leave.

Though she could sense that it was just a baby and deep into her sleep, Esmeralda didn't understand why she felt such a strong sense of danger from her, then she thought it might have been the nurse that made her feel that way; but when the nurse was ready to leave, the feeling continued and stayed just as strong; she watched silently as the nurse spoke gently to the baby and then turned to leave at last.

Esmeralda had the strongest urge to run over there right t that moment; she couldn't wait for the door to close and left too soon, that was why the nurse saw her furtive movement out of the corner of her eye; but she couldn't help it, Asmodeus and all of her senses told her to get over there and she could no longer ignore them and had to act.

She started forward and then saw the door reopen and the nurse return, and yet she knew she hadn't been seen, at least not clearly because the nurse was standing to the side and searching for something in the wrong part of the room, Esmeralda was on the leg of the chair and could see her clearly.

The feeling of danger became stronger then, and she was close to the vent and should have done what her instincts told her to do; run down the vent and come back another time, or wait out the nurse while hiding in there, but she as stubborn and stayed put because she had to know who the baby was and its significance to her.

The closer Esmeralda got to the crib, the more her feelings changed from being in danger to anger and rage; as it built up inside of her, she knew it had to be this baby; there was no longer any doubt of that, but the question of why still remained, it was a helpless child after all, and how could it hurt her except for maybe in the future, she wondered if it was a new witch whose power would one day surpass all others and maybe she would rule the evil in this world as Esmeralda thought she already did, she could think of no other possible reason and yet the baby didn't "feel" magical at all.

Then she got the idea that if she could get close enough to this baby and taste her blood, that it might help her to find some answers; maybe she would know what it was about this baby that tugged so hard at all of her senses at once, and yet she still needed to be cautious because of the nurse.

She knew that most of the women she'd ever known were afraid of spiders and would step on them as quickly as they could out of fear and ignorance; others would simply scream and leave the room in a hurry; and she hoped that this nurse was one of those but it didn't turn out that way.

She knew that for certain when she saw her coming her way again, she held a shoe in one hand and was looking under the chair where Esmeralda was a few moments ago, Esmeralda was thinking, "Go back to your other babies and leave this one to me!" and was trying hard to make her do that; and yet she knew that she would not do that; she would never leave this child as long as she was alive.

Maria thought she heard someone talking and turned around, and at that moment, Esmeralda ran up the back of her leg and jumped over to the other side of her; she never felt her on her leg until she was gone and had no idea where she was anymore, or what was going on.

"Stupid bitch!" she said, "I should kill you first!" she swore to herself, but this time she said it even lower so she wouldn't be heard, even faintly; "But first things first!" she said as she crept closer to the baby that she didn't know and yet hated so deeply already.

As she got ever closer, she still could not see her or know who it was that was lying helpless before her and she almost made it all the way over to her when the nurse knocked her off that path and over to the vent where she fell down three floors before she was able to stop herself from falling further and then found that one of her legs was broken but she had seven more so she just broke it off and tossed it aside so it wouldn't slow her down as it dragged behind her.

Dejectedly, she crawled back to her home, to the darkness where she found comfort and made her feel safe; but she cursed at the nurse that got between her and the baby and the answers she sought, and she vowed then that she would not forget her or the baby, but she needed to heal for a while first, so she stopped to take inventory of her wounds.

Aside from the broken leg, she cracked a rib as well, though she didn't know it until later when she was in her human form again and her body shifted and changed, she found a few other nicks and bruises but nothing else was too bad that she couldn't handle it; it didn't hurt when she was a spider so she changed back and went to sleep and heal.

After Maria reported the incident to the janitor, they sprayed something down the vent but they had to be careful not to use too much because the residents would be breathing it in too, and it never went down far enough that she even smelled it and never touched her, it wasn't enough to hurt her anyway, though no one knew that.

Knowing that she'd have to find another way in there, and that it would take some time too, because she just couldn't walk up to the nurses station and ask about her, she felt weak and needed to feed when she woke hours later, then she heard her last victim moan and try to get up, he was encased in her webbing and barely alive.

Crawling over to him, she saw Alberto's chest rising and falling weakly and she knew it wasn't long for him now; she crawled onto him then and his eyes opened, she could see nothing but pure pain and terror in them and it almost made her laugh.

He was crying dry years from even dryer eyes and was helpless resist or even raise his arms to swat her away; he couldn't move as he felt her feed on her eggs in his belly as she thought about the baby and that damned nurse.

She had remembered a story about a spider that paralyzed their victims and then laid their eggs inside, when they hatched they would feed and then leave, ready to take on the world; but as her "children" hatched and came out, she ate them and all around her were parts of her eggs sacs and legs and partial body parts of her children as proof of her ice cold heart and what she was capable of.

Maria woke up several times during that night, and every time she did, she would sit in the dark and watch that same vent; expecting to see the spider come crawling out in the open now that she knew about it, she thought it might even talk to her and tell her some of the things she needed to know; as ludicrous as that sounded, it made sense to her at that moment, though later she laughed at the thought.

Now she was feeling that she'd been born in the wrong time period, that she belonged somewhere else and she couldn't wait to find out if that was true as well; she felt she didn't belong here, that things and events in this time and place seemed so uncomfortably wrong, Maria was hoping that someone could tell her where she belonged and just as importantly; what happened to her nurse.

She already knew deep inside that it had something to do with that spider, that she caused something to happen and her nurse left because of it; and she also knew that whatever answers she found about that were not going to be answers that she was going to like.

Maria slept fitfully the rest of that night; and when the sun broke through the clouds in the morning and woke her; this time it simply hurt her eyes rather than gave her a small modicum of comfort as it usually did in the morning.

It took her a long time, but after she finally dragged herself out of bed, she went to the bathroom and started to brush her teeth, but she looked in the mirror, she saw that her eyes were now blood red and she had fangs, and it shocked her so much that she almost knocked her cup back into the sink where it would have shattered and the flying glass would surely have cut her deeply.

She was thinking that she was just tired when she looked again and it was gone, so she spent extra time washing her face and then she ran cold water into her palms and splashed it into her face and eyes and when she looked again she was normal once more.

But she leaned and looked even closer; she was making sire that there was nothing there, that they were clear and whatever that was wasn't going to be coming back soon because she didn't like the look or the way it made her feel.

As she dressed for the day, she tried to keep those images that she'd seen out of her thoughts, she got into her chores and then did her homework and kept herself busy and distracted all morning so she wouldn't give them energy and bring them back again.

She kept trying to convince herself that it had little significance in her life and wasn't important now; that it was all done, history and didn't matter anymore anyway, and yet, every time she thought he'd done it and got her mind clear of it, she would think about her nurse and wonder what happened to her; why she left if she did, or maybe she got married and didn't have to work anymore because her husband had money or something and he didn't want her to work.

Yet she knew inside that it was none of those things and that if her nurse was around here somewhere, as a nurse, someone's wife or just working at another hospital or facility that she would at the very least come by once in a decade to see how she was doing, that she wouldn't just abandon her baby to the fates of the world that way, and that made her sad once more.

She didn't get any big revelation or anything, but it was more from a feeling of deep dread that she felt in her heart when she wondered or tried to figure out what happened; and the closer she felt she was to getting to a solution and some of those answers she sought, the stronger the feeling of dread and gloom grew along with it.

Yet she had to find out; she had to know for certain what happened or the dread feeling would never leave; even though she knew she wasn't going to like what she was going to find out, Maria was her first real friend inn this cold world and probably her only friend at that time, one that really looked out for her and took good care of her all the time she was there.

The first one that ever made her feel loved and wanted, and now she was certain that something terrible had happened to her because of her devotion to a baby that wasn't even hers.

Later, the nurses were concerned because no one had seen Maria, she didn't come down for breakfast and no one could remember seeing her even leave her room that morning and there was never any reason to worry about her until now.

They checked with Morris and found that she hadn't left and then did a room by room search until they found her; she was in one of the third floor closets and appeared to have cried herself to sleep by the looks of her; she was muttering something about being frustrated and helplessness because she knew that something had happened to her and she blamed herself for it, though she'd done nothing.

She knew also that whatever it was, that it was bad; she felt as though she 'd already visited her grave and found out for certain; and she imagined it to be on a slope with green grass and rolling hills all around her, gently sweeping up towards the top of the hill that was her final resting place; the row of hills gently separated her grave from the next row of markers.

Then she saw the marker with the name "Maria Fonseca" and the date she was born alongside the day she left this world, but the re was nothing else; not a word that spoke about the kind if woman she was, or who she left behind; nothing about a family or what happened to her, how she lived and died, who she was in this world.

She saw herself standing there with roses on her hand, a steady rain that started when she got there and hadn't let up yet; she looked at the roses and suddenly they didn't seem to be enough; they were the wrong color, or she should have brought more, the wrong flower altogether and someone was yelling at her for getting it wrong, "After al that she did for you? You bring her these pathetic flowers? You didn't even know that she was allergic to roses, did you? She died for you, and this is the best you can do?" she was told.

"This woman gave her life for your pathetic ass and you don't even know enough to bring the flowers she liked?" she was asked, but as she looked around and tried to explain herself, there was of course, no one there; nothing but the wind that blew past her at that moment was speaking to her now.

She looked down at the gravestone again, while hoping that those voices would remain silent for her; but this time when she looked it showed her name engraved on it, the day she was born, which she'd only guessed at and felt that, though this was different than what she'd guessed at by looking at the records and guessing that she was about a month old when she was left there, she wondered if this was her real birth date or was someone having fun with her by putting her name and that date there.

For a brief moment, she thought that she saw something else there as well; and image of a flame that appeared to be what was left of a post or some kind of pole, but what really bothered her was that there was something burning brightly in that flame, it made her really start to pay attention because she was certain that there was a woman inside of those flames;and in the brightest parts of the fire she was sure that it was her face she was seeing in agony; and at the same time, the skin on her arms was starting to feel uncomfortably warm and when she looked, the fine hairs on her arms were singed too.

Then she looked back at the tombstone she saw that it was just a smudge on the surface of the headstone and nothing else; she wanted to look closer to be sure but she was afraid that this would be like the movies and if she did that, someone, or something would reach up and out of that grave and pull her down into it and she would not be able to break its hold on her.

Feeling silly, she stood back just the same and straightened her clothes and remembered that they had told her at the center that she was born on February nineteenth, and this showed her birthday as February tenth.

She looked a little closer and saw the other date this time, but she thought, "That can't be right, that would mean that I was going to die…today!" she said, almost laughing and then she started looking around her again, hoping that someone would be sitting out there in the middle of everything, waiting for her to ask a question so they could help her, and again, knowing how ridiculous this sounded, which made it perfect for everything else that was happening.

Suddenly, she felt as though she didn't belong there either; that she certainly wasn't welcomed there, and she couldn't get out of there fast enough though she didn't want to run and draw unwanted and certainly undie attention, the last thing she wanted at that moment because she didn't want anyone asking questions that she couldn't answer.

She turned to leave when her earlier fears were realized; she felt a hand reach out of the grave and grab her by the ankle, she thought it was Maria, coming back to blame her for her untimely death at the hands of someone, and as ridiculous as it sounded; the main suspects were a black widow spider and that damned cat that smelled like it was dead.

Reaching down, she was thinking to try and make it release her but it was already gone; she quickly crawled away from the grave; though she saw no grass disturbed and her leg was free, she didn't feel safe until she well down the path and far away from her that she could no longer even see the gate when she started thinking, "What black widow?" and then it came to her that it was the same as the one she saw near her crib so long ago, and what does that mean about the cat being there and on the street in front of her house.

Now she was trying really hard, searching her memory for anything that anyone might have told her about it; and she was fairly certain that no one did, that, at the time, they likely thought that she was too young to understand, that she would probably not even notice that she was gone, and it cut her heart deeply that they were right.

As hard as she thought about it, she couldn't remember why she left or even when she left; and she also knew that her nurse would have never have left her for a better job or something, maybe if she got married, but she would not have left her without stopping to say goodbye, and she decided that her next stroll down "memory lane" would start at that point.

As hard as she tried, and as much as she thought about it; she couldn't remember why the nurse left, or even a hint as to when it was, one day she just vanished and little Maria was all alone in the world once more.

Then she felt an old, and familiar feeling; waves of sadness washed over her and she could not help but break down and cry, and though she still could not understand what any of this meant, she knew that it was really important and she would not be able to stop thinking about it until she figured it all out.

Though these were feelings that she was familiar wit and felt that she knew quite well, feelings of hopelessness, of deep dread and at the same time; she knew that she was helpless to do anything about it, as if she was fund guilty of committing crimes against humanity, things that she would never have, even in her wildest dreams ever thought of committing.

She knew that she was all alone in this, and yet she felt that there was someone else, someone that was close and as of yet, undiscovered by her, someone that was important to her future, any thought of well- being and surviving, and yet she didn't know if that person was a good or bad thing yet either.

The question of whether it was a good thing or not was, in part, answered by the feeling s that she got from that direction; her instincts or something within told her that it wasn't evil or menacing; at least not at this point.

She thought then that it might be the spirit of her mother or father, or someone from another life that she shared her heart with, that seemed more likely but that might have been because it felt more romantic and at the same time, from a world far removed from this one.

That was another answer that she hoped would be revealed to her soon, before she lost her mind, or the visions went away and never came back and then she'd never find out; she wanted to find some way to peace with it; to solve the puzzle, yes, but more so to find those elusive answers that nagged at her, even while she slept.

Yet she knew that when she found the answers, that there would be something else there as well, something else that came along with it. A reckoning of sorts that might very well take her life and all of the people that loved or cared for along with her; and yet she knew that she must find out, she must know or even if it took her life, she would never rest; even while she was under the ground.

All of this was hurting her, making her feel like she had been selfish and inconsiderate because she didn't know anything, it was true that she never even learned anything about her nurse, and that hurt too, because it was clear that she was loved and she felt the devotion and dedication to her by the nurse and yet she couldn't for the life of her remember her ever saying goodbye.

HIGH SCHOOL CONFIDENTIAL

It is possible to store the mind with a million facts and still
be entirely uneducated.

-Alec Bourne

I WAS FINALLY STARTING TO FEEL as though I'd got the hang of things and
was feeling less like a new fish in the school, getting used to how things
worked and the quickest ways to get from one class to the other because
sometimes they were spread out so far that one was at the other end of the
campus and I didn't have a lot of time to get there.

It wasn't easy, maneuvering around all the others trying to do that same
without dropping my books or knocking anyone over, but I hated being late
and hearing about it in front of everyone and then I always needed a few more
seconds to catch my breath, it wasn't easy but it was starting to work at last.

I regretted the schedule they put me, I was given "second lunch" and
by the time it was my turn I was ravenous with hunger, and I don't know if
it was the idea that I had a break from all the things they were cramming
into our heads or that I could finally eat something without an instructor or
administrator running up and taking it away running up and taking it away
from me because it wasn't the right time or place to be eating.

It was probably just my imagination, I know, but the burgers they served
us seemed to taste better at first lunch, they were fresher and warmer, at
second lunch it felt as though we were getting the leftovers; food that was

made for the first lunch but they didn't buy it, so it was put under a heat lamp and saved just for me; now it was dry and a little crusty at the edges and just wasn't as good.

According to my schedule, I could go right after my P.E. class, which maybe was another reason I would get so hungry was I'd spent all that energy running around with the class at the whim of the teacher who was sometimes so angry about something that all we did the entire class was run the bleachers or around the track, and yet it had nothing to do with us so we never understood why he took it out on us.

So I found a way to skip through the gym and go straight to the lunch area; I knew it had to be damn near impossible for the teachers and staff there to know which of us belonged there and which ones didn't, and if I acted as though I was supposed to be they left me alone, but my argument was that it made no sense to wait another half hour to eat my lunch.

When I got there, I saw that the line for the burgers was already getting long so I ran and took my place there; in the front, someone would take your money and hand you what you asked for, milk, cookies, hamburger or cheeseburger, with or without secret sauce which was just ketchup and mayonnaise but you get the idea; once in a while they would make a mistake and it would actually taste...not too bad.

But I had an ace, the girl in the front who took your money was Caroline, and for some reason, she was so taken with me that she wouldn't leave me alone, though I'd made it clear that I didn't have time for her and wasn't really interested in dating, she wouldn't quit on the idea and it was getting worse.

She was pretty, had big blue eyes and pale skin, she was blonde and had the curves that my friends seemed to like so much that we were calling them "bumps" and if she was hot, as they said Caroline was, then she "had bumps" but I never saw her that way and didn't want to be her boyfriend but I couldn't explain why, it didn't feel right to me.

There were two windows, one where you paid, and then the one to the left where they gave you the burger; and the one that sat in the first window was Caroline; she was pretty, with big blue eyes and pale skin, with blond hair and "the bumps" but I wasn't interested, though when I was a lot younger I fell for her big eyes but she wasn't very friendly to me then so I gave up.

Now she had a crush on me, she would sometimes follow me around school like a little puppy, when I stopped, she would stop, and when anyone asked she would happily tell them that we were "going around" which sounds like we were arguing but I think it meant we were dating, even though we weren't, and I was sure that I would know if we were and isn't it funny how those things go in cycles.

When we were kids, I would have done almost anything for her; though we were innocent and neither of us would have known what to do if we'd somehow taken it to the next level; and yet, now that she could be mine, I didn't want to be with her.

Not that it kept me from taking full advantage of that; shameless as I am, there were times when I didn't even have to pay for my burger, depending on who was around and if anyone was paying attention to us; there were times when I would give her my dollar and she would hand it back to me with my receipt for the next window as if it were change.

It wasn't just her though, I had no interest in her or any of the other girls I knew in school; there were some cute ones and some athletes that I admired but I didn't want to date them, I just went to their games or events and supported them, I didn't want her the way she wanted me, and yet I went to her window; knowing that she would have one of those warm burgers waiting for me, she'd already paid for it and was holding it where I could see it, but even worse than that, I could smell it as well.

I caught a whiff of it and then saw her, she was smiling at me as always; and yet this smile felt different, though I had no idea why yet, and I was about to find out; she wore that "cat that swallowed the canary" kind of smile but I was so hungry while I was trying to keep an eye out for someone that might know I wasn't supposed to be there yet.

At that moment I was thinking that maybe I should have asked her if I could just skip the line and meet her at the side door where she entered; not because I thought I was better than anyone and didn't have to wait in line, but because then I could go and eat my burger without being caught by the wrong teacher seeing me out there.

Still, I knew that I was asking a lot and that she might want me to give her something in return for that and I didn't want to go over to her house to help her with her homework after school or anything like that, which was what I figured that she was going to ask me to do.

Though I'd told her more than once that I wasn't interested, she didn't seem to be getting the message and I really didn't feel that I needed to spend the time and patience to explain any better than I already had, I didn't want to overstate the obvious because to be honest, I really liked the burger and that it was occasionally free was nice too; I didn't want to give it up by being too honest or blunt about it.

Most of the guys I knew hated those burgers and most of the girls wouldn't touch them, but the guys were always too lazy to make their own lunch, or too caught up in the image that they felt they needed to show everyone and that didn't include brown bagging it; yet they never ate anything else either and were the ones constantly complaining that they were hungry.

They said that the brown bag didn't match their shoes or other things that made no sense like that; and that my burgers came either plain or with that yellow cheese that tasted like melted plastic, with the occasional pickle thrown in, almost by accident.

It sat in the freezer first, a frozen, preformed patty that probably came with a lot of things mixed in with that little bit of beef that it contained; and I would have to admit that it did taste like cardboard if you ate it without the bread or any dressing thrown on top.

Maybe that was something broken in me; but I loved those burgers and would eat them every chance that I got, but then again; it might just be further proof that I was very hungry and how difficult it was for me to wait for second lunch.

Caroline kept smiling at me, and she waved at me as I got closer to the front of the line; she seemed to be even more impatient for me to get there than usual, and that alone should have told me to turn tail and run but as I said; I was really hungry and it smelled so good that I was caught; even though I knew that something was up there was nowhere for me to go now but up there and face the dreaded music.

There really was no big deal about that burger except that she liked me and she knew that it made me happy, and I kept pretending that I couldn't hear her when she asked me for more, I kept cupping my hand over my ear but even I knew that she wasn't going to fall for this act for much longer.

Especially since some of the people close to me weren't seeing what I was trying to do and were either telling me what she said, or looking at me as if to say, "You really can't hear her?" and the, upon realizing that I could didn't understand why I was acting as though I didn't.

Then I was at the front and couldn't pretend anything anymore, it was time to put up or shut up and I was hoping I could do the latter but it wasn't going to be my day, "Are you going to Cindy's party?" she said, "It's this Saturday night and everyone is going to be there!" she said excitedly, "It might even be the party of the year, she even hired a band to play live music!" she said excitedly and then stopped when I mumbled something that she couldn't quite hear.

I was hoping that she'd heard me when I said yes, and that it would be enough for her to know I was going to be there; that she would now hand me the burger and I could be on my way, the party was three days away after and a lot of things could change by then.

But she wasn't done yet, and she wasn't going to let me off that easily; so she asked me again as I got closer, this time I told her I didn't know because I wasn't invited, and I hadn't heard anything about it; but that was a lie, everyone was talking about it and it was going to be epic, I was planning on going but I wasn't going to take anyone with me, "What kind of band and what kind of music do they play?" I asked, as if I hadn't a clue.

Then I showed her a weak smile that made me feel even more lame than I already did; but she wasn't listening to that either and was waiting with an answer for me, "I'm inviting you, silly boy!" she said and everyone around that heard was now laughing at me.

I looked around me then, as if I could find a sympathetic face or someone that understood and would help me, but no one was feeling sympathetic or helpful that day; but now the girl behind me wasn't doing her nails anymore because she was watching me and waiting for me to move, the two guys behind her almost pushed her aside because they were really impatient to hear what I was going to tell her.

Though I didn't know why they would have cared and thought they were just trying to intimidate me into a quick answer so we could all move on and didn't seem to care how embarrassing this was for me, or maybe they thought I might have a good answer that they could use if they were caught like I was.

Now I was finally at the front of the line, there was no one between us to hide behind or act confused about; she was holding my burger and smelling it as if it were the sweetest rose in history, I reached for it and she pulled it back, pretending again that it smelled like anything but cardboard and stale bread and waited for me.

I saw there was another one there as well, waiting for me, and then she asked me again, "ARE you going to Cindy's party on Saturday?" and held the burger as if she were weighing it; I could feel the people behind me getting impatient but I didn't know what to say to make her just give it to me and let me go.

Then I tried again, I told you, I wasn't invited!" I said, pretending that she wasn't trying to blackmail me into going with her, I reached for the other burger because she wasn't holding onto it but she pulled it back out of my reach, I should have just left then, cut my losses because even as hungry as I was; no burger was worth this much trouble; especially one that was only a buck and there was nothing special about it, but I felt weak and hungry and probably wasn't thinking right with the pressure of all those others behind me.

I felt that the line was divided then, one side wanted me to say yes and go with her, thinking it was romantic, but that was the girls and how they thought; the other side, the guys, just wanted to see me squirm and then hear how I was going to get out of it, but the smart money said I wasn't, and the thing they all had in common was that they all just wanted it to be over now so they could complain about the "cardburgers" as they ate them and then went to the next class.

"That's why I'm inviting you silly!" she said and giggled as if that was just a formality; "She told me that I could invite you, and I don't know what it was that you did to make her angry with you, but it wasn't easy to get her to say yes, let me tell you!" she said and smiled so sweetly that I couldn't believe a smile like that could twist my arm so savagely at the same time.

"What happened between the two of you anyway? Why was she so angry at you?" she asked me as if I was going to tell her; I heard her but my eyes, my focus was on the burger as she kept spinning it around the counter with her forefinger; I wanted to make her stop, she was going to cut a hole in the middle but I knew she wouldn't have heard me.

When it was clear that I wasn't going to answer, she stopped smiling and then asked, "So…are you going?" she said, just a little too sweetly as she pulled the burger back once more when she felt my fingers on it, I was so crazed with hunger now that I wanted to lick my fingers but the girl behind me cut in, "Come on man! Lunch is only half an hour!" she said, "Just tell her your going to the damned party and get the hell out of here!" she said, not sweetly at all.

I looked at her for a moment and was going to point out to her that it might do her some good to skip a few meals and lose that winter fat but I didn't want to get in that mud with her and just let it go, I looked behind her at the rest of the line and they all looked really pissed, most of them weren't talking, but if they were; it was about me Caroline and what I was trying not to agree to.

Knowing that none of them were going to help me, I turned back to her one more time and tried to reason with her, though I knew that she wasn't going to give in either; I knew her answer before I said it.

"Come on Caroline!" I pleaded with her; "You know I'm late for gym class and have to go, just give me my lunch, PLEASE?" I asked, as nicely and as patiently as I could, neither of which I was feeling at that moment, so it was a stretch.

I was begging now, which never came easy for me and I could see that it wasn't working so I was just hoping that I didn't sound as lame and moronic as I felt at that moment; everyone behind me groaned loudly as she smiled so sweetly at me and said, "Not until you tell me you're going!" and once again, put it under her nose and pretended that she was really enjoying the fragrance of warmed-over cardboard.

Then I took a moment and looked behind me once more and saw a lot of angry and impatient faces glaring back at me; I relented because I had no choice and then muttered "Okay" as the line cheered and clapped as they heard me, they were happy that I was going to get out of the way and I was again foolishly thinking that it was over and I could have my lunch when she said, "With me!" and my heart sank once more.

It was no use arguing and I gave in to her and the rest of the line was surging past me; I knew I was going to be late now and Coach Sanford was going to "Chew my ass off" because I made him wait and he had much better things to do; that's what he told anyone that had the temerity to be late for his class.

"Promise me?" she said, and again, she smiled so sweetly that it made me wonder how anyone could blackmail me so cold-heartedly while showing me such a sweet smile at the same time.

"I promise dammit!" I said to her impatiently, "I said I would, didn't I?" I almost shouted at her, "No burger is worth all of this trouble, and now I gotta get out of here before its too late!" I said as the rest of the crowd pushed me aside and surged forward impatiently.

That was when I found out that it was already too late, as I was opening my mouth to take a bite at last, out of the corner of my eye I saw her eyes flash wide open and then I heard Coach Sanford as he grabbed the back of my shirt and a large hank of my hair along with it.

"Am I wrong, or are you supposed to be here?" he said, "Don't you have a gym class at this time?" he asked as he shook me back and forth; he made a point of looking at his wrist but I wasn't going to be the one to remind him that he never wore a watch.

The crowd was cheering loudly now, applauding my capture and even more; the punishment that they knew I was going to be getting because everyone knew the coach and how he dealt with "non-athletes" as we were.

I tried to reason with him, "I'm sorry coach, but I was hungry!" I made the mistake of saying, "I was going to go right to the class after I ate this!" I told him, then I realized what I'd just said to him and tried to shift gears, but he wasn't having any of it.

He held onto my shirt as he walked us back to the gym and I tried to keep my feet under me as he dragged me along, "You don't make me wait!" he said angrily, MY time is worth something, even if yours isn't!" he said and again shook me by the collar of my shirt; I took one look back at Caroline and scowled at her before he dragged me off again.

She stuck her tongue out playfully, but I could tell by the look on her face that she was worried about what he was going to do to me; I was hoping that whatever it was, that I would have to stay home this Saturday night and do it, and darn it all and curse my luck but that would mean that I couldn't go to the party with her, I'd have a good excuse, caused in part by her holding out so long and getting the crowd into it that way.

But I could tell that she did feel bad for me and that made it sting a little less, though it was embarrassing to be dragged away like that in front of everyone; but it made all of them happy at least as they turned back to ordering their own pressed cardboard burgers with the occasional pickle and ketchup, tainted with thousand island dressing.

Through all of that, and as far as I was with the coach I could still tell that she wasn't sorry enough and was not going to let me off the hook; I was doomed to attend Cindy's party, with her dragging me along same as the coach was doing.

I knew there was a reason I didn't normally go to these kinds of parties, there were too many of the same people I saw all week for one thing; but this was going to be even worse this time, I was now going to be her date.

"I don't cate if you are starving to death boy, you come to my office and I'll call the damned ambulance, but you don't make me wait!" the coach said, interrupting my thoughts on the subject. He was still dragging me along by the collar, but he stopped at the door leading into the gym and said, "As son as you get your shorts on, you are going to run the bleachers!" he said, and when I didn't react he said, "That means for the entire period!" he shouted at me, "Am I understood?" he said, but he didn't wait for the answer, instead he opened the door and stepped through, leaving me on my own to follow.

I opened the door in time to hear him say, "If you finish before the end of the period, you keep running until the bells rings for the next class, and then you can stop!" he said, clearly angry; and yet I didn't think this was that bad a thing and he was over reacting, but I didn't tell him that.

"If I have to, I will hold your hand and explain to the next teacher why you're late for that class, I am sure they won't understand either and will want to deal with that in their own way!" he said with a smirk that told me he already knew that would not be sympathetic to me.

"Remember that if I look up there, and it happens to be the one time that you miss a step; either on purpose or accidently, if you slip and fall and gash open your knee but don't start again where you left off, and I promise you that you will be running those bleachers for the rest of this month!" but he didn't know me that well.

Most guys hated running the bleachers and would walk as soon as he was out of sight; or they would skip rows on purpose, but I didn't mind because it gave me a lot of time to myself; if there was anyone else near, they couldn't talk so it was nice to have the quiet and I loved the run, it was good for me.

I could be all alone with my thoughts as long as I kept my eyes on the steps in front of me; knowing that if I didn't and I fell that I would bleed to death before the coach would send anyone up there to help me. It also got me away from the jocks, and that was always a good thing; though it wasn't that they were bad guys and some were actually pretty decent guys, but the "superstars" that demanded the special jock treatment and slack the coach gave them because they were starters on the football team or something and they thought they deserved homage from us as well, some of us; such as myself didn't see it that way though, and I didn't even try to hide it.

Some guys didn't care about anything long as they got along and got through the day, they were used to being shuttled around like cattle, but those guys didn't matter either because the jocks took advantage of them, they tried to do stupid things to us like make us wait longer to get into the shower; sometimes by then the hot water was gone and you were lucky if it was lukewarm.

They acted as though we might contaminate them with our "normal bodies" and minds, and while we were trying to dress in front of our lockers they would shove their way past as if we were in their way, if any decided to stand up for ourselves, we would be outnumbered by at least four to one and that didn't count the coach who would also be there for them, he would always say that his boys would never do anything like that.

When they got away from that, from the other guys on the team and the school, they were alright; when they forgot they were supposed to be special, like everyone else, they had their moments too.

I had my day though, and I did hit the quarterback, and I know I hurt him because he didn't up right away and he didn't play the game for the next two weeks and he was first-string and all conference whatever that meant; his excuse was that he hit his head in practice, but everyone knew he hit his head on my fist and it had nothing to do with practice; and though no one said anything to me about it, I ran the bleachers those two weeks and then another just for good measure.

That day, he was walking behind two of his linemen; big, stupid as a bag of hammers guys that didn't know anything but to hit the guy in front of them; shoved me out of the wayand I guess I felt that I'd taken enough of it and I took my wet toweland squeezed it on his back.

He stopped and turned to face me, but his boys didn't hear him stop of didn't notice and kept going so this time at least, it was fair; he looked at the linemen but they couldn't hear him with all the noise going on in there and he thought I would see who it was and back down, that was because he didn't know me.

Reaching up with both hands, he tried to shove me in the chest, but I was ready and braced and hardly moved at all, he turned to say something to his friends who were now running towards us, bearing down on me.

I was quicker than he was though, and when he turned back towards me and raised his hands to fight I threw out a quick jab that caught him flush across his chin, I shot it straight out with my elbow locked and he tried to turn away from it, so it went from my right to his left with a perfect follow through, I knocked him into the lockers where he slid slowly down to the floor with a silly grin on his face.

His friends got there then and jumped me, and some other guys were in that mix but I'm not sure if they were trying to hep me or them because everybody was all tangled up; they got in a few hits, but because there were so many of us tightly packed in like that, they weren't getting full swings at me and they didn't hurt, they were mostly token hits though I covered up just the same.

They were all more concerned with Randy; he was the starting quarterback after all and it was only two days till the next "big game" was on, now his eyes were opening but he started blinking rapidly and drool was coming out of the corner of his mouth as it began opening slowly but if he was trying to talk it wasn't working and he wasn't saying anything intelligible.

A lot of the guys were still wrestling with me but their punches were hitting air and missing me entirely, it made me wonder if that was how they hit when they played football and no wonder we were having a losing season this year; then the coach ran and everyone stopped fighting "What the hell is going on in my gym?" he shouted.

"Are you boys having a party in my gym? On MY time?" he shouted across the room, and then the crowd parted, and he saw Randy on the floor; he was now starting to waken and was trying to get up but he wasn't ready yet and it wasn't working; he ran quickly over to him and I had to admit that I'd never seen him move so fast before, but he looked really scared.

He tried to help his QB up and then yelled at the other guys to help him get him on his feet, Randy was breathing normally, and he smiled at us then, so I knew he was still "loopy" and was clearly not all there.

Then the coach stopped and turned, looked to the rest of us suddenly and suspiciously and saw the guard and tackle still held my by the throat; when a fight broke out and any of his players were involved, if they were winning he had a tendency to look the other way unless it got serious; but god help the other kid of he was winning because he was right on top of it then and he never came alone either, he would say later that he didn't want his boys to lose their confidence or anything like that.

He looked at me then and saw red; "Son of a bitch, tell me that you didn't hit him! That you didn't sucker punch my starting quarterback before the big game, that you didn't slam him senseless into the lockers!" he said, and I knew he didn't care about the kid as much as the big game because he was scared he was losing his job as a football coach.

The problem wasn't the players, he had four starters returning on the offensive line, they'd been a unit for two years and were solid, his defensive front was strong as well, his QB had a cannon for an arm but didn't have the brains to use it right and the players were all tired of his "rah-rah" approach and were looking for some real leadership which he was fresh out of and that was the real problem; they were tuning him out and running their own plays.

"Tell me that isn't what happened! Did you trip him?" he shouted at me as they finally let me go and stepped back from me, they were as afraid that he as going to hit them as they were expecting him to get to me and deal with this.

By the look on his face he seemed to have lost it and was why they let me go as they did; they were afraid of him too, it wasn't respectful but that didn't mean I was going to be afraid of him as well; there was really nothing he could do to me that would bother me.

Though I wasn't stupid either; I didn't act as brave as I was feeling either, but then we were all kids, and I admit that I was scared by that look in his eyes as he walked towards me than I was of any of his linemen hitting me.

"Okay coach!" I said, "I didn't sucker punch your starting QB, nor did I trip him into the lockers to knock him out, I came at him the same way they come up the middle on your line, I came straight at him and punched him in the face and none of what you thought happened did in here!" I explained it to him nice and slow as I held my hands up to show him, I didn't have brass knuckles or anything else that might have hurt him.

Everyone else that was there thought that maybe I did and they were all waiting for him to deal with it; they were holding their breath because some of them thought that he would kill me for hurting his quarterback and they didn't want to miss it.

"I want to know, who the hell helped him because there isn't a boy in this room that is quick enough to get in a punch against this boy, not a one of you!" he said and looked around at them, daring the "culprit" to come forward and identify himself or point them out.

Then he noticed that Randy was struggling again, and now he wasn't smiling either, he was looking around as if he'd just arrived and didn't know what the fuss was about.

"Tell me boy" the coach said, "You take a look around this locker room and tell me who it was that tripped you, who did this to you, you point him out and we'll do the rest!" he said, "Just point out the coward that blind-sided you and I'll do the rest!" he said and looked at me expectantly.

Randy stopped then and looked around the room slowly, and his gaze even swept by me once or twice before he stopped and slowly raised his hand and pointed it right at me, he was trying to say something but his speech was slurred and drooled dripped again from the corner of his mouth.

The coach turned towards me again, angrier now that he thought I was trying to get away with it, Lord hates a liar, and if HE can't abide them, why should I?" he said to me, though I knew he wasn't waiting for an answer.

He started to walk towards me s he rolled up his sleeve and I was bracing myself for a hit when Randy grabbed at his shirt and tried to pull him back, he slapped at his hand but Randy refused to let go; coach turned to yell at whoever it was and then saw that it was Randy.

"Son, you try and relax, think about the game plan we talked about and let me deal with this, Thomas! Go get the nurse!" he shouted as he looked past Randy and then turned away from him.

"But coach" Randy said as he reached for him again, he stopped long enough to take a deep breath because just standing there was difficult for him, but he wasn't going to quit either, at least not until he spoke his mind about it. "He didn't trip me, and it was clean, not a sucker punch, I saw it coming but didn't move fast enough to get out of the way! It was fair and he caught me on the chin!" he said.

When everyone stopped and it was quiet, he said, "It was nothing more than a disagreement and I was out of line to start with!" he told them and then looked at me and then back at his coach.

Then he smiled at me, and I wondered how hard I'd hit him or that maybe he hit his head on the floor too hard because I thought normally he would just sit back and let the coach rip me a new one and then later tell him that I was innocent.

Later, I would joke about him, saying "It's not like you were a linebacker or something serious!" and we would both laugh about it, we actually became good friends after all the smoke cleared, I helped him into the stretcher that day but the coach never took his eyes off me, I don't know what he thought but he was looking at me as though I was controlling his QB or something and he didn't understand how.

So, once again, I was forced to run the bleachers, and even though I took the entire hour to run them, he made me run them again because he thought I was cheating him somehow, as it didn't take me as long.

As I ran them, I could see the others in my class, they were playing basketball this time, the weather was so nice we would be out there all week and a couple of them saw me up there and yelled to me; they were thinking that because they hated running the bleachers that I did too, they were jeering at me but I pretended that I didn't hear them and just kept running.

I slowed my pace a bit though because I didn't want the coach to be happy and even more importantly; I wanted him to leave me alone, though I did run them the way he wanted me to; from one end to the other and no skipping even a single step; when I was finally done, I let him know and then went to hit the shower.

Since I was actually feeling good and most of the others were already done and went on to the next class so I pretty much had the showers all to myself, and it felt weird, I couldn't remember that ever happening before and

I thought that was why it felt odd but I should have known better, it couldn't be that easy.

I remember thinking that "Things were just too damned perfect sometimes!" as I stepped into the still hot water, but as I stood in there and let the water run over my body I got the feeling that I was being watched, even though I knew I was alone because when I came in there I heard my feet echo through the almost empty locker room and there was no reason why those last "stragglers" would still be there.

"Things are just too perfect sometimes!" I thought to myself as I stepped into the hot water, I stood there for a few to let the water run over my body; it felt as though all of the muscle aches and whatever else was on my mind was washing away with the water as I stood there.

Then my thoughts were interrupted because I felt as though I was being watched again, even though I knew I was all alone in there; when I first came into the locker room everyone else was leaving and I heard my feet echo through the empty room after a few minutes, I thought I saw the last guys wander out as I went into the shower and thought I was alone.

Just to be sure, I turned the water off to listen, but all I could hear was the water running down the drain or dripping off the shower head and onto the tiled floor, I turned the water back on because I was getting cold, but I was afraid to wash my face because I couldn't shake that feeling of being watched, it was eerie and I didn't want to close my eyes.

As I sat down in front of my locker and was getting ready to dress, I leaned back and was trying to figure out what was going on, the aches I felt from the run had washed away from me and I should have been relaxing and feeling good about life, instead I was hearing and imagining things that weren't there.

I closed my eyes and then I heard that same voice again, calling out the name "Eduardo" which meant nothing to me; I thought I'd imagined it; or that I had my mind "open" to my thoughts about the wall and that window where I heard the voice, but then I heard it again, clearly calling for someone but I had no idea whoever the hell it was.

Then I was going to shout out to leave me alone, that whoever they were looking for wasn't here but it felt weird because I knew I was alone, then I saw the spider leg in my memory and got off my butt and tried to dress as quickly as I could, if that spider somehow followed me here, I didn't want to be alone when it found me here, all the time I was keeping an eye out for any arachnid legs or anything else that might jump out at me.

Because I was so scared, and having that, "hand at the base of your spine" kind of feeling; the kind where it's not quite touching your skin but close enough to let you know it's lurking there kind of scared, I was afraid to turn around and see who or what was calling out from the shadows and fell forward as I tried to pull my pants up, I think I was trying to do too many things at once and needed to focus or I'd never get my pants up.

I quickly looked around, though I was not afraid of being embarrassed, as if anyone saw me; but more so to see if anything was creeping up behind me as I lay there, then I thought it was waiting for me to fall like that so it could pounce on me while I was down and still confused.

Then I finally got up and turned all around me to see what was coming and almost screamed when I felt a hand on my shoulder and then fell again; my legs were too tangled up in my pants as I tried to run, and I almost hit my head on the hard surface of the tiles but caught myself just in time, though it felt as though I'd broken both my wrists trying to break my fall and save my face from that collision.

Then I turned again, expecting something to be ready to jump me so I covered my head as best I could, and then heard the coach say, "Calm down son, I'm not going to hit you!" he said, "I just need a word with you and wanted to remind you to come by my office for a pass to your next teacher!" he told me, looking closely now to see if I was doing drugs or something.

His look made me wonder what he was thinking, as if he was worried about my mental health or something, I muttered, "Thanks coach!" as he turned to leave, "I was hoping that you'd remember that!" I said, trying not to sound too lame or anything but I didn't want to be alone anymore and started looking for my shoes.

"So, coach, what's on your mind?" I asked him, sounding just like my counselor when I had a problem and he'd look up from his desk to see me there; I tried again to pull up my pants because its amazing how helpless I felt when my pants were down.

He looked at me for a moment and almost answered, then he thought better and said, "Finished getting dressed and come to my office!" he said and then dismissed me, he left without waiting to see if I'd heard or was going to do what he said, but since it was going to help me and wouldn't have detention for being late he knew I would.

I sat down again and wondered of it was the coach that was calling out that way; and why couldn't he have said something instead of creeping out of the shadows that way and scaring the hell out of me, and as I was thinking about that, I heard the voice calling out again, but this time it had a different timbre, it sounded as if it was dead or coming from deep in the earth, but which was worse, I thought under the earth because then I could at least run and have a chance, but if it was dead and in here it was a different game altogether.

Having enough of guessing and being scared that way, I grabbed my shoes; having finally wrestled my pants up and then I ran out of the locker room and straight into the coaches office, I jumped into a chair and started putting my shoes on and tying them as I waited for him to talk to me and pretended that nothing was wrong and this was all perfectly normal.

I knew that I broke the rules by not knocking before I came in, there was a sign on the door reminding us of that, but the coach didn't seem to mind or notice and to be honest; he seemed preoccupied as well, but I couldn't be sure because he wasn't my favorite instructor and I didn't like being around him.

Thinking about all of this as I finished dressing, I pulled my shirt over my head and then took it off because it was inside out, it looked as though he as having a hard time getting the words out, that he was embarrassed about something and that really intrigued me, now I had to know, and had no idea at the time or I would have taken advantage of it.

"So, coach, what's up?" I asked him, as I kept one eye on the locker room; I was half-hoping that someone would come out and start laughing at the look on my face as they pulled off that trick, but there was still no one there but the coach and I, and I knew for certain that it wasn't him, it sounded like a female voice, though raspy and evil sounding by its nature.

Having no real idea what this was about but I was glad he wasn't angry with me and going to punish me further for this "infraction" of his rules; and I was hoping inside that he was changing his mind about me and was going to let up, not jump on me so hard, and with both feet every time I stepped out of line.

When I looked back at him, he was still watching me as he thought about what he brought me there to tell me, I knew it wasn't just the hall pass, when he finally spoke he was still bothered by something and wasn't familiar with that feeling when dealing with students; he wasn't sure how to act now and still keep his tough guy image as he felt his job demanded that he become.

"Do you remember that aptitude test they made you take a few weeks ago?" he finally asked me, and I wasn't sure what he meant; he made me take a form and fill it out, general questions about my life and the school and I thought nothing of it; but now he was telling me what it was and now I was curious too.

"Yeah!" I said, you said it was a form that they were giving to everyone randomly, now your telling me it was something more, that it was an aptitude test and you were checking my answers against the national average or something?" I said to him.

"But I took that test a while ago, I guess that I forgot about it, until now; until you mentioned it, I mean!" I confessed, "What does that have to do with the P.E. class?" I asked him as I slowly began to realize what he was trying not to tell me.

"I remember, you sent me to Miss Patterson's class to take it!" I said, it was all coming back to me now, I liked Miss Patterson; she was every teenage boy's fantasy; she had all the curves and the looks to drive our hormones up a few thousand notches.

Some of us were asking her for help with things that we had no problem with just because she would lean onto our desks to talk to us; she was very pretty, with bright eyes and a killer smile, but we were all hoping for that really clear view down the front of her blouse, and she never seemed to notice where our eyes were, and if she did; she didn't seem to care.

He looked at me for a minute with a sheepish look on his face because he already knew about that and he could tell by expression what I was thinking about by the look on my face; it made me laugh that a teacher knew about it and wondered how he felt about it.

"You have a new schedule, with a different curriculum and you're out of this class now!" he said, and I could tell that he was hoping I wouldn't connect the dots and catch the irony of that; but then, he didn't know why I was stalling and trying so hard to stay in his office; he could see that I was distracted but he had no idea why and didn't try to figure it out because he really didn't care enough to look that deep.

"I'm a gym teacher and a coach, not a damned head-shrinker, I'm not a wet nurse and I ain't your mommy!" he said when one of his boys wasn't asking for help, and since I wasn't one of his boys I already knew the drill.

"I'm sorry, but I'm not getting it!" I confessed, and deep down, I think that I did but I wanted to torture him a little for making me run the bleachers again, even though it was good for me, at least until I got into the shower.

He took a deep breath then, and looked at the ceiling for a moment before he answered me, he was becoming even more impatient with me now; "Son, I don't know why, I think they made a mistake again, but they think your some kind of big-brain or something; that you haven't been challenged enough with the schedule and classes that you have now!" he said and then smirked before going on.

"Too easy and boring, and they want you to transfer to another class with some older kids, a special class for students like you, and that class is the same time as this class, so starting tomorrow, you will be going to first lunch instead of here!" and his voice trailed off as he got to the end of that sentence because he didn't want me to hear it, but the lights were on brightly and I knew what that meant.

"There!" he said, with finality; "It's out there, and if you want to be mad at me for making you run the bleachers when you didn't do anything wrong, then so be it!" he said, "You go ahead and be angry with me, it isn't the first nor the last time a kid was upset at me for doing my job!" he told me, but it was clear that it did bother him that he punished me, and I could tell that he loved that expression, "so be it" and used it whenever something went wrong; he lost the big game or it was rained out, for him, that expression was a blanket statement that covered everything, for him, it was the wise thing to say and it was as deep as he ever got about life.

He watched me, he was waiting for me to get angry but that wasn't going to happen; "They wanted to know how you felt about that, and Mr. Edwards asked me to talk to you about it because your counselor isn't here today, so, is that good enough for you? Does that work for you?" he asked, though he clearly didn't care and was just waiting for me to leave so he wouldn't have to admit that he was wrong.

"Sure coach!" I said, "I was just asking because I've never been in your office before and didn't know what you wanted!" I said as I looked at him and tried not to smile because this time I had him by the short hairs.

But this "voice out of nowhere" thing was bothering me, and it was making me nervous and I had the feeling again that something huge and deadly was going to charge out of the locker room at any moment and kill both of us.

For a moment, I thought about asking him to come with me and then, once outside, calling the exterminator but I knew he would never leave and as soon as he could he would call for the men in the white coats to come and take me away if I told him what I thought was happening.

This was really frustrating; he was the kind of official or adult that I should be able to turn to for help; and yet I knew that if I did; I would spend the rest of my life weaving baskets and chasing imaginary butterflies around my head and that wasn't how I wanted to spend my life.

Probably because of that and my over-active imagination, I suddenly got this image of him being found alone in his office later on; his emaciated body covered in spider webbing, and his long and boney finger was pointed at me, no matter where I would stand in the room, as if this was my fault that he wouldn't listen when I tried to warn him.

Then he got a look at my face; maybe a taste of my thoughts or something because he suddenly gave me a "What" kind of expression so I tried to explain, "Coach, when you went into the locker room to find me, did you, you know... hear something else perhaps?" I asked, not trying to sound crazy or tip my hand too soon, "Ile someone calling a name or anything like that?" I asked and then held my breath.

"What name would that be son?" he asked and then again looked at the ceiling, "Are you hearing voices now?" he asked me, clearly anxious for me to leave and this conversation to be over with.

They said he really was a nice guy and a good coach, but since he had no patience for guys like me, guys that he knew could play sports and be very good at it but chose not to, for whatever reason; in my case I didn't want to because I liked "freelancing when I played and didn't want the coach telling me where to position myself, I had a good feel for where the play was going when we played in the park and he'd heard about that from others that wanted him to put me on the team, but I refused, politely, but firmly.

He tossed me the excuse for my next class, as if he couldn't stand to touch it for a moment longer and then looked at me as if to say "we're done" as he waited for me to leave.

"Never mind, coach!" I said, "It must have been my imagination, or maybe it was someone outside the gym and close enough that it sounded as though they were in here!" I didn't believe it, but I thought it was what he wanted to hear.

"Get your butt over to Mr. Andrews, isn't he your counselor" he asked me, but he already knew, "I didn't hear anyone but you traipsing around the gym, and you had better have not left your towel on the bench when you left!" he said, a pet peeve of his that everyone knew about once we came into the class.

I remembered that I ran off so fast that I left the towel there, but out of the corner of my eye, I remembered seeing it fall on the floor. I was going to get it on my way out and put it in the basket, which would have made him happy and maybe given me a brownie point for being a good boy.

But that voice, and the fact that he made me run the bleachers when I was where I was supposed to be was stuck in my craw and In didn't want to let it go; even though neither of us knew that he was wrong at them time; I was determined to leave it there now, that he would find it and remember who left it there as a final poke at him for what he did to me; if he would have said "Sorry" or shown what his friend Johnny would say, "A modicum of remorse" it would have been different though.

"Yes sir!" I said crisply; I will check in with my counselor and then look at this class, I guess I'll be on my way then, if there's nothing else?" I asked, I felt as though he wanted to say something, so I asked; but I was still half-hoping for an apology or something that sounded like it, so it was a good thing that I wasn't holding my breath.

I knew that he wanted me to leave so I picked up the pass and reluctantly stepped out of the chair, I was ready to leave when the phone rang and I took it as a sign that I could stay a little longer; he snapped the phone up as if he was on fire and it was the hotline to the fire station.

"Hello?" he said into the phone, "Oh yeah, I was waiting for your call and was hoping you'd remember!" he said and then laughed, "No!" he said, "Not at all!" he laughed, "I was just taking care if this little pain in the ass kid that was in my class this period!" he spoke into the phone and half turned away from me, I wasn't sure if he forgot I was there or thought I couldn't hear if he did, but he didn't even bother to lower his voice.

"Yeah, you know how it goes, first they get the idea that they are something special and then some teacher gets her butt up about it and now he's trying to sell me the idea that he's hearing voices!" he said; and then he really laughed.

He stopped laughing when the caller spoke and then he answered, "Yeah, I miss the good old days; when we could swat their spoiled little asses into good behavior, they didn't "have problems" in those days, they just needed discipline!" he said, as if he was alone or I couldn't hear him, though he was glaring right at me.

I couldn't have told you if I was being polite or nosey, but I waited for a moment and still couldn't hear what the reply to that statement was but after a short pause, I heard the coach say, "Yeah, I know! No wonder tigers eat their young!" and I got up and left him laughing about that.

When I stepped out of his office I heard the voice again; this time it was shouting at me, "Edddduuuarrrdooooo!" and no matter what direction I thought to turn that I might escape was useless as well because it seemed to be coming from all around me this time and there was nowhere to run.

I was so afraid, I felt as though I'd jumped out of my own skin and I ran back into the coach's office again; and once more, without knocking or waiting for him to invite me in; and I felt even less welcomed this time when he saw me and then he stood up; clearly he was not at all happy that I was there once more.

Standing there, I tried to think of a reason to be there and then I asked him, Coach, since I have first lunch now, and I missed my lunch break, does that mean that I can go now and have my lunch?" I asked, I was trying to look serious, but it sounded funny even to me, "Or should I ask my counselor about that?" I said.

He looked at me for a long minute, and this was one of those times when someone looked so angry that you could cook an egg on their head moments; "You get your sorry ass out of here, and I mean right this minute; or you can forget about your lunch break for a few months because I will make sure you run for both lunches instead, how's that for an answer?" he said and then it was his turn to laugh.

That was enough and I back-pedaled out the door just as the bell rang and the next class came trickling in; they were talking about the game they'd just won or lost, I couldn't tell for certain, others were talking about girls but looking at them and hearing their words didn't add up and I knew they were making it up; the girls they were talking about would never do those things, at least not with those guys.

I went to my counselor and waited outside of his office until he called me in, he saw me smile and said, "For once, you're in here for something good!" and then he laughed.

It wasn't like I was a problem child or anything like that; it just seemed that I liked to challenge authority, though not aggressively, I just had a problem when I knew they were wrong and were not going to admit it; even when it's obvious; I used my smarts to make them see that I got it right, that I understood their game plan but not the plays they were drawing up.

As a result, he and I came to some sort of understanding; I didn't mind listening to him; he was my counselor after all, and there to help people like me get a better education, but I liked that he never once talked down to me as if I wouldn't understand.

"This class is a new idea, a fast track to a better education for guys like you!" he said, "This is actually a chance that a lot of kids would kill for and you are being invited, doesn't that make you feel good?" he asked with a huge smile on his face, "Just give it a try and see what happens, heck, you might even like it!" he told me.

If it was anyone else but him, I would think they were just trying to sell me on the idea, that they would either look good in the eyes of their superiors for it, or they would get a bonus for talking me into it; but this was my counselor, and I trained him right, others complained about theirs but we hit it off from the start and were almost like partners sometimes.

"It's actually a college-level class and it should be more of a challenge for you!" he said, "Something like this would stretch your comfort zone and make you think about the things we are trying to teach you!" he said, and then we both laughed.

When I left his office, I thought he was right, that I had nothing to lose by attending this class and seeing what he was talking about, I tried to keep an open mind, and the next day I entered the class nervously; the first thing I noticed was how quiet it was in there; no one was talking out loud about anything, they were all sitting at their desks and waiting for the teacher to come in and start the class; this was so different from the room I was in yesterday, which seemed like a zoo by comparison.

Some teachers, when they can't control the students, tried to ignore what they did; instead they tried to focus on the ones that were there to learn, the bright, eager-minded students that reminded them of why they started teaching in the first place.

At least they made the effort and focused on what they felt was important or worth their time, at least they made the effort instead of "force-feeding" us what they were supposed to teach us in that class, some actually made it fun to learn, to attend the class at the very least, but those were rare these days.

Teachers blamed on the parents for not teaching and enforcing good manners and behavior at home, or reinforcing what they should have learned at school that day and examining their homework; knowing what they did in school that day and what was next, involving themselves in their child's life.

The parents in turn; blamed it on the teachers and the school curriculum; that it wasn't challenging enough or the reward wasn't sufficient motivation; that the teachers didn't care anymore and were only there for a paycheck, that they never even really saw or got to know their child at all and couldn't understand them and what they needed to motivate them to better behavior and learning.

The students, caught in the middle, if they cared they were hurt by it; they had nowhere to turn and no one saw that they needed help, some just went on as if it had always been that way; or it was supposed to be that way, they would see it in their friends and others and eventually would come to see it as normal; others didn't care to blame anyone, and didn't even care that there was someone to blame; they only cared that they were not getting the full measure of their education and couldn't wait to move on to the next level where they hoped it would be better.

Some teachers spent their whole day trying not to lose it on some kid whose parents never spanked him or disciplined him in any way, "they spared the rod and spoiled the child" as the expression went; he wasn't going to get it at school either, their hands were tied and spanking was not allowed anymore, punishments were designed to be more creative and yet because there was no element of fear, they didn't care and became bored with the punishment and it was no longer effective.

The funny thing about all of that was that, sometimes those kids gave off the impression that were practically begging for someone to tan their hide for what they'd done; to show that someone at least cared about them and what they did; they would welcome someone to stand there and show them the line they weren't allowed to cross, that they needed that discipline that was lacking everywhere they turned.

Looking the other way might have been the way some handled it; but this room was already filled with students that were eager to learn and came with the smarts to get it done. My problem was that I was the new kid once more and had to earn my place in the room once more.

Because they were the "brainiac's" of the school, there were more than a few nerdy kids in there, but there were also a few of the so-called "cool kids" in there too; the ones that might not brag to their friends for being there but did well just the same and belonged there as much as anyone, they weren't going to apologize for being smart or different, but they weren't going to rub it in the others faces because they weren't there as well.

It was, as they explained it to me, a prep class, and it wasn't going to be the easiest to pass but that was what made it so challenging and most of these guys and girls had never felt that before in any level of school, and maybe not anywhere else in their lives either, they embraced this challenge wholeheartedly.

I walked up to the desk and handed the teacher the slip they gave me for the class; "permission to be a big-brain" was what I called it, but not there of course; I didn't know how to act in there yet and didn't want to get kicked out on my first day.

As she looked at the slip, I looked around the room nervously when I heard her say, "They told me you were coming, do you go by Juan, or John, or Johnny?" she asked me, which do you prefer?" she waited with a smile on her face that made me feel as though she really did want to get it right.

"I'm Mrs. Johnson, and you can pretty much sit wherever you like, as you can see, we have plenty of room and lots of seats to chose from!" she said, and as I looked, she was right; the other classrooms were almost all full, wall to wall students, but here there was a lot of room and it felt different too.

But I also lingered there for a moment as she spoke because she was easily the most beautiful woman I'd ever seen; so beautiful that she made Miss Patterson look as normal and plain as everyone else, pretty and alluring enough to make us forget Miss Patterson altogether but for the cleavage, which you never saw from Mrs. Johnson, she was not more reserved in her behavior but was there to teach bus and not entertain us in that way.

She had really long and silky-black hair and huge brown eyes and freckles on her cheeks and dark-rimmed glasses that somehow made her look even prettier and smarter, all of that behind such a beautiful smile that you couldn't help but smile back, no matter what kind of day you were having before you walked through that door and entered her world.

That day, she was wearing this little pink dress, and it made her look younger than she was; at first, I almost thought she was an aide or something; it was short enough to show off her athletic legs and yet it was long enough that it kept her on the good side of the principal and the other administrators who worried about such things.

It worked well for her though; she almost looked like one of us, and the more I got to know about her, the more I felt that she almost was, she didn't act like a teacher that was always ready to impose her will on us; but more like a friend that knew a little bit more than we did and was only looking out for us.

At that moment, she must have known what I was thinking because she winked at me then nodded her head toward the others and said, "Someone has to be the teacher and be in charge, so have a seat!" she said and then laughed.

She was still smiling at me as she politely waited for me to move, and though it was an innocent smile, I was again taken back by how beautiful she was; and because I was looking at her, I tripped over another student's back pack and fell hard, landing on my butt.

I felt my face flush and knew it was a deep red now, and I thought that I couldn't have made a better first impression if I tried; the rest of the class roared with laughter, and it seemed as though I was getting good at giving the others a reason to either cheer me or jeer at me, I recognized some of them from the burger line when the coach caught me out there.

But there wasn't a guy in that class that hadn't at one time been exactly where I was now; stunned by her beauty and feeling like that deer caught in the headlights, with the attitude that made her feel as though she was one of us; it was easy to forget that she was also one of them at the same time.

Though I never gave it much thought until that day, there were girls that I knew that I'd never considered them especially smart; it was not that I thought they were dumb; I think it was more that they didn't flaunt their brains, they didn't want to be treated differently because they didn't feel different.

But even the smart girls couldn't get enough of us making fools of ourselves in front of her; and they laughed the loudest when it was as obvious as it was right now. I stood up slowly and dusted off my pants and then looked back to where I normally liked to sit, there were two seats left back there so I started walking that way when one of those linemen that hit like a girl was sitting, and he gave me one of those "don't even think about it" looks so I took the other one, a little further from him.

It turned out that the seat I chose was much nicer anyway; it was in the left-hand corner and right by the window which was always open, clean air when there was a breeze and fresh air when it rained, I smelled the freedom of being outside while looking into the eyes of the most beautiful woman that I'd ever seen.

There was a park right next to the school, and I could see a large part of that park from that window as well; and my first thought when I realized that was what a dumb-ass that guy was; I would have fought for this seat, I wasn't afraid of him anyway, but this was a nice view and over there I likely would have had to smell him as well as endure his looks meant to scare me.

Again, I thought, "No wonder we were losing so many games!" for all I knew, next to the quarterback, who was still my friend though somehow absent from this class, this guy was probably the smartest guy on the team, and that thought made me laugh really hard whenever I looked at him.

I ignored him staring at me as if he'd read my thoughts and opened the book to see what kind of things I was going to be learning in this class when I heard the door open again, and at first, I didn't even look up; I was leafing through the pages of the book and thinking that some of those things looked really cool.

But when I did look up, it was because I thought I'd heard a familiar voice, a girl that I knew from another class or something because she seemed so familiar, though I couldn't remember the name, I almost shouted out, "Hi Maria!" as if we were old friends, except that I'd never seen her before and couldn't have known her name.

There were several times over the years that I'd seen in the movies and heard guys talk about love at first sight and thought about what a joke that would make, how can you look at someone and get hit by the "lightning bolt" as they called it, and fall hopelessly and helplessly in love with a total stranger.

But then, I saw her, and I understood exactly what they meant as I watched her stand there, changing the air on the room; which was now brighter and cleaner than it was about five minutes ago.

She was taller than most of the girls my age, yet she wasn't shy about it; or apologetic as some girls were, she made it with her attitude that she wasn't going to stoop down so that she could be the same height as everyone else; she stood tall and straight as if she was telling everyone that if they had a problem with her height, it was their problem, and not hers.

She had no patience for guys that were shorter than her and wanted her to wear flats or sandals that kept their height to a minimum because anything with heels made them feel inadequate, but it wasn't her problem as she saw it.

I would have to be the first to admit that I liked that kind of confidence and wanted to know more about her, I felt already as though I'd known her all of my life, as if we were deeply committed to each other for some reason; I knew that I'd never seen her before because I would have remembered her if I had; but that something familiar about her made it seem so strange, so good and so exciting at the same time, as if life was suddenly going to get much better.

As I was thinking about those things, I made a mental note to find Miss Patterson and thank her for making me take that test; especially when I realized that the only seat left was the one directly to my right, there were others in the front, but I was happy to see her looking past them as she waited for Mrs. Johnson to tell her what was next for her.

"Sorry for being late, but there's an excuse they gave me from the office in with those papers too, I am a new student here!" she said, as if that explained everything, and in a way it did; that was why I'd never seen her before, and why she seemed to be such a "breath of fresh air" in my life, but it didn't explain the feeling of familiarity that was so prevalent.

As her eyes swept across the room, I saw the greenest eyes that I'd ever seen; she had strawberry blonde hair and I knew that I'd already made a great impression on her as she walked towards that seat next to me because she leaned over to me and whispered, "Close your mouth!" and then sat down as she sat down.

I was aghast and embarrassed, but she looked over at me for a moment and then we both started laughed a little about it and that made me feel a little less embarrassed about it; she was teasing me and it didn't hurt my feelings or anything, and again I got that "I know her" feeling because it was as if we were already comfortable talking to each other; moments like this were not as much embarrassing as they were funny for both of us.

The feeling around her was so comfortable that I felt as if she knew what I was thinking and we both knew what we were feeling but I kept thinking that I couldn't be that lucky, I thought that anyone that pretty and smart would either be one of those girls that had no time for dating because they studied so hard for college and whatever was next for them, or she had a boyfriend already, some smart, good looking guy, a quarterback or something because things like this didn't just happen every day.

Looking at her dress, I liked her style too; and when she sat down next to me, she made me the happiest guy in the school; maybe in the whole world because it felt so good, if we were forced to be there because they made the rules and we jumped through the hoops they set out for us, days like this one made it so much more bearable.

I learned that her name really was Maria, and tried to pretend that was coincidental; and then I learned a few things not to do if you were trying to impress her; twice, she rejected the overtures of the lineman that didn't want me to sit there, while at the same time, answering anything the class was asked about the assignment that none of us knew where to find the answers and none of us knew what it was.

Natural smarts too, I was impressed even more; not that she was doing it for me, but it was funny to me that, while the rest of us were shuffling through our books to find any answers, she didn't even open her book and spent her time waiting for us to catch up, but she wasn't being arrogant about it; it was as though she waited for someone else to answer, to give us a chance until it was clear that we didn't know.

Then I heard the bell that ended the class that seemed as though it started a minute ago; I guess it broke my heart because I didn't get to talk to her enough to know anything else, and I knew that if I felt something, that spark between us; that there might be a chance that she would feel that as well, maybe not as strong, or hopefully even stronger but, from my vantage point that was asking a lot.

When I stepped outside, the quad was alive with activity, it was where everything was centrally located, the administrative office, the counselor's office's, the lunch area and where the main part of the student body seemed to gravitate to at that time.

As I sat down to eat my cardboard for the day, it felt weird, I felt foreign now because I could just sit there and eat it and no one was looking for me because I was supposed to be somewhere else, I could just sit there and eat it without feeling I was about to get caught.

I bit into the rumor of a burger as I heard a familiar voice say, "You're not really going to eat that, are you?" and when I turned to look, there she was; carrying her brown bag lunch that suddenly seemed to be cooler than buying and eating the cardboard, it gave her more time to enjoy it as well because she didn't have to wait in that line.

I wondered what it was about that, people will always ask you a question like that, catch you off-guard when your mouth is full and you can't answer, just like the waitress that pops out of nowhere to ask, "How's the food?" as she puts her hand on your shoulder.

She caught me with a mouthful so I couldn't deny it; but I think that I'd never realized how dry they were until that moment, when I tried to finish chewing it and swallowing it and then answer her before she thought I was too slow and would move on.

My heart raced when she smiled at me, first because it made me feel good that she smiled at me that way; but then, for a moment I panicked, I thought she as going to move on when she said, Well! It seems that you are!" and then she sat down and opened her lunch and started to eat it; making me feel that she was just as comfortable around me as I was around her, I liked that feeling, it was a trusting feeling and it felt good to me, I felt as though I couldn't stop smiling now.

Inside of me, I was jumping up and down excitedly and screaming "YES!" at the top of my lungs, pumping my fists in the air and doing a jog while thanking the heavens for this moment, but outside; I was still just another dumb guy asking dumb questions.

"How do you do that?" I asked her, and I think I regretted asking as soon as it was out there, but of course it was too late by then, but I couldn't believe how stupid I sounded and wished that it was someone else that said it.

"Do...what?" she asked me as she nibbled on a piece of bread, and I noticed that she always seemed to have a smile lurking at the edge of her mouth, ready to spring out and make the world a better place, and make me feel better about my place in it; which I was already hoping would always be right next to her.

I felt as though she as sharing her secrets with me; or maybe we just both felt that happy, that good that we were both laughing a lot of the time and the rest of the world had faded away, though we hardly noticed that either; we were so focused on each other.

"You have most of the answers in the class without even opening the book, I'm at least three steps behind you and I thought I was smart, I admitted, being honest with her.

"I don't have a lot of experience, but it seems that most guys are scared off by the thought or idea that I could be smarter than they are!" she said, and I had a sense of loneliness in that sentence, as if it hurt her, though she would never tell them that.

"They either back out of my life or they try to make me what they think I should be; as dumb as they are!" she said and then laughed, "The answers sort of come to me, they are the most logical, or they just seem to make the most sense to me somehow!" she said, and I liked that too; she wasn't pretending to be something that she wasn't, and she wasn't hiding from who she was or what she thought she was doing; it was out there, take it or leave it.

"Why does that scare them?" I asked her; "Why would they want to change you?" and then I stopped because I thought I'd cut her ff or said too much by the look in her eyes, but it was more because that was important to her, a "deal killer" because she wasn't going to change, no mater how much she might like him, she would change for her, to be better at something, but that was it.

"I couldn't answer that one!" she said, "I wouldn't stay around those guys very long and I think I like that about you, you're not scared, your just shy and that's cute; and you already know that I'm not changing who I am and you are still sitting here with that goofy grin on your face!" as if that summed up everything neatly for her, I liked it; and it made sense too.

So I spent the rest that day listening to her talk; I felt the sparkle in her heart that made me wish that we could sit there forever just like that; I could look into her eyes and get lost for a while; but that was alright with me too, I felt like I was already deeply in love with someone that I'd just met, and as crazy as that sounds; it worked, it fit and felt so damned good that it just had to be right.

After that, I could not concentrate on anything; I tried to study for the rest of my classes, and I was just hoping that I wouldn't get called on too much because I didn't know the answers and was lost in my thoughts.

If they looked, they would see that I was taking notes, but my notes had nothing to do with the class or the lesson of the day, I spent my time writing her name and mine in all kinds of different styles and all the ways I could think of; all over the inside of my notebook, sometimes I just wrote her name, other times I wrote her name inside of a heart, I was so lost.

I felt so silly doing that but I couldn't help it; I could not get her out of my mind and was constantly wondering what she was doing and if she was thinking the same things, that if I looked in her notebook I would see the same things in hers. I daydreamt about the two of us, doing silly things like playing pool, walking together while holding hands along the beach; and always talking and listening to each other, as we did earlier that day.

The next day, the guy that told me not to sit there was watching me with a keen interest now, as though he might have known what I was thinking about and he didn't seem to like it at all; he was looking at me as if I was interfering with whatever he thought was going to happen between them, ignoring the reality that she never even gave him so much as a glance when she sat down.

Looking past her seat one more time, I saw him give me the finger and it made me laugh really hard; and though I wasn't looking in his direction anymore, I felt him glaring at me, I knew that if we weren't in a classroom that he would be calling me out to fight him; it made me laugh because hew was a caveman; everything was settled with his fists or some sort of violent act; hitting the opposing team where it hurt the most or whatever, he didn't know any other way and I wondered how he ended up in this class.

I stayed focused on her and what was going on in the classroom, and I never gave him another thought; I already knew that if we did fight, that he couldn't hurt me because I already knew how he hit, I think unless he had pads on or was lost in the violence of the game he didn't have the guts to hit me or anyone else for that matter.

As my school day ran its course and we weren't together, I still kept thinking about her as not what was going on in the classroom, thankfully, no one seemed to notice and then we were given a pop quiz in some of the classes, but since they were mostly multiple choice I was able to find the answers without too much thought; I just ran them together in sentences and the ones that fit were right, they weren't that hard and I aced the first two and almost the third as well, but I changed an answer and the first choice was the right one, I should have left it alone for the trifecta.

As I was leaving the school that day; I was thinking that there was no way that I could get through the rest of this day without having her phone number or some way to contact her, to stay in touch after school and maybe go places together, doing our homework together, it was making me angry that I'd spent all that time listening to her talk and never asked for anything like that; I didn't even know where she lived.

It was on my mind to take her to a less hostile and bustling place such as almost anywhere on the school groundsand talk to her about how I felt for her and see if she even remotely felt the same; I was afraid to at the same time because I didn't want her to start laughing at me as soon I showed her my cards, but I really did want to know how she felt about me.

Then my heart raced, I saw her walking ahead of me and was about to call out to her when Caroline stepped in front of me and said, "Remember your promise!" with a huge smile on her face; "We're going to Cindy's party, and don't you dare pretend that you forgot!" and then her smile wavered a bit, maybe because she saw the look in my eyes, I was going to say I forgot because I did; before I met Maria; it was the last thing in the world I wanted to do, and now it felt even worse, I would happily go with Maria but felt ambushed and bush-wacked and whatever other term fit what she did to me and didn't like it.

"Don't you dare stand me up!" she said, "It starts at eight and if you let me down, I will pick my nose and put boogers in your burger, you look me in the eye and tell me you think I won't!" she said.

I thought about it, and could actually see her picking and planting and watching the line, moving it back from the others so she wouldn't give them "my present' from her, and then handing it to me with a smile; even the thought of it was making me green around the gills and now I was thinking that I would start bringing my own lunch anyway.

It didn't seem to me like she was joking anyway; probably because now I didn't have to hide when I went to her window because now I belonged out there; thought it still felt weird and uncomfortable because I'd been hiding for a while and I suppose I either got used to it or I missed it, which sounds funny to me.

In a way, this was a typical example of how I felt that my life ran; how things worked out and what I should have expected this time as well; I met a girl that I was crazy in love with and because of this other girl that I liked as a friend but didn't want to be with, I was not going to be able to get closer to her, to know whom she was and what made her smile that way.

Then, as I was thinking about that, I had a "flash vision" of a different version of Maria, she was a small child in a market that I felt I knew, because it seemed very familiar to me, and though she was quite young at the time, I am certain that it was her.

It was maddening, I felt as though I knew this place, as though I'd spent not just hours there, but days at a time, it felt so familiar now that I thought if I tried hard enough; I could tell you exactly how I looked from her perspective; the clothes I was wearing, how my hair looked and probably exactly what I was doing at that moment, it was when I first saw her smile and hoped she was smiling at me.

Without thinking about it, I remember how the sun felt on my face that day, I smelled the salt air as the ocean was not far from where we stood, I could even hear the waves as they crashed against the shore and the sounds of the market place where we were, goods being bought and sold, experiences of travel and life far away were traded as the day wore on and travelers came and went about their business that bright and sunny day, just as nice as thousands of days before it.

It felt as though I was reliving that past life as I watched her there; I had no idea of the events and anything of what have been my life at that time, and really didn't believe in reincarnation, and that was probably because I didn't know anything about it; but I did feel that it was one of those special days; marked by me as the first day that I ever saw her, and that smile that warmed my heart and made me feel for certain that everything was going to be alright.

That one day, everything would be set to rights and all that was needed from me was my belief in that eventuality, and the love we shared would give us the strength to conquer them and anything else that thought they could stop us, scare us apart or kill us off.

As I watched this vision of this little girl, I felt that it was more than just an image of a past life; it was a warning of something in this life, it was a wake-up call and I'd better not hit the snooze button this time because this was life and death.

It was insane, I could see her as she was that day, and knew that, there she was a live and real; I was too because I was sure that I was there too, I felt the warmth of her heart as she held onto a woman's hand and walked around the bustle of the square that was alive with activity, it was just as clear that she was oblivious to everyone and everything going on around her except for me.

Though the area was alive with those sounds and activities and it should have been confusing to me; I felt as though I knew more of those people around us besides her, I "used her eyes" to look around me and saw people there that I knew by name, that I did business with them, or went to school with their kids, it was very confusing and yet it was very clear at the same time.

I that way, I knew my house was on a villa at the north end of town; and my father was there right now; working the fields and trying to get a good crop out of the earth once more; my mother would be in the kitchen where the aromas wafted through the house, I could hear the sizzle of things she cooked for us, the wonderful dishes that my father loved so much; traditions passed down from their parents to them, and down to me to pass to my children.

I wondered how much of that came from my feelings for Maria; I knew that these things I saw were at one time real, and I didn't understand how she had something to do with the things I was seeing; if she made it possible for me to see her "back then" and showed me an old memory that was still familiar and yet so new to me that my mind was spinning around it in circles.

But her expression was a blank sheet to me as I watched, there was no way for me to know what she was thinking about as her face was a sea of beautiful calm and some understanding of what I was seeing; she was understanding things without them being told or explained to her; even as a little girl, she understood the psychology of the guys she would have to deal with and knew how to handle them, she knew that I could be trusted and she could tell me things without scaring me away, I wouldn't run off scared or be so amazed that I wouldn't know what to do next.

I felt as though I'd let her down though, I brought nothing to offer her in return, my entire world was turning all around on me; left was now right and up was down, and since I never felt love like this before in my life; I was thinking that maybe that was what this was all about, that my feelings for her, so new and unfamiliar that this other stuff was a "romantic notion or fantasy" that I felt for her, that the idea of knowing and loving her in another world long gone was a romantic thought or idea and that was all there was to it.

Little did I know what the warning was about, what was ahead, what we would have to help us and what we would have to do; not just to hold onto each other but to survive and live to see another day; and if I did get an idea of those things I might have gathered her and whatever family I could and leave the area forever, never look back and no trial behind that might lead anyone to us.

What I should have been focused on was who the hell we were trying to hide from; I was unaware of any threat to me or her, no one wanted to kick my ass for being with her; even the lineman could see the futility of that; maybe Caroline but I thought she could only flick those boogers so far and she wasn't prone to violence anyway.

There was no threat or danger on the horizon, and yet there was; I just couldn't see it yet, and until she stood there and tried to tell me about; there was no way I could have seen how bad it was about to become, and how much worse it was going to get before it was over.

She did try her best to warn me, though I saw a little girl I should have focused more on the message, on what she was trying to tell me about, but who could have blamed me for not seeing danger from her tiny little body and the say she was smiling at me.

THE SOCIAL HOUR

Everyone is born with genius, but most people only keep it
for a few minutes.

-Edgard Varese (1883-1965)

I WOULD HAVE DREADED NOT HAVING a choice about going to that
party, that night, even without being sandbagged with Caroline and
her blackmailing schemes; but the idea of going as her date made it so
much worse, and then you add to that fact that my mind was on Maria and
a blind man could see the dilemma I was facing.

It's funny, but I couldn't help but think that, aside from this; she really
was a nice girl and probably would be a good friend to have, she was cute,
and she as going through a lot just for me; to meet with me and make me her
boyfriend, no matter how I felt about it.

She wanted me to be a part of her life even though it was clear that it
wasn't what I wanted and it bothered me that no one ever bothered to ask
me how I felt about it; as if that was a foregone conclusion or something; I
resented the hell out of being forced into this situation.

But then, it was just how my luck seemed to run sometimes, it was ironic
that I met the girl of my dreams and we really hit it off nicely and yet, instead
of being happy with her as I should be, which is what my entire body was
screaming for, and I am stuck with someone that I can only see as a friend.

The guys having this party was the same guys that I'd known as kids, I knew them from, long ago; the days when they did the parties with milk and cookies; the wildest they ever got was either the pinata or pin the tail on the donkey games back then; the bright colors, the cake with your name on it, and the punch really was fruit punch.

But these weren't the same anymore, I didn't know a lot of them anymore because they'd changed so much, as we all did; there were some that I would see in my classes but we would maybe nod at each other in acknowledgement but nothing more; others I might see around school that I'd all but forgotten about because it's been so long.

They were all partying together now it seemed, but any resemblance between those kids was only an accident, and here they could let their hair down and be whoever they thought they were, not who they pretended to be when they were at school.

Some guys felt that when they were there, they couldn't be themselves and yet when they were here, and they "were themselves" they were around the same kids so it didn't make any sense to me, but that was what they chose to do.

They faked what they liked or didn't like depending on what, or who, was popular at them time; they thought it was the best way to fit in with the popular kids, and some had been doing that for so long that they forgot who they were and what they might have wanted out of life; those guys were sad and lost.

Although, since they chose that path freely, they must have gained something in the process but they'd lost so much of themselves that you couldn't blame them when they looked in the mirror and didn't know whose face was staring back at them anymore.

As we all got older and our priorities and views on life changed, things became more important to me than spending time with them, and I was pretty sure they felt the same because none of them went out of their way to stay in touch either.

It was almost as if we remembered the goofy stages we went through as little kids, and some of apparently didn't want to hang out with the ones that did; the cartoons we watched, the actors that we idolized, the music we went crazy over, the braces on our teeth, the times we fell off the bicycles, the school girl crushes; all of the stupid things we did, the mistakes we made as we grew up: those things that didn't mean we were stupid, it was more that we were human and prone to mistakes as we learned but some of us forgot that I think.

I was considered more of a loner now because I would rather curl up to a good book or go see a good movie, go body surfing at the beach or run along the shore; ride my bike through the woods, not seeing anyone out there for hours and feeling as though I was free, blazing my own trail through the woods.

But as there was no choice for me, I left the house with that you might call hopeful trepidation, I knew that it was either that, or risk the wrath of Caroline and her boogers. I dressed nice, but not too nice because I didn't want to give her the wrong impression; this was a date to her, but not to me.

I was more thinking that I was going to hang out with her and some of her friends, and somehow I'd got the impression that it wasn't so much that she wanted me, but that she needed to have a guy on her arm that night; to prove something to someone there, maybe make another guy jealous, but when I saw her face I knew that was wrong and my heart sank.

There was also hope that I wouldn't have to stay too long but I knew the chances of that were slim too; and then I hoped I would see some of my friends there, at least someone I could talk to besides Caroline and her friends.

It was funny, everything that I did now, Maria "floated" on the fringe of it; I was imagining that it was her and I doing things I did on normal days, only now they felt and seemed to be more special, they had a shine and bounce to them that wasn't there before I met her; they were more alive and there was even significance in their normality because she was a part of it. I was already so much in love with her and yet knew almost nothing about her, and at the same time I felt that I knew all that I needed to know.

Funny how love makes us so happy that we get stupid and ignore the bigger picture; and even when we do see that, we still deny with all of our might certain things that we know are there, we pretend that they aren't anything to worry about and rush head-on into whatever is next for us; good or bad, we don't care because it feels so good.

As I was walking, instead of thinking where I was going and what I was already dreading; I was thinking about that dream, that vision that I'd had of her in that marketplace and was feeling that it was important somehow and yet I could not see why it felt that way; even if it was her and I that day, it had to be so long ago that whatever significance it had must have expired by now, with the passage of so many years.

It was so long ago that the roads were unpaved dirt and gravel; that there were wagons with wooden wheels and small horses or donkeys that pulled them along to carry people or goods to the market to buy and sell things, it was the age of cars or engines, or anything like that, at least not in that part of the world.

I left the house that day, I remember that I kissed my mother as always, she'd taught me long ago to always tell her that I love her in case something happens and we don't get that chance again; and then I went to where my father was, then I went to the garage because I knew that was where my father would be; I was thinking about asking him for advice but I didn't think there was anyone that could help me; I needed to sit her down and tell her flat out how I felt and why this wasn't a good idea; why this wasn't going to work for either of us.

It was also hard for me to see my dad as a guy that chased after girls, unless it was my mother of course; but I got the feeling from him sometimes that she did the "luring" and he just went along because he was awestruck that she would want to be with him.

I opened the side door and entered, I could hear the familiar hum of his lathe machine, he used it to make table legs but not much else, sometimes to shape the wood into a design that he saw in there, he once even tried to make a bat for me, when I started playing baseball, but he worked so hard on trying to balance it and shape it that he ended up with a rather large tooth[ick, it was still on the wall in there somewhere, it was a great source of humor for all of us.

When I saw him, it took me a few minutes before I could believe or even understand what I was seeing because in all my years I had never seen him cry before, not once; but especially as hard as he was crying at that moment.

He was sobbing out loud, uncontrollably and I could tell that he was silently praying to the heavens above for a way to understand, to come to peace with what happened to my brotherand why he died that way.

I heard him crying about had sad it was, how much it still hurt to live with that, how violent and cruel his death was, the bullets and some fragments went through his face and they were forced to have a closed casket because he didn't want anyone to see him that way; it was heartbreaking not to have seen his face one last time before they said goodbye to him.

He looked up at the rafters and said, "His mother never got to kiss him goodbye!" and then sobbed loudly; then he started talking to my brother, saying that he should have known who he was dealing with, that he knew his father as he grew up and it was said that the son was much worse, more ruthless and cold-hearted, and this was proof that those rumors were true.

My father went to school with Stephon's father, though he was a full two years ahead of him, they crossed paths once before he started to come into his power, my father had some fight in him and knew what he was capable of but my father was not afraid of him, and he didn't respect him, but he saw how bad he became and saw it all happen as they went along the course of their lives.

They once even fought over a girl, my father liked her but he wasn't even trying to get close to her; she was attracted to my father and Stephon's father only wanted her for a little while, once he got what he wanted he was done with her, that didn't mean anything good for her and they all knew it.

One day it came to a head when Guillermo, Stephon's father, felt that she'd been teasing him along and was tired of it, he took what he said was his anyway; he kidnapped her during the middle of the day and dragged her out to the woods where he kept her until the next day; and whatever he did to her during that time, she would not, or could not ever bring herself to speak of; though she tried to live a normal life, everyone knew and even the ones that cared about her and wanted to help her didn't know what to do, they were helpless to reach her though they kept trying until her family moved away and they never saw her again.

After that, whenever they would pass in the hall, they would glare at each other until one day it boiled over and they fought a bloody and drawn-out fight that lasted three days before they were too tired and neither would gain the advantage, they came to an uneasy truce when they were tired to fight any longer.

Guillermo felt real admiration for my father because he never backed down, even when Guillermo's henchmen were there and could have jumped in; but it never went any further than that; they would never be friends and they would never be at the same table in any social event because my father didn't like his way of getting things done, but they knew each other well.

He even felt a bit of sadness, of remorse or something when he learned that is son killed my brother; but he never contacted my father to tell him that; when he heard that Stephon was killed, he thought about taking the family back home, but there were others there that would take up the slack and continue to sell drugs and use the locals to make it and help them distribute it and he knew it wasn't going to change.

I watched his shoulders sag and they began to shake harder as he wept, and before I realized what I was doing, I stepped even closer to him; I know that he didn't even hear me but I was at loss and I didn't know what to do; I was thinking that I should just leave him there and let him get through this on his own because I know it would bother him if he knew I'd seen him crying that way.

Because I'd never seen him this way before, I was also intrigued and I wondered what, if anything else he might say about my brother that I didn't know, he put his hands over his face then and wept even louder; it was so hard not to run to him and hug him; to tell him how much I loved him and would happily trade places with Flaco if we could bring him back, that I wouldn't hesitate or regret it in the least.

I saw something on the floor before him and when I saw it, I knew it was the photograph that he always kept in his pocket but never shared with me; as I watched, he was looking down at it and whispering something that I could not hear, every so often a word or phrase that he used often or I knew but most of the time I couldn't hear him clearly enough that I knew what he was saying.

As slowly and quietly as I could, I leaned even closer to him and looked at the picture that was dogged-eared, and I could see by the color mixture that had faded a bit that it was old, taken long ago in front of our home in Mexico.

He'd been carrying it for so long that it was worn, but it was clearly a picture of Flaco as he stood in front of a sign that said, "Arturo's" and smiling the same way that I'd seen my mother smile so many times; a smile that showed her joy and happiness at something that we all did together.

Standing next to him must have been Sabrina, she was beautiful, and they looked so happy and proud together that he felt like he would have been happy to see them together, she would have been welcomed in the family with open arms and the happiness in their smiles made me feel sadness because they should have been allowed to have that together; they should have grown old together and had many children and grandchildren.

Even though we'd never met, and there were not any pictures of him around the house because it still hurt them too deeply, and there were so many times that I'd thought to tell them that, the reason they were hurting so badly was because they hadn't let it go yet, they were holding onto their pain and anger and frustration about it, and should have instead focused on the good things, the happy memories that they shared and I am sure there were many.

They needed to get it out in the open and see it for what it was; and until they found a way to there, to find a way to come to peace with it and talk about it openly, this was always going to be an open sore, festering on their souls and it was only going to get worse.

They were old school and I knew that either they wouldn't listen, or they wouldn't hear me and they would keep going this way until they found their own way through all of the hurt and pain that they carried in their hearts; they would say I was too young to understand or that I didn't know him and how he was so how could I understand, but it was my brother and that was all I needed to know about him.

Now I also knew that I could see my father's face in his, and that was an odd feeling for me; sharing him with a brother I mean, but he did look very much like our father and it was especially clear in the defiant way he looked at the camera, he wore a smile but his expression was serious too.

He was proud too, I could see that clearly enough, my mother had once told me that his smile would warm the coldest of hearts and looking at him there, I could see why, she said that smile made them want to hold him and smother him with kisses.

I could our mother's sensitivity too; maybe that was another thing that made them want to hold him close, to comfort him against whatever was heavy on his mind; to feel that connection to the center of the world and share it with him, I looked deeply into that picture for a long minute; I was trying to imagine what kind of brother he would have been.

In the photograph, he looked as though he was about fourteen, which meant it was about a year before he died; I knew so little about him but seeing this photograph made him so much more real to me because I could now put a face to the stories that I'd heard.

Looking a little deeper, I could see touches of my mother in him too; especially in the way he dressed, my father was all coveralls and jeans with a t shirt or sweatshirt, depending on the weather; or he was in a business suit, which made him feel funny and made me laugh because he was so uncomfortable in it but he looked so handsome my mother didn't want to leave his side while he wore it.

The clothing style he wore in that photo made me think he dressed a little for her and a lot for himself; the pompadour hairstyle was my mother's idea, I knew that because she tried it on me too, but it never worked, my hair was full but not thick and it would not stand up, the curl in front that she worked so hard to get would fall flat before I left the house, but I still wondered how much fun it would have been to just hang out with him; to grow old together and share the kinds of things that only brothers could.

I wondered about the kinds of things he might try to teach me; especially about girls, and since I knew that he was an artist as well; it suddenly struck me that there might be some of his work around here somewhere, maybe something I passed in the hall and didn't know was his work, I was going to take a look around to see later, when I had the chance and they were at work or something.

The best time to do some investigating on my own was when they went out for their weekly movie, it would be easier to do then because I wouldn't have them wondering what I was doing and I wouldn't have to see that hurt look in their eyes if I had to tell them.

That was when I felt a strong sadness, and I didn't understand it; maybe it was the feeling of loss at having never met him nor even heard his voice, his laughter, I never got to know him and that hurt me from deep inside; I felt as though my soul was reaching out for him but he was no longer there, I felt the same sense of loss my father was feeling at that moment and I wanted to cry along with him.

Knowing my father, that would have been a mistake, he would have thought it made him look weak and he would be less in my eyes; but nothing was further from the truth and it only made me love him that much more, it helped me to understand him and answer some of those things that had vexed me for so long, I didn't understand, and yet I did.

Then he looked a the picture down there and stopped, put his hand over his mouth and stifled his sobbing though it was not easy, I could see that this was still tearing him apart; he reached down and picked it up again, as if he was embarrassed that it touched the floor, he kissed it and then put it in his pocket again, and then he looked around quickly as if he sensed me back there in the shadows, but when he didn't see me, he put his head down and began to cry again.

Again, I fought off the urge to run to him; I wanted to take the photo and have a good, close look at it, to hug him and cry alongside of him, but I knew that it would hurt him deeper because he would be forced to talk about it and he wasn't ready to; even after all this time, he hadn't come to terms with it or I would have never seen him this way.

That didn't mean I was ready to give up; I still held hope that we might one day be able to sit down and talk about it from all of our collective perspective, although knowing my father, he might have a hard time understanding my feelings on it; I wasn't there after all, even though he was my brother, my blood.

In the end, I left him alone out of respect, alone with his thoughts about it and his grief, I was helpless to help him or do anything else, my mind was a jumble of emotions about what could be, and especially what might have been.

"Whooo-peeee!" I muttered under my breath as I closed the gate and turned left to where Cindy lived; I was dreading this so much that I probably made it worse than it was going to be but I didn't feel like partying now and wanted to go back and talk to my father about what happened and how we can get justice for my brother but I know it's a different world once you cross that border and the rules change.

But knowing that he died that way, that he was taken from this world forever hurt me now as if I'd known him, the grief and feelings of loss and emptiness where that person used to be, we all needed to come to terms with that loss and I didn't feel that any of us was any closer to that place in our lives.

When I first heard my father talking about this, they didn't know I was awake and could hear them, but I thought he was talking about a gangster movie that he saw or something, but my mother didn't like those kinds of movies, she wasn't squeamish about them; she just didn't think the violence and murder and people going to jail for serious crimes just didn't seem entertaining to her; she was more of the comedy, which was okay, but she also liked the romantic movies and that meant my father did as well because she would never go out there alone.

For most women, they wouldn't go alone because they didn't want to be seen alone, it was just one of those things; they felt that they stood out and people would stare when she wasn't looking, but for my mother, it was because of what happened to my brother and the fear that it came out of nowhere and could just as easily do it again; you just never knew in this world.

I forced myself back to my thoughts about today and what was going on; I had known Cindy since we were kids, been to her house a few times because her younger brother was my age, we went to the same classes and were not real close but what you would consider friends.

There was that time when I had a crush on her, but I think it was the "older woman" mystique or some phase that I was going through at the time, but I quickly grew out of it because she was so ride to me then that I gave up on the idea.

Her brother and I would meet other guys that we knew and we'd go deep into the woods, until we could see nothing of the city and roast marshmallows and sometimes hot dogs over an open fire and tell each other scary stories until we couldn't stand it and would walk home as quickly as we could without actually running and admitting that we were really scared.

But as I remember those days, she always acted as though she was too good for me; and that made the crush, if that's what it was, fade fast, and I got over her in a hurry; I think that was why she didn't want me at her party, she thought I would ruin the mood or something; remind her of something that she would rather not think about; I wonder how much Caroline begged her to let me come before she relented and why the hell it was so important to her.

Through all of these thoughts I could still see Maria's face smiling at me; laughing at my predicament and the things that we did together, I could even hear her voice as she told me to find a way out of it if I really didn't want to go.

I saw my parents standing together and watching me with concerned looks on their faces, and there was Flaco was well; he was shouting something to me and then laughing really hard as he watched me, I saw him clap his hands together and then he pointed in my direction as if he'd just said or seen something so funny that he couldn't stop laughing about it.

Then I got an image of a huge black widow spider and "Sniffles" which really surprised me because I hated that sickly-sweet cereal and spiders were never anything to be afraid of, at least until now; but then they'd never been so big before either; spiders didn't scare me because they could run and jump and if they got close, bite, but one quick stomp of my shoe and it was over for them.

I remembered the leg in the window and I tried to look closer this time, thinking that since it was just a vision it couldn't hurt me; and that I might recognize the leg if I saw it again, but I couldn't get close enough to see the legs on this one, it was out of the frame of my vision.

It was the kind of thing that would make sense to no one else but me; but as I tried to look closer, the image faded a bit, and as I tried to bring it back to where I could see it, I stepped into traffic and was almost hit by a car that didn't even slow down.

That would have been the end for me, I would surely have been hit by that fast-moving car except that someone grabbed me from behind and yanked me back rudely, even though it ripped my shirt in the seam, I couldn't be upset because it saved my life; I heard the drivers horn as it blared at me and I knew that if I could see his middle finger it would be pointed at me.

It made me wonder what kind of man he was, what kind of father and what he might be teaching his children about life if he was that impatient and uncaring about others; I turned to thank my rescuer and when I saw that it was Caroline it made me jump.

"Are you stupid, brain locked, or just that desperate to get out of going with me tonight that you'd step out in front of a car?" she shouted at me, clearly mire upset than I was; and I had no idea how to answer her about that, but I did manage to mumble an embarrassed "thanks" and tried to check my shirt but she took my hand and said that it was fine and dismissed it as we started walking…together.

This might have been her plan and I was just now finding out, but now I was forced to walk the last three blocks to the party with her holding my hand; I knew that would tell everyone else that we were together now but I couldn't think of a reason to pull away from her and when I tried to walk faster she hooked the belt loop in my pants and pulled me back.

I looked at her again, wanting to say something but I just couldn't then; she was all smiles and talking a mile a minute and all I could think of as I saw that sweet smile was the idea of her sticking her boogers in my lunch, I tried twice to tell her how I felt but she never heard me; she ran right over what I tried to say as if it were a small detail and would work it out eventually.

I had an idea of how the party was going to be set up and there were no surprises when we arrived, I knew there would be a few people collected outside, either thinking that they are not cool enough to go any further; or the other side of that coin, that they thought they were too cool for that scene and waited outside so everyone could see them, either way, to me, they were airheads, worried about the things that didn't matter.

Out on the porch, before the door would be a few of the "hard guys" that waited out there and drank beer, pretending to be watching the door to keep the bad elements out, some would be drinking a "short dog" which was some of the worst tasting alcohol that I'd ever had the non-pleasure of trying, it would probably start your car if you ran out of gas but they loved it.

Those guys were actually cool when you got to know them, and I grew up with one or two of them, and some were a lot smarter than they would be acting out there in that crowd, they thought it would make them fit in better and they wouldn't get ridiculed by the others that would only be in that class if they were lost.

I would see some of them at church on Sunday though, and it always made me wonder what they did the night before that they were praying so hard; outside, in the real world they acted as tough as nails; ready to cut your heart out at the slightest affront, while inside the church they were pious and above that.

The next group would be the athletes, and the only really good thing about that room would be the girls there, a lot of the prettiest girls at school would be there, fawning over the starting quarterback or the point guard on the basketball team, the home run hitter in baseball, it never ended, those girls would never speak to guys like me unless they were being polite, it would never get any further unless I joined the team and got my first letter; to me, they weren't worth it and I didn't want to be that fake.

I would never fit in that group, I would never have enough off-color sweaters to wear, I did letter, in baseball last year; but that was for my father and I gave it to him and he loved to wear it because he was so proud that I'd earned it; I knew he liked to show it to his friends and brag about it.

Beyond those guys was the kitchen, there would be a mix of the groups in there drinking beer and playing beer pong games; the girls in there would be doing tequila shots; some to give them an excuse for what they already knew they were going to do; and some to forget what they already endured, and some for what might be awaiting them at home, liquid courage.

There would also be three or four girls in there, making jello shots and mixing the alcohol into the punch; they were what were loosely called, "beer tenders" but I didn't feel as though I fit in with them either although I saw a friend of mine rolling joints too, we smiled and nodded at each other but I didn't stop and he didn't call me over.

After that, it was out the back door and into the yard, that was where I would find the rest of the pot heads, waiting for my friend inside; they were there to seriously party and nothing else was important to them, nothing else held any meeting.

The funny thing about them was that, the only difference between them being here and where they normally would be found doing the exact same thing was the location, everywhere that they went, they would gravitate to a place where they would smoke and spend the rest of their time there; tonight, they'd be listening to the music, drinking beer and passing the joint along the line until it was roached.

They would always be completely oblivious to the cloud of smoke floating above their heads as it floated away with the breeze, but I knew that I could walk up to any of those guys and say "boo!" and they would all burst out laughing; no matter how many times I did it.

I always liked those guys, they were a lot of fun, but no matter how much fun they had, they would never remember what they did just five minutes ago; they forget how far they went or how they might not have made it to get to this day, they might end up crashing into a street lamp as some others sadly did during the course of our lives.

Every time I thought about parties like this one, I thought about Albert, a huge child in a man-sized body and a huge heart; he quit school early and yet was so intelligent that he could teach anyone what he knew about music and instantly make them a better musician or singer or whatever other talent they had and somehow in the process; make them a better human being as well, just by association.

He was naturally talented; he would gladly teach anyone what they wanted to learn and would never take anything back for it; because for him, the satisfaction came from helping others and that was more than enough; he could sing like an angel or get rough and gravelly at the same time if the song called for it, he was born with a natural affinity for music and all that it took to make it yours.

Everyone and anyone that ever met him knew and loved him, but in the end, he couldn't beat the speed he was addicted to, or the telephone pole in the center of town; but that wasn't their fault, they liked speed too, and these guys were always willing to share because "sharing is caring" as they would happily say and then they'd start laughing again.

There was a guy in some of my classes, they called him "Frito" because he was always fried on one thing or another, and funny but; he was the only guy in the school that I knew of that was absent more often than there, and always on something at any time of the day or night; and yet he was there on the days when we were given tests that determined our final grade and he always aced them with little or no effort on his part.

There were always rumors that he started the day on mushrooms and went through the entire school day whit no one except for a few close friends knowing about it, no one had any idea; the only way we knew was when those other guys were there, when he'd taken on a tough strain of acid or something and they were worried that he might flip out and not come back, but that never happened for as long as I knew him and he graduated three months early.

He was considered one of the smartest, graduated at the head of our class or damn near it, and yet he would always come to me and ask me to tell him a joke, any joke because he loved my humor but said he could never remember how to tell the jokes I told him.

"It's not that you can't remember the jokes!" I told him, "It's your timing, that's all you need to work on, and you'll get better at it!" I promised him.

But he would still beg me to tell him a joke, "Whatever!" he would say, dismissing my argument that he could do it, "Tell me a joke! Come on man, you always have the best jokes!" he said and started laughing.

This time, he pulled me over to his friends as I did my best to try and tell them that I didn't have any new jokes but they weren't hearing me either, instead, they were all complimenting me and agreeing among themselves that my jokes were the best, and I wondered who else they might corner this way and tell them the same things and that thought made me laugh too.

Without a word, they all closed in on me, getting closer so that they could hear me; all shutting up and all eyes on me from all around, they waited expectantly as they absently hit the joint and passed it along. I looked from one to the other and saw the same expression on each one of them, it was too funny.

I also knew that if I waited long enough, they would either wait until I said something, or start laughing as if I had; so I tried to think of a joke I hadn't told them, there were none and I was trying to figure out what I could say but my mind went as empty and blank as theirs was.

"Okay guys!" I said, as I leaned forward conspiratorially, "The other day, in science class, they gave us this big lecture about smoking pot, and what it does to your memory!" I said, "Didn't they show it in your class?" I asked them, all seriousness now, "I'm really surprised if they didn't!" I said, setting them up, even though I'd told them this joke before.

My friend, being a little sharper than the others looked me in the eye and was smiling; he said, "I think I remember that from somewhere, but I can't quite place it!" he said, and I knew I had him because he was in the class that day, sitting to my left when they showed the video.

Then a couple of the others said they had also seen it, though it was clear that they hadn't, they were just trying to blend in; one of them, when asked what he remembered said he fell asleep and missed it, which would probably be me as well, if I'd seen it, but I was making this up as I went along, same as last time.

Then they all leaned forward, though Frito and one of the others looked around as if they thought someone might learn the secret, they seemed to have forgotten that it was a joke and asked, "What did they say?" everyone was staring at me now, hanging on my every word.

"I forgot!" I said, and then waited for them to catch up as I walked away, whistling as I went and trying to keep myself from looking back.

It took them several moments after that though, either they were digesting it or they were waiting for more; and then they suddenly all burst out laughing, and a few moments later they were choking and gasping for air before they lit another joint in my honor, even then I knew that some of them would forget that joke and ask me to repeat it again later for some of the others.

I looked around, and there were several girls scattered all around the party that were clearly there just to dance, and they didn't need a partner to let their hair down and have some fun, some of them dressed the hottest and yet they acted offended if you noticed, especially if you said something about it that they thought was sexist, somehow they felt that we weren't supposed to drool when they showed that much skin so openly.

Then I went to look for the bathroom, went back into the house and into the room beyond the kitchen, where I'd turned away to go outside, and the music in there was so loud that you couldn't hear the person next to you; but it didn't matter since everyone in that room was looking to score; right in front of me, a couple that was walking in front of me stopped and shared a lip lock between them, oblivious to me and everyone else.

Caroline caught up to me as I was passing through that room, and I'd almost forgotten about her until I saw that some of her friends were in the next room, she snuck behind me and took my hand again before leading me to the table where the spiked punched was.

"Stay here! Wait for me!" she said, as if I was her puppy and she was training me to sit; I looked around the room and wondered what the hell I was doing there, none of these people even liked me; I dressed normal and would shave my head bald before I would colored and spiked my hair the way some of these guys did, some of those colors reminded me of Aunt Martha, and that wasn't a good thing.

I saw some of her friends were moving to the music, but they had as much life and enthusiasm for it as zombies, it made me laugh, and then I thought she was going to ask me to dance; there was no way thatwas going to happen; I was cursed with three left feet and nothing, not even the threat of "booger burgers" was going to change that.

Then I could hear people all around me asking others to dance, some girls started dancing together because there weren't enough guys in there but thankfully, they saw I wasn't in the mood and passed me by without asking.

"There you are!" I heard Cindy say, and I could tell by her tone and the way she slurred her words that she was already pretty drunk and feeling no pain, her makeup was running a the edge of her eyes because she was crying but she ignored that to give me her opinion of my being there.

"Caroline told me that she would find a way to get you here, and I told her np friggin' way! Yet here you are, damn!" she said, "Will that girl never learn?" she asked of no one in particular, I looked around and we were the only ones there.

I wasn't sure if that was a good thing or not, but I was pretty sure she didn't mean it nicely, so I said, "Nice party!" because I could hear my mother saying "If you don't have anything nice to say!" and letting me finish the thought in my head.

Even if they want to kill you, as I felt that she did, but okay, maybe she would have been happy just having someone throw me out, and rough me up in the process but not hurt me too badly; but she wasn't going out of her way to make me feel welcome; she was looking at me as though she knew I didn't really mean it and then she walked away unsteadily without another word.

I left that room then, forgot about the bathroom and went to find a corner to hide in; the trouble with that plan was that there was already someone hiding in every corner, and I ended up outside again, but this time it seemed more like my kind of crowd.

There was a band set up near the garage, they'd put up a stage and some steps and it looked pretty cool as long as it held up, but it seemed sturdy enough; I could see a nice set of drums, a double bass with lots of floor toms of various sizes, a set of top toms and then two fat toms; one at either end and lots of different sizes and styles of cymbals to play with.

Stacked up against the bass drum was a Fender Precision Bass, two different Les Paul's and a Fender Stratocaster and off to the left was a keyboard player with this huge box that was so big that it almost hid him, and it was set off from the stage because there wasn't room for it.

It was a square cabinet, with speakers on all four sides, and some kind of bell, or horn was set inside of the top, it was attached to a pedal that was at his feet, that triggered the bell and caused it to spin at various speeds that really altered the sound the keyboards made, sometimes it was almost a siren effect.

The front man was a singer, and it seemed as though they did a lot of songs by the Doors, which was a band that not everyone liked, they thought there was too much emphasis on keyboards but I liked them and thought they were hot, so I was happy to hear them play, I felt better for coming there now.

When they were ready, a few moments later, they open with a song called, "Love Me Two Times" and they did it really well, and now there was a crowd gathering at the front of the stage to watch them as they started the next song.

I saw a friend of mine, a guy named Andy as he staggered his way towards the stage, he was really drunk and clearly had no idea what the hell was going on as he would his way to the band so he could listen to them play.

Andy was a good kid, and one of my better friends as a matter of fact; one of those guys that would always stand by your side, if the numbers are against you, he's still going to be there because that's the kind of guy he is, but he as having a lot of problems lately and they were eating him alive; his parents were fighting their way through a bitter divorce, and he ended up staying with her because his father hadn't found a place yet and had no room for him while staying at this brother's house with his family.

His mother was having her fun, as she put it; she was making up for all of those years that she was married to the wrong man, she told that to anyone that would listen or that she thought might help her with that "problem" that she was facing.

Andy was having a hard time dealing with the kind of men she was bringing home lately; bringing them home with her never felt right to him either, she was still married to his father after all, and in the beginning she would date but not bring them home with her, and she never would have let them spend the night, and if she did, he never heard about it or they snuck him out in the morning.

For a long time, it was just men that she brought home, and a few of them stole things from her while she was asleep or too drunk to notice; he wasn't sure, but there was a morning he woke up and went to the bathroom only to find her asleep on the floor between a man and a woman that he'd never seen before.

He was certain that she tried to come into his room a few times during the night, the first time, she pretended that she was looking for the rest room but tried to come in, he never let her come in and he never told his mother about her either.

That was the point when Andy felt that he couldn't handle it anymore, he started staying away from the house, sleeping in the park, staying with friends, he even slept in her car while he knew she was inside with "one of her friends" and he didn't want to see them; after a while that meant that he was sleeping on the street because his friends couldn't sneak him into the house anymore.

There were times that he slept in the park, was rousted by the cops and then he'd go home long enough to shower and change his clothes but after a while he began to think that nothing mattered anymore; he was slipping down that slope faster all the time and for people like me that really cared about him, it was hard to see him that way.

As far as he knew, none of those guys hit her, or abused her in that way, but they were low life and well beneath his mother, yet she wouldn't hear him when he tried to warn her about them, she acted as though she was lucky that they even gave her the time of day.

It was really sad to see her that way too, the last time that I went over there, she hit on me and I was lucky that Andy didn't hear her; she was thinking that since it didn't work with Andy's father that she was well over the hill and not worth the time it took to get to know her.

This was bothering him a lot that day I think, because I'd not seen him that drunk unless it was something special, and this was a party but nothing special to him; he was drinking a lot after school and I wondered how he got the liquor.

He hadn't been caught yet and was starting to skip classes and he was found a lot of the time, hanging out in the park alone with his thoughts, or even asleep on the bench, though it was more likely that he was passed out.

Because of that, I hadn't seen him in a while, and when I did see him, I wondered if he actually did hear his mother hit on me because it was awkward, and as much as I was worried about him, I didn't want to lecture him about things that I could do nothing about; I couldn't change them for the better or worse, and he acted as though he was ashamed and dirty, even though he'd done nothing wrong.

I knew him well enough that, no matter how badly he might need it, he would never ask for help; but then, maybe he didn't know how to do that, he always thought it was the other guys problem if he couldn't get along, and he actually liked a few of the guys she dated; but as soon as that started to happen, something else would happen and the guy would be gone, and lately it seemed as though she seemed to be sliding down a bad progression of bad relationships that were getting worse all the time instead of better.

He tried to tell himself that he was glad that she was dating, but it didn't seem to help him or make it any easier to bear, before she started dating, she would come home from work and go straight to her room, alone; crying, drinking beer until she fell asleep, she was feeling worthless and as if no man would ever want her now, and it was hard to see her that way; he never knew what to say to her or how to help her.

Sometimes, he would go to her door and knock, try to spend some time with her but she wouldn't answer and the door was locked, he knew she was in there and that she was awake; he would talk to her through the door and then they'd both end up crying.

She was still beautiful though, and not just in his eyes, and she always had a nice figure though she didn't run or exercise; she just married the wrong guy and she probably knew it at the time but was hoping for better, and then Andy came along and she thought it would get better after that but it didn't.

After that, they went through something of a role-reversal then, Andy took a job after school and was paying the bills and buying groceries, making the meals and cleaning everything in the house, but then, his father kept telling him that the separation was nothing to do with him, he was lucky that the one thing his father did right was to make the child support payments on time.

The latest guy she was seeing didn't like Andy at all, though he pretended to at first; Andy saw right through him and so did his mother but she didn't say anything, and he was talking about marriage, and Andy could see it had nothing to do with heart; it was the wallet he was after; he couldn't understand why she couldn't see it but then he thought that maybe she did, but she didn't want to admit it.

He tried to point those things out to her and they would end up fighting and shouting at each other, he told her he was just trying to help her with things she couldn't see but were right there in front of her; she accused him of trying to deny her any chance at finding happiness.

As such, he was torn between wanting to see his mother find a way to be happy and really needing, and missing his father so much and that this latest guy was all bad news and even more on the horizon, there was no way this guy was ever going to be good for her in the long run and he was trying to make her see that without getting into another argument about it, but that was really hard because when they would start talking, he would come over as if he should hear it as well, and Andy didn't care to even hear his voice, especially at times like that.

He wanted to leave, but he couldn't leave his mother with him, he also could see that day, not far from now; where he would want to throw Andy out on the street and his mother wouldn't be able to stop it; maybe because she didn't know how, or maybe because she'd sunk that far down and thought he was going to be there forever and she could be happy with that.

As I was thinking about all of that and watching him staggering around, feeling lost and a strong sense of hopelessness was a dark cloud that hung over his head and followed him around; the potheads were calling me back, there were more of them now and they wanted me to tell the others the joke, but I knew Andy needed my help and went there instead, I told them I'd come back later but I was sure they'd forget, but as I went to Andy, there was Caroline, stepping in front of me again and thwarting my plan to help my friend, this time it angered me a bit because of her attitude, and I thought if she was like this now, what would she be like in a few if I gave in and became her boyfriend.

I was looking at Andy when I heard her say, "There you are! I thought you snuck out on me!" she said, with fire in her eyes, she was a little drunk too, and ready for a fight; it seemed to me, though I had no proof, that her friends must have told her what I was trying to say and she wasn't going to accept it, she must have felt that it made her "less" in front of her friends, who could see what she was denying.

As I looked at her, I saw that she held two drinks in her hands; they were filled with that foamy pink stuff that was soaked in seven different kinds of rum and whiskey and other things that made you crazy, and I didn't want to be crazy with her, I looked back at Andy but he wasn't going to help me either, he wasn't even aware that I was around.

But in her anger, she had spilled most of it while she was searching for me, and was even more angry now because there were splotches of the drink on her dress, which, under better circumstances I would have said looked good on her, because it did.

But I wasn't going to take advantage of her desire or whatever it was and use her as some guys would and then tell her I didn't want her anymore; so, I said, "Nope!" I said, "I just needed to take in some air!" and I took one of the cups from her hand and slammed it home before she could say anything else, maybe she was looking to see if anyone was watching us, she seemed slightly embarrassed as if she'd just realized where she was or something.

She looked around her and saw Andy near the stage and the band setting up and almost ready to start, Andy was still staggering around the stage, trying to talk to one of the guitar players about something but I couldn't hear him, she turned back to me then, with her nose turned up in the air because she didn't like Andy and she didn't like how this felt.

"You like this kind of music?" she asked me as they started up, "This is what you like?" she said again, as if she was trying to make sure but it was clear that I did, and I felt her laughter coming, as she didn't like it and even more so; she didn't like that I did.

I smiled at her then, I knew that I had her and my "out" and I knew what she wanted to hear but I wasn't going to lie to her just to make her feel better for a little while; I knew she would eventually see the lie and then I'd be screwed again, having to back-track or explain it to her, this was easier on both of us, or so I thought.

"Yeah!" I said and then waited a moment, "I really like the Doors, my second favorite band, next to anything that Jimi Hendrix plays!" I said delightedly, the music, the way they live their lives, Peace, love and happiness!" I said, making the peace sign and shaking my hips suggestively because I knew that would disgust her and I was on a roll, and it was time to spread some boogers of my own on her party cake.

"Let's get closer to the stage and check them out!" I said, trying hard not to laugh as I stepped around her and left her standing there with her mouth open, "These guys aren't bad!" I said.

On the one hand, I felt as though I was being mean to her, but on the other hand, she blackmailed me into this corner and should have expected some blow back from it; and I did try, as nicely as I could, to tell her that I wasn't interested in her, that I thought of her as a friend and nothing more but she closed her eyes and ears to anything that I tried, even her friends saw it and tried to tell her, that's what I thought.

One the one hand, I felt as though I was being really mean; but on the other hand, she did blackmail me into this corner and I kept trying as nicely as I could to point out to her that we came from two different worlds and, for me at least; all of this just further drove that point home.

As soon as I said what I thought she needed to hear, she crushed the cup in her other hand, though she hardly noticed as she stared me down and it spilled to the ground at her feet, she was trying to tell me that we should go back inside now; and in there, I could hear a record playing "This is a Man's World" by none other than the great James Brown, and I thought that if he were here that he would wink at me with that smile on his face and then tell me I was doing the right thing, I ignored her and went closer to the stage, and then I couldn't hear her even if she was shouting in my ear; I know, because she tried.

They followed with another Doors song; "Back Door Man" and their version had a lot of energy, they were really feeding the crowd now, they were rushing to the stage and trying to see the drummer, who was singing but he was on a riser so they couldn't see his face from that angle.

"What's the name of this band?" I asked her, working on her mind as much as I could to show her how different we were, I really did like the band; but I liked them a lot more because I knew that she didn't.

They were jamming the quiet stuff and yet I could still barely hear heras she sarcastically answered, "I have no idea!" she told me, and then she looked deep int my eyes as if the lights were going on and I was finally getting through to her.

But she said something else and I was disappointed, "Did you smoke some of that funny shit?" she said, "I heard that you were over there with the heads!" she said as if she was scolding me, and I wasn't sure which made me angrier; that she was actually thinking that she could scold me; or that she had people reporting to her what I was doing when I was out of her sight.

"Anyway!" she said as if that was the last word on the subject; "I don't like rock, its too damn loud and it sounds like they are strangling a cat, I want to go back inside!" she said, and then acted as though I was going to follow her, just because she said to, which if course, had the opposite effect; I dug my heels in and stood my ground; and on this night at least, this was a man's world after all.

She stopped when she realized that I wasn't walking behind her like a good little puppy and then I told her, "I'm going to stay outside for a while, I still need the fresh air!" I said, and I wasn't lying about that.

Crossing her arms defiantly, I thought she was going to laugh when she said, "But I want to go inside, where my friends are waiting for us!" she told me as she dug her heels in as well, though not as firmly.

"But I don't!" I said, I like this music, and maybe I might even smoke a little with the heads! What is that to you anyway?" I asked, "Isn't that what they call a personal choice?" I said, and then regretted my tone, but I unconsciously crossed my arms too, then I told her, "You can go inside if you want to, but I'm going to stay out here, at least for a while!" I said and then turned away from her, thinking it was done.

When I think back on that, I think that a big part of the problem was that her friends were giving her a bad time about me; they could see what I was telling her and that we were different, but they didn't tell her that, half of them (the girls) were telling her that she shouldn't give up on him, that if that's what her heart wants, then she should have it, the other half was telling her to move on and forget about him, that he wasn't worth all this trouble and heartache; but I guess she didn't want them to be right this time, even though she had to have seen it by now, she was just being stubborn about it.

As we were debating that point, the kitchen door opened once more, and there was Maria; she stopped there and was looking around for someone and I was just hoping that I was that lucky guy as I held my breath and hoped she would see me and be happy as about it as I was to see her.

Caroline must have seen my eyes suddenly open wider or something because she turned to see what I was looking at with that huge grin on my face, then she turned back to me and said, "You either come inside with me, and I mean now, or you can forget about us ever doing anything together again! EVER!" she said, with extra emphasis as she turned from me and started to walk away, I could tell that she was trying not to cry but not doing a very good job of holding it back and I thought that she made this a lot worse than it had to be, I wasn't trying to make a public scene, she was, it would have been less embarrassing for her if she'd just gone quietly, but she didn't see it that way or wasn't going to go out that way.

As she passed Maria, on her way into the house, she bumped hard into her and cursed her for being so beautiful that she took my heart away, but Maria hardly noticed and kept walking towards the stage, she was already moving with the music.

When Caroline opened the door, she turned and looked back at me and said, "You two deserve each other! You have your fun, and don't you worry about me, I will be just fine!" she said through her tears as she left.

As I watched the door slam shut, I felt bad for her, but then I never encouraged her, never gave her the idea that this would work out and spent a lot of time and energy trying to tell her that it wouldn't; if nothing else, this should have shown her at least that much; how different we are and how it might have been fun for a short while but we wouldn't have lasted long; I watched the door, waiting for her to come back out again because I didn't think that anyone that used boogers to coerce someone into a date wouldn't give up that easily.

Then I gave up, and screwed up the courage to go and talk to Maria, who was still standing alone and moving with the music, I was frustrated by all this unneeded drama and tossed the cup into a trash can and started towards her, but Andy saw me and waved towards me, he staggered then and almost fell.

I thought that he had the worst timing ever, my friend that needed my help, support and understanding was walking towards me and I was walking to her; but then she followed my eyes and saw him, and then she tried to help him into a chair because he was so unsteady.

For a moment, I stopped to watch her, I felt a pang of jealousy, even though she wasn't mine; but then I fought it off, she was just being nice and trying to help; and he was a good friend for so long, I thought it was good for him to see that other people cared too, he let her help him into that chair and then I smiled at him because he looked so happy.

Then he put his arm around her waist, to steady himself, I thought; but as she lowered him into the chair he grabbed at her, she felt it, but she had a choice to either let him have that cheap thrill or drop him on his ass, which was tempting, she was like most and didn't like being "manhandled" unless she gave him leave; but she wasn't that mean, yet she still dropped him into that chair a little roughly and then she backed away and straightened herself out.

He smiled at me again and said, "Women huh? She can't keep her hands off me!" he said, he almost left his lunch on his lap but managed to lean forward enough that he missed. She turned then, noticing me there, and she smiled, and I felt that was genuinely happy to see me there and smiled back.

Andy straightened up then and laughed, he wiped his mouth on his sleeve and laughed again, he was embarrassed, but he put his arm around her and said, "Hey man! Say hello to my new girlfriend!" and then he leaned over to her and whispered, "Hey sweetie, what's your name?" and then looked back at me because he realized that he'd said it too loud.

She recoiled as his breath hit her face, and then we both saw that Caroline hadn't given up yet after all when she said, "I thought you were going to join me?" she said, a little too demanding in her manner and then she looked around for someone to challenge her or something. Her eyes locked on Maria and though they were red and puffy; her intent was clear.

"I never told you that I was going in there!" I said, as I stepped in front of her, I was trying to keep her from confronting Maria, who seemed to be more than ready if I let her go there but I wasn't about to.

"But I do remember telling you that I wanted to stay out here, and you wanted to go in, but I didn't try to stop you!" I said, "But now you're upset with me and maybe now you can see where we would have never worked out, we are both different people that run in two different worlds, and neither of us would fit into the other's world, and why should either of us change to fit that mold when we'd never be happy that way!" I said, "You must know that by now, it must be clear that it would never work!" I told her as patiently as quietly as I could manage with all the noise going on around us at the time.

It was a lot more than I meant to say, more than I wanted to say, but I was really tired of this; there are times that I admit that I liked pushy women, to a certain degree anyway; this was not one of those times.

"Well then!" she said, "The hell with both you and her!" she spat at Maria as she passed her and headed towards the house, but I noticed this time that she didn't get as close to her as before, she walked a wider path around her, and either Maria didn't notice, or she was simply pretending that she didn't, but her ambivalence infuriated her even more than before.

Andy stood up at that moment and tried to say, "You can't talk to my woman like that! How rude!" he said, but then he leaned forward and slowly fell back and dropped into the chair once more; he was lucky that the chair didn't fold as it almost appeared to before settling into position underneath him.

"Well then, why don't you and your friends get the hell out of here then!" she shouted at me as she started to cry, and this time she didn't wait until she left. I looked at Andy, and he was snoring softly, he was sitting back in the chair and looked so comfortable it was sad to roust him, but we wore out our welcome and it was time to go.

Then I looked at Maria, to see if she was going to help me and felt my cheeks flush when she asked me, "Is that your girlfriend?" and then, "Did we do something wrong? Something that I missed?" she said, "Did she leave because of something that I did?" she asked, still serious, and then she said, "I just want to know, so I can remember what it was and maybe might want to use it again sometime!" and made me laugh really hard because I knew she was pulling my leg.

"No!" I said, "She wasn't my girlfriend, but I guess she wanted to be, that was never going to happen though, and she sort of blackmailed me into being here with her!" I said.

After a moment, when she didn't say anything, I said, I guess I should go and see what's going on in there, to apologize to her and then leave!" I told her.

"That way, you can stay here with your passed-out, drunken boyfriend!" I said, and then gestured towards Andy who snorted at that moment and added to the humor.

I realized at that moment, that there would be no more cardboard booger-burgers for me; I was going to be brown-bagging it for a while because I still liked to eat, and I wasn't entirely sure that she would actually dig her boogers out for me; that she could or would be that vindictive, and I didn't want to hurt her either, but I guess I didn't want to have to open the burger and look.

Maria smiled at me then and said, "She has you exactly where she wants you, you do know that, right?" she said and then laughed as if it was that obvious.

"She's crying those tears because she's hurt, but also because she wants to make you feel bad, but do you really think she's that hurt?" she asked me,

"She should have seen this coming, I know I would have and I don't even know either of you that well!" she said.

"But if you go in there right now, she's going to be sitting there among her friends, who are salivating, waiting there for a chance to kick your ass for making her cry like that?" she said.

"Do you really think she, or anyone else is going to listen to you while she tells you what a cold-hearted bastard you are?" she said, and then she started laughing at the expression on my face, and that got me going too, even Andy joined in after a moment, yet he never opened his eyes.

"If you go in there!" she said, "If you do that, then you really don't know or understand women at all!" she told me, "If you really feel that you want to, or need to talk to her about this, then you call her tomorrow and tell her, somewhere neutral!" she said, and then laughed as she said, "I hear Switzerland still is, and its nice there!" she told me as she looked away.

"Yeah!" I said, "I guess that you're right, nobody wins if I go in there right now, and I know that is isn't about winning or losing, I just don't want to give her any hope that it might lead somewhere just to pull the rug out from underneath her and have her hate me for the rest of her life!" I said.

"Come on!" I said, "We'd better take your boyfriend home!" I said, as I took one of his arms and waited for her to take the other.

"MY boyfriend?" she said, scoffing at me, "I thought he was your boyfriend?" as she lifted his other arm, and then all three of us began to laugh again, and then I interrupted that with another dumb question, but it was something that I wanted to know.

"So!" I said slowly, "That means that you're not his girlfriend?" I asked her and then I pretended to be serious; "Does that mean that…you are available?" I asked and then I laughed too.

She stopped and turned to look at me, as much as she could with his arm over her shoulders that way, and then she looked deep into my eyes and said, "If you're going to tell that you are finally ready to admit that you're sweet on me, then all I have to say is, again, you don't know women at all because I knew how you felt from the moment I first saw you!" she told me, and I knew she was telling the truth.

Andy interrupted whatever we were thinking by snorting again; she turned and lifted him, which forced me to do the same and she never saw the smile on my face, and as I said before; there were times when I liked pushy women, and this was one of those.

When we got him to his car, she drove and we sat him between us, to hold him steady but also because he kept trying to open the door and get out, we probably should have put him in the back but we lucked out and he never got sick and was snoring a few moments after we started off.

"You'll have to tell me where to go!" she said, as she shifted the car into reverse and backed out while watching for people walking behind or cars coming up or down the street while she waited.

"Helpless female!" I said, and then laughed as she pretended to lunge at me and almost hit a car that was parked across the street from the party.

"I'll show you a helpless female!" she said, grabbing me by the shirt, we were both laughing so hard as she drove us away that it was a wonder it was only one car that we almost hit, and no other close calls along the way either.

When we got to his house, we left him in the driveway, in the car with the keys locked in the trunk in case he woke up and was still drunk; I knew there was a spare key around the house somewhere and I was going to call him later to see how he was doing.

"Now what do we do?" she asked sweetly; we left him covered with a blanket and sitting upright so he wouldn't choke if he vomited and propped his head up to be sure before we left him there.

"I guess I should walk you home, and then go home myself!" I said, I was unsure of what else to say even though I did want to say more; I wasn't sure if there was a line or not, now that we were becoming more than just friends.

"What a romantic evening you had planned for us!" she said, "But at least you know how to get a lady home at a decent hour, after you had your fun with her!" she said, as we started to walk together.

"We had fun?" I asked her, and then looked at her out of the corner of my eye and tried not to laugh again, but it was fun being around her.

"Come on!" she said, taking my hand and guiding me, I live near Echo Park, so let's go this way!" and started us off.

Something about that name made me shiver, she thought it was that I was cold, but walking beside her, I had the strongest urge to take her hand, and I kept sneaking a glance at her as we walked, I kept thinking that I was dreaming, and I was afraid to pinch myself and find out.

As we walked together, I listened to the things she said, but more for the meaning of her words rather than the actual words themselves; because that would help me to understand her on a much deeper level; and the funny thing about that was, I felt as though that was an "instinct" or something that was passed down to me from my brother Flaco.

From that, I learned about the things that were important to her, about her faith and the few people she thought of as close friends, I knew what made her smile and what made her happy, I thought that I was just the man for that job and couldn't wait to get started.

Paying close attention, I watched the way she moved her hands when she was excited, how animated she would get about certain subjects, her voice would squeak a little higher and I guess at some point I realized that I was willing to listen to her say anything at all as long as she was talking to me.

There were times when I felt Flaco at my ear, saying things like, "Yes little brother, you listen to what she say's but look deep into her heart! That's where you look for the truth in what she means!" and other things that he might have told me.

Before too long, I realized that I was at the same gate as before, though this time there was no Morris, it was another guard and this time I wasn't lost, or looking for a voice that was looming out of the darkness at me, I hoped that meant there would be no spider either, but I kept that to myself.

"You…you uh, live here?" I asked her, feeling stupid for asking but again, it was out there before I could stop it, I will use the pressure of the moment ass my excuse but I didn't tell anyone that, I didn't know how she would feel about that and I didn't want to drive her away thinking that I was crazy.

"As much as anyone can say they live here, yes, I do live here, and then she looked dismayed, and I thought that this was something new to her, that maybe she didn't bring everyone here and was hoping for a different reaction when she told me, or maybe no reaction at all, but I knew I'd fumbled the ball and I had to get it back.

I also got the impression that however I was going to react to this part of her was very important to her, that it was hard for her to share this side of her with people that didn't know her, but they were those that she cared about.

It dawned on me then that she as taking my confusion, my hesitation as that I was possibly judging her or something, for being an orphan and living there, but of course, nothing was further from the truth than what, and I was trying to figure out a way to say that without putting my other foot in my mouth.

"Does that bother you?" she asked me, "Do you think less of me now? Feel sorry for me? Did I make a mistake in trusting you with this part of me?" she asked me, and she was looking deep into my eyes for the truth, same as I would have been doing.

Though I was pretty sure that she didn't want to ask that, or maybe she just didn't want to know the answer, but again, there it was; telling me that she was as confused as I was and that it was going tom be up to me to say the right thing, remembering to always be as honest as Abe when I did.

"Does it bother me?" I asked, though it sounded as though I was asking myself that question, then I said, "Should it bother me?" and then I looked at her for a moment, making sure that my next words were exactly what I wanted to say.

I think that it caught me off guard, because of the time that I was there before, and that time I didn't know how I got there, only that it was damned important that I did.

"I admit that I didn't know what to say, I was here once before, I was lost and found my way to this exact gate, and they told me that after I passed out, or whatever the hell it was that happened that day, that I was asking for two people, and one of them was named, Maria!" I said, and then waited for her to say I was certifiable and to get the hell out of there, but she didn't.

"It's really blowing my mind, that I was lost and had no idea where I was, got on the wrong bus and fell asleep and found my way to…you!" I said, and that last part really hit home for both of us.

"Wait!" she said, suddenly caught on that, "You were here before?" she asked, and then stepped back as if I'd been caught looking in her bedroom window or something; "You were looking for me? Why? How did you even know that I was here?" she asked me and was clearly a little nervous about this part of our conversation.

I could certainly understand that, but told her, "No!" I told her, "I was here, but I didn't know you were here, I was lost and got on the wrong bus from school; I ended up on this side of town and wandered around this area until I found my way to here!" I said.

"I will say this, I am pretty sure, because of what I know about you now, I know that you didn't plan or choose to be an orphan, that you must have some pretty serious feelings about that, and that's something that we can explore as we get to feel more comfortable around each other, and when you feel that you can trust me!" I told her and waited for her to look into my eyes to see the truth of it, but she didn't have to.

"But that's only if, and when you want to, I'm not trying to rush you in any way, I don't want you to tell me anything more than what you're comfortable with, and I promise to do my best not to say or do anything stupid or goofy!" and then we both laughed a little because we knew that would be a hard promise to keep.

"If you are asking me if it bothers me that you live here, or that you think I see you as anything less because of that, I will be perfectly honest and say no, it does not bother me and I don't think any less of you because of that, it doesn't what I think or feel about you, or how much respect I have for you; I think you are the kind of girl I can take home to mom and she'll love you and welcome you to our home, as will my father, I am sure!" I said, "If you ever felt comfortable enough to meet them!" I said, and then I noticed that she was holding her breath while she waited for my answer, and now she released it.

My answer made us both happy, I smiled at the thought of her and my father in the kitchen; though my mom might be there to tell her of my favorite dishes, he would tell her how to make them.

It seems to bother other people, there's a stigma to places like this I'm afraid!" she said, sadly, "I really feel that I can't trust a lot of people, very few, if any of my friends at school will ever know that I live here, they will never be here with me!" she said.

"I can see, and understand why it must have been shocking to you that day, and now; because you asked for someone with my name, and then you return later with me and find out that I was here all along, that alone has to be a shock to the system!" she admitted.

"When was this, that you were lost and ended up here I mean?" she asked me, she was clearly intrigued by the coincidence, if that was what it really was, "It was the first day of school, I fell asleep after getting on the wrong bus and ended up right here!" I told her nervously.

It was clear that this meant something to her, but I guess she wasn't ready to share that with me yet, but we were both trying to think of so many things all at once, she changed the subject though, breaking into my thoughts when she spoke again.

"I have never brought a boy here before, and I am very careful about who I trust enough to show this side of me, I cannot emphasize that enough, I am sorry for being redundant but I want to be clear!" she said, and then waited for me to say or do something.

"There is a day room where we can go and watch movies, they have popcorn too, and we can brink our own drinks, there are also games we can play or we can just listen to music and do homework, or talk about things!" she said.

Before I could answer she said, "I am not sure why, but I have been a little more…uncomfortable here, at home, more than I can ever remember feeling that way!" she said, "It has always been my home, but lately I feel as though I am a visitor and someone is out there in the dark, hiding for me to show my face out there in the open!" she said, and I could feel her fear.

I pulled her closer to me then, neither of us noticing until that moment that the rest of the world went away, there was no traffic, no one telling us where to go, and to keep a "respectable distance" between us as they would say if we were in school.

"Of course, you didn't make a mistake in trusting me!" I said, turning serious then and looking deep into her eyes, but that was not because I was looking for the truth, it was because I loved doing that now.

"But are you telling me not to tell anyone about it?" I asked, "Why would I? Why would this cause me to think any less of you?" I asked her, I am not a judgmental person to begin with, and not that shallow either, at least I hope not!" I said.

She was a bit stunned I think, maybe, as I hoped, it was better than what she expected from me, or maybe because she never thought of it that way before, but then she smiled at me and said, "Yes! No and No!" and started laughing, then she held me even tighter to her.

"Yes! Please don't tell anyone about it, and no, not to tease you about it, and hell no, not to think any less of you because of that!" I said, making sure I got the points down clearly.

"Yes and No!" she said again and then kissed me on the lips, softly and gently, as if she wanted to savor it for a moment, it seemed to me as though a huge weight was lifted off her shoulders now, it went better than she hoped it would.

"But you can tease me about it, it won't hurt me or bother me if it comes from you!" she said, as she started to leave, "I know it won't be done mean if it comes from you!" she told me.

I reached for her arm to pull her back and said, "As long as you end up right here, because it doesn't matter so much where you came from as long as we have this between us!" I said, as I touched my heart.

She knew right then that I was serious and that made her feel as happy as it made me feel, and to my delight, she kissed me again; this was brief but felt just as special as the first one, and I think we rushed that one a little because the security was watching us.

I walked her to the door to the elevator and stood there stupidly as the door swished shut in my face, I heard her say, "See you in school tomorrow!" as the door shut and then I realized that I didn't even have a phone number, or any other way to reach her except at school, I thought it would have been nice to hear her voice before I started to dream of her and I together.

Because it felt so good, I wanted to keep that feeling, the taste of her kiss on my lips for as long as I could, and yet I was getting the feeling now that I'd kissed her before, and funny as it seemed, that the time I kissed her before, there was someone we were worried that might be watching as well, and it had the same feeling, which made no sense.

Her kiss was probing, and gentle, as if she was holding something back, a little afraid to open herself completely to me, and yet I felt even then that she was more afraid not to open up to me, that she already knew that was a mistake and she had nothing to fear from me, only for me.

The feeling of "being there before" was so strong at that moment, that I stopped for a moment and touched my lips gently, I was trying to imagine how this was all possible, I know we never kissed before because I'm sure that I would have remembered that.

Feeling confused and yet joyously happy, I decided to simply enjoy the moment and not over-analyze it; I didn't want to get lost in the "why me?" club and yet I couldn't entirely escape it, it was not time for a pity party and I would have been the only guest if it came to that so I just kept walking as I thought of nothing but her and I.

As I got closer to the gate, I noticed that the guard was watching me closely now, I know that it was his job to be suspicious of anyone that he didn't know, for all he knew I might be hiding toilet paper under my shirt because he didn't know me, I smiled at him, trying to let him know I wasn't one of the bad guys but he never smiled back, he just kept watching me until I was outside the gate and not his problem anymore.

At that point, I was so engrossed in my thoughts that I never noticed that Maria was watching me from her room, she wanted to call me back and give me her number at least, but she also wanted another kiss, which I would have gladly run back to do had I only known.

She wanted to leave with me at that moment, and maybe never to return; but she knew that I couldn't hear her from there and they wouldn't allow her to go out again, it was too late, and yet she also felt a deep dread; she felt strongly that something was going to happen to us, and that it wouldn't have happened if we'd never met and found this feeling in our hearts, and she didn't know why, but she felt much safer when she as with me, she thought it was the love we shared that gave her that feeling.

But she was so happy that we worked out this way, she felt so many good feelings rush out of her heart and race to mine when ever she saw my face, I felt the same but still thought I was dreaming, she had so many good and loving qualities and she wanted to share them with me.

She couldn't understand how the feeling of something so good came with the potential to end up very badly, and to make it worse; she never before felt such a strong draw, such attraction from anyone or anything else in her life, she was confused as to why she felt so strongly about me, and felt such strength when she was with me, as if we couldn't be defeated, especially since it had come is such a short time.

When she saw me at the party, she was really happy to see me there, she saw some of what happened with Caroline and understood; she saw my body language and what Caroline likely saw but was still denying at the time, she felt sorry for me because she could see I wasn't happy there with her and didn't understand why Caroline couldn't see that and let me go.

It made her happy that she'd decided to come because when she heard about it in conversations with others or as she passed them in the hall, everyone talked about the band, how it was going to be such a great party and all, but she didn't want to go because she didn't know anyone and I never spoke of it, probably because I was dreading having to take her along, but she wouldn't have known about that part.

At one time, she was going to ask me about it, to see if I was going and maybe she could hang out with me, but we got lost in our thoughts and whatever we were talking about at the moment and she forgot to ask until later, when she went to bed that night wishing that she'd given me her phone number and then thinking it was too forward of her, that if I wanted it, I would have asked for it.

While I went home, I wanted to know what she was going to dream about that night, I was hoping that I would be in them of course; but she didn't know that, I was sure that I was going to be dreaming about her though, I was certain of that, and felt as though I was racing home to get to sleep just so I could look into her eyes once more.

But I never saw the other eyes that were watching me from the basement window, I never heard the voice calling to me again; but I was a little further away and it was whispered softly, as if they were going to allow us this moment without casting their dark clouds over it.

All the world could see how much I was in love with her, anyone could see that my feet never touched the ground as I put my hands into my pockets as I whistled some tune as if I hadn't a care in the world, as if the dark clouds that were on the horizon had nothing at all to do with us.

Those things would be revealed within a simple glance, and nothing was going to change that feeling unless it was to grow stronger and deeper within our souls; not for us, and not on this night, nor this time in our lives.

I thought about the guard and how he didn't recognize the feeling in my heart as I walked past him, I thought that it was sad that he'd probably never been in love, or maybe it was so long ago that he didn't recognize it anymore.

I was a normal guy I think, I liked some girls over the years, but there was never a girl I met lime this one; no one ever touched me so deeply in such a short time as she did, and we were just beginning, it was going to get a lot deeper and so much more intense.

"The English language was carefully, carefully cobbled together by three blind dudes and a German dictionary."

-Dave Kellett, Sheldon, 02-01-09

Gregor woke up suddenly, he was feeling as though he missed the Grand Ball by about three and a half years, as soon as he rose, he realized that he'd slept much longer than he liked to, he was hungrier than he'd ever felt before and on the edge of his consciousness as he woke uphe remembered thinking that there was so much more he needed to learn and he didn't want to waste any more time.

But he also felt that it was time to teach Jeremy a lesson about respect and humiliation, and though he knew that he would miss the boy; he was the only reason that Gregor was anything more than a shimmering mass in the attic, and yet Gregor would never give him that, he would never be able to look that deeply into it; he would never give Jeremy any credit that certainly was due.

The bigger problem for Jeremy was that he was no longer needed; Gregor didn't need the kids anymore either, he was as strong as he was ever going to be, he was also ready to see the world and to put his mark on it.

He crept down from the attic and went into Jeremy's room, this was a totally new experience for him, he was never in that part of the home without the fear of being caught or discovered before now, and now he didn't care; he actually welcomed the thought of being aught out there in the open, of having to confront whoever discovered him because there was no place or no time to hide.

Gregor looked down at the bed, and there was Jeremy, snoring softly, and the soft green glow on the clock told him that it was only nine-thirty, not very late at all.

He watched him for about five minutes, he was just listening to the quiet in the room, and then he stepped just a little bit closer; he was feeling the pull of the blood as it flowed through his veins, he fought the urge to rip him open then, he pulled up a wicker chair that was close by, sat down there and waited.

It was the kind of chair meant to make you feel as though you're on safari or something; it was noisy but comfortable as he settled into it and the strands stretched as it adjusted to his weight.

He leaned back then and smiled at the boy, he was not thinking about being quiet, or discretion or anything like that; but he was still thinking that he wanted to be discovered, confronted, caught in the open and this was his chance; he was going to wait until Jeremy opened his eyes and then he was going to show him the full measure of his power and the horror that he unwittingly helped bring into this world. He wanted to show him that there was no joke to be found here; and that his nightmares were real after all and not just his imagination as he'd been led to believe.

Gregor was thinking about the best possible way to send that message and to not think about that that pulsing in his neck, carrying the precious fluid that gave them both life; though not the same way.

He felt it, at times gently calling to him, at other times shouting at him to come and get it, as the boy slept so peacefully, and so to distract himself from looking at the neck, he started looking around the room, looking for anything else to keep him busy while he waited for the boy to waken.

As he looked around the room, he found out that Jeremy was an avid reader, or at the very least; a book collector, he had several of the books by Stephen King and his pseudonym as Richard Bachman, and Gregor was especially interested in "Salem's lot" because it was about vampires, so he sat down and opened that one.

He didn't read it page-by-page and instead he would flip through the pages for a while and then stop, find something interesting and then read about that part for a while before he'd start flipping through the pages again until he was done with it.

When he put that one back, he found Ann Rice's "Vampire Chronicles" and as he read through that one, he felt as though she'd written that book with people like him in mind, he also felt that it explained a lot of things, things that he couldn't manage like walking through walls or flying; or become invisible.

Then he found another book, and he knew that someone had done a lot of research when they wrote it; a study of vampires, listed as both lore and fact, in chronological order and started long ago, in dark times that were pretty much forgotten now.

He could see that someone came along every now and then and updated it, keeping it current as well as safe over the ages, and Gregor wondered how the boy came to own it because this was the original document and not a copy or something that you might find gathering dust in some library.

There was tape that held the edges together where it was especially worn and yet it was still falling apart, and there were burn marks along the edge as if it had survived a fire or two over the years, and he wondered why someone would want to destroy it.

As he leafed through the book, he found a story about a "contrary vampire" that was cursed by a gypsy when he hit and accidently killed the gypsy's wife, he was the leader or the tribe and there were rumors that she was also his mother, but nothing solid and no one ever cared enough to find out if it was true.

The story was, she and her younger sister were working the town, trying to tell their fortunes and make some money, the trouble was that they sometimes became too pushy and too aggressive; then they were asked not to come around, something that they were used to hearing; they would move on for a while, a few months at the most, but they would always be back, panhandling their way while trying to stay low.

That day, the elder woman had cornered a young boy, he didn't understand what she was trying to tell him and then, before he knew what was going on; she was telling him about his life as she caressed his palm, then she kissed her thumb and put it on his forehead before holding out her hand expectantly.

The boy still didn't understand, he had no idea of what she said to him, but he thought that he should at least be polite, and he took out a few coins and handed them to her, and then he turned to go on his way when she stopped him.

She stepped in front of him, then she started to indicate that coins were not what she wanted, and even though he'd given her all that he could, she wanted paper money, but he didn't have any and when he tried to tell her that, she became angry, she was like a crow hovering around his head then.

"That's all I have!" he told her patiently, and he started to walk around her, and again, she stepped in front of him with her hand out and her bearing more insistent as she again took out a paper bill and shook it at him angrily.

Then her sister/daughter/crime partner came running up, she saw that the old woman was angry and wanted to find out what was going on, but even from the distance she was already looking at the boy with an evil eye.

She scared the boy even more than the old gypsy and now they were both shouting at him, both angry at him and he still didn't know why, or what he'd done wrongbut it was clear that they were going to hold their ground and stay in front of him, they were trying to keep him there and hope that no one came along to rescue him, especially the local police.

As she got closer, he saw that the younger one was missing an eye, it was covered over with a white film and there were lines from a scar that ran from the middle of her forehead to the edge of her jawline. It was her curse, because no man would ever look into that face and see love; but then again, it was also her blessing because at times like this, she froze the boy in his tracks, it worked when she needed to be intimidating like now, it was perfect.

She stopped moving then, and raised her left hand over her white eye in the forked position as she prepared to curse the boy for his insolence, and he was near-panic upon seeing that, he needed to believe in it for the curse to work on him, and being so afraid, he backed away from her and ran into the other one, she fell and struck the back of her head on the asphalt, splitting it open, and she never recovered.

The other one ran forward just then and spit on him, he felt as though he couldn't move after that, and she was so angry that she bit into his neck, he felt that her spit was taking away his senses and sapping his energy to fight her off.

When he opened his eyes after that, he was in jail, awaiting trial for the murder of the old woman, something that was more of a formality because that had warned them to stay away after all, and the very nature of them told them who the aggressor was in this case, this was a chance to get rid of them legally, to formally brand them, "persona non grata!" permanently.

He was found guilty of accidental death, sentenced to one year of prison and then sentence suspended because they knew what happened, there were plenty of witness's that testified that it was a case of self-defense because of more evidence that was not yet presented.

The boy was not allowed to speak on his own behalf and was dazed the entire time of the proceedings, he never heard a word, nor entered a plea on his own behalf. He was confused as to what happened and yet aware that he was in danger, that he needed to get away as fast as he could, he felt that her blood had infected his mind and that he was actually dead now, and walking around at the same time in a semi-conscious state.

Now he was thinking that he had to find a safe place to sleep before the sun came up, which it would in a few hours; hopefully a place where he could sleep for as long as he needed without being bothered.

He would, like all vampires, feel the need to feed, to find new blood and take it, nothing else would give him any sense of peace or nourishment, and yet; unlike other vampires, when he drank the blood that he needed so badly he would immediately become ill and break out in severe hives and worse; he could feel the blood he took as it burned its way through his system, it closed his throat; this cycle continued until blood became both life and death to him.

When he discovered that it was a curse, he scoured the countryside looking for them; but then, by nature, they never left a forwarding address, and though they cycled through the same regions and towns at the same time of the year to take advantage of yearly festivities and they were very good at hiding when it suited them.

"Anonymity deflects more weapons than the strongest armor!" someone told them, and so his plan was to find them and explain to them why they should feel that the judgement was satisfied and they could remove the curse while retaining their honor over the whole thing, and failing that; he would feast on them and give them the same curse, and then they could all die together for all he cared.

When he finally found them, it was too late; the gypsy that could have removed it was so despondent over losing his mate that he took his own life a few months later, and as such, the curse could never be lifted.

He went through the rest of his life miserably trying to feed on others yet being so weak that they could easily fight him off and escape, and then he'd have to start all over again never gaining any sustenance and getting weaker with each passing night.

That meant that a normal feeding, which might have taken him ten minutes or so, not counting the hunting and taking of said victim; but now it took hours and sometimes he would get so frustrated that he would not be able to stop himself from tearing into them and then retching and vomiting all over them as they died.

It became so horrible for him, such a daily battle, a struggle to live that he wished he could die with them, but he doesn't have the courage to take his own life, and then he would start to feel as though his skin was crawling;

eventually, it drove him mad because there was no escape and then he walked
I to the sunlight and killed himself.

In actuality, he died of dehydration because he didn't drink anything
while he lay out in the sun, and the pain that he "endured" was more imagined
than real; he stayed out there for three straight days until he finally gave in
and died.

Gregor was bored, he looked back at the bed and Jeremy hadn't moved
any more than it took to breath and keep alive, his arms, his body was still
in the same position as he'd been in since earlier when they checked on him.

But he could sleep right through the loudest of noises, he once was found
sleeping on the floor nextto the waterbed as it was filling up, the stereo was
right next to him, blaring loudly and he was fine with it, never jumped when
the music did and slept right through the night, until someone turned it off.

Every now and then he would get up to use the bathroom, but that was
rare and he was pretty much sleep-walking when he did that; sometimes,
it was more of an excuse to get out of bed and stretch his legs; especially if
something was bothering him.

Gregor read about people like Van Helsing, and why he and Dracula were
enemies, and that there were female vampires that did more than just obey
their master, and some of those ran and hunted in packs.

There were times that he would wake up during the night and couldn't
easily go back to sleep even though he was so very tired.

He would force himself to sleep rather than wait for those dreams to
come, and then he would take what he'd call his sanity break, when he would
get out of bed and read something for an hour if he could stand it; or watch
the news on television until he fell asleep, have some warm milk and cookies,
a bowl of cold cereal with bananas, raisin bran, something that they said was
healthy and good for him.

Sometimes nothing would work and he'd be up all night, watching reruns
of his favorite shows on cable television, on this night, the thing that was
bothering him was that he smelled something that he would have been able
to describe as "dead" because nothing else seemed to fit.

He was thinking that maybe a rat chewed its way into a trap and died
within the walls and then worked its way into his dreams, but he also needed
to take a leak, and as he rose from the bed, he was thinking; This nightmare
is different, it feels real, and even closer somehow, but he hardly opened his
eyes because he thought it was his imagination.

What was happening for Jeremy was confusing him because his "half asleep state" made it all surreal, and yet it seemed both familiar, since he was in his home, and unfamiliar because of the feel of things that night; he kept thinking he should turn around and see who was following him, and then he'd laugh because he was in his room, but it was starting to frighten him.

In a moment of false bravery, he stopped and turned quickly; he thought he was ready to confront who or whatever it was, to demand an explanation but of course, there was no one there when he turned, nothing stirred in any direction, "Of course not! You're being silly!" he said to himself and chuckled, yet it was hard to believe that it was nothing and he was never easy to convince when he felt so certain about something, though nothing else ever felt like this.

Now he was outside and dressed warmly, though it had been unseasonably warm as of late; he was wearing a long coat and then he noticed that as it seemed to get noticeably colder though, and then, as he watched a fog was settling into the ground in front of him and then it began to drift towards him.

At the same time he was both fascinated as it seemed deliberate in its movement and he was deathly afraid because he felt the bite of the devil in that mist, he wanted in the worst way to turn and run but could not help himself; he felt that he needed to know what it was that he was running from.

Finally, he forced himself to turn away from it, he pulled up his collar because he felt a chill and then pulled his coat tighter around his waist, as if that might offer some protection; but protection from what, he had no idea yet.

He started to feel better then, as if he'd put some distance between himself and whatever he felt that fear from when he looked forward and saw a man standing there, though he was certain that there was no one standing there just a moment ago.

"But this isn't just a man!" he thought, because the man was unusually tall and he seemed to be growing even larger as Jeremy watched him; it was as if he was still trying to stand up completely, and now Jeremy could almost make out the man's features, even in the low darkness.

Now he thought he knew how a deer felt when caught in the headlights of an oncoming car; as hard as he tried and as much as he wanted to at that moment, he could not move though he felt that he was facing his worst nightmare and that even though he thought he was sleeping, this time it was real.

The man was standing there in the semi darkness, just staring at Jeremy, and though he held no weapon of any sort and didn't attempt to move come forward; Jeremy knew that the man held nothing but hatred for him, and that he wanted nothing more than to just rip into him and tear him apart; he was impatient with the idea of it and how close it was now, he could see it in the man's eyes and feel it as it emanated from him, and just as Jeremy thought he was about to start, a car approached them from behind Jeremy.

Jeremy felt a sense of relief, a feeling of safety for just a moment, as if the light was going to clear it all up and he would see the man for what he was, just a man that was out on the street, maybe he couldn't sleep either for all Jeremy knew; and he hoped for once that it was a cop, but it was just a car that was making a u-turn at the end of the alley where he stood.

Still, he was able to follow the path of the headlights as they pierced the darkness in front of him, he knew he would be able to see the stranger, who he now was thinking might be a statue of some sort because he still hadn't moved.

At the same moment, he was thinking about the lesson from "Pandora's Box" and then suddenly decided that he didn't want to know if the man was real or not, he was terrified to find out now and yet he could not tear his eyes away and followed the path of the headlights to his worst nightmare come true.

As he saw what was there, waiting for him, he knew that he was right, he was terrified because when he saw the man's face, he saw first the blood-red eyes that it wasn't a trick of the light and there was nothing but pure hatred for him in that glare.

Instinctively, he knew that the man's eyes were not always that red; but they turned that way when he was feeding; and the rest of the man's features, the palest skin that he'd ever seen, as if the man were made up of alabaster, or wearing too much makeup,

"OR DEAD!"

A voice jumped out of the darkness, and the man still hadn't moved, as Jeremy looked at him, he was not one to normally notice things like this but he did note that this man was easily the most handsome man he had ever seen, and for some reason that only added to his fears.

At the same time, he also felt as though everything was calm and peaceful and there was nothing to worry about, he felt that wash over him with almost angelic calmness, telling him that everything was going to be alright, it was going to be set to right in a few minutes and all I needed to do was trust this total stranger who scared the hell out of me.

Jeremy could almost feel the stress as it flew out of his body and all his troubles were magically solved, but he also felt another side of him; a side that seemed to be at war with the first half.

This other half hated anything that resembled calmness and a sense of peace; this was the side that, when he caught up to Jeremy would be very bad for the boy, he hated Jeremy because he brought out the feelings that it hated the most, and

"THE LIGHT!"

It shouted at him again, and this time the sound came from all sides at once, and it felt as though it wasn't going to wait, that it was already trying to taste Jeremy, to tear into him and see what his insides looked like.

He wanted to see how far he could get into Jeremy before he got sick, because he thought that he was the cursed vampire and not who he was before; now he was tired, and ugly and not very powerful, but as the car made that final turn away, Jeremy realized that he could also see directly through the man, to the markings on the other side that said, "No Parking" with stripes of black and yellow to make sure you didn't park there anyway.

The man smiled back at him then, but his smile held no humor; instead it spoke of things long dead, and when the man leaned his head back to laugh at Jeremy, his fangs elongated, changing from regular to canine as they glistened with razor sharpness.

He flicked his tongue over them because he knew that Jeremy was at that moment thinking he might yet escape; all of this was just his dream after all, and he was in control, and yet at that moment, Jeremy wet himself because he was so scared; he wanted in the worst way to turn and run, at least take a chance and not stand there like the sheep being led to the slaughter.

All Jeremy could manage was a sob then, he started to shake his head slowly from side to side as if he could deny what he knew was about to happen to him, there was to be no escape, no wake up and smell the coffee, there was to be no wake up at all; not in this world.

When he tried to speak, nothing came out but a weak "No!" and that was hardly audible enough for either of them to hear it sand then nothing else came out of his mouth as it opened and closed slowly as he tried to think of the right word; an entreaty that would make this thing change its mind and spare his miserable life.

Then he saw the man as he began to change, he seemed to be shrinking within his clothing and then Jeremy caught a shred of hope that he might yet survive this night, he was hoping the man would shrink away to nothing but a pile of clothes on the ground where he stood, like the wicked witch when she was doused with water.

Then he thought to run out of there, and this would have probably been his best chance for that; yet his muscles betrayed him and he couldn't move, it was as if he had to see what was going to happen next and couldn't force himself to move, no matter how hard he tried.

Then he saw the man had stopped shrinking, he was still moving around under his clothes, so Jeremy knew something was going to happen, but it was hidden from him for the moment; he wasn't being "held" by the man's gaze any longer and worked up enough courage to at least turn and look in the direction he might escape from, but then he heard a low growl that sounded like a very large animal and he wet himself.

He stopped and turned back, and was not able to do much beyond that because when he turned he saw was about three hundred pounds of a beast, sharp teeth glistened in the low light, they were made for the single purpose of easily separating tissue from bone.

The beast resembled a dog in most aspects, but for its size, it measured about five feet from shoulder to toe and was all muscle.

The eyes changed too, from whatever they were before to a blazing, bright red that seemed to come from a fire deep within it; a fire that had blazed for centuries and would still be blazing bright long after he was gone.

Then he heard that low growl again, and though it seemed to be coming from everywhere at once, he knew that he didn't have a snowballs chance in hell of getting away now.

He watched as the lips peeled back and then it snarled at him, foam was dripping from its fangs as it snapped its jaws together twice, as if to remind Jeremy that they were real and then it took another step forward, though it seemed to be waiting for something.

He could feel the force of its heavy paws as they hit the ground and imagined that it was leaving huge dents on the ground where they struck, and then once again, it snapped its jaws at Jeremy, it was taking its time because it knew that there was no escape for Jeremy; yet it was still waiting for something before it would attack and finish him off.

The dog seemed to sense Jeremy's fear and was feeding off it; it excited him and when he snapped again at Jeremy, he started to scream and that's what finally woke him up, he was shaking his head from side to side as he jumped up and pulled the blankets back as if the bed was on fire and he couldn't get out of it fast enough.

That was when he heard it again, that now familiar growl that was coming from just behind him as he stared at his bed, and then he realized that at least part of this nightmare was not just a dream and it was real, and it was there in his room with him; waiting for him to turn around.

Jeremy knew then that it was over, but he dropped to his knees, he was trying to find a way to plead for his life; as odd as it seemed and felt to him, he was going to try and pray and appeal to the dog for another chance; he was hoping against all sanity and reason that this was going to be alright; this was just a terrible dream and somehow it ended up real and in his room and now he wasn't sure if he was wide awake or still sleeping in his bed, he was praying that he'd never sat up and that he could awaken now; he would be cold and maybe shivering and maybe night sweats would be his only problem.

Instead, he was on his knees, crying his heart out as snot was running down his nose and into the corner of his mouth though he hardly noticed, he fell back then and raised his hands in front of him as if he could somehow ward off the danger, and he was willing to do anything, even reasoning with this nightmare in his efforts to make it go away and leave him alone; his mind screamed at him, "This can't be real!" and yet he knew that it was.

It was right there, live and in bloody color, it boggled his mind that somehow this nightmare chose his room to come into the world through, just his damned luck.

Now he was eye level with the animal, and he could feel its hot breath washing over his face and neck as he tried to squirm away from it, the fetid breath full of the promise of a painful and horrendous death that would not be quick.

"Up to you buddy, how do you want to check out?" he felt as though the animal was telling him to choose; and knowing how insane that sounded didn't make it any less real for him either, but then there wasn't much that happened in this day that could be considered sane in the first place.

"Quick and easy!" he heard, "Or you can just try and escape, see how far you can run before I snap at your heels, maybe rip open your Achilles tendon and see how much that slows you down!" and then he heard laughter, "Those are all the choices you get today, and no trading up!"

112

Then he began to laugh at the absurdity of this animal speaking to him and he lost it; "I would sing Dixie if I had to, if I thought it would save my life!" he said and then laughed some more.

But he stopped laughing when the animal stepped closer, he could see its mouth; it was closed, but the beast was snarling at him, then its gums began to recede, showing blackened gums that were curled into what might be mistaken for a smile, almost; but for the deadly intent that was embedded into it.

Leaning back on its hind legs, the animal suddenly lunged forward and closed the last few inches between them in a rush; those huge paws hit Jeremy full in the chest, knocking him back onto the bed while breaking three of his ribs and cracking two others; one of them punctured his right lung as he fell, and he coughed out a huge ball of blood onto his chest and stomach.

Then, deciding that he couldn't run, and it could take its time; the dog casually hopped onto the bed and crawled over Jeremy's prone body until its drool was running down onto Jeremy's face and covered it.

As disgusted as he was, he was afraid to move; he closed his eyes when he felt the animal's breath over his face again, he felt it lean forward and snap its jaw shut once, hard.

This was enough to sever Jeremy's head from the rest of his body in a flash of blood and gore; and as Jeremy's head rolled away from the bed, his lips still moved and you could hear him say, P-P-P-P-please don't hurt me!" as it rolled along, his life flowing out of his body and it finally stopped about three feet away from the bed.

His body twitched and convulsed for a few minutes as he fought against the iron grip of death, but it stopped after a few minutes, the blood continued to flow out of his neck, and covered the bed in a blanket of crimson.

Gregor was himself then, and he looked at Jeremy's body lying there and then he covered the bed with another blanket and went to sleep, the smell of Jeremy lingered on the bed and comforted him somehow.

Since he was used to sleeping in the cold darkness of the attic, this was a nice change for him, but his sleep was not all that restful either; he still had nightmares of his own, seeing bodies consumed by fire, and sometimes he thought it was his own body that was burning in those visions, and yet it didn't hurt him for some reason, which was probably because in the visions he was already dead but that never occurred to him.

There were times now that he was seeing someone new in the visions, a woman that seemed familiar somehow, he didn't know if that meant she was a friend or a foe so he didn't know what that meant, they were either indistinct or had been dead for so long that he couldn't see their features anymore.

Once, there was a woman who ripped out someone's throat as she straddled him, and the straddling part aroused him but then the blood that was splattered all over the place took that feeling away and he found himself reaching for his own throat, which felt raw for a moment; he woke up a few hours later in a cold sweat and decided that he was going to go out and make someone else suffer for this.

"If it's true that misery loves company, then let it sleep in someone else's bed tonight!" he said, and he never noticed that his voice changed in the middle of that, and for that moment, he sounded very much like Jeremy.

"For tonight at least, I will sleep in this bed alone!" he said, still in Jeremy's voice, "And woe unto those that disturb my sleep, you are all warned!" he said, as though he was speaking to children or something, and then he fell into a deep, and surprisingly restful asleep.

> Love is the only disease
> Love is the only disease that gives pleasure.

-Anonymous

As Maria prepared for sleep that night, she began what was becoming her nightly ritual, it was something that she started doing to help her sleep at night; it was something that made it easier to relax once she did all of the things on her list.

First, she checked all the windows, making sure that they were locked tightly, and then she checked the vent and made sure that it was closed, and then she put about thirty pounds of books on top to make sure that it stayed shut.

But as she went back to close the blinds on the window that was facing the only busy part of the street, she noticed a black cat that was crossing the street at that point, and there was something about that cat; a familiarity that she felt she could not ignore.

As she watched, the cat was walking onto the path of an oncoming car, and though the driver didn't seem to notice, the car was not slowing down as if they saw the cat on the road, and the cat wasn't paying attention to the car either, instead; it was looking up at her as if he knew the cat knew that she would be standing there a that exact moment.

It seemed almost deliberate, but that would be suicidal, but the cat stopped in the middle of the street and began to preen itself, she could see its long, black tail curled around it's hind legs and he was paying no attention to the car that was about to strike him right about shoulder height at a high rate of speed.

The car was so close to the cat that she could she shiny black hair on its back, with the headlights right on him, the cat lifted its right rear leg and began to lick it and then drag it across his face.

Maria started to pound on the window, she was trying to get the attention of the driver, or maybe to scare the cat away from there but they were both much too far away and her window was closed and not the kind that opened.

Then the cat finally stopped what it was doing and looked at her, it seemed to smile at her then, it waited there, as if it was making sure that she saw this, that it was being done for her benefit.

When the car finally got to that point and she turned away so she wouldn't see the car strike the cat, she heard the car continue, she heard a loud "thump" that told her that the tires hit and ran over the body; she closed her eyes and tried not to imagine how the cats body was tossed and spun around, the ribs crushed and the life's blood was flowing out of its nose and onto the street, but to her surprise; when the car went on its way, the cat was still there, and unhurt and unfazed.

It began to walk slowly and deliberately towards the building and Maria knew that it was coming for her, she watched as it stopped at the guard shack for a moment, and she saw the guard reach down and pet it instead of chasing it away as he should have.

She tried screaming at him, pounding on the window to no avail; he was still reaching to scratch it under the chin when a car approached and he went to check it, forgetting about the animal and doing his job.

She turned away from them and leaned back against the wall, she was trying to imagine what the hell all of this was about, what any of this meant to her and as was always the case these days, she was at a total loss when it came to any kind of understanding or explanation.

Looking out the window again, she couldn't see the cat, and then she thought that it might have run and was just then going into the door below, she tried to look down to see but couldn't get an angle to see that far down the wall.

Then she thought the cat must have gone around the building and would have to go through too many people and locked doors to get to her, but just to be sure, she put a chair in front of the door, angled it so that it would make a lot of noise if anyone tried to open it and it would surely wake her up.

Then she decided that she was being silly all along and pulled back the covers, ready for bed at last; she fluffed up the pillows extra high and then pulled the blanket all the way up to her neck, watching the door as she drifted off to a fitful and uneasy sleep.

She thought about me just before she fell asleep, and that made the room a little nicer, a bit warmer than it was before; and she thought it could have been her imagination and something of a romantic notion but she thought that was a good thing too.

Smiling in her sleep, she thought about that first kiss, and how soft and pliant my lips were when she kissed me; and that surprised her as well, she was never that forward before with any boy that she thought she lied, no matter how much she thought she liked him; with me, she felt comfortable and it just felt right, as if she'd been around me for a long time instead of us just now getting to know each other.

It was something different, like so many things that we shared between us, even things she'd done before felt new with me, it gave her the freedom to do things she'd never even thought of before and she had to admit that it felt good; it felt right because of things like that.

It helped her that I liked it too, that I wasn't trying to change that or act as though it was weird, I wasn't put off that she was that forward with me, that she didn't have to wait for me to kiss her if she wanted one.

She felt her face flush a little when she thought of that, the only kiss she could ever remember from before was in grade school, and that didn't really count; it was a boy that stole a kiss from her, and maybe because it was stolen, she wasn't sure, but it didn't make her feel all warm and fuzzy as this one did.

Then, just as she was starting to think that was a sign; that things were going to get better now, that was when she should have noticed the spider web that was high up in the corner of her room, directly across from where she slept, as if the spider needed a front row seat to her dreams.

Maybe she saw it subconsciously because she drifted off to sleep and whatever she was trying to get to; she was derailed, and her thoughts drifted back to Maria and that damned spider and she felt herself being pulled in that direction.

She fought against it, tried to make her mind go off in a different direction but her mind drifted forward to that day and away from the time she was trying for; she realized that she was powerless to try and change it or stop it;

she couldn't even slow it down, she decided then to just follow it and see where it went, where it would end up because that just might reveal something new to her, or so she thought.

She started seeing images that she thought must have been real to her at one point in her life; maybe memories of the things that happened when she was too young to understand, yet she felt as though they must have been real, there was no other way to explain why they came back to her just then.

Thinking of them in that way helped her to slip deeper into and farther back until she came to realize that they were, indeed, actual real memories of a time when she was very young.

She decided that she should wait and see, rather than try to wake herself up and start all over again; she thought that she might not be able to get back to sleep if she did and then she'd lose the thread, which, normally would not be so bad, but this one felt important, as if she needed to know and there was no other way to find out.

Then she saw the nurse, Maria, as she was preparing to leave for the night; she was still wearing her uniform but she was putting a coat on over it; her shift was over and the sun would be coming up just as she pulled into her driveway if she was lucky.

There was a full-length mirror on the back of the door, and she closed it so she could check her hair, she wasn't one to primp and fuss over her face and she hardly wore any makeup these days either, "Why bother?" she thought, "With no one to impress?" she told herself; the weather was so crazy lately that her hair was so dry and wild and she could do nothing with it.

There were other nurses there, coming in for their shift and one of them asked her, "How's that little imp of yours?" and they both laughed, as did Maria in her sleep because she knew instinctively that they meant her when they said that.

Then another told her, "It was pretty cold last night!" she said, "I'd put on a scarf if you brought one, but I have a spare if you didn't, you can give it back when you start your next shift!" she said with a smile.

"Bring an umbrella too, if you have one, I heard on the radio, a sixty-eight percent chance of rain!" she said, "It was getting dark and cloudy out there!" she told her.

"I have a scarf, thank you!" she said, "I'm parked near the building if its raining so I should be fine, thank you as well!" she said, and then went to her locker and took out the scarf she wore last time it was windy outside, she put that on and pulled her coat tighter around her to keep the wind out, she was always careful and tried to take care of herself.

As she walked out of the building, she was glad that she took them up on that advice; the first blast of wind would, have blown her coat away, "Someone in Kalamazoo would be wearing it next!" she thought and then laughed.

Her nature was such that she would have simply hoped that it would end up with a homeless woman that really needed it; that maybe their winter would be warmer because of her.

Maria smiled at the thought of that, of her nurse's coat flying away like that; floating through the air and ending up right next to someone that was feeling lost and cold, maybe even questioning their faith when the coat comes out of nowhere and it is restored.

She was thinking about that and praying for something good like that but as she was thinking that was "too funny" she felt that first strong pull on her heart that told her something was terribly wrong. Her heart began to race as she watched, ready to shout for help or run away if anything happened.

Then she felt her pulse quicken to the point where she was about to hyperventilate or something, she forced herself to see the image of herself breathing into a brown bag until she felt her heart slowing and that she was back in control again.

She started to feel a little better after that; she still felt a little nausea, though her head was clearing a bit and felt less like it was filled with cotton, all of this while lay fitfully in her bed and trying to sleep.

The feeling became much worse, a lot stronger once the nurse touched the handle of her door, as the nurse touched it, Maria saw visions of a horrible, fiery car crash and she knew somehow that her nurse was in there and still alive when those flames started,; that she was conscious as the flames crept towards her, but unable to escape in time.

Though she couldn't see her in those images, she knew for certain that it was her, she recognized the car as surely as she knew that it was a deadly accident, and that there were multiple vehicles involved, and a lot of those people didn't survive either.

She began to shake her head from side to side while she was asleep, and then she heard a voice shout out,

"WAKE UP!"

Yet she could not shake herself out of her slumber, she tried to say "NO!" to make it go away, but of course it would not, not now anyway, not simply because she wanted to goaway.

She got a dread feeling then, that this was what happened to her nurse, because as hard as she tried to remember, her nurse was just gone one day, with no explanation and no final goodbye, it would have hurt in any case, but not hearing at least that much hurt the most.

Now it was becoming obvious to her, there was a good reason why she never stopped to say a final goodbye; she never meant to leave her in the first place, and she felt better for knowing that, but felt worse for knowing why she was gone, and then she felt guilty for not even asking about it and simply accepting it as a part of life because people came and went all the time.

She watched her nurse as she did all of her safety checks; the lights, the mirrors, the seatbelt and the position of the seat, she checked all of those before she even put the key in the lock, even though no one else ever drove her car or would have moved the seat, the mirrors, or anything else.

There was another thing she always did, a quirky habit that she saw her father do when she was very young and did it "to remember him" as it always made her smile, which she did as she turned her lights on and off again.

When she looked out of the side view mirror, she noticed a large spider web clinging to the inside of the housing for her mirror, it was trailing over from the car that was parked next to hers; as if the spider jumped from that car to her mirror and that told her that the spider was somewhere inside the body of her car, as there was webbing on her car and not on the other car.

She took a tissue and scraped it off then, but she couldn't bear the thought of something so disgusting to her car so she walked back to the building and threw it into the first trash can that was outside and then walked back with a shiver.

Then, when she was finally ready, she backed out of the space and towards the guard shack and the exit; and as always, he stepped out and smiled at her as he waited for her to get to the gate.

He was a nice guy, he'd been trying to get her to go out with him for a while, and as she drove towards him and saw that smile, she decided that if he asked her again; she was going to accept this time, she knew that he wasn't going to give up, that he wouldn't accept no as an answer for much longer, and she did like him; he certainly seemed to be a nice enough man so why not, she asked herself.

Then she decided that she wouldn't wait for him to ask again, "Hey Frank!" she said as she rolled down her window, "Does that invitation to go out still stand?" she said, and now she was smiling too.

He smiled back at her and said, "Of course, but what was it that changed your mind?" he asked her, "Was it my new cologne? My clean, close shave? My endless persistence?" he said as he turned his cheek towards her that she could get a whiff they both started laughing.

It was a nice scene, that was what Maria was thinking as she watched them laugh so easily together; they were already comfortable enough that they could talk without embarrassing silences and they both had the same sense of humor.

Maria couldn't understand why she felt so scared when she watched them talking, they looked as though they would be very happy together, she heard the nurse say to Frank, "That would be nice, I haven't been to the movies in a very long time, I'm sure that will be a lot of fun!" she said.

"That idea, and your cologne won me over!" she replied and laughed, and then she handed him a piece of paper with her number on it and said, "Call me!" before she drove off.

He was thinking two things as he watched her drive off, though he couldn't have known that it was the last time that he would ever see her, first, he was thinking that he was the luckiest man in the world; and secondly, he was thinking that she was such a very nice lady, and very pretty too; and he was happily surprised that she was still available.

He smiled then, and waved to her, even though he knew that she couldn't see him anymore; she driven off thinking that he was such a nice guy and all and she was feeling good about giving him her number because nice guys didn't just fall out of the trees these days; he was always a gentleman and she would make sure that he remained that way or there would not be a second date.

Though it was a long while since she'd had any of "that kind of fun" and she felt that she was not only out of shape for that, that she wouldn't be enticing or alluring, but that she couldn't even remember anything but the most basics of it, she thought, or maybe she just hoped that he would be just as awkward as she was.

As Maria watched her nurse driving, she saw her turn right and hit the freeway; seeing the sing that she wanted, she took the five South, towards Orange county.

She was sitting in traffic, waiting for the meter light to turn green; she noticed a large black spider lowering itself into the back seat of her car, just at the edge of her vision as if it didn't want her to see and was waiting for her to be distracted to come out of hiding.

It bothered her so much that she started looking for something to swat it with, but at the same time, the light finally changed and the guy in the BMW behind her started leaning on the horn as if his pants were on fire, even though it had just changed.

Going into the flow of traffic, she started in the slow lane, but she was still thinking about the spider, how large it seemed to be to her; "It wasn't really that big was it?" she asked herself, certain that it was but still finding it hard to believe.

The impatient driver raced past her then, still blowing his horn and giving her the middle finger salute as he shouted some ignorant obscenity about women drivers.

As she laughed at him and his pettiness, she couldn't have noticed that Esmeralda was climbing up the back of her seat, crawling up from the floor so she wouldn't be seen and that she would be ready when the moment was right.

She was still being cautious as she didn't know if the nurse sensed her there and was going to pull over and find her, but so far, she hadn't even slowed down except for the demands of the flow of traffic and her plan was perfect to this point remembered

That was the same moment that her nurse remembered about the other spider in the vent and wondered how it could have found her because there couldn't be two spiders that large could there, she thought that there must be something else going on and was going to try and find out when she got back to work.

"Still!" she thought, "That one was very small compared to this one!" she thought to herself as she continued her drive home.

She changed lanes then, from the slow lane to the second lane and was now gaining speed, and thinking about what she was going to eat, if she was going to stop at a fast-food place or the store and buy something to make or just take it home and eat it there.

Esmeralda was almost in position and was looking at the veins pulsing in her neck; she bared her fangs then and waited for the right moment; she felt that it was soon but not yet, and she was having a hard time waiting, and yet she knew it had to be at just the right time or she might die again and who if she could come back again and find her if she could come back at all.

As the traffic ahead of her started to slow, she looked to the next lane, but there were no opening and every time she thought there would be, she would turn on her blinker and the driver in that lane would speed up as if to say "get behind me if you want this lane!" something always happened and yet still amazed her, to see how petty some drivers could be.

While she was so distracted, that was the moment that Esmeralda jumped and bit onto her neck, injecting a small amount of her venom into the nurse, she hoped it was just enough to slow her reactions down and make it harder for her to function.

She bit into her and then quickly backed off, because she didn't want to be swatted either; she felt, rather than saw the nurses hand that just barely missed her as she jumped down to the back seat and waited for the fireworks to begin.

She didn't have long to wait though, as Maria was trying to swat her away when she felt the bite, another car moved into the lane and cut her off, coming so close that she hit her brakes hard; with her attention off the road for the miniscule part of a second, she looked back just in time to see that the other car lost control for some reason and started fishtailing back and forth in front of her, it struck the car to the left and then swung back and bumped Maria hard on the left front fender, hard enough that it caused her to lose control and spin harshly to her right and into the other lane.

As she fought hard to regain control, a bobtail truck struck her on the other side, and it was heavy enough that it sent her flying in the other direction again, if she was lucky that day, she would only have slid forward, the car was crushed on the side, she was hoping that something would stop her momentum because her brakes weren't doing the job, she was hoping and praying that no one else would hit her as they swerved and avoided colliding with her, but luck was not riding shotgun on this day, not for her.

All around her, she could hear the screech of tires and the sounds of other cars as they tried to avoid hitting her and each other, it was made even more difficult because her car did finally stop, turned sideways and right in the middle of everything.

A lot of the cars did manage that feat, as difficult as it was but there was one that couldn't, it was caught between two cars that were careening out of control, in one of them, the driver appeared to be dead as he wasn't moving behind the wheel and his eyes were closed, the other was fighting for control as he flew down the lane, so his car, the middle one slammed into Maria's car on the rear fender and close to the gas cap, which caused it to start leaking from below the line that was compressed and eventually broke from the pressure while it spun wildly through the rush-hour traffic.

Sometime during all of that, her seatbelt came loose and she was holding onto the steering wheel for dear life while she was bouncing around wildly inside of the car as it moved from one lane to the other, at one point she was slammed head first, into the top of her car, the impact so severe that it caused her neck to snap with a series of loud cracks, she also broke two teeth in front, the least of her problems.

She was thrown across the seat and towards the passenger side of the car, she hit her head again, this time it was the back of her head so hard on the door that glass was now flying all around her and she almost passed out.

Now it seemed as though all around her was a world of broken glass and metal shards flying about her head, metal shrieking and the smell of burning rubber from all the tire tread left around her, other cars were slamming together and added to the confusion.

Then she thought she was losing her mind, or at the least she was delirious because she was seeing the other cars slamming into each other and all around her were demons, attacking her faith while threatening her very life; biting and lunging at her from all sides at once.

She couldn't explain it, but for some reason, she felt as though they were waiting for a sign, or some acknowledgement from her before they could finish her off, she paused long enough to cross herself and say a quick prayer, followed by others that she thought of at the moment; prayers of faith and promise.

As hard as it was, she even closed her eyes as she prayed as she was talking to the lord now and wanted to make sure that she got it right and her faith in him was absolute, she was certain that if those were really demons out there, fighting for her soul and that they would not allow her to live anyway, and she was going to do all that she could to make sure that they wouldn't win on this day.

The last of her windows shattered just then, sending more deadly shards of glass flying all around her once more; some of the larger pieces cut into her right temple, and more cut into her raised arm as she tried to ward them off, like shrapnel from a grenade they tore into her wherever they touched and she had no chance after that.

She fought against it, tried to get up and she thought she heard a scream of anguish as her car was struck again, slammed into from the rearby a car that managed to get three-quarters of the way through a complete three hundred and sixty degree turnaround when it struck her car.

At some point then, the main artery leading to her heart was cut and then the blood really began to flow, it was covering the dash and flying onto the steering wheel, coating the seat around her but she still had some fight left in her.

She tried once more to regain control; it seemed as though she was spinning around and bouncing around cars for what seemed like an eternity, she knew if she couldn't regain control and stop the car it would be over for her and then there would be no one to comfort little Maria.

Even in her sleep, Maria felt her breath catch in her throat then, touched beyond words that; even as she knew that she was going to die, and maybe even why it happened that way; her last thoughts were still about the baby that she loved so much, she thought about it and how much she enjoyed every moment of it as she applied pressure to the wound that was causing the most blood flow.

She tried to hold the blood flow with one hand, she tried to hold onto the steering wheel with the other and managed to pull herself over to the driver's side once more and felt as though she could manage this when she was struck by another large truck that smashed into the left rear side of her car and crushing it and now if she was going to be able to crawl out of the wreckage it wouldn't be from that side.

The impact from that hit sent her car rolling then, over and over until it finally came to a stop near the center divider of the freeway, the impact caused the car to slide up the retaining wall instead of stopping as it was meant to, and the car was mangled so badly that if another car hit her, it would knock her over the wall and onto the other side of the freeway with that traffic coming head on from a blind curve; they wouldn't see her until they were almost on top of her.

As her car finally stopped moving, she looked up, just in time to see that same large spider crawling away from her, as if it had been watching her from the headrest on her seat, even admiring its handiwork, but she couldn't believe that' she kept trying to think that it must be something else; she thought she was losing her mind then because she could swear that was what the spider was doing; she thought that it must be shock settling in and tried to think of what to do next.

Remembering her first aid training, she knew that she'd need a blanket, to raise her feet up, to keep calm, and all those things came to her mind but in jumbled terms, and she was already forgetting why she needed them.

Maria reached up again, trying to raise herself up from the seat of her car, Esmeralda jumped away from the window and Maria heard her say, "That will fix that interfering bitch!" as she jumped away, but she wasn't sure if the nurse heard her, because she never reacted.

She looked out of the window and saw a lot of cars in various positions, upside down, slammed together so tightly that they would have to be cut apart to tow them away, smoke and debris covered everything around her as well but it was eerily quiet as well.

Thinking that she might be safe and survive this after all, she heard a pop and then the car burst into flames, the engine was too hot and caught first, the flames spread slowly on the ground underneath her car where it had been leaking gas since this all started.

As she was reaching for the door, the car exploded into flames then, and if she would have made it there, she wouldn't have been able to escape because that side was damaged so badly that the door wouldn't have opened and she was already too weak to crawl out through the window.

When they cleared the scene, there was nothing left of her for the coroner to work with; coincidentally, he was the same man that misdiagnosed the boys death at the hands of Gregor, and he was not able to forget that boy; he thought it might be guilt for rushing through that and ignoring signs that he should have seen and known what to look for afterwards, and yet he felt that he didn't recognize them until a few months had passed and it was too late.

Now he was having nightmares about the boy, chasing him throughout his life and always popping up at the worst of times, and seemingly trying to kill him for getting it wrong.

He would have been more thorough this time if there was more to work with but there wasn't much left to examine and the cause of the death was obvious; her remains were so badly charred, it was difficult to extract anything of her remains from the car parts that were just as charred.

When they tried, her skin pulled away and one of her legs came off, and it was deemed a terrible accident, cased closed and no one knew the truth of it and what happened until now, years later.

Maria saw all of this and woke up with a gasp; she jumped off the bed as if her own legs were on fire and her lungs were burning from the same smoke and a fire that burned a long time ago; she sat down and began started to cry, she knew now what they'd kept from her, what they never told her about; but she had to remind herself that it might have been because none of them did know the truth.

They only knew that their friend and co-worker died in a horrible accident and that they would not even see her face one last time to say goodbye, and they probably wouldn't have told Maria what happened because they would have decided that she was too young to understand.

Maria cried for her nurse, the only one that cared for her so lovingly that it cost her, it put her in the crosshairs of her worst enemy when she chased the spider away that day, and that led to this, and as crazy as all of that sounded, she was sure that she was right; that she was deliberately murdered and the evidence destroyed along with everything else.

She never saw the spider escape, her attention focused on the nurse as she cried for her, but she hoped that someone saw it crawling on the ground and stomped its guts out, but she knew in her heart that no one ever saw it, not on that day.

Trying hard, she focused on those last moments and out of the corner or the nurse's eye she saw the spider when it flew from the window, it was swept along by the current of the traffic, her web was cast out and caught the antennae of and old, mint-green Buick Le Saber that was driving past.

Wilber Somersby was a retired postal clerk, living on a pension that never seemed to be quite enough to make ends meet and his one big expense was this car; but he loved the car so much, he was willing it through the wreckage, hoping that it wouldn't get even so much as a scratch.

He was hoping that his luck would hold out and no one would hit him, he was almost all the way to the other side, he bought this car right off the factory line and didn't want to lose her now, it was as if they'd grown old together.

"If I can make it over there, I can pull to the side and try to help!" he was thinking as he worked his way through cars crashed all around him and the others that, like him, were trying to avoid those cars and the bodies that were lying motionless on the road.

As he got past the last of the wreckage, he got out and tried to help and she saw Esmeralda as she jumped off his car and went into the underbrush nearby, Maria was sure now that she'd escaped and would have be dealt with one day.

She had no idea of where or how that would happen, or even how a spider could have managed all those things, but she thought maybe she would understand better when the time came, she wept for her friend who was so much more than just a nurse; beyond a deep friendship and far beyond where her duty ended, she was mother, sister and closest friend to her and was killed for it; and once again, there were those damned flames that seemed to be everywhere.

Maria ran to her closet and pulled out a broom and went to that corner and smashed the spider web, but since it was empty at the moment, it gave her no sense of satisfaction, and then she stayed up the rest of the night, cleaning her room and making sure that there were no other webs hidden from her view.

She heard others in the hallway and then realized that the sun was up, she was ready to run out there and challenge anyone out there and demand to know why they didn't tell her what happened, but again, she knew that she was being unreasonable, a lot of the people that worked there now were not there at the time, it was when she was very young and they had moved on.

She also knew that none of them had her "bird's eye" view of what happened such a long time ago, and there was no proof that it was really how it went, this was a nightmare and she tried to convince herself that it was nothing more but she couldn't, it felt too real.

It galled her that they went on as if nothing was amiss, as if she called off all the time or was so unreliable that they thought it was business as usual when she didn't show up for work the next day, "Life goes on!" as they would say, but god help the person that would have been dumb enough to say that right at this moment.

Still, she could not help herself and screamed at the top of her lungs about the injustice of it; she was angry and she demanded answers, and some of them came running but were confused, they had no idea of what she was speaking about and had kept nothing from her.

She had the feeling that some were ignoring her because they didn't know and didn't care enough to ask; but there were others that did know, and yet they weren't going to say anything either, maybe they felt that it wasn't their place or maybe they didn't even know how but they didn't stop to explain, or maybe even that she already knew.

The looks on their faces as they swept by angered her though, even if all they knew about it was that it was a horrible accident that took a good and honest woman in her prime, a tragedy that, as doctors, nurses and care givers they saw every single day.

"As careful as she was with her life, and as happy as she was, do any of you really think it was an accident?" she asked them.

She turned then, and walked away, certain that if anyone knew anything they weren't talking yet, though one woman did step out of her office and she tried to call Maria over, asking her, "Who told you that? How do you know anything about something that happened when you were young?" she asked.

But she ignored the questions and kept walking because she didn't want them to see her crying, she knew that they didn't want her to know what happened even though she knew for herself, she needed someone to confirm it but that wasn't going to happen, she kept thinking that she was murdered because she took such good care of her.

Some of those closest to her were asking the others who she was talking about, but they weren't getting answers either, she didn't stop to look back to see but she thought their questions fell on deaf ears as well.

Then she ran into Nurse Abigail; she was the senior nurse administrator because she had been here the longest, and was just a rookie when it happened, she knew and admired Maria and had worked alongside of her, had been helped along by her with timely support and good advice and she never forgot her or what she did for her; they had become more than just co-workers though Abigail was known to be somewhat aloof, and not a warm or caring person.

She felt a sadness at seeing Maria crying that way, she felt and understood what she was going through as she had gone through it in much the same way; trying to find elusive answers to something that she did have every right to know.

Abigail went to her then and held her close for a moment, even though Maria resisted and tried to pull away from her, she held fast until she stopped and then kissed her gently on the forehead; "I'm so sorry child!" she whispered to her, "If you go to Evergreen Cemetery in East Los Angeles you will at least find her final resting place, but no one was with her, so all we know is that she was a good friend and she died a horrible way!" and then she said no more, Maria could see that she was crying when she left though.

She thanked her as she left and made herself a promise to go there and take her some flowers and thank her for what she did, but she ran to her room and cried herself to sleep, and mercifully, there were no dreams this time, no visions that haunted her, and she never even noticed the web was back in that high corner again, empty, but for a couple of emaciated insects.

Since it was a weekend and 'free day" for her, no one ever bothered her, when they didn't see her they thought she'd gone out, or to the library or something and they thought nothing of it, some thought after what had happened earlier that she just needed to be alone with her thoughts.

They even thought that it was a good thing that she got out instead of stewing over something that happened a long time ago and that she couldn't change or do anything about it now; she was the oldest girl in the facility; all the other kids moved on in one way or another, even Monica.

What finally did wake her was when the phone started ringing, she woke up and stared at it for a moment; the ringing so unfamiliar as no one ever called her, and then she hesitatingly answered when it wasn't going to stop.

The only time the phone was ever used was to call out, check the movie schedule and the bus schedule that she could plan a trip to the mall and back.

"Hello?" she said, not even sure if she was in the mood for a conversation, she thought it was most likely a wrong number, the phone was still silent as she waited for answer and was reaching for a tissue to blow her nose.

Hello, Maria?" I finally managed to say, I knew it was her and was nervous about calling her because she hadn't given me the number and I wasn't sure how she would take that, I'd taken it when they were looking for someone to take me back to lost and found, I went to the desk and looked in the directory.

Since that day, I'd called her number and hung up three times, I was so nervous and scared for some reason and though it made no sense, I was being a guy and had to force myself to call her this time and wait for an answer, and now that she did I was kicking myself for being so foolish.

"Is that you Carlos?" she asked me, and that made me laugh because else called me Juan, or Johnny, or even Jon, but she liked to use my middle name, she told me that everyone else knew that name but few if any knew side of me and she felt it was more personal; it was a psychological thing she was doing to my head and I thought it was kind of fun.

I heard sniffle's in her voice and that made me sad as well; even though she tried to hide it from me, I just hoped that it wasn't a bad time to be calling because I really did want to see her, and I felt that if I didn't something was going to happen and it would be very wrong.

"I was um…wondering if you had any plans for today" I asked her and then held my breath, "But I am sorry if this is a bad time?" I said, hoping that it wasn't.

"No!" she answered quickly, "I don't always make plans for the day, sometimes I just go by the seat of my pants!" she said nervously and then giggled at what she'd said; she was feeling elation at the sound of his voice.

Sometimes I go to the library and go from there, see a movie at the mega mall, but I know how boring that must sound!" she said with a sigh. "I need a new life!" she admitted and then laughed.

"I was thinking today about going to Evergreen Cemetery, but I think I need to be alone when I do!' she said haltingly, as if she wasn't sure how I was going to take that and understand.

"Well, I trust you, and know that you don't need protection!" I said, "But I hope you don't think that I understand, I don't know what Evergreen has to do with you, and to be honest; going to the graveyard doesn't seem like the most fun or romantic placed to go with your girlfriend, so it must be serious, and if it IS serious, then maybe I should be there for you, in case you need a shoulder to lean on or a hand to hold" I said, hoping that she would change her mind and let me come with her, I wasn't sure why, but I really felt that she needed me there, that we'd both feel better if I was.

I guess that it worked and she decided that she didn't need to go alone after all, that maybe I could be the perfect support system because she knew that what she was going to see when she got there would hurt her, tear her apart from the inside, and she was sure I wouldn't be judgmental or try to "fix it" like a lot of guys would; I would know I was only there for support and not advice.

"There's another thing I need to ask you about!" I told her, "That kiss that we shared, I was wondering if you felt the same things that I did about it?" I said, impatient to get the conversation going again, though it was true that the kiss did spark something from deep in my heart, a deep and long-forgotten memory that was maybe repressed until now.

That bothered me though, maybe more than anything else I was thinking about, that it was a repressed memory told me that it wasn't a good one, and I wondered what could be bad about anything to do with her, when all the feelings from her were good.

I could sense that she was still digesting that thought, at first, she was thinking that I was going to be "a guy" again and ask her if it was good or not, if she liked it as much as he did, and she would have said yes without hesitation because she did enjoy it; but the way he said that made her know that he meant something a lot worse than that.

"Can we meet a t the library?" she asked me suddenly, and I almost felt as though a weight was lifted off her shoulders as well as mine; I liked the thought of the library as it was close enough that I could get there in a hurry and public enough that she would know I was being a good guy and meant her no harm.

"I sure can, and I sure will!" I told her, "What time is good for you?" I asked, though five minutes ago would not have been soon enough for me.

"Give me an hour, and I will see you there!" she said, and after a little more small talk, hung up and then ran to her closet to find something nice to wear, and then she smiled, thinking that being with me right now was just what she needed, something I would have been very happy to know.

"He'll make it better somehow!" she said to herself, "he can help me to understand some of these things and some of these feelings, maybe I can help him understand his too!" she thought.

Down in the sub-darkness of the basement, as Maria was leaving her room, Esmeralda was also trying to make some sense of things; she knew that she hated this girl, that there were unexplained and yet, strong feelings, about her ever since that day, such a long time ago that she crawled up the vent and went into that room.

She never forgot her, but it had been a long time since she'd had felt her this close, this strong that she knew the girl was close, she knew it was much as she knew she was no longer that innocent and helpless child, lying vulnerable in her crib like that day; she felt as though she'd missed her chance to kill a mortal enemy before she was strong enough to fight back, as she was now.

All of this time, Esmeralda had been distracted by her life, the things she went through and what she did to get to this point but Maria was always on the fringe of her thoughts, and at one point decided that Maria was the sole reason why she was drawn to this building in the first place, even though it was also perfect for her in all other aspects, giving her the darkness that she needed in order to grow.

Now, she was thinking that it was time for some new things, some changes in her life as well as her biology, lately she had been working on controlling her appearance and holding onto the human side of her personality.

Before, she was mindless in her actions, it seemed as though she was happy allowing the arachnid side if her to rule as it chose, now she was making her human side come out at will, or at least working on it, and making that last longer each time she got there; she was trying to remember what it felt like to be a woman and walk on two legs.

The thing was, it was as if she was at war within herself at that point, her spider side would become angry with her and attack that side of her mind by projecting the arachnid side of her into Esmeralda's mind, making her think that this was the proper face she should be wearing, that she was a true black widow and being a human was a mistake that nature had corrected.

When she would emerge from this "civil war" she would be exhausted and suffer through the worst headaches, because the two sides of her argument were within her, the term "splitting headache" really applied to her and how she felt when she opened her eyes.

She found that she did like the anonymity of her spider side though, she could go farther and faster as a spider, but then, it did nothing for her social life, she couldn't just change in the wink of an eye from one to the other so she had to plan her excursions and time them by how long she could hold on; it all came down to the fact that she missed the interaction that she enjoyed before.

Though some of those conversations about those people's lives bored her to death, now she longed for any conversation with anyone and she also knew that the bodies and stench were growing, and she needed to find something new soon.

The smell was so strong that it was getting to her now too, and it was a long time since anyone had slept in this area, even when it was raining outside or cold enough that people were dying of exposure rather than come there and have some sense of shelter.

She wasn't sure about what they called fashion these days, she found it distasteful and abhorred what she called the "stripping away" of a woman's femininity by making women wear pants and she felt that whoever started that fashion should be punished severely.

Then she started reminiscing about the fancy and elegant Balls they threw in the mansion, she remembered Tomas looking resplendent when he wanted to, especially when he wore the uniform of his office, the bright red sash that ran across his chest and the medals that he was given after the war, he cut a fine figure of a man in those days.

Then she felt a twinge of sadness at the memory of him in those times, she remembered him trying to make her laugh, acting as though he was sexy and falling far short, but they still had a good laugh; and then she felt anger at him, for making her kill him, simply because he wasn't strong enough to do it himself.

For a moment, she thought that there was really no reason to have done it, it made as much sense as why she killed Gregor, but there was no taking it back now; and it was at that moment that she realized that she truly was the ultimate black widow, killing off her mate even when she didn't let him have her.

She sifted through the things left behind, and the few bodies she could manage as she tried to find something to wear, trying to make herself fit the times and was upset that she could not find a dress to wear and if she did, it wasn't worth wearing anymore or much too small for her.

To make things worse for her, the only pants she found that she could wear were pants for someone very small, they were "Carpi style" which made her even more uncomfortable as she didn't know they were supposed to be short.

This all made her furious, and she almost shouted out; "They won't let us be women!" because she longed for the times and the fashion of her times, this was not beautiful or stylish, and she felt that it stifled her femininity.

She felt that she was as ready as she could make herself be, and this was going to be a recon mission, to scout out any enemies find a suitable place to relocate if she could, and then she tried to look for a mirror and because it was so dark, even when she did find one she could not see her reflection in it.

She felt that she looked horrible, not like her at all as she remembered herself; she turned away because she was repulsed by her ugliness, and she thought that this mirror was one of those trick mirrors because her reflection came back in dual images; almost interposed against each other so that one would be in front of the other but she could switch from spider to human easier.

As she watched, she could see her arachnid features, submerged just below her human face; the multi-faceted eyes that would fight to be in control because it gave her such a better view, especially if she felt that she was under attack.

She waited for the sun to go down that she could go out, thinking that the lower light would hide her face more easily, and as she waited, she worked on holding that human side longer, she kept at it until she felt that she had it under control, the two sides of her personality blending into one.

But she wanted the safety and comfort of the darkness in case she was forced to hide, she could run into the shadows more easily and if she was trapped in an alley, she could climb the walls and escape while they could not.

Before she felt she was completely ready to go outside, she climbed higher up the building to get a better view of how many people were out there, she hoped for low activity and yet the more people that were out there might have given her more anonymity and less chance of standing out or even being noticed.

But as she waited for the sun to sink further she cursed herself for being so careful and trying to get everything perfect before she would step out, because as she stood there and watched, she saw Maria as she left the building and walked towards the guard shack so that she could leave, and she looked as though she hadn't a care in the world.

It brought back a flash of anger, and she almost reverted back to her spider form to give chase, but it was still too light outside and she would be without clothes, undoing all the effort she went through to make herself fit in better.

Because of that, long after Maria had turned the corner and was well out of sight, she managed to get down to street level herself, without being caught and was still nervous about being outside, she didn't want any extra attention brought her way.

She'd spent all of her time making her face look human that she forgot about other things like walking on two legs and the coordination that it would take and she was a bit wobbly at times, her gait unsteady but she still managed to fool the guard and walk past him without any questions asked.

Not knowing where Maria went, she headed West and managed to find a park a short distance from the facility and thought that might a good place to catch her wind and observe people without being noticed herself, she had no idea of how tired she would be; how much energy this little trip would take from her.

She was doing all those things at once and it was hard for her, trying to adjust to the times; she found it quaint that they needed to reserve a small green place in the middle of the city so that children would know what a tree was.

As she looked around her, trying to catch all of the changes since her time, she saw other women that were she knew were practicing witchcraft, and this time she might have even reached out to one of them and asked for help, but she knew they were a different kind if witch; she didn't want them to see her though a couple of them did, they also chose to use her approach to this and turned a blind eye to her.

She knew they were "white witches" and she felt uneasy when they were around, and the word "Wicca" came to mind but she didn't know what it meant to these people though she'd heard it before, those times were so long ago that she thought these weren't the same as what little she knew of them.

Because of that, she was able to discover some things about this "new world" that she found herself in, but if she had looked the other way a little longer, facing East as she sat down, she missed Maria as she entered the library to meet with me.

The library was directly across the street from the park where she was but she didn't know; though she sat there for as long as she could stand it; she was as comfortable as she could manage and yet she noticed that people avoided her, she hoped that it wasn't because they had a sense of her true self; she hoped that it was the shabby clothes that she wore, that they would think she was homeless and would ask for their change in a time when there was no such thing as spare change.

As such, they gave her w a wide berth, and she didn't mind that at all; she closed her eyes to slits and thought "the better to see them with!" and laughed to herself.

They thought she was sleeping while she sat there and avoided her like the plague, and all the while she was playing close attention to everything that was happening around her, her senses so attuned to her surroundings that it was as if her head was on a turret and spun around quickly when something happened, yet she never turned.

She saw the little girl in the bright red dress and black patent leather shoes, the white lace frilly socks as she walked past with mommy and daddy, this after she spent the last twenty minutes jumping up and down, playing something she called "hop scotch" to her friends but it made no sense to Esmeralda.

The girl was about four or five, and Esmeralda thought she was so cute in that dress that she would make a nice snack, she was going to try and smile at her, but the little girl felt the evil in her and moved to the other side of her parents and away from Esmeralda who still hadn't moved.

The little girl never took her eyes off of her though, and looked back long after they were safely away from her, and then Esmeralda watched a couple that had sat on the far end of the bench; it seemed that they had never learned the word discretion because they couldn't keep their hands to themselves.

It started before they sat there, they were rubbing their bodies as they walked up, and now it seemed as though each was trying to swallow or absorb the other through their faces.

She was thinking that she would never get used to this new society as they sat there, in decent times they would have been placed in stocks for what they were doing, they would not be ignored as if it were normal as it was ignored now.

She was fighting against herself now because she wanted to kill them, "in the name of good manners and etiquette" if nothing else, but she managed to hold that in check because there were too many people around at the time.

It never occurred to her how absurd that was; that she would curse them for lack of good manners while she was thinking of them as food, and if they weren't out there with so many witness's lingering about she would have gladly shown them what she thought of their wanton behavior.

Deep inside, she was suppressing the feeling that she was as much jealous of them as she was angry; she was thinking that she'd never felt that kind of passion in her life; completely forgetting that the only time she ever did; she killed Gregor for it.

It bothered her moral sense, she was offended on one hand and aroused on the other, this was a society that she thought was really screwed up, something that she thought would never happen, not in her wildest imagination and yet no one else seemed to care so it must be normal, acceptable, but not to her.

She could imagine them in stocks, the people would over them with rotted fruit thrown in for good measure, she would be branded with a large red "A" on her dress, her hair cut short; and yet no one even gave them so much as a casual glance zas they went about their way.

All of this time, except for the little girl no one else seemed to notice her or bother with her until these little boys stopped when they were passing by, they thought they were going to mess with her, that was very old and she was sleeping and they were going to urinate all over her once they were sure they were asleep and they could escape from her.

She hadn't so much as moved a muscle in a while, they thought for a moment that she might even be deadbut they saw her breathing, and they didn't know that she was listening and she herself was waiting for the right moment, she knew what she was going to do before they even thought of what they were going to try to do.

One of them felt her eyes on him, even though they were still closed; he told the others that she had "bug eyes" and the others started teasing him about it, they were calling him chicken and worse, but he didn't care because the fear she put out was worse than anything they could have said or done.

"Look!" one of his friends said, "She isn't even looking in our direction!" and he pointed at her face, which did seem to be leaning a bit to her right now that he said that, but he still felt her eyes on him, and they felt hateful and evil.

He tried to tell them "her eyes" and they thought he meant both of her eyes, but he meant all of them, and he didn't know how to explain that because he felt that he was losing his mind; but for him, this actually began a few years ago, when he was awakened in the middle of the night to see a strange man standing over his bed, and when he sat up to take a better look the man jumped out of the window.

The thing about that was, it was upstairs, and there was shrubbery and branches to break his fall, but it still would have made a lot f noise and hurt like hell, it was a distance after all, and yet when he worked up the courage to look out there, the branches were undisturbed and there was no body lying there.

He went to his brothers bedside to make sure that he was okay and saw a small trickle of blood trailing down his neck, and yet; as he looked closer to see the wound and help him, it disappeared and he thought it was either his imagination or a trick of the light; yet it still scared the hell out of him.

He stayed up the rest of the night to make sure that the man didn't come back and that his brother was okay, he spent the rest of his life looking out for his little brother who didn't seem to remember anything different that night and never saw the man.

For a while he thought that it was just a dream but it never felt that way; he thought that it was either a warning or the beginning of something bad that was coming and that he'd better be ready, there were times when his brother seemed pale to him, almost anemic though he didn't know the term for it, but it went away after a while and he was fine.

There was one other time that he woke and thought the man was there again but when he was fully awake he found that they were alone and his brother was fine, yet he felt as though the man was there and was very close to his neck when he woke, he wanted to look under the bed but he was too afraid of what he might see down there if he did.

He also remembered that he felt the strongest urge to urinate, and he almost thought it would be okay, that if he told his mother about the man she would understand, but he knew that she would never believe him, she would tell him that he was making it up because he was too lazy to get out of bed.

Then he remembered a sting in his neck but thought nothing of it, and he never bothered to tell anyone about it either, and he felt that he wouldn't be able to sleep after that but was snoring away a few moments later; he woke in the morning feeling sluggish a little behind everything that was going on but at first, no one else seemed to notice that anything was amiss.

Then his mother saw it and took him to the family doctor, they thought he was anemic and prescribed more green vegetables and some rest for the day and left it at that.

Now, as he watched this woman sitting on the bench in the park, he felt the same fear from her as he dd from that man standing over his bed that night when he felt that he'd let his guard down and the visitor returned to find him sleeping.

He felt as though the other man had marked him somehow, that this woman and dead people, evil people would see him, that because of that mark, they would, see him more than the others as easy prey or something, it was something that he couldn't see, and he couldn't wash it away or change his clothes to get rid of it, they would still know him by it.

Then he thought he should try and warn the others, but he didn't know how to say it without sounding crazy and making them laugh at him, at that point they'd never take him seriously until it was too late; they would instead tease him about being afraid of an old lady.

The thing of it was, she did get a sense of him, more than the others, and she felt something on him as if he was wearing cologne or carrying a brightly lit neon sign, and in a flash; she knew that his name was Carl Lingstrom, and that he would grow up to be a good man.

Then she saw that something terrible was going to happen and that would change; not that he would become evil, but that he would become a man that lived "outside of the law" or at the very least, near the fringe of that darkness.

She felt both fear and loathing as he got close to her; she had to fight harder for control then, because she wanted to rip into him and kill him, to see what it was that was causing her heart to race.

As all of this was going through his head, she showed them that she was, very much alive, and that she had been watching them all this time, and not even close to sleeping as they thought.

She opened her eyes and then smiled at them, as if she were inviting them closer, to spend some time with her, and none of them could move for several moments; they all felt as though they were flies confronting the spider and armed with nothing more than their wings and their quick reflexes.

Though they all wanted to run as fast and far away as they could; they all felt that same fear in their hearts, they knew it started with her and yet they kept trying to remind themselves that she was just an old lady after all, not a monster or something that could hurt them.

Though they weren't saying anything like that out loud, she did "hear" what they weren't saying, those things that angered her even further, still, she seethed under her exterior and the smile was meant to show that there was nothing to fear at all.

Until she smiled at them that way, they thought they might be okay after all; but the cold smile gave them all a reason to run home and hide under their beds, and they should all hope that she didn't mark them too, and that they might be safe.

They never spoke about it afterwards, not even among themselves, and they never thought about abusing or hurting the homeless again for as long as they lived.

THE LESSER OF TWO EVILS

Men never do evil so completely and cheerfully as when they
do it from a religious conviction.

-Blaise Pascal (2623-1662)

Y OU COULD CALL IT A strange coincidence, but Gregor was at the same
park that night, though he was on the Southern edge and was the last
of them to arrive on that night.

He was out on the hunt for food when he found his way there, and he
was feeling a bit frustrated while he was there because that part held the least
activity, at least on that night; he liked that because if anything happened
there were less witness's and yet there were not a lot of options that night
either.

Gregor didn't know about the library though, and when he did find out
about it, that brought out the memory of a huge lizard, but he didn't know
anything else about it at the time.

The few people that were out there that night were couples and small
groups, they weren't alone and he didn't want to risk getting hurt, he preferred
to hunt single people because they were less trouble, he did once feed on a
couple but he was very hungry and the element of surprise worked in his favor,
it was what doomed them at the time.

They were drinking that night and decided that it was a nice enough
night to take a walk under the soft moonlight of that romantic full moon.

He forced her to watch in horror as he fed on a date though she knew she was going to be next, he was right next to her and yet he held her there with the power of his will, would not let her run from him, he enjoyed the power he felt from watching him feed.

Gregor fed on him and then tossed the body aside; he suddenly felt so powerful, so strong from the look of fear that he saw in her eyes, knowing that his will alone was holding her there, he felt invincible, ready to take on any challenge and all comers.

He gave her a small bit of hope then and smiled at her as he walked towards her slowly and sensually; as if there was something else that he wanted from her and his appetite was sated.

But she felt that shred of hope as it worked its way into her; she thought that maybe he was full now and he would spare her, but reality brought her back to her senses when she saw his fangs glisten in the soft moonlight, and since then he hunted mostly solitary people unless he was especially hungry, and then she knew that it was over and there was nothing she could do to change it.

He found that he liked women better than men, they smelled better and were softer and better tasting; but when he was hungry it didn't always matter, and he didn't always have a choice in that part of it and it was first come, first served.

Out of reflex, he looked up at the moon because he always thought of it as his friend, helped him to see it clearer and farther than normal, he saw that it was full and bright now.

But it was also different, and he didn't lime it at all; he winced when he looked up there because, instead of the cold-hearted orb that normally hung up there, the one that he was used to, it had changed on that night, and not at all to his liking.

This moon was something that he'd never seen before, this time it was a happier moon, it was one for the lovers of all time, the kind of moon that had already inspired a thousand poets to write a million poems and millions more to be written on the subject, it was bright, clear and especially beautiful.

Instead of visions of craters and green cheese he could see two figures dancing on it, they seemed to be frozen in some sort of embrace as they world watched; they weren't moving, and yet he felt as though they were laughing at him, dancing together now, and even worse than that; he felt as though they were mocking him in his anger.

He looked away quickly because it took his mind back to another time and memories that right now he'd rather forget, then he cursed at it and turned his back against it instead of following it and maybe finding some of the answers he wanted so badly.

Then he heard some activity nearby and found his first victim of the night, when he rounded the trees and found another path that circled around, he followed it from there until he saw a man that was walking alone.

The man was about thirty feet ahead of him and he was taking his sweet time because he had nowhere to go and no one to do anything with anyway.

"I'll give you something to care about!" he said as he quickened his pace and moved in closer behind the man, and then he felt that the man sensed him back there, his head turned slightly to the right and behind him.

Gregor could tell that the man was used to being deceptive because when he turned towards Gregor, most would have missed the slightest move but not Gregor.

It made him think that the man was possibly a police officer and this was s ting operation, a decoy to catch someone out there committing a crime, but this man felt different, not "official" as if he were a cop, so he didn't let go and followed to see where it would lead.

He tried to connect to the man, to will him to not be afraid or worried that he was being followed as he was harmless, but he quickly got the feeling that the man knew he was there and was not at all afraid of him.

Then Gregor got the impression that the man was possibly looking for some company on that night and why he was out there walking alone; he wondered what the man expected to fi d out there at this late hour, and then he remembered the men that enjoyed the company of other men.

He felt the alarms going off in his head then, and though it felt strange, it never felt dangerous and so, thinking that he had it under control, he ignored those alarms and watched as the man settled down on one of the benches out there, and he was waiting, and even in the low light, Gregor could see that a smile was playing on his lips as he sat there.

As Gregor approached, he asked for a cigarette and waited, and Gregor said, "No, I don't smoke!" though he said it somewhat impatiently.

He was not used to people that weren't of him, and speaking to him this way, this felt so odd now that he felt as though he'd become the prey, that the tables had turned on him somehow and he didn't like that at all.

Still, he sat down anyway and took his shoe off and pretended there was a pebble in it as he tried to sort this out, and the man slid closer to him as though they were old friends.

Gregor took his time with his shoe and watched the man out of the corner of his eye as he removed the imaginary pebble, there was no way that he would find easier prey than he found out there on that night, and yet he hesitated because sometimes when things appeared to be too good to be true that it usually was.

Though he'd had no experience with this kind of man, he'd heard of men that were drawn to other men, and it didn't matter to him in the least as he was hungry and there weren't many other candidates standing around, waiting to line up and become the blue-plate special.

Gregor looked around and didn't see anyone that might see them and then slid his shoe back on and then leaned forward as if he was going to kiss the man and then slowly went for his throat.

The man had no idea what he was dealing with, and he likely would have laughed if anyone tried to warn him, he turned his head slightly and let the man kiss and caress his neck, and he never felt the first bite until it was too late.

His thoughts were drifting off and he felt as though he was floating above his body now; and for a moment he panicked and tried to hold on, but then he felt that it would be alright and that it was okay to just let go.

He looked down at himself and saw the man nibbling at his neck and wondered why he couldn't do anything, he wasn't responding, he was trying to bring his hands up and yet they hardly moved, when he tried to grab ahold of something his hands slipped right through anything he grabbed at and he couldn't prevent himself from drifting away from his body and this world.

His hand did manage to reach out that time though, and Gregor thought he was resisting and pushed his hand back down as he fed, the man began to feel a sense of calm and peacefulness, he felt that if he looked down again, that he would feel a sense of regret, loss and sadness, so he kept looking away.

What saved him was a new policy that had been recently initiated by the new local precinct chief that started on that very same day.

He wanted to have his officers patrol the park and local neighborhoods on foot patrol as they did in the old days, this was meant to instill feelings of confidence and trust between the police and the people in the neighborhoods they served, and also to deter crime since the criminals wouldn't see them coming if they didn't have the cherry topped car.

Most of the crime lately had been centered around this park, drug deals that went well and others that didn't, there were fights, prostitution and then near the restrooms and then some used condoms and needles and now everyone was crazy about it and rightfully so.

He sent the word down and the patrol was set up to go right through the middle of the park; high visibility and a lot of publicity for any arrests that were made from it because it was an election year, and everyone was watching.

The chief was in trouble, the election wasn't going well for him, the challenger came up from the ranks and had the respect of the rank and file members of the force that he would be commanding, more so than the chief sitting there now, and everyone knew what was coming and they'd better choose sides wisely.

He told the press that they were on top of this small "crime wave" that was more like a burp as he called it, he said they would see a rise in the number of arrests and a lowering of the crimes being committed in their neighborhoods, that they would be safe again in their schools, parks and their homes.

"Think if this as a way to work off the doughnuts you eat while you're sitting on your ass in your cars!" he told them as he dismissed them that night.

"he just wants more for his fat ass!" observed officer Norton as they left, he always hated doughnuts anyway, because of all the cop jokes that started with them.

Norton was one of those guys that blamed everything on someone else, it was never his fault and everyone else should have known better, that he shouldn't have to tell them everything.

He was forced to work with another new partner, a kid that was fresh out of the academy, his name was Danny Nieto, and he didn't think there was any truth to the rumors about old-school training until he met his new partner.

Danny was a good man, one of those that went to church and he had always tried to live his life right, every Sunday, and he went to the classes the church demanded, and he knew the Bible well.

Not by chapter and verse, but he knew what it was and what it meant to his life; even when it wasn't the easy choice.

But Tommy Norton was as well versed as the local preacher, which only served to prove that you can know what the good book says and still not know what the good book says.

They say that even the devil knows the Bible, but knowing it doesn't mean that you live it, as much as you might have thought so, or pretended or fooled yourself that you did.

He heard daily scripture and word and what the Bible tells us about what's going on in the world; but he never really listened or paid attention because he held his own beliefs and he stuck to them, he knew what Tommy was telling him was not fact, but opinion anyway.

That they drew the first night of "crime walk" as it was called, was much to the delight of Danny, he loved to walk anyway and grew up near here, this was his neighborhood and he even played baseball in this park, but that was ages ago.

He tried to tell Tommy about it, but he wouldn't listen, he never heard a thing he was saying, he said he was trying to teach the kid the ropes and he wouldn't listen either.

It bothered Danny a lot that there was crime here, because his roots were here and he wanted to think it was still as he thought of it when he grew up here and ran these streets, and he was glad that he was chosen as one of the ones to do something about it.

"For the times I played catch out there with my dad!" he would say, "Or the times I was here with a girlfriend trying to get to first and then all the way home!" he said and then laughed at the memory.

But Tommy tried hard to talk him off the park that night, he had a premonition but he didn't want to tell the kid that, he didn't think the kid would take him seriously if he told him about that, but it was that more than anything that made him want to go somewhere else and roost for a while; he pretended that his feet were bothering him, and they were, but that was normal for him and tonight they were tolerable.

His feet hurt from the cold, and from not being used to walking at night, but it was that something else that was bothering him, something that he couldn't explain and didn't yet know if it was good or bad, though it felt very bad; something that he should have paid more attention to and maybe tried a little harder to understand what it was trying to tell him.

"Come on kid, let's go get a cup of joe and I can show you procedure and the best and easiest way to get your paperwork done at the end of your shift, I can explain a lot of the things you're going to see out there and tell you what to do ahead of time so you'll know and we can get through it safer as a team, what do you say kiddo?" he asked, though he could sense that the kid was already hot for the park.

"If I show you what I want to, the Cap will stay off your ass and things will go evenly and smoother for you, its something your going to have to learn anyway!" he said.

Danny said nothing for a few minutes as if he was thinking about what he said, he tried to appear as though he was in agreement when he was trying to change Tommy's mind while he was trying to talk to him about going to get some coffee.

Part of that was common sense, he didn't want to be sitting around in a warm coffee shop while his partner droned on about the what he thought the Bible meant, and how it related to what he was trying to teach him, only waiting and hoping nothing would happen to take them back out into the cold, he wanted to use that cold to keep himself alert in case something did happen.

"tell you what!" he told Tommy, I'll go through the park, a quick shot right through the middle to show we're here and you tell me where to meet you afterwards, no one will ever have to know, you can rest your sore feet and we can patrol the park as we were supposed to and keep the bad guys away for a couple of hours at least!" he said, he liked the plan and thought it would work, but he could see by the look on Tommy's face that he wasn't going for it, but was reluctant for some reason.

He was going to let the kid do exactly that, let the kid walk his nuts off in the cold, but he knew that if something happened to the kid, or he did something wrong that he would catch hell for letting him go alone, that he left him alone in a hostile environment.

He looked around as they approached the park, feeling as though someone was already walking over his grave and they were still talking about the captain as they got out to walk, but in truth it turned out to be night and really not that cold, and there weren't very many people out there at that hour anyway.

It didn't take them long to get to the far end of the park either, but Tommy still complained about it, and at first they saw nothing, though Gregor and his victim were right there, they were wearing dark clothes and blended into the bench and the darkness around them, it hid them so well that they were almost right up on them before they saw them there; they had to look really hard to see them and Danny made a mental note to talk to the cap about the lighting in this area.

They thought it to be two lovers and were going to break it up and send them home, and as they got closer, they were thinking to just leave them alone as long as they still had their clothes on, they were adults after all.

Gregor must have sensed them nearby or something because he looked up quickly at that point, and that was enough to make them both stop in their tracks as they saw the blood on his lips and the red in his eyes and both felt fear in their hearts.

The other man turned his head and groaned softly as Gregor rose to leave in a hurry, he was angry that they interrupted his meal but he was not yet ready to take on two men that were armed with weapons and had radios to call for more help if they couldn't handle him.

They looked at Gregor as he was trying to leave and ordered him to stop, but they first had to check on the other man, to make sure that he was okay, at least for the moment while they got him some help, they went after Gregor then but he had a nice head start on them and had already covered some distance.

Killing that man in the park was one thing, they would all make a lot of noise for a while and then it would die down after a few weeks, after they got tired of chasing their tails around and getting nowhere, but killing one or two cops was not so easy to forget and something that they would not let go of so easily.

In the meantime, he knew that the trail that would lead them to him would get colder and colder and he knew all of that, that they would never find him but he still didn't want to bring any attention to what he was doing, at least not yet.

They went back to the man who seemed to be asleep now, he was still on the bench and hadn't moved very much, they kicked the bench as they were frustrated and not used to feeling as they were at that moment; "Hey! No sleeping in the park!" they told him as they tried to wake him up.

When they couldn't wake him, they stepped a bit closer, but Danny was already at Gregor as he fled and he took out the radio, he was going to call for backup when Tommy stopped him.

"We don't need backup for one man, it's better if we catch him ourselves and get the collar!" he told him, though all of his training to this point told him the opposite, that backup would ensure that they would live to see tomorrow, but he hesitatingly gave in to his partner who was senior and "knew better" than he did about what to do or not to do in these situations.

Danny reluctantly put the radio back in his belt and watched as Tommy began to prod the man and push at him, and then they both saw the bite marks on his neck, though they were fading already, they saw the trail of blood that ran down his collar.

He knew what it was instantly, and Danny immediately crossed himself and said a silent prayer, because he was never so scared in his life, but that didn't mean that he was ready to turn tail and run; he heard, "What the?" as Tommy started to step back, this was too scary for him as well.

Then they both jumped and almost shot him as the man suddenly opened his eyes and said, "Something wrong officers?" and then tried to get up but was too weak and quickly fell back.

"NO sleeping in the park! Tommy repeated, this time much louder so he would get the message, he didn't mean to shout it so loudly, but this shit was making him nuts, he wasn't used to being scared and couldn't even remember the last time it had happened.

The man rose then and turned north first and then southeast before he finally left, they offered to call a cab or an ambulance for him, but he refused the cab and balked at the ambulance, "Don't need no doctor!" he said and then laughed.

"Hey Danny, what do you say we find that other guy and see what the hells going on? What do you say kiddo?" even though he was afraid, he thought that the kid was more afraid, being a rookie and all and that he would agree, and they could go back to the car and get warm again.

"Why the hell can't these guys feel this cold and stay inside?" he asked, though he knew that Danny wouldn't have the answer either.

They couldn't have known it, but Gregor hadn't left the area either, he was watching them as they spoke to his prey, he watched then as they turned in his direction and then headed the other way, towards Jeremy's house and away from where he was hiding from them.

He reached out to the man as they left, and he thought he got a hold of him when he saw him stagger, but then he continued the other way and Gregor knew he was going to get away because the cops were between him and the man.

Gregor knew that, even if the man hadn't had a drink all night that he was going to wake up in the morning with one hell of a hangover, but at least he would be waking up, and not be found in the morgue or somewhere worse.

Otherwise he would have followed the man again and caught up to him, finished what he started and when he saw Danny crossing himself he thought they might have an idea of what was going on but they weren't leaving so he thought they weren't as afraid as he hoped they were, as they would be if they caught up to him, he promised.

Gregor noticed that the other man didn't cross himself and was likely in denial of what he saw happening and there was a lost look in his eyes, even now, and even from this distance he could see that much and it made him smile, he knew he was still going to be fed on this night, it would just take a little bit more work and patience, but dinner was on the way.

Then Gregor heard as Danny called out to the local patrols, they wouldn't be ground units like Danny and Tommy were, but there were a couple of those nearby and ready to help, they were positioned as backup in case they ran into anything they couldn't handle something like this, one of them made an "unauthorized stop" and was actually too far away at the time, but then, neither of them realized how close they were to that table on the morgue at that moment.

Tommy grabbed the radio out of his hand and told them to stand by, that they might not be needed as he cursed at the rookie he was stuck with, and then he slammed it back into the palm of his hand and walked away, leaving the rookie dumbfounded and confused.

"I told you we can handle this!" he said, turning back and then turning away again because he didn't want to say more, but he couldn't stop himself from saying, "Dammit kid, why don't you listen to me?" he muttered to himself.

Though they weren't aware of it, the captain anticipated that they might need backup and had some units on standby, he sent them in as soon as the call went out from Danny, and now there were two more foot patrol officers in the area, three motor units and one canine unit in case they tried to run.

"Be on the alert for a suspicious looking man last seen leaving the park on the northeastern side" Gregor heard them say, and now they were becoming too much trouble in Gregor's mind, and he had no idea of how many more might be on the way or even from what direction, but he knew that it was a bad idea to wait around to find out, he felt them closing on him, even then.

He was able to circle around the first two, and was behind them as they headed north, the direction that he was headed in a few moments ago, before he heard the radio call and doubled back.

Now he was just thinking that she should just cut his losses and go home, the idea that he was flirting with disaster was getting to him at last; but then he saw something that shocked him so much that he was forced to stop dead in his tracks.

As he stood there watching, he saw the woman from the vision and his blood pressure began to rise; he thought for a moment that it was his imagination but then he was certain that it was the woman that cut open his throat and killed him such a long time ago, he was certain that she was the one that killed him.

How she came to be here at this time, he could never have guessed, but he knew that it was her as she sat there, seemingly without fear or a worry over anything, he was furious now.

At that time, she was thinking that she was getting tired of holding her face and worried that she might lose the image at the worst time, people would see her as she truly was and she was getting ready to leave when he saw her there, and if she'd left a few moments earlier he would have missed her entirely.

His hatred for that face boiled to the surface immediatelyand what made it worse was the two cops were between them and then two others joined them and now Gregor could hear them as they discussed what to do next, he'd circled around them and now because of that, he couldn't get to her.

It all came crashing back on his head then, now he could have closed his eyes and seen exactly what she did to him, and that hit him so hard that he staggered and he was forced to grab the wall to support himself or he would fallen and likely hit his head or worse.

All those things came back to him then; Elspeth, Eduardo, Esmeralda, the faces and their deeds swam around his head and it was almost overwhelming.

Then he began to see her face a lot more clearly in the images that he'd seen before, it was probably because some of the details were filled in now, and he could see her exact features and there was no mistaking that it was her.

She was there, much the same as he was; and the same as when they both died; yet something felt different, something that he couldn't figure out yet, but he knew that he would, and he stepped a bit closer; intent on studying her face, and that was the time that Danny chose to turn that way, he shouted at him, "Hey you! Hold it right there!" he said as he started towards him and drew out his weapon, he had hoped that his first day on the job would not end up in this way but he had no choice and was prepared to use deadly force if it was needed, and it sure looked that way at the moment.

Though the other man had not been hurt, he went home on his own two legs and they were both adults after all and they had nothing to hold him on, but there was something about him that gave Danny the creeps and he knew that this was a bad man and that he needed to be stopped.

Gregor stopped again, he was in a rage now, for being interrupted again; he was ready then to just kill the both of them and then her, but he knew that in the commotion of killing them, that she would hear it and be warned, and he didn't want her to know that he was there until it was well past too late for her.

He turned the other way, as hard as it was; and then he let them chase him away from her and in the other direction, she never got a clue that he was there.

"Officer's in pursuit, suspect now headed east, back across the park and towards the city!" he heard as Danny shouted into the radio, and once again, Tommy cursed him for it, though it was procedure and the kid was simply doing what he was taught at the academy.

The unit that was nearest to them heard it and cursed him as well, he was thinking that this was nothing to get all that excited about but now he needed to respond anyway.

"This had better be good!" one of them said as they got ready to leave the warmth and comfort of the squad car and answer the call.

As Gregor tried to leave, Esmeralda did see him, but he was so far from her at the time that she got a feeling from him but couldn't figure out why or who he was, what he might mean to her so she didn't pay any attention to him.

She felt her senses tingle and knew that there was some danger, or the potential of it; but she saw the police going in that direction and figured the danger was leaving with them, she thought he was a thug and that was why they were chasing him.

If she'd caught a scent of him, or any idea of who they were driving from her, she would have followed them as well and helped them to catch him, or even better; kill him herself, but she had no idea and was too tired to give them more than a cursory glance.

Truth of it was, she never gave Gregor much thought after the day she killed him, that it was so long ago that she didn't need to fuss over it, it was done and gone and nothing to do with her now, that's what she thought anyway if he ever did pop into her thoughts.

Gregor was not able to escape so easily this time, there was no window to jump out of, no mother to threaten and these were not kids with toy pistols that were chasing him, and because of the radio communication, they had him boxed in between the four of them and weren't sure of it, but they were closing in on him now.

He was running from two of them and almost ran into Danny and Tommy, who were still arguing about Danny calling for backup and what they should be doing, Gregor heard them from a distance as they approached, where as the other officer's were quiet in their pursuit, and harder to locate.

Then he changed his direction once more, but those officer's either anticipated that or were just plain lucky because they were there to cut off that escape route, and then he headed down an alley that he hoped wasn't a dead end.

This was a new area, he'd never been this far in this direction before and he was unsure of where it led to and even if there was a way out, but it was dark and they were close, he could hear them arguing again and was thankful for that and slunk further back into the shadows and waited.

After a few anxious moments, they passed the alley as if they didn't see it, and he hoped that was it, but he took that chance to explore it a little further and when he got to the far end of it, he realized that it was a dead end after all, and too high to climb up with nothing to help him get up there, he was trapped.

Then he hoped that they would not all come at once, covering each other's back as they did in the movies, he was tired and desperate to find Esmeralda and follow her to where she was hiding out these days so he could kill her and settle this anger and hatred in his heart.

He knew that she wasn't that far away from him, and he was tired from running but he was only half hoping that they would give up or just not come this far into the alley and maybe they would go home soon, the sun would be up in a few hours, but his other half wanted at least one of them to wander in there so he could teach him a lesson about interrupting his feeding.

Looking around him, he found the darkest corner and squeezed himself as far into it as he could comfortably manage and still breath and then he waited to see what would happen next.

From where he was, he could see pretty far into the alley, and the way it ran, it curved both left and right at slight angles, and he knew that if they came this far, they would have to come around that last curve blindly, and by then it would be too late to escape and he'd have them, while still being hidden from the street.

He didn't have to wait too long though, he heard them as they had circled back and were arguing about the alley because they saw it this time and were debating what to do about it.

"Come on Tommy!" he heard Danny say, "He has to be down there, we saw him go in this direction, the others are on the far end and we passed this alley once without checking it out, he must have gone this way!" he said.

Gregor was delighted when he heard their voices because he knew they were the ones that started this trouble for him and he would be able to settle with them, but the kid was pointing towards the freeway and away from there, they didn't think the alley was deep enough to hide him from where they were standing as they could only see to the first curve and didn't realize it went deeper.

It has been said, many times over the years, that good can find good in another, but then it must also be true that true evil can find that same evil in another in the same manner, without being told and merely by observation and the understanding of certain behaviors and values, the way they dealt with others and adversity.

From as far back as he was standing, Gregor could sense the evil in one of them, but he couldn't figure it out from there; only that it was "latent and undiscovered by the others" but was sitting inside his soul, waiting to come out and deal with his problems, waiting to change him into what he was meant to be.

He couldn't wait to taste his blood, to feel that evil as it entered his body and ran through his system, he couldn't wait to take him out of this world and find out what he'd done in his lifetime that was evil.

As he continued to "probe" them, he got an entirely different kind of feeling and reaction from the other one; he felt more spiritual, more in tune with the real world and Gregor even thought for a moment that such a man should be spared, but he could make no promises once the bloodletting started and he might lose control and not be able to stop himself in time.

"I think you're wrong, and he went down this alley, but I'll tell you what kid!" he said, You go that way and see if your right, grab the other two and drag them with you if it makes you happy, but I'm going into this alley and I will drag his scrawny ass out here and be waiting for you when you get back!" he said, "We can share this bust between us, what do you say to that kiddo?" he asked with a smirk.

"That alley dead ends, just this side of Sixth and Darcey Streets, why the hell would he go down a dead-end alley?" Danny asked, exasperated that they couldn't agree on anything on this night. "It makes no sense! He would know we could find him there and bring him in!" he argued to deaf ears.

He was sure that he was right about this, and that he was getting farther and farther as they argued about him, "Why are you so eager to split us up anyway?" he asked, clearly exasperated.

"Danny boy!" he said patiently, "I'm going to tell you this one more time, I have been on the force for twenty-seven years and I'm telling you, I learned that there is a science to everything!" he told him, "My science is telling me he's gone down this alley and is hunkered down there, thinking that he fooled us and we are going the other way, as you want to do, but I'm telling you, my gut is telling me that he's in there!" he said, almost shouting and jerking his thumb back at the alley where Gregor certainly was waiting for them and hoping that at least one of them, the evil one he hoped, would come in there and try to "drag his ass out" as he threatened to; "Are you coming or not?" he asked.

"Look at it this way, Danny boy!" he said, and Danny was getting tired of being called that but he listened because this was his teacher, at least for the day and he had to or face disciplinary action from the cap when he got back.

"Did you even stop to think that he might have run down this alley because he knew it was a dead end and that we'd know that as well and not follow him there, thinking it was useless? That maybe he counted on you to do exactly what your planning to do?" he asked, almost patiently now because he wanted to get this over with.

Danny turned and walked towards the freeway, sure that he was right and that Gregor had gone this way and was getting further away by the minute, they both knew that it was wrong to break up the team but he was getting damned tired of Tommy and his blustery ways.

"Okay Tommy!" Danny told him, "When we write up the report, I'll say you went around the other side to cover his escape, I'll cover your ass this time!" he said, "Maybe next time you'll cover mine!" he said, and then Tommy answered, "Maybe there won't be a next time!" and it sounded a bit morbid.

Now they both had a bad feeling about that alley, though neither was ready to admit that, Danny's sense of "live another day" won the fight for his soul and he went the other way, and even as he did; he knew that he would never see his partner again, but he thought he was going to die; he was so certain that Gregor had gone this way that he was gambling his life on it, ensuring that he didn't get away.

Tommy could feel the fear coming off the kid in waves, but he thought he was saving the kid's life by sending him off that way, as certain that Danny was that he had gone that way, Tommy was just as sure that he was hiding in this alley, "Cowering" is how he would describe it.

But maybe because if the fear he felt from the kid, he felt a little more fear of his own, but it made his Irish dander rise and he thought that he was ready for a fight, he was not ready to give up so easily, and then he thought, "Why should I?" as he watched the kid fighting against everything to leave him there.

There were many times over the years that Tommy was scared while he was on the force, and yet he was still here, wasn't he? He was doing the valiant thing, he was giving the kid another day, though he would never admit that he was thinking that way.

Then Tommy smelled something emanating from the alley; and to another man, maybe even another police officer it might have smelled of stale urine and old garbage that no one was ever going to come and get, but to him, at that very moment; it smelled of death, and even more importantly; it smelled of his death, and yet he continued on.

He started down the alley again, keeping his back close to the wall and standing in the shadows so that he would make less of a target, he checked his weapon and made sure that the safety was off and then he took one look back to make sure that no one was sneaking up on him.

At that point, he was about ten feet into the alley and already feeling as though he was going to explode if he didn't turn tail and run the other way; it was at that point that he felt the first real sense of the danger that he was in, it was almost as if he walked into a cloud of cold, there was no other way to describe it.

He felt it so strongly that he did stop, and he tried to look deeper into the darkness of that alley, as if he could bend his vision all the way back though that last corner and into the darkness beyond.

It was cold enough that he felt that if he touched his upper lip, he would feel a light sheen of frozen sweat collected there, and he could already feel the snot as it froze inside of his nose. He swallowed once and was thinking about turning back when he felt a hand on his shoulder and almost screamed, he turned around and was ready to fire when he saw that it was Danny.

"Dammit kid!" he shouted through clenched teeth, "Don't you ever do that again! I almost blew your fucking head off!" he said, and then laughed nervously, but entirely without humor.

"Tommy!" he said, ignoring how close he'd come to dying just then, "I got a bad feeling about this; let's call for backup and wait till they get here!" he said, looking back into the alley now as well.

He was pleading with him, which made Gregor even angrier; more determined and angry with himself for what he hoped the kid hadn't seen when he snuck up on him that way, he was trying to mentally check his shorts at the same time because he was really scared; as never before in his life.

"Listen you little piss-ant!" he shouted into Danny's face then, "YOU go to the end of the alley and wait for back up!" he stopped then and collected his breath, I am going to go down into the alley and bring out that little neck-biter and arrest him for being naughty in public with another man!" Tommy said as he turned away from him again, suddenly feeling braver than before.

"Dammit kid, it's only one man!" he shouted into the alley, "I am going down there and bring him out so we can have the damned collar!" he said as he shook his head and walked off into that darkness.

Danny looked at him one last time and then he did as he was told, he lifted the radio again and tried to make the call, but this time, there was a lot of static on the radio and he thought it was the narrow walls of the alley and thought he'd have more luck if he went all the way to the end.

"Hey Tommy!" he shouted, "I'm getting no reception in here, so I'm going to the other end and try my luck there!" he told his partner who waved him off impatiently and never turned back.

When he got to the end, it was the same though; he couldn't hear anything and wasn't sure if they could hear him eitherand was frustrated.

What he did hear were muted voices that faded in and out; they were so badly garbled that he couldn't tell if it was male or female that was speaking at the time.

As Tommy continued down the alley once more; he tried to whistle, to pretend that he wasn't so scared he was ready to soil his pants, but he stopped trying quickly because his mouth was so dry and he didn't want the suspect to know where he was.

He took out the flashlight that was on his holster, but put it back for the same reason, and he wondered why they did that in the movies, that if he were the bad guy hiding in that darkness and saw someone walking up with a flashlight he would know where to aim.

Unconsciously he reached for it once more and then stopped to screw up his courage that he could continue, after a moment of that he started walking again; and once again he took out his weapon and checked it again, and in all of his years on the force, he'd never felt the need to fire it, he never used his gun but he was not afraid to use it either.

He never felt that he needed it as badly as he did right now, and yet, a the same time; he also knew for the first time that, no matter if the safety was on of off, and no matter how many bullets there might be in the chamber or in the gun that it was not going to be enough to save him this time.

He was a big and strong man, he stood just over six feet tall and was always able to bully his way through any argument with anyone he encountered while on the job, using his size and intimidation go get his way; but that wasn't going to help him either.

After a few more anxious moments he was t the other end of the alley; and as he could see the end in front of him, he got the worst feeling that he should have listened to the kid and waited for backup, now it was far too late.

He felt his heart skip a few beats ahead and his breath caught in his throat, and it felt as though there was a large lump caught somewhere around his voice box that he would have to force down if he was going to keep breathing.

But now, as he looked, he thought there was something in the darkness after all; there was something evil that was hiding in the darkness that wasn't human anymore, it was too creepy and he couldn't force himself to take another step forward, so he tried to look deeper into the darkness without moving his feet and when he could see nothing, he called out.

"If you are hurt, or need help, right now is the time to let me know, to ask me for it!" he said and then waited for an answer, though he knew there would be none.

When he heard nothing after several more moments, he started to feel the hairs on the back of his head and his arms tingle, he holstered his gun and turned to leave then, ready to go the other way and wanted to run; would have sprinted out of there as fast as he could if he wasn't an officer of the law.

He fought off the urge to run because he knew that he couldn't outrun whatever it was anyway, and he stopped thinking about it when he heard a rustling sound, he had his hand on the butt of his gun when Gregor stepped up behind him and bit into the back of his neck as he said, "What do you say now kiddo?"

Tommy never got a shot off as he faded into the darkness of death; as he left this world, the last sounds he heard were of that damned kid talking on the radio and then calling out to him, "Tommy" You there yet? You see anything?" but he was already too weak and too far gone to answer him, what he did manage was a low moan, but Danny would have never heard it anyway, all he could hear was static.

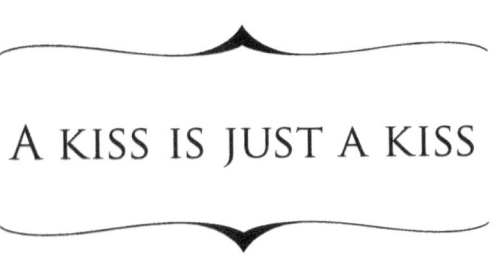

A KISS IS JUST A KISS

Love is the triumph of imagination over intelligence.

-H.L. Mencken (1880-19560)

ESMERALDA DIDN'T KNOW HOW CLOSE she might have been to her demise on that day, or at the very least, almost the fight of her life; but she was so worried about her appearance now that she felt stripped-away, as if everyone could see her true self revealed, and yet she didn't even know who or true self was, and she might even welcomed that fight, as it would stir up her help her get her aggressive feelings feel satisfied for a short while.

She thought that might also mean that they could se everything that she'd ever done in this world or the last, and who knew how many before that, no matter how small the wrong was, in her mind it was as if she was wearing one of those sandwich signs over her naked body with a list of all the transgressions that she'd committed in her lifetime.

The closer she got to her home, the harder it became to continue as she was; she was so worn out that all she wanted to do was to sit down somewhere; crawl under a rock or something and hide for a few hours; anywhere would have been fine because her head was swimming with the effort, but she knew that if she stopped now she would be discovered, there was nowhere for her to hide anyway.

With each tick of the clock, she felt herself getting weaker, as she walked, she shed her clothes and reverted to spider form again, she barely made it to the window and those bars that she'd bent when she first left the building, and now she felt that she was almost home.

If anyone had wanted to find her, they could have followed the trail of her clothes as shed them, but she was too tired to care and knew that no one would want to follow the trail of those clothes once they caught a whiff of them and the scent of the dead that was now in the fabric.

As she settled into the soft darkness, she felt as though she was not just stripping off what was left of those clothes; but that her clothes were just as eager to be shed of her as well, that they were shedding her at the same time.

They fell off her body and were left behind like a bad memory that neither of them could get away from fast enough, and she was thinking of nothing but sleep now and yet she was famished and stopped to eat first, she wasn't sure how long it would take to be back to full strength but she needed to think as well.

Gregor also went home, his thirst was slaked and he was feeling a sense of accomplishment; he'd found her, and best of all, she had no idea of his existence; no way of knowing that he was there at all, he could scarcely believe his luck at finding her that way that she didn't know he was there too.

He removed Jeremy's head and body then, and stowed them in the closet for now; but he didn't change the sheets because he didn't care about the blood, in a way it was soothing to him anyway, and he was going to change them later, but he did cover the bed with a fresh blanket and slept on top of that.

My day was better from the start, I was impatient to see her and got there long before she did because I wanted to see her face when she saw me; I wanted to see her reaction and hopefully know what was in her heart for me, I ran all the way there, but when I first got there, they weren't even opened yet and the doors were still locked, I was so disappointed but took a seat on a bench where I could watch the door.

My mother knew what I was doing and why I was going to the library the moment I told her I was going there, she sensed it by the way I walked, the smile on my face and that I spent extra time trying to make sure I looked presentable at least; she wanted to talk to me about the birds and the bees but thought my father should have done that by now, or would have to do thatsoon.

Instead, she walked me to the door, something that she didn't normally do, and then she smiled, and caressed my cheek gently, loving me with all that she had, as always; and there were a lot of things on her mind, yet she still watched me with great pride as I left.

I started walking and then began to run, I was feeling impatient and anxious to see her again, but the sight of me excitedly running to meet a girl brought back those memories of what happened to Flaco; she cried at that as it tugged at her heart.

She watched me until she couldn't see me anymore; and then went back to the kitchen to get her mind off things and pray that something that bad couldn't happen twice to the same family.

Then she started making chocolate chip cookies because they were my favorite; especially the ones she made, she was thinking that when I got home, we could eat them together with some milk and maybe talk about this girl and what she meant to me because she already knew that she was special to me.

Then they opened the doors and I went inside, and after a few moments of sitting and waiting, I took a book off the shelf and started leafing through it, but couldn't concentrate and put it back; then I took another one off a different shelf because the librarian was looking at me suspiciously, and though the library was pretty much empty at that hour, I thought that she could find better things to do than worry about me.

I flipped through that book for a while, trying to look busy or studious so she wouldn't throw me out, and ten minutes after that, there she was, walking in the door and giving me the biggest smile ever, and that sight, that vision of loveliness made me the happiest man ever.

As she came closer to me, I snapped out of my thoughts and rose to kiss her and hug her close to my heart; and once again I knew that I always wanted to have this feeling in my life; and it wouldn't be a life without her in it.

It felt so natural and then that feeling that we'd kissed before back once again in a rush; and then, once again I had the strongest feeling that I'd kissed those lips before, that I held her in my arms like that a thousand times, though I knew that it was not possible.

I was hoping that she wouldn't laugh at me for what I was going to say, but then I told her about what I was thinking, or that if she was going to laugh at me, that it wasn't too loud and for too long, but we were both so loud and excited that we got kicked out of the library by that same woman that was watching me suspiciously; she said we were too loud but we didn't care; she ushered us to the door with the sternest look on her face, but for some reason, that only made it funnier for us.

We walked away from there together, laughing, my arm around her waist as she leaned her head against my shoulder, it felt so good to me, though she hardly seemed to notice because it felt so good, so natural; and so right to both of us.

We walked that way, going around the park with no direction, sometimes we held hands, sometimes our arms interlinked but always laughing and smiling about something between us; and eventually we found our way to a bench and a table that was under the shade of this huge, majestic oak tree and sat down to talk, but this time the talk was a little more serious.

"Okay!" she said with a sigh, "What was it about the kiss you wanted to tell me?" she asked, "What were you talking about?" she said, as she sat down and started looking deep into my eyes.

At one point I know that I had a lot to say to her about it; I'd spent a lot of time thinking about how to say exactly what I thought and wanted to tell her, and I tried so hard not to sound crazy, but there was no way to sound a the very least, odd.

But now that she was in front of me, and I could say whatever I wanted to, that I could be open and honest and yet I could think of nothing to say, my mind was a blank sheet of nothing and my tongue was tied in knots.

Instead, I was looking into those eyes as she looked back at me, the feeling was so familiar and strong that my head swooned, and then I saw flames all around is, it was as if the world was on fire and we were trapped in the middle of the hottest flames.

I turned to her and she wasn't reacting, she wasn't seeing what I was seeing at that moment; and when I looked behind her it was all gone.

"What happened?" she said, and then she jumped up and began to look around her, and not knowing what I saw, but especially not seeing it made me feel as though I was losing my mind; I thought that if I told her right now, that she would run away from me, deciding that I was too crazy for her.

I was thinking that I was going to stall her, but I couldn't do it, I finally said, "I got this feeling in my heart, that ever since we shared that first kiss, I felt as though we did that before, but that's crazy huh?" I said, it sounded bad when I thought about it; but it sounded much worse when I spoke it aloud.

Then I told her that, as funny as it sounded, that we'd kissed like that, in another life, in another world far removed from this one.

"You aren't angry at me for kissing you first, are you?" she asked me, she turned serious because she saw that I was, and she wasn't sure where I was going with this.

"No!" I said, and then laughed nervously because it sounded funny to me, "Of course not, why would that make ne angry or bother me?" I told her, "I was glad that you did, heck, I was happy that you wanted to kiss me at all!" I admitted.

"It's just that I got this...I don't know, this feeling that we knew each other before, and I know that's crazy because we just met, but nothing else makes sense because it feels so real and I know we didn't grow up together, that we just started off on our road together!" I told her.

"There's no way I could explain it before any better than now because it makes no sense at all, and yet it does!" I said, "Its such a strong feeling that I know it has to be right!" I said, "I can't escape from it, or hide it, and I was kind of hoping that you could help me with it; that maybe your feeling some of the same things and had an idea of what I was feeling!" I said, and then shut up, thinking that I'd said too much.

She looked at me shyly and then smiled at me and said, "Then we should kiss more often!" and then she laughed, "We should test your theory and see where it takes us!" she said, "I know I'm laughing but it just makes me happy, I can't explain that anymore than you could have either!" she admitted.

I was happy that she was not teasing me, and I liked the sound of what she said and that she wasn't laughing at me either; but I also felt that there was a thin layer of fear underneath the surface at what I was saying, that was the first time that she'd made me think that she was seeing the same nightmares as I was; that gave me a great sense of "not being alone" but it also scared the hell out of me because it made them more real.

Though it sounded far-fetched and a little too much as though I was asking her for more kisses, she was more than ready to accommodate me; but it did scare her too; I was right about that, it instantly brought back the image of that damned spider once more.

But she shook that off, smiled at me, leaned over and kissed both of my cheeks as she told me, "You are so cute, and such a romantic! How could any woman resist?" she asked.

As my cheeks burned a bright red, I said, I am not being a romantic, I am so very serious about this, I seriously think there's something to this!" I told her even though deep inside, I liked the feeling it gave me that she thought of me as being romantic, and it was clear that she liked it too.

I looked deep into her eyes again, loving the way that they sparkled, the way they made me feel every time they were focused on me, as if we were the only two people in the world.

"So?" she said, "Are we talking about what I think we are?" she asked me, "Are you, are we…talking about…reincarnation?" she asked me, suddenly getting serious.

"I don't know what it is!" I admitted, "I don't have any answers myself yet, I just have this feeling deep inside of me that tells me that somehow, its really true!" I said.

"It could be a million things!" I said, "teen angst, puberty, finding out that I had a brother once, that was murdered by drug dealers in Mexico because he fell in love with the wrong girl!" I told her, "I don't know what's real and what could be true, but I do know that it could be real and its not going to go away if I ignore it, I think if I keep doing that, they will only continue to get worse!" I admitted.

After I said that, I closed my eyes because I was certain that she was going to call me insane; I thought for a moment that saying it aloud would make it easier to understand, it might make more sense, but it was far worse and not any better.

"You have nightmares?" she asked, "So do I! "But I can't explain them anymore than you could, and maybe it is all of those things that you said, added together, and for me; going to a new school in a world that I don't feel I have a place in, maybe it is all of those things and more, I don't know either!" she said.

"I know that I get overwhelmed too and feel lost and so alone in those feelings so at least its good to know that I'm not crazy, and if I am, then I am not alone in my craziness!" she said, and then she laughed, but it wasn't a purely happy laugh, it was more out of relief and I didn't know what else to do but hold her close to me.

I'm not sure if I was embarrassed, but men in my family didn't openly cry and I might have been hiding it by holding on a little longer and tighter, but it also felt good holding her close to my heart, and now I knew that those feelings would be returned as I gave them to her, and then some, I had no doubt.

But instead of making me feel goofy for crying, I realized that we were both crying then; and such a feeling washed over me right then, that I never wanted to let her go, not even if my life depended on it.

I held her that way until she tapped on my shoulder and in a muffled voice, I heard her say, "I can't breathe!" and then we both laughed as I let her go, we did our research after that, kissing a lot more and talking much less, but we should have taken it more serious, we should have been paying attention.

Because we were young and dumb, we didn't realize what we'd stumbled so blindly onto, we should have talked more about that, those nightmares that we shared, we had no idea of how similar the nightmares weshared were, that we saw the same things, not in the same order, those things that not only went bump in the night, but that were knocking down the damned wall with their intensity.

We should have spoken more about it, I should have told her about the spider and everything else but we thought that whatever bad was ahead of us and could stay there and wait for us as we held onto each other that way, that we could keep each other safe as long as we were together.

After a short while we forgot why we were doing our own study and started kissing just because it felt good, but that was alright with me too; even though it was still nagging at me, but she seemed to give it very little thought, if any and then we started to think that we should just enjoy the moment.

Later that evening, I walked her home and then turned to go, but as I approached the gate, I got the feeling again, but this time it was even stronger than before.

"Do you think that it didn't feel that way earlier because we tried to make it come back? Maybe it needs to be natural and on its own terms and we can't force it to, maybe that's why we didn't feel it?" I asked her.

"That might be it!" she said, I would think it might be anyway, because when we weren't thinking about it was when you felt it, and I think its when I do also; but you felt it much stronger than I did for some reason, why that was, I don't know, but I think your right about that, but I'm not complaining because this still felt good to me!" she said with a smile.

"I'm not complaining either!" I answered, "I like kissing you and holding you close to me, I was afraid to tell you how I felt and what I was thinking because it sounded silly to me, but now that I told you, I am happy that I did, that I trusted you; I know we will figure this out somehow and then it will be good for us, I think!" I told her, though in my heart I didn't feel as confidant as I was trying to sound.

We stood there and talked about that for a while, barely scratching the surface of our worst fears and nightmares, maybe we were thinking that what we found in each other was too good to bring "that" into our lives at that moment; we had no idea what a huge mistake that was.

When I left her there, I had a better feeling in my heart than before I told her; I ignored the dark cloud that was hanging over us and actually did think that it would be alright after all, though we still had to sort out the details, at least now we were on the same page and headed in the same direction and we were now together on it; I thought we'd be almost unbeatable, what did I know anyway.

When Maria went inside, she went straight to her room and either she forgot about it, or she just missed the web that was in the corner again; she was overwhelmed by her feelings and as much in love with me as I was with her; and she was a little confused because she never felt this in her life before now; until now, she'd never felt as though she needed anyone.

She had no reference point to measure this over because it was unlike anything she'd ever felt before, there were boys that she liked but never like this, so strong and intense; then she thought of Maria again, because she thought that she would understand and have some good advice for her, "She would have known what to tell me!" she thought.

But then she felt such emptiness, a terrible stabbing pain in her heart then; she wanted to share this with someone like that but there was no one left that she could have talked to about it.

She washed her face and then showered and prepared for bed, she knew what she wanted to dream about this time and was anxious to explore these new feelings so that she might try and understand them.

There were other things she wanted to study, and to look into as well; she wanted to see if there were any signs about us, and what they might reveal about our future together and any plans we might have in that regard; for once, she was looking forward to the promise of a new day.

As she lay down and then drifted off to sleep, she thought about the things that I told her, and for the first time since she head them gave them serious thought and then she concentrated on that kiss because, like me; she could still feel and taste it on her lips.

She concentrated on that feeling, and was happily surprised that it led her right to where she wanted to go, almost immediately, she felt her mid drift back to her early childhood then, but then she skipped behind that with little effort because that wasn't what she was looking for, those were memories that were too horrible to contemplate at the moment, she didn't want to see images her and the nurse, it would hurt too much and she'd focus on the pain, this time she wanted something that would make her feel better; she wanted some good news this time.

Wirth very little effort and one hard push, she drifted past those days and went further than ever before; and now she felt as though she were floating above her bed somehow, that if she looked down shew would see herself sleeping down there, yet she was open, and away from her body and it scared her but she knew it was the only way she could continue.

She felt odd being adrift that way, it was a bit frightening when she realized that the clouds had just parted to allow her to pass through and she didn't realize that she'd drifted that far or that high so quickly.

Then it went strange on her, everything went pitch black and there were sounds, but muffled, as though they were coming from under a blanket or something, or a very thin wall and then she realized that this was a vague memory of her birth, things were warm and comfortable and suddenly so cold and bright that it scared her and hurt her eyes.

She could still hear the muffled voices but now they were just a little clearer though she still could not understand what they were saying; everything was so clear and yet so blurred at the same time that it was hard to know where to look to see what was going on.

Then she felt a sting on her bottom and heard a baby crying, felt her tears as they flowed down her baby cheeks and knew it was her bottom that was smacked to make her take her first breath, and she whispered, "Hush little darling" because that was a song that Maria would sing to her when she was cared in the middle of the night.

Then she rolled over in her sleep and shoved the blankets away because it was suddenly too warm in the room, and then she was comfortable once more and relaxed, she felt herself drift even beyond that, and everything was so devoid of light now and she felt as though she was floating the inky blackness.

She could feel her feet and knew they weren't touching the ground, and she knew that she wasn't going to bump into anything in that darkness, she was both protected and safe, at least for the moment. Then she heard another voice and tried to concentrate on that one, knowing somehow that it was important, and the harder she tried, the clearer she could hear and understand what was being said.

She closed her eyes then and focused on the words, and she felt herself swimming towards that voice, she listened closely and felt that she knew that voice and that it was someone that she felt that she could trust.

Real recognition beyond that was slow in coming though, and that it itself was maddening, but she managed to hold on fast, and ever so slowly she discovered that someone was speaking to her and so she tried even harder to listen to what they were saying.

She could now tell that it was a male voice, and whatever was being told to her was being said with a sense of great urgency in what he said to her, so she slowed down everything even more and focused harder on what he was saying to her; no matter how long it took, she wanted to make sure that she understood it.

There was no feeling of malice in the words, or even the manner in which he spoke to her, and yet the words hit her hard, they seemed to almost slam into her chest and they made her sit up and really take notice to what was being said.

Then she knew that it was me, though I looked different and wore different clothes, she thought that it was from another life, a different time and place, and though my face and hair was different, she knew my voice and it was calming her just to listen to me.

She could almost see my hands moving as I spoke to her, and though she should have been listening more closely to what I said, she was lost for the moment in seeing me with a different face and all, and yet knowing that it was me was, in a word, weird.

The next jolt to her system came when I said how we would know each other in the next world; how we would find each other and that alone scared her; she could hear herself answering me now, and though that was another world, far removed from where she stood, her lips moved as she spoke in both the vision and from where she stood and watched it, and though her voice wasn't the same in the vision, neither was her face or the way she dressed.

From what she could see of me, I was wearing a white shirt that was normal in most aspects, a little rougher in material and the way it was sewn together, and obviously made by hand, probably my mothers, and there was a rope that held my pants up to my thin frame which would not have been proper in this world, that was what she might call normal.

But when she looked at her own clothing she was shocked, she was wearing a white night dress, it covered most of her body and was meant for comfort and slight warmth; but it was torn in some places and covered with what looked to her as though it was soot, or ash in a lot of places, and she could see bits and small pieces of fruit in her hair and on her clothing, and she was barefoot, though she didn't know if I was wearing shoes or not, she was shocked at seeing herself.

Interrupting her thoughts, she heard me say, "We will know each other by our shared kiss, the only one we had in this world, and when we find ourselves together again and our lips dare to touch, that is how we will know!" I told her, and I was so serious that she had no choice but to listen.

"We will be together again! I will find you, or you will find me; but we will! That is my solemn vow, and we will have our day!" I told her with great conviction in my voice. "This time they snuck up on us and took us unaware, thieves in the night as they were; this time, we will see them coming and we will be the ones standing when the smoke clears!" I told her and she believed that I felt that way, but she wasn't as sure as I was of that.

As strong as she felt that this was us in another life, that we were together there before, she also got the deep impression that when I spoke these words to her, we were both already dead at the time that I spoke them to her.

Though she felt somehow, that I could not see her when I spoke, she knew that I meant what I said and that it would somehow come to pass, she almost walked off the edge of that chasm between us in her excitement but held herself back just in time.

Being the giver, the person that she was; she never gave a thought to herself and why she might have been there, instead she began t worry that something terrible had happened to me in that world, that past life that we shared, and she began to wonder how many other lives we might have shared, it didn't seem as though this was the first one, and hopefully wouldn't be the last one either but you just never know and she had no control over that so she quickly dismissed it.

In her worst nightmares she could not imagine the horror we'd faced while we were there, nor could we have imagined the horror we would both soon be facing, or maybe we'd already unknowingly faced, and except for the loss of each other, it was something that didn't take our resolve, the will to be together.

At that moment, because she was only thinking of me, it was inconceivable to her that she might also be in danger, and that she was there at that time because she also suffered a horrid fate at the hands of someone else; the only certainty that she had was that these words were not spoken in this world, but on another level of our being.

She thought that at that moment, that we were probably somewhere that only two people that really loved each other and were so devoted to each other that they could reach this level of consciousness, if the love was pure as well as their hearts, that they might hit this level; this kind of commitment that would reach beyond everything; something between us that even the grave and the cold promise of death could not sever.

It was a rare and special place that we'd found together, she knew that for certain now and the tears flowed freely down her cheek even as she slept, and she wondered what had happened to us in that life, and why we were denied that bliss.

Were we foolish and somehow lost it? She doubted that, as she feel the bond between us as I spoke to her and she replied, this was a secret that she could not remember, and then she thought that maybe her mind knew better; that she was not ready for that yet, not ready to see my death revealed to her.

She wasn't sure that she wanted to know how I'd died there, but now she remembered that one kiss, though she could not see it in her dream, she could and did feel it in her heart. She felt the intensity of it, the passion in that tiny envelope of time; and she woke with my name on her lips, even though she called me "Eduardo" because that was my name in that world, she meant me in this one.

Now other things were coming to her as well, she was almost to the point where she could see us standing together, I was holding onto one of her arms as our lips mashed together in that passionate kiss; there was such a sense of urgency that it was almost clear that we knew in our hearts that we would not again have such a moment; she felt herself melded unto me, until our two bodies became one.

Our hearts were now blended together and beat as one, now there was no discernable difference between where my body ended and hers began, we were as one, and we always would be from that moment on, no matter what else had happened or who might have wanted to change it.

"Beyond even the black veil of death, beyond time, beyond even the most terrible pain that we felt in this world, we will be once more!" and now she knew that it was true, as much as she knew that I'd spoken those words such a very long time ago as if I'd seen it happen, and now it was happening.

Those memories came rushing back to her now, washing over her and reminding her of what we meant to each other in that world and how we found our way back to each other through all of that now.

She had no idea how it came to this, how we lost each other in that other world, except through death, hers first and then me or the other way around, those details were as yet, undiscovered as much as how we found each other this time and especially in this place, as if we were marbles, randomly tossed out the window and yet they kept ending up next to each other for some unknown reason; we found our way back and that was all that mattered for the moment; and she vowed to hold onto me and never let go if she had before; no matter what else might happen to us.

Like everything else in this world and maybe beyond; this was something that she couldn't have understood unless she could see it somehow, and unless she was able to come to some understanding of it, she was never going to let go as unsolved because it would drive her crazy to not know.

She knew that she would eventually find the answers because she knew that she needed to; she was pretty sure that we had both died at the hands of others, though she had a hard time imagining that we would do something so heinous that we were killed for it; that we deserved to die.

Thinking of that and the vow she made to hold onto me, she wondered what it was, besides our deaths, that forced us to let go before, she wanted to find out; she knew it was relevant to whatever we would be facing this time, and she knew that something was coming and it was bad.

Knowing that we would find the answers together gave her some hope though; a small candle against a mighty wind perhaps, but it was something, that I might even have some of the answers now, either knowingly or unknowingly; and that I could now share them with herbecause she was ready.

"Somehow, I know we will find them, and I hope that we endure!" she said as she turned in her sleep and then she fell into a deeper and restful sleep with nothing more spoken nor revealed to her.

When I got home, I walked past the garage as quietly as I could while listening for the sounds of my father, tinkering around in there, either building something or silently sitting and thinking about his other son; the brother that I never knew.

It bothered me at that moment that, even though I never got to know him; I never got to say goodbye to him either, there was no closure; he was one minute my brother and then gone the next, and we never shared a single moment because there wasn't time for it.

I put my ear to the door carefully and could hear nothing, I just wanted to know that he was okay and backed away from the garage then and looked at the upper level of the house where my parents slept and remembered that my father used to joke that he wanted that bedroom because he could see the world from up there, which he could have probably done until they built that big apartment complex a few blocks away that blotted out his view.

He said that he would know from there if I ever tried to sneak out in the middle of the night; something that I was never more aware of than at that very moment as I looked up there at the window into their room, I felt that it was looking back at me, daring me to come inside and see what was in store for me if I dared to enter the cool darkness.

In all the years I'd been in that house, there was never a time that I feared anything from it nor in it until that moment; I looked away for a moment, In thought that I'd made a mistake and was at someone else's house, but there was no mistake and it was very clear that night.

When I looked up there again, I could swear that someone was standing there now, just back enough from the light that I couldn't see them as they pulled the curtains back to invite me in; but I knew, even from there that it wasn't either one of my parents inviting me up there now.

If there was a mouth on it, it might have been smiling, as I said, In couldn't see it, but I did see two things, that there was fresh blood now smeared on my mothers curtains that she fussed over until she made them right, and that the hand that was holding them back had sharp claws at the end as it once again, invited me to come in, "IF I dared!" was whispered then and shivers went up my spine that I tried hard to ignore.

I looked away again, but knew that it was my parents room and if they were hurt I needed to help them, if they were still alive I needed to save them because there was no one else but me and there was no time to wait for help either.

Swallowing hard, I looked at the stairs that led to the door and they suddenly seemed to expand, and where they might have been a straight shot of about twenty steps now looked as though it was a hundred, and it seemed to take forever to get all the way up there, as well as sapping my breath and all of my energy in the process.

When I finally got to the door, the outer screen door creaked open slowly, and I tried to pretend that they didn't latch it shut when they went inside and that it was just the wind, but there was no wind and my father never forgot that latch, it was part of his security.

Ignoring that, and the fear I felt, I swallowed hard once more and stepped inside, only to find them both sleeping on the bed as normal; I turned to close the door and let them sleep when my mother opened her eyes and spoke to me.

"Que Quedes mijo?" she asked me, sitting up so quickly and yet so quietly that she didn't wake my father, I tried to wave her off, and tell her that it was okay but she was already putting on her slippers and shrugging her shoulders into her robe.

At that moment, I was instantly aware of how old my mother was at that moment, it really showed as she looked so frail and tired as she walked towards me that it added to the guilt that I already felt for waking her up, even though it was unintentional.

I led her down the stairs and into the kitchen where I knew she wanted to go and then watched as she worked her magic on the hot chocolate and she brought out the cookies that she'd made earlier, now I felt more as though I was ambushed rather than I went there out of concern for their safety, but I guess it was alright, this was my mother after all.

But it was a surprise to me what my mother knew about love, I never thought of her as a romantic until that day, and it was both fun and enlightening to me.

"Tell me son!" she said with that smile on her face, "How was your day? Anything special or unusual happen? Did you meet a new girl?" she asked me, getting to the point and laughing as she already knew the answer.

"Yes Momma, I did!" I said, "I can't wait for you to meet her and welcome her into our home!" I said, as if it was already decided that we would be family.

"You and Papa will like her, I think it won't be long, you'll meet her soon and then you'll see why I…like her so much!" I said, feeling funny about using the "L" word so soon in front of my mother.

I could see that she was excited and happy for me too, because she heard the happiness in my voice, and she noted the difference between when she went through this with Flaco he never told her anything about Sabrina as if she was his secret, though he didn't mean for that to happen, that we were openly talking about her and how I felt in the kitchen was what she thought of as a good sign.

Just Don't ever call me Eduardo

If you cannot get of the family skeleton, you might as well make it dance.

-George Bernard Shaw (1856-1950)

Maria woke up that morning with a new sense of purpose; she wasn't sure about the visions, she got some things from it but still wasn't sure what it was trying to tell her; what it was trying to show her except that she knew that she and I belonged together now, just as much as we did in that past life and who knew how many others that were far removed from now.

She never knew that while I was trying to find answers, and when I thought I was having no luck with that, I tried to divert my attention and focus on it from a different angle, some of the guys I hung out with were talking about a carnival that would be in town in a week, it was one that came to town every couple of years, and when it first started coming around and I was a little boy it scared me; gave me a sense that something was very wrong, even though nothing ever happened to my friends who didn't share my fears or even know of them and went without me.

As I got older, they didn't scare me as much, but something about them still made me a little nervous; and the fear was strong enough to keep me back; but they wanted to go as a group, even though they could all see that I never wanted to go there.

"What's the big deal?" one of them asked me, his name was Steve and he was my friend, the others only allowed him there because of me and they really didn't like him, though I never told him that; his boorish nature put them off.

"There's no big deal!" I tried to tell them, "It's not the roller coasters, or the fun house, none of the things you are thinking that are keeping me away!" I said, "I just never liked going to those kinds of places!" I said as if that was enough.

"What kind of places would that be?" Steve asked me, exasperating me beyond my patience, yet I held my tongue and kept it civil.

"I can't explain it in a way that you'd understand!" I said, "I don't know how to tell you what it is, its no big secret, its just a "thing" you know? Like some guys fear spiders or something, except that it's not fear!" I said, a little too gruffly for his tastes as his nose screwed up as if he smelled something bad.

"You think we're too stupid to get it huh?" he asked me, "Just because you get better grades does not make you smarter than the rest of us!" he said, sounding like a little girl to everyone else that rolled their eyes as he spoke.

"Did I say that?" now getting too impatient to hold it back, "I said I didn't know, as in even I don't understand, so if I don't get it, how the fuck am I supposed to explain it to you?" I asked and then walked away, shaking my head.

The others caught up to me and asked me if there was something more to it that I should just tell them all and then we'd deal with it, no judging, no laughter and no mocking whatever it was because it was obviously real to me and they only wanted to help.

"Fuck Steve!" they said and then we all laughed, "We can leave him here if you want, you're the only one that likes him anyway!" they said, looking back at him and laughing, he heard some of that but didn't get it.

"Naw!" I said, "It's not that I like him, its that I feel sorry for him because no one does!" and we all started laughing again but then he started walking back towards us and we had to stop.

"Okay!" I said, when he got there, "I'll tell you guys the truth, but I swear if I hear anyone snicker at what I'm about to tell you that I will kick your ass for it, I am trusting you guys, ALL of you!" I said as I looked at Steve who I really didn't trust but had no choice now.

"It was this gypsy-fortune-teller that was there the first time, when I finally went with my family!" I said and then waited for someone to giggle but no one did, maybe it was the mysterious nature of that name, but whenever we talked about gypsy's it was as though we were talking about magical mystics or something, people that knew things about your soul and who you were without speaking or knowing anything about you, people that could steal the rings off your finger while caressing your hand.

There was a carnival that year and we went as a family, we walked all over the place and the last place we saw that day, maybe I was tired, maybe it was late, maybe it was a trick of the light, I don't know but it scared me when I saw her!" I admitted.

"Saw who?" I heard someone say, and to be honest, he sounded as scared of what I was going to say as I was feeling the day I saw her, and that made me feel more comfortable revealing this secret of mine that I'd never shared before with anyone, "Why did she scare you that way?" someone else asked but I never turned to see either time so I didn't know for sure who asked what, only that they weren't teasing me and that the sounded as though they had something that happened that scared them in the same way, that they could relate to my fear.

"There was a woman, she would sit outside of this tent at the far end of the carnival or circus or whatever the hell they called it that year, she wasn't doing anything but sitting there, smoking a cigar and rocking gently in a chair, and maybe because her face was in the shadows or something that I couldn't see her face clearly but she just seemed…evil to me!" I said and then again waited for a reaction but got only stares back, some disbelief, but only because they couldn't believe that we'd shared the same fear and never spoke of it before, though my fear was enough to keep me away and they laughed theirs off, but then they didn't have my experience either.

"She was not there every year, but there was a time when I was separated from the rest of my family and was lost, I kept wandering around the grounds trying to find them as they were looking for me and yet we kept missing each other!" I said, and yet, whenever I walked past her tent, I would always see her standing outside of it, smoking something and waiting as if she expected me to be there at that time.

I felt as though she was watching me, no matter where I was standing at the time or how far away from her I was, I always felt that she could see me and hear whatever I was talking about, she had that power as long as I was within the boundaries of the fence around the carnival area; but anywhere outside of that little fence, I was safe.

Then, it was probably about two years later, and I went that year with some of my classmates, it was when I was about fourteen, and they dared me to go in there; told me that it was the only way to conquer my fears, that I had to face them head-on or they'd never let go.

Either I was gullible or off my game or something because I believed them, we went there, I paid two dollars to the scary looking Indian guy standing in front and then he parted the curtain for me, I went in slowly and sat down, no one else went in with me because they were even more afraid of her than I was; and they had no reason to be that scared, but they never told me that they were scared either.

She'd set up a table and chairs in that small tent, with tapestry curtains all around me; and while I waited for her I looked under the table, I lifted the cloth and looked to make sure there wasn't anyone under there; no speakers or microphones to fool me or to add "special effects" that would make me think she really was a fortune teller and had contact with the dead as she advertised.

There was nothing there, and no wires that I could see that would hide what I was looking for, and at that moment, the curtain parted and she popped in, and I almost didn't hear her in time to sit up and pretend that was all I was doing while I was there, I tugged at my shoelace as if I was retying it.

I tried to keep my face a blank so she would not read anything off of me, and I couldn't help but notice that she was doing the same; that she was reading me, but not looking directly at me, though I couldn't be sure because she had dark glasses on, and from what I could see of her, from the way she moved and all, she seemed so frail; I thought she was really old, close to "ready to lay down and die old," but that she was stubborn, refused to admit it and die.

Knowing that you aren't supposed to ask a woman her age, and how rude it was to ask; I couldn't help it, she looked so fragile I thought she should be in bed, living out her last days comfortably, "How old are you?" I asked and then held my breath, expecting a barrage of lecturing for that insolent question.

"It surprises me that you are so rude to someone that you don't even know!" she said, her lips puckered, and she looked quite funny at that moment, but I knew better than to laugh because she looked really angry and I'd stepped over the line.

"I am old!" she said, "Very old, very, very old!" she said, clearly angry that I'd asked, "I am old enough that my bones creak, even while I sleep!" she said, "I am old enough that I was young when you're mother and father hadn't met and of course, you weren't born yet!" she told me, and then stopped to catch her breath.

"But I am not so old that I cannot reach across this table and teach you some manners!" she whispered menacingly; and it looked as though she actually could, "I am in the shadow of my hundredth year on this planet, I am tired and yet I refuse to die!" she waited a moment and then said; "Does that answer your question?" she said and when I didn't reply she tried to take control of the interview.

"What is it you came for?" she asked, her voice dry and papery as though it hurt to speak, yet it came to my ears strongly and suggested that she was anything but weak. "What do you seek as you come unto me?" she asked.

"Can you take off your dark-glasses?" I asked, "So I can see your eyes as we speak? It will help me to believe you a lot easier!" I told her and waited.

"Would it make you feel more comfortable?" she asked me gently, "More at ease? Relaxed?" she said quickly, "Because I can, but I am not sure it will help you feel better!" she said, as she removed them and waited with her eyes closed.

"Yes! I believe that it would, but if you were really able to read minds, you would already know that!" I said, a little too testily for her tastes, here eyes snapped open to prove to me that it wasn't what I wanted.

Here eyes were white, but flecked with black spots and red lines, most likely veins crisscrossed over the orbs like little roadmaps to her heart; it scared the hell out of me because as terrible as they looked, I felt that she could still see me sitting there and was amused at my expression of fear, though I knew that she was blind by the way she moved and the cane; though again, that could be a prop.

I rose quickly and started to run from there, but then I thought it was giving in too easily, and I sat down, and then I knew she could see me, or her hearing was acutely tuned into whatever I did because she moved her head as if she could see me and knew exactly what was going on.

"You really don't know what I want?" I asked her, "Thought you read minds?" I said, "What am I here for?" I asked her and almost laughed because I was certain that she didn't know.

"You are so insolent!" she spit out at me, "You are here because you are a non-believer!" she said, "You think you are better than me because of where you live, or where you go to school!" she scoffed, "Yet is you that knows nothing of me!" she said and then she laughed, "Oh but I know of thee quite well!" she cackled and pointed a finger at me.

"You are here because your friend Steve egged you on until you gave in and are here!" she said, and took delight and pleasure from the expression on my face once more, "He is even more afraid than you are, but will never admit it!" she said.

"He is not true friend!" she told me, "He never has been, he both loves and hates you at the same time!" she said and laughed as she crossed her arms to let that sink in, "You know that it is true, is not first time you are told this!" she said as if she was there when others said it to me but I didn't believe it then either.

"What the heck does that mean?" I asked her, "How can he love and hate me at the same time? You are wrong about the love part though; we are just good friends!" I said, but the doubts started creeping up the back of my neck.

"He loves you! He envies you!" she told me, "He wants to be you, but he can't, so he hates you, while he follows you around and pretends to be your friend!" she said, "He was never a friend, not a true friend, he would steal your girl if you had one and weren't paying attention to her, and how many times has he already tried? He is not your true friend, as he pretends to be!" she said as she shook her head as if there was no other possible answer.

Then she started telling me other things, those things that she couldn't have known, I never told her and had never been there before and yet she knew, and as she spoke more about my friends and my past, it was making me feel more afraid as she went on, she started telling me my darkest secrets.

I would be the first to admit that my "dark secrets" were pretty tame in those days, compared to now at least; but to me it was as though I had been exposed, that I was the emperor was suddenly found to be naked in front of everyone and I ran from there as fast as I could.

Steve stood in my way and asked me what happened, but I didn't want to hear from him and I didn't have the time to explain it to him so I just ran right over him, knocked him down hard enough that he lost a tooth, right in front, when he hit the sidewalk face-first.

When we got there, I knew what to expect though I'd forgotten about her until today, when the carnival came back to town and then I saw her; I know it was the same woman that was there before, and I thought that couldn't be, when I was younger and saw her; she looked even older than before, but that would have made her well over a hundred years I thought, because of what she said long ago.

That reminded me of two things; the first was Steve, I'd seen him around school and some other places that we both liked to go, but we were never the same after that; we developed a "mutual hate" club and we were the only two members, yet everyone could see it though it bothered him more than me.

It wasn't what the gypsy woman told me, she was just a fortune teller at best, and even though she told me those things that she couldn't have known, until now; I would never have taken her seriously; it was because of the things he said and did when he thought others wouldn't tell me, things he couldn't deny because they were personal, yet he wouldn't say to my face; things that even the fortune teller knew because he'd told others.

But the last time I saw him I couldn't stop laughing at the gap in his teeth, it never grew back properly and he never forgot who did it to him; so maybe it was partly my fault that we drifted so far apart, from really good friends to what we were then, but I hadn't thought of him until I saw her, looking at me from a distance and then going inside to wait for me.

Maybe it was my imagination, but I could swear that if I looked inside, that she would be sitting behind that curtain, smoking one of those exotic, European cigars and really was waiting for me; and when she felt me coming down the road, she would rise from her chair, take her cane with the head of a wolf as a handle and then walk out there to see me; to welcome me; that she knew long ago that we would meet again, and likely when and where.

I was in a car this time, but I wasn't driving; one of my other friends was and there were two others there with us, they were going to the carnival to meet girls and have some fun; I just wanted to check out the rides and have my own kind of fun.

But when I saw her, all thoughts of fun stopped, I couldn't think of the Ferris Wheel or any of the roller coasters, even when I tried to ignore her, I felt her eyes on me and left the group to go and see her; though I didn't want to, I felt compelled to, that I had no choice and the knowing of that terrified me.

I left the other guys, though they wanted me to stay with them or got with me, they thought I was either meeting a girl or doing something that they might want to do as well; but I begged off, saying I had to use the restroom first and then get something to eat; I did need to pee, but I knew they ate while they were waiting for me so they wouldn't be hungry.

As she saw me walking towards her, though the lane was clogged with others going through that way in all directions, I know she saw me and that she knew where I was going because as soon as I saw her, she turned and went inside to wait for me.

When I got there, which seemed to take forever; she was sitting in the same place, smoking that thin cigar and holding onto the cane I knew she had, though I'd never seen it before and she didn't have it the last time I was here.

"Do you know what you want this time?" she asked, "Because I know, it shows that you have learned, become wiser since you were here the last time, you remember?" she asked, though she knew that I did.

"Don't you?" I asked, being insolent was something that I guess I never outgrew; I couldn't help it though, I guess it was a part of me and I wasn't trying to be rude to her, and yet I think she knew that too because she smiled at me; as if we were estranged family, or at the very least, good friends and she would let that pass.

I sat down and she asked me what I remembered about my past, and I started to tell her of my family; what I knew about my mother and father and where we came from but she held up her hand and stopped me, shaking her head almost violently when I didn't stop right away.

"I am not asking about this life, and you know this!" she said impatiently; "Tell me what you know about your past lives, how much do you understand and what do you remember?" she asked me.

This confused me, I did know deep inside that she wasn't asking about my life here, in California, and I'd heard about reincarnation but didn't know anything about it, and yet, between her and I it seemed to be alright; even though it went against my parents and everything I learned in church.

"You mean the nightmares? The dreams where I see familiar places that I don't remember ever visiting, are you saying that those are past lives that my mind is revisiting? Is that what you're telling me?" I asked her, suddenly very interested in what she had to say, I felt excited and scared at the same time.

"Didn't you come to me for answers?" she asked, acting a little surprised that I didn't know that already, "Isn't that why you came to me so long ago?" she said, and then waited.

"Long before I died, and now that I am here once more, you have come to me for the answers, am I not right?" she asked, but she didn't wait for an answer because the expression on my face told her all she needed to know.

I answered her with my silence, but it was because I didn't know what to say, I was stuck on the word, "died" and couldn't shake my mind off it, and she knew that; I could see that she counted on it and knew what my reaction would be, as if she knew my whole life, who I was and what I did; she was my guardian angel sitting on my shoulder and telling me not to pick the apple because she knew where it would lead to.

All of my life I'd had that feeling, I knew others that said the same before I confessed to it; that there was someone watching me, as I grew up, even before; when I was in my crib, I thought there were "others" that visited me during the night, when everyone else was asleep, though I must have known that they wouldn't harm me, because I don't remember being frightened in any way; but it didn't occur to me that they were never there in the daylight.

"Come!" she said, and rose from her chair, and though I didn't say anything, I noticed that she almost sprang out of that chair, as if it was on fire and she couldn't wait to get free of it, and her age wasn't an issue at that moment.

As if she realized that she did something wrong, she stopped and looked at me for a moment and then reached for her cane and went to the back in her "normal gait" and didn't wait for me to follow because she knew that I would.

She parted the curtain and I couldn't see her, but I knew she was holding it for me because it didn't fall back, I walked over, turned back one last time to see if anyone was behind me, swallowed hard and stepped into a whole new world.

It wasn't just different; I was somewhere in Europe, I knew that much for sure, but the tent was gone, and so was the gypsy-fortune teller that I followed there, and when I turned back, there was no curtain; all I knew was that I was outside, I was alone, it was night and I was smoking a harsh cigarette that made me cough and then hit it again.

I looked behind, and there was a bar there now, I was on the balcony and a heard lot of people talking drunkenly about the morning, it seemed that we were low on munitions and pilots, the planes were in disrepair and they were about to take on some of the new German BF 109 Aircraft, and if I knew my history, that would mean this was during the Spanish Civil war, it was 1937 and I was reliving history.

This was too much, I didn't understand, there was no history in my family of anything like this, I would have known if there was; I would have been proud of it, but as I listened to the other pilots and others that were there, none of them expected to return; they all thought it was a suicidal effort, that they would all die, but they were determined to take as many as of the enemy they could before they went down and none of them seemed even remotely afraid.

They knew they were going to die, but they had to slow the advance of the German Luftwaffe so that reinforcements could arrive and not be slaughtered as they got here, it would give us a chance and we needed that, things were not going well for us at the time.

I could hear music in one corner, an old phonograph with a record that was scratched and warped but played clearly enough that it could be heard over the crowd; it was French, and I didn't understand more than a few words of it, but I didn't think that I was an American either; they were all singing songs from their country and I recognized and joined in when it was Spain's turn, though I clearly was not fluent.

Not wanting to go inside and not know how to answer their questions, I looked in the window pane where I stood, the dark curtain behind it to blackout in case of enemy bombing made it an almost perfect mirror; there was not enough light to get a clear look, but I was able to see some of my face, which was different, I was older here, had a beard that was a few weeks old, my hair was cut shorter than I liked, it was a lighter color and now I had a lot of tight curls and was a little shorter too.

One of the others came out, called me inside and said they were all going to bed; some of them together, some like me; alone, but they wanted everyone to come and have one last toast, I tried to beg off but they wouldn't allow it and I reluctantly went inside.

The one that called me inside must have been a really good friend because he forced me to come in, but also seemed to be concerned about how I looked at the moment, he thought it was, "pre-battle" nerves and felt that at least one more drink would fix that.

"Are you still a bit nervous?" he asked me gently, "The plan is as perfect as we can make it, we've thought of everything; every contingency that might pop along, and we are ready for it, and you aren't going to live forever anyway, so you might as well enjoy it, make lemonade, as the Americans say!" he said and then laughed.

"Lemon…lemonade?" I asked, "Are you serious? How does that make sense, American or not?" I asked him as I stood back and tried to make sense of it.

"Well, as I understand it" he said patiently, "It has to do with attitude, that if life gives you lemons, you don't sit and cry, you make lemonade!" he said, and then the expression on his face changed because he knew I was teasing him.

"That's the lad I know and love so well!" he said, "A few more drinks, you'll sleep good tonight, and in a few hours you'll kill as many Germans as you can before you die a glorious death!" he said, and then paused for a moment and said, "Or, who knows? Maybe you'll be the only one left to tell our stories when this is all over!" he said, trying to be joyful.

"I…I don't want to be the only one that makes it home!" I said, going a long with his morbid thought but not joining in entirely, "What would I do without you?" I told him and then clapped him on the back.

"Well!" he said, trying to catch up to me, "At least you can tell my mother how I died, that my last thoughts were of her and my little sister!" he said, "Maybe you can marry her, take care of her because I won't be there for her anymore!" he told me.

"Marry who?" I asked, "Your mother or your sister, because I'll tell you the truth, as old as she looks from raising you, she's not bad!" I said and then ran a little faster because I knew he was going to punch me before I got away and I made him miss until we were both laughing.

I didn't want to join in anymore gallows humor so I found the others that wore the same uniform as I was; there were only four of us, I also noticed two British, three Frenchmen, three English, seven Polish and three Dutch pilots in the room, there were several others before, full squadrons; the proof of that was on the wall, there were framed photographs of them along the wall near the bar, with black arm bands stretched across the end from their funerals, if there was enough of them to bury.

I didn't have to ask why there were so few left, and when I looked closer at the photographs, I noticed that these all small black marks that ran along the corner of several of them, I stopped counting how many after it hit twelve, and someone said something about those being the kills they had before they went down.

The rest of us were still there, the photographs bright and clear, smiling hopeful and young men that stood confidently and eager to join the war, and I wondered how the ones that died felt as they were being killed off; especially after they started putting the little black bands on the corners, and if they got more nervous as the bands got closer to their spot on that wall.

I remember shaking hands and hugging people, I remember tears and I remember going to my room with a girl whose name I didn't even know, and yet we spent the night together, but when I woke in the morning, she was gone.

Walking towards the sound of laughter, I found the others; they were having some coffee before heading to their planes, I drank some and followed, hoping that I would know how to do this when I got to my plane, and then I saw my friend from the night before and walked with him, I thought that maybe he would lead me there and I hoped that I'd know which was mine as we went.

"I saw you leave with the barmaid last night!" he said, "I thought you said she wasn't your type?" he asked me, "Were you just trying to be coy? Pretending a lack of interest that she would want you that much more?" he said and then laughed.

"A good strategy! One I will have to remember, if I live through this day!" he told me and then saluted me, patted the wing of the plane where we were standing and said, "May her wings keep you up, your guns fire clean and true, and if this is our last day...well then, what the hell are we waiting for? Let's get it over with and find out, shall we?" he said and then walked off without another word.

I was right about getting to my plane, and everything else so far, but as I climbed into my cockpit; I still was not sure how to fly it, or even how to start the engine when one of the technicians came to my aid and spoke to me about the guns, that they were readjusted as I requested, he reached in and showed me how to handle the changes, and then stepped back.

My instincts or training took over then, I managed to start the engine and taxied off without anyone knowing that I didn't know what I was doing, and headed east, where the other pilots were going and to my destiny, whatever that meant for me.

I remember hearing the other engines as they revved up and took their places in line and followed, and there were some planes already in the air, but we could see the German planes on the horizon and coming in fast; I wanted to take off then, but had to wait my turn and it seemed to take an agonizingly long time before I was cleared to take off.

As I finally taxied in, I saw one of the others trying to tell me to hurry, I thought it was the battle that was about to happen and he was cheering me on until I felt it; one of the Germans was diving-bombing the airfield and saw me as I tried to take off.

He leveled his plane behind mine and lined up the shot and then fired as many rounds as he could into my plane, starting at the tail end and working forward, I looked back and saw pieces of my plane falling off, I saw the smoke trailing back already and yanked hard on the stick, trying to get enough speed that I could get off the ground and fight back but he was determined to get me and then he did, I felt hot lead ripping through me as I fell away, my last thoughts were of the girl whose picture was on my dash, I wondered who she was as I fell to the earth and died in a fiery ball of flame.

When I opened my eyes, I was in a hospital and thought Id survived after all, and was likely badly wounded or burned, but as I sat up, I realized that there were no injuries, no blood and the only sign of any injury was an IV that was hooked up to my arm as they gave me nutrients that I needed.

"Your friends brought you here!" I heard someone say and I jumped, "What?" I asked, What friends? Where am I and what the hell happened?" I asked him as I tried to get out of bed.

I was too weak and almost fell before he grabbed me and gently pushed me back onto the bed, "Hold on!" he said, "You aren't yet ready to get up and walk, though its good to see you trying!" he said.

"Your friends brought you here, said something about a carnival and that you went off on your own, do you remember anything at all?" he asked, "Were you robbed or hit your head on something?" he said as he took out that flashlight and looked into my eyes.

"If I remembered anything, I wouldn't be asking you how I got here or where I am, now would I?" I asked him, "Who, what friends brought me here and what did they tell you?" I asked him, thinking that would be a better way to get the answers we both needed.

"They brought you here after they found you, alone and wandering far from the carnival, you were near some woods and headed away from home when they found you!" he said.

"You fought against them when they found you, and they said," he paused for a moment and then looked around to make sure that no one else heard him.

"Your friends said you were speaking another language, and none of them knew what it was, except that they thought it was French or Spanish, though those two languages don't sound very much alike" He said and chuckled.

I fell back onto my pillow and couldn't stop my amazement from showing on my face, it must have scared the nurse because he stopped then and took my pulse again, "I might have said too much!" he told me as he checked my signs for rapid pulse but I was calm inside.

"Should I get your doctor?" he asked me, and then laughed, "I'm asking you for medical advice!" he said as he rose to leave and then asked, "Want anything? How's your water?" he asked and then started to leave; "I'll bring you some fresh water, that's urn has been here since early this morning!" he said and then winked at me as he closed the door.

I had a million questions to ask but could not think of a single thing as I watched him leave, so I started to think about what I might ask first when the door opened again and I thought it was him; "Did you forget something?" I started to ask, but I stopped when I saw that it wasn't him.

"Did who forget something?" the nurse asked me, this time it was a pretty woman with dark hair and dark-rimmed glasses that didn't hide the sparkle in her eyes as she spoke.

"The other nurse!" I said, the one who was just here, when I woke, he answered some of my questions!" I said, suddenly feeling nervous about all of this.

"Are you serious?" she asked me, and the look on my face answered her question, "I have no idea of whom you are talking about, I am the only nurse in this part of the hospital at this time because two others that were supposed to be here called off!" she said, and I could tell that it bothered her, and that she didn't mean to say that much.

"When was this?" she asked me as she took my vitals the same way, I almost pulled my hand back as it had already been done but her hand felt cool and strong, it made me feel comforted somehow, and I relaxed a bit.

"Just before you came in!" I said, probably a little too impatiently because she jumped back a bit, "I'm sorry!" I said, "Its just a little scary, the way you're reacting to what I said, he was sitting here when I opened my eyes, he took my vitals and asked me some questions and answered some of mine, why do you keep asking me? Shouldn't you go and ask him?" I said.

"Well, because, as I said before, I am the only one here that would be taking your vitals, if someone else did, I wouldn't need to redo it, now would I?" she asked me, "You say he was here when you woke?" she asked, and then she started to look around, maybe to see if he was still there or maybe something was missing or tampered with.

"You didn't see anyone leaving here when you came up to the door?" I asked, "Because he was here, I'm telling you that I am not imagining it or making this up, your scaring the hell out of me, please, PLEASE tell me that you saw someone!" I begged her, but she simply stared back blankly at me, understanding my exasperation but not being able to help me, she said, "I'll call the doctor, perhaps he can help!" and she got up and left me there, dumbfounded, and with even more questions now.

When the doctor came, he was of no help, and they watched me for signs of delusion or something that might indicate that I fell and struck my head on something, anything to explain my irrational behavior, they couldn't shake my belief that what I said was true, that another nurse took my pulse and told me things about how I got there and why I was there in the first place.

"He said that my friends brought me here, but he didn't know who they were, and that I was lost and wandering near the woods, but I don't recall any of that, but that's what he told me!" I said, maybe a little too excitedly because they were looking at me funny now.

"This doctor, um…excuse me, this nurse you said was here, he told you these things and then left? Did he say where he was going to when he left here? Did he hurry out because we were in the hall and coming here?" he asked me, as if I would know more and was holding back or something.

"Yes!" I said, "He was here when I woke, I don't know where he was before nor how long he sat there and watched me, I don't know if he took anything but my vitals, he said he was going to get my doctor, and I assume that's you, and then she came in and started again,!" I said, and they again started looking at each other as if I'd lost my mind.

"How the hell else would I know the answers to those things?" I asked him, "No one else has told me anything, and you all tell me that I was unconscious when I was brought in so how else would I know?" I asked them and waited while they tried to ignore me because they had no answers.

"I am your primary physician while you are here, you are under my care exclusively, we don't share patients, and if there was anyone else here taking your vitals, I am sure we would have known about it, believe me!" he said as he struck a needle in the line what went into my vein and put me to sleep.

As I drifted off, I remember calling him "Chickenshit" because I thought he was avoiding answering my questions, but they never heard me and it came out garbled anyway, as I slept I tried to remember what they guy looked like and could have told them then, but when I woke I was too drowsy from whatever he gave me that I couldn't remember anything about what happened before.

The last thing I did remember was the doctor telling the nurse to keep and eye on the door, just in case there was some poking around and playing doctor who wasn't supposed to be here, but it still didn't sound as though he believed me or anything that I said.

They thought I was dehydrated or something and set up an IV to get me fluids to help me feel better; I kept telling them I was fine and just needed to get home so they gave me more of something to calm me down, and that relaxed me so much that I fell asleep again.

Since I was too confused to help them when I was awake, they gave me more fluids, potassium and other nutrients and kept watch over me until I opened my eyes again.

They said the whole time I was shouting for two people, and they wanted to know if it was family, or a friend, someone that I was sweet on; they didn't know why, but they seemed important to me, so I asked the names of the people I asked for.

They said one might be easy, a classmate or something because when I said her name or "spoke to her" in my delirium I didn't seem as hurried, it didn't seem as rushed or excited, and they said that was Maria, and I knew a few Maria's in school so that made sense, but the other name was the one that made my heart skip a beat or two as I spoke it; "Elspeth" was the name they said I spoke the most often and that I shouted that name out as if she was in danger.

That was why they put me in restraints, "for my own safety" they said, as I kept trying to pull out the IV and get out of the bed, sometimes I acted as though the bed was on fire, they told me and they had a lot of questions that I had no answers for.

Then another doctor came in, and I had no idea who she was or why she was there, she asked questions and took notes, examined other notes that she'd written before, though whether that was while I was out and concerned me or notes from another patient I had no idea and she wasn't going to give me any answers, I could tell by the way she ignored my questions as almost demanded that I answer hers.

"What can you tell me about this? What do you remember last, before you found yourself here, and under our care?" she asked me.

"Has that mysterious nurse returned and asked you anything else? Bring you anything else?" she asked me, it was clear that she didn't think that was more than a delusion that I'd suffered and that I must have hit my head somewhere and didn't remember that, even though there were no bruises or "sore spots" on my head, and they x rayed me while I was out and saw nothing to make them worry.

"Do you have any idea of why you fainted?" she asked, "Do you have a history of this? She said before I could answer, "When was the last time you had anything to eat or drink, and do you remember what it was?" she asked me, and she never waited for an answer, as if she knew they weren't coming from me.

"I…I don't know!" I said, being honest, "I have different images, some of a party that looked like a movie set because it was old, and people spoke a language that I didn't understand!" I said, I was trying to clear my head and none of this made any sense to me, so I could only imagine what they were thinking.

"Who is Maria?" she asked, "Someone that your sweet on? Your mother's name? Is there someone we can call for you, to give us answers and maybe take you home?" she asked me as she turned to listen to someone else whisper in her ear.

I noticed that there was an older nurse, she wasn't asking any questions but was instead watching the monitor and saw it jump at the sound of the name "Maria" but noticed that it also happened when they said Elspeth, though it jumped a lot higher at that name.

"I'm sorry, but those people mean nothing to me, I don't know who they are and want to know why you would ask me that?" I said, though I felt inside that I knew the answers already, I guess I needed them to verify them for me and drive that nail home.

They exchanged puzzled looks for a moment before the doctor with the notepad shrugged her shoulders and said, "You kept asking for them saying that you had an important message to deliver to them, but you made no sense and as scared as you were, you would only give the message to one of them, and yet, maybe it was your confusion or something, the state you were in when they brought you here, but I guess that makes no sense either!" she said, dismissing it as unimportant or something.

"Why would you say that? I asked, though once again, I was pretty sure that I already knew the answer and was dreading the sound as they told me.

"Because you kept acting as though they were the same person!" they said and laughed at that, though it was more of a chuckle because they didn't want to offend me, "You kept saying you wanted to give the message to her, though at times you called her "Elspeth" and other times, "Maria" as if it was the same person, did we get that right?" she asked.

I sat up then and almost knocked everything over and had the closest attendant, nurse or whatever that was standing too close not had the kind of reflexes that she did I would have knocked her out for sure because I shot up so fast that it scared them.

"The same?" I asked, "I really don't know anyone named…Elspeth!" I said, though they noticed that I did speak her name with some reverence that time, "I know a few girls name Maria, two I think, but they aren't anything special too me, one is younger and in another class level, the other one I hardly know so there's no reason to fear her or feel fear for her!" I said, trying to figure out what was going on as well.

They exchanged puzzled looks which really made me mad, it was as if they were part of a club and wouldn't give me the high sign or tell me the secret handshake, and yet they had no compunction about sharing it between them right in front of me.

Without another word, they left me there and another nurse came in with a phone that I could use to call my family, someone that could come and take me home so I wouldn't be their problem anymore.

They took my from my room in a wheelchair, though I could have walked myself and felt embarrassed to be in that chair, they wouldn't let me, and insisted that it was just for insurance purposes, that I wouldn't fall and get hurt and they'd be liable.

On the way home, they sat me in the back seat, mom sat with me and dad drove; and mom kept fidgeting with the blanket that kept falling off my legs as it got hotter, the blanket was one of those "Mexican horse blankets" that was good for keeping the cold out but itchy to my skin.

Mom kept asking me about what happened and why they had to call me from the hospital that way; dad kept silent the whole way, but he kept watching me in the rear-view mirror, and all of this kept having that "Deja-vu" feeling to it, as though I'd done this before, but I couldn't remember when or even why.

As I tried to make any sense of this, two things happened to me, one was directly related to them because now I felt as though my head was a wad of cotton, I couldn't hear them clearly, it sounded as though they were in a long tunnel and I was on the far end of it.

Maria, for her part, grew up in that orphanage, life was structured and supervised, but that didn't meant that things didn't happen that they weren't expecting, such as the time that a girl named Monica was brought back from "trial run" as they called it when they sent someone out with a family and hoped it would take.

This time, it was a girl named Monica, and she was on her third trial run in a year, the other two weren't her fault though, one was a fraud and couldn't do all the things needed, couldn't produce the right kind of documentation to prove that they had a home and could take care of her, and the other suffered a horrible accident and the mother was killed by a drunk driver, the father was too distraught to attempt anything like raising someone else's child after that and committed suicide a day afterwards, so those were not her fault and anyone could see that.

The third attempt though, it was just bad news from the start, she went to a family that was having marital problems and stability was not something that they knew about, they were constantly fighting about everything but money, which they seemed to have too much of and they were going to use "this child" as a quick fix to their problems, he thought if he gave his wife a child to raise that she would not be on him all the time because she would be too busy and she didn't want to go through nine months of looking as though she'd swallowed a bowling ball (her words) and the stretch marks that she was sure that would remain after the baby was here.

Sometimes the kids, to deflect their own shortcomings would tease others when they were adopted for a short time and it didn't work out; they were brought back to try again with another family, and sometimes that was worse than not being taken out in the first place, it was more traumatic on the child.

It was always nice when people liked you enough to take you home and try to make a life with you, but you never knew how it would turn out, it was one thing when it was starting off new; but when the shiny gloss wore off and you saw things for what they really were, it could be somewhat disheartening to say the least.

There were times that the people that were most deserving of a child, that really and honestly wanted to try and raise a child but could not have their own for whatever reason and they could not afford to adopt, the legal fees alone were quite prohibitive and it was very difficult to even qualify, they were the opposite of the ones that thought a baby or child could fix their failing marriage, the only one that suffered was the innocent child in that situation.

Though Maria was a beautiful child and well-adjusted, she was never adopted; no one ever tried to even take her home for a trial run, and she was the constant brunt of jokes and teasing for that, and she always took it in good-naturedly, but this one time it was too much and Monica would not leave her alone.

Monica was riding her all day about that, and on this day she was especially mean in her attack on Maria, who had nothing to do with her being taken out or being brought back, yet she seemed to be the perfect target for Monica's ire that day. She felt as though she'd done everything right, behaved properly, she was polite and smiled a lot; things she thought would endear her to them, but when they got into a huge fight; he left her that day, vowing to never return and Monica was brought back in a taxi, especially humiliating for her.

When she saw Maria walking through the hallways with that ridiculous grin on her face, she saw red, Maria was always the perfect target anyway because she was always turning the other cheek and she almost never even argued back.

That day, she was trying to deflect any criticism or blame for her not being kept there and she spied Maria walking nearby and rudely stepped in front of her, almost knocking her over when she did, and though Monica was the smaller and thinner of the two, Monica already had that reputation as a fighter and Maria didn't; Monica was determined and told her, "At least they tried to take me home and make it work! You, on the other hand, have never been anywhere but here!" she scoffed at her as she spoke.

Although she herself had also been abandoned there, so it could be argued that Monica was rejected four times and she could also what good came from going to a home like that when it was never going to work out, everyone could see that when she left with them but no one spoke of it because they all wanted it to work, and they thought it if worked for her, it would one day work for them as well.

They were all in the same boat and no one had a paddle; as they saw Monica step in front of Maria, they knew what was happening and began to circle around the two girls, like sharks smelling blood in the waters.

Maria tried several times to step around her, but every time she turned, Monica turned with her and it was clear she was not going to let go this time and this time, simply turning the other cheek wasn't going to work and she would have to face her this time.

Maria was never afraid of a fight, she never looked for one, and she didn't have that rep because she always turned away or found a way to not get dirty as they wanted her to, but it was clear that this was not going to end any other way so she stopped trying to get past her and set her feet.

"You are much like the puppy that they see in a movie and think its cute, go out and buy one and then find out that's it's much more trouble than they anticipated and they brought you back the first time you shit on the rug!" Maria said as she threw her books down; showing that she was angry now as well, and ready to fight too.

All the other girls circled them even tighter then, encouraging them to fight and rooting for whoever they thought was going to win; a lot of them thought it would be Monica, she'd been here before and no one could ever remember her losing a fight and Maria had never been like this before, though s couple of them saw that look in her eyes and knew it wasn't going to be easy for either of them.

Monica struck first, she reached out and grabbed Maria by the hair and pulled her hard to the side and tried to yank her around by it, but Maria grabbed some of hers as well, and Monica had done her the favor of having her hair in a braid, it was the last kind thing the woman did before bringing her back, but it worked against her because most of her hair was in that braid and now it was in held tightly in Maria's hand.

Maria brought her to the ground that way, and as soon as she fell, Maria let go and began to rapidly punch her about the face, taking years of frustration and anger out on her until some of the others dragged her off and tried to stop the fight because it was getting bloody.

Monica saw her chance when they were lifting her off, her hands were held by the others as they lifted her off; she sprang to her feet and grabbed Maria again by the hair and pulled her hard away from the others.

By then, both girls looked frazzled, hair flying all over the place and Monica trying her best to breath because her nose was clogged with her blood that was also dripping down the back of her throat, she again reached for Maria's hair but Maria was quicker and knew where she was going; she stepped to the side and grabbed Monica's hair, and then it was her turn to pull hard, as she yanked at her hair, Monica's feet rose up and then she flew a few feet before landing on the small of her back, a hank of her hair still in Maria's hand.

That was when the counselor's and a few others finally got there and broke it up, that became the only bad mark on Maria's record while she was there; and yet you couldn't exactly blame her for that one, she was merely defending herself and was given no real choice in the matter.

As Maria sat in the office, she listened to the administrators argue those points for her, but none of them brought that one to the fore; no one mentioned that she was standing up for herself to her classmate who was clearly the aggressor this time, the only thing they said was that "Both girls should have known better and found other ways to deal with their differences!" and closed the book on the investigation with that statement.

Maria thought to argue that, but knew they wouldn't hear her if they even let her speak on her behalf; which they didn't, both girls were suspended from any extra activities for two weeks, but that really just meant that they wouldn't be sitting together for a while.

Though she showed a fat lip for a few days afterwards, and she also had a small scratch on her cheek; Monica's face was decorated with a black eye and some nasty bruises on her face, and Maria had a souvenir of her own; she kept that hank of Monica's hair and would take it out and shake it at her, and everyone knew that she had a bald spot that no amount of creative styling would ever be able to completely hide, shaking at her was Maria's way of reminding her that she could take more if Monica wanted to finish what she'd started.

After that single fight, they left her alone; they were now thinking that she maybe wasn't as shy or timid about fighting as they thought she was, for Maria, it was an eye-opener in that she realized that day that, most of the others seemed to be almost let down; disappointed that it was her that won that fight, and that she made sure there would not be a rematch by holding onto that hair; for Maria, that was okay though; she knew that she would never be let down that way, no one was going to stand up for her better than she would for herself.

She was beginning to think that might have a calling; some purpose for her that would reveal itself to her one day, she had no idea of what it might be, as far as she knew it could have just been some sort of romantic notion that she would outgrow one day, but it didn't feel that way.

I was now the son of a very successful hotel manager, they opened a chain of hotels and let my father run them, oversee all the business of each day, hire and fire staff as needed, expenses, all of that went through him, though my mother did most of the book keeping because she was better with numbers.

Elspeth as she once was, or Maria, as she is now, is an orphan that; in spite of her rather dubious beginning and the nightmares that we seemed to share; grew to be quite beautiful, both inside and out, she was happy and well-adjusted by the time she was old enough to ask about her parents, her beginning and have so many questions about life and how she got there.

Her questions were never answered though, and she spent many hours while others thought she was studying, as they were; but she was thinking about her parents, supplying the answers herself since no one else was willing to try and help her with those, she sometimes made them up as she went along.

Hearing others as they talked about the things they remembered, she made up her own memories or birthdays and holiday celebrations; her own life as she wished it could have been, and even though she never told anyone those "memories" because she didn't want to have to remember a lie later; what she didn't know was that some of those memories that she imagined were actually real, that they were put in and interspersed with her thoughts of how she wanted it to be.

She had glimpses of a past life, at least that was what she thought it was, and that it went against the grain of her teaching and what the others said, she was strongly curious about reincarnation, she didn't have my fears of finding out that it led to the devil and worse; and it wasn't that she didn't believe in god because her faith was strong, but it was more because her mind was open to things not studied or discussed in the classroom.

It was just that she knew certain things as if she'd been there, some things about history that the books had wrong, battles between European countries that Americans didn't fully understand, how they started and who started them, either on purpose or some act that sparked a war between them, those books weren't always right but she couldn't correct them and gave the answers they wanted.

But it was strange to them, and they would never understand unless they felt the same things; she would be reading a history book and then dream or drift off to another time and place, far removed from where she sat and functioned along with the others, and once found herself in Spain, during the Civil War and she was in a bar with others, drinking and laughing; listening to music that was playing on a very old gramophone.

The first time she saw that image, that was all that she saw, she followed the thread of her thoughts from what she was reading and it led her that far, but it scared her because she was with people that she didn't know, speaking a language that she thought was French, and yet she didn't speak French and was afraid she would say the wrong thing and get kicked out, it didn't make sense to her later, but that was how she felt that time; and she had taken so long to get there that any thoughts of "going back" were dashed when she found that it was time to get up for the day.

The next time, it wasn't as hard for her to draw the memory out and follow it back to where she was; she had an idea that there was a man she was supposed to meet, and since this was Europe, and during the war; it had a special intrigue; she wondered if she was a spy and there was a foreign agent and it made her laugh to think of it; she was reliving something that she'd seen in an old movie; she even saw it in black and white.

Her studies and life got in the way, so she didn't get back for a while; when her head hit the pillow she was out for the count; her studies and the sports she played after school took a toll on her energy levels but she thought it was good, because she had no bad dreams either.

But the next time she saw it, she was talking to a man, he was very mysterious, had spent a lot of time outside on the balcony, nursing his drink that was watered down when the ice melted away.

She didn't know who he was, or why he caught her attention, but she saw him before he went out there, he was standing at the bar and looking down as if the weight of the world was bearing down on his shoulders and he didn't know what to do, he seemed to be as lost and vulnerable as she felt, and she reached out to him with her mid; trying to get a read on what kind of man he was.

He certainly looked handsome in his uniform; she didn't know how, but she understood the patches on his sleeves, and the ones on his breast were indicative of the battles he'd fought in already, she saw that he was the leader of his squadron but not much more because that was when he went outside; just as she was leaving her spot to approach him.

Being oblivious to her and everyone else in the bar, he never noticed her there or when she stepped away from her seat, but he seemed to feel stifled in there and needed some fresh air; or maybe it was too loud, as the music was good, but also loud and the others had to sometimes shout over it to be heard.

She sat in another chair, across the room, where she could watch him without him knowing, and she didn't know why; but though she wanted in the worst way to approach him, to try and soothe his nerves and help him to forget whatever was bothering him; she wasn't thinking of sleeping with him, or anyone else for that matter, though a lot of people were asking her about that very thing, they moved on quickly after her rejection and went on to easier targets, it was almost enough to make her go home early but she felt that she had to stay; she felt that he needed some help and that she could somehow give that to him.

As she watched him outside, he seemed to be listening to what the others that were inside were saying, but he never reacted to what they said either, and it occurred to her that he didn't understand what they were saying because it wasn't his language.

Then, as she saw him coming inside; she thought that she could reach him then, to go over and ask him how he was doing and was there anything that he needed, but then she thought that sounded a little too suggestive and she didn't want to do that or give him that false impression.

She couldn't get close to him because that was when they all got together and began to hoist a few in the honor of the fallen and then she heard them morbidly say, "for those about to fall!" and other jokes about not living past tomorrow.

Working her way across the room, since she couldn't get closer to him; she decided that she would stay in a place where she could still see his face, read his reactions and he didn't seem as though he was listening to a lot of what they were trying to tell him; he was almost horrified at some of the jokes the others were throwing around the room.

Though he never noticed her across the way, she was staring intently into his eyes; trying to read his soul to see what kind of man he was, and yet he looked as though he was quite young, a boy in the uniform and with the attitude of a grown man; a seasoned veteran of some pretty nasty dog fights high up in the skies over Europe.

Then his friends pushed him and this other woman together, and after a few more drinks and some small talk; she began to kiss him and grind her body against his; she was disgusted for some reason, she felt as though she missed something special because she wasn't there for him in time, and yet, "There's always tomorrow!" she said with a laugh as she tried to dismiss it, and yet she knew that there wouldn't be a tomorrow, deep inside, her gut told her that, but she denied the feeling and went home alone that night, and he died the next day, and she missed their chance.

Because of that, she knew there was someone that was meant for her, and she would know him by the way it felt to have his arms around her and by the taste of his lips; she didn't know how or why, but she knew those things were true enough, because they felt too real, and too goodnot to be.

There were concepts that she had of life, those visions that she could not understand and no idea of their origin, and the ones that made sense but she still didn't feel connected to, like the dream about the pilot and that bar, it made sense how it was presented, as an old movie and not necessarily something that she lived through, but still those images stuck in her mind and made her wonder if that was a past life or just another romantic notion because she was being silly.

She thought about how she was named and thought that maybe her nurse might have steered her in this direction, and that it felt right, the feelings she got about Esmeralda and Gregor would stay evil because they were leopards that could not change their spots.

Maybe they deserved to be bugs for a while, giving the rest of us a chance to step on them and get them out of our world, but we all missed that chance and they made it here anyway.

I remember a question we were once asked about the choices we make, someone asked a clergy and it stuck in my mind for some reason, maybe because it made sense or maybe just because I liked the answer but it stayed with me over the years.

The question was, "If God is all-powerful and he can do anything, why doesn't he just snap his fingers and rid us of the devil and all of the evil in the world?" and the answer was, "Because he gave you a choice, he loves you that much, he gave us the power to snap the devil out of our lives, all we need to do is make that choice and he will help us make it happen!" but I think now that it would take more than a few snaps to get these two devils out of our lives; between the four of us, we shared those emotions and that helped to blur the line between us.

That was likely because of the events that happened before we died, the events that took our lives and the things they did to try and take away our hope; our shared dreams and desires, but those emotions were too strong between us to be killed by burning us in a fire or with acid, yet they might followed us into this world simply because they thought we weren't finished yet; that there was more killing and bloodletting to be accomplished and they couldn't let us get off that easily.

We shared a link because of our emotions, the bond that held us together or we would have never ended up in this place; all of us together at the same time; I could see not other possible explanation for it; all four of us here, and all of us oblivious to the others that were close by, we were all learning who we were and what our place was in this new world.

We were all blindly trusting and following our instincts and hoping that we were right; Elspeth and I, in our new lives were not entirely unaware of each other, we saw glimpses of each other in our shared dreams and nightmares but we never saw enough to help us figure out who was helping stoke those flames and who was trying to rescue us from them.

Esmeralda only had a sense of Elspeth, she felt a presence that was important to her, that felt dangerous but not why, or whom it might be, or even where that person might be found, and she wanted, for as long as she could remember, to find the source of that fear and stomp it out of her life, nothing else seemed as important to her, she fed by instinct and really had no control over that, but this one thought; this one goal stayed right in front of her all the time, and she was sure that she would find this person eventually and only one of them would walk away.

Gregor, for his part felt that same sense of Esmeralda being nearby; and again, not who she was or where he could find her; not even a direction to look as that sense of her came from all directions at once, but he didn't think anyone else would be here, certainly not Elspeth or myself.

Once in a while he would catch a vague glimpse of Elspeth and his heart would skip a beat, he felt the excitement but didn't have any idea of who she was or why she made him feel that way, for a time he thought she might be a relative; cousin or sister, certainly someone that he cared for but not why, and he sometimes felt waves of sadness rush over him when he thought of her though still no idea of why.

Esmeralda was wrestling with her own changes as well, she had her visions, though partial; of what once was and what she wished was still; unclear and shadowy images of that time and of things in her life as well as flashes of the journey to get here, and just like us; she was no closer to any kind of understanding of what they meant.

All of this could have been nothing, it could have been our over-active imaginations that were working against us and driving us crazy all at the same time, but it didn't feel like that to me, it didn't feel like nothing, it didn't feel harmless and it didn't feel like it would go away if I ignored it or rubbed some dirt on it to make it heal.

It felt dangerous, it felt risky, and it felt as though it was unavoidable, that there was no way I could escape it or that, whatever it was, good or bad, if felt bad, terribly evil and right in front of me though I could not see it.

Maria felt the same, she was wrestling with the same images and trying to decipher them, find out what they meant to her and why they wouldn't stop or go away; she felt the danger and that it was also right in front of her; yet whatever it was, it was not yet ready to reveal itself and let her know either.

Gregor was still trying to convince himself that he was a vampire; it felt right; but then it also felt as though he was making himself believe those things, it was a distraction from the bad feelings that the nightmares left behind, he knew that; but he also knew that whatever was ahead of him, he'd better find it before the danger, or whatever it was found him, and he'd better be ready because it was going to be huge.

Photograph by J.R. Gonzalez

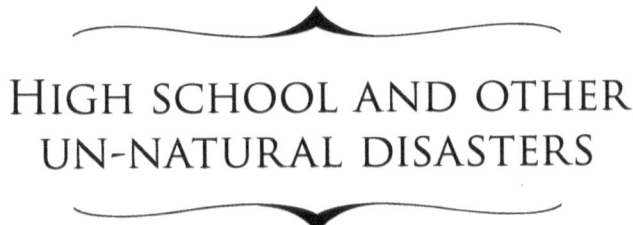

HIGH SCHOOL AND OTHER UN-NATURAL DISASTERS

IF A is success in life, then A equals x plus y plus z. Work is x; y is play and z is keeping your mouth shut.

-Albert Einstein (1879-1865)

WHEN I BEGAN MY FRESHMAN year of high school, I got that feeling, or what they might call a premonition of things to come, and I could not tell if they were good or bad things, and after all that we had been through, they could have simply been warning signs that I missed, because that was how they felt to me.

When I felt brave and trusting enough to ask some of my friends about it; they told me that they shared the same jittery thoughts and feelings, we all came to think that it was just new school jitters and I tried really hard to accept that and dismiss it as such; but again it didn't feel that way because that was just new school nerves and this felt deadly.

Maybe that's why some refused to talk about it and others were better at handling it than I was; but they did all seem to have more success in dealing with that and all the changes than I did; I felt that it would not leave me alone, even when I was awake.

I felt that I robotically went to all of my classes and did all the things that they told me to do, I shuffled along the lines between classes like cattle being led to the market; and in a way that was close to what it was; some of us would be successful and do well in life, some of might have been the ones that would find the cure for cancer before they were done, but in those days we just mindlessly listened to what they told us was best for our future.

It didn't take us long to figure out which of those teachers that were affecting our future forgot about us as soon as they clocked off and went home, and the ones that really cared about us and weren't there for a paycheck, and there was a world of difference between those two.

Which of the teachers was only there for that paycheck and the eventual pension, and that was never enough for what they needed and went through to get there, which ones felt passion for what they did and which ones were just putting food on the table while keeping an eye out for an easier profession.

We filled out the new student forms they gave us every year, with the same answers as last year, but by then, I was too busy to feel it or I just saw more evidence that it might just be those jitters after all and then tried to relax and forget about it.

I went through that first week in a funk, mostly trying to get used to where my classes were and how long it took to get from one to the next; how to adjust to the moods of my teachers and their styles of instruction that were being fed to us and this was not as easy at it sounds, at least not to me.

Though my mind wasn't in it; I thought I needed to, so I tied as hard as I could manage to keep my mind on what was going on in the classes, and concentrate on some of those other things in between because I felt as though something got a hold of me.

It was something that felt very close, and very strong because it was a feeling that I could not shake; and though it was, as yet, undefined, and as hard as I tried to understand it; to get some kind of an idea of what the hell it might be, it became more elusive, it slipped away from me and made it even more difficult for me to understand.

When I left the school it faded a bit, so I tried to convince myself that it was just the new school and all that entailed after all; dealing with, and understand the schedules and then my body changing as I got closer to becoming an adult, whatever that meant.

I was walking towards the bus stop that I was supposed to take home, and I felt that there was someone walking behind me, and when I turned, there were a lot of other kids out there but none of them seemed to be at all concerned with me.

The girls were all talking about school and homework and the cute guy in their classes, or the new gym teacher who was a hard ass on everyone that wasn't on one of his teams, he went easy on "his boys" as he called them, and that meant that the rest of us "non-athletic types" and the other normal kids were in for a tough year; lots of running the bleachers and setting up the field for the games, baseball and football.

As I was trying to make some sense of all of this, I got on the wrong bus and the driver didn't notice because it was a new year and she didn't know all of the faces yet; but she as leafing through a book as the kids got on, none of the others noticed either; but the motion of the bus as it rolled down the street easily lulled me to sleep in no time.

When I opened my eyes, it was hours later, and I knew right away that I was on the wrong side of town because I didn't recognize anything that I saw from the window of the bus; the bus was at the end of the line and the driver was cleaning out the back when she found me asleep back there and woke me up.

When I looked outside, we were going into the yard where they stored the busses overnight, I could see a ten-foot high fence that I was sure went all the way around like that, and if that wasn't enough to dissuade anyone from trying to climb in there, it was topped off with strands of barbed wire.

"Hey kid, you have to get off now, I'm going to take this bus into the yard in a minute and they won't like you in there!" she warned me.

"Did you miss your stop?" she asked me as I tried to wake up, and then she said, "I didn't even know you were here!" and then she walked away.

"If I hadn't done my last inspections, you might have ended up spending the whole night in here! They let the dogs out after they close the gates and those mutts aren't the friendly type, if you know what I mean!" she said as she got near the front of the bus, "Are you coming or what?" she asked, but she didn't wait.

I jumped up then and looked around, sure that the let them out early and the Doberman's were at the gate and waiting for me to step off the bus that the chase would begin, I asked her for some kind of directions, some way to get my bearings and know which way led to my home but she didn't have the time to help me.

"Hey kid, get off the bus, and I mean now! I got kids of my own to feed and care for myself; and a mean- spirited husband that doesn't understand!" she said, impatiently.

She looked as though she hadn't missed a meal in a long time, but I wasn't going to tell her that, but with that; she forced me off the bus and then drove it into the yard and never even looked back.

I stood there, dumbfounded and watched her leave and then turned around and tried to figure out what direction I lived in from there, I didn't even know what direction to start off in, so I headed towards the ware with the most noise, I was hoping to find someone that had the time to either help me or point me in the right direction.

But I was disappointed to find out that it was an industrial area, and not an area where you might find a lot of people about at that time of night, the noises I heard were the sounds of traffic that was going by too fast to flag down, and the machines that were inside the buildings that were locked to keep people out while they worked.

There were a lot of factories and warehouses around me but they all seemed to be closed except for the ones making that noise, there were three of them and I walked around the buildings a few times to find a way in but there was no way to call anyone, no bell at the only gate I found that was locked and was too high to climb.

There were not any places to ask for directions or to use the phone because everything was closed and all the normal people went home for the day and then I began to wonder what time it was and how long I'd been asleep because the sun was going down soon.

I found a few phone booths and got excited the first time, I thought I could call my house but when I got there the cord was cut and it was useless "as boots on a whore" as I heard someone say in a movie once.

It took me a while, but I finally found my way to the street, and wouldn't you know it; the traffic eased a bit and there weren't so many cars out there by then; the stores over there were closed too, but from there I could see a building with activity in it.

Because it was a few blocks away and I could only see the upper floors since the other buildings around me were taller and closer, but it was a beacon in the growing darkness, and I could see people moving in those upper levels.

I didn't know how far away it was, and I couldn't tell you why I felt a spark of hope, a familiarity of sorts and that it was what I felt that it was my best chance to get any kind of help, but I also felt that it was calling to me, telling me that there was a message for me there and that it was important that I get there really soon, so I began to run as I thought to myself, "How could anyone resist helping out a kid that was lost?" but then I remembered the bus driver and hoped I would find a more sympathetic ear next time.

Though I could see the building interspersed between the taller ones, it still took me a long time to find my way there, I ran into a lot of dead end streets out there and I wondered how people got around as I was on foot and couldn't seem to get any closer for what seemed to me was a very long time.

I could still see the people moving around up there, but was not close enough to see what they were doing and when I finally did get closer, I could see a solid wall that went all the way around it, too high to climb and no way to gain any footing if I tried, the all was at least ten feet high and I could see no openings where I might get inside either; I began to wonder if they went in and out of the building through some underground passage or tunnel.

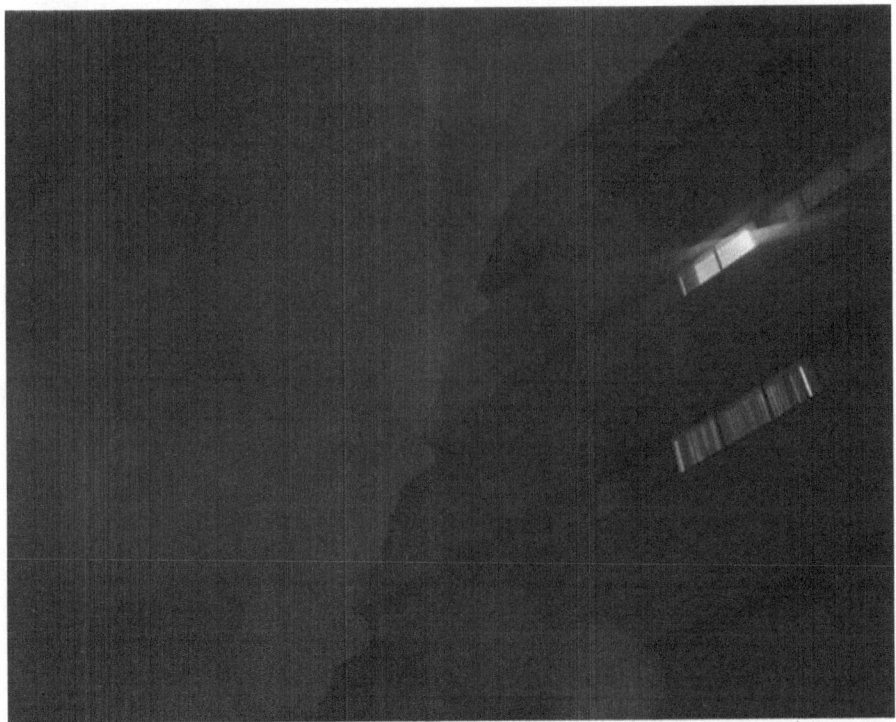

Photograph by J.R.Gonzalez

There was no indication of what kind of business they did inside the building, and now that I was closer, it almost felt as though the building was examining me now, instead of the other way around and it gave me the creeps.

I could see rows and rows of blank windows and then the occasional one that was till lit and active, but nothing that might tell me what kind of business it was; then as I finally got to one side of the building I saw that there was chain link fencing on that side, I could see that part of the block wall had fallen away and I thought that maybe they put that chain link there while they built the solid wall but there was no one around to ask.

Looking in both directions, I was trying to find an entryway but couldn't see it from there, I walked to one end with no luck, and kept running into that wall with no way to get past and felt that it was built to keep people like me out; and yet I meant them no harm, I was just trying to get home and kept getting the feeling that someone was behind me; watching from a distance and enjoying my predicament.

That part of the top of the fence was covered with concertina wire, and now I could see the top of the block was and there was glass embedded into that, and I couldn't have told you why, but it was suddenly very important to me that I get inside that building; but either for me, or someone that was close to my heart or important somehow; I didn't know if it was good or bad but I really felt that I needed to find out.

Because of that, I couldn't let it go and kept walking around, though I felt foolish for it; I knew that I had to find a way in because I was stubborn and wouldn't let it go until I did; and now, at least to me, it was even more important than finding my way home.

I went as far as I could to the right, but again, I came to a dead end, and all I found there were two roll-up doors that were locked of course, and when I pounded on them I made a lot of noise but no one heard me and all I managed to do was to hurt my hand, by the dust and everything that covered it, and how much rust there was that they hadn't been opened nor used in a very long time.

There was a shipping dock there, that sloped down but it also had the feel of being long-abandoned and was last used ages ago, there was trash collected in the corners; driven by the wind and ending in the recesses of the building as no one had cleaned this area for a very long time; rust coated everything that was metal and dust and dirt covered everything else.

As if all of that wasn't already making me feel as though I was all alone in the world and they were all conspiring against me, a strong breeze came out of the alleyway and kicked all of the dust and debris up around my head; it kept that up until I turned to leave, then it stopped suddenly.

I turned, disgustedly and walked the other way; I knew that there must be a gate that way since there wasn't one here; I was sure I would find it that way because they had to go home at night and come in the next day, I was hoping they did anyway.

That made me feel a little better, I thought that I was going to find out where I was at last; and then I could ignore that feeling of being watched because it wouldn't matter because I was going home, though I didn't want to be walking out here alone in the dark.

Just as I was thinking that, I heard a voice, and that chilled me to the bone; though it wasn't anything that should have scared me that way and should have meant nothing to me.

The sound was a voice, calling a name out softly, and so gently that at first I wasn't even sure that I heard anything at first, and yet I still looked around me to be sure, I was going to ask for help but there was still no one there, and then I heard it again, but this time a little louder, and it really got to me because this time it didn't sound human and it seemed as though it was closer than before.

It wasn't metallic, like some wacky, intercom speaker gone haywire; and yet it wasn't real, it sounded manufactured somehow, it didn't have a tone or cadence, not any trace of an accent and it was low enough that I could not tell if it was a man or a woman speaking and I silently thanked God there was no one close enough to make those sounds.

Then it was as if they were reading my mind or something and said, "Unless they are hiding on the other side of this wall!" and it made me aware of where I was standing; there was no one around to call out to me and yet I heard it very clearly, and that made the hair on the back of my neck stand up.

It came to me on the wind then, I heard someone's name called out in a raspy voice, "Eduardo" and the it was quickly gone, and then it was blissfully silent once more.

I would have dismissed it as such and forgot about it, they weren't calling my name after all; but then I thought that I saw something, just as it seemed to have darted into one of the lower windows, which were ahead of me and just beyond my peripheral vision so I didn't get more than a glimpse.

Instinctively, I jumped back because, even though I didn't get a clear look, I did see what I thought might have been an arm or something, and then I thought that it couldn't be; that it didn't look human.

It seemed more that it was segmented, and covered with coarse hairs; and I thought that for one thing, it would have to be a spider something that grew to obscene proportions, and denial still worked for me because I never got a clear look in the first place.

Using my over-active imagination, I thought about a bug that big, that it might have barbs at the end of each joint, and then I thought they'd need that to hold onto things; and then I wondered if they were to climb, or to hold onto its food while it was eating, or when it spun a web around it.

As I got closer, I thought that if it returned that it would give validation to my thoughts about its size and what those barbs were for might drive me insane, knowing that I was about to be consumed by a large arachnid and I felt as though I couldn't move until I found out what it was and if it was coming back this way; and yet, I was so scared that it might be real that I couldn't move.

Even so, I kept my eyes on that window, half hoping that whatever it was that it would return and give me another look, yet I was also dreading that because I wasn't sure how I would fight off something that big; I was used to the other end of that spectrum.

Then it came to me that I might seen the smallest part of it, and there was no escape if I stayed there much longer; and yet I had to go past it, but then I noticed something else; the farther I got to this part of the building; the lower the fence was, and at that point it was only about four feet high, it was partially torn or knocked down, and not yet fully replaced as they built up the block wall.

It was either go past that part of the building or die here wondering about it and what might be while I waited here for its return, and I wasn't going to wait around for that; it would be a lot smarter to be a lot farther away from it than I was right now and took the first step in that direction, as hard as it was.

That done, I don't know how long it took me to get to that window, and I couldn't tell you why I went that way instead of giving it a long berth and walking around it, but I did; and as I did, I never took my eyes off it; not for a second.

I even fought the urge to blink because I was sure that it was waiting for that, and that it would take that moment to run out and attack me; seeing an attack like that in the movies, I knew that it would be very quick and if I wasn't quicker I would be wrapped up in no time and then dragged back into the building, too stunned to even scream out for help.

When I got to about two feet away, I thought I heard a scratching sound for a moment; like someone that woke from his sleep and started scratching their back, it sounded lazy and unhurried; it was the sound of sharp nails scraping over a coarse hide, but it stopped when I stopped to listen and didn't start again while I was waiting for it.

Finding the strength I needed to keep going forward, I waited for several moments, all the time my mind was screaming at me to get the hell out of there; but I couldn't move, not yet, I was so scared that I thought I saw something dark and sinister lurking just inside the shadows while licking its chops.

My feet felt so heavy, it was as if they were encased in cement or something and so heavy that I couldn't raise them to take any more steps, so I dragged them in the direction that I wanted to go; as much as I dreaded being there.

When I was finally at the window, I found out that I was a few feet below eye level, and I knew that I could climb up there and look in but I didn't want to know that badly and stood fast, thinking that this was taking enough of a chance and I didn't want to push it.

Instead, I stupidly stood there and then found out that if I stood on my toes that I could look a little deeper into there, but I could see nothing that might be in there; the glass was tinted a dark shade and there was no light to pierce that darkness, I looked in at the mirrored image of my own face in there.

Then I noticed that it was also coated with a layer of dust that looked as though it hadn't been washed off in years and the only way to see inside that window would be if I cleared it away and then pressed may face up against it; and then my head swam with terrible images that I began to see at that moment as I was thinking about it.

I was feeling so scared that it was hard to think, I couldn't force myself to get any closer and expose myself to whatever might be hiding in that darkness as whatever it was in there waited for someone stupid enough to do exactly that; I thought that if I got that close, and cupped my hands over the sides of my face that I would regret that I made it so easy for it to get me, that it would simply crash through the glass and grab me.

Then I started to leave, but stopped because I thought I really did see something moving in that darkness, but more because I realized then that I was at the wrong window; this one was closed, and locked solid; there were steel bars in this area, but at the window to my right, the bars were still there; but were bent backwards and away from the building; it was clear to me that someone, or something escaped through that window.

I forced myself to look a little closer because I could see those coarse hairs stuck to the bars, as if they were scraped off when whatever it wasclimbed out through there, and I could see footprints on the ledge too; as if someone stepped up there and went through and this made me think that they were human hairs after all; a spider wouldn't stop there and wouldn't leave a footprint if it did.

That made me feel stupid again, and then I felt that I was safe and that I had confronted my fears by coming this close to this and then as I started to turn away from there again, the glass window just above me started to slide up, as of someone was trying to open it and it was stuck.

The movement was barely perceptible, as if they didn't want me to notice and I felt those stealthy fingertips sliding over the edge of my spine, brushing the bones to find the where the weakest point was and then break it.

That was enough for me, I turned and ran as fast as I could, I followed the fence until I came out on the main street again and the sounds of traffic and horns blaring at each other made me feel reassured somehow; the sounds of people meant I was safe for the moment.

Finally, I felt that I'd run far enough, I stopped and grabbed the wall to steady myself and the other was on my hip as I gasped for air, and then leaned forward and took several deep breaths until I finally felt I could calm down.

Then I heard that voice again, this time, it was a bit louder and seemed to be a little closer than it was before and it really scared me, the hairs on my neck tingling again, making me shiver; I thought I'd run far enough that I was safe, and now I felt as though I'd run in a circle.

As I started to run again, I suddenly got a sense that the spider was just on the other side of that curve ahead, mocking my feelings of being safe as it stood over there salivating and waiting for me to foolishly run right into it.

Then I heard it, behind me as I ran, "Eduaaaaaaaaaredo!" and I spun around as quickly as I could because I thought it was right behind me and speaking almost into my ear, but there was nothing when I turned, I lost my balance when my legs were tangled and fell on my butt, feeling all the time that it was over now, that I was going to die, but when nothing happened and I was able to force my eyes open, I saw there was nothing, got up and started to dust myself off, feeling foolish once more.

I managed to take a few more steps in that direction and instead of a huge spider or anything else that might hurt me, I was at the main gate, it was just ahead of me and just over there, on the other side of that gate was a little guard shack, I could see someone sitting alone inside of there, reading a newspaper or something.

Remembering times I'd been in this spot, I figured that he was probably sitting on one of those metal stools that are never comfortable for very long and was waiting for someone to break up the monotony of his day, I wondered how many hours he sat there with no interruption, no one driving into the gate or walking up to ask directions like me.

I imagined that they would be eager to see him there, ask him about his weekend and his family if he had one; and there would also be the others, who would be in too much of a hurry, or of too much self-importance to stop and lower the window, acknowledge him standing there, either they considered him hired help and were beneath them and not worth time to stop and say hello.

The first thing I wanted to ask was about the bugs in this area; if they were bigger than normal for some reason, but I decided not to ask and scare him off from helping me or even listening; I didn't know if he had a sense of humor and didn't want to risk starting off on the wrong foot so that he'd send me away with no help at all.

He was Morris Anderson, and he was actually a pretty nice guy but was going through "some shit" as he called it, but as whenever they coldly brushed past him or didn't "see" him there, that never bothered him, he thought it was their loss if they didn't have the time to enjoy their day; to "stop and smell the coffee" which was actually pretty good these days.

Though they didn't know, and a lot of them just thought of him as a badge at the gate that kept their cars from getting broken into; he could have performed a lot of their jobs, some even better than they could have, but he never pointed that out to them because he didn't want that kind of life anymore; that pressure to do better all the time.

He'd had his fill of that life already and felt that it cost him more than the blood, sweat, and tears of the job he did; all he cared about now was his teenage son that he was trying to reconnect with,having to fight his mother through a terrible divorce battle; he was trying to reestablish the relationship they once had but lost long ago, when he was busy working and bringing home the bacon.

Recently, he learned that his son was starting to hang out with the wrong crowd, some bad kids that were forming a gang that was moving up from night time burglaries to strong armed robbery and he wanted to get his son away from them before he got into some serious trouble or worse.

It was becoming difficult because they had a hold of him already; some of them went to the same school and they were friends for a very long time;

they grew up in the same neighborhood and even their older brothers went to the same schools, they drifted apart for a while because his son saw the bad coming and didn't want to be a part of it back then.

But his son was leaning back in that direction, partly out of rebellion against his mother and father and how he was torn between them and felt that his feelings, his needs were never considered as they "tore each other apart" in open court.

Then, another kid who was bigger and had friends that were just as bad decided he didn't like the way Reggie was acting and saw him as an enemy even though he wasn't in a gang and didn't do anything to threaten him, it was an excuse to beat someone and that was all they needed.

Reggie needed help with them, but he couldn't go to the school and "snitch" because then he would get beaten by others as well, the "little bitch" beatings they would give him for going to the principal and not handling it "like a man" and fighting back, but fighting back meant him and the other guy and his friends; to him that wasn't fighting like a man.

He wasn't afraid of being beaten in a fight, that would eventually heal and fade to a bad memory; but he didn't think these guys would stop with knocking him out and didn't want to find out if he was right by going there.

So he was stuck between the rocks and the hard places in his life, and the gang aspect wasn't what he wanted either, yet it was far preferable to being beaten up daily, to having your clothes stolen off your back, your shoes taken way because they were the wrong color or brand.

He didn't think he could go to his father for help because his father never had the time to help with homework, he was too busy for that, and beating the kids back would take even more of his precious time so he never thought to ask, and when he was living with his mother; he didn't know what his father was doing these days.

Now his father was back in his life; but to Reggie, it wasn't that he was wanted, he felt that his father only fought for him because he didn't want his mother to win, that's what she told him and since he couldn't ask his father about it, he thought it was true; especially after she said it in court and his father didn't do anything more than hang his head in frustration that Reggie thought was shame at him finding out.

If he'd known his father, he would have realized that it wasn't shame for himself that he felt at that moment; upon hearing her say things like that; it was that she would stoop so low that he didn't know who she was anymore, and he just wanted the "old her" to come back, and soon.

For Morris, the hard part was pushing his son too hard, because he knew that if he did, he would push back; simply out of stubbornness, a trait he inherited from his mother; but even the most devoted and loving son would resist and close his eyes if he thought his father was wrong and then he'd lose him for certain.

That meant that he had to calmly present a sound and logical reason for him to listen to his father, and the problem with that was that they could never calmly discuss any of this between them; it always led to shouting and mostly unfounded accusations.

It boggled Morris how his son ended up with those other kids; he knew the connection and all but they had drifted apart when his friends started getting too wild and risky in their "nocturnal activities" and because he knew better and was disgusted at what they did, something that Morris was happy to learn.

Because he was always smart and a good kid, and from the time he was young he was soft-spoken and gentle, the complete opposite the son that he saw these days; for Morris, it was hard to be patient; to come to grips with the changes in his son; he hardly recognized the angry and defiant youth standing before him these days.

He could have, at one time, made his son laugh by poking fun at those kinds of kids; but Reggie didn't want to laugh about them anymore; he didn't see the humor in it and would sulk off to his room without another word.

Morris couldn't understand it, he didn't know about the beatings but he still didn't see the need for gangs in his son's life; he knew that the lines of communication hadn't been entirely severed but they certainly were strained, and neither of them knew how to fix that, but only one, Morris, wanted to, and knew it was going to take a lot of work but he was willing to take the time and get it done.

What he didn't know was that his son did want to try and rebuild it, but he didn't know how to tell his father that without feeling weak and useless, he wanted his father to take the first steps but he wasn't going to tell him that either because in his mind; his father left him and it was up to him to let go of his pride and take those first steps.

He didn't realize because he was angry that his father had already taken those first steps and a few more; and Morris would gladly take even more; walk on those proverbial "hot coals" in his bare feet if its what it took, but his son was blind to anything but his rage that came with his frustration and confusion.

For Morris, it was never a matter of pride, nothing to do with that; he didn't care who reached out first but thought that he already had done that, he didn't realize that Reggie missed that entirely as he shouted back at his father, he only had love for his son and was trying to understand him.

He was trying to learn how to be patient and reach out to him again without being slapped in the face over it; he did truly love his son and was trying to find a better life for both than what those boys were planning.

Reggie still thought it was just blind-pride that motivated his father and kept him from seeing what he was trying to do, what he felt that he needed in order to stay alive in this world, thinking that pride was his problem, he was angry because anger wasn't what he needed from his father and he didn't know how to tell him in the first place, and then that he didn't think that it was his place to tell his father what he needed him to do.

Though he kept it to himself and actually did manage to hide it quite well; Morris was angry at being replaced by his new friends, Reggie didn't think he was replacing anyone; his father hadn't been in his life for a while now and didn't think that was going to change just because he was here in his home now.

Reggie didn't think he was replacing his father, he thought he didn't have time for his only son as always, and his friends did have the time and were happy to "hang" with him any time he felt the need, they had already shown that when they drove the other guy away by beating the crap out of him on the street and that took care of Reggie's problem, now he felt that he owed them for that.

When his son was much younger, they were very close, and spent all of their time together playing together and doing "guy things" that seemed to make them both quite happy, Morris tried to teach his son about life and tried to prepare him for the things he would be facing; much as he was now, and they spent so much time together that it cost him his marriage.

His wife, so sweet and caring when they met and through their courtship, he was seeing now the kind of woman she was, and the things that his friends warned him about when they met her; they weren't being malicious or mean spirited; they were simply looking out for their friend, they didn't know her before he brought her to their circle and were just telling him things they saw when she was around.

She went from sweet and demure when they started to pretty and small-minded and extremely jealous of the time they spent together; she felt left out of the things they did, the time they managed to find and spent without her, they were forming a bond between them and she didn't like it; the "boys club" had no room for a girl.

As much as they tried to bring her into the conversations and tried to do things that would include her, she only felt that they were deliberately breaking her heart, they were moving on without including her in their plans as she saw it.

If she would have been able to really open her eyes, to step back and see it for what it really was; she would have seen a man so happy that he had a son and that they had a good, strong and loving relationship that she could have been a part of that if only she tried; they left the door open for her but she closed it in her own face.

In her eyes, when they asked her to join them, it was a token invitation, that she was nothing more than an afterthought and they didn't mean it at all, and that was when she began to stray from the marriage, she rationalized it needed because of the neglect on his part; but when your heart and mind are not in the same mood, you can likely find rationalization for almost anything that you want to do.

To really drive the point home to her husband, she humiliated him further by cheating on him with the part-time, gas station attendant, down the street from their home and where they both bought gas; a man with no dreams or aspirations in life beyond the next paycheck and the alcohol that he could consume with it, he was already married; though estranged because his wife was hoping for a higher station in life and knew that he couldn't get them there.

How she came to be with him, to more value in a man like that and choose him over her own family, and the financial security that he gave her, and Morris demanded an explanation; but she had none, she didn't understand her behavior either and if she'd gone to her doctor and told him about it; they would have likely diagnosed her with post partem depression, and they would have been wrong because this was so much more and so much deeper than that; but she never had a thought to have told anyone how she felt until it was well past too late.

One day, he came home from work and she was already gone, along with his son and everything else that wasn't nailed down and not too heavy to carry out; some of the heavier things, they decided were too much trouble or they dropped them and then just left them where they fell.

Some special things that he bought her over the years were there, broken as much as his heart was now and maybe fixable if his heart was in in it but he no longer cared, and they had lost their meaning when she left.

It just happened that he was coming home with great news, and their troubles were going to be over; it was his best and most successful day as a worker bee, she broke his heart and ruined it all; he didn't care about the things she took, or the things she broke as she ran out of the house, it was losing his son that hurt; the one she had no time nor patience for, and she filed for divorce and left the papers on the counter for him to sign; he was crushed, almost beyond redemption; he felt that he'd done everything right and it still cost him.

He was so distraught over all of this that he never even read it, and never contested a thing; he hoped that if he didn't fight her, that she would come to her senses and call this off; come home and fix whatever was wrong between them, that was his hope; he gave her all that she demanded and then some, because he still loved her and held hope it would be alright and they'd be a family again.

She never did, he lost the fancy cars, the house that he told her was too big for them but she wanted anyway; and even the job he was so good at and made so much money; none of that hurt him as much as the loss of his son; he even tried to see him, to take him back as she never seemed to care about him before but the judge saw it differently and he never had a chance.

After that, maybe because she as scared that he would run off with their son; he wasn't allowed to see him anymore; even though he jumped through all of the legal hopes they set out for him, she found one excuse after another or just simply defied the court order and didn't show up.

She wasn't doing this out of concern for her son, or that she suddenly loved him; she kept them apart because she knew that it would cut him the deepest, he saw them tooling around town in what used to be his favorite car, and now there were dents and scratches on it and it looked as though it was leaking oil and she laughed at his expression when she saw him on the sidewalk.

On one of the few times he was able to spend any time with Reggie, it was when he was still young and he found out that his mother was making him call the new guy "daddy" and he gave him free reign to punish the boy if he got out of line, and he did; every chance that he got, even the slightest of infraction of the rules was severely dealt with, quickly and harshly, and his only explanation was "he should have known without being told!"

He was spanked with all the anger and vehemence that he could because it was not his son and he added resentment into the mix because he thought if the kid wasn't around, they could do more things and have more fun with Morris's money; they did as much fun as they could with it, drunken binges started every weekend and after a while, it didn't seem to matter what day it was.

Reggie was seeing adults at their worst behavior with no regard for the child that saw everything, and they used alcohol as an excuse for what happened, Morris had no way of knowing the hell his son was going through, which was another reason to keep them apart, she knew it was wrong, but it kept escalating and, in truth, she did enjoy some of that debauchery.

But he thought his father knew and either approved, or wasn't going to do anything about it because he no longer cared, he felt abandoned and on his own after that; his mother told him that he was a problem for his father and that he didn't care about him anymore; that he had a new family and they'd never see him again as long as he sent the money on time.

He would cry and ask her if he could see his father, was so desperate to see him that he demanded it; even though he knew he was going to be beaten for it, "I want to see my father!" he told her, "I want to ask him if I can live there, with him!" he cried.

"Your father has no time for you, little man!" she told him coldly, he has a new family now, he replaced you with two boys of his own and now spends all of his time with them, what makes you think that he even wants to see you?" she said with a sneer.

"If he wanted to see you, don't you think he would have asked by now?" she said, and she knew that she was cutting him deeply as well, that she was hurting her son with her words but she couldn't stop if she wanted to, she kept piling that shit on top of her son until something in him died; and then he buried the good times he spent with his father and how he felt about him deep inside where he thought it would never again see the light of day.

She never let him see his father, and lied to him, told him that he never asked to see his son, or how he was doing; or that Morris was using all of his available resources in the courts to that end; but he could not get a break because, at that time the courts always favored the mother, and in court she was clean and acted as though all she cared about was her son and she cried a lot.

Morris asked for help from the court but his pleas fell on deaf ears; all he got was an occasional grunt or nod of the head for an answer as they signed the papers that tore his heart out so they could all take turns stomping on it.

The final straw for Morris was when they asked his son, in the middle of the proceedings and with both his mother and father present and the new guy in the hallway waiting to see what was going to happen; the judge asked the boy if he wanted to see his father or stay where he was.

She fought tooth and nail to prevent this from happening but the judge said he needed to hear it from their son before he could make his final judgement and so she relented when the judge said he was old enough to speak his mind and that he needed to face his father when he made his choice.

Because she was looking at Morris when he saw his son enter the courtroom from a side door, she missed her son's first reaction, he almost fell because he was so happy to see his father, it was as if all the bad fell away from his heart at that moment and it was going to work out for them.

Morris was amazed at how much his son had grown in such a short time, it was years since he'd seen him and no one else would have recognized him after that long, but there's that expression about a wise man knowing his son and he felt relief and joy at seeing him; he had a hard time not running over there and hugging him tightly, as he used to do when got home from work.

When he last saw his son, he was short and chubby, wore thick, dark glasses and his hair was always unruly, no matter how hard he tried to control it, and the boy that stood before him was hardly a boy anymore; he lost most of his baby fat and wore thinner glasses that accented his good looks; a stark contrast to the smiling young man he enjoyed sharing his life with, and he almost cried then at seeing what they'd lost.

Reggie saw the look on his father's face and was angry, he knew then that his mother was lying all of this time, he was ready to forgive everything and try and start over with his father until he saw his father turn and whisper something to a woman that was sitting behind him.

There were two young boys sitting there, on her left, and when Morris spoke to her, they leaned in and laughed, as if they were all sharing a private joke, Reggie saw that and flashed back to the many times they did that very thing, that they spoke about things he needed to know about life and laughed a lot.

Now he thought that she was telling the truth after all and his anger came boiling to the surface, when he took the stand and her lawyer asked him a few questions to ease him into it because they were all afraid of what he was going to say; and then the judge asked him, "Reginald Evan Anderson, I want you to think carefully before answering when I ask you a question, please do not rely until you have given it careful consideration and you are sure that is what you want!" he said and then paused, "Can you do that for us?" he asked him carefully and watched him closely to make sure.

Reggie nodded his head and the judge told him he'd have to answer, for the record, so he said "Yes!" and nodded his head again and waited.

"Given that you appear to be intelligent and old enough to answer, to care for yourself as much as any man your age, please inform this court if you would rather live with your father or continue to live with your mother!" he said, "It is entirely up to you to decide!" he said and then waited along with everyone else, you could have heard a pin drop, it was so quiet.

The boy didn't hesitate, not because he didn't understand, or because he wanted or needed to think about it as instructed to do; but because he was being vindictive, he learned that from his mother over the years, and that it would be a dagger in his father's heart when he answered the question, he thought about the times they lost, and the look on those boys face as he spoke to them and couldn't wait for the judge to finish his instructions before he answered.

He looked his father in the eye and said, slowly and carefully; "I chose my mother, I want to stay with her, and as for my father, if that's who he is; he and I have nothing to say to each other, he has not been in my life for a long time and now I don't care to ever see him again!" he said, and if the court hadn't become so loud at that moment they would have heard his voice crack but it was drowned out.

Morris tried to say something but the judge dismissed Reggie at that moment and he walked out of the courtroom without looking at his father again; he knew that if he did, he would break down and cry so he couldn't get out of there fast enough, he saw his ex-wife smiling smugly at him; enjoying what she did much more than she thought she would, it felt wrong but it was also fun for her.

When she stepped out in the hallway, she found her boyfriend but couldn't see her son, he was in the men's bathroom, crying his heart out in one of the stalls while trying to keep as quiet as he could.

Morris walked out as the judge was talking and started drinking that day, he went to the nearest bar and drank until they threw him out because he was too drunk, and from there, he slid down that road fast as he tried to drown his sorrow, eventually none of his friends would talk to him anymore as they saw him going that route and didn't know how to help him beyond hoping that he would snap out of it and renew the fight for his son.

That went on for a while, until he lost everything and the he kept whatever was important in his heart which was most important; then he dragged himself back out of that gutter before it became too deeply embedded on his soul and turned his life around again, as his friends hoped he would.

It happened one day, he was walking, it was hot all day as the sun beat down on his head, and now that the sun was setting, it was much cooler, there was a breeze out now.

He was trying to find a place where he was going to be able to spend the night, and as he staggered by an empty store front, he saw his reflection in the blackened window when the lights from a passing car shone in his direction, he tried to shield his eyes but was too slow.

Because he was too slow, he saw in that reflection, what he never wanted to see, that he had become a failure in so many ways; and he knew that he was better than this, that it was up to him to make those changes happen and that it was well within him and most important of all; that it was not too late.

Before that, he had always been meticulously clean, and weighed almost the same as he did when he was in high school; he always loved to work out and stayed in shape, but the man he saw in the glass was lost, he was out of shape and the spark of life that had burned so brightly in his eyes was now nowhere to be seen.

When he looked to his heart, he saw his son and at that moment he thought, "He will need me one day, and I need to there, and ready when that happy day comes!" he said, "I can't do it like this!" he realized.

Looking down at his right hand which held the brown paper bag and the quart of beer that was inside he began to get sick, he handed it to another man that was out there and never looked back.

Knowing that he'd lost so much and would not easily get anyone to believe in him as he was; he knew that he would have to do this alone and started by working out the poison he'd been drinking since that dark day; it was going to be much tougher this way, with no one to kick his ass back in line but he knew he could do it because he knew it was for Reggie.

He kept thinking about how far down he'd gone, that he needed to drop down and see the bottom of that hole before he could dig himself out and know the true value of his life and his worth, and it all started and ended with his son.

That was what he thought about as he began the next, rising early and running in the morning to clear his head and sweat the toxins out of his blood; he ate nothing and drank only water for three days to get clean before the shakes became too much and he needed to check into a shelter to finish the cleanse.

He was able to save himself; to become a better man, every day he rushed home, checking for any word or message from his son but nothing changed, though it was tough, his hope never wavered and he never stopped trying to get stronger while he waited.

To his credit, he never once backslid; he tried so hard to be ready and fell into security work when he found a company that understood what he had gone through and believed him when he said he was ready to change, they took a chance on him and he rewarded them with dedication and a good work ethic and was offered, more than once, the chance for promotions but he politely declined, saying that he didn't want to influence other's lives and make decisions that affected them until he felt his own life was in order, then he'd be ready.

He found that he not only liked the work, but he was very good at it; he wasn't a hard-ass, and sometimes he went by "the feel of things" and if he caught a kid stealing something there and it wasn't too serious and the kid was "savable" he'd let him go, hoping that he did the right thing and the kid learned and chose a better path; but it didn't always work out that way.

There were times the kid was shot dead the next time he tried it in another store or a building that there was something inside that he thought was worth his life, he thought about those every once in a while but found that he liked the quiet time he had while he worked there, and he took the graveyard shift and took some courses to get better educated.

A few years after that, Morris was informed that his ex-wife had been shot to death, alongside her boyfriend and that his son was safe, that they'd been searching for him for a while and only found his address when they discovered that she had a secret safe deposit box along with some other pertinent information and a good portion of the money that she stole from him; they found it when the bank reported it as an abandoned account.

It was the gas station attendant's wife; that she wanted to reconcile their marriage but he told her he was making more money where he was and laughed at her, then he told her they could still have fun if he wanted to but she didn't want to share.

She followed him when he went home for lunch, which, from experience knew that it meant a "quickie" with her; then she waited in the car and watched the house, knowing that they were in bed, and when she could stand it no longer, she broke into the house and shot them both to death, loading and reloading the gun several times before the police arrived.

Reggie walked in after hearing the shots fired and was almost killed when she turned and pointed the gun at him and pulled the trigger but it was empty; he turned and ran out of the room while she reloaded and then went back to them, and it was Reggie that called the police.

They reported that when they walked up behind her, that even though they'd identified themselves as police officer's and were pointing their weapons at her she was still pulling the trigger and had spent all of her rounds, the many empty shells at her feet proved that.

They heard the dry clicks, the static from the television with a bullet hole in the screen and the sound of her labored breathing, and her softly crying were the only sounds in the room as they took the gun from her, put the cuffs on and helped her out the door.

Morris was ecstatic; not that his wife was dead of course, he was a much better man than that; but he knew that this meant that he was going to have his son at last; and he felt that he was ready, then he moved out of his single-spaced apartment that was more of a bachelor pad and took on a two bedroom apartment so he could inform the judge that his son would have his own room.

But he soon found out that they'd lost so much and that Reggie still felt that his father didn't want him there and only "got him by default" because there was no one else to take him in, he never knew that it was his aunt, Morris's sister and her kids that were there that day in the courthouse, and they had a father of their own who was at work, or he would have been there as well.

It wasn't his fault, when you hear the same things, over and over again and you don't hear from "the other side" you begin to think its true, no matter how wrong it feels or how outlandish it seems; it begins to take root in the dark recesses of your soul; he never saw that side of the family because they didn't want to see her and she didn't want him to see his son through them.

Reggie went through the "normal progression" that kids went through when they were in the midst of a bitter divorce struggle between the two people he loved most in the world; he thought it was his fault somehow; that he was a bad kid and his father couldn't love him, and all that he wanted was another chance to redeem himself and re earn the love that he wanted so badly.

It dragged down his sense of self-worth and he began to question many of the things in his life, the scars that he bore, both inside where they didn't show and yet burned brightly; and the scars outside of his body where he was beaten into submission.

Every day he heard the constant degradation his mother hurled at his father until it became real to him and especially when he heard nothing from his father; mail sent to him as well as birthday gifts, or even just gifts because Morris thought he would like them, they were never given to him and he never knew about them either.

Sometimes she would get the packages before Reggie got home and stop at a corner where kids were and leave them on the curb and drive off, other times, she gave them to other kids when it was their birthday instead of spending her own money to buy them a gift.

Reggie began to lack confidence in himself and thought that no one would ever want to be around him, he saw girls that he liked but couldn't work up the nerve to talk to them; they would have been glad to have been at least friends but it was even more than that.

He thought that he wasn't good enough to be around normal, good people, and it had festered and swelled up inside of him until it ate whatever good was left in his heart and replaced it with jealousy and resentment.

Reggie liked the gang because it gave him a sense of belonging to something, an identity and some brothers that he knew would stand with him and fight for him, and they weren't all bad kids after all.

That was what they'd argued about that very morning, Reggie told his father in anger, "What do you want from me? Want me to grow up and be like you? Have a son and forget about him? Become a rent-a-fool and spend the rest of my life guarding someone else's property?" he said, "You think they give a shit about you?" he shouted.

"You think if some fool shot you to death in the parking lot that they wouldn't step over your dead body and run to check their precious property first? Hire someone new that very hour?" he shouted, "Tell me, have you ever been invited to their houses? Inside for a celebratory drink on New Year's? Once?" he asked, "Ever get a birthday card from that company you care about so much that you risk your own life for?" he said.

He was angry at his father and angry at himself because he knew that his father was right, but he was also right about not pushing too hard and he did that anyway; if he'd thought of that it might have been a little different, instead of admitting that he might be wrong, Reggie dug his heels in deeper and refused to listen to anything that didn't sound like he was right.

He was certain that if he stung his father's pride again, and cut him deeply enough that he would get so angry that he would throw him out; that he would simply walk away, as he did before, he was sure that was how it would happen, it wasn't what he wanted, but he did want to know at the same time.

It was what he wanted but expected, he thought it was what his mother would have done too, once Morris was ripped out of her life, he wasn't needed any more and she'd stopped pretending that she cared about him.

His father shocked him, instead of being angry, he told his son that he took a lot of pride in his work; that it took honor and integrity to gain and then hold onto that kind of trust, and that, maybe he wasn't going to be invited into their homes, but this was his job and he wasn't there to be social; he wasn't trying to make friends.

But he also pointed out that it he wasn't out on the streets with his hands out, begging for money or stealing from others because he was too lazy to find a job; that sometimes just having a job at all was enough, it gave you a sense of worth and accomplishment, a good reason to drag his ass out of bed.

"When my day is over, I wash my face and brush my teeth before I say my prayers and show thanks for what I do have, and then I sleep a full, restful and guilt-free sleep!" he said, "Not every man is able to say that these days!" he said, "When work is hard to find and everyone is scraping to make it work.

"I can look at myself in the mirror now and almost like what I see in there, I take care of my own business now and the difference is so much better, I know that I did my best and I am trying so hard right now!" he told his son.

"Why don't you stay home today, son, and we can sit down and talk about this; work it out between us, are you hungry?" he asked and waited with a half-smile on his face, "I'll make us some eggs!" he said, trying to sound more cheerfully confidant than he felt.

When Reggie was younger, they both liked to have hot dogs cut up and mixed in with the scrambled eggs and potatoes in there, sometimes chili with grilled onions and sometimes with mushrooms sautéed in butter before they were thrown in; it was one of the things that he'd missed when they were apart, but now it was the last thing he wanted, it angered him that he even brought it up; this breakfast was never going to happen on this day, and maybe never again.

I have heard it said that you need to savor every good moment that you have in your life, every precious moment you can hold onto; because if you came back the next day and did exactly the same thing at the same time and with the same people it would not be the same, that this moment is gone and will never return so hold it close to your heart.

They'd lost so much of those special things between them, maybe forever except as faded memories of what once was; but Reggie murdered whatever chance was left for that when he spoke again.

"What the hell makes you think that now you can just step up and make it all go away? Make it better? That you can just snap away for all of the time you were having so much fun that you forgot about your son?" he asked angrily.

"For not being my father all of this time?" he shouted, "You think you can just cook up those fucking hot dogs and eggs and its going to atone for all of that? Are you fucking serious?" he shouted even louder.

Morris was not a prudish man, and he used more than his share of swear words in his life and then some; but he never expected to her them from his son, he himself was raised "old school" and never so much as said the word "shit" in front of his mother without profusely apologizing for it, yet his son didn't so much as blink when he did that.

"Son!" he said patiently, "Please don't use those words around me; those are words that anyone with little education and no imagination uses to hide their ignorance!" he said, "They hide behind words like that to make themselves seem tough when a lot of the time they are too afraid inside to let anyone see it!" he said.

"A man like that doesn't know to use his brains and will instead resort to his fists because he doesn't think there's anything better out there, but it's out there son, believe me on that!" he said and again tried to sound more cheerful and positive than he felt.

"Do you understand what I mean?" he asked, because his son hadn't spoken for several moments, he didn't react, nor flinch or turn away, and Morris thought it was because he as getting through to him at last; but he also felt that he'd rambled on too much.

"I ain't no fucking moron!" his son exploded suddenly, proving both the point Morris was making and showing his father how far he'd fallen, he could see that the words stung his father but he couldn't stop, even when he saw the way his father's shoulders sagged and then he walked out the door without looking back.

Morris thought his was stubbornly resolved to find his own way, he wasn't going to listen to him because he'd lost all respect for his father, that this was not from something that either of them did; but it was because of what she did, so he took this as "tuning out the old man" so that he could find out for himself.

He liked that he wanted to find out for himself in most ways, but not this time; he knew that he couldn't always be there to catch his son when he fell, because those falls might sting for a while but he would learn from them; he'd get up and keep going, but this was wrong, this was different and the possibilities scared the hell out of Morris.

This was different though, and not one of those things, Morris ran to the door while he felt that he'd lost the last chance he had to tell his son how he felt; but when he opened the door and looked out on the street his son was already gone, and he had no idea what direction he went in either.

As soon as Reggie was outside, he broke down and cried, but he didn't want anyone to see that even though he felt bad for the things he'd said; things that were out before he knew it and could stop himself, he didn't want to be mean, all those things just came boiling to the surface because they'd been held inside for so damned long, it felt good to get it out but he hurt the last person in the world that he wanted to; he wanted to hug his father but he didn't know how to from where they were at the moment and it all came out bad.

He ran around the corner and looked back in the direction of the house, and he saw his father looking for him, but he still didn't return, he didn't want his father to see him crying so he left and went to school, by the time he got there, the tears were dried but his heart was still heavy; but now at least, he hoped they could find a way past the anger he felt so strongly.

Reggie was so confused for a while though, and that led to more anger and frustration, and he had no idea that his father also cried when he left, he saw his son leave that day, but he didn't see the young man standing there; instead he saw his child, the boy that held onto his hand so tightly when he was younger, as if he knew they would one day lose this and he didn't want it to happen.

Morris cried at the sense of loss that he felt when he couldn't find his son, he knew they could fix this if they could both hold their anger in check and listened to each other with patience and an attempt at understanding, but it felt as though they'd lost all chance of fixing this at that moment.

Morris was thinking about that and not reading the sports page in front of him when a car pulled up to the gate, I could see him as he spoke to the driver through the window but I couldn't hear what was said, he allowed the car to enter and then I heard him say, "That's going to be over there, on the far left, and the visitors parking area in right in front of those double doors!" as the car left him there and I heard a female voice say "Thank you" as they drove off.

That was when he saw me standing there so I started walking towards him, and then he came out of the shack to see what I wanted, I could see the window was open and there was a small radio in there, I could hear it, and though it was small and sounded tinny, it was Sam Cooke singing "Down by the Sea" and it still sounded beautiful as he sang it; even on that little radio.

I was now inside the gate and feeling as though I was going to finally get some help and end this nightmare, I was about to ask him where I was and could I use his phone to call my mother who was likely frantic by now, when I saw the sign behind him, it said, "Saint Agnes School" and for some reason a very strong feeling came to me and I felt overwhelmed with feelings of what I wasn't sure.

It felt dangerous, and I thought about the spider, that maybe it was their "pet" or something, I felt love and I felt other strong emotional pulls in so many different directions all at once and all I remember after that is my head spinning and the same confusing images that I saw before swam before me now.

These were somehow inter-twined with new images, things I saw that I thought had nothing to do with me and yet they were very important somehow; they pounded their way into my memory and made me feel as though I'd seen them before; that it might have been my past life, coming to me in bits and pieces because I felt as though I'd seen them before now, that I might have lived through this somehow.

I must have passed out then, because the next thing I knew, I was opening my eyes and Morris was standing over me, and he was speaking to someone inside the building on his radio while he kept an eye on me; when I tried to get up he would hold a hand out and tell me not to try and get up.

Other than that, he showed no compassion, though he did seem as though he was concerned and he did roll up his jacket and put it under my head after checking me for injuries and then moving me to the shade; he put a blanket over me to prevent shock but it only made me warm while he waited for someone to come out of the building and take care of me.

Then two doctors, both women; ran out of the building and then one ran back and yelled for them to hurry with the stretcher, while the one than kept running towards me began to ask Morris for any details about what happened between gasps for air, for a doctor she seemed to be out of shape.

"He started off asking me about directions and I thought that he was lost, and as I tried to ask him things about where he lived so as to help him, he looked up to that window!" Morris said, and then pointed up there, where there was a light burning but otherwise there was nothing going on up there, nothing that they could see anyway.

"Then he asked me about someone that he thought was there, someone with a weird name that I've heard before, in a play or something, he asked for "Elspeth" I think!" Morris told them, checking things off in his mind as he remembered them, that was how he was taught, "report the chain of events as he observed them, not what he thought, but what he saw with his own eyes" and he was very good at it.

"Then I told him that I didn't know who he was talking about and that there was no one up there, because I didn't see anyone when I looked!" he told them and then waited.

"Is that all?" she asked him, "He didn't trip or anything and he as asking for directions?" she asked, as confused as Morris was at the way it happened, "He didn't hit his head at any time?" they asked.

"Yes!" he said, "I told him that there was no one here by that name or anything close to it and he looked up again and turned white, then he just fell backwards, but I don't think he hit his head, I checked for any bruises or bumps before I moved him!" he said, making sure they knew he did it by the book.

"Then I saw that he was unconscious and checked his pulse, I made sure that he was breathing, no obstructions and no signs of trauma, I put the pillow and blanket and then waited for you!" he said.

She leaned down and shined a flashlight in my eyes, and I turned away because it hurt and then I tried again to sit up, but they had more leverage and kept me down.

"Hello?" she said, "Can you tell me who you are? Or where you are?" I am a doctor she said, and pointed to her badge but I couldn't focus on it, then she said, "I am Doctor Crispen, is there someone that we can call for you?" she tried to smile but I think either she didn't know how or I made her nervous because it didn't work.

Then they put me on the stretcher and wheeled me inside because I passed out again, though I thought I said, "My mother, so she won't worry!" but they didn't seem to have heard a thing.

She called the other doctor back and together they checked my vitals and then they called an ambulance to take me to the hospital; they thought that I was anemic or was suffering from exposure, or maybe dehydration and they gave me fluids through an IV but they couldn't understand why I kept passing out and I couldn't give them any answers while I was out.

Funny thing though, when I did wake up, I tried to tell them that I was fine but they gave me something to calm me down and that knocked me out again, they fed me potassium and other nutrients and kept watch over me while they waited for me to open my eyes again or the ambulance to get here.

Then they told me that I was shouting for Elspeth and they had to put me in restraints for my own protection and I woke up to find them all standing around me with concerned looks on their faces; two nurses and a doctor, so I asked them, "What happened and where am I?" and then waited for them to answer as I looked around the room.

When I looked at the doctor after asking those questions, I noticed that she wouldn't look at me but she looked down at her chart and then never looked up, instead she kept scribbling her notes, then, still without looking up, she said, "You are being examined by Dr. Radison, he is the doctor on call tonight, and you were brought to us because apparently you fainted in front of St. Agnes!" she said and then finally looked up at me.

"What can you tell me about that?" she asked, "Do you remember what you were doing before you fainted? Do you have a history of this? Does it perhaps run in your family?" she said, "When was the last time you ate, and do you recall what it was?" she asked me in rapid succession, and then acted as if I was going to answer every question, in order once she stopped.

"I don't know!" I said, "I don't remember what I ate, it was something at school, but you never know what they put in that stuff!" I said, half joking, but none of them were smiling, "I think I was trying to find my way home and got on the wrong bus!" I said, a little sheepishly while trying to clear my head.

"Who were you asking about?" they asked, "Is it someone that you're sweet on?" she asked me, "Is that your mom's name? Can we call her so that she can clear up a lot of this? Take you home?" she said.

I noticed that there was another doctor or nurse, someone new that no one identified, not as though they all came and introduced themselves anyway, but she must have noticed that I was calm until they asked me that, and then she called the other one over when the monitor began to beep a little faster, and then leaned their heads together and whispered something that I couldn't hear.

"I...I don't know anyone with that name!" I said, suddenly scared for some reason, "You must be mistaken!" I said, looking from one to the other as if I could convince them but they wouldn't look me in the eye.

They exchanged puzzled looks when the doctor finally shrugged her shoulders and told me, "You kept asking for her, you fought against us when we told you she wasn't here!" she told me, "You said you had a message for her, but you said it was a warning, though you wouldn't explain what kind of warning or what that meant, but you were making no sense!" she told me.

After that, they waited a few more moments, watching me and checking my pulse and then they let me call my house so they could come and take me home at last.

On the way home, they sat me in the back with a folded blanket over my legs, provided by the hospital; mom rode shotgun while dad drove us home, she kept asking me what happened, why was I so far from home and what was I thinking, or even if I was thinking at all.

Mt father kept quiet all the way home, but he kept looking in the rearview mirror and his hands were tight on the wheel, since I was sitting behind my mother, I could see them clearly as if he could squeeze the answers out of it; but he said nothing the entire time and when we got home I was so tired that I went right to bed and fell asleep.

I missed the next few days of school, feeling as though I had a hangover or something; jet lag from the medications they put into me; it was what I imagined a hangover would feel like anyway, as though someone found me sleeping and decided it would be fun to beat me around the head and my stomach just for shits and giggles.

But I was groggy when they tried to wake me and when they tried to talk to me, it felt as though my head was a wad of cotton and I couldn't understand what they were trying to say. Their voices came through the fog but not clearly; it was as if I was in a tunnel or bubble and everything echoed around my head as I tried to listen to them.

My ears felt plugged and I couldn't breathe through my nose so I kept my mouth open and then was so parched that I felt as though I'd traversed a desert or something, and I know that nothing that I tried to say made any sense to them either, but all that I wanted to do was sleep, it was hard for me and frustrating for them.

Mom called the school and complained about the treatment I was given, tossed out and abandoned by the bus driver and she was talking about legal repercussions but she wasn't going to go through with that, she just wanted them to know that she was not happy about what happened and was warning them that it had better not happen again.

She stayed with me while my father reluctantly went to work, but he kept calling every few hours to make sure that everything was alright now, but he didn't much work done because he was so worried and he came home early to see me and make sure.

The school took the stance that they would talk to the driver but felt that she really did nothing wrong until she sent me away without trying to help, and I couldn't shake the feeling that my father knew something but wasn't ready to tell me.

He wasn't angry with me, I could tell that much, but he didn't like the way this was going or how it felt to him; we both felt that each of us was keeping a secret or at least something from each other, something that we didn't know how to explain or we thought it wasn't the right time, I don't know, but it felt that way to me as I saw how he looked at me.

Maybe because of that, but after sleeping those two days off, I still felt groggy and out of sorts, but lied to them and said that I felt better than I actually did; I felt the need to get out and get some fresh air, clear my thoughts and try to make sense of what happened, but ever since they spoke the name "Elspeth" I could hear a feint echo of someone whispering "Maria" right behind it, and I didn't know what the hell that meant it either but it scared me.

Though it was never a big deal to me before; I could take or leave school and it wouldn't have mattered a bit to me, but for some reason I felt that I needed to get there, I thought that maybe I might find some answers if I did, so I rose out of bed and was done with my shower before they knew what was going on, when they saw me, I asked them "What's for breakfast?" and my mother was just happy that my appetite had returned, she saw that as a good sign.

I was hungrier than I remembered ever being in my life; and for some reason, my mother came over to me, a concerned look in her eyes; she looked deep into mine and put her hand on my forehead, to heck for fever or anything that might still be wrong.

That was a "Mom thing" that she did, her "health check" for me, and because of her instincts or observations, there were times that she knew I was sick before I did; this time there was no fever and nothing was amiss, at least not enough to register so she let me go.

But then she stopped and looked back at me, tried to look deeper into my eyes but I turned away as if I didn't notice because I was afraid of what she might see in there.

She finally relented or was satisfied that I was on the road to health and then she went to make my favorite breakfast; something that I'd ordered a lot when we would go to a restaurant so my mother learned how to make it by asking me what was in it and then watching as I cut it open and ate it; I never left anything on my plate and that wasn't normal for me.

It was an omelet, made with fresh, sautéed mushrooms and onions, cheese and sausage; she knew that I would eat that, no matter how sick I was and even if I threw it up twenty minutes later, I wouldn't pass it up, she happily cooked it and watched me happily as the smells of her cooking drove me wild.

While she was cooking and not paying attention, I drank her coffee, taking sips here and there, I drank it a little at a time so she wouldn't notice; it felt as though I was waking up and coming out of that fog at last, and when she was done and I was eating my breakfast I pretended not to know what she was talking about when she looked at her coffee and it was almost gone.

"But Mom!" I said, "I don't drink coffee!" I reminded her when she asked me, and I even managed to keep a straight face while I did; maybe because I was having fun with her so it didn't seem like more than a little white lie; but she believed me and thought that she drank it while she was busy cooking.

I guess in my own way, I was trying to keep her from worrying, but I needed something to help me wake up, and her coffee was "black as a witch's heart" as she would say with a smile; but knowing her, no matter how simple or easy the answer was, she would not accept it and want to know the real reason.

There were more times after that, I caught her trying to look into my eyes, to see if I was trying to hide something and what it might be; but I wasn't hiding anything because I didn't have any of the answers that we all wanted so badly.

When I thought about it; school was actually the last place that I wanted to go, I knew that if I did, and then tried to sort things out in my mind, that I would be unable to because of all the things they needed to pound into my head that day; the driving need for those answers made me climb out of my comfort zone and go where I didn't want to be; because I knew that it didn't have to be a bad thing, it only felt that way right now; but that could have been because I didn't know what it was.

I left the house that day, knowing that I wouldn't find any answers in my room, but my heart was heavy; I didn't know what my parents knew about what was going on, but I knew that they knew something and they weren't telling me about it, a secret that I might not ever find out from them; but I was determined and would keep trying until they did, or I found out on my own.

Knowing their character, I knew they weren't criminals because I knew of the things they held in their hearts, we did things together or we didn't do them, there were no vacations without us all being there, and they worked hard in between those well-earned vacations, so whatever it was; I didn't think it would be that bad.

But that day, as I walked out of the house and down the street, I felt my mother's eyes on me as I left; I felt her heart reaching out to me and I could almost hear her say, "It's alright mijo! Things will be okay; all of this will pass, and it will be something we can all laugh about in a few years!" but I knew the truth by looking back into her eyes and would have known that in her heart, she wasn't so sure, and probably because of that, those doubts crept into my mind as well; clouded my thoughts and weighed heavily on my mind as I walked to school.

I knew that my parents set boundaries that I should never cross, some because they were good for me; and others because they still held superstitious beliefs and sometimes those were the hardest to follow, because to me; they made no sense.

The "don't call me by my first name thing" made sense, so di the respect that I would always give them; but I couldn't understand why they were so dead-set against the idea of reincarnation when nothing else seemed to make any sense; it felt so right to call it that, and I know they were just trying to protect me and it was done out of love, but I could never have imagined how this was going to turn out and the dark secret that terrified them both but they couldn't bring themselves to tell me about it.

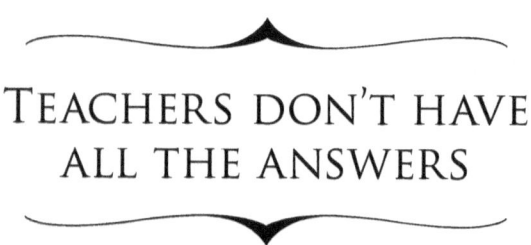

TEACHERS DON'T HAVE ALL THE ANSWERS

"I have never let schooling interfere with my education!"

-Mark Twain (1835-1910)

F OR HER PART, MARIA'S FIRST day at school was mostly uneventful, though she was, as the rest of us; nervous and excited by the newness of it, and she was overwhelmed by the number of new faces that she was going to see every day, kids that she would never see at the home.

She did feel the trepidation that they thought she would feel, but it wasn't as bad as they thought it was going to be; the only thing she wasn't prepared for was how loud it was; the home was never this noisy; even during the emergency drills that they ran once a month because the insurance demanded it, even then it wasn't as loud as it was here, and yet, everyone acted as though that was normal.

Then she remembered once, they thought it was a fire drill but it was an actual earthquake and everyone except for herself and a few staff that had been through worse shakes before; it was strong enough that it woke Maria from a deep and peaceful sleep; a rarity these days.

She jumped out of bed, not because it scared her; but because she thought they were shaking the bed because she'd overslept and they were trying to wake her; but as she rose from the bed she noticed that she was alone, then that the ceiling lamp was swaying and then that entire room was moving, books were falling off the shelf and joining others already on the floor.

She put on her robe and ran to the doorway and then waited while she put it on, and to her left she saw both staff and residents running all around like a Chinese fire drill, they were all shouting at each other and no one was in charge either, that was what they were arguing about; who had the final say in what they did.

When some of those people spoke to the others, it was clear that they didn't have the conviction to lead them out of there safely; they lacked the confidence and were scared and at least a few of them were already near panic; they thought the building was going to come crashing down on their heads at any moment and wanted to run out of there but were held back by the others.

That was when two of the female staff started a fistfight, they were grabbing at each other by the hair and both would have scars on their faces afterwards because they tried to scratch the other's eyes out, Mrs. Vincent; who was married to one of the teachers and thought she had all of the answers to life and we'd better start paying attention, before it got too late.

Whenever he tried to tell us anything, he made us go through so much to get there that we all felt that it wasn't worth it; and he treated all of his students, especially the "off-whites" as he called them, as if we were lucky to be in his classroom; and none of felt lucky whenever we saw him.

"Get out of the building!" she was screaming at the rest of us, even while they fought; "Run outside, follow the others to the safe zone!" she shouted at us, and a lot of the others were doing that, blindly following her orders without question.

Then she noticed that Maria and few of the others were still there, standing in the doorways and ignoring her and anything she was saying to them, "Outside, NOW!" she shouted and pointed, forgetting the other teacher who was trying to feel for bald patches where her hair had been pulled especially hard.

Mrs. Vincent put her hands on her hips, as if to emphasize her words but it only made her look funny to Maria; who couldn't help but laugh, "We were taught to stand in the doorways or under tables, but I can't slide under my bed, as you know; so I'm standing here until it's over!" she said, "They taught us not to run outside unless the building was on fire and to stay away from the windows!" she said.

There were huge cracks on the wall around her now, and some parts of the buildings would certainly be declared unsafe by the health department, but it held up well, all things considered.

As she started to tell Mrs. Vincent why she wasn't going to run outside, one of the overhead fixtures dropped down by one end; the other end swung around and caught her at the temple, ending the argument for at least the moment.

Maria paused to look at the ceiling, crossed herself and said a silent prayer before she went to her and checked her injuries, then she dragged her body to safety, sitting them both in the doorway while holding her head in her lap.

"Just because you're an adult, that doesn't mean that you have all the answers!" she said to her as she stroked her hair gently; "Sometimes you need to step back and take a good look at the entire thing before you can know what to do!" she told her as she kept monitoring her vitals.

Though she would wake with a concussion, she would be fine and when all was said and done, the two women were called on the carpet for fighting, one was put on administrative leave while the other was suspended without pay for a week.

The rest of us were given a repeat course in emergency procedures but all in all, they thought it didn't turn out as badly as it could have, none of the residents were so much as scratched or injured in any way.

After the quake stopped and everything was declared safe for the moment; Maria and some of the others went outside, everyone out there was talking about what they saw and how scared they were; one was a girl from the Midwest who came all way over here just to experience one, and she got more than she expected; her normally big eyes were huge now, as she was still trying to take it all in.

"I have never felt anything like this before!" she squealed delightedly but that was because she hadn't been there long enough to have anything fall off the shelf and break; the administrator on the other hand, had a different take on it; he had a large fish tank in his office, something that he took a great deal of pride in, and maybe that's why it happened; since even he say's that pride is a sin.

When the shaking was done, his prized fish were dead, the water had soaked into the carpet and would have to be dry cleaned, there were books on the floor as well, some ruined by the water, two lamps, one a floor lamp that was delicate, the other was on his desk.

But that girl was so excited, she kept babbling on about how much fun that was and when could we expect another, "It's a bit like a roller coaster, isn't it?" she asked of no one in particular, but she shouted that out and didn't mean to, she lowered her voice and asked again.

"Are you serious?" one of the others asked her, "Yeah! We know about that because we go to the theme parks every week and ride them all day and part of the night because we can't get enough of it!" the girl said, "The budget is tight and the economy is weak right now, but we have enough money for the really important things like roller coaster rides, as long as we don't care about things like shampoo and tampons!" they told her and then they all laughed.

A couple of weeks later, Mrs. Vincent returned to work with a supportive brace on her neck that made it okay for her to look down on us but also made her look ridiculous, but we weren't going to tell her that. The first time she ran into Maria, she stopped what she was doing long enough to take a second look at her but said nothing about what happened that day, ever.

She did acknowledge her, to a certain degree; she never shouted at her again, never got on her about the rules or what she might be up to; she pretty much left her alone after that, but she was the only one afforded that levity, she came down harder on everyone else as if to compensate, but she also knew that none of them would stand up to her as Maria did.

Until now, that was all of the excitement in her life, the noise level here matched that day in intensity and yet this was the normal, everyday, daily routine they were all used to and she would have to get there too, or feel left out; swept to the side with other debris while life, and the rest of the world flowed past her.

But that wasn't really what was on her mind that day, she was thinking about the Maria that cared for her as a baby; how hard she worked for a baby that was not her own, that had no real blood-connection to her, and then she started thinking about other things too; she wondered if that nurse would be proud of the way she turned out.

Thinking about her, she wondered how she would see her now; in a new school with kids her own age that she'd never met before in a world that she'd only seen on television and yet she felt as though she was at least holding her own and not doing too badly.

She knew that some of the boys had noticed her, new kid and she was quite beautiful after all; and some did wonder where she came from because they knew most of the other new students, but the orientations and the programs the school was implementing kept them too busy for anything like socializing and getting to know each other, that would come as they adjusted to the new schedules.

School can be a pretty tough place for new kids, and if the others smell a weakness or just feel that they are "too different" they will sometimes mercilessly jump on that with both feet, and yet they pretty much left her alone for some reason, they watched her from a distance, though they couldn't have told you why they did that.

The boys did some pretty dumb school-boy antics to impress her, but she hardly noticed, they didn't think she was snob because she answered when they spoke directly to her, but they knew that she was different, and they liked her.

But as they watched her confidently in the classroom and as she went through the hallways, none of them would have ever guessed that this was her first time in a public school, if they were clever enough to get into the files and saw her transcripts and other papers, they would have seen nothing about the orphanage or where she came from, just reports about her grades and how she was in school, medical reports and other papers that didn't reveal anything unusual; nothing to make her stand out.

She didn't make any new friends that day, but it was because she was used to being alone and didn't try, she would not waste time on boys anyway; she wanted to get the best grades that she could earn and then move on to whatever was next in her life, she was quite serious about her studies.

But it was that and much more; she felt as though she needed to get through this as easily as she could manage because she felt that there was something bigger on her horizon and she couldn't wait to find out what it was.

She decided in her mind that this was not going to be much different than the schooling she already did; since she was always independent and somewhat headstrong, she thought this wouldn't be much different than any of that and she felt that she was ready for it.

Her counselors, sensing a bit of hesitation at first told when they spoke of "what's next" told her to try her hand at college, that if it seemed too daunting that she could start at a junior college and see how she liked it; she could always transfer later.

Though she wasn't sure yet where she wanted her studies to take her, she was leaning towards a career in nursing; she wanted to touch lives as Maria had when she was a baby; she wanted to work with children, maybe a psychologist "Just because kids need someone to care for them and be on their side!" she joked.

She learned long ago that there were very few people that she could count on when things got tough, she learned that she had to fight for herself; but she liked it that way because then no one could ever let her down.

The only time that she ever felt that she was missing out on something was when she would see some of her friends with their new families, they always looked so happy, and so hopeful; and even when it didn't last it was a glimpse of the outside world and how things clicked or didn't.

When ever she tried to find out where she came from, anything about her parents, everything led to a stone wall, as if they never existed and no one wanted to tell her that; but all the trails left her out of the cold with no answers.

Part of the problem was that the orphanage didn't keep records for very long and there were limited resources at the time for her to find out any more than that; no one ever came looking for her and there was nothing about her on any public record or births that could give them any indication of who she was before she was so unceremoniously dropped into their lap.

The only thing that was left from that day was the handwritten note that she saved and kept in her diary; it was all that she had of her family and she treasured it, there was nothing revealing about it except that it was written in a woman's hand.

She would jokingly refer to herself as "Agent Double Zero" because they made a birth certificate after they took her in, using that date as her birthdate; and where it said "father and mother" it was left blank; it hurt her that she didn't have anything that told her what her name was but there was nothing that she or anyone else could do about it.

She knew that the birth certificate was just a formality and was not actually signed or anything, but she thought that she would have felt better if there were a few "not applicable" answers in there, those things gave her a way of laughing it off instead of crying as she sometimes did.

There were times when the others, to deflect their own shortcomings, would tease her because they at least were adopted for a time and taken in, only to have it not work out and then they were brought back to try again, and yet; as sweet and loving as she was, Maria was not taken for any "trial runs" like the rest, though some would show interest, they never followed through for some reason.

It was a nice feeling, at least she thought it would have been; but you never knew how it would turn out; when it was new and exciting it was one thing, but when the gloss wore off and you really got to see how it was; it could turn out to be very disheartening at the least.

There were good-hearted people that wanted a child but could not afford to adopt because the legal fees alone were quite prohibitive and it was difficult to even qualify; on the other hand, there are those that could afford it but were really only looking for a quick fix to the problems in their marriage; keep mom busy with a new child, but the child was the one that suffered the most in that situation.

Though Maria was beautiful and seemed to be well-adjusted, she was never adopted and no one ever tried to take her home or took her through that trial period with their families, but they stopped teasing her about it one day when she decided that she'd had enough and that it was no longer funny.

One of the older girls, whose name was Monica, and she had been after Maria all day, and on this day, she was especially mean in her words and the things she told others; she had been taken on three runs and they all failed, she was rejected three times by the time she was twelve and was especially angry about it that day.

Monica felt that she'd done everything right, that this last time it was going to work and she found her home, only to have her hopes dashed when they got into a fight and he left her; she didn't want to try and raise her alone because she would be too much trouble and would get in the way of her "new life" and so she had to go.

That time, when she got back, she was angry and frustrated and Maria was the first one she ran into; she always seemed to be an easy target because she never showed her anger and always turned the other cheek.

She was trying to deflect anyone that might blame her for her return to the orphanage when she saw Maria walking by that day and stepped in front of her and refused to move; Monica was smaller and thinner than Maria, but she was determined that day and told Maria as she pointed her finger in her face, "At least they tried to take me home!" she said, and you have never been anywhere but here!" she said and then laughed.

Although she herself was abandoned, and it could be argued that it meant that she'd been rejected four times and what good did it do to go to a home like that when it wouldn't take anyway; she was in the same boat as everyone else but was hurting that day and thought others should hurt as well.

As they saw what was happening, the rest of the girls closed in on them and circled around them like sharks, smelling blood in the water, they saw Maria try to step around her and go on her way but they also saw that Monica was not going to let go so easily this time; it felt like more than just light banter and they wanted to see what was going to happen.

"You are like the little puppy that they buy at the store and take home because they saw it in a movie, and it was cute!" Maria said when it was clear she was not going to move out of her way, "They took you home and decided that you were too much trouble, or got upset that you shit on the rug and take you back to where they found you!" she told her, her voice rising as it was clear she was not happy now either; she was ready for a fight as well this time.

Monica could stand it no longer, she reached out and grabbed Maria by the hair; Maria countered by grabbing hers as well, she pulled the taller girl to the side by her hair and then punched her hard on the face as she let go and Monica fell to the ground.

As she fell, Maria began to rapidly punch her about her face, taking years of frustration and pent up anger out on her until the counselors came in and broke it up; that was to be the only bad mark on her record, and yet you could hardly blame her for it; she was merely defending herself and really had no choice in the matter.

Both girls were suspended from any extra activities for two weeks, but that just meant that they would be separated and not sitting together for a while; and though Maria showed a fat lip for a time and a small scratch on her cheek and on her neck; but Monica clearly got the worst of it; she sported a black eye and some nasty bruises but Maria had a souvenir of her own; she had a swatch of hair that came from Monica.

After that day, when anyone tried to mess with her, especially Monica, she would pull out that hank of hair and shake it at her, she knew that Monica still had a bald spot that no amount of creative styling would be able to completely hide.

They left her alone after that, they left her alone, finding out that she wasn't as shy and timid as they thought her to be; and Maria knew at that point that she didn't have any real close friends because most of them seemed to be disappointed that she won and not Monica, but she felt that as long as she knew, it didn't really matter and she could spend the rest of her life without any of them.

That was when she began to think that she might be different; not special by any means, but not at all like the others, she thought that she might have a calling; some purpose that would reveal itself to her one day, she had no idea of what it might be but she hoped that she would be ready when it came along and that she would know it when she saw.

She thought that was why she was alone so much of the time, why no one came and claimed her and why she felt isolated from all rest; different, not bad or broken inside, to her it meant that she was simply meant to walk a different path than they were.

Though she didn't know what it was, she did instinctively know that none of the girls she knew at the orphanage, it wasn't their fault and just how things were in the way of the world.

She couldn't believe it was her when she thought about how angry she became with Monica that day she fought with her; when she thought about it, she felt as though she was with the others; watching as it happened rather than being in the center of it.

The looks on the faces of the others when it turned that violent was something she had a hard time accepting and understanding; it looked as though they didn't want just a fight, they wouldn't be happy just seeing blood, they wanted so much more and that thought scared her too.

Yet she would have to admit that things were better for her since she fought back; they all left her alone now, and privately some of them thought she was a little bit on the crazy side, but she liked having that "edge" when they saw her.

They all knew that she was different too, some of them liked that about her but didn't know how to say it and kept their distance in case the crazy side was ready to jump out again, being left alone was a good thing sometimes; but other times it wasn't, it kept people that she might have liked to have known better and become friends, but they were all scared of her now and gave her a wide berth in the hallways.

None of at the school knew any of this, but she spent the first day of school just as I did; filling out the numerous forms and even though she thought they gave her the same ones more than once, at the same time; she felt that feeling of being watched and had no more luck at ignoring it than I did, except for her it continued even to that night while she slept.

The few times that she looked around to see if anyone was paying her any extra attention to her but no one was even looking in her direction, everyone seemed to have their own agenda and though they looked like ants, scrambling when they are disturbed; there actually was order in the ranks as they all walked from class to class and went through their day.

She dismissed it as I did too; she decided that it was just "new school jitters" that were amplified by the fact that she'd never seen any of these people before, that she was being an unofficial ambassador of the orphanage because if she did well, others that were growing to that age would follow; she was in essence an "explorative experiment" and didn't mind though she felt the pressure from it.

As she was reciting her prayers that night, I was also in my room, I'd already said my prayers and was reflecting on my life; my experiences so far and the roots from where I started, the people that came from Mexico or thought that somehow their roots were stronger than mine because they spoke the language or were still "fresh" from there and hadn't adjusted yet to the new world; they were suspicious and sometimes simply envious of the "pochos" or people like me that didn't speak the language and looked white, didn't have jet-black hair and didn't dress the same; listen to the same music.

One day I asked my father what pocho meant and it really bothered me when he told me, I felt that they were separating me from my roots without asking me how I felt about it; or even knowing who I was inside, simply making that snap judgement because of how I looked.

Deciding that they knew me because my skin was lighter and my eyes were hazel instead of brown or black that I was different; though I never looked at them that way, never looked down my nose at anyone because I never thought I was better than them, though I did know that I was different; not special either; but because of the way my parents raised me, I knew that I didn't need to prove myself to anyone else.

Some people might have thought that it was funny, or that it was a name that fit some people, but it bothered me, I felt that they were punishing me because I was born north of that border, I didn't look dark-skinned or dark haired enough for them and I didn't think it was right.

I was Mexican Irish American Indian and thought of myself as pretty much normal, except for those nightmares that I couldn't stop, control or understand, but I still felt at odds in a lot of places; I didn't fit in with any of the groups or clubs that I was interested in while at school, I was either deemed "too smart" for some of them, or just not the right size, color or personality for them.

They would all ignore me until I got the message and left them alone, and it did bother me for a time but I guess you can get used to almost anything if you try hard enough, or in my case; you were forced to and have no other choice or option.

My parents eventually became legal, naturalized citizens and they were proud of that, anything that happened before that was something that they kept to themselves and were reluctant to talk about; even with me, and I didn't understand why they were like that with me.

The state was anxious for them to be legal because my father had become a person of influence in the business community and the political arenas as well; they were always asking him to run for office but he always declined and deferred that to the men that were "better equipped" to deal with those kinds of things, though he was flattered he wasn't interested, there were people that would walk behind him, all the way home if he asked, but he thought that was something that I might do one day.

I tried more than once to ask about my background, my heritage; and tried more than once to ask them why we moved here in what seemed to be desperation, I wanted to know why we ran away from Mexico in the middle of the night like thieves taking the silverware from the Governor's mansion.

Every time I asked, they gave me the stock answer, "It's better here, more opportunity; but I knew my father, and when he told me that, I could see that there was something else, buried beneath that story, though not too deeply; not deep enough that it couldn't be seen by me.

It felt too much as though it was a mantra, what they decided to tell me if I ever asked, and though it wasn't the entire truth, it was what they were going to color that truth with; what they were hiding from me was something that I could not guess, nor could I figure out why they would hide it from me, and every time I tried to dig deeper and find out what it was, they never let me get close enough to try and take a guess.

All of this meant that, though Maria and I had not met each other yet, we did share the same feelings of isolation and abandonment, though I think that my feelings were not as deep or profound as hers were because I had parents, and more of a sense of where we came from, more roots, even though mine were replanted.

We were as yet, unknown to each other, yet feeling the same exact feelings at the same time, though we were miles apart and in our own rooms; how we were in each other's lives and how we got to this point I had no idea; but we were bound together and headed for the same eventuality.

Neither of us knew what was ahead of us, and if we were able to see each other's faces we were even facing each other at that moment if we could have spoken but we had no idea.

My parents would tell me things if I asked, but I had to ask the right question and in the right way or they would stop talking or change the subject; and they would answer but they would not elaborate, tell me just enough to touch the tip of the question without going into depth or detail; they never gave me anymore, I always felt as though there was more, as though they were hiding a deep and terrible secret.

Knowing them, I knew that they would not do anything wrong; anything that might be considered criminal; the cops weren't going to bust down the door and take them away at any moment, but it was serious and felt bad to me.

That they were simply protecting me from something in the only way that they knew how, but they didn't realize that there are times when you hide or deny something from your children that they are going to be drawn into it even more so, more likely tom open Pandora's Box to find out her deepest secrets, to know what was behind the curtain for themselves.

I knew that to my mother, the most basic and yet important things in life were based on the "Golden Rule" which meant treat others as you wanted to be treated, not judge others by how they looked and give them all a chance to be my friend before making any decisions about what kind of person that they might be.

"As long as you live that way and keep God in your heart you can never go wrong, and remember that, no matter what else happens, I will always be here for you and I will always love you!" she told me.

I knew that my mother would never lie to me about such things and that she meant every word, that they came from deep in her soul and she would be here from beyond the grave if she was needed; that she would always be watching over me.

Those were simple words from her heart and yet I can't tell you how much those words meant to me; helped me through some tough times in my childhood, it meant that I would never be alone; and for maybe the first time in my life I was speechless, I simply reached for her and held her closed to me for a long time.

I rubbed her back as I held her, something that I'd seen my father do many times when she needed comforting, she leaned back to look me in the eyes and I saw tears swimming in hers, ready to over flow and run down the sides of her face.

"When a mother has her child, no matter what it is, boy or girl, and no matter how healthy and normal or sick and needful, a mother wants, needs to hold that baby close to her heart all of her life; to shield that baby from hurt and to protect them from injury, and no matter how old that baby gets, that doesn't change!" she said.

"In the course of our lives, things happen, and I can't be there, and I can't always find the words to make it right, to help make the pain go away; but some of that pain is meant to test you and help you become a better man through the process of hurting and healing!" she told me.

"But as long as you love me, and you know that I will always love you, we can always have that link, that bond between us that will keep us together, even though one day I will die, you will feel alone but I promise, I will always be here for you!" she said, and then pointed to my heart.

"Keep me in your heart and I can never be far away, and then she held me close again as she whispered, "I am so proud of you and I know in my heart you will grow to be a good man and you will always do the right thing!" she said.

For a long time, my mother only learned enough English to pass the citizenship tests, and sometimes we would all laugh because of her attempts to say some things, and maybe there were times when she was misunderstood because of that; but on this day, she said what she wanted to and was as eloquent as anyone born in this country.

She'd never told me these things before, so they held deep meaning for me; there were things I just knew, because of the way she was, things assumed but not spoken of until now, and it made me happy and feel so much love that I was overwhelmed.

Then she turned even more serious and said, "Don't you ever tell a woman that you love her unless you truly do!" she warned me, "You will break her heart because you were careless with it or the way you treated her, she might eventually forgive you but the world never will!" she said.

It took me a long time to actually understand that, what she meant by it; it made no sense to me at the time, but I thought that she wanted what every mother wants for her son; that he become a good man and responsible for his actions; one that respects women as well as everyone else that deserved it, to be a credit to my family and my race, and never forget where I came from.

I knew that it was important to them that I graduate high school and continue to college; that was their dream, I would be the first in our line to graduate from an major institution in the United States of america, as long as it wasn't a penal institution.

Though I knew nothing about the way I was born and where we were at the time, they never told me any of that, again, trying to protect me from what I didn't know, and I meant to sit down one day and talk to them about that, as you might imagine I had a lot of questions and very few answers.

Whatever she tried to teach me, whatever she thought important enough for me to learn I did my best to achieve; because it made her so proud and so very happy, and I knew she wouldn't try to teach me anything as useless as high school math.

There were times, I heard other mothers tell my mom that she taught me well; that I had good values and ideals about life, but she would always laugh and say that it was not her; that she was blessed with good material and a matter of good things put there by God that stayed with me through my life; that I was not her child, I was trusted by the lord with his child for safekeeping; like all mothers with strong faith.

My father was entirely different, the opposite of her; he was a very proud man and though he didn't finish school, he saw and felt how important it was to her and never spoke about his shortcoming, if that was what it was; he was still intelligent and it wasn't that he couldn't do the work in school; it was more because he didn't see where it was going to make his life any better and wanted to get out and work, make a living and put food on the table for his family, even at a young age.

As such, he was sometimes hard to read and understand; and he didn't always know the right words to say what he meant, he would say things and then assume that I knew what he meant; even when it made no sense to me at the time.

But I knew that he loved to laugh, and every day when I came home from school, the first thing he would ask when he saw me was what had I learned that day, and did I make any new friends that day. He'd done that for as long as I could remember, it felt as if he left work and ran all the way home because he couldn't wait to ask me, and I knew this question wasn't just about the lesson of the day in school; he was also talking about life, what had I learned about it.

If I had nothing to tell him, nothing new, he would be very disappointed, he wouldn't say it; in fact he wouldn't say a word for a while, as if he was trying to understand how I could spend an entire day outside and in school and not learn a single thing that day that I might share with him.

He would act as though I was holding out on him if I had nothing to share; and then he'd start thinking that it was a bad thing I'd learned and was starting to go down the wrong road or something, so I started making things up if I had nothing, expand on something that I'd learned but add my own thoughts to it; that way I found out of it made sense to anyone else except for myself, and to my delight it actually did.

My father was also a man that loved to work with his hands; and wood was something that he could work magical wonders with; we spent hours in the garage working on something he was building for the house, a rocking chair, a new dinner table because the old one was old; or he'd work on tuning up the car, replacing worn parts and we spent a lot of time talking about things while I learned how to replace the carburetor on a Malibu Classic, but I never got the hang of making furniture; he was so good at it that others would hire him to make them chairs and furniture but he would say no a lot of the time because he thought money tainted the pleasure of it.

They never understood that, and would either give him the money or give it to my mother and she would tell him; then spend it on groceries or something for the house, when things got too tough; he would take side jobs and build things for others; new cabinets in their homes, replace the wooden floors that had carpet over them for so long that no one saw the rot until it started to collapse.

It was more that he loved working with things, especially wood; and sometimes thought of his regular job as a nuisance; it was something that paid the bills but got in the way of what he wanted to do, it took too much of his time; he liked working with his hands and creating beauty out of a piece of wood, something out of nothing.

He once told me that if you took a piece of wood and stripped it down to its bare-naked soul; that it would tell you a lot about life and not just how old it was, but the things that it had been through; the history of that part of the world, that you just, "Needed to look deep into it, and accept what you saw in there!" he would say, wistfully; "It could tell you a millions stories, mijo!" he would say, but I could never see it as he did.

During those times we spent together I did learn things about my family; the things I learned that they tried to keep from me, I found out things when he was tired and he let his guard down, it made me feel guilty to get it out of him that way; but it wasn't fair that he was keeping these things from me either.

That was how I learned one day that I actually had a brother at one time; my father was drunk enough from a celebration at work that he blurted it out, and this time he did it without breaking down too much, my mother wasn't there and so once it slipped out; he acted as though it was something "just between us boys" which was really funny to me because he was the one that always said no secrets in the family.

Still, finding out that I had a brother was such a shock that I felt that I had to sit down; he said that they called him "Flaco" because he was really tall and thin at an early age, and though his real name was Anthony, it had been a long time since anyone called him that, except at school.

I knew it was hard to talk about, and I could see that just saying his name was hurting him deeply; "I have a brother?" I asked him, clearly both surprised and excited, but of course I also wanted to know all that I could about him; and the feeling I got from him, and the way he cried made me think the rest of it was bad news, that I had a brother but not anymore.

The look on my father's face when I asked that made my heart sink, and then my father did what he always did at times like this; he dropped into his "stone face" that meant he wasn't going to say anymore; it was what my other called his "El Indio" look because even she knew that when that veil dropped over his eyes he would not budge until he was ready to, that could take hours...or days...or weeks, you just never knew.

It told me also that this was the tip of the iceberg that was their terrible secret; that something bad had happened to him and it was something that they really didn't want me to know.

He told me that he loved the name Anthony, it was our grandfather's name, but he thought that Flaco was a name the defined him better, gave him more freedom to be himself; to be bohemian if he felt the need to, it was the name he earned and not what was chosen for him before he was born.

Then he told me that Flaco also had a great sense of humor, that made me think that in a lot of ways he was closer to my father than I was; they shared a lot of the same traits and personality issues which might have been why they had so many problems between them.

He said that they shared an intense love for each other but if they were together for more than an hour they would argue over the silliest of things, sometimes it didn't even seem to matter what the reason was; as long as they were on opposite sides and could shout louder than the other.

After that, it took me a long time to learn more because I got things a little at a time, here and there; things they "dropped" without realizing it, like the fact that he had the biggest brown eyes that women were drawn to, even when he was very young, and eyelashes that they said they would die for, whatever that meant.

My mother once told him that his eyes were so big because he tried to take in the whole world at once, as if he knew his time was short and he had to get it all in while he could; he was always trying to learn new things and seeing if and how they might apply to his life.

Along with all of that, he had an easy smile and a gentle way about himself that made them feel he wasn't dangerous and they could talk to him, then they saw the softer and more romantic side that they really liked once they got to see it.

My father told me once that he liked to see how things worked, what made people act certain ways and what he thought about things going on in the world, he wasn't a big talker and he didn't use words that were beyond his vocabulary, but he did have a feel for things in the world order and I liked to hear it.

"He could never ask enough questions to satisfy his curiosity about those things!" my father said, and then his voice broke, I think he was remembering one of those times, he was probably having a hard time fixing the car or something and my brother was bombarding him with questions and he wished he would go ask his mother or someone else; now I could see that he wished he was here to ask more now, and I saw the sadness wash over him like a dark cloud.

I wondered where Flaco was now and wanted to ask but this was tearing his heart out a little at a time and I felt as though I was torturing him just by asking about it but I wanted to learn more; in a way it was his fault anyway, by keeping so much from me for so long, in my opinion they drew it out that way, they should have just sat me down and told me the whole story at once and then it would be over.

Eventually, I found out that he was the reason why we left our home in such a hurry, why they risked having me in the middle of that move when my mother was so far in her pregnancy and left most of our possessions at home and fled to the land of milk and honey like thieves in the middle of the night.

Until then I never knew that I had history in Mexico, and now I knew why it bothered me so much to be forced to feel different, the "white of the egg" and called pocho, why I felt such a draw to go there and experience the land that my friends were going to on weekends with their families.

All of that "tough guy" stuff was okay with Flaco, he liked having the reputation because they left him alone and he really didn't want to fight, he was; as he said, "A lover, not a fighter!" but that didn't mean that he was going to back down from a fight either.

He would tell his friends that there was nothing sweeter or softer than a girl, that each and every single one of them was different than all of the others; he thought of them as an exotic flower, sometimes so wonderful, so sweet that he couldn't get enough of them; other times just too much trouble for his liking.

Those were the ones he said needed "too much fertilizer" and then that he didn't want to wallow in that shit, it wasn't his style, but most had their own sweet and special fragrance, learned how to wear their hair in ways that accented their best features; wore certain clothes that told you of their character, how proud they were and how much they didn't give two shits what you or anyone else thought about them.

"All you really needed to do was to listen to them, to look deeply into, not just what they say, but what they as well!" he said, "That's where you'll find the real truth of their words!" and then he'd laugh; take the time to get to know them and get to know them one delicious layer at a time, and each one so different, just like the Arista sisters!" he laughed even harder then, at some memory of them.

They were identical twins, sometimes even their own parents had a hard time telling the difference between them; and though they tested him many times, thinking that he was just lucky at guessing but he was never confused and never hesitated when he answered.

Though they were sisters and shared the same life experiences and had the same memories; each one still held their own opinions and emotions that went along with those memories; that was one of the ways he learned how to tell which one was standing in front of him.

He said he could tell because, though they both wanted to be loved and appreciated for who they were individually, that he learned about them simply by listening and then studied their words and actions, that would tell him who he was talking to and he was never wrong.

"Where one, Sandra was logical, cold and aloof most of the time, the other one, Erica, was always a sweetheart; warm and friendly, much easier to talk to and he considered her a friend, there were the things they did that couldn't be faked; when they switched identities, there were only so many things that they could pretend about.

Flaco would also get into trouble a lot for standing up for the smaller kids; and it didn't matter if he knew them or not, it bothered him when the bullies tried to take advantage of them; but in the end, all he ever really cared about was being loved by those that he held close to his heart.

Sometimes when my mother would tell him how much she loved him, he would tease her and say, "I know mom, but that's because it's in your contract!

You should have read the fine print!" he would say and then laugh, "Now you have to love me or your breaking the law!" he would tease her about that all the time.

It was obvious if you saw them together, there was a special bond between them; a deep commitment to each other that was meant to last the rest of their lives and then some, but there was a reason why he fought so hard to be loved; he always felt that he needed more, always testing the girls that said they loved him to see if their actions matched their words.

Even though he said that he knew certain people tat would never lie about something so serious, so sacred and important; this was a battle and a sense of loss that he fought and carried on his shoulders all of his life, always trying to do the right thing and not hurting people he loved and cared about and yet hurting some of those people the most.

In the end, you could probably say that being unloved was probably one of his greatest fears, being deemed unworthy of such a gift to his heart; and because he feared it so much, it was likely the one thing he could never put into words either.

That was a rare thing in itself because he was very good at using "big words" when they were needed and in the proper context of what he was trying to say, he could describe a rose in such a way that you wanted to rush out and find some that you might admire their beauty as well; he could make you feel as though you had never seen one before even though you were standing in a field of them that stretched as far as your eyes could see.

Yet, as eloquent as he might be, he could not describe nor explain that emptiness, that loneliness that he felt at times; there was nothing he knew of that he could compare it to. It was a flaw that he knew about and hated; something that he knew how to control or fix, and he didn't know how to turn it off either, ignoring it didn't make it go away and sometimes made it even worse because it felt like desperation.

There were other things that he would never talk about, things that haunted his good nature and made him feel dirty, broken and evil; he knew that these things were a part of him, but he never understood why.

As such; love to him was both the best, and the worst of emotions for him, it was the black hole in his heart, the empty void in his soul and there was no way to ever fill it or satisfy those needs, at least that was what he told himself when it hurt too badly; that he was born to be alone.

He hated those contrasting emotions because he wanted to always be open and expecting good, but he knew that this was something that he needed so desperately and the reason why he always felt so alone; so isolated from the rest of the world.

When he saw some of his friends with their girlfriends, especially if it was someone that he'd dated before, it would always make him angry at himself because it didn't work for them; he respected his friends and would never try to take them away, he couldn't help but wonder why it didn't click when it look so easy for them and he always felt that it was something that was wrong with him; that it was his fault and not hers.

It was even worse when the girl would look back at him with the same look in her eyes, that he knew that she was thinking the same thing at that moment; her eyes would accuse him of stalling and taking too long to make his moves, and sometimes they gave him the "see what you missed" look on their faces.

He would wonder if they ever looked that happy together, as if they belonged together, and then he'd feel even worse and more alone than ever, and even in his happiest moments he was always looking for the dark side of the silver lining; always waiting expectantly for the other shoe to fall and land square on his head.

Then, one day he met a girl that he thought was going to change all of that for him, and the moment he saw her he started to believe in love at first sight; he fell helplessly in love with her, he never before believed that could happen, not in real life; that it only happened in the movies.

The love bug bit his ass good and hard that day, and it took away his brains and commons sense as a trade-off, her name was Sabrina, and she was bad news from the start, though it wasn't her fault; she was knee deep in the shit before she got a whiff and knew where she was.

She was a nice girl, with a good heart that lived with her grandmother who was getting on in the years and not doing well; she was suffering from complications that were related to her asthma and getting worse by the cough, but her medication had recently gone up in price and it was already too expensive for her; she let the wrong guy into her life and then could not escape from him without seeing her grandmother hurt for it.

She was cute and perky and when he saw her smile his heart melted and he felt then that everything was going to be alright after all; he found his beating heart in her chest and enjoyed the feeling of hers right next to it.

The "bad news" was her boyfriend, his name was Stephon, he was the middle son of a local drug dealer that fiercely controlled the area, and even though he'd lost an older and a younger brother to the streets, Stephon was ready to strike out on his own, he wanted to become his own man without using his father's name to open those doors for him.

His reputation was bad enough at a very young age that there were polemen that would look the other way when he approached them on the street, if they drove past in their cars they simply nodded their heads in his direction but never looked him in the eye.

He also had an older brother that in a prison in America, he was there because he committed a murder; it wasn't a drug deal gone bad, or a snitch that he found that was giving information to the police about his dealings; it was nothing like that, he picked a man at random and shot him in the face just so he'd be sent there, he didn't even leave the area, he sat down and emptied the rest of the rounds on the ground as he waited for the cops to arrive and then he became the main source for most of the cocaine going through that area and to the rest of the states.

Stephon was a nice guy when they first met; very attentive and sweet, he charmed his way into her heart by pretending to be something that he could never be, and when it began to take a turn for the worst, it was too late; he had his hooks deep into her and knew that as long as her grandmother was around he had a hold of her, a way to keep her in line.

It turned really bad when Stephon got this idea and he ordered his friend Julio to make this sling for him; it would fit on his forearm and unless you knew it was there you'd never see it, and once you saw it at work, you'd hope you never saw it again, even in your worst nightmares.

The blade itself was razor sharp and almost fifteen inches of lethal steel that should never have fallen into the hands of someone like this kid; he took it from another kid, and couldn't wait to use it for more than the scare tactic he used to get it.

He was walking out of the schoolyard and he saw a small circle of kids that were laughing and having fun with whoever was in the middle, and it was enough to make him curious about what they were laughing about, and yet they never saw him there until it was too late.

There was a kid in the middle, he had the knife and was throwing it around, showing off moves that looked more dangerous than they were; looking at it, he thought they were disrespecting the deadliness of such a fine weapon, the light reflected off its surface would make most men turn away, or at least cover their eyes, but he stood there and took it in as if it were nourishing him somehow.

The kid was throwing the knife high into the air, and standing underneath until the last moment and then moving out of the path at the last possible moment, and the third time he did it was too much for Stephon, he shoved two kids out of this way and stepped into the middle of the circle and shoved the kid back and away from the path while the blade was still rising.

He stood there as the blade started to fall and never looked up to see where it was, he kept his eyes on the other kid, he told him, "If you're going to dance with the devil, you really need to get his attention!" he said, and everyone in the crowd went silent, all watching the blade as it seemed to take forever, and then fell in front of Stephon, close enough to touch him and yet it never did and he never flinched.

Then he took the blade, pulling it out of the ground and yet he still never took his eyes off the other kid, who was afraid to move or say anything because he'd heard about Stephon but had never met him before, and if he lived through this day, he hoped he never would again.

When his friends asked him about it later, he said that even though his eyes weren't blue, they felt icy cold as Stephon's gaze fell onto him, he felt captivated, as though he could not move until Stephon told him that he could, he was too scared to even breath without permission.

Stephon shook the blade at him for a moment and then said, "If you don't respect her, you don't deserve her, you aren't good enough to touch her, and I know you aren't going to argue with me, are you?" he asked as he tucked the blade into his belt and turned and walked away.

The harness that Julio made for him worked well; all he needed to do was bring his arm up quickly and then flick his wrist and the blade would snap into position, ready to let the blood flow.

Once it was set into place that way, it was as strong as if it were welded onto the bones of his arm and with enough thrust, he could rip straight through a man with very little effort.

Stephon was only ten years old when he first began to show his evil side, the side that he hid from Sabrina so well and yet it was the side of him that his reputation was built on.

He stabbed a total stranger while he was walking on the street, simply to watch him die, not for any reason or need, but to see it happen with his own eyes, and being a drug dealer's son with a bad reputation of his own, you'd almost expect things like that to happen all the time; a normal part of the drug world, but he was very young and should have been playing basketball or baseball with his friends.

To make it even more frightening, he was not angry at the man, he killed him because he was curious about the last things that happened when a man was dying; especially that way, but he also wanted everyone to fear him, and doing a cold-hearted killing in front of everyone was going to do it.

His victim was a man that was walking through the crowd that day, unmindful of the killer that was walking towards him that day, he was minding his own business and oblivious to everyone else that was out there on the street unless he had to step around them.

The man accidently bumped into Stephon and thought nothing of it; this was an accident after all, and as crowded as it was there were a lot of people bumping into each other on that street and then going on their way with no problems; he thought that as always, "Permisso" was enough and mumbled that as he kept on walking.

"Oye, puto! Come back here!" he said as he spat at the man who was still walking away from him and almost disappeared in the crowd by then, and the man was of course, insulted and turned quickly around, thinking that an adult was talking to him that way and he didn't like it.

But when he turned and saw the boy standing there, he made his second, and sadly; his last mistake of that day, one that was going to cost him much more than a simple "Permisso" and go on your way.

He saw the kid and laughed, "Why should I be afraid of a little kid?" he said, and then was laughing so hard that he missed the glint of steel until it was well past too late.

Stephon stepped into him and thrust the knife straight up and through the underside of his chin, the blade held his tongue in place as it rose up through the top of his head, then he grabbed the back of his head as the man slid slowly to the ground as if he was caring for him, looking right into his look of disbelief from inches away, he took the man's last breath as it expelled from his lungs, taking it deep into his own with a shudder.

He thought that it would take a lot more effort to slice through a man that easily, it sliced through him with such a sickening sound as he was surprised at how easily it cut through bone and tissue and blood began to flow then.

It came out slowly at first, coming out of the top of his head and then a little quicker as it ran down the side of his face, he'd sliced through some major arteries and blood ran down Stephon's arm as well.

As he felt the blood trickle down his arm, the warm sensation and all of the excitement gave him an erection that he didn't want everyone to see, so he held the man close to him until it passed and he was sure that the man was dead.

He looked at the blood as it crawled along his arm, then he touched it with his cheek and absently licked at it as he looked down at the body at his feet, the man had choked on his own blood with a shocked look of disbelief on his face, he couldn't speak but he tried, and with his eyes he pleaded with Stephon; he couldn't believe that this boy killed him over such a trivial thing, he thought about his wife and kids and wondered who would look after them now.

His life flickered out as he watched Stephon move away from him; it was clear that he was ready to stab him again if he wasn't really dead but he surely was, he looked around for another victim; he was a bit let down and disappointed that this was too quick and now he wanted more.

He felt as though he was the wolf cub that has taken the first bite of a tough kill and was ready to howl at the moon in triumph, except it was just after noon and the sun was high overhead.

Reluctantly, he looked around once more as he clicked the blade back into place; he was certain that no one was going to try and stop him, none of them would even look at him if he turned in their direction because no one wanted to remember his face or what he did.

Blood flowed out of the poor man's body and went down the street along the gutter line, it stained the front of his shirt a bright red, but he was too far gone to have noticed or cared anymore.

The police arrived about twenty minutes later, they were finishing lunch and didn't want to stop and let it get cold or the flies get to it; the first thing they did was ask for any possible witness's, and they thought they saw one of their own a few feet away, directing traffic as if this had nothing to do with him.

They found another seven people that were less than twenty feet away because of their shops and what they were selling at the time, they had a clear view of what happened but no one saw a thing; it didn't entirely surprise them because drug dealers worked this area and were not known for being nice when they dealt with their enemies, they were used to people not trusting them and the fear that the drug dealers held over their heads was enough to make them deaf and dumb as well as blind.

You really couldn't blame them for it, if the police knew they were lying, they would take them in for a few hours, maybe overnight; but they would have to release them and as long as the drug dealers didn't get any "surprises" while they were in there, their families were safe.

But if they raided the headquarters or clubhouse of the gang, then the rest of the family was in great danger, no one would be spared and then life would go on for the drug dealers anyway and they would be waiting to finish what they started when the police released whoever it was they felt snitched.

They were used to the ruthlessness of drug dealers and how they controlled the rest of the people, but this was one of them, and they were certain from the way he acted and what he said that he'd seen the entire killing but was not going to tell them anything.

"But I AM telling you the truth, patron; I didn't see anything!" he lied, "When the crowd parted and I could have seen something, the killer, or killers were already gone or blended in with the crowd!" he told his captain for the hundredth time.

The man was sweaty and overweight, and he had a knack for pointing fingers when the shit hit the fan; it was never his fault and he always had an excuse and wasn't popular with the others which was why he was sweating it out on the street that day; rivulets of the grease that he put in his hair to slick it back ran down the back of his neck and stained his shirt; the captain was disgusted by his appearance and didn't bother to hide it.

When he gave his report, he was pleading with his captain in a whiney voice that was highly irritating even under the best of circumstances; but now it was hot, and he was tired of hearing all these witness's lying about what they didn't see and he was angry and impatient.

The written report was in front of him, in spite of the man's crude handwriting he was able to read it and went over it more than once because he was sure that it was all lies and attempts to evade having to testify in open court as to what he really saw; he was simply hoping that if he confronted the man and asked him directly that he wouldn't be able to lie so easily, but it was not to be, he wouldn't even look his captain in the eye when he answered.

His captain had been around the block a few times himself and knew how to spot inconsistencies in his report; he was reading his reactions more than listening to what he said, "Dismissed!" he said at last; he spit that word out with disgust and would not say anything more because he could not stand this man for another minute; he couldn't even look in his direction and spun his chair around to look out the window, though the view wasn't what it used to be either.

Captain Pena was a good man, he was a no nonsense kind of leader who was a good cop in his time, he was a good leader of men and that worked well in the district where he came from but they transferred him here and he was working with new officers and men that he knew nothing about, and with things going really bad in this region; he had no time to develop any kind of rapport or relationship with them.

They in turn, had heard about him and his "no nonsense" approach but didn't trust him yet, the few good cops that were still there were holding back to see if he was a good leader or if it was going to be more of the same as it had been, and they were hoping for good but hadn't seen it as of yet.

Most of his men were corrupt like the one that just left; ready to take a bribe to look the other way or to inform the criminals what they cops knew about them and where they were looking now, but just as important and much more serious was that they told the gangs and others where the families were like and where they lived.

Of course he knew what happened, he saw it clearly because he was facing in that direction when it happened; he saw the kid moments before and knew he was up to something bad but didn't think it would be that bad, and when he passed him on the sidewalk he was just happy that it wasn't going to be him.

The officer was certain that he would never get that image out of his mind either; fist the look in the boys eyes, it was pure evil and it almost seemed as if they glowed with the heat of hell fire inside of him or something; it felt as though he was looking into the glass window of a furnace.

He was so shocked that he was still waving traffic along while he watched the poor man die and his only thought was; "Thank God it wasn't me!" as he crossed himself silently.

One of the witness's saw it in even greater detail as she was standing closer and decided that it wasn't worth her life, and those of her family as well, and left well before the other officers arrived, the area, which was so crowded when it happened was now almost clear of cars and pedestrians, they were all gone so they would not have to answer any questions about what they all saw.

He remembered the whistle as it slowly dropped from his lips and that he looked around to make sure that no one saw him deliberately turning away from the murder and he saw the woman that was there as she turned away but he thought she didn't see him, but she did and filed that away in case she'd need it.

To ease his conscience a bit; he told himself that there was nothing he could have done to stop it, since there was no crime, there was nothing he could do because the look in the boy's eyes scared him, he decided that there was nothing he could do but control traffic as he was scheduled to do and then go home to his family; he almost stared too long though, he saw the boy as he rose and started looking around for any witness's that he needed to fix.

He was so scared that he couldn't swallow, he thought he could imagine the boy's reaction to knowing that he saw him; he imagined that he was running towards him to shut him up forever; his knife coated with blood but was thirsty for more.

Being so scared that he couldn't turn, he thought, "That boy would probably fly the last ten feet between us and stab me in the chest as he landed on me!" and it felt as though it was already happening, he looked down at his chest to be sure and almost cried because he was so happy that he found no blood.

Closing his eyes as quickly as he could manage and praying harder than he ever had in his entire life; he was trying to be invisible to the boy as he stood there, and the boy wouldn't suspect that he'd seen anything at all. He knew the father and didn't want any part of this kid; the father was ruthless, and this kid was the apple that didn't fall far from that evil tree.

He knew that if he didn't report what everyone knew he saw, that he turned a blind eye to that as far as the authorities were concerned, especially as a police officer, that he would be well-compensated for his silence, the reward for something like this could be huge, and sometimes more than just money.

Because even he knew that he was not a brave man, and that he'd joined the force so that he could be in a situation to make this kind of money; and yet, now that he was there he felt that he was never so scared in his entire life.

As long as he lived, he would remember he could never forget the image of that boy, standing over that body with the blade still dripping blood as he held it, then licking the blood off his cheek as if he'd spilled ice cream; in all of his time growing up in this neighborhood, seeing all the different killings and the gangs that rose and fell on these streets, this was easily the scariest thing that he'd ever seen.

The look on the boy's face as he turned and looked, wanting everyone to see what he'd done and to remember him; that he was just a child, and that he could tell that the boy wanted more blood; he held onto that knife and looked so scary, so creepy with all of that blood splattered all over him.

It bothered him that he was afraid of a kid, though he didn't know his age, he knew was far too young to be killing a man like that and probably doing things almost as bad as a regular part of his day, business as usual for him, but he knew that there were others on that street that were just as afraid as he was; and maybe even more so because at least he had the protection of his badge and the other officers, but that didn't carry very far anymore since it was no secret that they were corrupt.

When they called him in to ask him about what he'd seen, he already knew what they were going to ask and what he was going to say, he'd been rehearsing it ever since he saw the kid turn and leave and thanked God for the hundredth time.

He told them that there was more traffic than usual, which was true, and that he was very busy with that didn't hear nor see anything until he heard a woman scream and brought his attention to it; and though he pointed out that it was him reporting what he did see that brought them into the investigation; no one else could remember hearing a woman scream when they were asked about it.

Stephon hadn't expected to kill anyone that day, and yet it turned out perfect for him; he had the notoriety and knew no one would testify, for who would feel safe, even snug in their beds after this; he knew that he was far younger than anyone else than ran the streets and that it would fade into the background after a while, with no witness's and nothing but the dead man they'd have nothing to follow.

If you saw him and "his boys" as he called them, it would make you laugh, or you'd think he was out there with his older brothers or something, they were mostly older than he was except for those in his inner circle, and yet they all did what he told them without question; if you were dumb enough to laugh when you saw them you never lived long enough to apologize for it, and if you tried it fell on deaf ears.

The word of what he'd done spread almost as quickly as the fear of him, and some of his "boys" were already looking for a way to escape him, the problem was their families, there was no way to uproot and move thirty people or more without drawing attention and they weren't strong enough to kill him so they really had no choice anymore; they knew that he was crazy and this just proved that if there were any doubts.

There were two of them, not the youngest of them and yet they should have known better than to speak aloud about this; they joined the gang because they thought it would lead to more girls and would a nice change to not be afraid when they walked down the hallways that were at times, a gauntlet where the bullies ruled with ruthless impunity.

They were trying to convince their families to move when he found them and they were dragged back in, he stood them in front of the others and called them cowards for trying to run away, "You think your better than us? That you are too good to be one of us now?" he asked, "That you can just take off and run away without even think of asking me first? You think you can run far enough and fast enough to be safe from me?" he shouted, "Even now, you think you're going to walk away from this, I can see it in your eyes!" he said and then back-handed the closest one.

The other started to cry, and that made Stephon even angrier, it was likely the worst thing that the kid could have done at that moment; he might have even had a chance until that moment, but now he sealed the fate of both of them.

"What the fuck are you crying about?" he asked, incredulously, but instead of waiting for an answer, he reached for a gun from one of the others and shot him in the temple.

As he fell, he looked at the other boy, who was about to plead for his life, his mouth opened but nothing came out; he already knew that mercy was not something that was not on the schedule for today, that no matter what else happened; Stephon was out for blood and there was nothing going to stop him from killing him; that even if, by some miracle, the cops burst in just then and saved his life, Stephon would catch up tom him after killing off his family anyway, he was just hoping that he would be satisfied this way and not go after the rest of the people he loved and cared about.

It wasn't Stephon that shot him though, it was someone else, that was standing behind him; he didn't mean to pull the trigger, he was just so scared that it went off and then he realized that it was him.

Stephon, angry that he was cheated, shot him in the chest and then went back to the "traitor" and shot him again, just to make sure that he was dead.

He looked quickly at the remaining guys, and some of them were at that moment thinking about how to get away, but you couldn't tell it by looking at them, no matter how close you looked; none of them showed the slightest bit of emotion, they showed him just what he wanted to see.

"Respect is something that you earn, that is true! But then it is also something that you can take from a man and cover yourself with it! Much as I took this man's life and now my blade is covered with his blood because I taught him to respect me!" he said, with fire in his eyes as if he were reliving it now.

They all raised the bottles and shared a drink in his honor, and, once again, it might have seemed normal under most any circumstances, but these were all kids, not much older than he was and now they were trying to be as cold and ruthless as he was so that he wouldn't shoot them too.

They were there out of fear of him, but also because there were no other gangs in the area strong enough to stand up to him, the odds were stacked against them, they would either have to join him and fight alongside or have to fight him on the streets on their own, an eventuality that they could not escape; and they already saw what he did to his enemies, two were lying on the floor at their feet.

Though it wasn't his fault, or something that he'd tried to do, he couldn't have chosen a worse man to turn into his mortal enemy; he had no idea at the time and by the time he found out it was too late, but at that point, he might not have been able to stop himself anyway; just because this time it felt real and he thought she'd healed him enough that there was no hole in his heart anymore, and that realization made him cry like a baby.

That was something that he thought he'd never have and never understood; he knew that he was really happy most of the time, and really good now; but he would have walked away even then if he knew what was coming and he could have saved her life; he loved her that much and this was for real.

He knew that he was in love, and it felt so good, so deeper and stronger than ever before and it was still new; he knew that things would change when they "got comfortable" around each other, that this was how it always started off; but it felt better than ever and he knew this was "the one" he'd searched for all of his life, and he never saw a guy nor did she ever talk about one either; she became his hearts desire the moment that he first saw her.

That was the day, he was going to the park because he was bored at home and was going to see if any of his friends were out there, playing carom's or basketball, maybe a game of over the line, this park was close to his home, on the southeast part of the city and where he learned how to ride a skateboard when he was younger.

It was a good place to hang out, most of the time, the carom boards were always set up and you needed to check out the sticks and markers to play but that was easy, you only had to ask. There were ping pong paddles that almost never seemed to be used for that game, and other things to paint or draw; those were for the aspiring artists that came around later.

Sometimes there was a pickup basketball game at the far end of the park, but Flaco could see from there that no one was out there at the time; the baseball diamond also stood silent and empty, the only movement was caused by the dust that was blown up by a passing breeze.

He thought that maybe they were getting ready to play and he couldn't see the guys so he walked past the first building and the restrooms before he could see the entire basketball court, but they were still empty and that kind of spooked him a little bit because the park was never this empty unless it was raining or there was something else going on, but there was nothing that he remembered, no holidays or celebrations either.

He was ready to give up and go home when he saw her, she was walking on the other side of the street; deep in concentration, she didn't see him or anyone else as she walked with her head down, and he was ready to turn around and go the other way if she turned away; but she was going in the same direction now, so he followed her, shadowing her to see where she was going and just for fun because she was ignoring him and he could tell she was really worried about something and he wanted to help.

She was thinking about something that one of her friends told her about Stephon, something that she didn't want to believe was true; and yet in her heart, she knew that it was true as she heard the words, but it was told to her by someone that always thought she was better than everyone else.

She was the kind of person that if you looked better or seemed to be happier, looked for the chinks in the armor of your happiness to exploit them, expose them and make herself feel better about her own shortcomings, that made it doubtful that she was telling the whole truth.

It wasn't even a first-hand account, it was hearsay, she'd heard it from her cousin who heard it from his aunt whose best friend was supposedly there and saw the whole thing, and was still frightened by the look on Stephon's face as he left the street that day, covered in blood.

At first, Flaco thought that he might scare her, following her that way, since she didn't know who he was or anything about him; so he made sure that he wasn't so obvious, and then he noticed that she was going into an area of the park that he'd never been to before.

During the school year, the wood shop and auto repair classes were held in this area and he didn't take either pf those classes so he wasn't sure where she was going until he saw her enter a classroom and when he looked, there was a sandwich sign that said "Art classes!" and had an arrow that pointed into the doorway that she'd just entered.

Without hesitation, he followed her into that art class and pretended to be another student; he acted as though he didn't see her and then sat next to her as though there were no other seats even though there were plenty of places to sit.

She noticed him when they were on the street but thought if she ignored him he would go away, she knew that he wasn't a student though, even though she did think it was cute that he would go so far just to sit next to her in the art class; yet she knew better than to encourage him, that would end up being very painful for him and it quickly brought back a sad memory for her.

That was about the time that the first signs of the real Stephon began to show, when he found out that she talked to one of the other boys in one of her classes, they were just friends and she told Stephon very clearly that he was not interested in her that way, and that he was a nice boy; they were simply talking about school and nothing personal, she thought it would be okay until she saw the look on Stephon's face when he found out about it.

He had his friends hold him while he beat the boy mercilessly, he was beaten so badly that they ran out of town as soon as they released him from the hospital, they refused to return, and told the officer's that they would not be testifying about what happened, though everyone knew.

It was so embarrassing for her, and she didn't know how to react when her friends first told her about it, when she asked him about it, at first he wouldn't listen, but after a while he admitted that they "roughed him up" a bit but that he was fine when they left him, "He was still breathing!" he said and tried to laugh.

Then he suddenly changed his bearing, the way he looked at her; he was different that moment, and she felt as though if she touched his skin it would burn her hand, he looked at her and said slowly, "You are mine! Every other cabrone has to know that, to understand it and to let you be!" he seethed.

She didn't want to risk that happening again and hadn't talked to another boy since, she knew that she couldn't live with herself if she did, but also that if she didn't break away from him it was never going to be better and it was only going to get worse; but on the other hand, she knew that she could not just break up with him because there was more than her own life to think about and even if her grandmother was well enough to make a trip that far away; she would never give up her home, she would rather die in it; have it fall down on her head in flames if it came to that than to surrender it to someone like him.

He changed for a while, and he would even beg her to stay if she threatened to leave and no one else was around, promising to change, and he would; but only for a short while, and every time she forgave him and let him back into her life that short while became even shorter.

If she thought this was going to go anywhere like that with this new boy, she would have told the instructor that he was bothering her and wasn't a student, asked him to be removed so that she could save them both a lot of pain.

Flaco was a natural artist, had been ever since he was four, he never took a class in his life and yet, using his mind's eye and his imagination he could draw anything at all, and no matter what it was that he drew; you would swear that you never saw it before, or never so clearly and in as much detail as he presented on that piece of paper, and armed with just a pencil.

As the instructor was introducing himself and talking about his "artist philosophy" as he liked to call it; Flaco kept himself busy by drawing the wings of an insect, probably a fly; but it could have been any bug, but when she saw it, she gasped at the reality of it and he wasn't showing off, he was just staying busy because it was hard for him to sit still.

Then he turned the paper over and looked at the basket of fruit that was in front of them, a few grapes, a banana an apple and a large grapefruit was sitting in a bowl, waiting for the students to draw them once the instructor stopped pontificating about his accomplishments.

Flaco began to draw the fruit, but he never looked up again once he started; and while he drew it, he quietly tried to make small talk with her, he told her a few jokes that a twelve-year-old would have found boring and yet she couldn't laugh when he told her, they were so simple and silly that she could not help herself, and she needed to laugh so badly and hadn't even realized it until that moment.

He made her laugh while he never stopped drawing, and then he shifted the pencil to his other hand so that he could shake hers, and still kept drawing, he said, "My name's Anthony, and I refuse to let you sit this close to me any longer unless I know your name!" he said.

She laughed and shook his hand, she almost expected him to kiss her hand and was a little disappointed that he didn't, but he was being funny and though he thought of it, he didn't want to push it and scare her off before they had a chance to know each other.

After that, she pretended that she wasn't listening, but she heard every word that he said, and he was so funny that he made her laugh more than a few times, in spite of herself; again, she couldn't help it and she really did need it.

When the class was over, it seemed as though they had just sat down because it went so quick, he jumped up and said, "See you tomorrow!" and ran off without his drawing.

She tried to call him back and tell him that, but her voice was stuck due to so much time without being comfortable talking to other boys; knowing how crazy that made Stephon when he found out, he would get jealous and mean and even she didn't feel safe anymore; so she kept quiet and didn't call him back.

She thought about that then, hoping that she hadn't encouraged him or anything, and remembered that when he first sat there, she refused to say anything to him, when he asked her something, she pretended not to hear, or would get up and get some supplies or ask the instructor a question and not answer him.

Then she would answer him only out of politeness or because she had to, she told him several times that she needed to concentrate and asked him to be quiet and he would; but then he'd start up again a moment later and make her laugh. She tried to absorb herself in her work and so she would not be hearing him, but it didn't dissuade him in the least, and after she looked at the drawing he left behind, she had to sit down, because it was that good.

He put things in that fruit basket that were from his imagination because some of what he drew wasn't there; the fruit in the basket looked old, as if it were taken from the trash as unfit to eat but okay to use for the class; and he made it seem so fresh and clean that you almost wanted to take a bite, he drew water droplets slowly running down the sides too, as if they were fresh picked and washed, ready to eat.

She looked closer and now those grapes looked fresh, and sweet, she imagined taking one into her mouth, or the succulent, gritty taste of the pear; and though there was no apple on the table, he remembered to add one, with a leaf attached to the stem; every detail was perfect; every freckle on the pear, the lines in the center of the apple, he didn't miss a thing.

But even more than that, he drew her into the picture; standing behind the bowl, trying to decide which piece of fruit to eat first, and though he never stared at her, never seemed to give her more than a cursory glance, even when he shook her hand; he some captured the easy parts, her beauty and her essence; but even her honesty was apparent.

She looked back at the street again, where he was headed and was amazed, "He doesn't need this class!" she thought to herself, "He could probably teach it!" she said, and then laughed.

Looking back at the drawing again, she half-expected to see it change into something else, but it was still there; the fruit looked so real that she felt that it would slowly drip off the page if she took a bite. Then she noticed that he took extra time when he drew the pear, her favorite fruit, though she'd never told him that; she was looking at the freckles on the yellow skin of the pear and the stem that was still attached.

With little effort; he'd made her feel like a little girl again, and then she remembered that she would twist the stem off and recite the alphabet to see who her boyfriend was; she wondered what letter it would have come off on and almost reached for it but then remembered that it was just a drawing.

What eventually broke her down was his persistence and his sense of humor; his lack of pretension and how he didn't seem to care what anyone thought about him, good or bad; that his sense of self-worth was enough, and she'd never met a man with so many funny ways about him.

He made her smile and then laugh and then the walls came crashing down, all of this happened slowly but surely because she didn't realize until then how much she missed the sound of her own laughter, her life had been empty until now, though she couldn't remember when it started being that way.

There was no humor when Stephon was around; no real happiness, it went away as he became more hardened by his other life, the life he led on the streets and the nature of that business; how cold-hearted and ruthless he had to be in order to stay alive.

Stephon didn't trust anyone anymore; he was suspicious of his friends when they weren't close by, and he didn't trust her, though he wasn't following her around, or having her followed as he did some of his friends, he thought the fear of what he would do was enough to keep her in line.

Then for a time, she though he'd found out about Flaco because he suddenly started trying to be funny, that he was trying to do what Flaco was doing; but he didn't know how to be funny, he didn't have the timing down or something, she forced herself to laugh to be polite but she really didn't understand his humor, very few did.

She knew that the funny comedians used what they called timing to tell a joke, and that timing was just as important as the joke itself; but Stephon hadn't learned that yet and no one was going to tell him and risk his anger.

Though she was afraid, she couldn't help herself from feeling excited when she thought of Flaco; and that made her more afraid of Stephon than ever before, she was happy that he was very busy most of the time and hadn't had any time for her; there were a few times that he went to her window, and tossed some small rocks at the glass to wake her as he'd done before, but she ignored it as if she never heard him until he quit and went home.

At the same time, she was beginning to see the signs that her Abuelita was getting older and more frail with every passing year, and there were times now that she heard her coughing all through the night, cough syrup didn't help, nor did warm water and lemon, the only thing that worked was getting her to gargle with salt and warm water, but it took a lot to get her to do that, it made her gag but it cleared up a lot of the coughing.

The cold seemed to settle deeper into her bones in the winter, and she knew that if she was gone there would be no one to care for her and at the same time, she wasn't trying to look forward to that day, but she knew that her grandmother was not going to last much longer, it made her sad, but it also made her think that she could get away then, there would be nothing else to hold her there.

She thought that maybe he might try to hurt Flaco, even though he looked as though he could take care of himself; he had friends too, but in a fair fight it would not be a problem for him, she thought that as ruthless as Stephon could be, that Flaco was smarter and quicker and would kick his ass.

Then she remembered that Stephon never directly threatened her or her grandmother; he only pointed out to her, more than once, that there was nowhere that she could hide from him; and that no one was safe if he wanted to get to them, that his enemies had family and that was leverage, and she knew what that meant without being told.

This was one day when she finally confronted him, asked him about the rumors and what he did when they weren't together, because she noticed that even when it was just the two of them, it was never just the two of them; there were always several of his "boys" hanging around, staying back, but clearly following and most likely because he was getting threats or things were going bad in his business and he felt threatened when he was out, she didn't know, nor did she really care as long as no bullets flew.

Until she met Flaco, she felt that happiness was something that would elude her forever; that she would be stuck with Stephon until he grew tired of her or someone killed him, which was not what she wanted; but she was resigned to that life and now felt a glimmer of hope that grew each time she saw Flaco's smiling face once more.

"How do you do that?" she asked him once, "How do you always look at me as though you haven't seen me in a long time, though I saw you yesterday?" she asked him with a curious smile on her face.

"Because every time I see you, it's like I've never seen so much beauty, strength and intelligence in one person before, and my heart soars when I see you, you must know that by now!" he answered her, being as honest as he could because he knew that was the only way to be with her.

She liked to wear the blouses that were now the rage in California; they called it a peasant blouse, but she didn't wear it for style as much as she wore it for comfort; it had nothing to do with anything South of the border either, because she'd been wearing them for years.

Hers were made of coarse cotton and they kept her cool when it was hot outside and yet it kept her warm when it was cold too, which made it practical for the weather in Mexico, when the temperatures would at times soar to one hundred and twenty, and that was considered a cool day.

This blouse was a bright white, it had green and red trim around the yoke, and it was sheer enough that her Nana made her wear a t shirt underneath it or she couldn't leave the house; and it was one of three blouses that she wore that weren't given to her by Stephon, this one was her favorite.

When Flaco first saw that blouse, he couldn't take his eyes off it; especially the thin red thread that held it together in the middle, though she knew that what he wanted from her was not at all sexual; she was still flattered that he noticed that, of all things.

She was no longer trying to ignore Flaco either, she liked the way he reacted when she poke of her Nana; he didn't treat her like a child when she spoke of her, or any of the other little things that excited her; those little things that were important to her, that she literally begged for someone to listen to and understand, and now someone finally did; she didn't see him dismissing it as "girl stuff" which meant "she the hell up" about it to her.

He didn't have time for those things, he told her to talk to another girl named Gloria about it; he said that she was a girl and would understand, that she would want to hear about it and would know how to help her; but that would never do, it would never happen because Gloria was his old girlfriend and not a friend of Sabrina's in any way.

Sabrina knew that Gloria would twist her words around to suite her own needs and make her look better, then she'd run to Stephon and she'd tell him about it; and then they wouldn't be secrets anymore because all of her friends would have a laugh over it, though she would feint empathy when she was asked to listen and maybe help.

Stephon didn't want to hear about her feelings because he didn't understand them and didn't know how to deal with them and return them; he would never invest the time and effort to figure them out; whenever he wanted to have sex with her, Sabrina would say it was her period or some other excuse and she knew that when she did that, he always went to Gloria, and that was okay with her because she wanted nothing to do with that kind of "activity" as she called it.

He never wanted to heart about the things that made her feel happy to be alive, and if she wanted him to leave her alone, all she had to do was start talking about her day; or she would tell him that "her friend was visiting" and he'd leave.

They went to that class together for about three weeks and she was impressed that he was that patient with her; that even though they'd never touched, and as badly as they both wanted to go there, he was just as patient and considerate as before when he might have thought that was possible; but she cared more about herself, about her body and what she did with it than to give it away so freely.

She never asked him about that, but she felt that he respected her for that, that he liked that she was selective and discreet about those things and not given to jumping in and out of the bed as a lot of girls were doing these days; he was all of the things that Stephon could never be.

Though she fought against it and denied it as much as she could, she fell in love with Flaco; but then, she could not have stopped herself if she'd wanted to, and instead of making her heart race with joy and anticipation; this filled her heart with dread, it made her sadder than she ever felt before in her life.

Instead of the joy and elation, the racing heart beat while you wait for your love to smile back at you and tell you that everything's going to be alright with simply that smile; she felt at that moment, more hatred for Stephon than ever, she was clearly impatient with him and never laughed when he was around anymore, he wouldn't have noticed but no one else was laughing with him anymore either.

She jumped when he tried to touch her and then he began to suspect that something was going on, that had never happened before; and when he told her that he was too busy to come over for a while she didn't try to change his mind as she always did before.

When she went to sleep a few days after that, she began to dream about things that never occurred to her before; she saw a rival drug dealer kill Stephon over some territorial dispute, and when she woke in the morning, she found that she kind of liked that idea.

It was not that she was mean-spirited or anything like that, but she knew that she would never be happy with him and she also knew that he would never let her go, "Not while he's still alive!" she said to herself.

A week after that, the art instructor realized that Flaco wasn't registered for the class; he could attend, it was free and all, but he needed to be registered and this came out while they were arguing about a slight difference of opinion; Flaco thought that abstract art could go on the same page as "non-abstract" images and the instructor disagreed vehemently, he said they needed to be uniform to be accepted in his classroom and neither would budge so he threw Flaco out.

It started when they were drawing a nude woman who came to pose for them, he noticed Falco's drawing was exceptionally good and brought him to the front of the class; he was thinking that Flaco learned at least some of what he did in the class, and he wanted Flaco to tell everyone that.

Flaco was told he should always be honest, it was how his mother raised him and he wasn't going to lie just to make the instructor feel any better, so he told them the truth; that he learned from watching and then copying what he liked, and over the years had developed his own style, and that, in short, he'd taught himself, exactly the opposite of what the instructor wanted them to hear.

This offended the instructor and he told Flaco that it was not possible, but Flaco told him that the only influence came early, that he found a "steamboat Willy" cartoon and that helped him a lot but after that, it was all his own inspirations and ideas that led him along.

For Mr. Faltenberg, this was going all wrong, he was a stickler for certain things that he thought were sacred and inviolate; rules that should always be obeyed unless you were world famous and then of course, you could do whatever you wanted.

Any illustrations with letters in them must be uniform; anything abstract was not allowed on the same page and that came about because he didn't like abstract art, it was too random and what he called "Willy-nilly" and he didn't like it; he tried to interrupt Flaco and tell him that but one of the other students was quicker and louder and asked Flaco another question.

"You're telling us that you taught yourself how to draw like this?" he was asked, "You were never in a class like this before?" a girl asked, she clearly thought Flaco was cute and had tried several times to get his attention but he clearly only had eyes for Sabrina.

As they argued about the merits of "self-teaching" versus the conventional way, some of the students began to look at Flaco with renewed interest because some of them had been thinking the same thing; that he was restricting them too much with his rules, they were all ready to walk out with Flaco at that point, which would have been funny to Flaco since he never thought of himself as a leader.

Flaco was having a lot of fun with it and began to feed the flames of dissent and have some fun with it; "Yeah, it's true that I didn't learn a thing in here either!" and they all laughed at that, which didn't go over very well with the instructor.

If it had been only one or maybe two of the students asking him questions, it might have been alright, or different; but as Faltenberg tried ordering him to stop, four of his favorite students all asked the same question about his ideas and he felt that he couldn't allow any more of this, that was when he ordered Flaco to sit down.

He stood with his mouth open for a moment because in his entire life; no one ever gave him this kind of stage and now he couldn't believe the rug was pulled out from under him like that, when they started asking him things, it was a really nice surprise, he was as honest as he could be while also trying to have a good and solid answer when they asked him things.

When Faltenberg showed him the door, he turned to say something when he saw that Sabrina was going to leave with him, then she took his arm and started laughing with him as they both left.

They were so absorbed in each other and spent so much time talking that before they knew it, they were in front of the local hangout for kids after school; and some of those other art students were right there behind them, trying to catch up.

The store was located on the corner of Main street and Revolucion Avenue, they had tables and chairs outside in the front and on the other side in the patio area when the weather was bad, or it was too cold to be fully outside.

On that day, for the rest of the world it might be horrible, raining buckets where everyone else went home for the day, but for these two, it was a beautiful day to be alive, and especially to be in love; it was actually very bright and sunny, with a slight breeze that drifted by and was just strong enough to cool the air as it touched their skin.

It was a small place, but the kids adopted it because they could sit outside and listen to the jukebox as it played American Rock and Roll; they also made shakes by hand with real milk and fresh fruit, no one else was doing that in the area but then they had recently added a banana split that was "to die for" as they advertised it.

The place was called "Los Hermanos" but they called it "Sangrona's" and though it had been called that for as long as anyone could remember, no one could remember why they called it that, they liked the sound of it for some reason and then it caught on; no one cared why or what it was called, even the owners, because the money was good and constant and business was good.

They didn't have a stove, but they made sandwiches to order that were actually pretty good; the prices were right and if you didn't want onions or tomatoes or anything like that and ordered it without it didn't really matter, they came with them anyway; most people simply learned to pick them out and throw them away or ate them anyway.

They did have a small oven for heating things up, not big enough to cook a whole goose or turkey yet this all worked out well for everyone, they could get creative too and make cakes and things but they usually kept to the sandwiches and shakes that were the most popular.

That time they went there, they sat there for about an hour, just talking and holding hands while looking deep into each other's eyes, they were avoiding it, pretending that they didn't want to take their relationship to the next level, but it was inevitable.

They found in each other the love that very few in life ever touch at all; some people find it but deny that its for them, they think they don't deserve it or it wasn't meant to be and move on without finding out, it was not a matter of two horny kids, trying to satisfy their lust; but they felt so much passion and that they needed to finish what they started on that first day that he saw her.

Things were building up inside of both of them for some time and it followed the natural progression and they both knew what they wanted and felt that it was time and there was no reason to hold back; she felt that it was right to give herself to him because she would be with him for the rest of her life, and they tried to hold onto each other and make the rest of the world go away, at least for a little while.

But then, out there in the open and on the main street that ran through the center of town it's hard not to be noticed; it's even harder when you are the envy of the people walking by, seeing you together and so happily in love, everyone that saw them wanted to feel that happy again; to feel that special to at least one person and feel that alive for the first time in a long while for most of them.

They eventually found their way to his house and as she went there, she knew what was going to happen but she couldn't believe that she was doing this; even though it felt so right, and so natural and he wasn't pressuring her at all, but it was also what she wanted to do; and the more she thought about it, the better she felt about it.

She felt that she wasn't forcing herself to be anything or anyone other than the woman she always was, she knew that even after this, that he would still love her just as passionately and attentively as before, nothing would change except the bond between them, which would always grow stronger and she never felt happier or more loved in her life.

That she could be her true self and be loved for that was so much more than she ever really expected from life; ever since that first day in the art class when she noticed him following her; she knew in her heart that this was going to happen, but she related to that with her heart and not her brains; she thought that since everyone in town knew who Stephon was, that Flaco did too; that he knew the risk and knew what he was doing.

Still, deep in the heart of her heart she knew this was going to end badly; there were times that she thought he knew, or that she should make sure that he did, but she didn't want to lose that feeling that she'd found in his arms.

She hoped and prayed with all of her heart that this would have the best possible outcome; something that they could all walk away from and feel satisfied that it worked out as it did, and she meant Stephon too; she wanted him to be happy as well; she just didn't want it to be with her.

Flaco, for his part, never felt so complete; he was not just in love for the first time in his life; but he was also being loved in return, he knew that this was the love that he'd been searching for all of his life; the heart that was meant to beat next to his belonged to her.

When he held her in his arms it felt as though she belonged there; even as though she'd been in his arms before, what he knew the poet's called a past life; but he wasn't thinking about that, he was too busy feeling good, that she belonged there as if they were molded together because they fit so perfectly, it felt so good that he never wanted to let go.

But if you asked him, Flaco didn't know Stephon from a Klingon; he'd heard about the murder on the street but as much as he knew her; he knew that she would not willingly be around people like him and he was a little younger than her so he didn't make the connection.

Even if he knew, by that time he was too far gone into this feeling to turn around and give it back to someone that clearly didn't appreciate it or she would have never have fallen for Flaco in the first place, but he had no idea of the danger that he was in or things might have ended differently.

She liked the clean and quiet neighborhood that he lived in, as opposed to hers, where it was closer to the main streets and there was more traffic; she also liked that it was obvious to her, knowing him and seeing how he changed things, Stephon hadn't sunk his hooks into this part of town yet.

His family lived in the front of the house, and alongside the left side there were stairs that led up to his room, it was private, one way in and out, one bedroom, living room and bathroom, but nothing to cook on unless you counted the microwave that his mother put in there one day while he was at school.

Flaco and Sabrina went there three more times in the next month before Stephon got wind of what she was doing, or at least that she wasn't going to her classes anymore, he'd been out of town for a while and even busier than usual and they hadn't even talked on the phone for some time; long enough that she began to have hope that he'd met someone new and forgot about her.

It also occurred to her that maybe it wasn't just a dream and he really was dead after all; but he found out when one of his boys told him that she wasn't going into the ark when she left "for her class" as she told him, that was going somewhere else but he lost her in the crowd when he tried to follow.

Stephon went to the class and waited for her; when he didn't see her enter but heard Faltenberg speaking to the class he knew they'd started and walked in to see if she was there ahead of him; some of them knew who he was right off, they pretended that they didn't see him and kept drawing as if he wasn't there.

Faltenberg felt afraid of him, though he didn't know why, yet he still tried to ask him what he wanted when Stephon held up one finger as if to say, "Wait" and he actually stopped, mid-sentence, and waited as Stephon turned and looked through the rest of the class, luckily for them; he didn't know any of them and left on his own without another word.

Faltenberg watched as he left and swallowed hard, he felt as though someone had just walked over his grave and he was lucky to be alive.

A few days later, he waited outside of her house, to see where she would go, and when she came out she almost saw him but he was quicker and she didn't expect to see him out there and wasn't looking for him as she should have.

He followed her all the way to Flaco's house, watched her walk up those stairs as if she was home and knew that she was going to his bed and yet he waited for her to come out; if he came out, Stephon was going to kill him in front of her, and then maybe her, but he didn't think he would.

Seething in rage and anger; Stephon hoped that none of his few remaining friends would pass by there and see him out there, he would die of shame at being betrayed this way; but he knew they wouldn't come this way because none of them lived around here or hung out over here.

But it was more than that, though he didn't want to admit it because even saying it made him feel weak but he did love her, he thought that he was going to be the mother of his children; he was going to grow old with her; all she was supposed to do was to wait long enough for him to take his business to where he wanted it to be, where it could run itself, then they could have anything that they wanted and go anywhere in the world, but now that was a shattered dream that he would never tell anyone about.

He didn't see this coming; he thought she understood, that even though he never told her that she should have known, but then he thought he should have told her, but he had a hard time talking to her about how he felt; it went against his grain because men in his family never did that.

That was also because he hadn't realized how cold and uncaring he'd become, how thoughtless and inattentive he was with her and he thought that everything was fine because she'd stopped complaining about those things.

Then it came to him, that the reason why she wasn't complaining was because she didn't need them from him anymore, she found those things in someone else and even though he'd betrayed her with Gloria a number of times; he didn't see it that way because she would do the things for him that Sabrina wouldn't.

He was so furious now that after he checked his watch twice he took it off and threw it hard against the wall and it shattered; and then he started to cry, though he didn't really understand why; the watch was a gift from his grandfather who died long ago, but he refused to believe that he was that weak that he would get sentimental like that.

Yet he cold not help it, nor could he stop himself and then he thought that if anyone did see him, that he would have to kill them on the spot; so he moved further back into the shadows and let the tears flow for the first time in he didn't know how long, and as embarrassed as he would have been, it felt good to let go.

Then he tried to put his mind on other things while he waited for her, he remembered that she asked him about the stabbing one day, and he replied to her with a question of his own, "What kind of man do you think I am?" instead of answering.

His mind was racing ahead of her answer because that was now his calling card; it was what made him, set him apart from the others and kept them in line because it showed them what he was capable of and how far he would go to get what he wanted.

"Well...I...I guess I don't know!" she stammered; "But everyone say's that it was you that did it; that it showed your...crazy side!" she said, afraid to say that because it made him angry to hear it, then she quickly added; "They said you killed a couple of your own men because they were going to turn you over to the police!" she told him and then went quiet.

That was the first time that she was afraid of him, she saw and felt a flash of something that felt horrible and yet undefined, it flew away from him and though her in a rush and she felt it burn her soul.

"Okay but...IF I was that guy, I wouldn't be asking you to believe me, I would instead be asking you who said that about me, wouldn't I?" he asked her, and the look in his eyes made her realize that it was exactly what he wanted to ask her about.

On the outside, he hadn't changed his expression and he looked very calm, but underneath he was quite angry; he was trying to figure out a way to find out who said that but didn't know how without betraying how he felt at that moment, he felt that his trust was violated and he wanted to know who warned her about him and who else they might have told.

She saw none of this as she looked him in the eye, though she felt it, she wasn't sure because he looked so calm, she thought she saw a nervous twitch or something but it was gone before she could be sure that's what it was; the expression that she saw on his face made her think they got it wrong, and she felt bad for believing them; she told herself all of the things that she wanted to be true but deep inside she knew that they never would be.

How much of what she felt and saw in him came from her needing to be loved and thinking that he was the right one and how much was flat out denial was anyone's guess, but either he fooled her or she fooled herself into thinking that he was very attentive and sweet to her and she liked that, she never felt that before from a guy and didn't know that he was faking it; saying and doing what he thought she wanted to see and hear, nothing more because he was a sociopath and didn't know what love was unless he looked it up in the dictionary, except that he never learned how to read more than rudimentary words.

Now she'd spent a lot of time with Flaco, and she was certain that he wasn't acting and that she'd seen his true heart; that his words were true and real and came with meaning in them, that he wouldn't say things to her that way unless he meant them.

His words took her to different places and she imagined things that she thought she'd never have in her life; that if she'd only waited a little longer she would have maybe met Flaco and this would all have been someone else's problem, that she wouldn't be feeling that black cloud that was hanging over her head and getting darker and more ominous every day.

Flaco never seemed to notice it or feel it, when he looked up in the sky it was simply to point out to her how beautiful it was; and he was so happy all of the time that it was contagious, she couldn't help herself and noticed that others around them were starting to envy them; they sometimes even joined in the conversation because they felt they were happy and approachable.

Some of her friends warned her about Flaco too though; they'd seen him sweet-talking girls before and she could see things in what they said but she thought he'd grown out of that and was ready to settle down with her, it was what he said and also how he acted with her.

She was not sorry that she'd flowed her heart, even though she must have know what was going to happen next and how she couldn't control it; when Stephon first saw her go up there he was struck with how comfortable and familiar she was that she just walked right up and opened the door as if this was her room.

"Hija de la chingada!" he swore at her and then spat at her in disgust; he could see that she was easy with him, that she'd changed in ways with him that she never would have without him; and that made him angry too.

He saw her now as a confidant woman, and he'd never seen her like this, and that hurt worse than anything else, he stepped further back into the shadows and squatted down before he lit a cigarette and waited for her to come out.

He wasn't yet sure what he was going to do when she did; he waited for her in the dark and smoldered, much as the cigarette in his mouth; the only time he ever smoked these days was when he was extremely angry, or as now; when he felt a deep-down hurt, such as recently when his father was gunned down in the streets by his own bodyguards and a few corrupt policeman that were paid more by his competitors.

So he was smoldering the same now, because of his feelings for her; he was feeling as though he could hate her now, and the only real surprising part of this was his patience; he wanted in the worst way to climb up those stairs and kill them both as they lie together in that bed; he would empty his gun into them and then reload and empty it again until they felt the pain that he was feeling right then.

It was that he could see now, everything was tainted in different tones of angry red, he wanted to wash his face in their blood as they died, and he tried not to think about what they were doing up there and yet he didn't want them to have anything more together after this day.

So he waited, hunkered down in total silence, the only sign that he was there was the occasional flare up of his cigarette the only sign that he was still there; he took out his gun and hefted it in his hands and checked the rounds to make sure that it was ready, he flicked the safety on and off again.

Then he flicked his wrist and felt the blade poke out; then he slashed at the air in front of him, he was imagining that he was slashing her throat and slicing his head off, this was not the same blade that he used to kill that man so long ago; this was a new blade, and one that he liked much better.

He felt that this was his blade, he found it while he was out walking at the edge of town, in an area that he normally wouldn't be out alone like this, but it was old and rusty and he spent hours cleaning it up; but he felt a special call from it and kept working on it until it looked new again.

The funny thing was, the more rust he cleaned off; the better he felt, it was as if cleaning the blade so lovingly was cleaning his souls at the same time, and the night that he found it, he was passing an alley that two bars and a restaurant when he heard what could only be two men fighting over something that meant a lot to both of them, and each of them thought it was theirs and were willing to fight to the death over it.

Normally, he would just keep going, he was alone but for some reason he thought he should check it out; he followed the sounds in carefully to make sure that he wasn't walking into a trap when he found them.

He saw two men struggling in the darkness, one of them had a knife and the other was trying to wrest it away from him, Stephon stopped to watch them, it always fascinated him when someone was killed, it was never too gory or gruesome for him; if anything it was over too quickly.

When the man with the knife finally won, he shouted at the other man as he brought the blade up high and was ready to strike, "You want the blade? You think its yours? Here, take it then!" he said as he thrust it into the man's chest and through his lungs; the other man gasped as he grabbed his throat and began to choke on his one blood and then died.

Stephon had seen enough, he stepped out of the shadows so quickly that the man hadn't seen him and was still looking at his victim, lying on the ground, and he was surprised to see Stephon standing there, and though he didn't know it was, Stephon took the blade from him and stabbed him through the heart.

"This isn't your blade either, pendejo!" and then he spat in his face in his contempt, something that he was starting to do to his victims as his trademark.

He took the blade home and almost threw it away, he wondered why they fought so hard over a blade that was so covered with rust and scale, and yet once he started on it, he couldn't stop; and then he found an intricate design on its surface, the etching started at the base and wound its way around the blade and for some reason, he thought that made the blade scarier and even more special; deadlier than any other blade, he thought it was made to steal the soul of its victim as it took his life.

He also felt that the blade was speaking to him as he cleaned it, telling him what a good job he was doing and how much fun they would have spilling the blood of his enemies with impunity; for such a knife would never lead the investigators back to him; he thought it had a lot of hidden powers or magic that the right hand would entice to come out and play.

People were always afraid of him, but they seemed more afraid of his knife than the guns he brought; he knew if he brought them both out and held one in each hand, they would be looking at the knife more than the gun.

Maybe that was because a knife is more personal, a bullet flies through the air mostly unseen, delivering a lethal blow; but a knife, you had to have it in your hand to use it, you had to be closer and you could see it coming with its promise of pain and bloodshed; maybe they thought they'd have a better chance to dodge the bullet.

Stephon really needed at least one good friend in his life; someone that he could confide in without worrying that he might be considered as weak or cowardly, someone that could keep his secrets from his enemies and not use them against him.

He felt that he never could though, that there was no one, outside of Sabrina, that he could trust like that; and now that was gone too, he realized then that the control he held over his men wasn't from respect or friendship, not honor, but fear controlled his men, and once that fear was gone, he would be too, because they would kill him for what he made them do, what he molded them into with his insanity and sick, twisted mind.

Even that was slipping away from him, so much of his life that was looking so good a few weeks ago was now falling apart all around him.

He smoked that entire pack of cigarettes before she came out and broke the rest of his black heart, the butts spilled all around him as proof if it was needed; he dropped the last smoke and stomped it out as he watched her walk down the stairs and a huge smile played across her lips.

As she approached his hiding place, he thought for a moment that she would smell the smoke and know that someone was near, if not him, but she was too preoccupied with whatever they did up there to have noticed, and he slithered back into the shadows where she couldn't see him, but then she wasn't looking either; she'd already found what she wanted.

She never looked around her as she walked, either because there was any danger that might be near by or she was just so happy and so fulfilled that she didn't care to look; adding gasoline to the fire that raged inside of his heart; the huge smile on her face infuriated him, she looked so beautiful under that full moon that he could almost forgive her, but for that smile on her face which didn't come from him, but from another man that she wanted to take his place.

Stephon watched her as she left and watched her as she walked down the street, and when she was far enough he wanted so badly to go up there; he could imagine it as if he'd already done it and he knew he could get away with it because he wouldn't be expecting anyone and there was no one between him and those stairs.

He "saw" himself as he opened the door, same as she did, and stepping inside to find that cabrone smiling and asking, as he looked up from his bed, "Did you forget something or came back for more?" he said.

Then Stephon saw himself as he raised the gun slowly, the look of happiness on Flaco's face replaced by one of surprise and fear just before he put a bullet right between his eyes, instead, he headed home, feeling beaten and lost, and knowing that she thought they were safe, at least for now, but that would change, and very soon.

There was a gym that he owned, he hadn't been there in years, in fact, ever since he killed the owner and took it from him; but he stopped there on the way home, most of the guys would go to that gym and workout so he knew there would be someone there most hours of any day.

Once he was inside, Stephon didn't bother to change his clothes but began to use the jump rope and then tried lifting heavy weights to ease his pain, the he started to hit the heavy bag; back and forth it moved and he stepped into each punch and hit the bag as hard as he could while trying to assuage his anger and pain.

He hit the heavy bag for about twenty minutes, and in his rage, his shirt tore and he ripped it off without slowing down because he imagined it was the two of them he was hitting and couldn't hit it hard enough to make himself feel any better, but he did notice that the room was emptying at the same time, they were seeing his rage and the smart ones left right away, not even changing from their sweaty clothes as they ran off.

It didn't help him much in that regard; but hitting the bag did feel good but he needed more; he went over to the ring and put the gloves on while telling some of his men to "strap 'em on!" and waiting for them to do what he ordered as he knew they would.

Though he was not known as a fierce fighter and used his men to do that dirty work most of the time, he was more of a dirty fighter and they weren't worried at first, but that was because none of them looked into his eyes or they would have been afraid, he didn't look the same at the time, but they were used to looking away when he turned towards them, out of fear and respect.

If they had, they would have seen that this time at least; there was good reason to be afraid, and it would not take much time before they would find that out and the rest of them would sneak out the back door and run through the alley all the way home.

They started to see it in the ring, when it was too late; and he sparred almost six full rounds before he knocked out the first one, sent him flying across the mat with teeth falling out as he flew from a vicious uppercut.

Stephon saw him fall and stepped over his prone body; thumping his chest and shouting at the top of his lungs as if he'd knocked out the champ and pulled off an amazing upset; then he began a long string of obscenities until he collapsed into the ring and once again, began to cry.

It didn't matter, he was alone again; even the staff was smart enough to get the hell out of there by then, he let it go again and was surprised that there were still tears left to shed and yet he couldn't stop himself this time either; a lifetime of holding back those emotions and tears left him as he lay there.

He knew what he had to do, the last thing in the world he wanted to do, and yet he could see no way around it; but he escaped that eventuality when his uncle needed him to go to New York and take care of some business because there was a problem with a rival gang that was moving in on them.

They had recently killed the man that was running the operation for Stephon's friends and there was a meeting set up, they were going to try and settle it diplomatically and not retaliate over it and start a war on the streets, his uncle didn't want to send Stephon, he wasn't known for his diplomacy after all; there was no one else and he had no choice, though he should have kept looking for someone else, but then he didn't see him before he left, he looked terrible, as though he hadn't slept in weeks.

Stephon's mind was circling around the many ways he wanted to punish Sabrina for betraying him with Flaco; he wanted to kill him first and make her watch, then he thought it would be more fun the other way, to savagely kill her in front of him; he thought about letting his men have her and making him watch, but that would bother him and he'd start to hate them for doing that to the woman he loved, even with his permission.

Because of that, he wasn't thinking of taking the gloves off and playing nice; he was thinking that he wanted to send a message once more, that he was out for blood and nothing less would do, the benefits were his either way, so he really had nothing to lose.

When he went to the meeting in New York, the entire time he had no other plan; the only thing on his mind was to get this over with and get home, settle this business with that back-stabbing bitch and kill my brother but he had to go, for his uncle he was told to listen to what they had to say and go from there.

Though he was given free reign and listen between the lines, he didn't care what they wanted or what they had to say; he walked into that meeting alone, thinking that he was going to die but he didn't care; he would take all seven of them with him if he could, one way or another, this was going to be settled for good on this day.

He counted on the element of surprise because that always worked well for him in the past; walking in alone would make them think he was going to extend the olive branch as he was told to; but of course, not what he was thinking at all and he took out his gun and shot all seven of them to death before even one could draw a gun and fire back, he came back without so much as a scratch.

He was planning it all along, and yet they still had a chance, while he listened to them outside the office in that warehouse he couldn't get over the attitude of "these guys" as he referred to them, "They think this is the movies or something!" he said as he made up his mind.

They opened the door then and he pulled his gun and started blasting away as he entered; he killed the first three he saw and then the other four as they ran in to see what was going on, they all died without firing a shot, and the same surprised look on their faces.

The middle one, a guy that he liked was killed first; the bullet through his chest and bounced around inside of him, ripping into his vitals before it bounced out of his neck, just above the shoulder.

The man in charge never moved, never blinked and knew it was over when the first shot was fired; he was resigned to it as he watched the others fall one by one; he was tired and almost welcomed this end; he actually smiled at Stephon as he pulled the trigger twice at close range.

The first went straight through his heart and took the smile off his face; the other went through his collarbone and struck the far wall on the other side and kept going, he turned and fired as the door was opening, he hit the first man as he rushed through the door and then realized that he was out of bullets when the door was pushed forward once more.

He quickly jumped down and grabbed the wrist of the man lying there, raised it up and shot the other man twice and then a third time because he was still trying to fire his weapon; he shot him through the forehead and ended the fight.

Stephon thought he was done when he heard something in the other room, there was a guy hiding in there, either low level or maybe some kind of book keeper or clerk for that gang but he wasn't armed and thought that meant something, that he was going to get away but none of that mattered to Stephon, he was an enemy; a bug that needed to be stepped on.

The first shot took him down as he begged for his life; he began to crawl on his belly and crying as he tried to get further from Stephon, he thought if he stayed low and tried to move away that he would be spared and yet he knew that Stephon would not leave him behind as a witness or for possible retaliation later.

During that entire time, Stephon showed not an ounce of remorse nor compassion for any of the men he killed; he knew that his uncle would be angry at first but in the long run it was heading off what would happen down the road anyway, they looked weak and that guy thought he could take advantage of it and that couldn't be allowed; they had to make a show of strength.

BACK TO SCHOOL

ARIA WOKE WITH A START, she couldn't wait to see how true any of this was, and now she felt that they were more than just dreams, she showered and dressed as quickly as she could and then ran all the way to school.

We were both eager to see each other but in school we were kept so busy that we didn't get a chance to see each other until we got to the class we shared, for me the day dragged on so slowly until then, and it seemed to take a lot longer than usual to get to that class.

I felt as though I was running through my classes until I found her there, though I did the racing part to get there and then to the next class, the rest of the world seemed to be on "molasses time" or something because they moved so damned slow it was driving me crazy.

There were times that I remembered answering some of the questions during my classes but was only there to endure that time and get through them, I couldn't have told you if I was right or wrong about anything I said or did while rushing through there though.

I was feeling strangled or smothered or something and was having that same feeling that she was, that we shared between us something that was beyond the time we'd spent together here, that with the deep feelings we already had in such a short time, that this was just the tip of the iceberg and there was a lot more to discover about this and what our part was in it, why we were lost in that chasm.

Feeling frustrated, I kept having to remind myself to slow down, that just because I was in a rush didn't mean that anyone else was, the clock was going to tick along just as slowly either way, and in my haste I went to the wrong class more than once; I ended up in the Home Economics class and the girls in there laughed so hard at seeing me there that I left in a hurry.

As I went a long, I thought about her, I knew that I loved her since the first time I laid eyes on her, that I fell so fast and hard and that feeling of being safe and comfortable around her came to fast for it not to have been right.

It bothered me that I held nothing back from her, I let her know what I was thinking and how I felt about her, a little of my history too; I would have said more but I thought it was boring and I told her that I was never really alive until I saw her, but I knew very little about her, that wasn't her fault though, she had only clues to her past too, and that was from what we both had to agree was another life, and we weren't sure if it would help us in this life, though we knew a battle was coming; we still had no idea of how bad it was going to get.

We had no idea of what her family would have been like, or where they might be now, or what made them abandon her as a baby, although I thought that turned out alright since we were together now; we might not have found each other in this world if they hadn't done that.

It was funny to me, how we felt each other's hearts well enough to trust in each other in such a short time, as if we'd been together for years instead of a few weeks, as it truly was.

Although there were other girl's I thought I liked before; it never felt this way, this right, and I felt as though her love was returned to me long before I ever told her how I felt. Those kinds of things told me that my heart was where it belonged, and now I knew that love at first sight could be real; but I guess it only worked if you were lucky and your eyes were open to it.

That day, I got to class early, even before Miss Johnson walked in, and when she got there, she was surprised to see me sitting there, even though she could probably guess why when she looked at my face.

As the rest of the class drifted in, she started talking about the lesson of the day, but when Maria walked in, I didn't hear her anymore and it was probably obvious that my heart skipped a beat, and I could see by her expression that she was happy to see me too.

We went over old business; things going on in school and in the world, where there was a lot of things going on and things like that, and then she saw something in my eye when she asked about anything that was "closer to home" and so I told her about something that bothered me before that class, earlier in the day and in between classes but near the quad, where everyone liked to hang out and catch up.

Everyone else seemed to have moved on and forgotten about it by then, but it stayed with me ever since it happened, a stench that lingered in the air even though fighting among students to fight with each other between classes; it was sometimes over the most trivial of slights, at least as far as I could tell, none of what I saw was worth punching somebody in the mouth, but then no one asked me either.

For most of us, I thought it might be the specter of Viet Nam that was hanging over our heads, especially for the seniors of the class, if they didn't get into college they would almost be assured of being drafted into the Army to fight and probably die a couple of thousand miles away in a "police action" that almost assured everyone that the minorities would be dying, and in greater numbers all the time; as if they wanted to get rid of us and that was the best way to accomplish that.

"With so many fights happening every day, what is it about this one that bothers you so much?" Miss Johnson asked me, "I mean. Not that its okay, but there are always fights, with so many minorities squeezed into small classrooms as you are, why does this bother you so much?" she asked, "I'm just curious!" she said with a smile.

For me, the funny thing was that, until that moment; I thought that I was thinking to myself, that I hadn't given voice to that concern until she asked me and caught me off guard.

"Well, it was a fair fight when it started, I thought Hector started it, he pushed Darwin because he acted as though he was in his way, but Darwin hadn't seen him, so he never tried to go around him, but he didn't know he was there!" I said.

I noticed out of the corner of my eye that some of the others on my right were nodding their heads, they agreed with my "assessment" of what happened and wondered what I was going to say next. One of those sitting there was Darwin's sister, but I forgot she was there, I didn't say it for her benefit, and I think she knew that.

Regina was beautiful, and even at a young age she was a very strong woman, but you'd better not call her that because she had become such a radical that she would take that as a slap in the face, and then she'd kick your ass every time she saw you for the next week.

She was also highly intelligent, everyone knew that about her too, she wanted to be seen in that light, and not as beautiful, she thought anyone could be beautiful if they tried hared enough, and if that didn't work; there was always makeup.

But there were those of us, mainly me, that had known her for a long time and could get away with stuff; we thought she went over the edge with her radical thinking and started called her "ugly" instead and it worked, she laughed about it too.

She would still become hostile around people not wearing a peace button or had their fist raised high in the air, she wore military style khaki's and shirts, always green with a black t-shirt underneath.

Darwin was smart too, but not as smart as his sister, and he'd always taken a lot of flak for his name, but that wasn't his fault and I didn't really care about that; Hector could have picked on someone a lot easier to pick a fight with and I thought that Darwin was cool, he lettered in three different sports but he had a hard time hitting a curveball though I heard he was getting better, that his father hired a batting coach.

The other students, further behind and to my left didn't agree though; I knew that without looking over there, and though they didn't care about Hector; they weren't trying to hide that they felt as though I'd sold out my race because I called it as I saw it.

I knew that Darwin was there too, but I forgot where he was at that moment, though I also knew that he likely turned and scowled at me when he first heard me talking about it; but his sullen expression changed quickly when he heard the rest of what I said.

He knew what I was talking about, but he didn't know that anyone else knew, or that anyone would come forward and be thought of as a "race traitor" by his peers, and now he knew that at least one guy would, but I was taken from my thoughts when Miss Johnson asked me another question, one that really stirred up the pot.

"Did it seem that it was racial to you?" she asked me, "Is that what bothered you about it?" she asked me innocently enough, but it angered some of the other students in the room, the loudest was of course, Regina, "Damn right it was racial, and damned right it was wrong!" she shouted and looked at me as if I was on the other side now.

"I'm sorry, Regina! It isn't your turn to speak, so please, sit down and wait for your turn!" she was reminded by Miss Johnson, "Please!" she said again; she said in a firm voice but with no hostility; Regina saw that and returned the favor by sitting down, but it was clear by her expression that she wasn't happy about it either.

She was more vocal about her feelings and politics than anyone else in the school and was not above stopping the students in the middle of school, only to get them riled up about things; to make them see how it was wrong to even be there in the first place.

I understood her idealism though, not because I was a part of it, or I wanted to be; I was raised to see everyone the same until they proved me wrong, so I gave everyone a chance to be my friend, but no one ever asked me what I thought.

"Honestly, I think that what bothered me most about happened at the end, how it ended I mean!" I said, "In the beginning, everyone stood back and let them fight, it was fair then, no one else tried to get a hit in or anything!" I told her.

"I thought then, that it was a good thing, I mean, not that they were fighting, but that it wasn't a bunch of guys fighting a bunch of other guys that really had nothing against the others, no one was jumping in!" I said, and this time, even Regina shut up.

"But after a few minutes of that, the teachers heard about it and came to break it up, and one of them, whose name I can't say because that would make Mr. Vincent seem racist!" and then everyone started laughing because we all knew that he was, he was the only one that thought he wasn't, probably in the whole world.

"Anyway!" I said, "He jumps in there, without checking to see who's the aggressor or anything and grabs Darwin in a headlock, and it seemed to some of us" I said and looked around to blank stares all around, "Okay, it seemed that way to me that he was a lot more forceful than he needed to be!" I said.

"Then he dragged him into the office, but what about Hector?" I said, "The guy that started it gets to walk to the office as if they are sorry to bother him, something about that, at least to me, isn't right, and that ain't selling out my race, that's telling the truth!" I said, and that started off another round of debates.

It took Miss Johnson several anxious moments to do it, but she finally got control of the classroom and though she was only trying to make us see things in a different light; she almost started a riot.

A lot of us shared the same views about it; the same ethics and upbringing as the others, or the ones that some of us thought as the others; either because they were forced to, or they felt that the situation called for it for whatever reason.

But it became really clear to a lot of us that day; we all shared the same fears and felt the same devotion to our families and friends, regardless of our own race and ethnic backgrounds.

Then she dropped the bomb that no one expected that day, maybe it was her way to distracting us from killing each other, but she said, "Today, we are going to explore something new, and something that will hopefully be exciting for all of us!" she told us with that smile on her face again.

"It will force all of us to look deep inside of ourselves and use our imaginations in new ways, at least I hope they are new, though some of you might have already tried this!" she said, and then looked around her classroom.

"Today's assignment is for each of you to write a poem or sonnet to someone else, it doesn't have to be a real person if you want to write it that way, but the feelings you express during this exercise might surprise you!" she said.

All I ask is that it's your original work and since there's some of you that might not be entirely comfortable doing this, so there is no limit, no minimum of words, it can be just a few words that maybe mean something to you, or a lot of words that work for you if that's what you want, it's entirely up to you!" she told us.

Everyone was grumbling about it and they all started looking around, some of them complaining loudly about having to write a poem, and as they spoke about that, she interrupted them again by saying something else.

"Oh!" she told us and then paused, "The other thing about it is that you have to turn it in by the end of this class!" she said and then sat down and pretended that it wasn't a huge thing that she should have said a little sooner.

"Have fun with it if you like!" she said, without looking up, "You can even write about how unfair it is for me to force you to do this as long as you keep it clean! Write about the puppy you got for Christmas when you were five years old, the red bike you got when you were ten, how your grandmother used to make the best cookies from scratch and never even knew what a cookbook was!" she said, and then she smiled at me.

"It's up to you!" she said, "You have the entire hour to do this, but you're wasting it if you're still looking at me!" she said and went back to grading papers.

Though this was considered a "brain class" no one outside of the two guys that sat in the back, on the corner who were both musician's; no one had ever done anything like this before.

As such, she expected the usual moaning and groaning about having to something like this, something that took them out of their comfort zone; but she was encouraged when she saw some students actually embrace it and jump right in, it didn't escape her either that while they were all debating the unfairness of it, that I took out my paper and started on it right away; and then she didn't have to think very hard about who I would be writing my paper to and she couldn't wait to see it.

She never liked to play favorites with her students, that wouldn't be fair to the others and she tried really hard not to; but she felt there was something different about me, that we had a bond that started on that first day as well; she knew that I was lacking in self-confidence but was eager to learn, she didn't understand why I wasn't quite ready to believe in myself even though there were several times she thought I knew the answer but didn't shout it out because I wasn't sure.

"This is going to be an important part of your grade for this quarter, so follow the example of some of the others in here and get to work!" Miss Johnson said.

Some of those "grumblers" started to look around, to see who was already writing and at the moment, I was the only one with my face in my work, and they started calling me "teacher's pet" which kind of made me laugh because a lot of those guys saying that wished they were her pet.

"Of course, HE would be writing already, I heard one of them say, "He has no life, no friends and nothing else to do all day!" and then wasted the next ten minutes bad-mouthing me before another one of them pointed out that I wasn't even listening; when the class ended and everyone was filing out and turning in their papers, she noticed I was still sitting there and Maria was waiting for me.

I was still working on my paper, feverishly writing and ignoring the others as they left, then she looked at Maria, who was patiently waiting for me to finish so we could leave together, that caused Miss Johnson to smile, she also knew that we were good together and liked seeing the love between us, it took her back.

"Come on Juan!" she said as she winked at Maria, "You don't get special treatment in my class, you know that, no one does, turn in your paper and be on your way!" she told me, firmly, but without conviction.

She thought she saw a look of relief then, that I would have to stop and leave with her, and she remembered the impatience of love, when two people feel so much between them that they felt they would spend their lives together and couldn't wait to get started, but life gets in the way.

When I was finally done, I jumped up and started towards the front of the class, but I was still reading it and stopped a couple of times to correct something, erasing it and then putting a better word in there, and there was at least one time I was stuck for the word and kept trying to figure it out while making them wait.

After we left, she took out my paper and read what I wrote, and she was impressed at how easily I expressed my deepest emotions, she noticed that, at least on this paper, or maybe it only worked with Maria, but it was clear on that paper that I wasn't shy with her, it again, took her back and brought tears to her eyes for a moment, she put an "A+" on it and read it again.

Then she sat back in her chair and stared at the far wall for a while, as though she was thinking about, or measuring every memory that she'd ever shared with a boy, she thought about every lover that she'd ever had and measured them all by "the one" and then there was her husband, and why she went by "Miss Johnson" when it should be Mrs. Yates.

Then she looked at my poem and read it aloud, as if she wasn't alone and wasn't feeling very alone at that moment.

As the flower that blooms only when under the moonlight

I live only for those moments that I get to share with you

As the sun shines on days your hurting and you must hold on tight

I want you to be at my side when all of my days are through

As water finds its own path through granite rock and oak tree

I'll always find you, my one true love; I know your heart is true

When times are tough, and I wonder who might be there for me

Its your loving, sweet face that I know I will see

Knowing that you gave me your heart gives me a feeling of pride

As the smallest seed reaches for the sun and the sky

My arms reach out and long to hold you so tight

Your love caresses me, gently, as the softest of sighs

Telling me to hold on with all of my might

As the journey, though long, begins with a single step

I turn my feet, my heart and soul to your door

I need your love, and the promise kept

And my love for you is like none ever before

She sat there and looked at my paper for a long time, it wasn't the best poem that she'd ever read, and she could tell that last line bothered me, she could see where I'd erased and rewritten several words there, but she was seeing into the words rather than at the ink stains they left behind.

That reminded her of a man that she loved that way once, and sadly enough; it was not her husband, though she would never tell him that, but it caused some problems for her, and she tried to explain it to him more than once but it never actually came out, and then it became one of those uncomfortable things that they agreed never to talk about.

He was a good man in most respects, but even he knew that he wasn't the most handsome man that she'd ever met, or most appealing; but he loved her with all his heart and that really should count for something, she thought.

Yes, she did love him, and yes, if he asked her, she would have married him and not ended up where she was now; not a bad place to be by any means and she was happy, but when it came down to it the married him, and not the guy he was so worried about; there was just that part about how she felt about him, at least at one time; and the fact that he was still around somewhere.

She was certain that he knew how she'd felt and that she didn't want nor need to be reminded of it; he was happy with the way things were now, though he still kept in mind that he was second choice he didn't dwell on it, "Can't worry about things I can't control!" he said to himself and then he tried really hard to let it go.

When he came home from work, it was just the two of them and nothing else mattered to him, and many times she wondered about the simplicity of that; how he felt in his heart of hearts and what he believed was important, what was real.

There were many times that she wished she could feel that strongly as he did; and though she never once strayed from their marriage, there were several times that she could have and there was at least one time where she almost did; but she stopped herself in time, before it got serious, or even very far.

That was because she could not bring herself to hurt him that way, and she promised herself as well as him on the day when they married that she would not have another man as long as she was, "No one deserves to feel that kind of hurt and emptiness!" she said to herself, as if she didn't know what that felt like from both sides of the table.

While it was true that her first choice, her first kiss, her first in a lot of things was a man that she could never have, and that wasn't because he was married or anything, but because he could never return the love she felt for him; he thought of them as very deep and close friends, but nothing more, and she couldn't accept that, not that it was all or nothing but it couldn't be all her and nothing him and she lost.

When she showed her heart to him, he balked, he told her to quit rushing him and pressuring him into decisions that he wasn't ready nor willing to make yet; he wasn't a strong man, he had no convictions, no purpose in his life beyond whatever today held for him, and this day ended badly; her husband was simply the guy that came along when she needed someone the most, and he helped her to pick up some pieces.

He held her hand and waited patiently with no expectations until she was ready and he was sure that he wasn't going to heal her and simply lose her to another guy, and when he was strong again, he came around; and when she was past crying over him, though she knew that she would never forget him; he just hoped that she didn't call out his name in the dark.

Miss Johnson marked the paper with a smiley face and wrote "Good work!" as she wiped away her tears, she decided that she would talk to me about it tomorrow in class and put it her briefcase, and then she looked around her classroom and sighed; she was wondering if she still felt the same passion for teaching as she did when she first started, such a long time ago.

Thinking hard and looking closely at it, she knew that she hadn't strayed too far off that point; she still enjoyed seeing the young minds opened to new thoughts and ideas, she lived for those students, so she was still a good teacher no matter how you looked at her.

The other thing was, she wasn't old, not by any means, a lot of the boys were calling her a "milf" and though she wasn't entirely sure what that meant, she was glad they didn't say it to her face and thought of it as a kind of compliment, though not something she would ever act on, ever.

She would ignore the things she heard until it became too much and something she could no ignore and then she made sure that they knew that it was never going to go there, she was a good teacher, after all.

When she examined herself closely, she felt that the only part of her that showed her age was her hands, and that bothered her a little, she would look at the wrinkles in dismay because they spoke of cosmetic surgery for the eyes, the mouth, the neck and the stomach, but never the hands.

Then she thought about it, when she started off teaching, she thought that she was going to change the entire world, one young mind at a time.

Through the years, that gave way to silent optimism that there were always going to be kids that were open and ready to learn and there were going to be others that couldn't, no matter how hard they tried.

Things changed over the years, things that once were taught at home were not being taught anymore and kids needed to learn respect and manners from the teachers; they were more rebellious than ever before and they became harder to control, they didn't see the need for a good education and most of them were simply there because they had no choice in the matter; it was either that or be out on the street, and they weren't ready for that harsh option, it was too cold out there.

Discipline sometimes went out the window, and every now and then a teacher was forced to remind themselves to keep calm as there was a lot at stake; the schooling, training and the education that it took to get them where they were, more often than not more than ten years, all that could be thrown away in a fit of rage if they lost it with a rude or unruly child.

They learned to look the other way sometimes, to fight only the battles that were worth fighting and that they knew they could win, and they had to choose them carefully.

At one point, even she was ready to give in to the gloom of the new world they all saw on television, in the newspapers and everywhere else you thought to look for news of the world, wherever you found senseless violence and bloodshed.

The future look was so bleak with more of that in the future and she was feeling overwhelmed; but then, every now and then things would happen that made her feel alive, to feel that shred of hope for the future of the world.

She wasn't yet ready to look past the bad things in her life and pretend that they happened to someone else and try to dismiss it until it stops at your door and you have nowhere to hide.

But she had been thinking a lot about doing something special for her husband, though lately she'd felt distant and somewhat cold to him, she knew that he'd deserved better and it was time to accept things as they were and move on.

There is nothing like the feeling of new love to bring out the best in the world after all; flowers are brighter and more colorful, the songs birds sing seem much prettier, babies still make you laugh and smile on the worst of days.

She thought about how they started off and how he cared for her, and because she was trying to get over that sense of loss, the sudden transition from being "with" someone to being left all alone in the world.

That was something she didn't like to admit; that she needed to be loved, to feel someone else's gentle touch and see a across the table from her at mealtime; someone that made it all worthwhile.

She thought about her parents then, and all the things that they did to make them a close-knit family, the hardships they endured and those things that made them stronger, and how they always found a way to stay together, no matter what happened.

They always had the time to show each other that they were loved, to give that love to each other at the end of the day when all was said and done.

She remembered that, though her father never spoke to her of religion, that he was the one that told her that "the Lord never gives us more than we can handle!" when things got tough and it looked bleak.

When her mother caught an illness and eventually died from it, that was when she felt the strongest test of that belief because she thought that she would never get over that pain and emptiness; then she fell away from believing for a while after that, she turned her back on her faith because she felt betrayed when her mother died, and that she couldn't wait to leave this world.

She blamed the lord for taking her mother away, and when someone told her that "God needed her more than she did" she went after him and almost killed him, being selfish at the time, and she was blindly reaching out in her pain, and that night she could also see it when her father came home from the hospital and he was never the same after that.

He was "broken" and seemed well beyond any kind of repair, and though he still functioned; he went to work and did all the things that they expected him to do, until the day that they found him at his desk and no one could remember the last time that they spoke to him or that they saw him out of that chair, when they spoke to him, if at all.

They found him sitting in that chair but he'd been dead a long time by then; they didn't know the cause of death but they knew that he died when she died, while its true that love changes the world in so many good ways that it makes sense that it has to do things in bad ways as well, the other side of the yang.

Photograph by J.R. Gonzalez

Revelations and Second Chances

I have only e superstition. I touch all the bases when I hit a
home run.

-Babe Ruth (1895-1948)

W E LEFT THE CLASS AND Miss Johnson behind, but I was really
anxious and nervous for Maria to see the paper, more than the
grade which I knew was important, I wanted her to see it; to read
it and give me her grade on it, that was just as important to me.

I have to admit that I was a little embarrassed about the feeling s revealed
in it, and I wasn't really even sure how I did it but it was something that I
did for her and I thought she'd like it, I thought that she wanted to see it too,
though she probably had different reasons than I did.

Though the pen was in my hand, the words just came to me, all I did
was try to make them rhyme, but they started coming faster then, and the
faster they came; the faster I wrote until it was done, but even then I thought
it needed more work, I'd never feel satisfied with it and would always want to
rewrite it; especially the last part which bothered me.

At the end, when they were both waiting for me, I was debating as to
whether or not to throw it away and start all over again, I knew that it would
mean a lesser grade, that I'd have to do a make up exam or something for
it, I also thought about copying it to show her what I wrote but didn't have
the time.

When I ran out of time, I gave in and submitted it, and I had some fun doing that because Maria tried to peek over my shoulder a few times as I turned it in, I kept moving it further away from her until Miss Johnson picked it up and ended the game.

I figured that I would show it to her after we got the grades, and then I wondered what she wrote about and laughed because it didn't have to be about me just because I wrote about her.

We skipped the rest of our classes that day and headed to Winslow Park, which was nearby, just so we could talk about things, we wanted to talk about our future together if we were going to have one, we knew that there was something in our past that was looming over us, even though we tried to ignore that for as long as we could, hoping that it would go away.

Yet we felt that we were stronger now; that together we could defeat it, whatever it was; even though we didn't know how bad it was, we felt strong enough to beat anything that was coming and that was far better than ignoring it and hoping that it would go away.

"Okay!" I said, "What's the big deal that made you want to skip all of our classes?" I asked her, even though I'd rather be with her any time or place rather than going to school, I wanted to know because she sounded scared and serious and I had to find a way to comfort her and calm her, to le4t her know that it was going to be alright.

There were a million things racing through my mind about what she might have to say, and because of what I felt for her and how insecure I was, I had a hard time waiting for her to say what it was.

"Remember what you said after we kissed?" she asked me, "The first time, I mean!" she said, and she was looking deep into my eyes again for the truth, she wanted to make sure that she said it right; but she also wanted to see my true reaction.

There was a chance that I might just tell her what I thought she'd want to hear, but as soon as her words hit my ears she would know if I was just being nice or telling her the truth, so she chose her words carefully and never took her eyes off mine; even as she reached for my hand.

I was, at that moment, thinking of how much I loved her, and that I knew two things right off; the first thing was what she was doing and why, and secondly; there are times to be nice and there are times when the truth is all there is, and this was that second instance.

But I could get lost looking into those eyes and never be seen nor heard from again, and that would be alright because I would still be the happiest man in the world, I felt that I could endure any kind of pain or suffering as long as she was there at the end of it to take me home.

"Yes!" I said, "Of course I remember, I told her, though now I was nervous again, thinking that she was going to tease me about it because she hadn't said anything about it since the day I mentioned it.

"I want to tell you, no, I needed to you to tell me everything that you feel and that you remember about this, even if you think its silly or trivial or even unrelated!" she said, "I want to know what it is, and I need to know what's on your mind!" she told me and then waited.

As I looked into her eyes, I could tell that she was either scared, nervous, or maybe even both in equal parts, she wasn't smiling nor smirking at me as if she was about to break out in laughter, she wanted answers too, and then I got the impression that maybe there was something about it that she hadn't told me yet.

I was excited about the chance that we'd both felt it; that would validate my own feelings and give us a starting point to start our research of our past lives that we might have shared, "I don't know what it was!" I admitted to her.

The only thing I know is that it was very real for me, and I felt it very strongly, as if the kiss we shared that day was one that we'd shared before, in some really bad times; and it seemed to be a very long time ago, and since we've never met before this year, I don't see any way that we might have kissed as children, and it didn't feel like a childish kiss either, it wasn't a "kid kiss!" I told her.

But it was enough that it scared me!" I admitted, "It brought new thoughts into my head that I think I was not entirely prepared for!" I said, "Not that I regretted it, not a moment of it, I am very happy now, and the world even smells like a better place now!" I said, and we both laughed at that, but I was nervous and that was what I did when I was that way.

"I was hoping that you felt the same, and yet the thought that you might not was something that I wasn't sure that I wanted to know!" I said, I was blabbering now but still thought being honest was the best way to be, and I knew she did too.

"My Grandmother Mary used to tell me all the time, "I would rather tell you the truth than try to remember a lie!" and just as she would have, I put all my cards on the table because I already knew that I could trust her.

"But then, when you didn't say anything, I thought it might just turn out to be wishful thinking on my part, delusional wishful thinking at that!" I said and giggled, and if you didn't feel anything then none of that bad stuff really happened and maybe I am watching too much television!" I said, and now I was really feeling bad about all that I'd said.

"But after we shared that kiss, when I went to sleep that night, it hit me a lot harder; there were even more images and things that I saw in my sleep that night, and none of it made any sense either; it didn't help me to gain any understanding but I think that together, we might be able to figure out at least some of it, maybe piecemeal it together and figure out the parts that are missing and make some sense of it!" I told her expectantly.

"Then I kept thinking that all of this proves that we've met before, but to be honest, until now; I've heard of reincarnation, but I never thought it was real, and yet, nothing else makes any sense!" I said, sounding as frustrated as I felt.

"All arguments and debates within myself and any research that I could do let to that same conclusion; and I was hoping that you and I could share those thoughts and exchange ideas about what it was, what it means and what we should do about them, because I don't really think that either of us can rest until we know the truth of this!" I said and then waited for a reaction and thought that I'd said way too much, but it was out there and no taking it back now.

She stared at me for the longest time, and while I was talking, she never moved, and there was no expression on her face and spoke not a single word so I thought I blew it, that now she knew that I was really certifiable and was going to call for the white coats and would be reminding them to bring the straight jacket with them.

Or even worse, that she'd already called them because she knew and they were out there in the buses, waiting to spring out and get me, take me away to happily make baskets and chase butterflies for the rest of my days.

Then she surprised me by saying, "Last night, I had the most amazing dream!" she said with a wistful smile on her face, "At least I think it was a dream, I have to call it that because I don't know what else it could have been, until now I mean; and now I'm thinking that it might be related to what your saying!" she said.

"In this dream, you and I were talking, we were somewhere dark and "wide open" I think is the best way to describe it, as if there was a huge chasm before us that prevented us from getting any closer, and since I couldn't see us anywhere in this, I thought that maybe we had just died or something terrible happened to us, I don't know but it sure felt that way!" she told me excitedly.

"Or, it could have been that one of us died…and maybe we were sending our last thoughts, a promise to each other somehow! I think it was almost without words being spoken as well, if that makes any sense, but then if that doesn't, how does the rest of this make any?" she said, and I could see her mind spinning around it, she was doing the same things I did when I was confused like this.

Then she bit her lip as if she'd said too much, "Though I couldn't see your face, I knew that it was you, and if I'd closed my eyes and tried to imagine it; I could see how you moved and have further proof if I needed that it was you, speaking to me in earnest about any chance we might have to find our way back to each other and to hold onto each other far stronger the next time we faced this; and that there was no doubt in your mind that we would face this again, and that next time we'd be ready and we'd be the ones standing triumphantly over their dead bodies!" she said, and almost laughed at the sound of that.

"You were talking about when we'd meet again, and I believed you, the conviction in your words told me that it was true and that it would happen, that it would come true, and it has!" she said, "Here we are!" and then she waited for me to reply but I was numb because it was so much at once and it confirmed my worst fears.

"I couldn't understand why we couldn't just stay together then, that we could find a way through or around that hole in the ground and just hold onto each other until it passed us, but I thought that maybe something happened to you, something terrible and I'd lost you for a while!" she said sadly, and then she stopped as if considering that possibility once more was too much to bear.

"But I knew that it was quite important to you, and to us in the long run; it was really important that I understood and even agreed with what you were trying to tell me, your "plan for our future" is what you called it once!" she told me.

"Those are the things I was trying to tell you?" I asked her, because it cleared up things for me, though she was vague because the details eluded her as well as they did me; it "showed me" the other side of the discussion now; on some deep level of my sub-consciousness, I knew what she was going to say next and I was anxiously waiting and dreading it at the same time.

"You told me that when we got together again, that we would know each other by that kiss that branded our souls together!" she said, "That no matter what they did to us in this life; that we would find each other and make it right again, for us!" she told me.

"That our shared kiss would open doors for us, doors to the past and to the future if we were going to have one; that we would have our time together, and I remember you said "our time" with emphasis, as though it was ordained and there was no way to stop us!" she said with so much love in her eyes I almost cried.

I felt as though the wind was now swirling around us at a rapid pace and picking up speed; as if the trappings and our very existence in this world were being stripped away from us and another world opened up as the old one fell away from where we stood.

But I could also hear my voice as I spoke those words to her, and while it was true that my voice sounded different than now, it was clearly me, I heard myself say those things now, word for word as if it were yesterday, my head began to swim and I felt as though I was about to pass out, I forced myself to slow down for a moment before I could listen to any more of the things she was telling me that we did.

It was so vivid that I felt that I could see where we were at that moment and what we were doing; I saw the deep and dark chasm that was between us, saw myself kick a rock over the side that never landed because it was so deep; and I knew that she was right, that those words were spoken from our hearts at a time when we were already dead and yet we were still trying to reach out to each other.

A lot came back to me then, in a flash, I heard myself repeating those words to her, or maybe it was the chasm and it was an echo, or maybe it was repeated in a vacuum through all those years that had passed since then and it was now catching up with me.

She was right though, even as we stood there in Winslow Park, I felt as though that was the most important message that I would ever deliver in any life that I might have lived, and all of this was so overwhelming that we both stood silent for a few moments, to absorb it and not question it so much.

It worried her that she could see thoughts swirling through my head and certain things on my face that made her nervous; things like recognition, bewilderment, amazement and maybe even some kind of comprehension.

Now she knew me well enough that she could also see some kind of shock as well, followed by relief because now I knew that she felt and saw those things too; and then I asked her, "What do you think we should do now? How do we find out how much of this is real and how much of this is a romantic notion that we both feel and want for it to be that way?" I asked her, but I didn't expect her to have an answer any more than I had any answers, so I guess I was "spit-balling" or using her as a sounding board.

I thought that was the answer anyway, I wanted to hear what she thought about this, and how much she knew and remembered if anything, and then she smiled at me and said, "Let's try again, right now; while we can clear our minds of anything else that might clutter these images and confuse us; while our minds are open to the possibility and willing to discover what it was and what we can do about it!"

This sounded like a good idea to me, starting with the kiss and then seeing where it led us, and so I leaned forward to give her a kiss and my hand accidently touched her bare knee and in the blink of an eye we were both back in the dungeons once more; except this time we were spectators.

We were standing together, and off to one side as if we were watching a high-speed film of the things that we endured in this past life; as if we could be innocent bystanders in this new version of the hell we went through, and though I could not feel it, not anything else at that moment like cold or discomfort, it still was very painful to watch as others were tortured and bludgeoned to death for no reason, other than that they were there and they were too weak and couldn't fight back.

I stood behind Gregor and watched her as she died, dancing in those awful flames as they licked at her bare feet, her legs kicking as if she could jump high enough to escape the flames that licked at the wood underneath her feet.

From there, I could hear her screams of shock, pain and horror as she died, I saw the flames consume her body as she died, and we were both taken aback when the crowd began to cheer as she finally gave way to the smoke and intense heat, I heard that final scream as it was choked off when she died.

She looked at me, and she must have remembered now that it happened just that way, I felt her body trembling and wanted to hold her but I didn't know what would happen to us if we were caught and just squeezed her hand a little firmer and hoped she'd know what that meant.

As we stood there, I could now smell smoke on her but the look on her face told me that she knew her suffering was over, but the look on her face told me that she knew that I was next; that even though she didn't know what happened to me because they killed her first and publicly while my death was held before a private audience for some reason; probably because they weren't sure how it would work, how thorough it would be in eliminating the evidence.

Though she had just witnessed her own death, as horrid as it was; she was now more concerned for me; she hoped that I didn't suffer, that I didn't see my death creep up on me as she saw those flames rise up and sweep her life away, she didn't want to look, so she buried her face in my chest as I watched in shocked silence.

I saw Esmeralda as she tried to sway me away from my love; tried to convince me to join her and then my adamant refusal though we both knew what that meant for me, and I felt her squeeze me tighter when I did that, because she knew that I held onto the promise of her love and risked everything to have her, just as she did for me.

Then, I felt a lot of emotions running through Maria then; and I felt things as well, but I could feel somethingin her change, something that I couldn't describe but I knew that if I was her enemy and got even a whiff of what she was feeling at that moment, that even as formidable as I might be, and whatever weapons I brought forth: I would think twice about taking on her as an enemy combatant; that made me proud of her as well.

She refused to give them any more than they'd already taken from us, "Not one more inch!" she promised to herself.

Finally, she thought that enough time passed that it was safe to look but when she did, she saw that my legs were burned away by the acid; she could see the look of agony and bliss in the confusion of my death, being slowly deprived of my senses and then being acutely aware of what was happening because the pain woke me in a hurry and there were not enough drugs to stem that burning all over my body.

She turned away when she saw the clean white of my bones and heard me screaming as I died, screams that I'd heard in my nightmares but didn't know what they might mean to me until that moment, I didn't even remember screaming like that.

We both saw Esmeralda doing her victory dance and then the rape and murder of Gregor, the two strangers that died along with them, all of this was passing before our eyes as if we were watching a movie and no one seemed aware that we were even there, some of them even passed through us where we stood and never seemed to notice that either.

Though we both would have liked to change the view to a better and more entertaining site, we both knew that we needed to see how this ended together, what we might do next as a way to possibly ease and understand the nightmares, find our way to be together in peace with nicer dreams somehow.

We both had an idea of what was going to happen, but neither of us was ready to give those thoughts a voice yet, to make them real; we both felt the fear in our hearts, we knew the pain of what had happened and were weighing it against the pain we knew was coming our way, and that was the pain we couldn't give in to.

It made me wonder how many lives we lived through before this one, if we were together in any lifetime before this one and after the one we were seeing now; if we were searching for each other as we lived our lives out; did we get it wrong and die in the arms of another, someone that we settled for because we gave up instead of waiting until we got to the same place in that world.

That was enough to drive me crazy, and then I remembered the old lady in the carnival and I wondered if she made it to two hundred years old or not, and I wondered for a moment if Maria was there too, because I know she wasn't the girl I'd ended up with, at least I didn't think it was her, that was just drunken passion and knowing that it was my last night on earth, not the passion I felt for Maria.

It made me laugh, I wondered if we had been living in a cave at one time, running from T-Rex and other carnivores as we discovered fire and other new and interesting things to make our lives better.

I knew that if I thought of us in that context I might lose it, thinking of the many lives we might have led, how we lived and died and if we were together at any point; I guess it was meaningless now because that was in the past, and I was fairly certain that what happened with the flames and acid only happened once because those images never changed, there was never anything different in the background when I could see it; they might become more gruesome or violent, but I was certain that they never changed location, and it was always the same blurred faces sweeping by with very little, if any definition.

Images flashed by us of spiders attacking and eating each other, feeding off their young; we saw vampires and werewolves; all of these intermingling together and rushing into each other with such a force that even though I knew it was a vision, I still felt its immense power, and through it all, everything that I saw and every living thing was being consumed by flames that rose up from the ground as if all the world was on fire and it started with the two of us and spread out from there.

The flames rose so high that they threatened to burn everything away before we could read any of the clues, which to us meant that we couldn't see how all of this related to us, what it had to do with either of us because we knew we didn't deserve this and it wasn't from bad decisions we'd made and had to atone for our sins, as hard as I tried, I could not imagine any sins committed by either of us that would call for this.

We were just two kids who should be spending our time kissing and getting to know each other, making plans for our future and choosing the names of the kids we would have together, holding hands as we walked, holding the pinkie finger sometimes because life is fragile yet ourbond was strong.

Instead of that, we were seeing images of horror and death beyond comprehension; it all seemed so predetermined and yet so senseless, and so much blood that it covered everything and was everywhere.

We knew that this wasn't the end, as much as we knew that something was ahead of us, we just didn't know where it was coming from, or when it would be here, but the flashing images had a renewed sense of urgency now; telling me at least, that it wouldn't be long now, and we'd better be ready this time.

But we'd already been given a lesson in how cold and ruthless they could be, how they abused whatever power they held over us and twisted things around because they couldn't have what we had between us, and when they couldn't take it from us they murdered us.

We saw the murder of Alberto in the basement, but from the perspective of Esmeralda, but Maria recognized the building and connected the dots, she realized that it was the same spider that came into her room that day, the same spider that somehow plotted and then killed her nurse and was now after her, it sounded so absurd to her that she was afraid to tell me, she wanted to try and figure it out a bit, make a little sense of it and then talk to me about it, not realizing what a huge mistake that was and how that helped them more and did nothing for us.

She saw the web in the corner of her room, as if she was sitting up there and watching herself sleeping on the bed a few feet below; and then it was Esmeralda herself sitting up there and watching her as she slept, and we were both looking up at her.

Without saying a word, Maria squeezed my hand again, and then she put her head on my shoulder, I thought that it was because it was hard for her to see these things, but she was thinking about what had happened to her nurse, I felt her sobbing gently against me but didn't pull back to look at her, I just held her a little closer instead, I thought that was what she needed.

Both of us were there as my mother delivered me into this world, I could smell the dirt and choked on the same dust as they were, I felt the heat from the sun bearing down on us, she was born and then placed on someone's porch, or near the front door, we couldn't see clearly enough to be sure.

There was water and it seemed to be at least semi clean and away from the house even though the house itself seemed abandoned and empty at the time.

I felt the indignity of being born out there in a swirl of dust and again felt the heat of the sun bearing down on us; it was all vivid to me now, and seeing what my parents went through to keep me safe gave me an entirely new perspective of them and how much they loved me; what they felt for my brother and how much it ripped their hearts out with so much pain that it almost killed them as well.

We saw the images of a homeless man, sitting on a park bench and we knew right off that there was something wrong about him; even though he was doing nothing more than just sitting there and watching everyone walk by until he fell asleep.

Suddenly, he sprang up and changed from the homeless man to one whose face was contorted with pain and anger; his eyes red and black rimmed orbs now, and fangs that were already dripping blood. I could see ashen white skin and that he was looking for someone to feed on.

We saw all of that in an instant, and were both so overwhelmed by what we saw that we both passed out as we held onto each other; anyone that saw us out there might have thought we were making out or just talking about things important to us and left us alone.

After all, we were destined to be together, right? It was ordained, was in the cards, whatever fit to describe it best and there was no arguing that now; but there was no turning back either if that was what we wanted, but neither of us thought of going through that again.

At that moment, it felt as though the rest of the world was gone and it was now just the two of us, my parents couldn't help us; they didn't believe in reincarnation and wouldn't have let us explore it, no matter how convincing any argument we might have presented in our defense, to them it was wrong and that was that they would see until it was too late.

We felt that the world could go on without us, that we might be forgotten and left to each other that we could be happy, but at the same time; we knew that it was never going to be that easy for us.

Death was coming for us, and it could take us once more, or we could take a stand and fight this time, we knew that we were right this time, as much as we were last time, except that we believed in the good of man then and now we knew better, there was no one going to save us except for us.

Death was coming again, but this time we were going to send him packing, empty-handed with the knowledge of how it felt for us, death would leave without our souls once more, we just didn't know how we were going to do this yet.

Gregor woke with a nasty headache, he felt as though he'd somehow fallen asleep upside down again; he didn't like that when he tried it before but thought he was supposed to while he slept, it didn't work and felt the same as it did just now.

Among other things, it played hell on his sinuses, but this time it wasn't that, this time it was because Jeremy had drank more than just a few beers that night; and then added that champagne, and he'd "hoisted a few" with that cop named Tommy who died that same night, "snapping one off" before he came on duty because he knew Danny would not approve.

Jeremy came home and got drunk, and Gregor woke with the hangover, if it wasn't for what happened to Jeremy it would have been funny.

As he prepared to go out again, he felt a tremendous thirst raging through his body, something that seemed to be happening a lot more these days, he was thinking that he was finally ready to leave when he heard footsteps coming up the hall.

He knew that they were headed towards this door, there were only three doors at the end of this hallway; one led to another apartment that was empty at the moment, the other was a supply and broom closet, and it was too late in the evening for a cleaning crew so he stood still and listened, waiting to see whom it might be.

Then he heard someone stop at the door, at first gently, and then he heard a girl's voice saying "Jeremy, its meee!" and then a little laughter before she knocked a little harder.

It was clear from how she slurred her words that Jeremy, Tommy and that stranger were not the only ones imbibing that night, but Gregor still didn't know why he had a headache, and in the "old days" he was sure that he'd had one or two and woke up with at least a bit of an ache, but since he didn't drink anything but the blood that was tainted with alcohol he didn't think it was that.

He knew who she was, he had seen her a few times around the apartment, sometimes wearing very little if anything at all, and other times "dressed to the nines" as Gregor heard Jeremy say to her, and he had to admit that she did look resplendent when she dressed like that.

There was a time when Jeremy was gone, hadn't come home from work or something, Gregor came down from the attic and was surprised to find her there, she was taking a shower and was oblivious to the danger she was in.

He turned to leave, a little embarrassed by her nudity, but when he realized that she hadn't seen him, he stood to watch as she lathered her body; it was very erotic for him, something that he enjoyed and would not forget.

There are those that say that the imagination is the only real erotic zone and that you can conjure up images of whatever perversion you desired if your imagination is good enough; that was what Gregor did after he saw her that day, whenever they made love; he couldn't see them but could hear everything down the rustle of the sheets as they made love.

A moment later, there was another knock, this time a little firmer than the first time, a little more impatiently as she said, "Jeremy! Hey Jerry honey!" she cried out, "Please answer me and open the damned door, pretty please?" she begged.

"I am very tired and have no time nor the patience for games, come on honey!" she pleaded with him, and then whispered a little loudly, "I really have to pee!" and then she giggled.

Gregor stood silent by the door and waited to see what was next, he wanted to open the door but he thought that she might scream if she saw him because she would have expected to see Jeremy there instead of him, then he heard her say, "Jeremeeee!" You are making me work too damned hard!" she said, "Are you going to open the door or make me dig through my purse to find the key you gave me? You know how cluttered my purse gets!" she said as he imagined her rummaging through her bag for the key.

"Open the damned door!" she pleaded again, and then he heard her drop her purse and then another string of cuss words that erupted from her mouth as she bent down and picked it up.

Gregor smiled on the other side of the door, "How nice!" he thought, "Food is delivered, right to your door and you don't even have to ask!" as he laughed and then shrunk behind the door and waited for her, "looks like I don't need to go outside tonight after all!"

Finally, he heard the key slide into the lock and then she said, "Okay! Ready or not, here I come!" with a smile on her face, "This is not how your going to get me into your bed tonight mister!" she said, and then giggled again."

"Okay!" Gregor whispered, with that same kid of smile on his face, "This is too easy!" he thought, as he saw her peer into the hallway and then she said, "Jeremy baby? Are you even here?" she asked as she walked in; her heels clacking loudly on the tile floor as she walked in and went back outside and then dragged her bag in and closed the door behind her.

"Hello?" she said again, and this time she tried to say it louder than when she was in the hallway but she felt suddenly afraid, she felt as though something was terribly wrong, that he would be upset if her found her there while he'd been gone and yet she'd been there often enough that she knew the smell and the feel of the rooms; she was comfortable in his home, he always said she should make herself at home, and that was why he gave her they key, so why she felt that way was something she couldn't understand why she felt that way but she couldn't help it, and she was really scared.

She thought it might be the silence, it had never been this quiet before, even the clock in the hallway that clicked so loud was quiet, that meant he hadn't rewound it, something he never forgot to do, she took the key and wound it after setting the hands at the right time just to kill the silence and then she felt a tad better but it didn't help her much.

There was always a radio on in one of the rooms, a football game that was played earlier but he liked the team and hated who they beat that day and would watch it several times over the next few days, or maybe a game or something else that he'd missed so he recorded it to watch when he got home.

She remembered how much fun it was to tease him because everyone else knew the final result and the score of the game, but he wouldn't let them tell him, it was one of her favorite quirks of his, "Jeremy?" she said again.

Her voice sounded so sad though, as though she really did need to see him, to feel his arms around her and let him comfort her as only he could, she wanted to be pampered and spoiled by him for at least a little while, because the visit didn't go as well as she'd hoped it would.

She went further inside, and noticed that the blinds were drawn, which made it unusually dark in there as well, it was now impossible to see anything so she tried turning on the lights but nothing happened when she flicked the switch, "Honey!" she said, "Did you forget to pay the bill or something?" she asked and then giggled again.

As she looked down the last part of the hallway, she felt the fear return again, that led to the bedroom, and when she looked in there, all she could see from there were the green lights of his alarm clock; blinking off and on like the lights of a crosswalk, but this time it wasn't indicating the time; it was shouting at her to run, but she didn't see that.

When she stepped into the bedroom at last, Gregor was right behind her, he watched as she walked, ready to pounce on her if she turned, and there was a small bit of light that was trickling through one of the blinds, she followed that bit of light into the room and then noticed the smell, but couldn't identify it right off.

"Maids year off too?" she said, but her laughter was choked off quickly when she saw the pool of blood on the floor where Jeremy's head rested, and then she slipped on part of that puddle and landed hard on her butt with a loud grunt.

"I am going to so kick your ass if this some stupid game that you are playing with me, especially if this shit doesn't come out of my dress! What the hell is this, anyway?" she asked him, still not sure if he was there or not because she had a sense that someone was there.

Gregor almost giggled himself as he waited in the darkness behind her, and she thought she heard something, but she still couldn't see a thing.

She looked down to see what she'd slipped on and then almost screamed when she saw it was caked on her hand and she realized that it was blood, a LOT of blood as a matter of fact, and though most of it was dried, she could swear that it was smeared all over everything from where she sat.

She started to say, "What the f" but that was all she had time to think of saying because that was when she saw Gregor out of the corner of her eye; she thought it was Jeremy, she tried to turn towards him; her eyes adjusted to the darkness a little better and then she could see Jeremy's head as it rested in the closet; his eyes rolled back until she could see the whites if his eyes, and his ashen tongue poked out from between his lips.

It was as if he was mocking the terror she felt in her heart at that moment, and then she tried to scream but that was when Gregor stepped forward and choked it off when he grabbed her by the throat and he began tearing into her, and as she died, her mind was flipping around and she thought it was Jeremy that was killing her; she thought "I thought he was the one, even my father liked him; he was always such a nice guy!" as she choked on her own blood and died with her eyes locked on his head in the closet.

Gregor kept tearing into her until her struggling stopped and then he tossed her body aside with a satisfied burp.

He looked around the roomand wondered how much longer he would be able to stay there; this girl coming here was proof that there would be others following them, coming here to see why they hadn't been at work or wherever they were missed by their friends, family or colleagues, and there would also be the woman that came here once a month to clean the apartment, he was due in a few days he thought.

When he wasn't sure, he knew that it really was time to leave, but he was thinking about Esmeralda, she was his first priority; he needed to know where she was hiding and then think of a plan to deal with her, she was never far from his thoughts these days, and though he wasn't hungry; he went out to hunt anyway, just because it made him feel better.

Though he didn't know it, Esmeralda was going out at the same time, though she was impulsively going in the other direction this time and away from where he was, and for a different reason; she wasn't hungry either, and wasn't hunting for food; she was looking for a new place to hide, she felt this one had outlived its usefulness, people were staying away now as they felt her evil presence and she knew it.

She was getting better at leaving the building undetected, the last two times she tried to leave, someone had almost seen her and she went back inside and waited but they had more time than she did and she was forced to give up and stay there, the other time someone almost saw her but they didn't get a solid look, this time she made it out and there was no one anywhere near.

It was easier for her to "hold her face" as she called it, and appear to be human for as long as she needed; it still took her energy and made her tired as hell, but it was worth it; she found out a lot of the things she needed while walking among them, even though they feared her and kept their distance, her hearing was very good and they unknowingly spilled all their secrets to her as they went by.

She was actually getting tired of her life and how it was stagnated; she missed the conversations that she'd had so long ago, and she missed people in general; she missed conversation, she'd never realized what a social creature she had been back then either.

She was working on attracting her prey with her mind now, making them see what they wanted to see when she was out there; that way it would be easier to lure them to a less populated area and then feed on them and take her time.

But this time she struck gold, as she was walking around the outside edge at the far end of the park where she'd never been to before, she found what she needed more than food; though she almost missed it because she was looking the wrong way; it was small and dark and there was nothing to flag it so she thought most people missed it too, unless they were maintenance or something and they knew it was there, there were weeds and undergrowth that needed to be cleared away and they hadn't been there in a while, another reason she almost didn't see it.

Photograph by J.R. Gonzalez

Then she went closer, and saw a small tunnel or opening in the side of a hill, it was almost too small for a child to get into, but she easily managed it and went deeper inside, feeling excited because she knew it was perfect already and she'd not even been more than five feet past the opening.

She looked back to see if anyone noticed her crawling in there and waited a few moments, but no one came along and told her "Get out of there! There are spiders on there!" and she laughed about that as she turned to go further into the tunnel.

It was so low that she had to stay on her knees for about ten feet before she could finally stand up as it opened up more and widened out as well, she stood up and took a good look around her from there, and saw that there were several paths that led off from there, with no sign or indication of where they led to or what they were, she assumed it led to different sewer lines or something like that.

Then she found a series of underground tunnels that led off from those first tunnels, she found other tunnels and caves that were both larger and smaller than where she started off, there were so many paths that they seemed to lead everywhere and nowhere all at once, and after that first ten or so feet, it sloped down for a while until the opening seemed far behind her and above her head though she could still hear sounds from there, they couldn't have seen her.

Since she had all the time in the world, she started following tunnels and paths until they ended, and found out that from that one central hub; she found several different ways to get to almost any part of the city, undetected and faster than any kind of emergency response team; police, ambulance or fire department.

This was perfect for her needs, there was nothing about it that was not to her liking; and she knew already that most people would not follow a sewer line as far as she was now, unless it was their job but the area didn't look as if anyone had passed through there in a while, there were footprints there, but there were old and almost filled in with silt, dirt and debris.

That meant that she would be pretty much left alone down there, that made it perfect, it was so deserted and abandoned that she spent a lot of time exploring the outer recesses of her new home; she wanted to know where all the exits were in case she was chased or discovered in there, where they led to in case she had to make a quick escape.

There were a lot of tunnels that were identical in size and seemed to be going in the same direction though they would peel off left or right after a while, or they would lead to storage area where tools were kept, but they clearly hadn't been used in ages either; she saw webbing all over them and smiled as she said the word "snacks!" and looked for the spiders that left it but they weren't there anymore.

There were several times she needed to back track the way she'd come because while one pipe might have led outside, its twin led to a dead end; pipes that were sealed off or seemed to be incomplete as they simply ended and there was dirt around it but no sign of workers in a long time.

At one point, she found a cavern that she could tell from her home in the basement was used by the homeless, to get out of the rain and the bad elements, there were footprints and sings of people that had camped there; there were rags scattered about and it was filthy here, the rags were rotted away and the smell of urine and excrement were strong to her, but probably not to anyone else as even that was stale.

She couldn't see them because they were smart enough to stay back from her, but she could also hear a lot of rats in this area and that made her laugh, "The creature comforts of home!" she thought to herself.

Then she heard a soft sneeze behind her and turned around with her claws out, ready to kill whoever or whatever made that sound; her face a contorted mass of anger and rage beyond human comprehension until she saw that it was her beloved Asmodeus, that he came home to her.

When she turned she was ready to kill him, yet he never flinched and never seemed to be scared of her, and it never occurred to her that she didn't take him along when she left and he shouldn't have even known where she was, and yet he did, and then he looked bored and went back to preening.

She could not have explained why, because she still hated pets, but she was especially happy to see him for some reason and rushed over to pick him up and then she brought him to her face and asked him if he wanted some milk, and then, smiling at him, she turned his body left and right with hers as if they were dancing partners.

He still hated the touch of any human being, and didn't see why she should be the exception because for him, there was nothing special about her, certainly nothing endearing if he were looking for that when he found her; but when he found her, he saw the darkness in her soul and knew she was a witch, someone that was already evil and capable of doing the things that he could never have done without her, and though she didn't know it; she needed him much more than he needed her.

There were times where she was asleep, or he thought she was, he would go out into the woods and search for the things she needed for what she was going to do because he knew what she was going to do, long before it was even an idea in her simple little mind.

As she danced with him, her unwilling partner was imagining that he could take out his claws and show her what that was like, cut deeply into the soft tissue of her nose and cheeks, then rip into her throat as much as he could manage before she would pull away or throw him across the room to escape him.

In his minds eye, at that moment that was what he saw, her face shredded, her blood covering his face and the fur around his neck and chest as she fell to the ground, though he knew that even if he did, it wouldn't have killed her because she was very powerful, but he also knew that it would each her to think twice about rubbing her nose against his and thinking it's cute and that he was enjoying it too.

After a few moments of him thinking that way, she must have sensed something was wrong, there was something she smelled that was dead, she looked around her then, trying to figure out where it came from and thought a demon had found her and was sneaking up on her; she held the cat out on front of her as if he were her weapon and then laughed when she realized that, she hugged him closer then and that was when she smelled him and knew he was dead, and then she put him down, not so gently.

He landed on all fours and his tail began to twitch again, he turned from her and walked away into one of the tunnels that she hadn't explored yet, and she made a note to see where it led later when she was done here.

As she watched him walk away, she told him, "I shouldn't be surprised to find you here!" she told him, "After all! You were always here when I needed you before!" she added, she was trying to apologize to him without actually saying it, trying to soothe his nerves because he was just a cat after all, and because she needed him and they both knew it.

He did look back at her, once, his expression said that he was bored, but he was waiting for her to finish what she was saying, he hoped she understood that he still didn't like her and would not let any other human get as close to him as she did.

She laughed as she watched him, nervously; she was trying to imagine him with hurt feelings and it just didn't fit; she tried to imagine why she got that feeling but forgot about it a few moments later because she was so happy that he was there, even if he wasn't so happy about it.

Then she turned and walked further into the cavern, and she didn't see him; but she could hear him walking behind her, she noticed that the further they got away from that cavern with all the feces and litter, the better it smelled, even though she was certain that she was far underground at this point.

Still, wherever they went that day, as long as they were underground, or at least, out of the sun; they could not escape that feeling of "winter cold dampness" and a musty odor from somewhere close by that made it feel as though the area was covered in wet mud, it reminded her of a very large grave for some reason; but she didn't mind that at all, she was at home with the dead.

But then it started to get warmer in there, by then, she wasn't how far underground they were, but now she could hear water flowing nearby, a strong current of a fresh water stream that slowed down in a bend near where she was, the water was warm and not very deep though.

It made no sense when she thought about it, and she couldn't explain why she felt that way; and yet she felt as though the water sensed her confusion and that was why it would quickly go from shallow to very deep with no warning, and fast enough that it could knock you off the rocks and then carry you away.

As far as they were into the tunnels, she knew that they would not see another soul down there and began to shed her clothes, absently taking them off and dropping them into a bag on her shoulder.

She was practicing holding onto her human face as she walked, it was getting easier for her to do for longer periods of time, and when there was enough light, she would look down at her body because she knew that was where she showed her age these days.

Not being able to stop herself, though she didn't want to; she looked down at her breasts and then remembered how Tomas liked looking at them, he would stare at them from across the table when they were eating dinner, and a lot of other times she would catch him looking down there when he stood over her, and that always amused her.

She hated the bustier, what she called a torture device, and other things that they made her wear in those days, and she was glad to see that they were in fashion here; there were some women that had the body that she thought they might have been wearing one, but she didn't think they were, she thought it was how they were built.

At the same time, she kind of missed them now, the way they elevated her breasts until it seemed as though they were going to explode out of it, but as much as they were sagging now, she thought she needed the help, they had no life or tone to them anymore and she felt that it was gravity; that it had killed whatever life was in them before.

"What else should I have expected after almost two hundred years!" she said and then stopped trying to look at them, she was never a mother and had no use for them anyway, unless she needed the favors of a man; but she never understood their fascination with them.

They finally came to a larger opening, it seemed to be the focal point for all of the other caves and tunnels, it was so wide and so many tunnels came to that point from all directions that it made her think of Grand Central Station.

She put her bag down and brought out some candles and other things that she'd brought with her for what she was going to do next.

It made sense, the way the tunnels led through this area, that most of the spirits and wandering souls that she could use would also be using these tunnels to travel unseen across the underbelly of the city; they likely hated the sunlight as well because it reminded them of what they once were; and most people would never see them unless they laid their eyes directly on them and in the right light; and then then most people would pretend that they didn't see anything that wasn't ordinary, that was out of simple fear, with that in mind; she used "Grand Central" as her own focal point, and it worked well for her.

Now, most people believe that you can just go anywhere and practice witchcraft and black magic anywhere, and maybe that's true to a certain degree; just like a lot of people know that you don't need a church to pray to God, or even just to speak to him, he spoke to us on a rock after all.

But for some things, the really detailed and intricate ceremonies for example; the things you wanted to make sure you got right because it was something that you really wanted or desired; something that you just had to have, or see done to your enemy, someone's untimely death, sudden wealth or suddenly being cured of an illness that should have taken your life; and for those important things she needed to purify the air first, and she brought several candles for that reason.

She also had several kinds of scented oils and incense to chase away any of the wrong kind of spirits that might be lingering around, ready to attack the unprepared or insufficiently trained; even as she stood there she could hear some of them running by, scurrying like rats towards the hint of escape from their world.

With that in mind, she went to work quickly and quietly; humming to herself as she went along, but then she'd done this so many times before that now she was doing most of it without even thinking about it.

Then she had to move some rocks around until she found a place that she could use as an altar and placed more candles there and then she lit those immediately while some of the others weren't ready yet or it wasn't time to light them.

She placed three of the largest candles there and spread the rest out in various places as she went along, and though it might have seemed that they were randomly cast out there, there actually was a purpose to each candle and the position it was in.

Each candle was selected for its color and the fragrance that it emitted while it burned and what it was made of; some of those she made herself because she couldn't find exactly what she needed to make things work for her, and then she found that when she made them they worked better, the spell was stronger and more effective.

The next thing she did was to take out some white, chalky powder and spread it out, she drew a pentagram on the ground and some other symbols around that, and the powder might have looked innocent enough, but the main ingredient was human bones, ground into this fine powder; and if she wasn't as careful as she was and accidently inhaled some of that white powder there would be a good chance she would go mad and eventually kill herself.

This was also mixed in with some dried blood that was not as old, and some of that was Susan's blood, but then she began to chant, and her body swayed with her incantation as she worked.

It seemed as though something in the air shifted or changed then; it was not easy to see before, the only light in there was provided by the candles she brought after all, but now, she could not even see the walls around or nor the ceiling above her at that time.

Then it got even darker, as if someone tossed a silken veil over her and the room, and then another until it was almost impossible to see, she kept working and hardly noticed the change at all; it was what she expected to happen, but also because she was so intent on getting this right and what she was doing to make it that way.

She reached into her bag and took out more large, black candles that weren't as large as the ones she placed on her altar, and they were also a bit thinner, but she placed those in each of the five points of her pentagram and lit them in reverse order.

At that same moment, she couldn't see where he was, but she could hear Asmodeus as he began to purr, softly, but not contentedly because this was for pure evil and he was doing his part; it almost sounded as though he was growling as he stood to the side and never moved, he kept his focus on one point in the pentagram and waited for her to do what she needed to do.

When she first began to fully realize her power and how she might use it for her own means, she wanted to talk to Mamma about it, but she was sure that she really was dead because it had been so long and no word at all, without even so much as a rumor that they were in the region, and she thought to try and call out her mother but had no idea how or where she was that she might do that.

She felt herself being drawn in the darker parts of that world, and though she tried not to think of it that way, she could do nothing about how it felt in her soul, she kept telling herself that good intent mean that she was at least trying to do right, but she couldn't convince herself and gave into it.

On a rumor of a chance that she might gain some new knowledge, she went deep into the Balkans, she wasn't sure what she was looking for but she felt the pull and followed it, she was hoping to find better ways to make her spells and potions, enchantments that she needed to "further her cause" and knew that certain evil demands certain names and formulas, and she knew she couldn't get those at home.

Why she went in that direction is anyone's guess, but in her mind she thought it was something that came from Mamma, but that was maybe because she wanted to believe it was, but she kept going, when her horse died she continued on foot, climbing over mountains and through valleys, never stopping because she knew she wasn't there yet, but she was supposed to find something or see something, she wasn't sure, but kept getting a feeling that made her feel that was why she was there.

While she was on her trek, she discovered that there were tools that you could use for certain spells, and they could be used for both good and evil, but for the "darkest of evils" as she called them sometimes, these tools, if she found the right one and used it properly would boost the effect or power of the spell she cast, making it a lot more effective if she harnessed it right.

There were also, always those risks, if she rushed herself, or if she used the wrong amount of something or didn't cover all of the options presented with that spell; she might end up bound by the spell instead of her enemy, it would backfire on her.

She also learned that there are certain skulls, based mostly on their shape and how they were killed would be of help to her as well; she'd heard about the tribes in Africa that ate their enemies in order to absorb their knowledge and power, and then she heard about something called a "skull collector" that piqued her interest, but it turned out to be more of a "bounty hunter" that reinforced curses or something and she didn't think she could use it.

Still, the idea of an invincible "monkey" or whatever it was from the descriptions she was given, was one she thought about a lot, she wondered how it was made and where she might get one of her own but gave up when people stopped talking about it with her.

She brought four of those skulls with her, and she placed them in strategic positions across the room and making sure that all four of them were facing south.

The skulls she found had been from a collection that someone else had amassed over the years, she passed on others when she found these and would have likely brought more if she could have carried them but she knew the ones she found had power because she felt it when she picked them up.

When she found these four, they were of special interest to her as she felt two of them calling to her, the others from one of the enemies that they had conquered, and she thought it was long ago because of the condition of the skulls.

She placed two more on the outer edges of the area that she would be using and then was careful to stay within her boundaries that only she could see and was aware of, then she went to the other edge and placed two more skulls there, the one on her left was an old Spaniard, an officer that was slain in battle when his skull was crushed in from the right side of his head, and three of his front teeth were broken.

The other was a murder victim, she was killed by a serial killer who was just starting off on that path; his first victim, this was an innocent woman found outside in the wrong place and at the wrong time, and yet the evil that was done to her; the way she was raped, murdered and mutilated, the evil remained in the fabric of her skull, Esmeralda could feel it whenever she touched it, which at first was often as she took delight in the poor woman's suffering.

This would be the last time she would use that one though, when she was done here, she would crush it and grind it into powder and use that for something else, if the pandemonium that sometimes broke out at times like this didn't blow everything away from her in the process it would be "boosted" after this and the powder would be stronger.

When she placed the Spaniard officer's skull there, she felt that it was representing her authority, telling any that were lingering that she was in control and if they stayed too long would be taken in by it and subject to her will, she was warning them because she didn't need them this time.

The other skull was to remind her to take her time and carefully carry out her plans and make no mistakes, she needed to focus in everything she did within that circle, using exact formulas and incantations and the correct time while facing in the right direction, calling the name of the demon or demigod that she did want to come there and do her bidding.

But while she was in the Balkans, as she came over one huge mountain that took her several days to pass, she found herself wandering in a desert, she had no idea where she was at the time, had been lost for about three days but she felt she was still being drawn out that way, that it was not her that chose this direction nor was it her that was pushing her feet this way either, someone else was in control, and she only hoped that they were not there to enslave or injure her in any way.

As she continued on, she ran out of water and hadn't eaten in a few days, she was starting to hallucinate when she stubbed her toe on something hidden in the soft sand at her feet; and though it was just a knife, and she couldn't see all of it because most of its surface was still submerged in the sand, she felt that it was special, and that holding in t her hand would give her immense power somehow.

Maybe it was her delirium, but she thought that it knew her name and called to her, that it was hidden in the sand and waiting all these years for her, not just anyone, but her to find it there, that it wasn't out in the open where anyone could see it, and that maybe if she weren't as out of her mind as she was at the time she would have turned and gone back home, no better off than before she left and truly and utterly disappointed that she'd found nothing for all of her troubles.

When she found it, she was at the base of the mountains again, though just prior to that she thought she was further away from them and lost to the world because she couldn't see them from where she was, but as she got closer to it; she felt as though she was right where she was supposed to be all along.

As she looked around her, she could see other ruins of old structures that were worn away by years of dryness and neglect, and it had clearly been picked clean by scavengers and people looking for lost civilizations that came here and left long ago, taking anything that was of value and yet they somehow missed this knife because it was meant to be hers.

Some of that stuff was being sold as artifacts in the open market because they didn't know the power or value they held, some of the more obvious precious stones and other items would find their way to private collectors and museums all over the world, but no one bothered with any of the skulls, and had all been left to rot in the sun, even the commander, maybe they felt the evil within and gave them a wide berth, she had no idea but it was their loss and her gain.

When she managed to find the strength to actually touch the knife, she instantly felt the evil in its inner body, she thought that it felt as though it was forged in hell and made magical by the devil, and that it cut and stabbed its way through a thousand victims to find its way to her, its one true master was here to claim it.

She felt as though it was waiting all those years for someone with a black enough heart and soul to use it properly, and she knew that she was just the woman for that task and was ready to start that moment, but she was all alone.

As she sat there, thinking about all of that, everything suddenly flashed a white so bright that she had to shield her eyes and it still stunned her for a few moments; she could see nothing, and kept waving her hands in front of her face as she tried.

As the brightness slowly receded, she started hearing noises, the sounds of shouting and fighting, yet there was no one in front of her and no one fighting, and then she saw them; first it was one or three or four men, they were all violently arguing about something.

But as her vision cleared a little more, she could see more and more of them, those first few men were joined by a thousand more, and there were even more on the hills around them, anxiously and impatiently awaiting their turn to join the fight.

All around her now was the clash of steel against steel, men trying their very best to kill each other; and even though some of those men were very close to where she stood, once in a while a stray arrow narrowly missed her, or passed right through her without inflicting any damage or pain, nothing those men did would hurt her, and she never felt a thing.

She sat back to watch, thinking that this was fun and exciting, entertaining even as she watched and studied the things that men did to each other in the heat of battle; and then she noticed these two men, they were from opposing armies but both seemed to be especially adept at killing and maiming their way through the fight without so much as a scratch on any part of them.

One to the other, they fought and worked their way towards each other, though she didn't think it was their plan, that it just happened that way; and in a few more swipes of their swords would soon be close enough and would face each other.

She thought they were Asian in their features and the way they dressed, with primitive armor covering as much of them as they could manage, the other side seemed to be waring nothing more than a simple loincloth and carried a shield and a spear or sword, and for some reason, she thought they were the invaders; they seemed to be more aggressive.

All around those two, men slashed at each other and were being killed, they cut off arms or legs, and every so often a head would roll past the blood that was pooling and soaking into the ground; with the promise fresh blood on the way.

Yet those two seemed oblivious to everyone but whomever they were engaged in combat with, sometimes two or three men at the same time; yet they couldn't be taken down by anyone, and then finally, the one with the armor pulled off his helmet and tossed it aside, the heat of the battle and the sun high overhead was getting to him, clouding his judgement.

Even as he threw his helmet, at the same time he thrust his sword into abdomen of another man that was charging at him; then he turned and saved the life of one of his men by cutting into the middle of the back of the man that was sneaking up behind him, intending to cut off his head.

He fell forward as his sword was shattered and then the other man pulled out his own sword and raised it high above his head and was about to bring it down on his enemy, the armored one, Chi Luu, sliced the back of his enemies leg open when he tried to kill him, then he helped his friend to kill the man as he writhed on the ground.

His enemy was holding onto the back of his leg and screaming at him, that it was unfair, a sneak attack because he could not face him and defeat him, but those were his last words as they both stabbed him repeatedly even long after he stopped moving.

The defender was almost naked now, most of his clothing torn away as he fought, his chest and arms were covered with the blood of many others; and then they were facing each other at last, it was inevitable they said, because one of them turned when he made a killing and the other was turning towards him at the same time.

They began to circle around each other as they both looked for an opening, carefully stepping both over and on the dead and dying because neither wanted to fall and give his enemy an opening. There must have been well over four thousand men on that battlefield, and yet when these two; the best killers from either army faced each other everyone else stopped to watch and cheer on their champion, some quietly hoping that their champion would win and that would be the end of it, no more reason to fight, others couldn't wait for this part to be over so that they could continue the carnage they wrought.

Chi Luu then took off the rest of his armor then, he didn't want his enemy to have a speed advantage over him in a fight like this, he tossed everything aside as his enemy watched and waited, though he never took his eyes off him.

Instead, he aced from left to right and then back again, circling and waving his blade in the air as he built up his anger and frustration as he waited for the chance to kill his enemy and end the battle.

Finally, they were both ready and the fight started, Chi Luu was quicker and leapt at his enemy with both feet, he struck him square in the chest and knocking him to the ground, he was smaller and needed that kind of advantage over his taller and more muscular enemy.

His momentum carried him past his enemy when he fell though; not what he expected and as he fell back, he struck out at Chi as he passed over him, both men inflicting wounds, and though Chi's were deep, they were mostly superficial; he sliced out with a very sharp knife that was hidden in his waistband.

The knife gleamed a brilliant white when he pulled it out, and though it didn't seem to bother anyone else out there, it was so bright that it hurt her eyes; as if she was looking directly into the sun, and she began to sneeze until she finally got it under control at last.

At that moment she felt another change, imperceptible to most but she sure that she felt it when it happened, it felt as though it took its power from the sun and that was why it was so brilliantly white, why it hurt her eyes so badly that she still saw a small white square on the edge of her eyeball that was hard to ignore; it gave that power to the man that wielded it.

She stood transfix; fascinated by the spectacle as it transpired before her unbelieving eyes, she saw Chi as he rolled over and came to a fighting stance when he turned to face his enemy once more, ignoring the blood as it flowed from his wound and the pain that was nothing to him.

He got himself ready, stood on his toes and bent his knees as he was coiled to spring at the other man, he leaned forward on his hands and growled at his enemy.

His enemy jumped to his feet as soon as he felt the blade slash at his sternum and then passed just inches from his face; he was angry because he didn't see the blade until it was too late, and it almost cost him.

As it was, the blade did nick his chin, and just above his right eye, he felt that one did more damage than he thought that it should have, it was not that deep after all; he was used to the hot sting that he would have expected from such a wound, but this one felt as though it was burning its way into and through his body.

Reaching down gently, he touched the wound carefully, and his hand burned where he touched it, and in the places on his palm where he could see the blood were hotter than the rest of his hand.

Then he looked at Chi and snarled like a wild animal in his rage because he knew that he had painted his blade with some poison because he knew that he could not defeat him in a fair fight. He rose up and took a spear that was dropped near where he stood; it was broken, but he didn't care as he pointed the broken, sharp end at his advancing enemy, his momentum carried him forward until the shaft was thrust into his gut and then they were eye to eye, the end of the stick went straight through to his spine and then it slipped and bounced all the way to the left before going all the way through.

They both stopped then, fir what seemed like an eternity, the men on both sides of the conflict suddenly quiet because no one had a clue as to who was winning; it was eerie how deadly silent the world became at that moment; one minute the clash of steel on steel, the next moment it seemed as though even the wind was afraid to make a sound; it made her wonder who these men were and why they would have any import in her world.

The man holding the spear could not believe his luck at dealing such a deadly blow, he started to raise his hands triumphantly when he saw the look on Chi's face; he expected to see shock and surprise, to hear him plead for his life; as if that would have done him any good, instead he saw that Chi was not yet ready to quit the battle, that he still had some fight left in him.

Chi grabbed the shaft of the spear where it was closest to his gut and pulled hard, drawing the spear further into his stomach and bringing his enemy closer as he was shocked and wouldn't let go.

He didn't know what else to do, this was madness and he didn't know what else to do, he stared back incredulously at Chi as he held onto the spear, as if letting him pull it all the way through was admitting defeat and he couldn't give him that.

Then Chi took that moment to raise the knife once more and slashed the throat of his enemy and then watched as his lolled back and the skin of his neck tore away as he fell.

For a few more tense moments, no one moved, or made a sound, it was as if everyone was holding their breath and waiting for confirmation that it was real, that was when he fell forward; the blood flowing freely from his neck a he died with a shocked and surprised expression on his face.

Then one of the men stepped forward and dealt Chi that fatal blow, he bashed in the side of his head with a large hammer and then he died a moment later when someone else ran a sword through his back and through his lungs before it cut his heart; and then all hell broke loose and she watched the rest of that battle from her ringside seat.

But she did take notice that they both died with wounds that were mostly inflicted upon each other, the bashing of his head aside, Chi had several large wounds by then and was hemorrhaging a lot of blood, leaving puddles of it as he moved.

The battle raged on for about a week and showed no signs of letting up, and after a while she got bored with watching them as they maimed and destroyed each other, eventually she fell asleep while waiting for the outcome, the clash of steel and shield music to her ears instead of annoying to her, the sound of wild animals killing each other in any way that they could.

The armies fought long and hard into that last night, and in the morning, when the smoke cleared enough that she could see anything, there were thousands of men lying on the battleground, only a handful of men were left; she wasn't sure if either side could be counted as the winner, but it was clear that the men that died there went through hell before they died, there was nothing else that cold be done with them.

Then, time seemed to speed up or something, because either from the scavengers or the passage of time, she watched them go from freshly dead to rotted carcasses, just moments later they were broken down so much that they were absorbed into the ground; their weapons rusted and corroded way beyond recognition or salvation as the sounds of that battle faded away with the wind that gusted by.

She heard someone calling her name then, and though she knew that she was alone, she looked around her once more to make sure that there really was no one out there before she returned to her gem in the sand.

The sand beneath her feet was so hot that it burned her feet through her sandals; yet she could not stop herself, even though she heard sounds of battle coming back and then fading away; echoing all around her.

The glow of the knife was blinding her once more as it shown brightly in her face, yet this time she could not shield her eyes nor turn her face away, this time it burned itself into the back of her skull, she thought if she looked away this time, or tried to cover her eyes it would disappear and then would be lost to her forever.

After what seemed like an eternity, she managed to look down at her feet because they were smoldering, she thought that was hot as the sand was, they should have been on fire by now, she thought it was safe then and reached down with her bare hand and picked it up.

For a moment, the saw that it was white hot and thought it would burn her hand but was very surprised that it was cool to the touch, she lifted the blade, and instantly saw more of its history in vivid detail.

It wasas if the entire existence of the blade flashed before her; letting her know what she was dealing with, or possibly warning her about what lie ahead if she continued and claimed it for her own, and she was fair game for it either way at this point.

Now she could see that it was forged and created for evil right from the start, the man commissioned to design and fashion it was murdered for his hard work, though he did exactly what was asked of him, they didn't want anyone to know about the knife or who owned it.

It was made for a man who was a professional assassin, he knew that when he was asked to build it but didn't care, his money was good and he didn't care what he was going to do with the blade or any of the swords and other weapons that he made were used for, he knew that if he didn't take the commission that someone else would and his family would go hungry.

The man that killed him was a thief, and he was also murdered in a most hideous manner; he was disemboweled while still living and his body found floating in the river, he was barely alive and it appeared as though the fish had been feeding on his open wounds, but he died as they were pulling him from the water with no strength to speak and the knife was lost.

Eventually, the assassin found it and took it back, and then he was killed in another war; the legend of the blade grew that way, sometimes in battles that were fought over the possession of it because of the power that was said it held within, its history, the blood that was spilled both by it and for it were legendary.

"Now you are all mine!" she said as she caressed its surface lovingly, then she started dancing in circles because she felt so joyous, "Your power is all mine too!" she said, she felt it killing and shedding blood that way for years upon years, and she could swear that it still dripped that blood as she held it in her hands, though that was long ago.

She looked closely at the side of the knife for the first time and she thought she could see that faces of its victims reflected back at her, as if their very souls were trapped within its cold surface forever, woven into the fabric of the steel now, and one of the things that gave it so much power.

Then she ran her hand along the edge of the blade carefully, and though it was razor sharp, it didn't cut her, she looked at the blade lovingly and noted that it was bent at an angle, almost like a boomerang though she knew it wasn't meant to be thrown that way, and she wondered about that.

She thought that maybe it was designed that way to cut under the armor that the other man would be wearing, to work its way through it and cut him, but that was just a guess, she had no reason to believe that it was true.

There was another thought that came to her one night, she was asleep and dreaming of nothing special, when a voice broke through her thoughts and told her that she needed to know something about the knife that she was so enamored with now, and as odd as it sounded, she thought it was the knife itself that was delivering the message.

"You must know!" she was told, "Though you know the good of it; those things that you like, the power that you feel from my surface, and you have already risked your fingers on my edge!" she was told.

"Yes" she said, and then laughed at the absurdity of this, and had to remind herself that she was dreaming and it didn't need to make sense; "So, what is it that you feel that you must tell me!" she asked, expecting anything but what she heard.

"It is the one blade that can kill you!" she heard and then nothing for several moments, until her heart hammered in her chest, and then it went silent again until the next beat.

She jumped from her bed then, and took the blade from the nightstand next to her bed, as she put her feet on the ground, she heard the echoes of that conversation and then looked down at the blade once more; as if it was the first time she'd ever seen it.

As she held it, she felt the power of it thrum through her hands and ran through her body, she felt that it was giving her new knowledge, but that as it gave things to her; it also took from her, knowledge and power traded for knowledge and power, it felt odd to her and a little frightening, but it was exciting too; and made her feel stronger for it so she didn't mind at all.

But now, she was ready at last and took that knife from her waistband where she always kept it but she needed some of that power, she started turning counter-clockwise and pointed out from the corners as she spoke, whispering and invoking her demons while chanting softly in a long forgotten language.

Though this part had to be done exactly right she also did this part out of habit, without thinking about it too much and yet making sure that she got the names and points right, that her body was in the right direction and she spoke the right words because anything nearby would be able to swoop in and take over if she did it wrong, said the wrong name at the wrong point or even mispronounced a single word in the spell, they would be able to take control of her and she would not see it coming or be able to fight it off, then she would be at its mercy and under its control.

As she spoke, her words grew in their volume and intensity and she felt a powerful wave of high voltage electricity surge through her and give her even more energy and strength, she never felt it this strongly before in her life; she closed her eyes to take it all in, every pore of her being was open to the sensation, she raised her hands high and stretched out as much as she could, reaching to the skies above the cavern.

When she felt that she was ready, she went back to her altar and pulled on a black robe that went from head to toe if she wore the hood, which she didn't, and left the front open because she wasn't worried about being naked, but that was also more of a formality.

She lit two candles in front of her, the large white one first and then the black one, she was making sure that there were no doubts as to who was in charge that dayin the way that she lit them and what she whispered as she did it.

There were certain "white" powers that she would need for this and she was paying them tribute; she knew they would never come no matter how she summoned them if she didn't do that part right, and she got a sense that she did right away, she was so happy that she allowed herself a slight smile as she worked.

But she also had them under her control now; and as she spoke, Asmodeus stretched out slowly and then lay on his belly, by then he was bored and gave a quiet yawn, stretching out his front paws as he watched her with detached interest.

Most of his part in this was finished, a few more details that he'd need to wait for, and he knew that, but he was bored waiting for his part and fell asleep.

Then a fire sprang out of the rock on the ground in front of her, first just a spark, and then two that flashed low in the dark; it looked as though there were two pieces of rock being struck together to spark a fire but there was no one holding the rocks and you couldn't see anything but the spark, and yet she continued as if that was what she expected.

It started smoldering, then a small flame rose up and grew until it spiraled about three feet off the ground and stayed there as if it was watching her and waiting instructions.

Asmodeus sat up then and was paying attention, the hair on his back was standing up straight now, as if the air around him was charged with static electricity though it didn't seem to hurt him.

She was watching the flame, and though there was nothing on the ground to burn, it was clear at its base as if natural gas from the center of the earth chose that time and place to gently pour out and pay her a visit, then it rose about a foot higher and began to pulse lighter and then darker for a few moments.

Leaning back, she raised her hands high again and began to chant once more, not loudly, but as she spoke a mist began to form on the walls around her, it slid down to the ground and joined together as it slithered low to the ground until it all came together with the flame.

Then the room became even darker at that point; smoke began emanating from her then, pouring out of her nostrils and her ears, it reached the other smoke and twirled around, mingling together and creating something from the nothing that was there a moment ago.

Soft hisses and small flashes of light came forth as though two sides were battling for control, this went on for several moments, continuing until a shadowy form began to take shape in the middle of the pentagram.

It got even darker and then it was as if a curtain was parted or something, she got a sense that something opened and a when it did, what stood before her stepped through and into this one; it slowly stepped out of the flames as it solidified.

It might have been a man at one time, or a statue of a man, it was now all dark and gritty as if it were formed from the sand, and indeed it was; then it opened its eyes and began to search the room, and though he couldn't move at the moment; he could speak, and was trying to do that but was struggling as he hadn't spoken in a thousand years, he was trying to understand why he was summoned.

He was muscular, very tall and naked, and though he had only the soft edges of a face that was eroded away, the eyes were clear and that made him more frightening because the rest of his face, his nose and mouth and any other features were worn away by time; but none of that mattered to her, she wasn't bringing him there to kiss him and hold hands.

Speaking in several old languages, he tried to speak to her once more; struggling as he tried to find the right words before she finally understood what he was trying to say.

Getting impatient while she waited for him, she spoke a few words to him to help him along; his mouth began to mimic and copy the movements of her words until he got it and they started chanting the same thing in unison; though the voice was far from human and sounded as though he was grinding huge pieces of granite together.

The sound it made and by its expression, she could tell that it was painful for it to speak, but again; she didn't care, she kept at it long enough until she was sure that the spell was set in motion, now it sounded so dry it made you want to run to the fountain drink an ocean of water, and it still might not be enough.

She stepped back from the altar and began to "un-bless" the air as she walked around with more of that dry powder, remembering to cover her mouth to make sure she didn't inhale it, she never took her eyes off that form of a man as he waited for her to tell him what to do.

Then she started walking around the pentagram, going counterclockwise, each time making sure that she didn't break the lines of her pentagram, she took out a flask and took a long drink of the inky black fluid it held.

She fund the flask about a year and a half ago, and thinking about how she found it made her smile, she was wandering around at three thirty in the morning in Hollywood, near Western and Santa Monica and she was not getting a lot of business at that late hour, it was especially cold that night as well.

But she probably hadn't yet earned enough money to go home yet, and what intrigued Esmeralda more than anything about her was the flask that she took out, every so often she would take a drink from it and then hide it in her clothing, Esmeralda thought it to be alcohol, in an attempt to keep warm.

Every time she raised it, Esmeralda felt a draw to the flask, as if it were calling to her, same as the knife had in the desert, absently, she caressed the handle as she watched the hooker getting drunk.

After a few moments of that, she couldn't tell you anything about the woman, other than that she was female, about five feet tall and very slightly built but not where she'd seem to be anemic or sick, even though she kept wiping her nose as if she had a cold.

Esmeralda tried to look closer at her, trying to decide if she was a witch herself or not to be in possession of such a powerful tool, but she quickly realized that she wasn't a witch; that she had no power and no business with it, Esmeralda decided that she was simply holding it for her until she got there and claimed it for herself.

As she got closer she was able to see more of her, and she saw a reed this woman from Chickasaw Mississippi that was chased off those streets when the sheriff was trying to get re-elected and she found herself here one day, she liked the weather and the customers were cleaner and not so mean to her all the time.

Except for the occasional beating she took which she thought of as a risk and part of her trade, it wasn't all bad here; but lately the customers had been staying away and the cupboards were getting bare, and the weather was getting colder too, the jacket she wore to "entice" the customers wasn't warm at all and it was getting worn out as well, and to add insult, she couldn't pay her rent and was kicked out of her tiny crappy little apartment.

She was even drunker now, and the cold wasn't bothering her as much, she didn't see Esmeralda as she closed in on her because she was thinking about her mother and then she began to cry because if her mother was still alive and knew what she was doing they would both die of shame.

If she were not so preoccupied with her thoughts as she walked, she might have noticed Esmeralda following her because she made no effort to conceal herself as she followed, or she might have seen the flask, for the first time since she found it was glowing softly in her hand, this gave Esmeralda a clear path to follow, a beacon in the dark.

When she found the flask, it was sitting in the window of a pawn shop that she passed almost every day and had never noticed until that day that it flashed as she passed, and it caught her eye. When she looked closer, not knowing exactly what flashed at her, she was looking for glass or some sort or jewelry and almost kept going when it didn't happen again, but then she saw it and immediately wanted it.

Though she was working and someone was calling to her, she ignored him and went inside, it was sitting there between a violin and a snare drum on display, and when she asked the clerk for it, he looked at her suspiciously because he thought she had no money, then he said, "Fifty dollars!" with a slight smile on his face, knowing by the looks of her and because he'd seen her on the street, he was fairly certain she wouldn't have and she would leave his store so he would work with the real customers.

She opened her bag and there was exactly fifty dollars there, money for food that she couldn't afford to spend; and even knowing that he jacked up the price, anyone else might have paid half that but she paid it anyway without trying to bargain for it as she should have.

Though she didn't understand it, when he handed it to her at last, she felt its power, she felt as though she'd been searching for an old friend for such a long time and now her efforts were rewarded, she almost cried as she left the store, caressing it lovingly and holding onto it, caring for it until this day when her true master came calling for it.

At the moment she was thinking about the last time she saw her mother, just before they chased her away, it was something that she swore to her mother that she would never forget; and yet, by her present state and living conditions, she obviously had forgotten that message and a lot more.

"I did forget momma, I backslid a bit, but that's over now, I'm going to clean up and straighten out my life, I promise momma, I'm done with this and will make it better momma, I will, you'll see!" she said, and though she meant it, and it was what she wanted to do, she knew even then that it was too late and the forgotten promise didn't matter anymore.

"I forgot momma!" she said and began to cry, "I know...I know!" she cried, "But I promise momma, I'll get clean and straighten out my life, I promise momma, but please don't look at me like that!" she said, "Please momma, please don't turn away from me momma, I can't stand it when you do that!" she pleaded.

She didn't know that he mother died long ago of a broken heart when she saw her daughter on the corner one day, it was the same day the sheriff escorted her out of town, and he never bothered to tell her that her mother was in the critical ward at that moment because he didn't want her to stick around; he took her to the edge of town and told her to stay away, or being escorted out of town would be the least of her troubles; she kept talking to the shadows as if her mother was there.

Then she either heard footsteps or she sensed her back there but she turned and saw Esmeralda as she walked towards her, and maybe because she was drunk; maybe because she wanted to see her mother so badly that she looked at the deadly face of Esmeralda and thought it was her mother, come to claim her daughter home, take her off the streets and clean her up one more time, "I'm ready momma!" she cried to Esmeralda, "Take me home momma, I'll be good, you'll see!" she whispered as Esmeralda closed in on her.

Esmeralda was surprised she was called "momma" and took a step back for a moment, then she stepped forward again and spoke a few quiet words to the poor girl who instantly feel asleep and never woke up again, Esmeralda caught her body as she slumped forward and dragged her back to the alley they'd just passed, she searched her pockets, found an old gum wrapper with a solid wad of gum inside, a key and three one dollar bills and then the flask; "This flask was not meant for you dearie!" she told the girl, "It has too much power for you, for one that is ignorant of the power within and how it must be used!" she told her, "Or even what it was made for!" and then she poured the liquid out over the girl's body and then left her there.

She couldn't wait to get back and play with her new toy, and all the way home the flask kept telling her that she did the right thing, that it was a misuse of its power to be in her hands and now that she was holding onto it, there was no limit to what they could do together.

Looking at it closely; she could now see that something was intricately cut into the surface of it, the arts that glowed in the low light; she wondered if it was always there and she'd just noticed it or, as it felt; that it just decided that she was ready and let her see it, she followed the design and discovered that it was cut inside of the flask as well, and wondered at how that was done.

The way it was cut, if you followed it from one end to the other; it would seem as though you were following the dragon into the flask, and she wondered if she followed it in, would there be a way to return once she was ready to leave or would she become trapped inside, it was something that she felt a strong curiosity about but not strong enough that she was going to follow it to try and find out.

She thought that would also mean that if you poured the proper liquid into the flask, the blood of an innocent perhaps, that the power of the dragon would then be absorbed inside of her, it would be hers to command after that, and dragons were always thought of as a mystical source of magic and powers that gave the right handler or owner unlimited power over their enemies if she harnessed it properly.

As she looked at the surface, there were four large heads cut into the side of the flask, they were spread out just enough so that when you held the flask properly, your fingers would be on each of those heads, maybe that was what would protect you from the bad side of dealing with its power; there was also a spot for the thumb, to complete the circuit of your grip and the cap made a fifth head which gave you the power of all five when you drank from it that way.

She mixed her potion and carefully poured it into the flask, and as she did, she felt a surge of power that was so strong, it was as if she'd grabbed live wires in her hands and was trying to connect them together, she felt it surge through her and then it burned into her soul.

There were plenty of times that she examined the flask from top to bottom, always making sure she didn't get sucked inside of it; and yet, this time when she looked, there was another carving; this one was on the back, it was a carving on an intense battle between devils and angels; and it seemed to be particularly bloody; she thought it must have taken a lifetime to carve all of that in such great detail on the side of the flask.

Now she was standing at the base of her altar, she put the flask away and leaned back, then she called for her succubus to come to her, though she never spoke a word.

He didn't move for several moments, maybe because he couldn't, yet; maybe because he was trying to make sure of what she wanted, but most would win the bet that he did know exactly what she wanted and was trying a way not to comply with her "request" which was anything but asking, even as a long dead being, a carcass it disgusted him, he was trying to find a way to refuse her if only he could.

But he was given no choice, and in truth, she didn't care a bit what he felt about it, she said all the right words and did her part to ensure that she was in control and that he could not refuse any order that she gave him, and then she saw him take a small step forward and knew that he hadn't missed the message.

Then, as she watched, he slowly started walking towards her, very stiffly at first because the muscles in his legs had not been used in ages, and once again it sounded as though gravel was grinding against gravel as it moved.

The more he moved, the easier it became for him, and as he got closer to her and the altar his muscles loosened and his movements showed he was more limber, his gait was as a normal walk now, and he made a noise then, a low moan, because he couldn't stand to be that close to her, his rest disturbed for this, but again; he had no choice and was forced to obey.

As he stood before her, he began to speak again, but this time he knew what language to use and didn't waste time, in a voice that would make you or I want to clear our throats because it sounded as though the earth was moving as he spoke.

"Who calls on me?" he said, "Who has the nerve to disturb my sleep after so many years?" he asked a little angrily, "What would you ask of me?" as if he didn't know, as if he wasn't sickened by the very idea of having to touch her and then pretend that he liked it.

"I am Esmeralda!" she answered, slowly and clearly, "Of the line of Grandura, and the witch Besthmesda, though you may know her as Lyndreika; and it is I that summoned you, are you prepared to do my bidding?" she asked him, as if that was an option. Then she slowly shrugged off her robe and laid back on top of the altar, watching him and waiting for the words to sink in.

He stood there for another moment, as if he was weighing the names she used, and then he slowly stepped forward once more; but this time an erection rose stiffly out in front of him wagged obscenely as he walked, though he showed no emotion because this was duty after all; part of the penance for his sins.

Once again, by strange coincidence, Gregor decided on that same night that he study and pursue women, stay away from men from now on; the women were so much nicer and always smelled so much better.

He loved how soft women felt, how some of them took care of themselves and how they looked, and he saw that some of them were copying the style of the character "Vampira" that he saw in one of Jeremy's books, he would have to admit that he liked that leather look with the high heeled boots.

Then he tried to remember how one vampire made another, because everyone that he killed was just dead, with no chance to ever return, but then he thought that maybe if he didn't take all their blood, that maybe that was the secret, he wanted to try and find out for himself, this was a night for experimenting.

In most of the books, he remembered that they said that you had to be bitten by someone that was "born into it" and not just pretending or imagining that he you were a vampire as he was, and the vampires that he read about had a class or distinction of their own, even the lower levels that did nothing but feed and then move on, following the darkness and pretty much obeying the vampire among them that they feared the most, he held the power.

Gregor was thinking that he missed the beaches, the things that he used to do in the daylight; walking in the park and enjoying the things that others took for granted, all those warm comforts, though he knew that he never fully appreciated them when he could have.

At that moment, he saw two lovely young women walking together and he decided to follow them, to see where they went and what they were going to do; he was drawn to them because they were young and attractive, full of life; they seemed to be having fun as they walked, oblivious to Gregor so close by and the danger he presented; they were living in the moment.

He stood in the open and they walked right past him on the street, he thought that they ignored him but they never saw him, but they gave no reaction to him as they strode past, he stood quietly in the shadows but they weren't that deep and they should have seen him out there.

Gregor stepped in behind them and matched their stride; he thought that these two would be a good place to start, he would make them his and help them to be reborn as vampires, just like in the movies. Bela Lagosi was popular at the time and though those were more conservative times; he still had a bevy of beautiful women at his beck and call, he thought that these two could be the start of his harem, he thought with a laugh.

As he walked behind them, he was checking out their clothing and though he was never a slave to fashion in his day he was aware of what women wore and what was considered proper; and as he watched these two, he wondered how long it had been that women walked the streets as near-naked as these two were, he thought for a moment that they were prostitutes but they didn't act or speak that way, "Why do they bother to put on anything at all?" he asked as he watched them walking before him.

From where he was, he could see more of them than any of the women he saw in his lifetime, and he wasn't even trying, he looked closer at them and thought they might be in their early twenties, one of them was wearing a tight skirt that kept sliding up her thighs, she reached down every few steps to pull it back down to where she liked it but it wouldn't stay there.

The skirt was probably meant to accent her legs but it left very little to the imagination, wherever they were going, they were in a hurry, yet he had no problem keeping up with them; he followed them for about another two blocks before they turned right and then went straight for a few more blocks.

"Perfect!" he thought to himself, "Not into the park or too close, and yet near enough that he felt that he knew this area now; he let them get a little further ahead of him as he listened to their conversation and it was annoying him, he kept following the clicking of their heels on the sidewalk so he wouldn't have to stare at them.

This was a fertile killing ground for him now; especially since he had to stay away from the park for a while at least, after he killed that cop in the alley they were patrolling the area more often now, roving patrols so when you thought they were gone and missed you another would pop up and you never saw them coming.

There were posters on the telephone poles and everywhere else with a vague description of him and a phone number to call if he was seen with a warning not to approach, as he was considered extremely dangerous.

He laughed at the description because it was so vague that it cold have covered anyone over the age of eighteen, as long as they were male and considered secretive or someone that didn't seem to get along with others, a loner who went out mostly at night; it was clear that they didn't know who they were looking for as even the cop that survived that night, though clearly shaken at the loss of his partner, but even he could not tell them what Gregor looked like.

They were getting a little further from him, so he stepped up his pace and got a little closer again, close enough to move in fast when the opportunity arose and he knew it would be soon because of where they were but he didn't want them to get out a scream if he couldn't surprise them, if they saw him coming before he was ready.

Now he could hear them talking about a boy they both liked, and were in friendly competition for him as they spoke, they were at that moment talking about how cute his butt was and laughing and Gregor was stuck on that, "What is cute about a man's butt?" he thought but dismissed it as girl stuff and not very important at the moment.

The one on the left was speaking then, "I really like him, but he's so serious about his music, he's in that band and say's he has no time for anything else!" she was complaining, "But I want some of his time too!" she admitted and they both laughed because of what she meant.

She didn't notice because she was laughing so hard and thinking about that, but the look on the other girl's face showed that she wished that he had time for her as well, he seemed to be popular with the girls they knew.

"While I think he's cute too, and being a drummer...well, you know what they say about that driving beat, that rhythm!" she said, and again they laughed, "But that band stuff won't last, they always break up when they are sounding so good, one guy gets jealous of the other guys because he's not as cute, or older, or his attitude puts them off and he blames the others for his shortcomings, something always happens, the lead singer gets a new girlfriend who takes up his time, or she doesn't like someone in the band and they fight!" she said, "What will he do then?" she asked.

"You have to think about your future and if its with him, then what are you going to do then?" she said, "Because he sure ain't going to be thinking about you and those kinds of things, you can bet on that!" she told her friend, a little too excitedly.

They were approaching the corner of Seventh and Western, and he was trying to think of where he should take them down, he was thinking of the street ahead of him, though he couldn't see it yet as they were too far; on that corner, it became a three cornered street, because those two met with the street they were on, Madison, so he closed the space between them a little more and was surprised they didn't sense or hear him back there because they were moving fast but not quite running, and he was breathing hard.

He remembered that one of those streets ran at a sharp angle to the others, and that area was filled with a lot of little shops, they would all be closed at this late hour of course, but he knew they sold antiques, recycled clothing and old books, all from an earlier age, "Just like me!" he thought and laughed.

There was a bookstore there, he'd been walking through there about a week ago and saw it, and it had to be new because he'd never seen it before in countless trips through the area, not just to hunt, but to window shop; to see what was popular and going on in the world at the time.

This was an area that he knew well, and though the other shops were closed, this tiny little bookstore was open, he could see the lights on and the little sign that hung on the inside of the door said "open" but there was no one moving around.

Gregor went to the window and looked in, then he saw an old man at the far end of the store, he was so far away that he looked tiny, like a little boy; and yet he moved as though he was well over a hundred years old, and he turned then, and smiled at Gregor as if he knew he was there and had been waiting for him to show up, that he even knew he would be there that night, at that very moment.

That, and someone coming up the street that didn't sound friendly was enough to make him leave, he ran around the corner and escaped but when he came back the next night to check out that little old man in that seemingly ancient book store that was squeezed into a tiny space between two large building, it was gone, and no trace it of ever being there, not even an opening between the two buildings where he thought he'd seen it just hours before.

Now as they passed it again, he felt an involuntary shiver run up and down his spine, he looked there and where he knew he'd seen a very old door and that very old man shuffling about was still nothing of the bookstore, but there was a note pasted on the wall there about a bookstore, "Coming soon!" but nothing else about it.

The other thing was, though he didn't know it, Maria lived on the far end of that street, a few blocks past the hair salon they sent her to when she wanted to cut her hair; there were other stores scattered around there too, a store that sold make up and did nails, a small bakery, a dress shop, and a few other stores that were empty at the time.

Maria would walk through here sometimes, on the way to see a movie or to visit some of these antique shops because they fascinated her, she would sometimes look at a dress or something and imagine herself wearing it and walking with me, and the funny thing was, she could really see herself in it, and there were pretty good odds that she had worn something very much like it, if not that dress in that time, maybe she sold some of them in her shop; they just seemed familiar somehow.

Once she found a ring that was quite beautiful, and very expensive and she knew she couldn't afford it but tried it on anyway, "Just for fun, just to see how it feels and looks on your hand!" the clerk told her.

"I do that all the time!" he admitted, "When the new stuff comes in and we haven't put it out yet, or sometimes after hours, its just fun for me, I pretend I lived in those times or maybe I was adopted by my parents because my family is weird!" he said, embarrassed then, and then he laughed nervously, because he'd said too much again.

He was laughing so hard that he didn't notice until then that Maria wasn't laughing with him, the word adoption was something that she still felt a little touchy about sometimes, she wondered if people saw that on her somehow, that when she walked in this door he knew that she was abandoned that night; but her attitude changed and she said, "Of course! What harm could it do?" and then she slipped the ring on her finger.

A strong current of energy flew through her in a matter of moments and took her breath away when it left her, she passed out from that and the clerk panicked, he called for an ambulance as soon as her head hit the floor as he hoped that she wouldn't get blood on the new carpet.

He ran around the counter then and saw her, she was bouncing all over the place as if she was on fire, her body was shaking so violently that he thought she was having a seizure, but it was nothing like that.

She woke up in the hospital and could not explain what happened, how she got there or even where she was when it happened, she knew nothing of the store or the clerk or any ring, all she knew was that she was hungry and wanted to go home.

Gregor knew none of that of course, though it meant that he was a lot closer to her than he ever would have dreamed possible, he had no idea that she was there as well.

He was focused on the girls, he followed them around the corner, his plan was to take both girls in an open doorway and bite into one as he held the other by the throat; preventing her from screaming, but if he needed to; he would kill one and take the other; it was just as well either way, he wasn't sure what the hell he was doing anyway.

Concentrating hard, he was trying to decide which one to take first when he saw Esmeralda, she was just across the street, dropping out of a window and stepping out onto the sidewalk, and though she was almost directly in front of him; she couldn't see him because traffic on that side was facing her and the light was in her eyes, making her turn away, but if it weren't for the lights, he would not have seen her climb out the window and then he wouldn't have been able to see who she was.

For a moment; he didn't see, nor hear her after she jumped from that window, he was hoping that she hadn't killed herself in the fall and cheated him of his vengeance; he hoped that she was lying on the ground, she would be vulnerable and he would have the element of surprise but then things happened and everything changed in a hurry.

One of the girls sensed he back there and turned her head, then they both stopped, the way her friend stopped, she thought that maybe she'd seen a cute guy or something and wanted to see who it was, she was so totally unprepared for the last thing that either of them ever saw in this world; she wanted to scream, her first reaction was to jump away from him but Gregor grabbed them both by their heads and smacked them together as hard as he could.

The clacking sound that it made as their skulls were smashed together that way made a very loud and distinctive sound in the silence of that night, he hadn't planned on that of course, but he forgot all about his plans to turn them and abandoned that in his rage at seeing Esmeralda again.

Both girls collapsed and died with a scream in their throats and surprised expressions on their faces, there would be no more cute butts for either of them; when he saw Esmeralda, he forgot about everything else except how much he hated her for the way she killed him.

It bothered him that she left him behind as she did, and for being here without him, and obviously without the slightest regard for him, he stepped over the dead bodies and towards her; his hands open claws that he was thinking about using to rip her throat open with when he saw the police cruiser on the other side of her, doing a slow crawl with a searchlight reaching out through the darkness as they searched for him.

If he stepped back into the shadows right then, they would almost surely pass right by and not see him hiding there; but the bodies were still in the open and would be very hard to miss, lying on the sidewalk like cordwood.

Gregor looked at them now, and under the streetlight they looked very much like two life-sized dolls that some child forgot or abandoned on the street; he reached down and scarcely had enough time to pull them into the shadows with him when the cruiser went by, so close that he could hear the static on the radio and it crawled by.

Gregor could see both officer's facing forward and talking about something when the officer riding shotgun and closest to him turned his head and looked right at Gregor and the two girls.

The officer opened his mouth and started to turn and to say something just as Gregor gave him the most evil look he could muster; a look that he would remember to the day he died, his mouth clacked shut and he never said a word; not even to his wife when his shift ended, though he always shared whatever happened, good or bad, he didn't say a word that night, went to bed without stopping to eat dinner that was waiting for him as usual.

His face turned an ashen white and he was barely able to hold his bladder but his partner hardly noticed as he drove on, as his partner drove on, the other officer thought about the job in the pharmacy that his brother offered him when he first became an officer, now it didn't sound like such a bad thing.

Gregor turned to see where she was, but Esmeralda was gone now; he looked both up and down the street but he could not see her anywhere, and he thought that might mean that she was headed towards the park but with the police patrols that were centered through that region now, he knew that even if he did find her, there would be no surprising her if he was running from the cops.

But now he thought at least he had an idea of where she lived, a place to find her while she still had no idea that he would be there waiting for her when she got home.

He picked up the girls and dragged them into the alley and fed on them absently as he thought about these latest developments; it bothered him that they were dead, he thought he was missing the struggling and the crying noises they made as they died, that without that it wasn't as much fun for him.

But it didn't bother him enough to stop him from feeding on their dead bodies, even after he realized that they tasted different when they were dead, he dropped the bodies in a large trash bin when he was done.

If they found the bodies soon enough that the bite marks would still be there, this would all point directly at him and intensify the efforts to find him, he knew that this would mean that he'd have to move on soon but he was never going to leave until he was able to settle with her.

In his heart, he knew that he hated Esmeralda, but in a much deeper sense he knew that he loved her too, and that a lot of this stemmed from his anger at being abandoned that way so many years ago; that she left him behind that way and now she'd not even invited him to the next dance.

He had nowhere to go now that he'd fed, nowhere to hide from the sun that would be up in a few hours; he looked at the moon and figured that he had about threehours before it would be gone and the sun would rise.

Esmeralda did go to the park as he thought, but there was so much going on there at the time that she couldn't do what she wanted and left feeling disappointed and for some reason she felt left behind too, as much as Gregor did, though she didn't know that.

All of the cars racing up and down the streets, bright red and blue lights flashing and sirens wailing as they rushed this way and then back the other, it was clear they were not sure where to look, let alone what they were looking for.

She didn't know what the commotion was about, but Esmeralda but she could see the cops beating the bushes and kicking up the dust all around her, yet they ignored her as they thought she was a harmless old lady.

It was about that point that she started to get a premonition that there was something wrong, and though she had no idea of what it might be, she put her senses on "high alert" but didn't get a whiff of Gregor or else she would have kept moving and maybe moved into the caves on the very night, she surely wouldn't have gone back to the cellar.

She thought whatever it was, that it had something to do with the park because that's where most of the activity seemed to be; there were more cops in the area, and they were busier there than anywhere else in the city.

It was bad enough when she was home and she felt that she had to sleep with an eye open because there was too much activity nearby, but now she felt suffocated even out there in the open, as though everyone was watching her now; that they all knew who she was and what she did.

She could see them circling her now, ready to spring out at her and tear her to pieces, but of course, none of that was real, it was just her imagination, fed by her guilt over the things she did over the course of her life, so instead of going home and running into Gregor, she went through the park and then deep into the caves to sleep.

Esmeralda felt better once she got there, the musky odor soothed her and she drifted quickly off to sleep, and she drifted off with thoughts of great parties that they held in the mansion; especially when Tomas first became governor, and when she thought about those days, she felt a sense of loss because he was gone, as if she forgot that she was the one that killed him.

The night that he won the re-election, he thought that he did it al by himself, he had no idea of what Esmeralda had done for him, he thought that when all was said and done, that he was the people's choice after all, and now everyone was lining up to kiss his ring and a certain part of his anatomy.

She could close her eyes now and see it if she tried hard enough, the main hall was decorated with bright and colorful bunting and green and red flags, the state colors and there were beautiful flowers everywhere; the air was sick with their sweet fragrance.

The hall was built to accommodate at least eight hundred was filled, and the three gardens outside that surrounded it as well, and beyond that, there were people outside of that waiting just to get in but there was no room.

Suddenly all was forgiven, and they all wanted to be a part of the celebration, that really made her angry though because she thought that if they had shown that kind of support before, she never would have had to do what she did for him.

The truth of that though, was that she enjoyed what she did, the things she went through to get them done, the effect it had on the one man that had a chance against her Tomas, those things would make anyone with a conscience feel bad didn't bother her in the least.

Every kind of meat and dish was served, roast pigs with apples in their mouths, gigantic swordfish; whole sides of beef, row after row of food and then there were almost as many different dessert dishes as well.

The wines flowed freely as well, the parties went on all night and through the next couple of days and it might have gone on for even longer but as she remembered it, they closed down the party after the wine ran out and there was no more to be had.

Then she remembered sadly that it was the last night they were ever together like that, and even further, as much as they were partying and having fun with all those people; that was also the night that she decided that she was going to have to kill Tomas, she couldn't wait much longer for him to find the courage to do it himself.

It came to her in a dream, that she would be walking alone and would have to find her own way without him; she saw some things that later did come true, but not as clearly as you might think; images of faces and places that she's seen before, though she hadn't visited them yet, but she planned to one day.

"Oh Tomas!" she cried, "You were such a fool!" and though she could not see it herself, she truly did love him, and she missed him as well, more than she ever thought that she would.

Then she remembered the first time that she ever saw him, she heard some of the women in the crowd say that he was a pig, but he was gentle and not very demanding, and that was what she told herself that she needed, and when she first laid eyes on him, she felt that he was going to be very powerful in politics one day, if she steered him in the right direction.

Once she got to know him, she agreed that he was a pig, it was hard to keep his hands off her, but he never went too far and he did have a gentle soul underneath; she thought he was a boy in a man's body and wondered what kind of a teenager he was.

When Tomas first saw her, he was in love instantly and would have given anything to have her, something his friends didn't understand as she wasn't particularly beautiful; she looked deep into his soul and saw the wrong image for a man that meant to lead the people, she also knew right off that she had a lot of work to do.

It was the first and last time she ever let him kiss her passionately, until the night she killed him, but that was not the first time she'd caught him in bed with another woman; inly the first time she confronted him about it.

Though she was furious about it, in truth she had to admit that she drove him to it and could not blame him for it, she'd denied his lust from the start and, being a man; he had to go somewhere for what she denied him.

She remembered what she did, but thinking about the last time they were together and happy like that brought a real sadness to her heart, and that surprised her because even she thought that she didn't have a heart anymore, that there was nothing she really cared about beyond her own needs.

I DO NOT REGRET A SINGLE ENEMY

I do not regret one professional enemy I have made. Any actor who doesn't dare to make an enemy should get out of the business.

-Bette Davis, (1908-1989), the Lonely life, 1962

THE VERY NEXT DAY MARIA and I agreed to meet and discuss what we needed to do next, to come up with a plan, but we promised to be serious this time, no more kisses. We felt that it was time that we got real and I was only hoping that we hadn't waited too long to do this, though deep inside, I had a feeling that we were way beyond being just a little late.

We both knew that what we were thinking about at the time was no a popular or mainstream idea, it was the thing that would have pissed off both of my parent if they knew; if they even thought I just said the word they would be equal parts hurt and upset, something that they would never understand, and if they knew what we were doing they would have probably blamed her for making me think about reincarnation in the first place.

We were both sure that our friends would laugh at us, they would say the notion was romantic and nothing else, but somehow, we got the feeling and we knew we were right that this was life and death for us, that we were risking it all and could not lose.

Maria told me that she'd found out about a woman that taught a class at the local junior college that might be able to help us, at the very least give us some kind of answers, or some place that we might go and find out things for ourselves if she couldn't help us.

She was teaching a class, was an expert on things like dream interpretation and reincarnation, some of the other things that we were both experiencing and didn't understand; she talked to her on the phone about some of the things we were experiencing and that were bothering us.

Maria said that she was skeptical at first; that she had seen her share of fakers and people that pretended to be experiencing reincarnation, others that thought she was doing the devil's work, and those extremists that wanted to kill her for what she did in the name of research.

There were terms laid out before we could meet her, she said that we both needed to be together and she didn't want anything that we couldn't back up with evidence or witnesses; we needed to be prepared to be interviewed both together and separately to determine the veracity of what we said, there was a lot of that legal "mumbo jumbo" that we didn't really understand but we agreed to it anyway so we could get into the meat of this thing.

One of the first thing they asked us about was how we would feel if we were ostracized for what we were doing, that mainstream America wasn't ready for this kind of thing, that we would be called devil worshippers and worse just for being there.

I looked at Maria and we both had to admit that we hadn't thought about that, but we both admitted that it wasn't a popular subject, alongside the word "exorcism" and other things that were not spoken of in polite company.

The doctor we were there to see was Samantha Contreras; one of the leading experts in the field despite being younger than most of the people that were above her and controlled her fate in the field.

They didn't like that she was teaching reincarnation and were only allowing it due to her reputation and standing in the field, it made them look good to have her there even if they didn't consent or agree with her or what she was teaching.

She had been spending a lot of time studying in Europe and abroad, it was easier to find schools that would be open to her teaching there; she felt that no one took this teaching seriously in The United States, that the origins of this kind of thinking could never be found here, even with the kind of compelling evidence that she was finding every day.

It was a surprise to her that they came to recruit her, they told her that people were more receptive to her, new and unusual ideas and studies, they opened their wallets to her and were ready to fund her studies, and yet they still asked that she keep everything about reincarnation as low key as she could about that.

In the last few years, she had written two best-selling on the subject which led to us finding her, she was at the time, searching for subjects to study, and she was doing her research for what would eventually become her third book.

As we waited for her to meet with us, they were in the next room, watching us on a monitor because they wanted to see if we had "ulterior motives" for being there, because it was amazing what people would talk about when they thought they were alone, this was a plan that saved her a considerable amount of time and money.

When we walked in, we saw a building that was bustling with excitement and everyone was rushing around trying to get things done, clearly they were just moving into the office and not everything was working yet or put in its place, there were a lot of boxes and machinery sitting around, we were a little lost when we ran into a woman that we hoped was the doctor we'd come to see, or at least someone that might tell us where her office was so we could meet her.

"Oh!" she exclaimed when we explained ourselves, "You are the two kids that Sam was so excited about!" she said, "At last, we get to meet you and get started!" she said, "I am sorry to inform you though that Sam left early this morning, something about a conference in San Diego that they keynote speaker took ill and they needed someone with her expertise on the subject!" she told us and saw the look of disappointment in my eyes.

"She was very sorry that she was forced to go, she really does want to meet you both and she was very excited after talking to you!" she said, looking at Maria, "You are the one she spoke to, am I correct? She said she really liked you, that you were honest and willing to answer any questions we had to make sure that you weren't fraudulently making this up!" she told us.

"Don't worry!" she said, patting me on the arm gently, "She will be back soon and we can get started on the things she wasn't going to be a part of anyway, the forms, the permission slips, all of the legal hoops we have to jump through in order to be valid and sound in our findings and presentations!" she said, as if that made it all clear to us.

"We have a good feeling about you two, a very good feeling about this!" she said as we sat down together; "Though you are a lot younger than most of the subjects we get in here; its nice that you are so open minded and willing to help us as we might be able to help you find some answers at the same time!" she said.

"You must remember that whatever we say between us, whatever is revealed in our studies and conversations on the subject is something that might end up in my next book, and we need to know if you have a problem with that, we can keep your names out if that's what you're worried about, you can contribute your experiences anonymously as well, if that's what you want!" she told us and then waited.

When we didn't do anything beyond look at each other for a moment and then she nodded her head at me to say it was alright with her if it was alright with me, and maybe we didn't know better but we thought it didn't matter too much if we were in the book or not.

"While I cannot guarantee that someone that you already know if your life might be able to recognize you from your story, or maybe that it would go the other way and they won't know who you are from the book, but I need to know if there's a problem, what are your thoughts on the subject?" she continued.

Of all the things we talked about before we went there that day, we never thought nor talked about that; I couldn't talk to my mother and father about it they would never consent because of the subject matter but I also knew they would never read the book so I thought I would be safe from them finding out that way.

But then she was called out of the room for something technical, "Do you want anything while I'm out?" she asked, "Water? Coffee?" she asked, "There's a coke machine around that corner she said as she pointed to the left, but we both declined politely, and she left us alone for a few minutes.

"Are you sure we can trust her?" I asked Maria, "Please tell me you didn't just pick her out of the phone book, that you know something about her!" I said, something about her made me nervous and I couldn't figure it out yet, I was hoping that asking Maria would bring it out and I would know.

I knew that I could trust that whoever she found, and even however she found them would be someone we could trust and would be helpful, but I guess it just kept jumping out that my parents would find out and be very disappointed in me, and then it came to me that maybe I had seen her before somewhere, or read about her somewhere.

There was no way that I could have known it, but the reason she felt so familiar to me was because she was one of the doctors my parents took me to see a long time ago, she was the doctor that spoke of reincarnation, the one my parents ran from and my father didn't want to pay to support her "devil work" as they saw it, it would have amazed me to know that because we had come full circle and I was in her office once more, waiting to see her, and my parents would really be furious if they knew that too.

"No cara mia!" she told me patiently, "Before I asked you about this and before I even made the appointment, I went to the library and looked her up, and went to some of her classes and watched her at work, asked some of her students about her and they all said she was a great teacher and they learned a lot from her and the classes she taught and lectured in.

"She has a book in the library, but you have to ask for it; they only have one copy and they don't keep it on the shelves!" she said as she touched my cheek tenderly, "It's like they are acknowledging that it is a real thing and yet they are trying to keep it secret and not let everyone know that its there!" she told me.

Just hearing her call me that made my heart melt and I knew we weren't going to debate this any further and I did have a good feeling about this visit and all so I decided to just see where it led us when the door opened and she was back.

This time she brought a pad of paper and a couple of pens, along with some kid of recording device, but I didn't mind, we were ready for that and expected it anyway.

"Things are so hectic right now!" she explained, "I'm so sorry to make you wait this way, running in and out, you must think I'm not all here!" she said and laughed at her joke.

"Everyone is excited about the new developments for the book, and then I heard your voice on the phone and your excitement is contagious!" she said, looking at Maria and then me with a huge smile on her face.

"But with so much going on, believe it or not I have to break in new research assistants to handle all the information we have been getting, background investigations, and I know that's not your problem, but I was forced to fire a couple of my staff recently when they were found to selling some of my material to another writer for his book!" she said, as if we would understand how that felt.

"There are people walking around here and working in my building that I don't even recognize!" she aid and laughed again, I have no idea where they came from and they are asking personal questions from my staff that I wouldn't want to answer because they are so personal I'd be red-faced to ask, let alone have to reply to them!" she said, again as if we could understand, but we simply stared back and nodded politely when it seemed necessary.

"We have all of this going on while we are moving into this new facility and haven't ironed out all the bugs yet!" she admitted, "As such, we have normal investigators here as part of the process now, and let's just say that I am glad it isn't my job to ask them, to dig into a normal person's life and dig through their closets and trash cans to find the skeletons they buried!" she said and shook her head.

"So, when will she be here?" I asked, "We really aren't trying to be rude, you seem very nice and have the answers so far, but we really needed to talk with her, when will she be back?" I asked anxiously, I wasn't sure why but suddenly I felt stifled in there, as though I was going to suffocate and needed to get going.

I couldn't explain that, or why I felt as though we didn't have a lot of time left, that things were going to start happening soon and we'd better be more ready than I felt we were at that time, it was very hard for me to hide my exasperation at not being able to speak to her now.

"We really don't feel comfortable waiting for her and would gladly walk from here to New York if we could meet with her that much sooner!" I said, "You saw the data and you know that we are being honest, we aren't quacks or whatever else you might have been worried about and we need real help, and we need it now!" I said, hoping she would hear the desperation in my voice and help us out.

"I'm so very sorry!" she said with sincerity in her voice and bearing; "I do know that she was very excited when she heard what you shared with us already; you have the background and information that she has been searching for, even before she wrote the first book!" she told me.

"Maybe in her excitement at finding you she missed how desperate you are for help or she would have been here, I am sure of that, but it was unavoidable, it would have set the research back and made this whole study and all the participants look incompetent and we couldn't let this all go to waste!" I am sincerely sorry for that!" she exclaimed.

"You must understand that, we don't always get the chance to talk with living witnesses with such vivid memories and such attention to details before you two came along and dropped these gems into our laps!" she said, excitedly, "Your memories are very good!" she said and then stopped as if she said too much.

She was saved from any further explanation when the phone and apologized for the intrusion, "I'm very sorry, but I have to take this!" she said and excused herself for a moment, answered the phone and spoke quietly to someone about something that was making her sound impatient.

"I'm so sorry, but I have to leave you once more, but only for a moment I think!" she said as she excused herself, we were pretty disappointed as we waited for her to return, when she left I tried to tell her it was okay, and that we understood, but I don't think I convinced her or myself.

"Its okay!" I told Maria, "We might have more time than we realize, especially since we are learning more about what happened back then!" I said, "I think that this time, we can see bad things coming long before they get here, because of what happened before, at least I think so!" I said, I was feeling desperate because I didn't know how much time we had and it didn't seem like enough, no matter how much time we had to get ready.

I managed a smile when I said that, and I think it eased her concerns at least a little bit, even though I couldn't convince myself of that because I wasn't feeling it in my bones.

Then I went to the door that she went through because she didn't fully close it after she left us there, I could see her talking and going over some case notes or something as she spoke on the phone; then I heard her ask someone, "Is Sam there? I mean, is she nearby where she can come to the phone for at least a moment?" she asked, and my heart leapt, I was hoping that she was, that she would know we were here and leave right away to come back here and meet with us, but of course, our sense of urgency didn't mean she would feel the same.

"Okay, I'll wait!" I heard her say, then I saw her sit down at the edge of the desk, and after a moment, I heard her start talking again, though I didn't know to whom she was speaking, only that it was about us.

"What?" she said, "Oh, okay, I understand, believe me, but you remember those two kids that you wanted us to look at, the kids with the shared experience?" she said, as if that would remind her who we were and why we went there and wanted to see her.

"I am not entirely sure why, but they seem desperate to see you immediately, they said they would walk to New York if they had to, so that they could see you straight away, they are very keen on that!" she said and then waited for an answer.

"No, I am sure they are serious, and they feel its important!" she said, I was happy to hear that she was arguing our case very well, and then I heard her say, "Okay, I'll fetch them so they can speak to you, hold on!" she said, sounding a little more relieved than she should have so I thought she was really trying to help us and not just paying us lip service while we were there, especially since she didn't know we could hear her.

She came back to the room and didn't see me as I ran back to Maria's side and sat down, but she looked as excited as I felt when she told us, "I have good news!" she told us, looking from one to the other, "Sam is on the line and she has agreed to speak with you, but she doesn't have long!" and then she held the handset out for one of us to take and say something.

"Sam?" I said as I took the phone, I looked at Maria to make sure it was okay if I spoke for us and when she nodded I knew it was alright, I was still impatient to get started, I was still hoping that she could cancel her plans and rush back there to help us which was more important than any seminar, but that was just from my perspective and I knew that she wouldn't feel that the same way as we did; she wasn't wearing the desperation cologne that we were.

"I am so sorry I wasn't there to meet with you!" she said, "But I am glad I got this chance to speak with you, even for a moment, it's always much nicer hearing a voice to match with the information you gave us!" she said happily.

"As I understand it" she continued, "What you shared with us so far, that is just one small part of the things you remember, that you both experienced, is that correct?" she asked me.

"Well, yes, that is true, we have experienced a lot of things, and both have the same visions and scares as the other; we both feel that things are going to get worse soon, if we don't get answers and prepare for it, that we will die just as horribly as we did then, with no help, nor reason for it to happen, and no easy way for us to stop it!" I admitted, trying not to shout at her as I tried to convey my feelings of frustration.

She asked us then, independently, I had to leave the room so she could describe the most frightening of our visions and, then when it was my turn, we both described the same thing; even though we didn't talk about that before, not knowing they would ask, but it impressed her that we both spoke of the same thing, with the same fears and concerns for the other, we weren't afraid to die, we were both more concerned for the other than for ourselves.

She asked us both at the same time, the details about what we remembered about how that life was ended and what we thought the images might mean.

"We don't know!" I admitted, I mean, we can tell you what we remember, but we have no idea what the hell it means!" I said.

"Well, for what its worth" she said, "I like you two, I feel that you have been more than patient and very honest with us about what is going on in your lives!" she said, "In spite of what you might think at not finding me there, I am very anxious to speak with both of you, to begin our studies, and I am positive that we can find some good and solid answers to some, if not all of the questions you have, to help clear things up and hopefully any misconceptions you might have at this time!" she said.

"We both feel desperately that we need to know what was going to happen next; that if it was good or bad as long as we got an idea of what it might be and hopefully be ready for it this time!" I told her.

I wasn't ready to let go of that and asked her if there was any way that we could go there and meet with her, get a face to face meeting for starters, even if it was brief because I felt that her excitement almost matched ours, and yet she didn't have the time to come here and then go back and finish.

We were going to help her tremendously in her research; we had answers she needed and could prove things that were, until now; simply theories that she could not prove, that had no evidence to back up until now; but it didn't seem like that was enough of a reason for her to abandon this and come to us.

"I'm so sorry that I can't leave right now, you two sound delightful and I would want to know you even if it weren't for the study, I will be here at least one more day, maybe two, but I will say this much; if you can manage to get down here I would be glad to meet you, though I can't promise much, maybe we can have lunch!" she said, sounding hopeful.

Though I wasn't sure yet how we would get that part done, I agreed before I thought about that; I was just excited that we made some progress, at least I thought of it that way as I hung up the phone; but she had already given her assistant a number to call when we got there.

"She said it was okay to go there and meet with her, so how do we get to where she is?" I asked her as I took a pad off the desk to write it down.

"Well!" she said, "As it turns out, she is not far from here, only a few hours drive as a matter of fact!" she said, "In a town called "Vista" she told me and then gave the directions while I wrote them down, and then it took us a while to find anyone that would drive us there, even though we would provide lunch and gas money for them.

Just when we were ready to quit and go home, we struck paydirt when one of my friends wanted to have some "alone time" with his girlfriend and loaned me his car, I was afraid to drive it and made sure he as okay with it, I didn't have a license but knew how to drive, at least I thought I did, it didn't seem that hard to me.

But this wasn't "just a car" to him or to me, it was a classic; '64 Malibu, it was silver, with a four-speed transmission with 327HP under the hood, moon rims and black leather upholstery, and best of all, it was a convertible which would make the nice ride a lot nicer.

But it came with a warning: "I'm telling you, right now, if there is so much as a scratch on it, anywhere, you pay for a new paint job and repair any bodywork on the entire car! EVERYTHING!" he emphasized and made me wonder why he was doing it if he was so worried, but I didn't want to change his mind and agreed with it, even though I had no idea of how much that would cost or how I would get the money for it.

It seemed to take forever to get going and then even more to get out of the city and into the highway and then to find her once we did, but I felt better as soon as we got to a decent speed, not sixty-five, which was the posted speed limit, but around thirty five to fifty miles an hour, which was better than nothing.

Though neither of us knew how to drive, I never told her that and I guess she just assumed that I knew how since my friend trusted me with such a beautiful car, she thought I knew what I was doing, and so did I, but I was learning on the fly.

To me, the time with her like that was really special, and maybe because of what we were doing or because we were supposed to be somewhere else at that time, we shared a "nervous good" at first, but as we got further out of town and away from anyone that might question us or become upset about it, we both began to relax and enjoy the time and the drive together.

As I weaved and drove through traffic, I kept looking over at her, and she kept smiling back at me, and more than once we heard the sound of the car behind us, blowing the horn because we were kissing and the car in front of us had finally moved until she came close and leaned her head on my shoulder and we held hands.

I couldn't help but wonder how we did this in that "other world" we lived in, or other worlds, which was mind boggling to me, I again wondered if there were other lives and how we did, if we found each other before we left that world, I was thinking about that as I watched the road ahead of us; it would not do to get this close to the answers we sought only to die in a car accident on the way.

There were times I would stop for gas and come out to find her asleep, I knew it was the long road that lulled her into it, and I took advantage and enjoyed the moment; watching her sleep so comfortably, her head to the side while a slight smile played on her lips, I hoped it was because of me.

I stood there and watched her sleep for as long as I could, until some guy in one of those little rice burners drove up with his stereo on loud enough to cause quake damage and it woke her up, so I pretended that I'd just got there and wasn't watching her sleep and pumped the gas.

The second time wasn't as nice, there was an accident as we came through Oceanside, two cars collided when they were racing each other on the freeway; one of them ran into the guard rail and it was spun around and directly into the car that he was racing, with three teens in the first car and two others in the second, along with one little brother along for the ride, they were all having fun until they died.

Traffic went from a robust crawl to less than five miles an hour and then stopped altogether when another two cars became impatient and tried to do an end-around run, one of them rear-ended the other when he stopped suddenly upon seeing the highway patrolman in the lane.

She fell asleep again and I reached over to touch her hand and it felt really warm, I thought that for a moment that she'd caught a fever, I thought that maybe we should just give up and go back, it was as if things were stacked against us on this road and our search for those elusive answers.

I looked closer at her face then, and put my hand on her forehead to check if that was warm too and she opened her mouth to scream, yet she was so terrified that it seemed to take forever for her to breath again, I thought her lungs would explode in her chest and she would die and it scared me.

Desperately trying to soothe her, I tried to hold her close without making her feel as though I was smothering her, I tried to comfort her as she tried to fight me at first, but that might have been a good thing because she stopped trying to scream as she fought against me.

I was able to hold her until she was back, asking me what was wrong and why we weren't moving; I let go and she started looking around the car, expecting to be closer or possibly parked somewhere while I got some rest, anything but being in the same place as when she fell asleep an hour before.

The good news was that traffic broke at that moment; I felt her nightmare, I felt the fire that consumed her in that other life and all that I could do was to hold her hand and pretend that I was making a difference, I hoped that I faked it better than I felt it because it scared the hell out of me.

Showing his impatience to get going, the driver behind me leaned on his horn and I had to move and I thought I saw the highway patrol a little look at me a little suspiciously but it might have been my imagination, then I saw something that really made me think I was imagining things because that officer looked a lot like Diego, someone that was important to me and I knew his name but not why or how I knew it, why it came to me at that moment; than to prove that it was more than just a bad thought; he took out his baton and began to wring it back and forth in his hands while he watched us drive off.

He had the same exact look as he did that night in my cell, and that almost distracted me enough that we would have ended up as another statistic of the long weekend and the accidents that took life, limb and loss of property as they say in the fine print.

I swerved around him and then drove away from there, the nightmare fading back as I saw his shrink back into the recesses of my rear view mirror, and yet as far away as we were and as quickly as it took us to make that distance; I felt that even now, he could still see me, through the few miles and all the other cars that were between us.

Because of the feeling that gave me, we couldn't get there fast enough now; the cool air flowing through our hair as we traded time for the miles we had to travel, I pulled up to the place she told me to find and got someone to help us in a few minutes, all while fighting the urge to look behind me to see if he might be following us.

The clerk checked her messages and then told me, "Yes!" she said, "She is staying here, and left instructions that if you came here in time for lunch to meet her at a place called "Uncle Tony's Italian Cuisine" and since your not from here do you need directions?" she asked.

I admitted that I didn't, being from out of town and all, so she gave me directions and said that it wasn't far off the freeway that I just fought my way through, "The address is 770 Sycamore Avenue, it's suite H in the shopping center, southeast corner and very easy to find, a really nice place to eat if your hungry!" she said, a little too cheerfully for me.

We found the place easily enough, as she said; and she was right about the food being good, it was served nice and warm, just as I liked it, though we hardly ate because we were talking so much and we too excited at finally meeting her and getting this thing started.

She must have felt our excitement and thought we were having doubts or second thoughts though and tried to soothe our concerns as much as she could, though it wasn't needed.

"Any questions you might have about me, my background? Any concerns about your possible place in the book?" she asked us.

Maria had some definite questions for her and I was surprised at how candidly she spoke to the doctor about our feelings for each other; how she thought our growing feelings were feeding the nightmares and intensifying them; how she felt about our past life and what we could and should expect from our future if we were going to have one that is.

Uncle Tony himself came over to our table then, he was a big man and hard to miss, yet he had a gentle way of making you feel as though you were welcome in his second home, he was a gracious host with a lot of good food offer as long as you behaved.

After we ate our lunch, or rather, after I pushed my food around the plate for a while and listened to them talk, comfortable as old friends already, we went out to the patio and she had some Chablis and for some reason I thought the wine looked very inviting for some reason.

"Dr. Contreras, thank you for meeting with us, for taking this time out of your busy schedule to have this talk, I certainly appreciate it and I am sure he does too!" Maria said.

"You are so very welcome, it has been very pleasant meeting the both of you!" she said, "I know that many times, people make the mistake of not taking you serious, I certainly don't intend to make that mistake, which is why I agreed to meet with you!" she said.

"My time here is short, and yet I felt this was important as well; I could sense it was for you, at the very least we could find a way to get comfortable around this "touchy" subject and get the dialogue started between us!" she told us, "To start our relationship in a good and relaxed situation rather than clinical and legal!" she said as she shrugged her shoulders as if she was dismissing what she considered a necessary evil.

"But please, call me Sam!" she said, "Juan already has!" she said and then winked at me, telling me that it didn't bother her, but it didn't escape her either; her one act of being an adult while she was around us.

"I like to work with my staff informally than runs strictly by the rules, and I feel that if we'd met under different circumstances, we would have been good friends, but then again, maybe we already did!" she said, using some of her reincarnation humor.

"So!" she said when we stopped laughing, "How is it that you think that I can help you today?" she asked, "I mean, I'm sure that you understand that all my equipment, all of the things I need to do this right are in my office in the facility where you went to meet me!" she said.

I took the chance to look over at Maria, I was hoping that she would bail me out, but instead she smiled at me, ever so sweetly and nodded her head at me; I guess that I was going to be the only skeptic in the room that day.

"Did they take you on the tour?" she asked, "We have a state-of-the-art facility, I'm sure when you see it, that you will agree!" she said, certainly happy at the way things were going.

"Everything we need to record your dreams, the brain activity while your asleep, your thoughts when you wake up, we can keep you there overnight if its easier for you, or we can just keep gathering data as we go along; either way works for me, but the continued monitoring is quicker and easier to read, and more exact than starting and stopping again!" she told us.

"It works better when things are recorded "live" instead of you telling me about them later, your body reacts internally in ways that you aren't aware of when you are in danger, your reaction time and your system changes to whatever your facing!" she said, checking things off in her mind as she spoke.

Then I told her all that I could remember, making sure that I forgot nothing in my excitement, but I started talking about the beginning, the first nightmares that I'd seen and what I could remember of them; and as I spoke I saws Maria's jaw drop a few times, I felt that now we could sit side by side and finish the dialogue that the other started because we were seeing the same things; some things we had spoken of but others we never had, but it really bothered her that we shared them, as bad as they were for each of us; the memories so real and vivid that we both shuddered at the same time.

In forgot that we'd never discussed some of the more brutal images that we'd seen, even though we both had seen them at one time or another, each of us from a different perspective though, but we smelled and heard the same sounds.

Sam made me start and stop three times; she wanted to make sure that she got some details right, but as a habit; she was also making sure that I digress in any way from my earlier statements but that was easy to see and I figured it out.

Because we both knew that we needed to trust her, I held nothing back, and since my memory has always been pretty good, it took me a while to get through some parts, but I never hid my eyes or looked away while I spoke so she would know I was speaking true.

Though her expression changed a few times and it didn't always look good for us when she did; she sat there for the most part, taking notes and listening patiently, writing something down that she thought was important.

There were some things I said, when I'd kept them to myself I'd forgotten about, but saying those things and some of the more gruesome details and saw how she reacted, that all helped me to feel better, and it made me feel that we weren't wasting our time in coming to her.

There were times, such as when I got passed that part, where she stopped writing and simply looked back at me and said or did nothing for the longest time, but then something that I said made her react with surprise and delight.

"Did I say something important? Significant?" I asked her, then waiting for an answer but I thought she would say something that I didn't want to hear and held onto Maria's hand while I waited.

"No!" she said and smiled at us, you haven't said anything new that you didn't already say, but in a different way!" she said.

"Different way?" I asked her, "What does that mean?" I asked her, suddenly feeling as though I needed her to clarify that, explain it to me because it sounded important.

"Well okay!" she said, shifting gears, "Let me explain that in a different way!" she told us, and then she shifted in her seat to face us both while she leaned forward as if she was confiding a deep secret with us.

"As I am sure that you know by now, we screen applicants for certain signs, things that tell us if you're yanking our chain or you are for real; something that we don't like to do, but we feel it is necessary in order to stay effective in this business!" she said, and then waited for that to sink in; maybe making sure she chose her words wisely.

"There are certain words, they trigger alarms, bells and whistles go off in my head, not always in a bad way though, but sometimes, just enough to grab my attention, you understand?" she said.

I didn't know what to say, so I just nodded my head and then she said; "When you say things in casual conversation, you are more likely to be open and honest about your feelings and what you went through!" she said, "Different than you might say in front of a stranger, or even a professional like myself, partly out of fear and partly out of not understanding what it is I need to see or need to understand!" am I right about that part?" she asked me, and then waited.

Out of the corner of my eye, I saw Maria look at me so I turned towards her thinking she had something to say, it was as if we were making some sort of unspoken agreement between us right at that moment; we both felt that we could trust her, but we also knew that we had no choice now either, but we knew she was going to get us the answer, one way or another.

"Listening to you two as you talk, there are certain things you've said that you feel is…unrelated or irrelevant or that have nothing at all to do with this, study!" she said as she could see that we were understanding her.

"You are so very wrong in some aspects and so very close to what you're looking for in other parts, you are so close to figuring out your part in all of this, I can't see it but I can feel it, things that happened back then will soon become clear to you, I think!" she said, excitedly.

We spent the rest of that time talking about all those things and more, until it was time for her to go and she left us reluctantly, but we understood and agreed to meet her the next day, at her office.

"I really want to, I need to ask you more about that flashback, but I want to do it when we get back to the lab, as I said, all my equipment is there and here all I have is my notes and what I think about them!" she told us; looking genuinely sad about it.

She told us before she left that most people can't remember things like we did in such vivid detail, especially when awake and lucid; that they normally need to use sessions of hypnotherapy and sleep studies to get that deep and that kind of detail; that the process normally takes several months before they get to anything useful.

"This was much more than I hoped for when you first came to me, and it is such a welcome surprise that neither of you know anything about reincarnation!" she said, and then when she saw my expression she almost laughed, "It's a good thing, it means your mind isn't sent on a certain bent where you have these misconceptions about the subject, your minds are open and not cluttered with false information or overloaded with the truth!" she said.

"The things you might have read about it, there are times when people are thinking something about what they saw, they read a book about it and it taints their thoughts and sometimes even changes how they perceived it, they think that what they felt or saw should have been more like that experience rather than what they really did see and feel about it!" she related to us.

"They forget that what was real for someone else and that it was as unique to them as it was to everyone else in that situation, shared and yet unique to each of us!" she told us.

"It was real for them at one point and yet it was now changed; influenced by the experience and words of the others, she said and then became quiet.

"In your case, your experiences, your thoughts and ideas about what you have shared have not been tainted as such, and that alone excites me because of the possibilities!" she said.

"This is something that I cannot stress enough, it is my good fortune that you both came to me, that you have shared experiences that validates your claims even with your different perspectives!" she told us.

I have to admit that a lot of this pleasantly surprised me, I thought she was going to tell us we were crazy and show us the door, that we would have to fight this thing alone, with no knowledge because while we were trying to find whatever it was, it would find us and then it would be over.

But when she said that, I felt as though a huge weight was lifted off my shoulders, and when I looked at Maria, I could see that she felt it too.

"I'll need a couple of days to set everything up, to make sure that I have my best staff working on this and have all the permission slips signed and filed so that everything is covered!" she said. "We can start filling out the forms when we meet tomorrow though, at least that will be out of the way!" she was laughing then, as if this really was the best news she'd ever received.

"As soon as we get all of that, I will need you both to spend a couple of nights with us!" she said to us and then paused for a moment, thinking about everything she needed to do.

"We'll be monitoring your sleep and see things you might have missed as you sleep, the data and your testimony will be of tremendous help to the study and I am fairly certain that you will find your answers there as well!" she told us.

"How can you promise us that?" I asked her, suddenly the skeptic again, "I mean, if the study is going to be done while we sleep and you aren't yet sure of what you will see, how can you promise us that with such certainty?" I asked her.

"If you want to go by scientific evidence alone, all I have is what you told me, what you have already shared with us, but my years of experience and that information added to my gut feeling which has never been wrong; I will say without a doubt that you will get your answers, what you're dealing with and how to get on with your lives normally!" she said, emphasis on the last word.

The look on her face told me that she never said things like that unless she meant it, so I thought we could believe her and something about the look in her eyes made me feel that she believed it too, so I backed down and asked her what we could do next, anything to get the ball rolling.

"So, you think we can get this done? Can you do those things I asked?" she said, "I have some permission slips with me, I c them in my briefcase because you never know, but I will need both your parents to sign these before we can continue!" but then she stopped when she noticed that my expression changed, "Is something wrong?" she asked.

Since she was looking at me, probably because I was "the skeptic" and since Maria didn't answer, I thought it was up to me to tell her, even though I knew I was lying on the first part, "I can get my parents to sign this, and bring it to you tomorrow if you need it, but Maria doesn't have parents to sign it, is it okay that it's just an administrator or someone in authority that signs hers?" I asked for her.

I felt her anxiety as soon as I said it and felt bad; she felt that emptiness before when people would talk about their families, I'd seen it though I never spoke to her about it, but this kind of brought it all home and I think the way I said it made it sound even worse than it was.

I looked at her and whispered, "I'm sorry!" and she knew what I was thinking and squeezed my hand a little tighter before she handed Sam a card with a name and number on it, "Call this number, ask for her at extension 1122 and they will give you permission or whatever you need!" she said.

"Okay then!" Sam said, "I need to know what, if anything you may or may not know about reincarnation, as much as you know, or think that you understand about it; and I want to know your opinion, not your friends or your families, or anything that you might have read about it, or seen anything about it in a movie, okay?" she asked us.

"I don't know much about it; I am not even sure how to spell it!" I admitted to her, "Because of my catholic upbringing I was always scared of the church's views and opinions on it, I know its forbidden, they don't want us to know anything about it, to study it or even talk about it!" I said.

"But I think that isn't because they think the devil will jump off those pages and take possession of us, I think it's more so because it's like the Spanish Inquisition; an embarrassment to them because they did it and it got out of control and you, of all people, should know that we know a lot of innocent people were killed before Napoleon put a stop to it, we know first-hand how that went!" I said and shuddered as I looked away.

"But reincarnation takes away the control they need to scare you into being good, if you can "wash your sins and mistakes away" and get another shot at it, you can have your fun and eat your cake too if you get my meaning!"

I said, and they both laughed at my mixing up of metaphors and that broke the tension I was feeling.

"To me, it seems as though when we die, we go to one place or the other, there is no "in between" purgatory, I think the church made that up but can't figure out why, but I think we go to heaven or hell, depending on how we lived our lives of course; and if you went to heaven, maybe they thought you were "close" but no cigar, so they decided to send you back and give you another chance to get it right, or you take an extremely long punishment for getting it all wrong!" I said, and then stopped to take a breath.

I looked at both of them, and they weren't saying a word so I thought it was okay to continue, "I think that if you're lucky enough or good enough that you get to return here, that your brain, your memory and all of that gets scrubbed clean, all data erased and you get that proverbial clean slate to start all over again with!" I said and smiled a little.

"But I think that sometimes the scrub doesn't "take" and there's stuff that stays with us, small things that pop up once in a while, mostly when something similar happens to us and it reminds us that "we were here before" in that way, a face, a song, something that triggers it!" I told them, "You have memories of a life that you don't remember living!" I said and went quiet so they could reply or add to my thoughts.

We both looked at Maria, to see what she had to say, but she told us that was thinking along the same lines, that she didn't think of some of those angles that I did, but they made sense to her and they did clear up some misconceptions that she had, she admitted that beyond what we were saying about it now was all that she knew about it.

Finally Sam spoke and cleared the tension in the air, I was still thinking that my ideas were a little "out there" and they would laugh at my conclusions and throw me out, continue the study without me, but when she said what she said I felt better.

"Those are supremely honest answers and I like that!" she said, and then she stood up and walked over to the window where there was a spectacular view of the ocean and the cliffs nearby.

What she told us then was what I thought she considered her "stock lecture" but I think it was easier for her to explain it this way, the best way that she knew of to help us to understand.

"History has shown us that the really strong objections on the subject by Orthodox Christianity!" she said, "The one voice that was pro-reincarnation was Origin, of Alexandria, who just happened to be one of Christianity's theologians, even though they knew that he believed in reincarnation and the transmigration of the soul, also called metempsychosis!" she went on.

"History has shown us what the Egyptians and what they taught about the transmigration of the soul, that it travels from one body to another and that's why they started embalming their dead, so it could journey with the body, along with Ka, and that makes the subject older than the pyramids; but it started long before that in my opinion; and the Hindu's have strong beliefs about it as well!" she said.

"So why does the church have such a problem with it then? If their greatest theologian was all for it and espoused his beliefs on it, why would they object?" Maria said, "Wasn't he considered a great proponent?" she asked Sam.

"As far as I can tell, it was during the early centuries that they held five main objections or arguments on that!" Sam told her, "They felt that it minimizes the idea of Christian salvation, as Juan said, it takes them out of the equation or puts them on the sidelines!" she said, and then she winked at me, remembering what I said about that.

"They feel that it conflicts with the resurrection of the body in Christian morals and teachings, it goes against them and that's all they see, it doesn't "jibe" with their teachings and so it must be wrong!" she said and then laughed.

We must have looked confused about that because she paused for a moment and then almost laughed again because, though we hadn't said anything and weren't looking at each other now, Sam told us that we wore the exact expression on our faces.

"They felt that it caused an unnatural separation between the body and the soul!" she said, "And that's too much speculative a use of the Christian principles and that there is no recollection of a previous life!" she said.

We went back and forth over those points for several hours arguing both sides of it; and it made me think how we thought about it before, as opposed to how we felt about it, we were playing it by ear with no basis of fact to help us better understand and yet we were, as Sam said, a LOT closer than we thought and we were right about those things I thought to be outlandish and absurd, that made the least sense, those things were clearer to me now as well and now I felt better.

As we left her that day, we'd spent much more time than she thought we would talking about this, but she liked us and thought the subject and what we (especially me) thought about all of this and how we were so damned close without her training and help astounded her and made her want to know more.

The one thing that was still bothering me was that I said she had no parents and I was feeling that it was her place to say that and I shouldn't have, that I went too far, and I apologized for it.

She turned to face me then, and I saw tears swimming in her eyes and then felt even worse until she spoke to me and made me feel so much better; "Ay cara mia!" she said gently, and then she hugged me tightly, "You are my only family now!" she said, "You are all I want and have in this world and I would much rather trust in you to speak for me on such sensitive matters than anyone else, you knew that I would have started to cry and then wouldn't be able to say what I was trying to say and you took over and I appreciated it!" she said with a sniffle and a smile.

"Mi Corazon, te quero mucho!" I whispered into her ear as tenderly as I could, because I felt so much love for her at that moment that I felt I would hug her so tightly with that much feeling in my heart that I would smother her, but I held on tightly anyway, because it felt so good.in to my fears

We walked together to my house and we spoke to them, I wanted to be the one to tell them before they spoke to anyone else, I decided that it would be best to tell them and get it out of the way, rather than wait for them to find out about when someone read the book and recognized me in it.

But in the end, I gave into my fears and told them only what they needed to know and said nothing about reincarnation; because they didn't believe in it and wouldn't approve, but knowing that they would never allow it I lied to them.

I told them I was taking part in a school study that would get me extra credit towards college, but they were so happy to meet Maria and make her feel welcome that they hardly heard a word of what I said, so it helped me that she was there.

It was clear that my mother loved her right off; and my father too, he was falling all over himself trying to be polite and doing everything right, he even winked at me when he thought she wasn't looking to tell me that they approved.

I honestly hated lying to them, but I knew they would never allow it otherwise, and I didn't think there was any other way to get help and without help we were surely going to die, and again; if they thought that Maria was behind it they would likely forbid me to see her and I couldn't allow them to put me in that kind of corner; it was important to me that they accept her because she was going to be their daughter in law someday and then we'd be giving them grandchildren to love and enjoy with us.

I knew that they equated reincarnation with devil worship, but we didn't see it that way and were fighting for our lives, I thought that once they saw that, they would come around and see why I had to lie to them; why we had to do this, with or without their permission.

They were both nice to her though, welcoming her into our home with open arms, I don't remember a time when I saw my mother smile that much and when my father winked at me, she saw it and squeezed my hand to tell me it made her happy.

It was all too perfect, and I guess deep in my heart I must have felt that it wasn't going to stay perfect unless we were ready for it; I was ignoring that dark cloud hovering over us and succeeded for the most part, but it persisted and never really left my thoughts.

The rest of the time that we had to wait for them to be ready and start the study went really slow, it felt as though it was dragging along; one tedious day at a time, with the only good coming when we were together.

The next day, we went back to Miss Johnson's class and with all of the kisses and interviews for the study, I forgot all about the poem until now, but I never expected Miss Johnson to be excited about it but she obviously was; she seemed to be almost as excited as if I'd written the poem for her and she couldn't wait to share it with the world, yet I still didn't think it was any big deal.

Maybe because when I thought of poetry, I thought of the works of Edgar Allen Poe and others that wrote so beautifully and I knew this, my first effort was amateurish at best; but I didn't see the big deal and thought at most I'd get a "C" for my efforts, and maybe a "plus" on it, but I never expected any excitement over it.

I thought that maybe Maria would get excited about it, but then it was to her after all; to me it was too basic and simple, and there were far better works in the world than anything I could ever write.

"With your permission, I would like to submit this for some honors programs and maybe even possibly get you a scholarship, what would you think about that?" she asked me with a smile on her face.

"Honors?" that word really jumped out sat me, and then "scholarship" and it made me wonder if she'd read the same paper that I left on her desk or was I getting credit for someone else's hard work; I kept thinking that it wasn't that good, and she was pulling my leg.

Everyone else in the classroom turned and looked at me then; as if they had never noticed me sitting there before, and thankfully, she didn't make me read it to the class but she really gushed over it, she made it very clear that she thought I had the potential to be a writer someday.

I guess that I never saw it before, but the spark of those few encouraging thoughts and words made me think that I should take a much harder look at that, I hoped that if I did, that I could write something better next time, but those things she said gave me the spark to think that it might be possible.

The rest of the day, I was making jokes about being big-headed now, that I was a "star" and wouldn't be able to get my head through the doorways at school anymore, it was fun and we both laughed about it.

After we got out of there, one of Sam's assistants came and found us, said that we had to take a physical and sign more release papers and thankfully, none that my parents needed to sign that said anything about reincarnation.

It was more formalities in most cases, making sure we crossed the T's and dotted the I's and make sure that everything was in order, it took some explaining before I could understand all of the legalese that was involved, but with a lawsuit happy society I guess that was just how it worked these days.

Still, it made me laugh that we needed to pass a physical before I could do a sleep study, "Does that mean that I have to be in good shape to sleep here?" I asked, only half-joking.

"That makes as much sense as telling me that I have to get some sleep before I take a nap!" I said, and then laughed some more, though they didn't see any humor in it, I couldn't help it and ran with it some more; "Go home and get some rest so we can see if you can sleep!" I said.

When the big day finally came, we walked there together and maybe because we were more than just a little nervous about it, okay, outright scared is more like it; we stopped in front and started talking again, and we began to make promises that only make sense to those in love, but even more; because of what we already remembered and that seemed like more and more all the time, we were making sure that we both were ready for whatever we would be seeing and possibly reliving on the other side of those doors.

But as we sat there talking, I noticed a sign that I had missed before; maybe because I was so nervous that time and this was all new, but neither of us had seen it before. It was a sign on the front of the building, and it said:

"You will understand the past through the present, and conform the present with the divine teachings revealed in past eras!"

And just underneath that it said:

"Teaching 366:29, the Book of the True Life"
(The Third Testament)

As we were going through all of the preparations and the steeling of ourselves for what we hoped would not be the last time we opened our eyes together in this world; Gregor decided that he could wait no longer, that he needed to get to her that night because he felt the police closing in on him; as if there was nowhere to hide anymore.

He felt as long as she was still breathing, that he could not rest easy, and he was angry at having to wait there all night and he didn't see her return, he wondered if there was another way in and out and cursed himself for not thinking of that sooner.

But then it occurred to him that maybe she had already moved on, that she discovered that he was searching for her, even though he doubted that because he was pretty sure that if she knew about him, she would have paid him a visit at his own door, that meant that it must be something else; just her dumb luck most likely.

He walked around the compound, much as I did that first day, making sure which windows had no activity and where the employees checked in and out as they checked in for their shifts, and he knew that it was probably his imagination but he felt that he could smell her stronger in certain areas of the compound; as if she'd passed through here recently; but that only made him feel lonelier, gave him more of a sense of being abandoned and all alone in the world.

Yet he also noticed that her scent had changed, somehow mixing the old Esmeralda with the new one, but he couldn't figure that the other part out because he hadn't see her as a spider yet; to him, she smelled musty and earthy more than soft and feminine.

He did make it into the building, but he couldn't explore it completely because he didn't want to be discovered, and as he went into the lower levels he was trying to find that window that she dropped out that first time he saw her, he was hoping to find the window so he would begin his search from there; but he knew deep inside that it was far too late and she was already gone.

As he walked back in the direction he thought he'd just come from, he found a large freezer in the middle of his path; he was thinking that it would lead to another doorway or stairwell, but the freezer looked too big for him to move; he angrily kicked some boxes out of the way and since they were empty they fell over easily.

Thinking that he'd made too much noise, he stepped behind some boxes, in case someone came to investigate and almost fell down a stairwell that he would have missed had he left, and no one came to check on the commotion anyway.

It was so dark down there and the chain the prevented anyone from falling in was gone, and as he looked to those lower levels he saw that the stairwell went almost straight down and he would have surely broken his neck if he hadn't caught himself or just walked in blindly.

After his eyes adjusted to the darkness down there, he saw that there were other floors below this one, several in fact, then they leveled off before they went down even further.

Now he was being careful again, he thought she might be sleeping down there and it wouldn't do to wake her before he found her; he wanted to surprise her, even though he thought his footsteps pounded loudly in that darkness.

It was so dark at that level that he kept having to stop and check his bearings and retrace his steps because he'd end up somewhere that he'd already been; the steps were deceptive in the darkness and he was afraid to fall and hurt himself, he couldn't see two feet in front of him now because the only light came from the emergency exit signs that glowed softly in the darkness.

That might have given someone comfort if they were working down there and now could find their way out by seeing that dimly lit sign; but to Gregor they were simply red flags that told him to get the hell out of there before she was able to sneak up behind him and kill him again before he had a chance.

It smelled wet down there, as if the plumbing sprung a leak somewhere and the water settled and fouled or soaked into something and it became mildewed and was rotting the wood underneath; it just smelled wrong for some reason.

That was when he smelled something else, something that was worse than wood rot and mildew, and likely a lot harder to clean too, but in the pitch darkness, it might have taken him a few more minutes to figure out that it was the same smell he'd created at Jeremy's; the smell of dried blood, rotting corpses, it was the smell of death.

He was thinking that it was the same scent he smelled when he crawled through that window, though it was no intermingled with so many other odors, the smell of fear and some other things he couldn't quite figure out, he thought maybe she left them there to confuse him or anyone else that might be trying to find her lair.

The scent was stronger in some areas, and he felt as though he could close his eyes and follow that scent, but he couldn't in the dark without falling over something, and it was just his imagination because he thought he could feel her blood pumping through her veins and smell it as well.

He looked around as much as he could for any other clues or evidence of her; but all he saw was furniture scattered all around this level, some of it weas covered with old, tattered blankets that were covered with layer upon layer of dust; the blankets were falling away as time ate at them, sad remains of what they once were but were no longer useful.

There was a lot of other things scattered about the room, as people might have come through here and shoved things out of their way; or maybe they were looking for something and threw the things in their way in frustration at not being able to find it.

But it also seemed as though there might have been some fighting here more than once; or maybe someone was chased through that room, it was hard to tell now, but he thought that the only thing that would make someone feel that much fear had to be Esmeralda and now he knew he was close.

He looked around and found one hell of a collection of spider webbing and he could smell her scent a lot stronger now; he thought he could smell her sent better in there because they were linked, because of the way she killed him, but that was just a thought that came and went quickly because it didn't matter.

Following that scent for a while longer, he noticed that when he did that, it became darker down there and the smell was much stronger as well; and then he found some of the emaciated bodies that she'd drained and left behind.

Some bodies were dangling from the ceiling, others simply wound up in webbing and scattered about the room as the furniture was in the other room, he could see one man that fought back, his hands were still up as if he was reaching for someone or something when he died.

There was still a snarl on his face, though he was long dead; and Gregor saw a large, empty hole where his stomach was, and when he looked closer he could see that his eyes were gone too, the empty sockets glared back at him where he stood.

His skin looked dry and leathery, and some of his bones showed through his clothing but Gregor moved on from there and found more bodies hanging from the ceiling and felt as though some of those were still barely alive, though he wasn't going to help them so he didn't care and moved on without getting any closer to them; he thought he could hear a slight heartbeat or something, though feint and slowed to a crawl, he could do nothing for them as they were nearly dead.

A lot of bodies that were dried out and forgotten as the world moved on without them, the occasional empty eye socket and body parts missing as though they were chewed off by rats or something, and if it was bigger than a rat and not Esmeralda, he didn't want to know what that was.

This was confusing to him though, he still was unaware of her spider side and wondered if she'd made a huge, monstrous spider her pet, maybe something that she'd brought from another world and made it her guard dog, he looked around quickly to make sure it wasn't sneaking up on him at that moment.

All around him he saw the dead and the near dead; all wrapped in that silken thread until they could no longer resist, or move because they were too weak to even cry out for help; he felt their eyes on him, pleading with him to kill them and end their misery but he had no care for them and kept going.

He could tell that they gave up any hope they held onto a long time ago, they just wanted to die, they had no illusions of escape or rescue anymore and just wanted to end it, some were so near to death that they didn't react when he walked by, it didn't give them any hope of rescue or the end to their suffering.

They all seemed to share that one common thread; the smile they wore on their faces, they all bore the exact same grimace of pain kind of smile that held no humor and nothing nice could come from that.

Now he was getting angrier, she still didn't know that he was hunting her and yet he now knew for certain that she's already moved on and was no longer here and wasn't coming back anytime soon; his fury grew with each discarded body he found lying there, he was angrier now, knowing for certain that he was too late.

She had moved on, he was right about that part; but it had nothing to do with him as he was thinking at that moment, she just had that instinctive feeling that it was time to move on; all the dead bodies were bothering her as well, though she had no conscience to make her regret what she'd done to them, she felt their dead eyes on her while she slept and thought she could hear them cursing her for what she'd done.

Gregor finally gave up and went back to Jeremy's to wait for the sun to set again; this time the smell did bother him, he thought that it put him in the same place as Esmeralda with her skeletons in the webbing and didn't like the image it projected into his mind.

He opened the door to the bedroom and saw both bodies lying together, he went to the closet and picked up Jeremy's head and placed it next to hers, "Lovers! Even in death!" he said and tried to laugh but couldn't because it reminded him of Elspeth and me, and he didn't like to think she was still "with me" even though he had no idea that she truly was.

As he came to the door, he found several of those annoying little yellow post it notes stuck to the door that told Jeremy several of his co-workers had come by to see him; as well as some of her associates and family because they hadn't been seen nor heard from for several days and were worried, Gregor was sure that he would also have to move on and find new digs because the smell would give him away if their friends didn't.

What Esmeralda liked about her new hideout was that now she could have all the privacy she would ever need to carry out her nefarious schemes and plans and rituals she needed to perform without being interrupted, if anyone was foolish enough to follow her down there, she thought she would see or hear them long before they got close enough to harm her and she felt that she could literally get away with murder because no one would hear them scream.

"Home sweet home!" she said and laughed, then she looked at Asmodeus, and the cat seemed to agree with her, she thought he was smiling now and went to pet him, but he ran off before she could.

She also discovered that this part of the caves or tunnels went back a lot farther than she thought, and there was another escape route if she needed one, even though she was sure that no one would follow her and she knew if they did, they would never return to tell anyone else about it.

If she didn't find them in that darkness, they would likely become lost and never find their way out, nothing was marked to help them if they wandered in there were no signs that told them to go left or right to exit, not even a sign for the bathroom.

She'd spent most of that day gathering firewood, collecting as much as she could carry and stacking it in a pile, and when that became too much, she moved it to another room where she could pile them even higher, and then it was stacked so neatly that it resembled the pyre that they killed her on so long ago, only on a much smaller scale.

It wasn't deliberate, or because she remembered what she did to Elspeth; though she did see that in swatches of her visions, but it must have been in the back of her mind because she even looked up to see where the smoke would go because it would not do to die alongside of her.

The last thing she wanted to do was go through all that trouble, then watch her burn to death, delight in her screams of pain and anguish and then die alongside her of smoke inhalation or something while she celebrated the part of her prophecy came true and she killed her.

The odd thing about all of this is, at the time, I was in the middle of civics class, giving my report on what we were studying at the time; and we were discussing freedom of speech and debating how the government limits that, what we can say and write, even when it's true.

In the middle of my argument, which I was winning, I was arguing against a guy that was pro-government, and as I was talking, I fell down, face first into the carpet, so hard that I almost broke my nose in the process.

Everyone that wasn't rushing to the office to get me some help was trying to clear away the furniture and anything else I might hurt myself with as I thrashed around on the floor, but also to give them room in case I was having a seizure, which I wasn't; and to make sure I was still breathing and my blood was still being pumped through my heart, and thankfully; it was.

When they felt they had it under control, whatever it was; they asked me what I remembered about what happened, and what was the last thing that I remember doing before I fell.

I told them I remembered that I was walking forward and went to shake someone's hand after being victorious, but in reality I heard her, and I saw both versions of her at that moment; first, her dancing in the cell with me while my love was about to be burned at the stake, and even from the distance and through the walls that separated us; I could still hear her screaming, though in this version she was curing my name and blaming me for all that had happened to her; my heart was exploding with pain as I knew that it wasn't true, and yet it was, because of the love we shared; if I had denied her they might have let us live, and yet I couldn't bring myself to do that anymore than she could have; a love so strong that we were murdered for it.

In the other version I saw her building that pyre in the caves, and then my love was burned again atop of it; murdered for the second time in just as horrible a manner as before, this time she was standing next to me and holding my hand as we both watched her die in those flames, and just as the last time, I was just as hopeless to stop it or do anything about it, just as she foretold.

They said I was feverish, that I was screaming about the flames and trying to get help to put out the fire, I thought I was trying to pull away from

Esmeralda and, knowing it was too late, I was going to join her in the flames and die alongside her as I tried to before; and that was when I woke up.

I had no idea of what happened when I opened my eyes again, a feeling that something bad had happened but not what, or even to whom it might have happened to; but then I saw my mother and father talking, and Maria came out of the bathroom while drying her hands.

It might have been funny under normal circumstances, but it seemed as though my mother and Maria both raced to my side at the same moment; because both were overjoyed that I was back and they both wanted to hold me; mom was closer and had the edge in angle and distance; but Maria almost beat her there anyway because she thought that she'd lost me again.

They all heard me call out names while I was out, they all agreed that the "Maria" I was calling for was the one they'd just met; that I seemed to be trying to fight to save from something terrible, but the only one with a clue as to whom Elspeth could be was Maria, and she wasn't going to say anything either.

Still, when Maria heard that name she jumped, and the only reason that my parents didn't see it was because they were both looking at me.

Photograph by J.R. Gonzalez

LAST ONE TO THE BAR BUYS

Believe those who are seeking the truth.

-Andre Gide (1869-1951)

BEFORE WE COULD DO THE real study, they wired us and tried to help us to relax so we could sleep restfully while they monitored everything from brain waves to heart rate, respiratory and even muscle tone was going to show up on the graphs, and they wanted us to sleep there for two days, we could go home and go to school or do whatever we needed to do before we went to bed for the night.

They said they wanted even more days than that, more would give them consistent data to track and note any changes when they brought out the heavy stuff later; the meat of our story and all that we went through, what happened to us.

It took me a long time to relax and let go, but when I finally did, I slept like the dead, which I hoped wasn't a premonition, but I never stirred, I did change positions every now and then; but there was no sense of urgency, as if I was running in my dreams or something like that; my blood pressure stayed even and right where it was supposed to be, no spikes and apparently, no nightmares either.

The only thing I could remember of those two nights was that I went out to a field of tall, green grass; at least two feet high in most places, I was walking alone, slowly, so I thought that I was safe and no one was trying to chase me or kill me.

I laid down on my back and was looking up at the clouds and they were so clear, bright and beautiful; huge and puffy white interspersed with the brightest blue behind them, I think I even remember thinking that it must have been a glimpse of heaven.

I got up after a while and started walking again, feeling as though I was missing something, but again; it didn't feel dangerous, the grass here was not as high and the blue sky was still calling to me from up there so I lay down once more, I was thinking that if this really was heaven; that my brother Flaco was there, and I could almost see and hear him laughing at me as he waited for me to get there; and that was they would find my body a few hours later; it was as if I just decided it was time to die, and then I did.

We didn't tell Sam about that part because we didn't want to cloud up, or muddy up the study and put off finding our answers even longer; we foolishly made that decision because we didn't think it was relevant, it nothing to do with flames, murder or anyone dying except for me, and that seemed to be a peaceful passing, which was how I'd want to go, except that I would want Maria there, holding my hand.

I felt a sense of urgency that I couldn't explain but I couldn't tell Maria about that because I thought she already had enough to worry about.

The second time, maybe because they were going to try and bring some things into play while we slept, stimulate the process as I heard one of them say, to try and force my mind to more activity that they could record and study, and they gave me medication to help me because this "stimuli's" was going to make it harder to relax.

They called this phase, sleep-induced reincarnation, it was going to help us get to that state and study our reactions, but this was different than the first time because this was going to allow them to see a with that and feel what we did, as if they were there alongside us when it happened; they would record the way we dealt with that stimuli, both physically and emotionally through our brain waves, heart rates and other physicality.

That we might also relive experiences that we could not have knowledge of in this life, they could check them and verify the timeline by how we described things, that those things could come back to us as we slept, or at least some parts might be revealed; but they couldn't promise if it would be good or bad, or even that they could clear up anything at all, but it was a chance; and there was no other way that we could think of and we were desperate.

From the time second we went to the room and they wired us, to the time we were leaving the building that morning, we were going to be recorded on tape and watched on several monitors mounted in the rooms and high overhead.

All of that would be backed up with both audio and video recordings that they were all sure that they would not miss a thing in either room, we weren't even going to be able to get up to use the toilet, there were attendants with bed pans at the ready and that was awkward for me, I didn't ask Maria how she felt about it but I'm sure she didn't feel anymore comfortable than I did.

We were given a sedative while they attached the wire from head to toe on us, and I joked with the techs and said I felt like a toaster oven now; but they tired to ignore me and stay serious and none of them laughed, but I did see one of them turn her head to the side so I wouldn't see her laughing.

I wasn't sure if I said it wrong or they had no sense of humor; I always tried humor when I was nervous or scared, but I knew this time it wasn't going to help me at all.

After that, they left me alone and I tried to sleep but kept thinking about the dreams and images that they would be monitoring and I couldn't wait to see what they got but it still made me nervous thinking that they were going to be inside of my head, I wondered at the things that scared me, how would they be perceived by these guys with no sense of humor, all of my secrets spilled out onto those monitors; I wondered what else I might say or do while I was under, but it was too late to back out now, if I'd wanted to.

What if I started talking about Maria and how I felt, it would probably make them laugh, those were things I couldn't stop thinking about and were keeping me awake.

I couldn't see the techs anymore, they were on the other side of the glass and watching the monitors, and I knew that they could hear me but I also knew that they weren't going to answer me, even though they could push a button and I'd hear them too so I didn't bother to ask them.

Every now and then I would see them as they walked by the window but they were so intent on what they were doing that they never even saw me unless it was on those monitors; even if they looked through the glass and directly at me.

I might have been trying too hard to get there first again; but this time it wasn't just so I could see if she was happy to see me waiting for her; this time I didn't know what was going to be waiting for us, I didn't want to be thinking about arriving during the kiss we'd shared and coming out in the middle of a fire.

But maybe it was all of that and the underlying fear that I wouldn't like what we found out after this, I couldn't relax enough to sleep, but I was sure that they were going to wait me out, they were going to wait until I was so tired that I couldn't keep my eyes open; they were getting paid by the hour anyway and had all the time in the world.

My thoughts were interrupted by the click of the intercom and the metallic voice that said, "Do you need another sedative?" making me think that they read my anxiety on the charts.

"Only if you think it will help!" I said slowly, I didn't know what else to say, they were the techs with the brains, and yet, they were asking me what they should do.

They ended up giving me two more and then a shot in the arm before I could relax enough for them to get started, the last thing I remember was a guy showing up with a short, stubby needle and a long tube at the end, filled with some yellowish fluid.

They strapped my arm as they injected me and then told me to start counting backwards from one hundred; I think I made it to ninety-six before I succumbed to its spell, I also remember that same tech smiling at me and waving as I went under because this stuff never failed.

I opened my eyes, and I was back in hell again; I was in my cell and could smell the stale urine, the sweat, intermingled with fear and blood, with the smell of desperation, hopelessness, and death.

There were a number of other prisoner's in those cells, and it seemed that from every direction at once I could hear the screams, I could feel their pain and suffering and I knew how real it was; the pain of what they did to us came rushing over me in waves.

I looked down the hallway and it seemed that the cells, which numbered eighty-three when we were there before now stretched on and seemed to be limitless, it went on for as far as I could see, and it might have just been my imagination but I thought it started to curve down not too far from where I was.

What scared me the most at that moment was that I saw, farther down that limitless hallway to hell was a figure that resembled a man in most aspects, but it was much larger than any man I ever saw, he was huge and muscular; and he was naked but for some filthy rag that was tied around his waist.

He also had a long, wicked-looking whip with steel barbs at the end that were meant to rip into the flesh of the unfortunate that drew the wrong kind of attention.

Maybe he was trying to show me, or prove to me what they did, he flexed his wrist and the whip snapped up and when he brought his hand forward I saw the whip fly through the bars and strike a man that I thought would normally be asleep until he felt the sting and screamed loudly, not in protest but in pain because protest would only bring more of the same.

As I looked at him then, he became angry at me because he looked harder at me and snorted, I tried to stand back in the shadows, I even turned away and pressed my back hard against the wall, I was doing my best to hide within it because I heard and felt the thunder of his hooves as he approached my cell.

Then I heard him snort again, and I knew that he was just a few inches away from me, he couldn't see me and I tried to keep my eyes closed but I could see his breath as it expelled from his nostrils and wet the area above his upper lip.

Then he cracked the whip crack as though he was warming it up to use it on my back and as I was praying that he would leave me alone until I saw his tongue flick out and then he turned in the direction that I was hiding, telling me that he not only wasn't going to leave, but he also knew exactly where I was at that moment; he didn't actually need to see me, to know where I was.

I tried to pull back even further, but ai was in corner and there was nowhere else to go unless I ran out of my cell, which would have revealed my hiding place, even though it wasn't working anyway; I was at the mercy of his whip because I'd already seen him flick it through the bars.

His tongue was reaching for me again, it was almost close enough to touch me and I could feel him trying to stretch it further, to touch me with it, but I was too far for that, he fell short and I could hear his frustration and exasperation; I heard the whip crack again and then another man's scream before there was another crack and I thought this should have awakened everyone in the prison by now and everyone would think that it was my fault because I didn't let him tickle my hide with that whip.

Being that close to the wall, I could hear large rats scurrying through the walls, along with the low moans of the men that were waking at that moment and cursing my name; and then I was visited once more by that ghost-dead man that came before; his eye still dangling from his face and his tongue still flicked out every so often like a bad habit.

Despair was the most pervasive odor, through my cell and everywhere else I thought; the smell of fear and the stench of death, the smell of men that had given up any hope they might have held onto at one time; though by the looks of them, that must have been a very long time ago.

The man in the next cell started screaming then, he couldn't bear his pain any longer and wasn't able to keep quiet about it, I remember that his crime was trying to pass through town, asking the wrong questions of the wrong man, though he thought he was safe asking a priest, but everyone was afraid of strangers now.

For his transgression, he was stretched out on the rack and tortured for three days before they decided that he was innocent after all: but even when they knew that, they didn't want to stop there and kept going until he was babbling incoherently.

Then they dragged him back to his cell to think about it and were going to release him in the morning but they never told him that and, during the night he made the mistake of waking one of the guards because he was hurting so badly.

The guard sat up with a snort and looked around for the source of the noise, then he kicked the cot that his partner was sleeping on, "Hey chingon! Its your turn to shut them up!" he said.

When he didn't reply or get up, his friend kicked the cot again until he finally started rubbing his face while still trying to wake up, "Son of a bitch!" the guard swore as he rose from the cot.

He was in the middle of a wet dream and was not at all happy that he was interrupted, and he let his friend know that, "All right, ALL RIGHT!" he shouted, "If its too damned much to ask that I am allowed to sleep in this world as the rest of you are doing, I will get up, but I swear on the bones of my mother that someone is going to pay for this!" he seethed as he left and went to find out who he was going to give the bill to.

They started arguing about it, and almost broke out into a fight but it was his turn after all; as he left the room, he felt that threads and tatters of that wet dream leaving him and adding to his anger and frustration about all of this.

He came back and took the flask that belonged to his friend and took a long pull on it without asking, enjoying the look on his friends face as he felt the warm liquid surging through his system, he gave his friend one last nasty look as if he didn't already know how much this angered him, tossed the flask to him but his friend was already lying down and missed the face, though he caught the flask.

He turned left and walked towards the cells, from there he could hear the man and he was getting angrier as he walked, it wasn't as warm and cozy out there as it was in that little space they called their room, "You would be wise to shut the hell up before I get there!" he said, the cold air was grating on his nerves now too.

All were meant to suffer here, no one was spared no matter their standing or station here; it was the sole reason for them building this prison in the first place; not to coddle the prisoner's whether they were innocent or not; it was to make people like me suffer for crimes they imagined that we did.

There was no justice in the world then and we were never given an opportunity to argue our innocence or state our defense, they would not allow it and if they ever heard it, they refused to accept it; it was clear from the day they brought us here that we had no chance, that we were betrayed by men that came from the church where we prayed so hard; that they could prey on us in return while officially, the church looked the other way.

The guards were made miserable, and since they said that shit rolls downhill that meant we would surely feel the wrath of that anger, they would make us suffer all the more for it; though it was not our fault they took the position, but then, jobs were rare and money wasn't easy to find these days so they didn't have many options.

If the prisoner's made too much noise, we were beaten; or they died without permission, that would cause their cell mate to be punished for it, since they couldn't hurt a corpse and he didn't keep him alive so who else would they punish, and sometimes even the quiet ones were killed, because they weren't liked, they spooked the guards by never complaining or crying out about the injustice as everyone else did vociferously, every chance they got.

It went on and on that way until someone died or went insane and then ended up dead anyway because they would end his misery after that, there was no reason to keep him there now, because they would beat them as brutally as ever and he would laugh and ask for more.

I felt that if anyone ever needed a vision that they might paint what hell looked like, they could come here at any time of the day or night and cover this place from any angle or position and get that accurate vision to inspire images of such evil works.

If the guards ever forgot why they were there, they were rudely reminded that they were also guests in this place that could never leave either, again, they made it feel as though that was our fault.

He finally arrived at that man's cell and stood for a moment and watched, enjoying the man's suffering; the poor man was trying to get comfortable to get back to sleep but everything hurt, he was all stretched out and the parts that hurt weren't going back to their normal state anymore; no matter where or how he laid on that straw mattress, it still hurt him somewhere.

After a few moments of watching this and savoring the man's pain; he took his key and opened the door slowly, as if he wasn't there to cause even more pain, then he spoke to the man gently, as if he really cared, "Do you require a healer? Leeches? Want me to summon the physician for you?" he asked, mocking his pain now.

The man stirred in his bed then, he was unaware that he even had a visitor until that moment; and then he tried to sit up and reply, but the guard put his foot on his shoulder and pressed down hard, knowing how much pain that was going to send screaming through him.

The man was already delusional from the pain, it was so great and showed no signs that it would let up soon; it hurt just to breath, but then the guard punched him hard in the stomach and told him to shut up, "Take the pain and shut the hell up! Go back to sleep so that can, or you will not live to see the sunrise!" he threatened; and the man knew he meant it but couldn't help himself.

The guard was rewarded for his anger by the prisoner's foul breath as it flew into his face and disgusted and angered him so much that he struck him two more times in the gut, just for spite; he heard one of the man's ribs break and caused him to scream even louder.

The guard stepped in closer and covered his mouth, choking off his scream and blocking the air he was trying to draw in, "Go ahead and scream!" he whispered menacingly; "I will kill you before the sound hits my ears! You just try and tell me I won't!" he said as he drew out a short, stubby knife he carried in his belt, it glowed softly in the low light and he saw his face reflected in the blade to add to his fear, now the blade was "branded" with his face and he felt as though the knife was made just to kill him.

He dared him to scream but he didn't, he turned his face into the straw and began to cry, he thought that since he stopped screaming that he would be left alone.

The guard was angrier then, crying was against the rules, or maybe he was just angry and hadn't released enough of that to get back to his straw and try to sleep, dream of that gypsy girl again, though there weren't any gypsy's in the region and hadn't been for a long time; ever since their witch was killed.

The guard reacted to him turning away as if he were being dismissed, he reacted with even more punches to the exposed kidneys, hitting him faster and harder and taking out years of frustration on the poor man, he hit him everywhere that he could until he was too tired and back off for a moment.

He stood back, panting and covered in sweat that stung his eyes and made his nose run which further irritated him; he raised his hands and they were covered with the poor man's blood, "NOW you need a healer, pendejo!" he shouted at him.

"Would you like for me to get one for you now? Or are you going to finally shut the hell up, Hijo de puta!" he spat at the man and then he walked out because he didn't need an answer from him.

The prisoner sobbed quietly for a few more moments, and he died a short time later because one of ribs broken ribs punctured his lung and nicked the edge of his heart, and as he moved around and tried to get comfortable or at the very least, minimize his pain and that was when he punctured his spleen and then bled to death internally, all quiet at last.

I watched all of this happen and I prayed for the man, and began to wonder which circle of hell and I noticed that it was getting hotter in there now; and then I heard another man scream, the kind of drawn-out scream that spoke of intense pain, which was normal for this place, but not usually at night.

This was the kind of pain, the scream that you hoped you never felt or heard in your lifetime, but thankfully the oversized guards were gone though I never saw them leave, they were suddenly gone and I wasn't going to ask because I knew that I wouldn't miss them.

I tried to look down the hallway, to see what else was going on but then I was forced to shrink down to the floor and cover my ears because it was suddenly so loud in there that the sound found its way into my ears anyway; I was hoping this was all a bad dream but was having a hard time, it was a tough sell.

That scream kept going and it was so painful that it was taking away all hope because you knew that you could be next, and the way things happened in here, it could very well be your scream that you were hearing and your mind was denying it; it was too much to bear.

I was worried about Maria then, but in my mind, I thought "Elspeth" instead, and that was weird; thinking of her with that name, even though it was her seemed unnatural in this other world, it did to me anyway.

There was no way that I could have known it, but she was having it much than I was; she was seeing herself at home and talking with her father about family history, they were in the stable and her father was at that moment, tending to a beautiful mare, the sun was shinning brightly above them and there wasn't a cloud in the sky.

She was asking her father about her mother, what she was like; how they met and what they hoped for on the day they married, what kind of plans did they make, "girl things" of that sort.

"What made you fall in love with momma?" she asked him, and I could see her; she was sitting on a rail, happily swinging her legs underneath her and watching him as he worked.

He thought that maybe this was one of those "after church" kinds of discussions because she was wearing a beautiful, frilly white dress, with lots of lace and extra stitching on it, probably with the white ankle socks and gloves to match, she wore boots on her feet but it just seemed too formal for everyday wear, which made him think it was Sunday.

"The first thing?" he asked her with a slight smile on his face, she knew that he liked being funny and mysterious, and even romantic and was overplaying it and he probably knew the answer before she asked the question.

He was trying to be serious, yet she could see the slight smile as it played on his lips as he thought about her mother; "It was her smile, Mija!" he said at last, when he couldn't make her wait any longer.

"When I first saw that smile, to me, it seemed as though the good lord opened up the heavens to show me what paradise looked like!" he said and this time his smile was more wistful than playful.

"It made me want to know what made a woman smile like that, if it matched the smile on her heart; I knew that if her heart was as beautiful as her smile that I'd found the woman I wanted to spend the rest of my life with!" he told her as he looked away in the distance, maybe trying to see it once more; what was lost when she died that horrible, dark night.

Before this, whenever she tried to ask him about things like this, he immediately brought the wall down and closed the doors about any further discussion on the subject; for him, it was too hard to think about and feel that deep sense of loss again, and yet this time; he was more than happy to talk about it and held nothing back; he didn't break down and cry either, a great relief to her.

"What was your first date like? Did you ask her, or did she ask you first? Did you have to ask her father's permission first or did you just go out?" she asked him in rapid succession, probably because all the other times she stopped him before she got that far.

"Aye Mija!" he said, as he shook his head and then laughed, "You ask too many questions that you're giving me a headache!" he said.

She quickly asked him about their wedding, what kind of reception did they have and where was it held, what her mother looked like that day and how he felt when she told him he was going to be a father, those things that she'd always wondered about, things she imagined had happened.

In the other room, things were wired so tightly that they could tell the temperature on any part of my body as I slept and did my prison time while I revisited the nightmare that was.

On the one hand, I was happy to be in the midstof this, I imagined that in the other room the needles were jumping all over the place, and they would have plenty of data to study and figure things out with; I tried to turn my head to see their reactions but I couldn't see them when I did.

I didn't know it, but in the other room, the only time the needles moved at all was when I moved my head or tried to turn in my sleep, otherwise they heard nothing but the soft hiss of static on the tapes, everything else with needles or lights that was set up to record all of this, all of those devices were as still as death.

There were no alarms, no bells nor whistles, no bright flashes; nothing to indicate what was going on inside of our heads, most of the technicians had fallen asleep while they waited for something to happen and the one that was awake could barely hold his eyes open, his feet were on the desk while he was trying to read a book, but he kept nodding off.

Elspeth was still sitting on that rail and talking with her father when she felt her gaze being drawn behind him, to the far horizon where she saw a cloudbank approaching from that direction; it was coming her way and moving very fast against the wind.

Though her father was happy and talking excitedly, and yet she felt a sense of impending danger; she knew there was something evil about those dark clouds, and then she realized that he couldn't hear her anymore; though he hardly seemed to have noticed.

She was suddenly very frightened, and she tried to warn her father but the wind blew her words back at her and he didn't seem to hear or notice either, and kept talking as if he was sharing something special with her; he kept laughing and gesturing excitedly, he didn't see anything alarming in his daughter's face.

In fact, he didn't seem to notice much of anything at that moment, then he turned and walked towards the barn and speaking to her as if she were following closely behind him and nothing was amiss.

She had this feeling then that something evil that had been sleeping for a long time was now awakened; that it sensed this tender moment that she was sharing with her father and couldn't allow it to continue; was coming there to put a stop to it; that it could not be allowed; we could not be given that moment of comfort in this sea of madness.

Then she felt as though their time was short, it was running out on them and she had to ask whatever him whatever it was that he'd come to find out because she was sure that the information window was about to be slammed shut in her face.

She looked back at him, and he was still walking away from her slowly, he was still speaking to her as if she were walking alongside of him as he left; but she still couldn't hear the words he was speaking to her as the wind swirled around her in stronger gusts, she had to climb down then before it pushed her over.

The horse that her father was grooming turned away from him then and began to stomp her foreleg and raise her head up and down while looking at her; then she felt the tether around her neck give way and she rose up on her hind legs and began striking at her.

She couldn't tell if it was fear or hatred as the horse tried to get to her, but she knew that it was trying to hurt her and she moved further away from it, her eyes went back to the darkening sky, and now she thought she could see a face forming in those clouds, it was malevolent as it seemed to be searching the ground for her as it was swept along.

Debris began to fly all around her then, branches seemed to reach for her and tore at her arms and her dress as they swayed with that strong wind that was growing stronger by the minute.

Now there was clearly a face in those clouds, and it seemed to have found her and was glaring at her before it moved on quickly; she felt as though it wanted to stay there and hurt her badly but it had other, more important business to take care of, but she noticed that, everywhere the clouds passed, things under it turned a shade darker and plants and flowers withered under its intensity.

She turned back to her father again, but he was gone; and so was the horse, so she walked towards the house thinking that he'd gone into the house and she'd find him there; she wanted to know that he was alright, though she should have known better.

As she got closer to the house, she saw that it was in ruins now, the front door hung off the hinges, the entire house was faded, cracked, splintered or hanging off to one side.

The white-picket fence in the front of the house that her father always took great pride in was broken and falling over in more than one place; the once bleached-white white paint now faded and cracked as well, it was the same all over the house, everything was flaked off and peeling away.

The curtains her mother used to take down once a month and beat the dust out of over the fence were in ruins also; covered with dust and streaked with spider webbing.

Every window that she could see was broken and at one time it had been boarded up, but someone smashed through those too; as if someone fought hard to enter but then she wondered if they fought that hard to get in, or were they possibly trying to escape, and that thought bothered her even more.

She paused for a few moments, trying to decide if there was anyone in there at the moment, but the house was too old and dilapidated to allow anyone to live in there, she could see that from where she stood then and thought it wouldn't hurt to get a closer look.

Though she must have been aware that the time between when she was there before and now was a great chasm of time, in this vision, her father was not any older, and then she remembered that the house was fine just a few minutes ago when she was out there talking to him, before those evil clouds arrived and changed everything.

She jumped then, she could hear a cat meow from the woods nearby, and though she couldn't see it; she thought that it didn't sound like a normal cat; she knew that it was Asmodeus, but the possible reason for him being there was what scared her the most about that; she decided to move on anyway, and she heard it again, though this time it was a long and drawn out noise, as if the cat was yelling at her.

She walked through the door and hardly noticed it fall off as she passed through it, and because it really bothered her that this was her house, and it was so lost in deep decay; cracked or broken and covered with layer upon layer of dust.

But as she walked, she got the feeling that if she backed up and retraced her steps, that the farther she got from it, the more it would be restored to its former luster; it would revert from the decay she saw now because she was the pariah that brought death to them all.

That it could all be normal again if she would only leave them alone, she was reluctant to go because she thought if she did, she'd be abandoning her father and she couldn't bring herself to do that and she thought that she could somehow save his life and she had to try; she didn't know what else to do.

Yet she was afraid too, because she didn't want to see the house with all her memories, she felt a cold hand pressing at her back, though she could see no one there; she knew the house was urging her forward impatiently and she'd better move on.

She could also hear that damned cat, his meow was bouncing off the emptiness of the house, when that stopped, she reached for the door of her mother's room and found her mother snoring away on the bed as she got closer to her.

Though everything around her was dark, dead and greyish, that sound gave her a false sense of hope that was snatched away as soon as she took another step into the room.

She saw them both there, mother and father, lying together in a loving embrace on the bed, both were long dead and were now only bones and tatters of clothing they once wore.

Then her mother woke; she sat up suddenly as if she realized she had a visitor and turned towards her daughter standing there, in her room.

As she turned her head, Maria could hear the bones in her neck snapping and popping as she turned, and the many layers of dust fell away from her.

Maria wanted to scream, she wanted to run and hide somewhere, or wake herself up to get away from this; anything would be better than seeing them this way, but she could do none of those things, she was frozen to the spot; waiting for whatever was next.

"Y-y-you won't hurt me!" she said pleadingly; "You're my mother, you… you can't!" she cried but knew in her heart that she was wrong and fooling no one.

Her mother pointed a long and boney finger at her then and said, "You brought this upon us! Why couldn't you simply give in and marry Gregor!" she screamed at her, "Get OUT! You brought nothing but pestilence and death to this house, get out, GET OUT, GET OUT!" she screamed over and over again, and louder each time she repeated it, the walls shook with her anger and vehemence, dust fell from the ceiling as she shouted at her daughter and then the wall cracked and began to fall away.

She tried to say "mother" because she'd never known her but she couldn't speak, she looked to her father for help and he was covered in maggots though he must have been as long dead as her mother, they were squirming out from his chest as he tried to speak to her; nothing came out of his mouth except for more maggots, they refused to give up the corpse, and then felt as though the entire house was falling down on her now, she called out to her mother once more to no avail.

A support beam broke and fell towards her, she put her hands up to try and protect herself and thought it was going to crush her but that was when she finally woke up.

The new day was arriving, the sun was bright and shining down on everything and the study was over for the night, she could hear the technicians coming down the hall to remove the wiring from her head and body and though she'd seen her mother and father and all that she'd lost, and couldn't wait to find out what they saw on the screen and what they were able to record of it.

With all that we'd seen and experienced that single night, and all the frightful visions, the scary things we saw and some that we'd never seen before, they didn't get a thing, the tapes were blank but for that static his, the needles never moved to record anything significant, no data to study, nothing to analyze, as my mother would have said if she was there, "nada" but they didn't tell us that, they thought it would be delayed and would show up somewhere eventually, but they didn't know for certain because no one had been through this before and been so vivid in their memories, some of them previous "studies" were thrown out because it was obvious that the participant was "missing" parts of their memories and would "fill in the blanks" with things they thought happened, or that they wanted to happen, though they didn't, it invalidated the study.

Because of the sedatives, she was a bit groggy and unsteady as she tried to get out of bed and they had to support her until she felt steady enough; but I was even worse because I'd needed more of that "see you later" medicine than she did.

I was still dreaming that I was lying on a strange bed, though I think this was not in the time we were in Spain, it seemed to be an entirely different place, everything was strange and unfamiliar to me.

But I was awakened by the sound of men marching in step past my window, I ran to see what was going on and saw them; a long procession of hooded people walking side-by-side in two rows like soldiers with a purpose in their step.

They spoke no words, the only sound was the crunch of gravel beneath their sandaled feet, and I looked around and no one else seemed to have heard them as they marched along a trail that ran behind the house I was in and into the woods nearby.

I could see that they were wearing dark robes, like priests, but they didn't feel or seem like priests and they seemed to be up to no good from their bearing, they clearly knew where they were going without speaking to each other, and they never glanced left nor right as they marched to what end I could not imagine so I decided to follow them and see what they were going to do, it felt scary and exciting, but I guess not scary enough to keep me from following them from a distance.

Though they weren't in a hurry as they went, I thought if I stopped to find my robe and slippers it would take too long and I'd lose them, so I threw on my slippers and climbed out the window and I almost lost them anyway as they turned and were into the woods by then, the ground was softer and made less noise as they walked so it took me a few minutes to find them.

It helped that the front ones carried torches, as well as the ones in the rear; but they seemed to be guards, though as the others they kept their eyes forward as they went, but they were spaced a few feet back from the rest of them, and as I chased them, I almost laughed because I thought that if I'd worn one of those long caps that I would probably look like Ebenezer Scrooge when I ran out that night, chasing the ghosts of my past.

As I entered the woods, I was trailing not too far behind them and I could hear them as they began to chant softly, in rhythm with their footsteps, all spoke the exact same words and it made me feel as though they were sending out a warning to anyone, like me; that was foolish enough to follow them and see what they were doing.

I ran behind them but at times I would not pay enough attention and I'd be running alongside of them, and I thought that since they wore those hoods they didn't see me, I wasn't that close, but I thought I stepped on a few branches as I ran; though they never turned their heads in my direction.

But then I noticed that they were carrying something in the middle on them, on a stretcher or something, and there was someone lying on it; they didn't seem to be injured or dead because they were moving slightly, and every so often, he would twitch or move, as if he was trying to get up.

Since they were carrying him and he didn't seem to be putting up much of a fight, maybe he was drugged or wounded but I couldn't see anything for a time, and then I thought he was blindfolded, or that he couldn't open his eyes, that was because when he tried to raise himself up, he spent a large part of his efforts reaching out in front of him, as if he couldn't see, or he was imagining something that wasn't there for the rest of us to see.

For some reason, though I couldn't see much of him, I felt that I knew that person lying on that stretcher, he seemed familiar and yet I was trying, but couldn't get close enough to see; I thought that it was maybe someone from school, maybe this was a hazing incident that went bad, now I really had to find out what they were doing.

The only other movement I saw was when his leg fell over the side as he tried to pull himself up again, the man walking alongside of him reached down and gently placed it back without breaking stride or even turning his head.

Then they finally stopped walking, without a word or gesture, all at once they stopped and then after a short pause they began to fan out around a clearing; one by one they all stepped up and took their place, making a perfect circle around the stretcher that was placed in the center, on top of some other rocks so that it was waist high to the man standing silently next to it.

All of the others were now shoulder to shoulder, with their backs to the rest of the word and me, and then the man in the middle began to speak to them, but he kept his voice and his tone low and I couldn't hear what he was saying.

I thought that I might be able to get closer without being caught so I crept forward from tree to tree until I thought that he heard me because he turned suddenly in my direction; but then after a moment he turned the other way and I thought it was part of his ritual.

But for a brief moment of terror, I thought that he'd sensed me there and sent someone to root me out, it was really hard for me, but I managed to turn around and found that there was no one behind me at all.

Then the man went back to the center, he spoke a few words to the man in the stretcher, and then he took a knife from his sash, raised it high above his head and then paused for a moment, gathering himself before he shouted something at the top of his lungs and then brought the knife down quickly.

He struck the man that was lying there in the stomach and the blood immediately flew from the wound and then his blood struck him across his face and his chest, both hands came up as if to ward off another blow, but he moved too slowly and when his arms fell I thought he was dead.

But it seemed that he wasn't done killing yet, he kept raising and lowering the knife, repeatedly stabbing the poor man, and, as the knife came out; blood followed the path of his arm, arcing and spraying him and everything around him until all was coated with it; his face a shining mask of red, his hair was matted with it, his bright blue eyes wide open, he had the look of a madman.

I heard the poor man cry out one more time and wished that I was quicker and could have done something to save him, and though the man was not that far off from where I stood; the scream sounded far off and behind me; I turned quickly and almost screamed myself, again, I thought that they discovered me as I hid in the bushes.

Then, in a sudden flash, I realized that it was my scream that I'd heard; and that it was me dying on the table, and all of that pain and suffering that could be found in that long, piercing scream was mine.

Through all of the visions and horrible things that we'd seen, though they weren't exactly the same, we both felt that we were running for our lives long before all of this started to come out; and now, as we lay in our beds we thought that they had more than enough data for their study.

We both saw and remembered the horror that we felt before, and on that night and thought they had plenty of evidence; enough to study for them and get the answers for us, yet the machines failed us once more and the monitors were silent, we seemed to have slept through the entire night, as everyone else did, with no problems or visions.

I woke then and felt panicky, I tried to pull out the needles before they came in because I was impatient, my nose was plugged and the snot was caked over half my face and it was hard to catch my breath; we were supposed to sit down at this point to write down whatever we remembered, or speak it aloud to have the recorders catch it and then they could study it.

At that moment, I fell off the bed and frantically grabbed at the microphone began to speak into it, telling them as much as I could remember of the things I saw when they finally came in the door and began to pull the wires off that I'd missed.

As I described what I saw, the techs in the next room began pouring over the recordings of the night before; checking for any indications from the graphs and charts, but they were blank, or the lines were flat with no indication of any activity at all, nothing out of the ordinary.

Sam walked into the room at that moment, she took them aside and she began speaking to them, watching them as they checked their work; she was listening to me through all of that, amazed at the details I was able to recall, she wasn't at that moment, looking at the charts so she didn't know they were blank yet, she was excited about what I told her and couldn't wait to read the data.

All the techs could think of was that they were in a lot of trouble, she didn't know that they slept through the night and were just hoping that someone didn't screw up and forget to plug something in or push "enter" before they closed their eyes.

The data should have recorded everything it was set up to; it didn't miss my reactions and the changes I went through because they were inattentive and asleep at the time, it just didn't get what it was supposed to do; what it had done before with others that they studied, so there was no reason it didn't record, but they didn't know that as they scrambled to find the answers before she found out.

But there was always the possibility that they were so conditioned to what they did as a routine that they might have overlooked something they thought they covered, that's what they were thinking at the time; though they were professionals, they were still human.

As they ran through the checkups, they found that there was nothing unplugged, or wired incorrectly, nothing was waiting for them to push the start button and they were now dumbfounded, they had no answers to why there was no data on any of the things I spoke to them about, my dream or nightmare or reenactment, whatever the hell it was, they eventually had to tell her that there was nothing, that they only had my memory to study.

"Everything was working?" she asked, the shocked look on her face told them that at least she wasn't angry with them, wasn't blaming them yet, but of course; she wanted to know the answers as well. "You checked all the connections? Ran diagnostics?" she asked, though she knew the answer and also figured that they'd probably checked before they came and told her because she was big on accountability and they knew it and had always reported the facts to her, even when they messed up; it was why she hired them and didn't fire them at that time.

She had to ask anyway, as a matter of procedure, but also because everything was being recorded as normal procedure, and then she turned on the tape to listen to the last nine hours of my life and was rewarded with that soft hiss and the occasional snore that didn't last long, as if it bothered me to hear it and I'd made myself stop.

The three of us were supposed to meet for breakfast in the cafeteria downstairs afterwards; to discuss anything we might have forgotten or missed, any questions we might have about the procedure so far, things of that sort, but now she was hoping we wouldn't ask about the data, at least until she found out why and what she could do about it, if the data was somehow found and possibly retrievable.

This wasn't to "save her ass" or anything, she was genuinely concerned as to why it was missed, since I obviously had some things happen while I was out, and she never called them on it, but she knew they slept because two of them did snore, but she didn't mind; she knew the machines were running themselves at that point and they worked hard, and there was nothing for them to do at that point anyway but watch us sleep and who could stay awake watching someone else sleep, I didn't think I could have either.

I knew that it was too soon to be going over any findings, but I tried to ask anyway, I was jumping out of my pants with excitement and the chance that we at least opened the door to the vault with our answers inside, and I couldn't wait to get in there, as you might imagine.

"Did they find out anything that might help us?"I asked her, anything new or different, besides my marching dream? Anything that you might not have seen before that you can share with us?" I asked her.

"it's too soon to know anything at this point!" she said, a little too quickly, which made me think she was waiting for that question with that answer before I asked, and it made me nervous but I didn't push it because I didn't think I could.

"I still need the technicians to go over the information, discuss some things with my colleagues and others that are key to my studies; a lot of that doesn't concern you, it's just that we want to make sure that we do everything right, as much as we asked that you do!": she told us, "It's all procedure, and I think that we did well for these first runs!" she said and then laughed nervously, trying hard not to tip her hand and reveal they had nothing but us as before, and hoped we didn't catch that.

"But they got data, they got readings off what we saw, right?" I asked her frantically because I got the feeling that something was wrong and I couldn't let it go without asking about it, even though I was pretty sure she wasn't going to tell me whatever it was; it was really making me nervous and jumpy.

Sam assured us both that everything was fine, and she was adept at lying to people while looking them in the eyes because she looked as though she actually believed it, that they had enough to get started with and hopefully would have some answers for us in a few days; and if we were lucky, maybe even less than that, but we'd have to wait.

I don't need to say how I felt at that moment, disappointed, let down, but that was wrong; I had to remind myself that just because we wanted the answers yesterday, didn't mean that they would be here today, or even tomorrow by the sound of her voice.

As we left, I could tell that she was trying to wait until we were gone and thought we were out of earshot; it came out in a rush when she called out to one of her assistants that was trying to tell her she got a call from her publisher about a rough draft of her new book. It wasn't a "bad" question, it was just a bad time to ask about it.

I looked at Maria, because I knew she's heard it too, and I felt her trepidation mixing in with my own, and I asked her what she was thinking; she shrugged her shoulders before she answered me.

"I think that we have gone too far now, to turn around and start over somewhere else!" she said, "I think we should stick with her, I still trust her, so let's see where it goes! I mean, its not like we have a lot of options to chose from, and I for one, am damned tired of those fucking nightmares!" she said at last, her frustration boiling over as well.

Hearing her cuss like that told me so many things, as I said before; she would answer any questions in any class and not get this frustrated, she always seemed to be the one that thrived under pressure; it scared the hell out of me, but I wasn't going to tell her that.

"I think that you're probably right!" I said, "That makes the most sense to me too, though I think you said it a lot better than I could have!" I admitted and then looked away so she wouldn't see me laughing.

"You're such a guy!" she said, and then laughed along with me, she started chasing me around the sidewalk for a while until she caught me and then gave me another kiss, that was one thing that always made my day so much better, no matter what else was going on.

After I walked her home, I once again had that feeling of being watched, and at first I thought that it had been going on for a while, but I didn't "feel" it as strongly because I was with her and my focus was elsewhere, but now that I was alone, I felt it coming in waves, as if someone was running sonar at me or something like that; as if they were searching for my exact whereabouts.

Because of that, I took a different route this time, it wasn't because I was lost or desperate as I felt; okay, maybe I should admit that I was desperate at that time; but being "a guy" as she put it, I tried really hard not to show her that, and when I left her I felt how wrong that was, I was frustrated that I didn't.

When I got home after that, I felt as though I'd failed an important final exam or something; I felt that I'd let her down and was so let down and disappointed, but maybe I was reading too much into it; I thought that the answers would be easier to find once we let them look at our nightmares, I thought we'd at least know something by now.

Being desperate, and since I could think of nothing else that it might be; I went back to the center, to try and think of; maybe ask them what they thought, I knew it was after hours now and closed to everyone, including me; but I had nowhere else to go.

I saw a bench outside the building, it faced the front, and I sat down there, trying stop my head from spinning around in circles over this, I felt so confused and overwhelmed; inside of there, I knew they were still going over the data, "collating and deciphering it" as she once said, but I also knew what the data should say, and I wanted to talk to them about it, maybe clear up some questions they might have for a change.

When I got on my feet, it felt different to me, I saw a screen ahead of me and felt I had to walk through it, and then I turned and saw myself sitting there to make it even ore confusing; there was a life-sized version of me sitting there on the bench, looking confused and maybe a little angry at how things were not turning out.

I felt as though I could step back into the screen and everything else would be normal; I'd be sitting there on the bench, trying to make sense of this, I guess that I wanted to find out why I was back in my cell more than sit there and the bench and wonder about the answers and would they ever come.

As crazy as it sounded, it made sense to me; I was thinking that there might be a ghost or two that I'd missed; something terrible that hadn't been inflicted non my mind yet, and as frightening as that sounded, I still had to know, and going there was the only way that I could find out.

I took a deep breath and turned around then, felt my other self, reaching for me as I did but I kept going anyway; I was hoping that they wouldn't hurt me for real this time, I knew that last time, my escape was dumb luck and not much more, but I felt that this was television after all; and I was the movie of the week, and I knew that if it went well and everyone liked it, there would be a series and they couldn't kill me...yet.

Then I heard a voice, it was someone announcing the crimes of Elspeth, crimes they alleged that she committed, and I remembered what was next and I knew that I needed to get out of my cell; I thought that with what I knew from before, that I could find my way to her this time, and save her from what they were doing or die alongside her; once again I thought those were the only choices I had, and I was determined to get to her this time, no matter what.

As I turned towards the door to my cell, the scene shifted with me as I moved; and now I was alone and walking in the woods, though what woods they were and where I was, I could not say.

There was a mist, or a low fog that covered the ground, the air was damp and misty, I couldn't see much of anything from where I stood; and yet again, it all seemed familiar, as if I'd been there before.

I heard a voice again, "You still believe in your god?" he said to me, mocking my faith as if nothing had changed since the last time that he'd entered my cell.

I knew who it was, and I didn't want to see that evil face again; but I knew there was no choice, so I turned towards him and said, "My faith in him is stronger than ever, you cannot take that away from me, no matter what you try, what you show me or how painful you make the rest of my days, even the rest of my eternity for all I know, my faith will be just as strong as it was when you started!" I said to him with real conviction in my voice that he couldn't miss.

He stood there, in a robe that seemed to shimmer as he moved, but as he stepped into the moonlight; I saw that it wasn't shimmering at all, rather, it was made up of the souls of a countless number of people; they were somehow caught up, or woven into the fabric, it was made that they could see out, stretch the fabric so they could partially see out, but they couldn't escape, they were given a constant reminder of what a normal life was; what they would never have again.

As I stood there and watched, they were climbing over each other and shouting at me; they were pressing against the wall that separated us but even they knew that it would only bend, and never break, and I couldn't hear what they were saying anyway.

Maybe it was the fabric, maybe it was because they were all shouting at the same time, but if I leaned closer, I could hear something muffled and indistinct, as if they were in an envelope or vacuum. He smiled at me then, almost graciously because he knew what I saw and that I knew what he was now, and even worse, I saw what would have become of me had I given in to him and his temptations; he turned then and showed me the tomb and the rock that covered it.

"he died, and yet he lies there still!" he said and then laughed, as if I was going to believe him just because he said it and showed it that way, and when I looked where he was gesturing, all I could see was a dark hole in the wall.

"Lies!" I shouted at him, pretending to be braver than I felt at that moment, "You feed me a banquet of lies and deception, nothing else!" and then I started feeling as strong as I pretended, almost strong enough to keep him away from me.

"I show you what you need to see!" he started to say that and more, but he stopped because I interrupted him and started shouting at him once more.

"NO!" I shouted, HE rose from the dead and beat you, He cast you out of heaven and sent you to the eternal fires of hell, where you belong!" I said, "He resisted you and never gave in to you!" HE did what his father asked, He did it for us!" I shouted at him again; and by the look on his face, I knew what I was doing was the last thing he expected, and he wasn't prepared for it.

"You know NOTHING!" he shouted back at me, "You were not there, what do you know of what happened?" he asked me, "What little you know was reported by men, written by men, men who see things as they see fit, to their own end and to suit their own needs!" he hissed.

"Are you trying to tell me that the Bible is a pack of lies?" I interrupted him again, which seemed to have the effect I wanted, and made him angry.

"I am simply saying that it was written by men and men make mistakes every day, I count on that!" he laughed at me.

"Well it is true that I admit to not knowing how to read the Bible, and I guess that means I have to admit that I don't always live my life by its precepts either, I have done a lot of things that I will have to one day answer for!" I said.

"But it also true that I have been good in most respects; I have tried not to hurt anyone and I mean, especially not just to make them feel pain, but mostly when my good intent went wrong, or I didn't see the whole picture and how it affected those that I loved the most, and thusly, hurt the most.

All the time I said that, I was being honest and maybe that was wrong when your dealing with the devil and I should have just shut up and let him speak his piece and be gone, without my soul, I felt as though he might have understood the things I did on both sides of that fence better than I did, and that bothered me as well.

Then he again showed me images meant to could my judgement, to sway my thoughts and feelings about the state of the world, that he was testing me somehow, trying to circle around to my flank to try another angle to attack me from.

I saw the sickest images of children being abused and murdered, their tiny little bodies tossed aside like so much garbage, it was heart wrenching and yet I knew he would not let me turn away.

I saw images of hard drugs being sold near schools, crack houses and the addicts that lived inside of them, if you called that living; there was prostitution being committed and used needles laying in the playgrounds where the children would be playing if it was safe enough for the parents to let them out.

All of these images flashed before my eyes as if he thought he was somehow going to appeal to my baser instincts or something; maybe he was showing me the changes man had gone through over the centuries and yet we were still killing each other for no real reason, and every year we found new ways to kill each other faster and more efficiently, and then it was not for the good of man, or to protect our freedoms or our way of life; but to control man, just for the power of it.

The last image he showed me was of the stone, rolled away from the opening and the body of Jesus was clearly gone; replaced by a goat with red eyes that glowed in the darkness of the cave. It was meant to frighten me, but also to make me believe somehow that the devil himself took the corpse and that's why the tomb was empty.

I suppose all of this proved that he could only bend, or distort the truth; but he could not change it, or present it in a way that he was satisfied with when he saw me smirk at it, and then it was gone, even though he hadn't given up yet.

"Do you really believe that he rose after all that they did to him?" he asked, "They stabbed his body with spears and water came out, you know what that means?" he laughed, "The things they did to his body and mind to make him suffer that way until he died, and that he could come back from all of that?" he asked, shaking his head sadly, as if it was too much to believe.

"You really think that if he is as great as you think he is, that he would go through all of that pain and suffering and misery, just for you?" he asked, as if that were the biggest joke or deception of all; he was getting impatient that he wasn't getting through to me, I could feel it from where I stood.

He was angry that I was not bending to his will and not on my knees, begging for my life, "Look at the headlines, on your television screens!" he shouted at me, "See what man does every single day in the name of your god!" he spat out that last part at me.

"See how ruthless men have become over the years and they call that progress!" he said, "Every time they were given a chance, ever since they crawled out of that darkness they have found better ways to kill each other, you know its true!" he said, as if we were both on the same side now.

"Man will always take or at the very least covet what his brother has, without regard for payment or consequence, and then they call themselves good Christians!" and again, he laughed at me, "You men will sometimes surpass the evil I cold ever hoper to put in their hearts without my help!" he said with a smile as if he admired us for that, for our killing efficiency.

"It's not about what you hear about, or what you might read in a newspaper account; and its not what they tell you the television at night, or even what any of our friends of any of this!" I said to him.

"It's not even so much as what it say's in the Bible, I told you that I don't know how to read it in the first place, I don't know how to understand all of what it says, because I am not ready to, in my heart my mind; though my faith is strong!" I said and then thumped my chest confidently.

"It's about what you know inside and feel in here, as well as in whom and what you place that trust in!" I said, gaining confidence with each word as I spoke; feeling the weight of my words and the conviction I was feeling for real this time.

"It's in those things that you know are right and wrong; those things you know the true of from deep in your heart, and the weaker ones don't listen to that voice, even then!" I said, feeling guilty for my own sins now as I thought of them.

"THAT'S where my faith is, in HIS promise! He defeated you, more than once; and HE conquered death for all of us, and even now his very name makes you tremble with fear!" I said then, the words were coming out of me in a rush.

"My belief also tells me that you must leave when his name is invoked, so leave me now, you foul thing! You might have power over the men outside of this cell, but not in this cell, you have no power over me! LEAVE ME NOW!" I shouted at him.

He looked suddenly saddened, or embarrassed; as if he was the party crasher found out in the middle of dinner; exposed and ready to be dismissed, then he rose up to his full height, and he was huge; he seemed to block out the rest of the room and half of the space in the hallway, and then he spread his arms wide, claws extended and ready to tear me to shreds; I felt the heat of a thousand miles of flame building up inside of him, ready to incinerate me as if he was a dragon.

But I felt nothing but faith in my heart and no fear at all, I shouted again, at the top of my lungs;

"LEAVE ME NOW, IN THE NAME OF GOD!"

Even though I myself could not hear it, he brought those wings down on me with all of his might but then he vanished and I was alone again, the quiet was so eerie, it was almost worse than his terrible voice and the empty promises that he spoke of.

I still felt what I could only describe as his filth running through me for a moment, I felt nausea; as if I was falling through a very large chasm to my death, a chasm so deep that my body would drop for a very long time before I got anywhere close to the bottom, it might even take years.

But I was standing there with my eyes closed, and my faith told me he would be gone and so I expected that, but I didn't expect the sudden silence that followed in his wake.

When nothing happened, I opened my eyes and then noticed that the in my cell, the air was suddenly cleaner, and I felt a shred of hope as I headed for the wide-open door.

I stepped out into the corridor and the men were running all over the place, wildly shouting at me, they knew that I'd died already and didn't understand; they thought they were seeing a ghost.

"Why are you here? Am I mad? DO you want to die again?" they shouted at me, it was madness, they were saying those things to ne as if they made perfect sense.

I could not see them, but I knew that they were talking to me; I could hear steps as they came up the hallway, their weapons jangling loudly as they approached.

For a brief moment, I thought they came to help me, that they were going to release me, that reason had prevailed after all and they were coming to bring me to her side, but as they got closer, I cold see that they weren't in any kind of good mood at all, and they sure as hell weren't there to let me go; that was abundantly clear to me.

Their footsteps were booming loudly in my head now, bouncing off the walls as they got closer; I saw an army of those large, "steer men" marching down the corridor with murderous intent, now they were in sight, and just three feet away from the gate that meant my escape or my death at their hands.

But I think if you saw it through our eyes, death and escape were one and the same because either way it would finally be over.

I saw that they were escorting six men of the church; those men were dressed in official garb, with heavy, solid gold crosses that hung at their waists, almost as an afterthought, as if they needed a badge of that sort to give credence to what they were about to do.

Everything all bright and shiny as they walked, sometimes it seemed as though the more colorful the uniform, the more removed they thought they were from the violence, from the blood and gore that the rest of us were forced to live in, each and every day.

Those things that almost became everyday events that we became too familiar with, in ways that we never asked for, I doubt they ever heard the crack of a whip just before it ripped open their flesh; or felt a man's life slip away after a fight because they were immune to the brutality that they brought on those of us that they considered below them.

They also wore a white cloth as a part of their blouse; I saw them being covered with soot as they walked and I wondered what other stains they wore on their souls and very few that knew of the stains lived to tell about it.

As I looked at the leader of them, his face was distorted, a swirling mass of nothing solid, he didn't look at all human, nothing identifiable, the second one was scarred in a terrible fire and yet he was the one carrying the torch.

From where I stood, I could see that the skin of his face had been burned away, and his right eye rolled as he turned his head and when he wasn't moving, it leaked some white fluid that seemed to burn a trail along his cheek bone where it touched him, and the other eye was exposed and black, and bright white bone gleamed from his cheek.

I could stand it no longer and turned away before the others got there; I felt them as they stopped in front of my cell, three abreast and facing each other stiffly now.

The one that went to open my door had maggots covering his face, and as he put the key into the lock, it seemed to take forever before he finally pulled it open, all the metal parts echoing loudly in my cell.

Then he stepped back as if he was inviting me to join the party, but they never spoke a single word as they stood there and waited for me.

I knew there was no escape and that if I didn't come out and surrender myself to them, that they would come in there and drag my ass out by the short hairs if I didn't, but as I closed my eyes and stepped through the door I was suddenly back at the bench, sitting there, seemingly admiring the building.

There were traces or tendrils of them reaching for me; I heard them bellow in rage and frustration as I'd escaped them but when I opened my eyes, that was what I saw as a couple strolled past me, arm in arm and very much in love.

That was enough and I got up and ran back to Sam, I wanted to tell her what I saw, and especially what just happened as it was still fresh in my mind, I thought we could add it to the data they already had and maybe it would help.

But when I walked into the reception area, normally that was the hub, everyone came and went to their respective places from there, retrieved mail, messages and other "work related" issues but this time it was empty and there were no sounds that didn't come from me walking in there; I called out once, and then again a moment later and a lot louder, "Hello? Anyone here?" but no one was around to answer me.

I thought about when I was in a store and they were ignoring me like this, and I looked up at the camera and said, "I wonder how much I'd get if I just dropped this lamp?" and looking at the camera, in case they couldn't hear on that camera, I imitated that movement and a few moments later someone rushed up to helpme, I thought of doing the same here but if there were cameras in this part of the building, I couldn't see them.

I stepped in a little further and when no one answered, I went in a little further, I had that creepy feeling that I wasn't going to like what I found when I got past this other door but I couldn't have stopped myself then, even if I'd thought of it, I had to know where everyone was, and was just hoping they were still alive and this bad feeling was just that, a bad feeling.

Because of that feeling and not knowing what I was going to find, I crept forward a little more, slowly, quietly, I wanted to call out again but was afraid, it wasn't that I wanted to hear their secrets or spy on them; it was because I had this dread feeling that they were all dead.

I finally heard one of the techs talking to her from the next room; they had no idea that I was out there, or they would have either shut the door in my face or asked me to come in and then not said what I heard them say, but they had no idea I was out there.

"How could we have missed all of this?" she asked the tech, "It was right there in front of us!" Sam said, and then another one said, "Because we weren't expecting that, and we weren't set up for it!" she said, "It wasn't meant to take in that kind of data, and to be honest, we are damned lucky that we got anything at all, and that we thought to try this when the other methods had failed us!" she explained to Sam.

"What do you think it is?" they asked Sam, "Is there anything that you can think of that would make all the readings go flat like that?" they said and waited for an answer as if she'd know.

"Yes!" I said, "What do you think of all of this?" I asked, as I entered the room and they all jumped at the sound of my voice, the frightened looks on their faces almost comical, so scared that I thought they were all going to rush out the door at once.

"Sorry, I came to the door and there was no one out there, and I waited but when no one came out I came here, so what does that mean?" I asked her, daring her to lie to me or tell me that I didn't hear what they knew that I heard.

I walked past them and saw they were looking at two monitors, one of each room, on the beds, and we were both sleeping peacefully; no sign of any danger or nightmares that I knew I was having at the time, though I didn't know what time I had the vision and when this was recorded so I couldn't figure that out; I knew they were supposed to record that stuff but now I had my doubts about the whole thing.

But when I looked a little bit closer, I could see that both our heads were moving very fast and acting out both sides of an argument or something, we would yell out something that was one side, and then turn our heads the other way and argue the other, our expressions either softening or hardening as we argued back and forth.

The odd thing was, if you could have seen both our faces side by side, you would see that we "shifted our faces" as we changed sides in our arguments, you could almost see the same words coming out of our mouths at the exact same moment, as if we weren't arguing with each other, we were arguing against someone else, together, though they couldn't see who that someone was.

The other thing was what was making them all so jittery, I looked at the monitor in her room a little closer then, because in her room was the shadow of a huge spider, you could clearly see the shadow of eight legs and a fat body, and even on the shadow, you could see the hourglass on her belly; looking down on her as she slept while weaving something with her forelegs.

In my room, there was also a shadow, but mine seemed to be of a man; he was pacing back and forth angrily watching me as I slept, hatred oozing out of his pores as he forced himself to hold back because he was also just a showdown and his hands passed through me when he tried, every so often he would stop as if he was listening to what I said and then he'd either start pacing again or trying to rip me apart.

I got the impression as he snarled and growled at me that he wanted to change the rules about being a shadow and not being able to touch me, to stop being a shadow and just kill me, but he couldn't.

One of the techs shouted, "Brian!" and when Brian turned, the other one cocked his head to the side in my direction and then nodded towards the monitor and he realized I wasn't supposed to see that, at least not yet and he quickly reached up and turned it off.

"What did you see?" How much of what we said have you heard? How long were you standing out there?" Brian's friend, Stan asked me, but this time, I was as determined as I was scared, and I wasn't going to give them anything until they gave me something first.

"You know, I asked you guys a lot of questions, told you some really funny jokes…okay, they were moderately funny and none of you so much as smirked except for her!" I said, gesturing to someone standing there and doing nothing but listening at the time; she looked down, a bit embarrassed that I saw her, and the others gave her a stern "told you he saw you" kind of look that made me feel as though she was either new here, or just not popular with the others who wouldn't let her into their little clique.

"Since I consider myself a fair man, I will give you guys another chance to play nice and make friends, answer some of my questions, such as; what the hell was that?" I asked, "Why did you lie to me, tell me that the monitors were flat screened and then I see this?" I asked them and none of them would look me in the eye at that moment.

Sam decided that was her chance to regain control and asked me, "Juan, I don't mean to sound rude, but what are you doing here?" she asked me.

I still felt that I needed to tell her, to get it out and see what an expert might say or think, and I still wanted so badly to trust her but she wasn't making it easy, though I think she was just trying to be an authority, an adult.

Maybe it was her that I trusted and not her aides and staff, so I tried to tell her what happened, I remembered every detail perfectly as usual, no one interrupted me once to clear up a point or ask me a question, they all stood silent and sometimes aghast at what I reported to them, and when I was done, they all looked at each and tried to hide their feelings, but I saw or felt surprise and excitement in their bearing, as if this didn't happen all the time.

All except for Sam, "Are you telling us that you experienced all of this… while you were essentially awake?" she asked me, and she didn't even try to hide her surprise as I nodded my head slowly.

"In my experience, this is a very rare thing that almost never happens, I am sure that somewhere, there is a study that might explain some of that, but I doubt that there will be much, its not like we see or hear of this every day!" she said, delightedly.

"Usually, the subject is incoherent when they come out, sometimes complaining of severe headache and nausea, they need to sleep and rest their brain for several days afterwards to recuperate, so it must be very taxing on the body and mind, and yet you are here, coherent and ready with vivid details as if you'd just seen a movie playing down the street and you thought we might enjoy it as well!" she said.

"To answer your question, and for the record, the images that you just saw, those were recorded on a separate monitor, a spectrogram imager, and yes, its new and we aren't fully trained in its use and function, obviously, and therefore the findings are unreliable at times, and that's why we didn't look there before!" she admitted.

"We found these images just before you walked in and we obviously have not had time to look them over and analyze any data that they show us!" she said, and I felt bad for calling them lairs, but they did lie to me when they said they still had to study data when there was no data they could have studied and they knew it.

Then they noticed my voice was hoarse and gave me some water and asked me to sit down for a minute at least, I was so excited at seeing that, and scared at the same time, true, but more excited so it was hard for me to sit even that long but I tried.

But as I sat down there, I went back again, but this time I was one of the guards and on the other side of those bars and not as a prisoner. I was walking down the corridor between the rows of cells, the keys jangling at my waist as I walked, and once again the smell of death was strong in the air; it sickened me and yet I had to move on.

Then I caught one of my sandals and almost tripped, as I stopped my fall, I saw a river of blood running through the center or the corridor and wondered why it hadn't already soaked into the ground, and then I thought it was because there was so much of it, that maybe it had soaked into the ground; and yet there was more, fresh blood, fresh bodies daily.

But I had the feeling that this river had stopped before and recently restarted and wasn't in the mood to stop anytime soon, now that it was going so strong, now that it had been primed with new blood.

I stopped in front of one of the cells as the door was opening by itself, very slowly, and I stepped in and heard myself, talking to the prisoner; then I started kicking and lunching him as he lay there helpless, I was disgusted by it and yet I could not stop.

It made me sick once more, I could hear his labored breath wheezing in and out as I struck him repeatedly, and even though he was defenseless every punch landed with a satisfied grunt as it landed on him.

I felt his blood splash against my face and yet I still cold not force myself to stop, when I finally got tired of hitting him, I turned to leave and then stopped, giving him one final warning before I left him there; with as much hatred and venom as I could muster, I was ready to pounce on him as I spoke to him, or he so much as moaned in his pain.

But as looked down at the man lying on that mattress, I was shocked to see my own face there; bloodied and broken, staring back at me and begging for mercy that wasn't coming that day, and that was when I woke up again, and since there was no one around me now, I left to find Maria and make sure that she was alright.

There were going to be no answers for me that night, I had no idea what those images meant, and no real idea if they were related to us or some residual ghosts or nightmares from their earlier studies.

Either way, that had told me all that they could, or were willing to tell me at the time; it was frustrating to me because they were the so-called experts in the field and they didn't know any ore than I did; they made their bread in those ovens and yet they could tell me nothing about the loaf that came from it.

All those toys, those gadgets, all those bells and whistles and yet we were no further along in the study or answers and now I felt as though we had wasted all of this time; that maybe we were just certifiable and none of this meant anything at all, and it never would.

Photograph by J.R. Gonzalez

IT ALL COMES OUT IN THE WASH

Actions lie louder than words.

-Carolyn Wells

Maria was back in her own version of hell; her mother and father, Gregor and Esmeralda, and even I was chasing her through the ruins of her house, each of us dead, and in a different level of decay, and everyone was laughing except for Maria.

She saw the ghost that looked like me and turned so quickly away from me that one of my legs fell off as I tried to turn with her, and then I fell face-down into the dirt, but I was trying to get up and get back in the chase.

The others knocked me down again as they tried to step over me and then they stepped on me, breaking more bones as they stepped on me and she ran out of back door then and out of the house and towards the woods behind it.

As she got to the edge, she stopped to turn and see if they were close behind; she was sure they would still be following her and would follow her all the way to hell before they'd give up the chase; three of us were fighting to get through the door, I was dragging myself on the floor but there was a barrier at the door, and we weren't allowed to pass through it.

She tried to run to the barn, she was thinking that she could maybe get one if the horses and escape us that way, at least get some distance between her and those damned clouds that were messing with everything.

But even as she ran, she wasn't sure if there was anywhere she would find something that she consider a safe haven from this madness; she thought that no matter where she went to try and hide, that we knew her secrets and would know how she thought and thus, where to find her.

She also got a feeling that the reason we were chasing her was that in catching her and killing her, whoever did that would get renewed life, but it could only be one of them, and then they would take her place.

But when she got to the barn and found the horse, she found that it too had changed, and she should have expected that but for some reason she thought it would be different this time and that everything wouldn't be working against us.

Where this horse was once beautiful and so gentle, it now had razor sharp teeth and eyes that blazed a fiery red at her when he saw her, and then it began to rise up and strike at her, she could feel both its power and hatred as it tried to get at her, it was pounding the door that held it back to shreds as she stood aghast and tried not to scream because she knew that it wouldn't help.

She turned away from there before he escaped and ran once more towards the woods and now she was feeling that if she didn't escape soon, that she would be trapped with us in that house for all of eternity, they would be eternal guests of this decaying house and the long-forgotten dreams they once held sacred, and now they would all be joined together, chasing humans to escape.

As she finally entered the woods, she thought she might be safe, and tried to take solace in the cool darkness, she hoped that we might be tired and would leave her alone; but she thought she could hear us, whispering and calling out her name softly as if she would listen and come to us.

She started walking backwards, she was confused and so afraid that she didn't want to take her eyes off them for fear they would escape and come for her; as she kept backing away, she came to a clearing in the woods, and in the middle of the clearing was a very dark and long dead tree.

Turning back again to see what we were doing, she saw back there, her mother and father side by side, I was still on the floor, trying to get up; we were all looking longingly at her as she stood well beyond our reach.

We wanted to get to her, she could feel that from where she stood, our hands were opening and closing, we couldn't stand still and kept hopping from one foot to the other as we waited for her and hoped that she would come back to us.

We were still at the doorway, what was our boundary, unseen, and yet we could go no further, no matter how hard we tried, as if we were forbidden to leave the house, and all they could do now was to reach out to her, though she was too far out of reach.

She turned around again, thinking that we saw something or someone that she hadn't seen yet; some menace in those woods that even the dead feared, but when she looked, there was nothing between her and the woods except for that one dead tree.

That was when he began to feel something from the tree; something that made her feel as though she was being watched, as though the tree wasn't so dead after all; she stepped a little closer then, and she heard something that sounded like humming, it as coming from the tree.

It gave off a feeling of intense power that came from the tree, and the closer she got to it, the louder and stronger it felt; and then it started to shake her all the way to her bones.

She looked up high into the tree, thinking that someone was hiding up there, that maybe that was why she felt such a fear and loathing from the tree, bit there was no one up there of course.

As her eyes swept over the surface of the tree, she wondered how it could be dead and yet still have life, how it still could be standing there, and for so long; she saw that the bark in some places as was lot darker than the others, she could tell that it was burned, that it had survived a fire, or maybe

"SOMEONE TRIED TO BURN IT DOWN! TRIED TO KILL IT MORE THAN ONCE!"

She heard a voice shouting at her, and it made her jump, but again, there was no one around her but for the three of us still reaching for her sadly and drooling at the thought of getting our hands on her.

There were other marks on its surface as well; it appeared that someone, or maybe more than a few someone's had tried to cut the tree down; she could see gouges cut into its bark at different points and levels as it grew to its present height, and where it was cut that sap that oozed out of it was black and seemed to have burned its way into the bark; to seal the cut and stop the bleeding.

Walking around the trunk of it slowly, she found one of those two-man saws, it was still embedded into the trunk of the tree, she wondered how the men that were using that saw were stopped, and just thinking about that; imagining the men as they lay dead at the base of the tree, their bodies rotting in the sun because everyone was afraid to get close enough to retrieve the bodies.

Just thinking about those things scared her, gave her such a feeling of unease that made no sense to her; it was just a tree after all, but she also felt that if she got too close, those black, twisted, branches would stretch out and grab her; as she thought it had happened to others before.

It was a really tall tree, she couldn't see the top of it from there, but even as tall and as old as it was, there were no leaves anywhere on it, and on the ground around it, there were no flowers and no grass would grow either, and she had a sudden thought that maybe the tree wouldn't allow it, nothing green would survive that close to the base of it.

She looked closer at that soil and it was blackened and didn't have any kind of "earthen texture" to it, it didn't feel like dirt or sand, and yet she didn't know how to describe how it felt to touch it, and that spread out from the base of the tree, it looked like tar was coming out of the tree and spreading out, she took a step back as a reflex.

The roots of the tree looked like long, boney fingers where they touched the ground; they were moving and clutching at the ground, but not for support, it felt more as though they were trying to squeeze the life out of it, taking it for its own use.

Then she noticed that there was a stone path that wound around the tree, it seemed as though it was meant to surround it, but not to touch it, and she thought the steps were coated with something because the "fingers" of the tree would touch it and then recoil quickly, she knew that it was meant to keep the fingers of the tree from spreading out too far, and maybe they counted on the intelligence of humans not to get too close because there were no warning signs posted.

It appeared that they weren't all that smart though; when she looked a little closer, she could see human skulls scattered around the base as well, some were partially submerged, she felt as if the rest of the body was still there, just below the soil, and that there were likely a lot more under her feet or where she couldn't see them at the time.

All around her she could see spinal cords, ripped from someone, and arm and leg, three or four hands but no feet, she thought that maybe they were caught and then held by that tarry liquid until they died of starvation or thirst and then they were slowly absorbed into it.

She looked back at the house again, and we were still there, watching her hands still reaching for her and her mother's mouth would snap open and shut loudly as she looked at her daughter, they swayed together and hummed with the tree, she looked from the tree to her mother once more, maybe thinking to ask for help or some explanation, but she only stood, slack-jawed and drooling at her.

Maria couldn't help it, she felt so overwhelmed that she wanted to give up in a moment of weakness, but she knew she could not, that we had to fight for what we wanted and not give in to them, but she could not understand why she never got the chance, why she never had a mother when everyone else did, and now that she see's what she can only guess is her mother, all her mother wants to do is kill her.

Even a bad mother would have been so much better than no mother at all, and now she was thinking that she'd had two mothers that she knew of, yet she knew nothing of either one, she began to wonder if she could speak to this one, that maybe she might find some answers.

As she was thinking about that, her mother's head snapped up as if she'd heard her or caught the thread of that thought; she snatched it out of the very air and wanted her daughter to try, "Yessssss dearie!" she hissed, "Come and try that! Let's sit down, right here and talk about this, I will tell you all that you need to know!" she said and then laughed as her daughter's confusion.

A hole opened up where her mouth used to be, it was probably a sad attempt at a smile, but instead of mirth, or any good cheer it might have once held for her; it frightened her, she tried to coax her to come forward anyway, she cooed softly at Maria, "Come along darling, would a mother hurt her own child?" she said softly.

Maria knew as she looked at her that her mother didn't have a warm and comforting embrace in mind, instead she was offering her the chanced to see the eternal fires of hell and the damnation that went along with it, and Maria wanted no part of it.

She turned back to the tree and entered the circle of stones at last, feeling that she had no choice and there was no other escape; as she did, she a scream that might have come from her mother but it sounded as though it came from all three of us at the same time; there was a lot of hatred in that scream, it was as if she couldn't believe that he daughter had escaped from her.

But she couldn't hear for too long, the minute that she entered the circle, the sound outside was lessened considerably, it was almost like a feint echo or vibration now and she couldn't hear much.

The light also changed, as if it shifted somehow to something else; everything inside of there was either white or grey, there were no colors allowed, even the clothes she wore lost their color.

Then she felt something in the tree stir, as if something inside was awakened by her coming there and she felt as though it was watching her now and shivered involuntarily.

But she also felt that she could see things outside of the clearing a lot clearer now as well, and much farther than before; crystal clarity with an unlimited view. She took another step towards the base of the tree and everything outside of the circle began to shimmer, like it was a mirage and making her feel as though only her and the tree were real now, the rest of the world was made up of her imagination, it was just them.

She got the feeling that up there, above the tree birds would likely avoid the area, would fly around it and avoid it altogether, and that if she rose above the clearing and looked down at this tree, it would be like looking into the eye of a hurricane, the calm in the middle of the storm that was the rest of the world as it flew by in such a hurry.

Though she could not see more than a few feet in front of her if she looked back, and she knew that somehow that face in the clouds was busy re-arranging things outside of the circle she was in, and she wondered about her father, would he still be alive, would she ever get to see any of us again, she had her doubts at that moment.

She walked around the tree a little more, she felt as though every time she did, the tree would grow in girth and show her a little more, spill some of its secrets out to her; and then she saw a skeleton hanging from its branches and she knew it wasn't there before.

It was swaying gently as if a breeze was pushing it around and yet there was no breeze in there to speak of, everything about that tree spoke and felt like death and the promise of a lot of pain.

She thought she heard something and for a dreaded moment thought we'd escaped the house and snuck up behind her, but there was nothing.

Then she turned back to the tree and the skeleton and it had turned around now and was facing her, then the jaw unhinged, and she heard it say:

Beneath your bones and into your blood

One last chance I will send to thee

Get away now, lest you be lost for good

And for your soul, the devil will be very pleased

It's a fool that thinks he has a chance to get away

Yet ye might have time for a quick and simple prayer

But don't waste your last moments with talk, there's nothing to say

Just a quick word, the last between you and your savior

Because your soul is mine at the end of the day

And whatever it tastes will become my favorite flavor

As it stopped speaking, the mouth clacked shut hard, so hard that the jawbone fell off and he went slack again, swaying in the wind as if nothing happened, to a wind that hadn't existed inside that circle for who knew how long.

She felt something else than, as if someone, or something was approaching now and that whatever it might be; it was important that she see it, though she didn't know why or how she knew that, she hoped it was not something that meant to take her resolve away or hurt her in any way, take away the little bit of courage that she had left.

With that in mind, she turned to wait for it; she looked in the direction she thought she'd heard it from because she could see nothing and then she waited for it; after a few anxious moments, she heard something and she hoped it was louder and bigger than it sounded and that it was just the dead air inside that was making it echo and then drop off so suddenly.

She now felt as though she was trapped, or even just hiding in some kind of miniature dollhouse or playhouse and that damned cat was just outside of it, waiting for her to come out and play with her; and she couldn't see it, but she knew if she came out, it wouldn't be her doing the playing or even enjoying it.

Then she felt the tree shift again, and she felt as though it was watching her and waiting for that exact moment, that it would catch her off guard.

As she looked around to see what that might mean, she felt it grab at her ankles and it weas dragging her towards the trunk, and then she saw a mouth open as it waited anxiously for her, the darkness inside was hungry for her life, for her very soul as she screamed and reached for anything to stop her from being dragged into it.

"Maria! Wake up!" she heard me say as I shook her out of her sleep, I didn't know what was going on inside of her dreams but it didn't look good, so I probably shook her a little harder than I d=needed to when I woke her but I was scared.

She sat up and saw the concerned looks on our faces as I stood there with two of the nurses from the floor, she wasn't sure if I was the demon that she saw in her house or the guy that was trying to save her from that and it took her a moment to make sure.

"What?" she asked us, "What's...wrong?" she stammered, "Did something happen while I was asleep?" she was clearly confused and I wanted to hold her but couldn't, "what happened?" she asked again because of the concerned looks on our faces.

"Look at yourself!" I told her, "You look as though you have been running for your life, you're all covered in sweat and your legs were moving as if you were running from something in your sleep!" I told her and then looked at the others and they simply nodded at her.

She looked down and saw her legs were tangled and covered with blankets, and now as the tendrils of that dream faded, she thought that must have been why she thought the tree grabbed her, but she was still a little confused and not sure what was a dream and what was real.

One of the nurses stepped forward and said, "I'm sorry, we were going to try and wake you when it seemed you were in distress but were afraid to; that it might further traumatize you and add to your fears or whatever you were feeling, but it seemed very frightening to us!" she told Maria gently.

"But I thought that if we didn't wake you, that you might never wake up again!" I confessed, and when I said that, she almost agreed with me, she thought that even though it was a dream, that if those branches had dragged her into its base that she would have been lost forever; maybe there would be a body sitting in the bed, functioning by breathing and all, but essentially dead to the world, much like a coma.

But she also felt as though she'd run a marathon and then she told them, "I do feel dirty and in need of a shower now, it must have been a bad dream and if you will allow me a few moments I will shower and get dressed!" she said, and then waited for us to leave her there.

When I first got there that day, they were asking me questions and none of them knew or even understood why I felt that I needed to see her immediately, they argued with me about it as she was still asleep and as far as they knew, there was no problem.

But I knew differently, though I couldn't have explained why; I just knew that she needed t wake up and soon, or something very bad would happen, and since I wasn't privy to her dream, I didn't know what it was, only that it was very bad; they likely would have kept me out there for too long had it not been for her scream that brought us all running to her room.

I was still waiting for her and thinking about how she looked when we first got there, and I am not sure what they saw and wondered if they heard anything of what I heard.

She was speaking to someone in a language that I'd never heard before, it was so strange and it sounded as though she was saying the right words, only she was saying them backwards for some reason that I could not think of nor imagine why.

Her eyes were wide open too, but instead of the soft brown eyes that I loved to look deeply into; these were icy cold, and they seemed to radiate and spread that cold out from her and across the room, I even rubbed my arms without thinking about it to try and warm up as her coldness flew across the room and tried to get into my heart.

As she spoke, a thin vapor trailed out of her lips and into the air around her, it seemed so cold that if I reached out and touched it with my bare finger, that my hand would be frozen to the spot, and then I thought it would spread from there until I looked like an ice sculpture, frozen solid and lost to this world forever.

When she was ready and finally came out of her room, I was waiting for her in the hallway and I tried to tell her about what I saw, what happened when I was on the bench and everything else, but I must have been too excited or spoke too quickly because she kept trying to calm me down so she could understand what I was trying so hard to say.

"You need to see the tapes they recorded of us!" I told her, still too excitedly "There are things that we need to study and understand, something that you need to know about, maybe its what will lead us or get us closer to the answers that we need to find!" I told her at last.

We left there after a while, talking about what we both saw; and we decided that the best thing would be to go back to the center and see what they would allow us to see; find out anything new and tell them what we went through to add it to the other data that they didn't have, it was crazy all the things that were going right and wrong for us.

It was driving me crazy that I was seeing all of those things happen while I was awake, while I functioned in this world and I wondered what the people that didn't know what was going on thought of what they saw; and even what they saw while I was gone.

We were so excited about these developments that we never saw the shadow that was following us, instead of keeping an eye out for the danger we should have been looking for and aware of; I was at that moment, lost in her eyes, I was enjoying the sensation of holding her hand in mine and how soft it felt; how natural we fell in step as if we hadn't a care in the world.

Esmeralda had seen us in the park as we were walking, we walked right past her without noticing her there, even though I did get a sense of something foul in the air at that moment, when I looked for the source of that scent I saw her and dismissed her as homeless and not something she could help, I almost stopped to give her my spare change but remembered I didn't have any and kept going; unaware that my sense of danger had been activated and ignored.

She almost jumped when she saws us, but then remembered where she was, there were others around, and on the far side of the park; she could see two officers standing and watching everything in case Gregor showed his face there, she couldn't believe how happy we looked, how god things must have been going for us by the way we walked and smiled so much.

She of course, already knew about Maria being here, though no real idea of who she was in this world or how she arrived here; but then Esmeralda thought that maybe Elspeth did have some magic in her soul after all, that was what she thought when she saw me there, it wasn't magic that connected and brought us back together; it was love, pure and simple, denied to us in another world and yet ours once again, in this world.

Anger replaced any good or positive thoughts she might have felt then; even as briefly as they floated in and out of her mind, she never expected to see me there with her, not in her wildest imagination, and yet, there we were.

She'd hardly given me a thought, maybe because she didn't expect me to have found her this way, maybe because she was consumed with thoughts of finding Maria and killing her again, that would have been just for fun; now it was to prove that she meant what she said those many years ago; that if we somehow found one another again, that our joy, our happiness together would be short-lived because as soon as she found us, she would fulfill her promise to me; that she would snatch her from my arms and kill her in front of me, horribly, and there would be nothing that I could do to stop her.

The first time it was because she defied her, she was the one true enemy that stood up to her and defied her, even unto death, she would not give one damned inch and that infuriated Esmeralda to no end; she thought if word got out of that, everyone would laugh at her and think her a powerless fool that only thought she knew magic spells and potions.

This time it would be to prove to them that she meant what she said, that her power was vast and limitless and she would always find them no matter where they went and how safe they thought they were; that she, and she alone controlled their destiny and would not allow it to be happy and filled with laughter or flowers, that affront to her would be stomped out quickly to prove her power to anyone that thought different.

Of the four of us, she thought of me as the weak link until she met me in my cell that day; she thought that I was only as strong as Elspeth was, that if she gave in that I would fold like a cheap suit and she'd have us, and somehow she forgot that I also defied her and stood up to her; but even then she thought it was false courage and that once Elspeth was gone I'd have no reason to hold on or hold out and stand up to her.

Seeing us together that was such a shock to her system that she almost screamed at us in her fury when she saw us walking so causally in the park, she was trying to blend in with everyone else and not doing a good job of it, but enough that it didn't make me stop and check her out as I probably should have.

Maybe she would have gotten to me then, but Maria could have escaped and sent for help, or at least she would have known that Esmeralda was here and maybe could have done something about it.

She stood out a bit because she was wearing warm clothes and everyone else was in shorts and t shirts, but the homeless look worked for her, though that wasn't her intent; she dressed in what she could find after all, but everyone else gave her a wide berth and hoped she wouldn't ask them for spare change or anything.

It was just our bad luck that she saw us out there, she had been walking on the path that wound around the outside edge of the park and was tired, she sat down on that bench only ten minutes before we got there and would have left to go elsewhere in another had she not seen us.

She held her breath as we walked past her, just a few feet away, and though she noticed when I caught her scent or something, she saw that I was too involved in Maria to pay her too much attention and she was happy for that distraction of my thoughts.

Thinking she could sneak up behind us now and take us both, she looked around and there were too many people so she decided it would be best to follow us and see where we went; wait and see if an opportunity presented itself, she didn't want to kill either of us right off, but if she had to, it would have been Maria because she hated her, she still saw me as a tool she could use.

She was going to make me watch as she killed Maria again, she would make me watch her burn and as before, be helpless to do anything to stop it; all of this simply to prove her strength, to show others what happened when they thought they could beat her and to fulfill that prophecy she'd made so long ago, to teach us both that defying her would cost us every time we thought we were safe from her.

If she was thinking right, she would have given a thought to Gregor then, she might have thought that since we were both here together, that he might also have found his way to here as well, but she hardly ever gave him a thought anymore and it made sense that he wasn't here with us, he would be the third wheel and that would never sit well with him.

Her thoughts were consumed with images of killing Maria and eventually me too, she was the ultimate black widow after all, and she could not change her hourglass anymore than the leopard could change his spots; she hated me enough to kill me at that moment because I was so happy that I wasn't even looking out for her as she trailed behind us.

Gregor was out that day, he was looking for a new place to stay and missed the stability of Jeremy having his home that he would hide in, he was in an area close to the park that he could see people and get an idea of what was going on, but not close enough that he would be caught by the police patrols that he could see from there were still in the park.

They had eased up a little, maybe thinking that he'd left town with all the people searching for him, but he still didn't feel safe or comfortable within its manicured lawns and trees; and it was also a blind stroke of luck that he once again found Esmeralda, because of the police he was never on that side of the brush before, and he was angry that the police forced him out that far.

He saw her at the same moment that she saw us; though he didn't know right off what she was doing, he read her body language and didn't know she was following us, only that she was intently looking at something and he thought it must be something like food.

Every time he thought she was going to stop or turn around he ducked behind a tree or something else so she couldn't see him and come after him, with no idea that she was following us at that moment.

Then he did notice us in front of her, and he got a sense of something but he wasn't sure what it was; he thought the cops were coming and looked behind but they weren't there, no one was, he looked at Esmeralda and she was still looking ahead of her, and that was when he realized that she was following someone, but he still could not tell who it was; he was staying behind her far enough that she wouldn't get a sense of him or he might have figured it out.

Then he thought the police did find him because he heard the radio send out a call, but it was nothing, he stayed back until he could hear nothing, seething furiously because he had to stay back while we were all still walking forward, and though we weren't walking fast, it wouldn't be long before we would be in an area that would have several options and would take a few minutes to find which path they might have taken.

He couldn't find us after they finally were far enough that he felt safe to come out, and as he searched for us he found himself in front of the center where we did the sleep study, and it was confusing him because of the images that floated out at him, he saw the four of us, in this world and then back in that one, as were then, but not as we were now because he hadn't seen us, but those images swam back and forth across his mind until he had to sit down to get his bearings, and by another odd coincidence, on the same bench that I sat on that day that I "went back" to the old world.

It would have been funny, or "poetic justice" or something if he would have had the same thing happen to him at that moment and he would have gone back too, it would have made me think it was a portal or something, a window into the past, but he didn't have any flashbacks as I did, maybe his mind wasn't as open because he wasn't trying to find answers to the same questions we had, I don't know but he found his way there and didn't know it yet.

Though he had no idea what it was, he looked around and it made sense that if se came this way, we went into that building for whatever purpose and she was either around here, outside and waiting or she followed us inside, but he was going to wait and find out.

What he didn't know about her was that Esmeralda broke a window in the back area and waited to see if anyone would react or come running to investigate, but when no one did she climbed through it and didn't realize that she'd cut herself when she did.

It was not a deep cut, and if she would have been her spider half it would have shaved the coarse hairs on her hide but not cut her, it was just enough that it left droplets of blood as she went, she didn't notice because she was focused on us so intently.

Gregor was growing impatient and walked around the building twice to make sure we didn't escape from the back door or something and then he finally saw the glass shards that twinkled on the ground where she'd broken the window.

He looked closer and saw her footprints in the soft grass and the little bit of mud under the window from recently being watered and they stopped at the window, telling him that she must have come in this way and we were all together inside, he could see her blood trail as clearly as if he'd brought a flashlight.

The last thing he wanted to do was not rush in there blindly while she was waiting for him there in the darkness, ready to kill him once again, he smelled her blood too, making it easy to follow her but he still had no idea why she was here.

Esmeralda entered the building through the basement, that might have been out of habit but this time she sensed where we were in the building and was walking along underneath us, and of course we had no idea as we were a few feet above her, and sometimes even more, yet she still held onto us as if we were linked with a fine thread.

As she walked through the floors below us, she followed us, her sense of us so strong that she could follow us and know what we were doing at any time, she kept going until she found a stairwell that led up to where we were, and then she decided to wait for the right moment before she would jump out and reveal herself to us.

When we stopped walking for whatever reason, she stopped with us, but now she knew we were going to stay in that area for a while, she never took her eyes or her focus off us that she might lose the thread and have to frantically search again while we might have left the building with Elvis.

As impatient as she was to spring her trap and laugh at the surprised and shocked expressions on our faces as she did; "This time for good, I'll remove your head with a spell I found just for that purpose, just for you!" she said with a sneer, "There will be no more lives for you, instead your body will spend eternity searching for your head, which will be in a bag so that you cannot see where you are and help it!" she laughed at the thought of that but not very loud as she wasn't sure how sound would carry from there.

Gregor almost stumbled into her in the dark, as she was hiding and watching the ceiling, he came around a corner and through a doorway just as she was stepping through another, he got a glimpse of her just before a door closed behind her.

In that brief moment, he saw us on the other side, though she wasn't close to us, he got a sense of who we were in that moment, he almost blew the surprise he had in store for her when he did, he had to sit down for a few moments to catch his breath and absorb it all.

Now he knew why she was following us, and it shocked him to see us both there as well; and though we didn't look the same and he might not have known who we were if he hadn't seen us with her, but he got a sense of us now and there was no mistaking our identity now, and he could put faces on those images he was trying to understand.

He started thinking that this was his good fortune, that this would be the best way to settle all scores at the same time and take control of everything; he would kill Esmeralda first and then me at last, and then he would have Elspeth, she would be his bride as he always wanted and dreamed about, the shock of seeing him in her new world would be enough to overcome any objections that she might have.

Because he knew that Esmeralda would kill him in a heartbeat if she had the chance, so there was no choice there, they could not both be in the same world at the same time, she would have to die or he'd have no chance at a real life.

He didn't want me there to interfere with his plans either, he still thought he could convince her to fall in love with him, especially when she'd have no choice but him, he forgot somehow the many times she'd already done that, even without me in the picture; he thought it was only a matter of time, "Once we are rid of him!" he promised her in that darkness.

"We can start all over again, we will be together as promised!" he said, "As it was meant to be, As I told you long ago, you will be mine, and mine alone!" he hissed.

It never bothered him enough to see us together that he wondered why we were there, together that way, though he was certain now that we didn't know she was following us or she wouldn't be hiding in the stairwell and waiting for something to happen as she was.

In his heart, it was bothering him that we were together this way and he wasn't even invited, not even an afterthought this time, and as he looked at Maria, he never really saw her as she was, but as Elspeth, as she was, wearing the same clothes and speaking the way as she had before, and he still loved and desired her so deeply.

He saw it, but he denied that he could see those old parts of her fading away as these new parts of her became more comfortable, that they became her as she would be from now on.

The worst sting came from another realization though; that through all of this death and mayhem that crashed down on our heads so savagely and all the time spent searching and rediscovering things we lost; she was still very much in love with me.

Even through his hatred he could see that, it stung his eyes and he could feel it too, and he did a slow burn over that, he still told himself that once I was gone and we were together she would forget about me in time.

It caused him tom fly into such a rage and maybe that just slightly skewered his plans enough that they were doomed to failure, though he didn't see that or even give it a thought because he was too deep into his own insanity by then for anything like reason to come to mind.

At that time, we were both headed back to our rooms for further study though I was against this, they had lied to us and had nothing from the last two sessions, I didn't see the need for another but Maria talked me into it; she said she was going to do it either way and then we agreed that it was the only real chance we had to find out, little did we know what that meant this time.

This time we could talk to each other through the extension, part of the intercom which meant that they could all hear as well but we didn't care, neither of us were sure that we would be opening our eyes again once this started but we had no choice.

I was scared this time, more than ever and I didn't know why; this time it didn't feel at all as it had before, the slight bit of trepidation because of the unknown element but this time I really felt my heart was hammering in my chest and about to explode.

There was a deep-seated feeling gnawing at my mind that this was going to be the final act, that we were really going to get the answers we fought so long and hard for, like it or not, we would have our answers soon.

Whatever was going to happen, I felt that this time it was going to be really bad, or maybe it could happen if we let it, I was determined that nothing was going to happen to Maria, I could die and rest in peace as long as I knew she was safe and Esmeralda's prophecy didn't come true.

The funny thing was, it was about that time that I was finally buying into the whole idea of reincarnation; I thought that if I was able to find her in this world, that I would be able to find her in the next as well, as if it was going to be that easy, even if we were both born again in the same world, there was no guarantee that we would meet or feel that love between us.

Because of that, I tried to be brave when I spoke to her, and I was hoping I sounded at least a little braver than I was feeling as I said, "Cara mia, remember that whatever happens next, that we found each other here, and we will do it again if we must!" I paused then, to think about that, but it was more to catch my breath than to reconsider it.

I knew that we'd already walked through the fires of hell together so what could they do to us that was worse than that? I didn't think there was anything they could have but then, I was never as cold-hearted as they could be without trying.

"To find you, I would search through all of the stars if I had to and never feel tired!" I said, but then the image of "Pandora's Box" popped into my mind and how they felt when it was opened and what happened to them.

Remembering the lesson of that story and I could not help but wonder how we would feel after we opened this box of secrets, of our unknown future; or even if we were going to have one.

When they saw that I couldn't sleep, this time they gave me the shot right off instead of wasting time with the other sedatives and hoping they didn't mess with my liver too much, I think this time I made it to ninety-eight before I went under.

I remember the technician waving at me as before, but this time it was a different tech, I guess it was something they all thought was funny; I think I was trying to be polite when I tried to laugh as she was acting like I was a baby as she waved me to sleep, my last thoughts were of the shadows I'd seen on those earlier tapes and I wondered what they could see on them now.

Then I thought, "Were they blue-grey, or grayish-blue?" as if that made sense and I had to know the answer as I went out, Sam was here this time, so no one was going to sleep except for Maria and I; she was going over her notes, reading about the things I'd told her aboutwhen I was "awake" and still left my body.

She knew by how we repeated our statements that we were really seeing and feeling what we reported, we couldn't make it up and never had a chance between us to talk about it without them knowing so she knew we were real, she just didn't understand why they missed so much.

But as I went under, she heard me call for "Elspeth" and not Maria and wondered then about the difference between her then and how she was now; and then she noticed something new, something that was not any of the other tapes and it had happened then as well and they missed it, and then she wondered if it happened when they were sleeping and they could have seen it even though the machines didn't catch it.

What she saw then was that, though we were in separate rooms and the intercom between us was off and we could not speak to each other, we were in fact, doing exactly that now.

Through the wall and the distance between us I could hear what she was saying and would react to it and answer her, and we kept going that way as we went deeper and deeper into our past life, though the banks of machinery and the new toys they brought in this time, we could hear each other clearly.

There were times when I would refer to her by both names, and she would respond to either the same; as if she knew who I meant or that was somehow normal, Sam thought it might be because I was Elspeth at one moment, and Maria the next, and maybe I traded back and forth as well but she didn't call my name.

We spoke low enough that they couldn't hear us, but Sam was pretty good at reading lips and our reactions, but they were scrambling to find out why they couldn't hear us; "Not again!" one of them said under his breath; he knew that he'd done everything because he triple checked his work as a habit, and now was thinking that the overtime he was getting wasn't worth all of this trouble, and he wasn't the only one that felt that way.

She added that to her notes about us, another thing that they had never seen before; we were obviously closely connected and knew each other so well that we could communicate on a different plane, something that most people were denied, though they spent their entire lives searching for that kind of commitment.

That we had that ability as well, that we could see it but didn't recognize it for what it was, and we let it pass without ever exploring it because we feel that we are not worthy of that kind of love and devotion.

As if we felt it was reserved for the rare ones and we didn't belong; the ones that felt things deeper and stronger than most of us, that were connected to the earth on a different level, those few that could love that deeply and give themselves completely to one other person exclusively.

For the first time since she'd read her first book, she felt as though all of this new data was going to give her studies validation; after this, they wouldn't be able to deny her the respect she felt she'd earned long ago, she was elated and giddy over the thought of that and yet, for reasons that even she couldn't understand; she felt a great fear in the pit of her stomach.

It had been growing for a few days, getting stronger as she tried to ignore it as much as she could but there was no denying it and it wasn't going to go away if she kept ignoring it.

These were her pet theories, and the rest of the leaders in her field were one of those "old boy" networks, and as much as she had accomplished; they refused to acknowledge her, kept her out of the inner circle as much as they could without being too obvious.

"Now they'll have to open that door, and I never had to take off a stich of clothing, or sleep with some idiot that would forget my name before I left the room!" she said to herself with a smile.

Though her ideas were not original this was going to be the first time that she had solid evidence of her own and it was indisputable, and would soon be validated by experts, people that would pore through them and verify that they weren't doctored or altered in any way.

She made a mental note to stay in touch and invite us to dinner a couple of times a month, to stay in touch yes; to also clear up anything that might pop up while they went over the data, help them with the finer details; but she was also thinking beyond that.

She was thinking that since we were in love and, things taking their course, we would one day marry and then have children, and maybe they would be something to study as well, make contributions of their own, she already had a name for that volume of her work, she would call it; "The Seeds of Reincarnated parents!" at least that was her working title until she came up with something better, something that rolled off the tongue a bit easier.

She'd spent the day going over the earlier tapes to make sure there was nothing else that they'd missed, she had transcripts made up of what they had anyway, at least that data was there, but it made her laugh to think of it as a "solid shadow of evidence" as it seemed.

It wasn't something that she thought would help, but she was a big believer in going over things again to see if they might reveal things she missed later, they verified her thoughts and what she already knew to be fact now, but it would at least give them a baseline to work from.

But the last time she listened to the tapes, she heard something that no one else had heard before; she was sure of that because no one else said anything about it, and they surely would have if they'd heard it, but it seemed to have been left there for her ears only.

She heard a voice on the tapes, it called her by name as it rode in the background of the other voices on the tape, mainly ours, but once in a while one their voices would come out because they left the monitor on or something.

But to her, this was the same as the shadows in our rooms, the spider in Maria's room and the vampire in mine, though no one knew who the vampire was, they thought it was just a man that hated me enough to want to kill me; and this voice, which spoke her name and told her to "STAY THE HELL OUT OF MY BUSINESS!" and she heard it clearly enough, though no one else did, even then, and it chilled her to the bones and scared the hell out of her.

Without thinking about it, she'd learned a trick from a man in her travels and slowed everything down in her mind, the tape still played at regular speed for everyone else; but she was no longer hearing it because she heard the whispering so clearly now that she started to cry.

"STOP what you are doing, do not listen to me, turn everything off immediately or you will suffer the most horrible death you could imagine!" it warned her over and over again until it became more than a whisper and then she shut off the machine because she couldn't stand it any longer.

As you might imagine, in her field there were a few times that things happened that frightened her enough that she thought about backing off or taking on a new career path, but she convinced herself that the "risk vs reward" was worth it and continued; but none of those "experiences" ever made her feel this threatened, it knew her name.

Once she was heard of a tribe in South America that was said to have many experiences of reincarnation; a missionary that was travelling with them as a doctor and when one of them broke and the treatment started they started speaking a different language and acting differently, it was recorded her findings and one day Sam found the book in the library and was intrigued.

She convinced the school that she'd worked for The University of Southern California, a prestigious school of course, but not one known for that kind of study, they didn't condone it but they funded it because they liked her enthusiasm and thought she was onto something.

That led to her going to find that tribe in South America, and because she was relatively new to that part of the game, she fell for a number of schemes and had accidents that almost killed her entire party, eight left and only three returned with her.

They became lost when the guides left them during the night, taking food and supplies with them, though they didn't need them, they would sell them to other "explorers" that would be coming to follow her and see what she'd discovered.

They ran out of food a few days alter and then fresh water wasn't far behind, one of them wandered off a cliff and dropped three-hundred feet to her death; they thought she was delirious because she'd been dragging her feet all day and then suddenly perked up and shouted, "There it is!" as she ran off the edge without screaming as she fell, they could hear her laughter though.

As quickly as they ran to help her, they hoped she'd caught a branch or fell onto a ledge that they could bring her back up, but they could see her body way down there, the blood spreading out below her and onto the rocks around her body.

When they got further into the jungle, they thought she'd gotten off easily because they found the tribe they were looking for, but another tribe caught them and took them back to their village, when one of the men tried to resist, he was quickly cut into pieces and his body parts salvaged for later, the rest fell in line but would have preferred to fight and die than what happened next.

They were placed in a hut that had no walls, it's tightly woven strands were strong enough that they couldn't get out, it was made for observation, and all of the tribe's people, including the women and small children paraded by and watched them as they huddled together.

As they passed, they spoke of what they thought of the people inside, they were essentially sizing them up and making their choices as to whom they wanted to have for dinner, not as a guest, but as the main course.

It became clear when they took one, a guy named Deacon, who was also the largest of the group, they came in with knives that they threatened the rest of us with while they dragged him out by the hair; they wanted the rest of them to fight, they were ready for it but it didn't happen.

As more of them began to arrive, it seemed they were from other villages or something because one of them was different; he stood apart from the others and they seemed to defer to him, as though he was special somehow; they thought he was another leader or some kind of royalty.

He stopped at the front of the cage and nodded his head slowly at us; then turned to his right and spoke softly to the man that was waiting there, they knew that the man he spoke to was the leader of the tribe that captured them because of the way they acted when he spoke, especially when he was angry.

They were hoping that they had just come to see the outsiders and they were the entertainment for the night; that they would get tired of it after a few days and let them go; but that changed when they brought Deacon back, naked and embarrassed as they shoved him forward and he tried to cover himself.

One of them shoved him too hard and fell down into the dirt, face first; they laughed at his face covered with dirt, and then they stepped forward and began to piss on him to wash away the dirt as they laughed at him and he screamed at them to stop.

Then the leader of the visiting tribe stepped forward and extended his hand, to help Deacon up, and as he rose to his feet, the tribal leader walked around him, appraising him from all angles as he went, speaking to the others, poking and prodding at the man as he went around him twice.

For the next several hours they cooked and ate two more of the group and then started to celebrate, they were all drinking and jumping around and one of them dropped a knife close to the cage but didn't notice it, or the man that saw it and grabbed it before someone else saw it and took it away.

The party continued that way for what seemed like hours, they would come by the cage and talk about whatever they thought, excitedly pointing at the people inside and then going back to the celebration until they got too intoxicated with whatever they were drinking and eventually feel asleep.

When they were sure that they were deeply asleep, the others began to talk among themselves, they knew what was going to be for breakfast and didn't want to be a part of that; they dug and clawed their way out of there, they cut a few of the strands and the others fell away as they were wound so tightly that they almost snapped which would have woken someone, but they were careful and had thought of that before.

Although the full moon t]lit the cage fairly well, in the back there were too many shadows so they couldn't be seen that way, there was a guard out there, but he was also sleeping while clutching a spear that still had blood on it.

The last of them crawled out and they were well past him, but in their haste to escape they went the wrong way, the first one, Arlene, was the fastest of them and she was running ahead of everyone else because she panicked, she was overjoyed that they'd escaped and she was still alive as she ran, but the guard that was sleeping did waken, and he saw her running, stepped up and launched his spear as she was about fifteen feet away, he hit her right between the shoulder blades with a perfect shot.

She did turn and tried to reach for it, and then she fell into a river that we didn't even know was there, and then she became lunch anyway for something that was swimming just below the surface that looked like a dwarf crocodile because it was broad-snouted and boney looking, the last they saw of her was her trying to reach out for them or something to pull herself out of there, that one hand came up and then she was dragged down deeper and then gone.

They strangled that guard with their bare hands and threw his body into the river as well, taking satisfaction that they got even for Arlene though she would no longer care, the rest escaped and were asked to tell the story but none of them wanted to talk about it, another of them, a woman named Serena killed herself a few days after they got back, she said told the others she felt guilty for surviving when the others didn't, and that she couldn't get those images out of her head, even when awake, and then she went to the bathroom, took tranquilizers that she found in the cabinet and slit her wrists.

They knew it bothered her more because she was the one that talked Arlene into coming along, telling her that it would be a great experience for her, the guilt ate at her until she could take it no more, all of this explained in a note that she left.

The voice that she heard on the tapes was the same voice as that leader from the second tribe, the timbre and dialect were exact, the way he spoke, she could swear it was the same voice though it had been years since that happened.

Sam was concentrating on that so hard and t5rying to figure that part out that she missed what was going on with the monitors behind her and to her left; if she'd looked, she would have seen us both jumping on the beds frantically, as if we were in a skillet and the flame was high.

This time, the techs saw it, and they tried the intercom to let Sam know about it because they were really excited except that it wasn't working, it would click over but no one could hear anything from the other end except what sounded like a voice a the far end of a really long tunnel; they sent a runner to let her know that this time was different.

None of them knew the feeding habits of a spider, let alone one with as voracious an appetite as Esmeralda brought to the fore; and today she was ravenous with all the hunting and secretive, furtive movements that she went through; and by the time they found that out, it was far too late.

When the runner first tried to open the door, she thought it was Sam, that she was blocking the door for some reason, and they had recently installed and activated the cameras in the hall and over the door, so she looked up there, to wave to her boss and let her know it was her, but the camera was covered with webbing and dark, coarse hairs, so much they they couldn't see the lens.

She finally pushed her way through the door and tried to call out to Sam, and saw Sam there, but also two other techs; Brain and another guy whose name she couldn't remember because he was new, but her voice was choked off when Esmeralda rushing towards her, she pushed the poor tech out of the way as she entered and climbed up onto the far wall and then to the ceiling and then stopped for a moment to watch them.

Esmeralda wore a grin at that moment that was both so beautiful and yet filled with so much evil the tech, whose name was Molly; actually stopped and smiled back at her, she'd clearly lost it, the others thought as they tried to get her to come back to them; she kept stepping forward haltingly.

"Molly!" they said, "Come back here! What the hell are you doing?" they asked her, and though they reached for her; none of them would step any closer to where Esmeralda waited for them.

They couldn't see it because she was looking the other way, but her expression wasn't of fear, but instead of wonder and you would have thought she was looking at a beautiful flower or something, a damned sunset except that she was inside.

She was the first of them to die, Esmeralda lifted her off the ground and she never fought her; she picked her up with her forelegs and bit her head off and drank her blood as it spurted out until she stopped twitching altogether, then she tossed her aside and turned back to the others.

The other two were so stunned by her appearance and what they'd just seen her do right in front of them; they couldn't force themselves to move until that moment, one of them finally broke at that moment and made a mad dash for when Esmeralda caught up to him.

She grabbed him by the head and rolled onto her back, then she pulled him with one of her legs and pushed back with another, and then two more came up and pulled at his back until they heard a loud snap that meant she broke his back, as she tossed him aside, she turned towards the last tech as she stood there, still to afraid to even move.

The girl knew it was hopeless to try and escape, she saw how fast Esmeralda could move and she knew that when they put that camera in the hallway to watch this door, they also key-coded the lock on both sides; she was thinking that if she tried to run it would be over quickly while she tried to remember the code for the day and hoped they hadn't already changed it again.

She'd watched while her friends died, she didn't want to; she tried to shield her eyes, tried to get them to stand together and fight; that maybe they'd have a chance that way; her mind was telling her that none of this was true, that it couldn't be real and she was losing it.

Though she couldn't manage to cover her eyes entirely; she did manage to cover her ears, but that didn't help her much, the scream that Esmeralda made when she attacked got into her head and there was no way that she could shake free of it.

Her mind did snap then, and she began to laugh uncontrollably, she had no control over anything of herself; she gave herself to the death she knew was waiting for her, she dropped her hands to her sides and waited as Esmeralda grabbed her by the sides of her neck, twisted her head back and bit deeply into her throat.

She fed on them for a short time, even though she hadn't tried to change her appearance all the energy she'd used to get to this point made her so hungry she couldn't help it.

The adrenal rush and the need to get to us prevented this from being much more than a quick "feed and run" because we were hiding somewhere in this building and she couldn't think of anything else.

Under normal circumstances, anyone would have a hard time believing what they saw, they would never live to tell about it either; but as she was mostly spider in her appearance at the moment, her body and legs, but the head was still Esmeralda, covered with blood and tissue that ran down her chin and soaked into the fur below that.

Gregor was locked onto them too now, and now he was not going to let go, no matter what else happened and good lord help anyone that got in his way now.

He wanted to get Elspeth of course, to be with her and find a way to her heart, and that of course, meant that he had to eliminate me; but even in his fevered mind he knew that there would be no future with Esmeralda, she'd already proven how ruthless she was the first time she killed him, she was a black widow.

We were both mortal and could be found again if we escaped him, but there was no way that she was going to, he knew one of them was going to die and was just as certain that it was not going to be him.

He felt a new sense of what Esmeralda was now, and she was different, she was other-worldly now, and he knew he needed to be even more careful than ever before, there would be no second chances to gain the advantage of surprising her.

For a brief moment he thought that she might be, at that very moment killing us, and as much as he loved Elspeth, he didn't care at that moment because he was so tightly focused on Esmeralda and what she did to him and at the same time he was steeling himself for what he felt he must do next; but he was so frantically "out of the loop" because he was alone in this while thought there was at least that connection that brought us here without him.

The witch must die, above all else, and she must suffer at his hands, those were "givens" and he couldn't wait until the moment when she would see his face, and then she would know that he'd come all this way just to kill her and avenge his own death at last; he'd had almost two-hundred years of seething and planning for this day, and now it was almost here.

Photograph by J. R. Gonzalez

He stood down there in the darkness, his gaze upward, his hands up, opening and closing as if they were already wrapped around her throat and he could hear her struggling for breath.

The claws came out too, striking at nothing and then retracting again; at the same time his jaw clenched and loosened, the fangs elongating and then also retracting; gleaming under the soft light down there.

His tongue slid out then too; it was forked at the end and slithered out as a snake would, his eyes went a deep black as he fought against the urge to run up there and kill everything that moved.

I was awakened then by the strong urge to urinate, they must have thought I was cold or that I would sleep better if they turned the heater on, that was why I thought I was so thirsty and my throat was so dry and parched that it hurt just to breath.

The urges were stronger than my desire to sleep a little longer and I sat up and started pulling the wires out while I squeezed my knees together so I wouldn't pee all over myself.

I muttered "Sorry guys, but nature calls and you're always too slow with the bed pan!" and in my mind, I was imagining the bells and whistles going off in the other rooms, and I thought that even if they were sleeping again, they would be awakened by that and come running.

Then I jumped of the bed and waited a minute, not because I wanted to see them rushing in, but because I was still weak and a little light-headed from the sedative and almost fell twice.

After a few more anxious moments of no techs running in to shut off the alarms, I felt brave enough to walk out into the main hallway, I remembered there was a restroom just outside of my door and to the right and hoped it was the men's room and that it was working because they told me that the one in my room had been backed up for a couple of days.

I forgot that I was wearing a hospital gown and nothing else and my bare ass was hanging out when I did notice that it was a little cooler out there than it was in my room.

Taking care of business, I was still keeping an ear out for the techs that I still thought were on the way, I knew that something was wrong and while I was still fighting off the cobwebs I went back to my room and got dressed, all the time I kept my eyes on the door as much as I could, only taking them off to look for my shoes; but that was as brief as I could manage it.

Though I was normally shy about my body, this time I dressed in front of the one-way glass so they could see me and let me know that everything was alright and they were just being lazy, though I think deep inside, I already knew that no one was coming; at least, no one that I would have wanted to see.

As soon as I was done, I ran to Maria's room and shook her awake, she tried to push me away, mumbling something about her homework, but I kept it up until she opened her eyes and I was sure she wasn't going to go back to sleep, but I was sure that at any moment, someone was going to rush through that door and kill us both were we stood.

"Why do you keep looking at the door?" she asked me, "What's wrong?" she asked, seeing the look of concern on my face, she sat up suddenly and before I could answer she touched my face and told me that she was dreaming that we were married and she was having our baby, and that vision gave her a feeling that everything was going to be alright after all.

She didn't tell me that as the dream was fading away, she remembered seeing Asmodeus at the edge of the lawn, he was cleaning his fur and acting innocent; she knew that there was never anything innocent about that cat.

In her sub-conscious thoughts, she wanted to know who this cat was and why he was always there, and she wanted to know what his being there might mean now, what bad tidings he was bringing along with him this time.

She looked at me then, thinking that I should at least be happy from some of that news, and I was happy that she saw that we had a future together, but I whispered as urgently as I could to her, I wanted her to hurry but I didn't want to scare her too much or cause her to panic.

"Something is VERY wrong!" I said, "Please get dressed, we need to leave, PLEASE!" I said as I turned to give her some privacy while I watched the door.

She dressed quickly then, without another word, and when she was done, she came behind me and wrapped her arms around me, hugging me close and kissing my ear as she reminded me that everything was going to be alright.

"This!" she said as she squeezed me a little tighter, "Was meant to be, there's nothing they can do about that, nothing can change it!" she told me, "We've done nothing wrong!" she said, almost desperately, and then she held me closer.

I turned around then and looked her deep in the eyes for a moment and saw the truth in them, and then I held her close for a moment and said; "I have this deep-seated feeling that when I died back there; I loved you then, as I do now, and as I will for all of time!" I whispered in her ear.

"Something makes me feel that I promised you back then that I would always love you, and I think that, from that time so long ago, to this time I've spent my entire being searching for that look I see in your eyes and no where else, I searched for that kiss on your lips and the love I can only find in your heart, which was made for me, as I was made for you!" I told her.

Although I was scared before and started to feel better as we spoke together; I tried to pretend that there was some sort of meeting or something, and that would explain why they were all so quiet and not here yet, at least I was hoping that was what it was.

But even I had to admit that the entire place had an empty and abandoned feeling about it, and now we both felt it, and scared us; yet neither of us was ready to speak of it; speaking of it would make it real and we weren't ready for that yet.

We stepped out into the hallway and tried to ignore the eerie quiet, or to pretend that it was supposed to be that way but even the elevator music was off and though the carpet was thick; we tried to be just as quiet as everyone else was.

I felt as though every single step we took echoed loudly through the walls, announcing our location to anyone or anything else that was inside the building with us.

We finally got back to Sam's office and found the door closed, just as it should have been, but for some reason I took her hand and held her back for a moment; seeing that closed door made me feel that it proved that something was wrong, I looked around us and then behind, and then I felt brave and knocked softly on the door and then pushed it because it was open.

This time, there was no one in the outer office, and I was going to turn and leave but Maria stepped past me and went into the other room, where she thought she heard something and thought it was Sam.

I tried to hold her back, tried telling her that something was wrong and that we should leave now; before it got any worse, but the look that she gave me told me that she already knew but also knew that we couldn't run fast enough to escape it, "We need to see what happened and maybe help if we can!" she told me.

Then I told her, "I think that you're right, but we shouldn't both go, you should go for the police, get us some kind of help!" I said, "I'll go in there and see if there's anyone I can help!" I said, but she wasn't going to stop.

"There is no way I am going to just leave you here!" she said, "We face this together, we have strength to beat it together!" she told me with such conviction and determination that I felt some of her strength surge into me from her hand to mine and all through my body.

"If we separate, they can kill us, but if we stand together, that's out only chance, and I would much rather die at your side than anywhere else, if it comes to that!" she said.

"Okay...okay!" I said, "You're right, I was just doing the guy thing and trying to protect you, I don't know what's out there; I have no real idea, but I feel like its going to be very bad!" I said.

She took my hand and squeezed it harder as she said "together" and squeezed it harder, then she pulled me towards the door and whatever awaited us on the other side. But now I felt as though we had a chance, that we could conquer whatever it was, but never, in our wildest imaginations could we have known that the nightmares that we shared were at least partially coming true.

From where we stood, I could see that the other door was at least partially open, and I could see the top of her head as she sat in the chair at her desk, though she had her back to us, it was a great relief to see her there, finally some good news.

She was watching the monitors in her office, they were flickering all over the place, jumping as if they were resetting every few minutes; messages about waiting for buffering and other things, signal lost, it kept flashing on and off.

Just to our left, we could see alarms going off as we entered the room a little further; and though the sound was turned off, all the lights were still flashing and the needles were jumping off the charts, they tore through the paper in some areas where there was a lot of ink.

I could also see that some of the tapes had run their course and were no flipping over and over as we stood there, the voices and other sounds on them were warbling as it played over the same spots, and I knew right then that no one was coming to change them.

Maybe I was being too hopeful but I was still thinking that Sam was sleeping because all of this was going on and yet she wasn't moving; just like in all of the horror movies I'd seen over the years and was screaming at myself to run, for us to get the hell out of there because I knew what I was going to find if we didn't.

"Hey Sam!" I called out, as if I felt confident, which was anything but true; "What's going on, where is everybody?" I asked her gently but was answered with nothing but that same eerie silence.

I took a look around the room again because it didn't feel right, I felt as though I was going through my father's liquor cabinet or something and didn't belong there; I felt as though we were missing something important but I couldn't figure out what it was.

Finally, I could stand it no more and I reached over and spun her chair around, I thought she was asleep or something since she hadn't responded to us being there yet, then I saw that she was quite dead after all, and I laughed then because I remembered Joe say, "I hate it when I'm right!" and smacking his head as if he really did.

It stopped me cold when I saw her body so emaciated already, it was as if Esmeralda put a straw in the top of her head and sucked all of the life out of her in the last few minutes, her devoid and dried out that it seemed as though it had been ages.

Her blackened skull grinned back at me, mocking the screamin my throat, Maria took that moment to turn on the light and we saw that the worst nightmare we could imagine had come true, the thing we feared the most, Esmeralda had been hiding below the desk when she heard us coming this way.

A lot of things were slammed home in those few moments, I knew now whose leg I saw outside the orphanage that day, and whose voice was calling to me out of the darkness, the shadow over Maria's bed as she slept in it, and why there were so many spiders in so many of my bad dreams and I should have remembered the man standing over mine but this was too much to absorb all at once and I wasn't thinking of myself, I was trying to imagine how I could save Maria.

When she heard us in the hallway, she was feeding on Sam, sucking the life out of her and watching her features as they faded from supple and young looking to something that had aged a few hundred years in the last five minutes.

Maria hadn't seen her until the chair rotated around another time and she moved closer, and she tried to scream but she was afraid to, and then she just fought it off because she knew that it wouldn't matter; that we needed to keep our wits about us this time or we were doomed.

"She thought she knew me!" Esmeralda whispered to us, "She thought she knew what I was, and that she could control me! Can you imagine the nerve, she wanted to study me!" she said and then laughed, her voice shouted it s way around inside of my head and I was near panic now.

This was madness coming into our lives as we stood there, finally I grabbed at Maria's hand and tried to pull her away from there but she wouldn't let me; the harder I pulled the harder she fought against me because she knew we couldn't outrun this thing that killed Sam.

I heard Esmeralda whisper something else behind me and I knew then who she was and why she was here, I looked into those insect eyes and still knew who she was, and that she was here to fulfill her promise to snatch Maria away while I stood helpless to stop her.

It brought back memories of her dancing naked, hopping from one foot to the other in joyous celebration at what she'd done to us, the witch spun a wicked web and danced as we died; we were both caught in it back then, just as we were now.

I felt her hot breath dripping slime on my shoulder and hoped it wasn't going to poison me, get absorbed into my skin or even burn where it touched me, I knew she could sense my revulsion for her but I wasn't going to try and hide it anyway.

All the things she warned me of were coming true now; except that this time we weren't prisoners and we already knew what kind of terror and worse that she was capable of; we'd both seen and felt her handiwork.

She didn't have all the cards stacked in her favor as she thought she did though; at least I hoped that she didn't, that she forgot some important detail and this was all going to blow up in her face but I couldn't imagine what that might be, and I didn't know that Gregor was there with us, though I knew he wouldn't be an ally, I did think he would distract her enough that we might escape and form a battle plan to use against her, find a way to fight her on our terms and not hers where she'd have the advantage; I was hoping that they couldn't win all the time and that this time it was our turn.

I looked around for something to use against her when she shoved Sam aside and jumped across the room, screaming with delight; as she flew over me, I thought I was ready and braced myself for the hit; I was hoping to deflect her from us somehow but I hadn't counted on her way and she was so powerful that I was nothing to her.

She knocked me across the room and the quickly jumped on me and injected her venom into me before I could react or get up, it stunned me enough that she knew it was working, I was helpless now, aware of what was going on but I couldn't even move my hand to fight her.

Esmeralda picked me up and wound me around in her webbing until she was sure that I couldn't easily break free and then she hung me, upside down, from the ceiling. Then she did the same to Maria, and then she picked us both up and carried us both, those fangs of hers not far from our faces as she walked, a reminder that she would use them if we fought against her.

Though she didn't know it, I was trying to, but couldn't move, the venom weakened me and the webbing held me fast, but I felt it loosen as she walked with us and our bodies swayed with her steps, though she hadn't noticed.

She carried us effortlessly while thinking that she was going to kill anyone that we ran into, right where they stood, then she found two bodies and brought those with her as well, slinging them over her back in case she got hungry along the way.

"I warned her, I told her to leave me alone and stop watching us, did she tell you that?" I heard Esmeralda's voice inside my head, it was scratchy and loud, and I tried to ignore her, but she only got louder when I did.

"I even sent her bad dreams when she didn't back off, but she wouldn't listen, like you two fools, she didn't believe me until it was too late, but I bet she knows now!" she said and cackled at her little joke as if we would join her in it.

"I warned you both!" she hissed at me, "I told you both what would happen, and you never listened but you will learn as well, NO ONE can stand against me!" she shouted in my head.

Sam never told us any of this, but I knew that she wasn't lying to me about it; I would have asked Maria but, that would have to wait until after we got out of this, which I still wasn't sure we would be able to do and it didn't look good from this angle; yet I knew I couldn't give up hope.

I looked at Maria and knew in my heart that it wasn't over yet, that somehow, we were going to win this time and this was our round to win; I promised her with all my might and tried to will that same confidence into her but I don't think she heard me and then I thought she might be in shock; but as bad as things were, it might have been the other way around and I was in shock and she was the one still working to save us.

It couldn't end like this, we weren't food or toys for her to play with at her leisure, we weren't done yet, and I kept trying to send that feeling to her but couldn't tell if she felt it, heard me or even believed in them because she never reacted in the least way.

Thinking it was best, I kept sending those messages and thoughts to her because I didn't want to leave her alone in the darkness that way; I had to let her know that as bad as it looked, this wasn't the end and she wasn't alone in that darkness, and that, as she told me; together, we could do anything, if we only believed that we could.

HAPPENSTANCE AND CIRCUMSTANCE

We must believe in luck. For how else do we explain the success of those we don't like?

-Jean Cocteau, (1889-1963)

Gregor sat in the darkness and surprised even himself as he was so patiently waiting for his chance to spring out and reveal himself. He stood back and watched all that had happened he didn't know exactly how, or why, or even the change in Esmeralda but he did feel her power, even from where he stood, that alone was maddening for him, waiting and yet it was all that he could do.

It took him a few minutes to get over the shock of seeing all three of us, though he hadn't yet seen Esmeralda as she was now; he wanted to go outside and calm himself down, pace it off as he liked to say, but he was afraid he would lose us if he did, or that someone might see him out there and maybe recognize him from the posters and call the police.

It finally paid off for him when he saw her leaving the building with us in tow, he should have been shocked to see her in that form, but maybe he was ready for the unexpected by then because he wasn't surprised at all, but he didn't think it was her, he thought it was her "pet" and it was sent to fetch them for her or something, he thought she was around somewhere, controlling it, so he was especially careful when he stepped in behind to follow her.

When he first saw her carrying us, he thought that she had killed us after all, but then he saw my eyes move and knew that she'd only stunned us, he couldn't see much of Maria though so he wasn't sure what she'd done, only that she had us in her clutches.

He dropped in behind her and followed from a distance, as closely as he dared because he didn't want to lose her now; though she was so intent in her purpose that she hardly ever looked around and never once looked back as she went along.

But then, something about her bearing or they way she walked made him realize that it wasn't a pet and that it was her all along, and he marveled at that.

There was no one outside that night to see our little parade of the once dead and soon to be once more, but had anyone been unlucky enough to have witnessed that, I doubt that they would believe what they saw with their own eyes.

As we all got closer to the central section of the park, Gregor got a little nervous because it was right in the middle of the shift change and that meant new officer's with fresh eyes would be out searching for him, luckily for them, they weren't out there yet be would be soon.

He was looking in that direction and almost missed her as she went into the sewer line but he saw the last of her duck through just as the grate closed behind her, he admired the beauty of that as he saw the broken lock inside the hole; it was a perfect hiding place, right out in the open, and in the middle of the city; and he never would have found her without following her.

But he also thought it would be easier to follow her in there, even though he couldn't see in the dark because the sound carried, he could hear the rustle of our bodies as she carried us along and tried to move slow enough that he made no sound and yet quick enough that he wouldn't lose his way and be lost down there forever, or come around a blind turn only to find her standing there, waiting for him.

He was able to stay back a bit as he tried to think of a way to save Elspeth and kill Maria, he didn't even give me a second's thought.

Even though he'd never been to these tunnels before, he marveled at her finding and making it her own, he knew from the odors in the air that it was her killing ground; he slowed down even more then, he thought she must have left some kind of surprises that she might have left behind, and after a while he relaxed a little because he knew she didn't expect anyone to follow her down there that far, and if she found anyone that did, she would deal with them then; he thought that would be her way.

But she held all the advantages down in those tunnels and he didn't like that, but as he didn't think of that ahead of time, he had no plan to deal with it either and that bothered him too, he was finding out more and more that he had little patience for surprises.

He stayed back and followed her as she worked her way through the maze of tunnels, too late, he thought that he should have marked the walls as he went along, so that he wouldn't get lost, now it was important to make sure that he could see her and he needed to be faster and less cautious.

He stood back at what he was sure was the last turn because he saw wavering light that meant torches or something down there, a regular light would be solid and constant, this one wavered and was weak, he was near her altar, and when he saw it, he noticed how much it resembled the one that she accused Elspeth of using in the woods.

He saw the candles then, and the bodies of the techs thrown so casually aside; and he knew that, even though Esmeralda was the one presenting the most damaging evidence, even before she took the stand he knew that she led them all where she wanted to go; she manipulated them all like puppets, and she held the strings and worked us as she liked.

But he could see where she was now, and where she was going and so he stepped back a little further into the darkness, to keep an eye out for anything else that might come along and to make sure she didn't escape and to watch what she was going to do to us and lastly because he wasn't sure how good her vision was down here and would be able to figure out the best way to surprise her and kill her.

Though he wouldn't have cared about it, I was also watching her and waiting for my chance; as bad as it looked at the moment, I knew my shot would come and I knew I had to be ready when it came because there wasn't going to be a second; I was at that moment, trying to raise my hand or at the very least, move a finger because I thought that might be the easiest place to start.

After what felt like a couple of hours, my right hand moved, it was not much more than a twitch, but it was a start, and other than my eyes, nothing else was moving and believe me, I tried.

I could see Maria though, hanging to my right side like two sides of beef in the window of the market where my grandmother used to buy the meat for the family and ordered in quantities.

Feeling desperate, I tried to will my thoughts into her mind; to tell her that it wasn't over; that this wasn't the end, but no matter what I tried, she still was non-responsive and I was just hoping that she hadn't been over-medicated and wasn't going to be coming back.

Gregor and I were both watching her as she set out new candles and then lit some of them, placed others at points inside the pentagram but she left them unlit for the moment.

I hoped that it meant that we had more time, I didn't know what she planned either except that she meant to kill Maria, burn her in that pyre she set aside for it; it made me wonder how long she'd been watching us and planning this because it clearly wasn't done in the last few days; I knew what she was planning and even if I didn't care for her, there was no way I wanted to watch or hear that happen again.

Now I was remembering what she'd said before, and though it seemed very much as though the odds were in her favor and that her words would come true; I set my mind to the fact that if it happened again, it wasn't going to be easy and it would cost her this time, as long as I was breathing, I promised.

Then I got a glimmer of hope because my hand moved just a little more freely, I was feeling the numbness wear off my face and especially my nose, things were starting to look better again.

Gregor saw the pyre and noticed also how much it looked like the other, he was wondering why she built it, why she'd go through so much trouble and not just kill her and be done with it.

"She must have some special planned!" he thought, "Some evil plan that only be satisfied with a horrible death!" he thought and then laughed a little.

He thought it might be something that she tried to do the first time and maybe it didn't come out right, maybe something to extend her powers, which were already too much to handle or they wouldn't be here once more.

It will eventually destroy her! Even if I don't!" he prophesized, and he almost left then, was going to let her find out for herself; but then he wanted to be the one to take her out of this world.

He decided that he would stay back, watch what she did but he would step in and kill her before she realized her chance, her renewal of life if that's what this was, he would step in then and kill her and then end me and whoever else was in the way.

Though he didn't care about me, he wondered what she had planned for me; and he was wondering how long he should stay there in the dark and wait for his chance and what the hell were the candles for; then he smiled at the thought of taking her as she did t him, and then ripping her apart as she did to so many others during her lifetime.

His thoughts were interrupted when he heard her chant softly, he thought it was for some of her demons, that she was summoning them, he shivered as he imagined some of them standing next to him at that very moment.

He risked a look at her, and saw that she had taken out a long knife and was pointing it at the northern corner and then another to the eat as she chanted, she must have sensed a lover nearby or something because she stopped changing long enough to say, "Not this time my pet!" as she smiled and whispered softly.

Then she felt other spirits, she saw some of them too, both good and evil; some wanted to be used for this, others wanted to be a part of it because it had been so long that they felt that they were worn and beaten down to almost nothing.

There were others that had no one to talk to in so many centuries that they forgot the words because they'd had no one to talk to, once they were eloquent, now they wept because they forgot, and they kept moving away.

Then Asmodeus joined in, suddenly springing out of the darkness unannounced, he watched the parade of the dead with detached interest, and though Gregor had forgotten about him, he was at least glad that the cat hadn't come his way, or sensed him back there in the darkness, he thought that maybe there were too many different scents in the air.

Setting things out in a certain order, making sure she was at the right position; the right point at the exact moment, she had always been good at making sure those things were carefully done; she was always so precise and that she knew the right words before she ever lit the first candle and the ceremony began.

Though she always knew the rituals, the proper names to invoke and when it as the right time; the proper incantations and the best time of the year to use certain spells for the most effect, there was always the chance that when you opened a door, even if it was the right door and you opened it just a crack; the wrong thing might chance through that opening that you created and it might just ruin all your best laid plans, and though Asmodeus was always a welcome friend, this time, he arrived at the wrong time.

He was just enough of a distraction that Gregor saw his chance to strike when she turned towards him, and Gregor moved into a better position as quietly as he could.

Maria was still in a state of shock, but she was a little more aware of what was going on around her, and she couldn't move yet either, though she hadn't tried as I did.

I knew that if she didn't get help soon, that she might lapse into a coma and die, and I hoped that she was fighting as hard as she could to hang in there until I got us out of there.

Esmeralda got a sense that Maria was coming around now, but that wouldn't really change her plans because she wanted to have some fun with her before killing her and this would just make it that much more enjoyable for her.

She stopped again and looked at me as though she'd forgotten I was there and then a slight smile played across her lips, as if she was remembering that time we spoke in my cell.

As she watched me I thought that she was reading my mind, and knew what I was trying to do, but she was thinking about other things, the past, the promise she'd made to me and how this was all working out so well for her.

We humans, we always want those things we can't have, those things we want the most and that we can't have the most, the untouchables in our lives that the poets write about; those things that were deemed unobtainable.

Her thinking was still so twisted that she thought that if she killed Maria on front of me again that I would give in, that I would see the hopeless futility of resisting and then give in to her.

She was sure that I wouldn't die once again for Maria, and that if I fought her, she would just have to oblige me and send me to my death as well, and then wait for another two hundred years if that's what it took.

As she worked so hard to prepare for the last part of her ritual, Esmeralda never saw or heard Gregor as he crept up behind her; he was still watching and waiting for the right moment, and he knew that it was going to be soon.

She carefully pulled the webbing off Maria, and then raised her up by her right arm; like a child that was carrying around her rag doll and then, with surprising gentleness, she carefully placed her atop the pyre and then stood back to admire either her handiwork or Maria's beauty, I couldn't tell from where I was but I was glad she was looking away from me.

She didn't have a watch on, and there was no moon out there, and yet she knew that it was seven minutes to midnight on February seventh, and she was almost ready; it was almost time, everything was in place and she was going to come and wake me then; she thought that I should have come to on my won, she hadn't given me that much venom.

Then she lifted me up and said, "Do you see my darling? Do you have any idea of the luxuries that await your acceptance?" she asked so sweetly that I wanted to throw up, then she said, "Do you know what I will do to you if you say no to me again?" she hissed into my ear.

I tried not to, but I looked at her insect face and then I did throw up, something about her face so close to mine that way was so disgusting that I couldn't help myself. She tossed me aside and moved on, forgetting about me for the moment; but from where I stood I could very well see what she had planned for us; and I had more movement in both of my hands now, though not with a lot of strength if I had to fight.

Then I watched her skitter to the far side of her altar then, her fat abdomen bouncing along as she went, she looked like a happy chef at as the banquet was about to begin; she changed to her human face for the next part because she had to speak again.

She removed a torch from the wall and as she walked towards Maria, but then she stopped and asked me, "Any last words for her?" though she knew that I couldn't yet speak either and she was just gloating.

Because she was enjoying the moment, she didn't see my foot as I kicked at hers when she turned away, and then she fell forward, the torch fell away from her and went out after it landed in a shower of sparks.

Still, showing amazing peed, she rushed towards me angrily and pulled me as close to her face as she could, showing me how angry she was, the rage she felt then, it was burning the tiny space between us.

"Do NOT make the mistake of thinking that you are not expendable! It could cost you more than just your life this time!" she seethed at me.

That was the moment that Asmodeus jumped up, he distracted her again because he saw Gregor; or maybe he sensed him back there as he approached her from behind, he sent out the alarm, but he was much too late.

Gregor felt that he 'd waited long enough, he thought she might present a different chance for him, but when he saw her turn away like that, he thought that it was now or never and sprang at her though he was a full twenty feet away when he did.

He was hoping that he could get close enough to her before she turned so that she would be shocked enough that he would be able to move in and kill her quickly before she recovered.

When I tripped her and he saw her fall, he thought that was his chance but even he was surprised when she got up that fast, he would have seen him coming and had time to get ready for him.

He closed the space between them in a blur, knocking her down again and kicking the torch away from her as he kept running past her.

The torch was now rolling towards Maria, each time it rolled over it went a little slower and I wasn't sure if it would stop before it got there, and I knew that the torch went out, it trailed sparks behind as it rolled and then I saw that the wood she had there was very dry and it wouldn't take much to ignite it.

Esmeralda was caught off guard by the attack and she had no idea who it was or where he came from; he hurt her really bad when he crashed into her, he hit her really hard when she was vulnerable and hadn't seen him coming, she was trying to regain her senses, she wasn't trying to get up yet, and then he turned his attention to me.

"Are you trying to save our Elspeth again?" he asked me with mock seriousness, "Have you not learned the power of those you so foolishly stand against?" he was enjoying the moment now, his turn to gloat I suppose.

But I was getting more movement now, I just didn't want them to know it yet, I was now the one that was waiting for the right moment.

He also raised her by the wrist and when I saw her face, I knew that she was at least, still alive, though she was going deeper within herself and I didn't have a lot of time.

Then he raised her a little higher and shook her limp body at me and said, "Or maybe you can sit there helpless and watch me drink the life's blood out of her!" he said, with a laugh.

As his fangs came out, he was thinking again about how a vampire made a another and then said, "Maybe I'll drink most of hers and let her change and then I can enjoy watching her drink the life's fluid out of you, watch you die at her hands? Doesn't that sound like fun?" he said, and then he laughed at me.

I was struck by how lonely he sounded then but dismissed that quickly because I thought that anyone that was that evil deserved to be lonely, as he was evil, pure and simple, his motive and driving force.

While he was shaking her around like that, I saw the greenish, yellow eyes of Asmodeus as he crept closer on the ledge above us, he was close enough to see everything that we were doing and yet high enough up there that no one could see him but me.

Knowing that he wasn't there to help me, I didn't say a word as I saw him spring out as he tried to scratch out Gregor's eyes or bite deeply into his neck; Gregor felt him as he landed and then bit him; he reached back and grabbed a handful of fur and then threw the cat as hard as he could into the far wall.

Asmodeus shredded his neck as he was pulled away and I imagined that must have hurt, even though he was already healing, and the only evidence was the blood that was still on his collar.

The cat hit the wall hard and it probably broke his neck, but that was when Esmeralda was regaining her senses, she saw it happen and was angry, that was her only friend these days; she changed to her spider form, knowing she would be quicker and use her many limbs to grab and hold onto him as they fought.

She also felt that as a spider her heart was hardened, though doing the things that she did was never a problem for her, those decisions were made quickly and easily, and it never bothered her, no matter who it was.

But she knew that voice and was stunned t find him here, she knew that they way he came at her, that he was only there to ruin her plans and she had already been set off her timetable by his intrusion; "There would be hell to pay!" she vowed, and she was going to give him the bill.

Then she remembered the first time that she killed him and knew what her mistake was, why he was able to be there and that it was her fault that he found her; she drank of his blood in what she thought of as the final insult.

She might have even been glad to see him, but that was before he attacked her and killed her cat, and though he hated her touching him; she knew that he was always there for her, even now, that he would pop up at just the right time to save her life, and she'd never thought about it until that moment, now that he was dead, and she was even angrier about how it happened.

When she looked over there, she could see his body lying still on the ground, a trail of blood where his body hit and then slid down, fur was there as well, but she thought there should have been more blood.

She was going to kill Gregor, and this time there would be no tasting of his flesh or drinking of his blood; she hoped that this time, it would sever the link between them forever; and then even if he did find his way back to a world where she was, he would never know her in that world.

Gregor heard Maria say something and he turned towards her and Esmeralda saw her chance and jumped at him then; if she'd waited any longer, he might have taken Maria off the pyre and make my job a little easier.

She struck him as hard as he hit her, she thrust herself forward like a linebacker hitting a running back, and then she ran him into the far wall and slammed him hard into it, breaking his nose when he couldn't raise his hands fast enough.

But he also sprang up instantly, he bared his fangs at her and hissed as even in the low light of that cave they glistened white-hot with his anger and hatred for her, his eyes burned as red as coals, and that line that sometimes gets blurred in the heat of passion.

If he thought about her in the old world, he never really loved her, he thought she was there because the killing made her want to behave that way; and in the new world he hated her because of how she left him behind, and hatred was the wrong emotion right now, any thoughts of love were being cast aside.

She glared back at him with her multi-faceted eyes that gleamed a bright red and dark blue at him, he could sense something else as well, that she was fighting within herself or she was trying to confuse Gregor, because she kept changing from spider to human and back again as she walked; sometimes walking on eight legs, and other times on only two.

At one point, as she circled him, I saw the knife dangling at her waist, for the moment it was forgotten as she concentrated on Gregor and looked for an opening, and as she got closer, she bared some fangs of her own, and then she circled to her right and I saw a flash as it fell from her waist, she didn't notice because he was attacking and she was trying to ward him off.

She shrieked again and then ran towards Gregor, seeing her opening, she ran on all her legs and stunned him with her speed and might; she knocked him back and then ran quickly past him.

He couldn't see her, but I saw her crawl up the wall as she waited for him to come over there, trying to find her in the darkness, and I could also see that he was stunned; she hit him hard enough to knock him out, and any normal man would still be lying on the floor, but now his senses were returning to him though he had no idea where she went.

Staying as still as I could, I watched as he looked towards the south wall for her, but she was higher up and on the right side, not where he was looking; part of me wanted to warn him, and even felt a little sorry for him at being so overmatched, but the other part of me remembered his treachery, and the fact that he would likely kill me and not give it even so much as a moments pause.

I had a better idea of where she was because I saw when she went up there, but it was still hard for me to find her, I think it was the gleam of her eyes that helped me the most, otherwise she blended into the shadows.

He walked closer to where she was, but she waited until he was about eight feet away from her, he was trying to shield his eyes to see where she was better and then he thought he heard something the other way and turned away from her.

She sprang at him out of that darkness right then, her fangs bared, she was moving in for the kill which was what he was waiting for when he pretended that he didn't know she was behind him, he actually did see her in the shadowsand now turned to spring a trap of his own.

He counter-attacked as he turned towards her, he grabbed one of her legs and ripped it off and then tossed it at her, she screamed at him in anger and then ran off to the far side where it was especially dark and she could hide from him a lot better.

Knowing that she was hiding in there but not where, he wasn't going to walk in there blindly; he circled to his left, and then back to his right, like a boxer trying to make her come out of there and face him, while she waited like the fly that walked blindly into her trap.

Then he panicked and thought that she'd escaped into that darkness, he thought there was an exit back there that couldn't be seen from where he was, and then he knew he would have to go into that darkness after all.

As he was trying to screw up his courage to do that, he heard a noise off to his right, it sounded like something was scraping against the rock, and he was sure that it was her; that somehow, she'd snuck up behind him again.

He was sure that she was there, he thought that maybe since he pulled off her leg that she was losing her balance; that she might have slipped, he ran over there as quick as he could and was ready to pounce on her when he saw that it was only Asmodeus, he was doing the only thing that he could have to help her.

Asmodeus was dragging himself along the ground as she would have if he had hurt her, he was distracting Gregor long enough that he wouldn't see her or know where she was until it was too late, and she would have him.

Then She did, she jumped at him, screaming out of the shadows and she knocked him down; he couldn't turn fast enough and was facing the wrong way, she grabbed the back of his head and slammed his face into the ground and then again to make sure he was at least stunned; she raised him over her head once more and then slammed him down and she skewered him with a piece of rebar that was sticking out, and in her anger she drove it right through him.

She bit him twice more, injecting all of the venom that she could into him and then with her claws, she ripped into his neck until his head flew off and then waited to make sure that he wasn't going to get up and searching for it but he never moved.

When she was satisfied that he wasn't coming back from that, she returned to Maria and dragged her back to the pyre and placed her body there, this time, maybe she was still angry, maybe because her timetable to get this done was seriously off, she didn't place her on there as gently as she did before.

While she was searching for the torch, I was still not able to use my legs, but I was dragging myself along while they fought, using my arms like a soldier, I crawled around in that darkness until I found the knife that she'd dropped, I didn't know what she used it for, I had no idea that it was special or anything else, I just thought that since she had it, it might be useful.

As I lifted the blade, it burned my flesh, I think that I wasn't supposed to handle it but I didn't care, I felt it of course; but it wasn't going to stop me; and then it spoke to me, trying to warn me off, showing me its history of bloodletting and murder.

It told me that it was a demon's knife with a will of its own, a way of inter-weaving itself into the mind of the person wielding it, it would begin to change that person until they were no longer who or what they were, because it was forged in the fires of hell.

Finally, she found the torch and then she started to look for me, it would not do to go through all of this trouble and not have her audience after all, she wanted to make sure that I had a good view and see that I was once again, useless if we fought against her.

She laughed when she saw me crawling there, "Got some use of your limbs huh?" she asked, and then she smiled at me, and for one micro-millisecond of a moment she looked like the Esmeralda of old, the one that was innocent and was happy to go and play with her friend until she murdered her; that knew nothing of black magic and the casting of spells.

Some might even say that this was long before the darkness came and took her soul, but then, there are others that would say that her soul was black before she took her first breath in this world, that possibly she'd lived a previous life where she was even worse.

She dropped the torch then, and it caught quickly on the lower parts of the pyre and was working its way up quickly, I tried to look at Maria, to call to her but she wasn't moving.

She was going to watch her burn, and she was going to make sure that I watched as well, that I didn't try to turn away or escape just to show us what she was capable of, as if we needed a reminder.

As Maria died, Esmeralda would burn her soul into mine and then we would celebrate our union by making love on the remains f her body, cover ourselves with her ashes, this was the plan she had in her twisted little mind.

Walking towards me then, she started shedding her clothes as she came; as she did, she was trying to make herself look human again, but her head wouldn't cooperate and for that reason she looked anything but human, she looked horrible.

With surprising strength, she lifted me up and carried me on her back to the altar and then I could see what the candles were for, she intended to use her magic to make me see her as something else; hiding her ugliness in one of her deceptive spells, she might even make me think she was Elspeth and that we could escape together now, and I could smell her wetness now and it was disgusting.

She dropped me on the altar and rolled me over on my back, and since she did it so roughly and she was so strong, it was easy to use the momentum when she turned me so harshly and I raised the knife and thrust it into her right shoulder, just below the neck, I was aiming at her heart but she saw the flash of the knife and moved.

Then I used my own anger and frustration and raised it up again, striking her once more before she knocked me back; her blackened blood spilling all over me as she gasped and tried to recover.

It was so hard to cut into her because her hide was so tough and the knife still burned my hands when I used it but I didn't care, I was either fueled by my anger or the determination that I felt to end this with both of us standing intact, I hit her again, this time I must have hit her in the right spot because this time the knife went in and cut her deeply, surprising her, as she thought she was damned near invincible now.

She was, under normal circumstances, but this blade was different, one of the few in the world at the time that could have cut her or even hurt her at all; it was one of the few weapons that had that kind of power, it would kill her if it was delivered correctly, as it was that last time.

Esmeralda knew it was over then, she felt her life force slipping out of her like fine sand falling to the bottom of an hourglass.

The way the blade was bent helped me too, it caused more damage and went deeper at vital organs than a conventional blade would have, if it could have cut through her hide.

But the wound to her shoulder blade dropped below the collarbone, inflicting serious damage to her lungs and the tissue around them, and it barley missed her heart.

My arms were now covered in her blood and I could see that she was feeling light-headed as well, but she managed to shake free of me and then she ran off, back into the shadows where she had a better chance than I did.

But she left a trail of blood drops where she went, but as she moved away from me, she kicked at me with one of her legs and I fell, it broke my jaw when I landed and my skull was fractured and one point from her tossing me around, but all things considered, I was still in the fight.

She tripped on the torch as she ran from me, and I saw it rolling again towards Mariaand that it would reignite the flames that went out before, I didn't know how but was grateful that it did.

Out of the corner of my eye, I saw that Maria was now struggling to get up, I think she saw me there and was trying to get to me, to help me somehow if she could.

Esmeralda saw that, and kicked at the torch again, trying to make it spark the fire again but she tripped over Gregor's lifeless body and instead, she landed on the pyre and knocked Maria off as she was still trying to rise, she landed on top of me as Esmeralda took her place up there.

I managed to sit up a bit while I held onto Maria, my legs were coming back but would not hold my weight yet, they wouldn't cooperate when I tried to stand but now I could see that the wood caught fire once more, but we were still not safe, we were at the base of the pyre.

We were close enough to see that Esmeralda was caught in the fire that she meant to kill Maria in, it caught on the coarse hairs of her legs and body and in her death, she was changing rapidly from human to spider, trying to do anything to escape the flames but it didn't help and she shrieked in agony as her legs kicked at the empty air above her.

I turned Maria away so she wouldn't see but could do nothing about the sound, I pulled her close to my shoulder but she heard the screams as Esmeralda died, and in her mind; they sounded exactly as her own did those many years ago.

Esmeralda's stomach burst open then, and it was over for her, but I thought the screams and the shrieking, the nightmare of her would be echoing in my mind for years to come, I managed to pull us away and to a safe distance but then I was exhausted and passed out.

I woke up, about three days later, and found myself in a hospital, the first face I saw when I opened my eyes was the officer from the park, I saw the name "Danny" on his chest and smiled, though I didn't know who he was; then he told me that he was the one that chased Gregor from the park that day and lost his partner for it.

He still looked as though he was in shock, but I could see that he was back at work because of the uniform and I knew he was going to be alright, he wanted to know if I knew who Gregor was and why he did what he did, but I didn't know what to tell him, I didn't want him to think I was certifiable and yet, who would believe me if I told them, I know I wouldn't have.

Then he smiled at me and said, "Well, either way, you gave us a hell of a scare for a minute, but it looks like you're going to pull through after all!" he said, my name is Danny and I'll try and ask you more later when you feel stronger, maybe you might remember something that isn't on your mind right now!" he said cheerfully, "First, I will go get your doctor!" he told me, and then he turned to leave.

But he stopped at the door and smiled for a moment and said, "You're going to have one hell of a tale to tell your grandkids one day!" he said, and smiled, "Oh, your parents are here too, I'll let them know that your awake!" he said and then disappeared around the doorway.

I looked around me and then tried to speak but couldn't do much more than raise my head off the pillow a little bit, and then I fell back.

Another officer was sitting there and he filled me in on the details while I waited for the others and the doctor to show up; he said that they saw Gregor was he was going through the park, but they were trying to follow him until they got sufficient backup that he wouldn't escape or kill another or their number, they lost him for a moment when he followed her into the tunnels, but they heard something and found him there, they didn't realize how bad it was until they saw her on fire and then they called for more backup because it was getting serious then.

Danny Nieto was the first on the scene, he'd been trying to finds the killer harder than anyone, he wore a haunted look on his face until then because he felt that he should have fought harder to stay together and then his partner might have had a chance.

He was having nightmares now that his partner left him because he knew he was going to die and sent Danny the other way to save his life, and in another nightmare; he kept seeing Tommy rise out of his grave and come after him because it was his fault.

Danny had followed Gregor into the caves and saw what was going on, he had to leave the area and go back outside because the radios wouldn't work in there, he got no reception, he could almost hear that someone was speaking but he couldn't tell what they were saying.

As soon as he went back in, that was when all hell broke loose, all Danny could do at that point was to watch and try to understand his disbelieving eyes, and it was all over so quickly that all he could do was cut the webbing and get us out of there when backup finally arrived.

Then there were two officers standing over my bed, they were talking about what they saw, I tried to ask about Maria but I couldn't move my jaw which was still wired shut, and until it healed enough to take out the wires I couldn't raise my voice above a whisper, they couldn't hear me anyway.

In my somewhat confused state, they said I asked for Elspeth, and they of course, had no idea what the hell I was talking about, and when the doctor showed up they left, a little too relieved, I thought, and were somewhat grateful for the interruption too, I think.

I tried to ask them about the cat too, though I couldn't remember his name and couldn't have explained why I was asking, but I was just curious; they thought that they gave me too much medication and decided to cut it back.

The doctor that was examining me didn't say much, he was looking at my face, closely into my eyes, shining that bright little light into them and telling me to stop looking away; he touched my ribs and checked to see if anything was especially sensitive or maybe injured; then he checked my vitals once more before he stopped and took another good look at me.

He must have understood what I was trying to tell them because he finally left me for a moment; went out to the hallway and came back a moment later whit a wheelchair and waited for me.

I tried to wave him off and tell him that I was strong enough to walk but he laughed at me and said, "You are too weak to walk, so it's either this or you stay in your room! Nor arguing, its doctor's orders!" he said and then gestured for me to climb in, which I did.

"Ready to go for a walk?" he asked and then I must have given him the nastiest look because he broke out in laughter, and then, without waiting another minute, he helped me out of the bed and put me gently into the chair; someone else brought a blanket and he wrapped it around my legs to keep me warm and then we wet out of the room and he began to whistle.

We went out of the room, turned right and went down the hallway, I looked at him once; wondering where we were going because he never said, but he kept his face straight and his eyes down the hallway and never said a word.

I thought that he might have been taking me to see the other cop, or another doctor, maybe to take some tests or go through some therapy, but I was too tired, and too wired to stop him and ask, but all I really wanted was to ask about Maria, how she was doing; was she still here in the hospital or was she home now, those kinds of things that inquiring minds wanted to know.

Three doors down from my room we entered another room, it was just like mine, probably like all of the others in the hospital, but for Maria they added special touches to make her feel more comfortable, they said they were doing this because she wasn't responding as quickly as they hoped she would; as quickly as I was and she was still basically in a coma.

The other thing was, there were so many flowers in her room that they had to put a lot of them on the floor, along the window; I knew that it would make her happy to know that so many people cared about her and wanted her to hurry back as she was missed.

On the far wall to my left, there was a poster of some cartoonish alien, winking his eye out at us and saying, "Everything's going to be alright!" as he gave you the thumbs up sign.

She had a television on a cart instead of high on the wall as mine was; making it seem more homier to her, she had blankets from home on her bed, and she wore pajamas, even the curtains around her bed weren't the same as everyone else's.

Maria was lying there on the bed stiffly, too rigid in her position to be sleeping; I looked at the doctor and he told me, "She's still in shock and though she's not physically ill, we need her to come around soon, the longer she stays under, the worse it will be for her, the less her chances of recovery!" he whispered to me.

He pushed me a little closer to her bed and then he left us alone there, but he said, "Maybe the fact that she can see or feel you here, maybe that might help bring her back, you never know!" he said, "I'll let your parents know your over here!" he told me.

As soon as we were alone, I took her hand and held it close to my face and then kissed it a few times, I was trying to will her back to us; her hand felt cool to the touch and yet there was no resistance when I pulled at it.

"Please, cara mia!" I whispered to her, I was crying then but I couldn't help it, "Tell me that you're going to be okay, that we can be together now like you said!" I pleaded with her.

"We beat them this time!" I said to her, "We won, they lost, they are gone; please don't make me celebrate a moment longer without you!" I cried into her hand as I held it close to my face and then kissed it again.

Then I heard my parent as the came up the hallway and entered the room, my mother rushed to me and hugged me tightly, crying into my shoulder while my father stood back with tears swimming in his eyes but he didn't know what to do next; all he could think of was that he almost lost his other son and he had no idea why.

I reached for him, and then he came over to me and hugged me too, we cried together for a while but it was okay, we were together and we were not going to hold anything back now, I told them that it was going to be alright, though in truth I didn't think it would be until Maria was back with us.

Then I felt someone squeezing my hand and thought it was my mother until Maria said, Okay! I'll tell you that it will be alright, that we will be... what else did you ask me to say?" she asked and then smiled weakly.

I guess that meant the doctor was right, and maybe she was just waiting for me to come there so she could come back, all I know was that it was sure good to hear her voice again,we all had tears running down our cheeks now, but they were happy tears.

Feeling overwhelmed, I laid my head upon her chest, I wanted to hear the heartbeat of the woman that I loved so much; the one that beat the same as mine.

But there was something that was bothering me, nagging at my mind and I couldn't let go; I wanted to take stock of what happened, now that we could step back and take a look at the whole picture; but I had my love now and everything should have been fine.

Something didn't feel right, I leaned back a bit and let my parents talk with her, seeing she and I together made my mother very happy again, she knew that this was the one for me, she could see it in my eyes and now she wasn't seeing her little boy when she looked at me, now she was seeing a man looking back.

I started looking around the room, and my eye caught the poster of that impish alien again, and now something about it didn't seem right, and I wondered if she had a poster like this at home in her room, or did someone put it up there thinking that it would help, it was hard to say and he didn't know who to ask.

It wasn't art, after all, and I didn't remember her ever speaking about anything like that and I thought that was why it was bothering me so much, but then I noticed that it didn't seem the same as before when I first saw it; I thought it had changed somehow, or it was a trick of the light but it looked different, as if it shifted its stance, turned its body a quarter of his body to the left and away from me.

This wasn't an alien anymore, and I pushed my wheelchair over to it so that I could see it up close; I wanted to figure out what was really bothering me now about it.

I could hear them asking me where I was going, but it sounded as though they were a million miles away, or in a tunnel and the sound wasn't carrying very far; they could have been talking to me through a tin can with a string attached to it for all the good it did.

The closer I got to it, the more I felt as though it wasn't just a harmless poster after all, and if that was an imp, that was one without good intentions, his fun wouldn't be fun for whoever he was laughing at.

Now it took the shape of a skull with its eyes intact and looking to the right side, away from anyone that might be looking at it from where I stood at that moment; from the other angle, over by the bed, you could see nothing but the imp that I saw on the way in, but from there I could see that skull in great detail.

The teeth were bared in a grin of death, its skin rotted away and completely gone, and there were a few wisps of hair here and there, but they eyes were the frightening part because they were so clear and they looked so real, as I looked a them, it seemed as though they were focused on me.

But when I looked again, it was as if they had shifted away to try and deceive me, yet they could not be real, they were just an image imprinted on the paper, or maybe it was a hologram after all I thought, but it still didn't feel right to me.

I was now about a foot away from the poster then, and I looked at it again, hanging from a crazy angle and looking so harmless and innocent, and then I took one end and pulled at it; I wanted to seen what was on the other side and why it felt as though it might be a window to another dimension or something.

Now I was scared that things like that might pop into my head for a long time after what we went through; that I might be suspicious of everything and everyone for a while, I was feeling silly for being afraid of a silly poster, but again; I couldn't help it.

When I flipped it up and looked underneath it, I saw that there was nothing on the wall and that it was just a poster after all, and I almost let it drop back, but then I noticed that it had a signature; someone had signed it, there was an autograph, and I wondered whose it was; if it was worth any money.

The name signed on the back was "Ronnie" and though it was just a name, a signature on the back of a poster, for some reason that name scared the hell out of me, I don't know why; but I thought it had been signed by the skull in the front of the poster; and as I let it slip back to where it was before, the eyes did move towards me and I screamed.

Photograph by J.R. Gonzalez

"The End"

If you are still reading this far, then I must thank you again for reading my work, and I hope you had as much fun reading my story as I did in the telling of it.

Just in case you're wondering, the next book is a story about a family that bought the wrong house in a good neighborhood and find that something dead is living beneath the house, something that they wished they'd never woken.

They lose mom to it and spend everything they hold dear to get her back from Izak, who has no intention of giving her back. Ever.

So, yeah, it's a love story, but if you liked this one well enough to read it all the way through, give it a look and see what you think, it can't hurt, right?

It's called "The Lingstroms" and is unlike any other story you have read on that subject, I promise you.

ACKOWLEDGEMENTS
(FOR BOTH VOLUMES)

"Gloria" by Them with the excellent vocals of Mr. Van Morrison
"Dead Man's Party" by Oingo Boingo
"The Crypt Keeper" from "Tales from the Crypt"
Bela Lagosi, the great and renowned actor.
Christopher Lee, also a great actor.
Rod Serling, and "The Twilight Zone"
"The Great Pumpkin from Charles Shultz and Charlie Brown
The Los Angeles Lakers
Ann Rice and her "Vampire Chronicles"
'Joust" by Midway "Thank you very much)
Sam Cooke "Down by the Sea"
"Klingon Warrior" from Gene Roddenberry
"Vampira"
Warner Brothers Cartoons
AND
Bugs Bunny

www.ingramcontent.com/pod-product-compliance
Lightning Source LLC
Chambersburg PA
CBHW051552100726
47898CB00001B/63